FANDANGO

MICHAEL ZIMMER

WARNER BOOKS

A Time Warner Company

WARNER BOOKS EDITION

Copyright © 1996 by Michael Zimmer
All rights reserved.

Cover design by Elaine Groh
Map art by Karen Wimmer

Warner Books, Inc.
1271 Avenue of the Americas
New York, NY 10020

W A Time Warner Company

Printed in the United States of America

First Printing: January, 1996

10 9 8 7 6 5 4 3 2 1

For Mary Huebschman,
who never lost faith in her brother

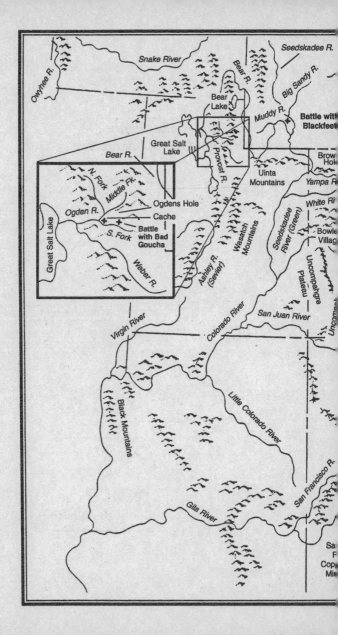

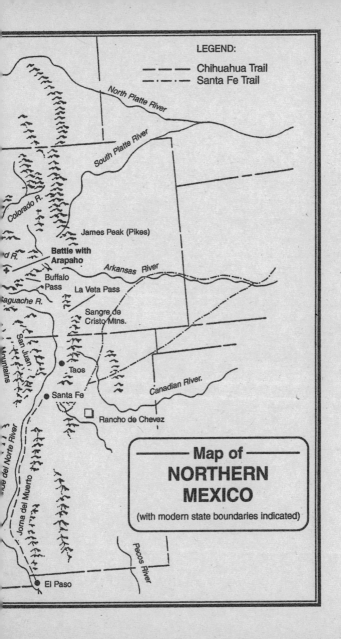

FANDANGO

CHAPTER ONE

St. Louis, August 1828

There was no breeze, and at the tall, multiple-paned windows, the lacy curtains hung motionless. A fine cloth mesh tacked over the windows kept the droning horde of nocturnal insects at bay, while the unrelenting discordance of cicadas and tree frogs raked the muggy night air.

Standing self-consciously before one of the windows, Eli Cutler stared wistfully across the high stone fence at the lower end of the yard. Beyond the iron-spiked crown of the limestone wall, the lights of St. Louis sloped steeply toward the broad, moonlit band of the Mississippi. Eli had forgotten, in his years among the cool parks and snowcapped peaks of the Rockies, how loud and irritating the sounds of a Midwestern night sometimes became, or how utterly miserable a hot summer evening could be.

A slender, fragile-stemmed goblet of imported red wine was nestled carefully in one of Eli's callused brown hands. Sweat beaded his face. His father's old broadcloth suit chafed at his crotch and under his arms, and hugged his shoulders with an uncomfortable tightness. Although at five-foot-eleven he was less than an inch taller than his father had been, he was broader through the shoulders, filled out and hardened by his years in the wilderness. His face was square but well-defined, tanned to a deep walnut hue, and his green eyes were rimmed by a webbing of crow's-feet that deepened into shallow canyons when he laughed. He wore his curly chestnut hair long and combed back, falling to his shoulders, but was clean-shaven except for a small, neatly trimmed mustache. He was twenty-seven, but looked ten years older.

Eli forced his attention back to the stuffy dining room, staring past his reflection in the wavy panes of glass to survey the distorted images of the men and women behind him. At least a dozen guests still lingered in the long, high-ceilinged room. The men wore dark broadcloth suits and silk cravats, their pudgy cheeks glistening with perspiration above scratchy, cardboard-lined collars. The women wore light-colored gowns that, if they were young enough (or thought themselves so), revealed bared shoulders—inviting targets to the tiny drillers at the window.

Here were the elite of St. Louis, Eli knew, the movers and shakers, the financiers and entrepreneurs. He recognized old Sylvester Girardin easily by the high sweep of his thinning gray hair, the slightly rigid stance, and the unmistakable sway he held over his guests as he ushered them from the room. A trio of middle-aged black women—kitchen slaves, Eli guessed—were already clearing off the table. Cups and saucers made a soft, comforting clatter as they were piled onto a mahogany cart. Eli saw Girardin make a slight motion with his hand, and an old black man with snowy hair moved away from the wall, leaned close for his master's instructions, then strode purposefully across the room. Eli turned to face him.

"Suh," the black man said, coming to a stop and bowing stiffly. "Mistuh Girardin has asked me to escort you to his study. If you would please follow me."

Eli nodded and obediently fell in behind the old man. Girardin had by now herded his flock of dinner guests through the door and to the right, where the men and women would separate—the former to a den where cigars and bourbon awaited, the latter to a sitting room across the hall, where Girardin's wife would entertain with lighter drinks and cakes. The black man turned left, away from the shuffling crowd, and led Eli down a narrow, unlit corridor. He pushed a door open, and Eli entered and paused.

"Please make yourself comfortable," the black man said, directing Eli's attention to a plushly upholstered chair with a slow wave of his hand. The chair resided in front of a huge desk cluttered with letters and invoices. A copy of that morning's *Missouri Dispatch* was perched on top of a stack of ledgers, folded open to the page containing Eli's interview. It was a long, rambling piece that ran several columns, focusing largely on what he had seen and heard around the Mexican settlements, as well as his own adventures and plans for the future. Although Eli was no authority on Mexican politics, he was an eyewitness source to those distant, exotic lands, and the *Dispatch*'s reporter had been quick to seek him out when word of his arrival in St. Louis got around.

"Mistuh Girardin will be right with you," the black man said as he retreated, pulling the door closed behind him.

Eli studied the den thoughtfully, trying to glean from its furnishings what kind of man old Sylvester Girardin was. It was a small room, lined with shelves that were beginning to sag beneath the weight of books, ledgers, and stacks of paper, some yellowing with age. A painting of a steamboat hung above the wing chair behind the desk—the *Lucy Della,* which Eli hazily remembered had burned and sunk above Memphis five or six years before. Three other portraits were hung around the room, all of steamers plying the rivers between Independence and New Orleans, Pittsburgh and St. Louis, but none was as prominently displayed as the *Lucy Della*.

The *Lucy Della* had been the real start of Girardin's shipping empire, Eli knew; before purchasing the steamer, the old Frenchman had operated on a much smaller scale, using keelboats to ship goods between New Orleans and St. Louis. The *Lucy Della* had been his big gamble, but it had paid off handsomely. Only recently had Girardin begun to venture after some of the overland markets. He had sent a caravan of wagons as far south as Chihuahua, Mexico, last summer, and another, larger train to Santa Fe this year. Rumor had it that he was also trying to establish a more direct link with the fur and robe trade, financing illicit trading posts close to the Osages, the Sac and Fox, the Otos and the Pawnees. Eli didn't know how much credit to attach to such rumors, but he wouldn't have been surprised to learn that they were all true. Nearly anyone of wealth in St. Louis had some connection to the fur trade, licensed or otherwise.

There was a window here, too, and from it, through the same kind of fine mesh that covered the dining room window, he could see a portion of the riverfront. Even at this late hour the quays were busy. A sidewheeler nosed into one of the scarred and splintered wharves swarming with men and oxen; winches powered huge crates from the hold and set them on deck, where cursing, sweating stevedores wrestled them onto drays to be carted to nearby warehouses. From those same warehouses, honey, lead, tallow, and lumber from the Missouri backwoods; furs and buffalo robes from the mountains and plains; and gold, silver, copper, wool, and leather from Mexico would be shipped to other, larger warehouses in New Orleans, Philadelphia, or New York, from where much of it would eventually find its way across the Atlantic in one form or another. It was a big business, and a complex one, Eli knew; sometimes, trading a hank of glass beads from a factory in Venice, Italy, to a Cheyenne along the Cache la Poudre or the Laramie for a prime beaver pelt, he wondered how many men really understood the intricacy of such a simple transaction. Could the Indian comprehend the international intrigue, the political and financial savvy that was required to bring such gew-gaws to the frontier? Did he know that, half a world away, Venetian factory workers were being killed for revealing trade secrets? Or could the artisan, sweating at his furnace, fully appreciate the danger and labor involved in the exchange of his product for the hide of an animal? Eli had once overheard a woman decry the injustice of trad-ing beads that cost only pennies to make for a plew that would fetch five dollars in St. Louis. But he knew it was more complicated that that. Men died and others went broke, and in the mountains, the In-dians thought the white men were foolish to trade something so valu-able as a bead for the skin of a beaver.

Eli emptied his wineglass and set it aside without turning from the window. Girardin's house sat atop the bluff overlooking the town, a grand, two-storied brick affair with cupolas and slate shingles. Eli didn't find it ironic at all that Girardin had located his private study here, near the rear of the mansion, where he could keep an eye on the comings and goings of his business enterprises.

A whiff of the riverfront—of damp decay and sooty exhaust—strayed up on some vagrant breeze too slight to feel. The curtains, cut from the same cloth as those in the dining room, remained limp, but the odor sharpened for a moment, filling the room with a dis-tasteful pungency, then slowly receded.

The thumping of hard-soled shoes on the carpet outside the door tore Eli's concentration away from the window. He turned as Gi-rardin entered the den.

"Mr. Cutler, how good of you to wait," Girardin said graciously, flashing a smile. He spoke with the clipped precision of a man inti-mately familiar with a foreign language, but not totally comfortable with it. Motioning toward the same chair the old black man had indicated, he added, "Please, sit down."

Girardin circled the desk and sank into a well-worn leather chair. He reached almost absently behind him to pull a gold cord that disappeared through a small hole in the ceiling. From somewhere deep within the house a bell tinkled, and a moment later the old black man reappeared.

"Would you care for a cigar?" Girardin asked Eli. "Perhaps something to drink? Bourbon? Or brandy?"

"Bourbon'll do."

"Hiram," Girardin murmured. The black man glided toward a sideboard without further instruction.

"I must apologize for the unrelenting questions of my dinner guests," Girardin continued with a trace of a smile. "I am afraid everyone in St. Louis is hungry for news from the mountains."

"I've become used to it," Eli replied as Hiram returned with a cherrywood box filled with cigars. Eli chose one, and allowed the black man to light it for him from a taper. Hiram went through the same ritual with Girardin, then returned to the sideboard to fetch the bourbon. There was an iron and glass ash stand in front of the desk, and Eli slid it closer.

Girardin was silent a moment, his eyes narrowed in concentration. Then he gently tapped the newspaper on his desk with a slender forefinger. "I read your interview in the *Dispatch* this morning. It said you planned an immediate return to the mountains."

"With the next boat upriver. I'll outfit myself in Westport."

"Your destination is still Taos, then?"

Eli regarded his host curiously. When he'd first received Girardin's invitation to dine with him that evening, he'd imagined the old Frenchman had merely intended to ask him to carry dispatches back to the Spanish settlements for him. It wasn't an unusual request in a country with such a haphazard postal system. But as the hours dragged by, Eli began to realize that Girardin had something else in mind. There had been a sense of urgency within his subtle probing at the elaborately set dining table, an undercurrent that carried over into this quiet, closed-door meeting. Girardin had seemed to gauge Eli's every move, his every response, with an almost analytical thoroughness. Eli felt himself warming to it.

"Yeah," Eli replied laconically. "I figure Taos."

Girardin jetted a cloud of smoke toward the ceiling. "I suppose you are wondering why I asked you here this evening, why I have forced you to endure such a stifling occasion, as these affairs have an irritating tendency to become. I will come to the point.

"As I am sure you have heard, Girardin Shipping and Transport has recently expanded its operations into the Santa Fe trade. I have sent two wagon trains of goods to the Mexican markets so far, and intend to send a third next year. The returns have been marginal so far, due to difficulties along the trail, not the least of which are the Indian tribes inhabiting the country between our two nations. The Comanches in particular seem to have a penchant for stealing mules and shooting oxen, sometimes just for the sport of it, I gather. In spite of that, I am convinced the Santa Fe trade offers a golden opportunity. I hope to open stores in both Santa Fe and Chihuahua within another two years, and in time perhaps penetrate even Mexico City itself."

The trace of a smile, no more than a slight uplifting of the corners of his mouth, crossed Girardin's face. "I can assure you, my intentions toward the Southwestern trade are well known in St. Louis and New Orleans. Those cities, both centers of western commerce, are quite abuzz with speculation. I like that. It provides a distraction I hope to use to my advantage against the competition. You see, there is another arena I wish to enter at this time, an arena with which you are well acquainted. I speak of the fur trade, of course. The price of beaver rises every year, with no sign of leveling. I feel the time for investment is ripe."

Hiram brought their bourbons, setting Eli's glass on the desk in front of him and Girardin's within his master's reach. Stepping back, he said, "Will that be all, Mistuh Girardin?"

"I believe the fan, Hiram."

"Yes, suh." Hiram paced to a far corner and wrapped his bony fingers around a cord dangling there. He pulled it down and let it rise of its own accord. A wave of smoky air washed over the desk, and Eli glanced up to observe a large reed sweep bracketed to the ceiling.

As if unaware of the sudden but ineffectual passage of stuffy air, Girardin continued. "I have a man in Santa Fe now, procuring the necessary permits and visas. He is a former sergeant of the Dragoons, a very capable and efficient organizer. But he lacks the experience of a mountaineer, what the local press calls a mountain man. I need someone who knows the fur trade intimately, who is familiar with the country and the natives, and who is capable of leading a brigade of trappers into them, as well as bringing them out alive. I think you are that man, Mr. Cutler, if you are interested."

Eli leaned back and hooked an ankle calmly over one knee. But inside he felt a sudden exhilaration, a gut-deep excitement at the opportunity Girardin had so casually dropped in his lap. "And if I am?"

"The job would pay one hundred dollars a month, plus three percent of the furs taken. Perhaps, in time, a partnership. A successful hunt could prove quite lucrative."

"I've never led a brigade before."

"True, not for a company. But you have led others like yourself, free trappers who band together for protection. Your reputation precedes you, Mr. Cutler. You are a known and respected figure in the mountains. Additionally, according to my sources, you have an education, always an asset to a company. But I shall admit there is another reason, one we shall delve into only if you are interested up to this point."

Eli nodded slowly. "Go ahead."

There was no change in Girardin's expression as he went on. "Have you heard of the Reed party?"

"Big Tom Reed? Yeah. Word is that he and maybe a dozen men were jumped by brownskins somewhere on the Colorado River. I haven't heard many details yet."

"It happened early last spring, as I understand it," Girardin supplied. "There was supposedly only one survivor, although legitimate verification has been hard to obtain." His head tipped back and his face hardened, offering Eli a glimpse of the real Sylvester Girardin, the man who had built an empire through hard work and determination. "The Reed party was a GS&T venture. We financed it in hopes of establishing ourselves quietly in the mountains before the larger companies became aware of our interests there. My son was a clerk with Tom Reed."

"Ahhh," Eli sighed. "Hell, Mr. Girardin, I didn't know. I'm sorry."

"I am a businessman, Mr. Cutler, and I have never lost sight of that. But I am also a father, and I do not wish to think Antoine died under questionable circumstances. Word arrived from my man in Mexico just a few weeks ago that there may have been some treachery involved on the part of Mr. Reed. Understand that I do not put much stock in rumors, but I do wish to know the truth. I want to know *why* my son died."

"You said treachery?"

"Supposedly only Reed survived the massacre. Now I understand a Mexican has turned up in Taos with a different version of what happened on the Colorado. I want you to find him and see what he has to say. And if Reed is guilty, I want justice administered. Do you understand?"

He meant mountain justice, Eli knew. He wanted Big Tom Reed killed.

"The Spaniards are notoriously indifferent to crimes against American firms," Girardin went on. "No matter how much they desire our financial influx, they do little to encourage it. But I will not tolerate such an affront against the GS&T, no matter how Mexico feels toward the subject. Nor will I tolerate the murder of my son through deception."

"If Reed is guilty, he won't last long in the mountains," Eli said bluntly. "It's a big country, but we take care of our own."

"I am counting on that, Mr. Cutler." He leaned forward, his dark gaze boring into Eli. "You are familiar with the Shoshone chief Bad Gocha, sometimes referred to as Mauvais Gauche, or the Bad Left-Handed One."

It was a statement rather than a question, and a muscle in Eli's arm twitched; the curved ash that had grown on the end of his cigar fell against the ashtray and tumbled to the carpet. Neither man looked at it.

"I know him," Eli replied tonelessly. "But he's not a chief. He's a renegade among his own people, a leader of other renegades from other tribes. Even the Shoshone don't want any part of him. They're a bad bunch."

"You were with Etienne Provost, on the Provost River." He pronounced it as a Frenchman: *A-tea-n Pro-vost*, rather than *A-chen Provo*, mountain fashion. "Between the Utah Lake and the Great Salt Lake in 1824."

Eli nodded stiffly. "I was with him."

"It is my understanding that the same methods were used with the Reed party on the Colorado, that it was in fact Bad Gocha's very band that perpetrated the deed."

"In cahoots with Reed?" Eli looked doubtful.

"Find out for me, Mr. Cutler. Your first priority is trapping, of course, the taking of beaver pelts. I do not want you to lose sight of that. But find out for me if my son was sacrificed for another man's gain."

"Gain?"

"According to the Mexican whom my man in Taos uncovered, Reed cached a large number of furs somewhere north of the Colorado River. Perhaps as many as ten packs, which would represent a sizable return." Girardin's voice softened for the first time. "Those furs belong to the GS&T. I don't want Tom Reed to have them, under any circumstances."

"And this Mexican knows where the furs are cached?"

"He knows their approximate location. He managed to hide during the slaughter, and was forced to stay in hiding—among a clump of willows within the Indian camp itself, if his story is true. After the renegades left, he wandered through the camp looking for food and a weapon. He found some papers which he brought back with him. Most were of no consequence, but one gave detailed directions to the cache from the fork of a river. I believe this Mexican can lead you to that river, and from there you should be able to locate the furs with the aid of the map, assuming they've survived the winter." He leaned back, steepling his fingers above his chest. "So, Mr. Cutler, the story has been told. Are you still interested?"

Eli didn't reply immediately, but he already knew he would accept Girardin's offer. He'd been in the mountains a long time, and he loved them in his own way. Their pureness and size, the wild and unfettered life among them, appealed to his own recklessness. But he'd also recognized that he would never be a part of them the way others were, never give himself up to them so completely that he would turn his back on ambition, or a desire to elevate himself beyond what he already was. If he had been running when he'd first gone to the mountains, he wasn't anymore. His father's death had convinced him of that. And Girardin was offering him a second chance, an opportunity he had thought was stripped away for good by his father's stubborn Old World attitude of birthright. Nodding abruptly, he said, "Yeah, I'll lead your brigade, Mr. Girardin."

The old Frenchman's smile was jubilant, revealing, for the first time that evening, the polished ivory of false teeth. He stood and they shook hands across the desk. "Splendid! Just splendid," Gi-rardin said. Lifting his bourbon in a salute, he added, "To success, Mr. Cutler, success and justice. May they go hand in hand."

Chapter Two

They pushed a little as the light of a new day spread across the dry, rolling hills. In the west the pine-darkened slopes of the Wet Mountains rode low on the horizon, still a full day's journey away. To the north of the Wet range the bald, craggy shoulder of James Peak glistened under a cap of fresh snow, while to the south the Spanish Peaks heaved into the pale morning sky like white-nippled breasts.

There'd be a heap of water up there, Pete Meyers reasoned as he eyed the far-off mountains. He pictured it in his mind, tumbling fresh and icy cold from between sheer-rock canyon walls, spilling into marshy valleys where the grass was still green and rich, the elk just now coming into their prime.

"Seal-fat and sleek," Charlie would call them, and Pete mumbled a curse as he pulled his arm from the shelter of his serape and wiped a dirty shirtsleeve across his cracked lips. He tried to push the image of cool mountain streams and languid beaver ponds out of his mind. The Arkansas River was just a few miles to the north. There was plenty of water there if he wanted it badly enough—that and maybe the dozen or so Pawnees who'd trailed them into the dusk last night. Pete figured if a man wanted to risk dying slow and losing everything he owned or loved to the brownskins, then the Arkansas might be the way to go. But he wasn't willing to give up his hair just yet. Or anything else, he thought, glancing ahead at the others.

Charlie Williams led, riding a thin-maned appaloosa mare he called War-Heels, a title more descriptive than affectionate. Charlie rode hunched forward in his saddle, a slim, wiry man of medium height, with coal-black hair that fell below his collar, and a scraggly, drooping mustache that curled down on either side of his narrow mouth. Charlie wore an old black hat that was grimy with dirt and grease, the brim broken and pushed up in front, but sagging like an old man's waddle elsewhere. He carried a knife and a brace of pistols on a belt wrapped around the outside of his red blanket coat, and a shortened fusil across his saddlebows.

Red-Winged Woman, Charlie's Cheyenne squaw, tagged close behind—a slim woman of lithe grace, stabbing black eyes, and fiery temperament. Her head seemed to swivel constantly as she tugged on the lead rope to one of the pack mules, scanning the horizon behind them, and to the north and south. And always, before looking ahead again, she would let her gaze rest briefly, warmly, on her children. They had three—a boy still nursing, carried in a cradleboard on her back, and two girls who rode double beside their mother.

Annie, Pete's woman, trailed behind Charlie's family and a string of loose pack animals. She was a Comanche, Annie was, a full-blood, she claimed, although Pete sometimes had his doubts. There was a hint of wave in her glossy black hair, and an olive fairness to her complexion that made him suspect Spanish or French blood somewhere in her past. She had seen maybe twenty winters by her reckoning, fifteen less than he had. She was a short, comely woman with an oval face and a bright smile when she wasn't annoyed with him for some wrong, real or imagined. She was feisty at times, occasionally hardheaded, but always gutsy. Come hell, high water, or Pawnee, Pete knew Annie would stand beside him, as unfailing as the Rockies.

He had traded a couple of good ponies, a rifle, some powder, lead, and trinkets for her about five years back, on the Mora River where he'd spent the fall season trapping beaver with a handful of others out of Taos. At least trading was what the white men, the *tabbahos,* called it. Pete knew it was a little more complicated than that from the Comanche point of view. To a brownskin's mind, Pete had offered Annie's father the horses, rifle, and all the rest as proof of his ability to care for a wife. In return, and as a way of showing his love for his eldest daughter, Annie's father had given her the two ponies, and three more besides. Others—relatives and friends—had offered additional gifts—saddles, lodgeskins, kettles, knives, cloth and bedding—everything a woman needed to become a proper wife.

It had been a touch and go thing when the Comanches discovered them on the Mora. A lot of the younger bucks had wanted to kill them all right off, but Annie's grandfather, old Cordaro, coveted friendship with the *tabbahos,* and he'd persuaded the others to hold back. In time Pete learned it wasn't actually friendship the old warrior craved, but trade with the Americans. Better to fight the Mexicans, who were forbidden by law to bring guns and ammunition to the Comanches, than the whites, Cordaro had finally confided to Pete.

It was at Cordaro's lodge that Pete first saw Annie. She'd been called something else then, something long and hard to get his tongue around, and, translated, had turned out to be obscene, to boot. After they were married in a brief Comanche ceremony, he changed it to Annie, the name of the first girl he'd ever imagined himself in love with. His first Annie had been a whimsical, heavy-breasted corncracker down the road from his pa's farm back in Indiana, and he'd never regretted turning his back on her. But he liked the name. It brought back the fledgling feelings of adolescent love he'd felt then, a fragile tie to a past that hardly seemed real anymore.

His love for Annie, the Comanche, wasn't anything at all like what he'd felt for Annie, the towheaded farm girl. Hell, it hadn't even been love at first, he thought, smiling at the memory. It was the stirring in his loins that had first attracted him to her, her ability to tan a robe and keep a lodge that convinced him she had potential. Only with time had his feelings toward her softened into something he hadn't yet put a name to. She wasn't his first woman by a long shot. He'd had plenty of others—squaws and greasers, even a few powdered whores back in St. Louis, before coming west to be a mountain man. But he'd never felt for them what he'd eventually come to feel for Annie.

In spite of Red-Winged Woman's constant watching, it was Annie who spotted the Pawnees first. Perhaps she'd felt her husband's gaze on her back. Or maybe it was some sixth sense warning her of danger. Whatever the reason, she glanced to the rear, and Pete saw her eyes grow wide and her mouth part in a silent O that her hand quickly covered, lest her spirit flee. He twisted in the saddle to follow her gaze, and the muscles across his flat, hard stomach tightened.

"Hold up," Pete called ahead, swinging his little cream-colored buckskin around to face the half dozen or so Pawnees who'd topped a sandy rise nearly a mile behind them. He saw a puff of powder smoke blossom into the sky above the Indians, and heard the faint but distinctive boom of a smoothbore.

Charlie jogged War-Heels back to Pete's side, his expression grim. "Hard luck's doggin' our trail," he grumbled wearily.

Although Pete was inclined to agree, he remained silent as the warriors fanned out into a gallop. Even at this distance he could see the long fringe of their leggings and hunting shirts popping in the wind. The early morning light glinted off their shaven, oiled heads, accenting the grease-stiffened roaches that rose like black hedges from their foreheads and ran down toward the backs of their necks. He felt a twitch of annoyance at running into a bunch of Pawnees here, along the Arkansas and so close to the Rockies. This was Cheyenne country, rightly, though shared some with the Arapahos, Comanches, and even the Kiowas to the east. It was a long way from the humped-earth lodges along the Loop River, north of the Platte, that the Pawnees called home.

"The others can't be far off," Pete said at last, glancing toward the broken line of sandhills to the north that separated them from the Arkansas Valley. "Not if they meant to signal 'em with that shot."

Charlie drew a deep breath. "Well, best we cache while there's time."

"We could outrun 'em," Pete offered without enthusiasm. There was a chance they could, he knew, but it would likely mean losing most of their mules if they tried. They couldn't drag the pack animals along on lead ropes and make any time, and left to their own hook, the mules would just slow down until the Pawnees overtook them. He and Charlie had been out for a couple of months now, rambling the Front Range of the Rockies hunting deer and elk for their hides, and the mules were carrying full packs, several hundred dollars worth of buckskins, if they could get them to Taos. They had swung east, on their way to the Mexican settlements, to hunt buffalo along the Arkansas, needing, according to the women, better robes for the winter season.

"Reckon this child'd rather cache," Charlie replied solemnly. "There's broken country up ahead. Might be we can find us some canyon to duck into."

"Wagh!" Pete grunted in a fair imitation of a grizzly's warning snort. "Let's ride, amigo."

They whirled their ponies and set out at a hard gallop. The squaws rode before them, lashing the mules with their quirts and sharp, scolding tongues. The curs they kept mostly for the pot ran with them, dodging in and out among the flashing hooves, occasionally nipping at a hock or yipping shrilly when struck by an iron shoe.

From the top of the next rise they spotted a piñon-covered ridge flanking the mouth of an arroyo a couple of miles away, and Charlie whooped lustily. "Canyon country," he shouted. "By God, this coon knows the lay of the land, or he wouldn't say so."

They streaked down the long, gradual rise, raising a fog of red dust. The Pawnees topped the hill just as the trappers reached the bottom and leveled out toward the arroyo. The gap between them had closed by maybe a third now, and the Pawnees were whipping their ponies savagely in an effort to catch up. But the arroyo was less than a mile away, and Pete figured they would make it without trouble; their own ponies were strong and deep-bottomed, and there would be plenty of time if one of them didn't step in a badger's hole.

There would be a fight before the morning was out, and no way around that now. When they had been able to dodge the Pawnees until darkness covered their trail last night, Pete had figured they would gain such a lead the Indians would never catch up. He hadn't counted on poor luck putting the brownskins right back on their track before the sun had even cleared the horizon.

Pete ran his hand along the heavy, iron-mounted flintlock rifle cradled across the saddle in front of him. His fingers caressed the scratched and dinged curly-maple stock. It was funny, the sentiment a man could feel for a good rifle, one he knew well and trusted. In many ways it was a bond stronger than any other, stronger than what he felt for a horse or a dog, or even his woman. Pete had decided a long time ago that it was because a good rifle was what separated him and those he loved from the elements, that protected them all from marauders and thieves—two-legged or four—and kept them alive and warm through the harsh winter months. A man in the wilderness could survive without a horse or a dog or a woman, but his days were short-numbered without a good rifle. And his was a good one, a .54-caliber that was, he was fond of saying, capable of driving a nail at fifty yards.

"God*damn*!" Charlie bellowed, reining his appaloosa over to Pete's side. He pointed north with his fusil. "This child ain't never seen so much hard luck pounded into one skedaddle."

Pete's heart sank a little. Pawnees were spilling over the distant crest of a hogback ridge. Forty at least, he thought, and the arroyo too far away now, certain sure. "We ain't gonna make it," he shouted. "They'll cut us off before we get there."

"I can see that, goddamnit."

There was a tinge of panic in Charlie's words. Pete felt that same fear within himself, but forced it down. He didn't want to think about the odds, or about what would happen to Annie and Red-Winged Woman and the kids if the Pawnees got them. The women had quit hazing the mules as soon as they spotted the larger band of Pawnees, and pulled their mounts back to flank the short-coupled mustang ridden by the two girls. They were lashing at the pony's croup with their antler-handled quirts, still racing forward, but darting quick glances over their shoulders at their men for some sign of what they should do.

Pete hauled back on the buckskin's reins, drawing the gelding down to a lope. "There're too many to outrun. They'll drag us down in relays the way a pack of wolves drags down an elk. We're gonna have to hole up right here."

"Bring 'em in," Charlie shouted, motioning the women back. "We're gonna fort up."

Pete slid the buckskin to a halt, dropping to the ground and jerking his rawhide reata off the saddle. He looped one end around the buckskin's rear hock, then ran the rope around the saddle horn and down the near side, drawing the horse's leg up. It wasn't the first time the buckskin had been thrown that way, and he went down easily. Pete quickly hog-tied the gelding's legs, then cut the excess rope with his knife.

The mules pounded up, driven in by Charlie and the women. There wouldn't be time to throw them all. Those animals not used to it would fight too hard, burning up time they didn't have. Pete grabbed the halter of one of the pack animals and jammed his knife into the mule's throat. Blood spurted warmly over his hand and ran down his wrist. The mule squealed and reared back. Pete, keeping his grip on the mule's halter, jerked it roughly into position as the animal crashed to the ground, dead before it struck. Charlie threw his appaloosa and Pete tossed him his reata and grabbed another mule in the same motion. He slashed the animal's throat, guiding it down beside the first one. Annie threw and hog-tied the black-and-white pinto her father had given her, then quickly jabbed a second pony in the throat with her knife.

Pete could hear the growing thunder of the Pawnees' mounts as they swept down on them, the two groups merged into one now. The warriors were already yipping triumphantly. Red-Winged Woman cut her pony's throat, and it fell close to the horse Annie had killed. The baby swung wildly on Red-Winged Woman's back, wide-eyed but silent. The two girls, Magpie and Blossom, were frantically cutting the packs free and dragging them over to close the gaps between the dead animals. Pete dropped to his stomach and slid his rifle over the sloping withers of a dead mule. The Pawnees were still a little more than two hundred yards away, coming at them in a compact bunch. Pete held his sights high and slightly windward, and squeezed off a shot. Rolling onto his back, he thumbed the plug from the throat of his powder horn and tipped the spout over his palm.

"Yeow!" Charlie shouted, bellying down nearby. "That's makin' 'em come, by God."

Pete poured the dark granules of gunpowder into a cupped hand and funneled it down the rifle's muzzle. Next he thumbed in a round ball without bothering to patch it, and with his ramrod, drove the charge down the barrel. He pulled the cock holding the flint back to the half-cock position, and sprinkled priming powder into the pan. Snapping the frizzen closed, he called "Loaded!" and rolled back to his stomach. Charlie's fusil boomed, and a pony's front legs buckled, tossing a painted warrior over its head.

"You put one afoot," Pete said loud enough for Charlie to hear over the ringing in their ears.

Charlie laughed as he whipped his ramrod out. "This child can make a fuzzee shine, short or long," he crowed. "Just back me up the next time I see Sublette."

Pete grinned as he nuzzled the rifle to his shoulder. He knew Milton Sublette would never acknowledge Charlie's skill with a smoothbore. Not even if he saw it himself. It was a long-running but amiable feud between the two of them, going back to a three-hundred-yard kill Charlie had made on an elk several years before. It had been a scratch shot, pure luck, and no one had been more surprised than Charlie when it happened. But he wouldn't admit it now, and Milt wouldn't let it drop.

The Pawnees were still over a hundred yards away. Pete sighted on a broad, coppery chest near the front of the throng and set the rear trigger, then let his finger rest lightly on the front trigger, set to a hair's-breadth's pull.

"Loaded," Charlie called, and Pete stroked the trigger. The rifle rocked his shoulder, spitting out a roiling cloud of gray powder smoke that obliterated his view. It didn't matter. Charlie would tell him what he needed to know.

Annie scooted into the shelter of a dead mule and slanted the long-barreled fowler Pete had given her across her knees. "Load it with shot," Pete instructed in Spanish, the language they used most often with each other. Annie had learned it from a Mexican slave her father had captured from south of the del Norte, and Pete had picked it up around the Spanish settlements; he spoke only a smattering of Comanche, and Annie refused to learn English, claiming it hurt her jaws to shape such odd words.

"Do not waste words with foolish orders," Annie returned in Comanche, which she often reverted to when angry or frightened. "It is my gun. I will load it as I wish."

"It doesn't matter whose gun it is," Pete said, thumbing an unpatched ball down the muzzle of his rifle. "Just make sure you load it with shot. Then don't fire it until they're close enough to smell."

"I already smell them," Annie replied, wrinkling her nose. "A Pawnee stinks like dung." She tipped the powder horn over the muzzle and poured it directly into the barrel.

"Goddamnit, you're gonna overcharge it that way," Pete told her sharply.

"Now you tell me how to charge my gun. Do you think I am some foolish Mexican who does not know anything but to bob his head and jump like a puppy?" She slung the powder horn back on her hip and dug into her shooting bag for her shot pouch. That, too, she tipped over the muzzle.

Pete heard the trickle of buckshot rolling down the barrel and shook his head in exasperation. "If the Pawnees don't get you, that load will. You're gonna blow the damn barrel that way."

"It is—"

"I know," Pete hollered, ramming his ball home, then sliding the hickory rod clear. "It's your goddamn gun." His gaze swept the tiny fort. Red-Winged Woman was huddled beside Charlie, holding one of his pistols in both her hands. Blossom and Magpie were crouched behind her, while the baby cried indignantly from beneath a buffalo robe between a couple of packs. Pete's gaze returned to Annie, and he felt a moment of regret. All of a sudden, half a dozen dead mules didn't seem like much of a defense.

"Bastards ain't splitting," Charlie said tersely. "They aim to run right over us."

"I'm loaded," Pete told him.

Charlie must have heard something in Pete's voice. His finger eased off the fusil's trigger and his head swiveled toward his partner. "Hell, hoss, don't look so all-fired glum. If this coon's gotta go under, he can't think of any man he'd rather go under with." Then he flashed a grin. " 'Sides, this *baile* ain't over yet. Could be we got us another dance or two left."

Pete eyed the Indians dispassionately. They were less than a hundred yards away now, and closing fast. "It just sours my milk to get rubbed out by a Pawnee, is all," he said. "I never could abide the two-tongued bastards."

"Well, we ain't rubbed out yet, and this child aims to take him a lock or two of Pawnee hair 'fore he is." Charlie tucked the fusil against his shoulder. "Even as sorry a scalp as Pawnee hair—" The fusil roared, drowning out the rest of his words.

Pete laughed. "Skewered him clean, by God," he shouted. To the Pawnees, he added, "Wagh! Come on, you coyote-foaled sons-abitches. I wasn't wantin' to live forever anyway."

A rifle blossomed smoke from near the center of the charging Pawnees. Arrows began to flash across the sky and thud into the ground in front of them. A few struck the dead mules with soft, wet *thups*. Several fusils boomed in a ragged volley, and the air above the trappers buzzed angrily.

Pete fired, tumbling a warrior from the back of his pony, then dropped the rifle and pulled his pistol with his right hand, his heavy, long-bladed butcher knife appearing magically in his left. He could see the Pawnees clearly now—the whiteness of their teeth as they screamed their war cries, the obsidian glint of their eyes, the greasy sheen of their shaved scalps. Their faces were grisly with war paint.

Jumping to his feet, Pete howled his own war cry. *"Owgh, owgh, owgh, owgh,"* he screeched, dancing defiantly from one foot to the other. "Come on, you shit-tongued bastards. I'll set to with ye." He laughed as he leveled his pistol on a garishly painted warrior about forty yards away. An arrow pierced the coarse weave of his serape; he felt a sharp, slicing sting along the side of his right leg, just above his knee, and the warm trickle of flowing blood, but he didn't look down. Charlie's fusil and Pete's pistol roared as one. Then Red-Winged Woman's pistol barked, and Charlie pulled his second pistol and emptied it at the surging line of warriors. Their fire dropped several Pawnees, but it was the thunder of Annie's fowler that broke the charge. It bellowed with the deafening blast of a cannon, the barrel bursting as Pete had predicted it would. Shards of hot iron flew in every direction. Red-Winged Woman screeched as she dove to cover her children, and Charlie swore as a finger-sized piece of the barrel drilled into the dirt beside his knee.

But it was the Pawnees who suffered the brunt of the fowler's explosion. At less than twenty yards away when Annie pulled the trigger, the lead shot and iron barrel fragments cut a deadly swath. Three warriors were blasted from the backs of their ponies, and two horses went down, screaming hideously in pain. Other horses began to buck, forcing their riders to drop their weapons and cling desperately to their rough-framed wooden saddles. A handful of Pawnees, only a handful, paused long enough to rescue those who were unhorsed or only slightly injured. The rest wheeled their mounts and fled in terror. In less than a minute the prairie before them was empty except for the dead and seriously wounded.

"Jesus Christ," Charlie murmured in awe, standing to peer after the retreating Indians. Red-Winged Woman was comforting the girls, who were crying at last. Annie lay on her back, staring dazedly at the sky. Pete knelt swiftly by her side and laid a hand against her shoulder.

"Annie? Annie, are you all right?" He switched to Spanish and repeated the question.

Annie blinked and rolled her eyes toward him.

"Are you all right?"

"*Qué?*" Annie said, the Spanish word for "What?"

"I asked if you were all right," Pete said, louder.

"Goddamnit gun no shoot good."

Pete blinked, then a smile spread across his face. "You spoke English."

She glared at him, shaking her head. "*Qué?*" she repeated, but Pete just laughed. He retrieved his rifle and began to reload, patching the ball with a thin piece of greased antelope leather this time.

The Pawnees had regrouped about four hundred yards away, sitting their ponies in a tight group and talking angrily among themselves, hands flashing with agitation. A couple of boys, no more than fifteen or sixteen, left the main party and circled wide around the trappers. The mules that hadn't been killed or thrown had stampeded, and were standing about a quarter of a mile away, their huge, floppy ears canted forward as the two Pawnees rode toward them. The youths gathered the mules and drove them back to the main group.

"Goddamn traitors," Charlie grumbled. "If it was me tryin' to round 'em up like that, they'd just stand there like fence posts. Either that or run."

"You just ain't learned to sweet-talk a mule yet," Pete replied. "There's a knack to it. Maybe someday you can get a Pawnee to show you how it's done."

"This child'd rather swallow a handful of elk shit than anything a Pawnee laid out," Charlie flared.

The Pawnees began to break up. A delegation of six or eight older warriors rode toward the trappers at a walk. They stopped just out of rifle range, and one of them stood in his stirrups to sign by hand, asking permission to retrieve their dead.

Pete laughed, answering with his own hands: *You give us our mules first.*

No. We will keep mules. Too many of our men have died.

Pete replied, *We will take the scalps of your dead, and they will wander forever on the Other Side without hair. A warrior without hair is like a man without balls; he is like a woman.*

The Pawnees conferred among themselves for a couple of minutes, then the warrior stood in his stirrups once more, signing, *You may keep the scalps. We would rather have the mules.* That said, he reined his pony around and galloped back to the main party with the others.

"Now see, that's what I was talking about," Pete said dryly, butting his rifle between his moccasins and watching the Indians drive the stolen mules toward the ridge of hills to the north. "A Pawnee ain't got no more honor'n a snake."

Annie was sitting up, rubbing her shoulder and staring skeptically at the ruined fowler lying beside her. Red-Winged Woman tossed the robe off the baby and lifted him out of his cradleboard. Pete watched silently as she cooed to him, then lowered a shoulder of her dress to expose a milk-swollen breast. The sound of the baby's nursing filled the little fort.

"Wagh," Pete murmured.

Charlie grinned. "This coon's thinkin' Little Pete might grow up to run buffler with his ol' daddy, after all."

"He might," Pete acknowledged, turning once more to watch the Pawnees disappear into the hills. Aye, he might at that.

CHAPTER THREE

Eli Cutler halted his sorrel at the mouth of the canyon and stared wearily across the village of San Fernandez de Taos, sprawled gracelessly below him. Evening shadows softened the squared-off adobe buildings, shrouding the narrow, winding streets in gloom. Tiny pockets of window light punctured the darkness, reminding him of splatters of butter against a dark canvas. A breeze, blowing off the purpled sage plain to the west, carried with it a lingering trace of the day's warmth, along with the scent of the village itself—piñon smoke, livestock, dust, manure, green hides, exotic spices, rotting meat, and bubbling chili. It was, after the clean, sweeping zephyrs of the plains he had just crossed, a rank and bitter stench, but familiar, and comforting because of it.

It was good to be home again.

He lifted the sorrel's reins and said "Hup" in a dry, cracked voice. The horse splashed across the shallow Taos River, the two pack animals following compliantly, without lead. The trail widened as it neared the village, becoming a rutted street. He passed a few homes—small, squat adobe structures set back among the cottonwoods that flanked the river—surrounded by tethered goats and pecking, complaining chickens. Oxen, burros, and an occasional mule chewed sleepily on handfuls of dried corn shucks inside picket corrals behind the houses. Mangy, half-wild dogs barked frantically at his passing, but barking, snarling dogs were as much a part of the daily routine of Taos as the choking dust of summer, and no one paid them any mind or came out to see what the commotion was about.

Eli followed the hesitant strumming of a guitar to a small, box-like house on the outskirts of town. "*Qué pasa,*" he said to the gray-ing Mexican who sat with his back to the adobe's wall, guitar in lap.

"*Buenos noches,*" the Mexican replied. Taking in Eli's slumped, dusty appearance and the stock, gaunt from their long trek across the plains, he added, "You would like a drink, perhaps? A little *pulque* to wash away the dryness."

"*Gracias,* no. Just some information. I'm looking for a man named Silas McClure. He's putting an outfit together for the mountains."

"*Sí,* I know of this man. He has rented a building and some corrals north of town. A clerk, I think. Always writing." He made a quick, squiggling motion through the air, in imitation of a man using a pen. "North of the plaza, *señor*. The east side."

"*Gracias,*" Eli replied and started to rein away.

"You have a place to stay?" the Mexican inquired. "I would offer my own poor home, if not. My woman is a good cook. *Fajitas* and *tortillas* and *chili colorado* that warms a man like good *pulque*. Only *dos pesos* a week."

"I'll keep it in mind," Eli said, nudging the sorrel with his spurs.

"It is a fair price," the Mexican called after him. "You will find none cheaper."

Eli kept riding, and after a minute the soft strumming of the guitar picked up again, a little stronger now, a little faster.

Nearer the plaza the casas were built closer together, bigger and better made. Most were hidden behind heavy wooden gates and high adobe walls crowned with a thorny ridge of prickly pear to discourage scaling—a remnant of the days when Taos was raided frequently by the Apaches and Navajos. These were the homes of traders, merchants, and politicians—the upper echelon who could afford to hide the plain, mud-bricked walls of their houses behind coarsely-woven sheets of *jerga,* or dull layers of milk paint.

The iron-shod clopping of Eli's animals echoed hollowly between the high walls. The sorrel's ears pricked forward when they came in sight of the plaza. A few vendors still lingered near its center, hawking their wares in the flickering light of torches, but most of them had already packed up and gone home, taking with them their strings of peppers, their trussed chickens and corded piñonwood and baskets of wheat and maize. Nearest Eli, bundles of *hojas*—the dried leaves and shucks of corn that furnished the people of Mexico with the paper they fashioned into cigarillos, fodder for their stock, and the stuffing they crammed inside their *jerga* mattresses to soften the hard-packed dirt floors of their homes—were stacked carelessly close to a sparking fire over which tortillas warmed on a flat griddle.

Eli halted at the edge of the plaza, his gaze lifting past the old crone watching over the tortillas to take in the rest of the square. The cherry glow of cigarillos dotted the blackness beneath the porticos, and the hitching rails in front of the cantinas and monte parlors were filled. Laughter erupted from across the plaza like the rattle of distant gunfire, and a trio of drunken *soldados* staggered out of a cantina and weaved their way down the street. Eli eyed the cantinas wistfully for a moment, but finally turned away.

Several blocks north of the plaza he came to a long, low-roofed building set back from the street. A pole corral butted to one side of the warehouse churned liquidly with milling animals, and a number of horses whickered curiously as Eli rode into the dark yard. Through an opened doorway he could see a short, round-bellied man in a blue military jacket and forage cap sitting within a wavering pool of candlelight, scribbling in a leatherbound ledger. From time to time the man would pause in his writing to stare reflectively across the room, then dip his quill into a smear of powdered ink and go back to writing.

McClure had been a sergeant in the Dragoons, according to Girardin, but had resigned after his transfer to the Quartermaster Department in St. Louis. Before that he had spent a good part of his military career on the frontier of a burgeoning nation. He had ridden with Major Stephen H. Long to the Rocky Mountains in 1819 and 1820, had escorted peace commissioners to the Comanches, Kiowas, Osages, Caddos, and Wichitas, and helped run down the cutthroat whiskey peddlers who were constantly slipping into Indian Territories to trade their contraband poteen for furs and horses. He had spent considerable time patrolling the Santa Fe Trail from Leavenworth to the Mexican border on the Arkansas River, and knew that part of the country intimately.

"A skilled and efficient man," Girardin had insisted. "A man of integrity and remarkable energy."

Listening to the old Frenchman expound on McClure's abilities, Eli had envisioned a man of strapping, rough-hewn strength and un-

flappable character. Watching this stubby, barrel-framed man with
his pudgy, whiskey-reddened cheeks and quick, choppy movements
brought a smile to Eli's face. But he was reminded also of his
mother's old adage: Never judge the strength of a man by his physical appearance.

McClure must have sensed his presence. Or perhaps the stirring of
the remuda inside the corral finally caught his attention. He looked
up abruptly, his gaze seeming to penetrate the thick evening shadows. Eli dismounted and looped the sorrel's reins over one of the
poles at the corral. His long, heavy-roweled spurs jingled musically
as he walked across the yard to the door.

McClure was still sitting at the table when Eli entered, but he'd
moved the candle to one side so that it wasn't shining directly into
his eyes, and his right hand was hidden from sight.

In one of the far rear corners, a boy of fourteen or fifteen was folding buffalo robes from a mountain of loose hides and stacking them
alongside several bales of beaver pelts. Extra gear—saddles, traps,
dry goods, all the things a brigade would need to spend a season in
the mountains—was arranged along the walls in neat piles. A narrow
cottonwood-framed bunk and a corner fireplace with a tin coffeepot
sitting on the hearth constituted the living quarters. The dirt floor
was hard and clean, the rafters free of cobwebs. Eli's gaze swept the
room once, then came back to McClure.

"What can I do for you?" McClure asked.

"You Silas McClure?"

"I am." There was a trace of suspicion in McClure's voice, but
nothing uncalled for. Taos was a rough town, and a smart man didn't
take anything for granted.

"My name's Eli Cutler, just in from St. Louis." He pulled a package wrapped in oilcloth from the fold of his buckskin jacket and laid
it on the table in front of McClure. "Maybe you should read that top
letter first," he said.

But McClure didn't pick the package up right away; he didn't
even glance at it. He examined Eli with the same probing intensity
that Eli had studied him with a few minutes before, taking in the
trail-worn, fringed buckskin trousers, the smoked, Indian-tanned
jacket that extended below his hips, the faded calico shirt and the
plain, rawhide-soled Pima moccasins. His gaze seemed to linger

longest on the dusty, broad-brimmed wool-felt hat that had been white and stiffly new when Eli left the Missouri settlements.

Apparently satisfied with what he saw, McClure brought his right hand from beneath the table and shamelessly set a five-shot pepper-box pistol beside the ledger. Without speaking, he unwrapped the oilskin and broke the wax seal of the top envelope, fishing from it a single sheet of foolscap. He scanned the letter quickly, noted the date and signature at the bottom of the page, then went back to the top to read it a second time. When he had finished, he slowly refolded the letter and put it back in its envelope.

Eli watched McClure curiously, wondering how he would take this news of his demotion and the unexpected introduction of a new boss. But McClure seemed as unmoved as he had been at Eli's appearance at the door. There was a white, ornately carved clay pipe sitting beside a leather tobacco pouch at one corner of the table. McClure picked up both and calmly filled the pipe's bowl. He lit it with a sliver of pitch ignited from the candle, then leaned back and hooked his thumbs in the waistband of his wool trousers.

"Well, I won't deny a certain degree of regret," McClure spoke at last, tipping his head back to avoid the blue curl of smoke that rose from his pipe. "Although I knew Mr. Girardin wanted a more experienced man to lead the brigade, I was rather looking forward to the opportunity, if it came to that. A new adventure, I suppose. But!" He stood and extended his hand. "Welcome to the Girardin Shipping and Transport Company, Mr. Cutler."

They shook, Eli with relief, and McClure motioned toward a chair sitting against the wall, straight-backed and uncomfortable-looking. Eli hooked it around and sat with his arms folded over the back.

"A drink?" McClure asked. "A toast to the GS&T, its entry into the Rocky Mountain fur trade, and the glorious days to come?"

"*Bueno,*" Eli said, grinning. "I reckon a drink would cut the dust some."

McClure brought a clay jug and a couple of tin cups from an open-topped box beside his chair. "From El Paso," he explained with overdrawn seriousness, pulling the cork with a shallow *pop*. "I feared the worst when I found only *pulque* and that hideous brew the trappers call Taos Lightning served at the local taverns. Then I discovered Pass Brandy, and decided the frontier would be endurable after all."

Eli chuckled, accepting the cup McClure offered. He took only a sip, letting the brandy settle like a solid ball of warmth in his stomach. It had a slightly sweet taste, and was weak when compared to other whiskeys, but he hadn't eaten since a light noon lunch, and he knew it would pack a punch on an empty stomach.

McClure drank deeply, with a soldier's appreciation of rare luxury, but set his cup aside without emptying it. Returning the pipe to his mouth, McClure said, "I'll need to read the rest of Mr. Girardin's dispatches. Most will probably pertain to the Santa Fe trade, and be of no concern with the trapping interests of the company." He hesitated briefly, then added, "You realize that although you'll command the brigade, I'll still outrank you in company matters."

Eli studied the brandy in his cup, swirling it with a gentle dip of his wrist.

"Understand that I have no intention of undermining your authority with the men," McClure went on. "But my primary responsibility is to the company, a sort of overseer, if you will. It's what I was hired for. You'll need to consult me on a daily basis as to your intentions. I'll want to know—"

"Uh-uh," Eli interjected without looking up.

McClure paused. "Uh-uh?"

"Not on the trail, Mr. McClure. I was hired by Girardin to guide a brigade of trappers into the mountains. I won't have my decisions questioned by the company clerk. You'll keep a journal, tabs on where we go and how well we do. Consult that at the end of the season and make your judgment then. But on the trail my word is the law." He looked up then, meeting McClure's scowl without emotion. "The only law."

McClure's lips thinned. "If there is some question concerning my position within the company, I can assure you I have Mr. Girardin's complete confidence."

Eli made a flat, cutting motion with his hand. "Ain't a question of position," he said. "I was hired to do a job, and I can't do it without free rein."

"I was also hired to do a job," McClure said stiffly. "I'm chief agent for the Western Department of the GS&T. That includes all levels of the Western Department. My orders come directly from Mr. Girardin."

Eli nodded toward Girardin's letter. "Reread it," he said flatly.

They locked gazes, and for a moment neither man spoke. Then McClure's face relaxed, his lips curling slightly upward in what may or may not have been a smile. "No, there's no need to reread it. Mr. Girardin was, as usual, typically vague. It's his method of delegating authority without granting carte blanche. So command as you see fit, and I'll stay out of your way unless I deem it absolutely necessary."

Eli shrugged. It wasn't much of a compromise, but he decided it was probably as close as they'd get. Surprisingly, he found himself admiring McClure's stubbornness. Changing the subject, he said, "Who have you signed on?"

McClure leaned back in his chair. "I'm afraid most of the old hands have already committed to other outfits."

"You've got a few, though?"

"Some." He backpaged through his ledger until he came to a list of names written on a single page. He stabbed the top of the list with a blunted finger and slowly drew it down the page. "Caleb Underwood, a freetrapper I've hired for wages. Remi LeBlanc, Cork-Eye Weathers, and an Iroquois half-breed named Johnny Two-Dogs, all working for a percentage. Those four plus a Frenchman named Pierre Turpin, who'll cook and help care for the plews, and Juan Vidales." He looked up questioningly. "I assume Mr. Girardin told you about Vidales?"

"He the Mexican who survived the Reed massacre?"

"He is, and it took some persuading to convince him to go out again."

"Well, it's a small party, all right," Eli conceded. He had hoped for at least three times that many men. "Maybe I can turn up a few more. There're always some who'll come dribbling in from the summer hunt too late to put out with the bigger outfits. We could use more swampers, too. Vidales ain't gonna be able to keep up with his chores and take care of all the plews the boys bring in, not even if Turpin helps out. You got mules and ponies enough?"

"All but Turpin and Vidales will furnish their own mounts. The company has half a dozen horses and twenty stout mules. You saw them in the corral outside. I'd like to have another half-dozen pack animals to bring in the furs Reed supposedly cached."

"You doubt Vidales' story?"

"Unfortunately, no. I made some inquiries about Big Tom Reed while I was in Santa Fe, and I'm convinced he's capable of such action. Reed is a cold-blooded man who has traded in scalps and Indian slaves. Furthermore, Vidales would have nothing to gain by lying, and everything to lose. Certainly Reed would make a formidable enemy."

Eli was silent a moment, considering the implications. He found it hard to believe a man could betray his comrades the way Vidales accused Reed of doing. But greed was a powerful influence, and the mountains attracted a rough crowd. It was possible, he supposed, no matter how distasteful. "Where is Reed now?" he asked.

"He turned up in Santa Fe last summer, guiding a trader's caravan to Chihuahua. He passed through Taos again a couple of weeks ago, with a license to trap the Gila River country. He had three men with him. At least two of them have reputations as hardcases—scalp hunters from the Sonora region. The third may have been a Mexican servant, a swamper. They took traps, and four pack animals apiece."

"Four?" Eli cocked an eyebrow. That was about two more than a man usually needed during a season, even with good luck. Taking along a couple of extra head wasn't unusual; the mountains were hard on stock, and any outfit generally lost a few head to starvation or the brownskins, but Reed had taken along too many to be accounted for that way.

It puzzled Eli a little that Reed had bothered with a license at all. Although it was required by Mexican law, it was something most of the smaller outfits chose to ignore. A license cost money, plus it assured taxes would have to be paid on the returned pelts. As a rule it was easier and cheaper to just slip out of town without telling anyone where you were going or when you'd be back. Not that a license meant that much. A man could turn off just about anywhere after leaving the settlements. Likely that was what Reed had in mind, Eli thought. It would be a handy dodge to throw off suspicion, and account for the furs he brought in, as well.

"That much is reliable information," McClure continued. "I turned up some additional news that's interesting, although I couldn't verify it. Reed apparently had a Shoshone squaw that some say was either a sister or sister-in-law to the renegade Bad Gocha. If that's true, it would provide a link between Reed and a known killer of whites. It would also lend credibility to Vidales' story. Reed claims he never knew who attacked them, but Vidales says it was Bad Gocha's bunch, and that the trappers were in their village at the time."

Eli's fingers tightened around his cup. That was just about the way it had happened with Provost, too. "Does Reed know about Vidales?" he asked.

"Not as far as I know, although it's possible. Juan and Cork-Eye are at the village of Río Colorado, purchasing pemmican from the Mexican buffalo hunters up there. Reed was only in Taos a day."

Eli was quiet a minute, putting it all together in his mind, what he knew of Reed himself, and what old Sylvester Girardin had told him back in St. Louis, as well as what he'd learned from McClure tonight. Mostly it added up against Reed, but there were still a few pieces of the puzzle missing, things that didn't add up.

"Juan says the furs were buried near the Salt Lake," McClure intruded softly. "He says they trapped through the parks first—Bayou Salade and Middle Park, then up through New Park to follow the North Platte out of the mountains. From there Reed led them almost due west. They trapped the Green and the Bear rivers for a while, but kept running into Ashley's old crowd, Bill Sublette, Jed Smith, and Dave Jackson's outfit now, so they cached what they had and wintered near the Lake. They were on the Green River, south of the Uintas, when the massacre occurred. Are you familiar with that country?"

Eli nodded. There weren't many parts of the Southern Rockies he didn't know well by now. "I've tramped it a time or two," he replied.

McClure nodded and drained his cup.

"Have you got the paperwork straightened out in Santa Fe yet?" Eli asked.

McClure grimaced, as if the brandy had turned suddenly sour. "Yes, damn them," he rasped. "I felt it was important to maintain honest relations among the local politicos, in the interest of future growth, so I applied for all the necessary passports and permits." His nostrils flared. "There is more honor among bandits than there is within the local government."

Eli laughed. "How much did it cost?"

"The usual fees, plus fifty pesos as assurance the applications wouldn't become lost in bureaucracy."

"Fifty pesos ain't bad. Some of the bigger outfits have to pay a percentage."

"It was hinted at, I can assure you. But I thought it would be cheaper this way. Do you disagree?"

"No. Not necessarily. Less trouble sometimes to pay a percentage, is all. How we fixed for supplies?"

"A little short," McClure replied with a wry smile. "But nothing a side trip to the Cimarron wouldn't cure."

"*Bueno.*" Eli nodded approvingly. It meant McClure had cached some provisions on the east side of the Sangre de Cristo Mountains before reporting to the customs house in Santa Fe, to avoid paying a tax on them. It was a skinning to the local government, but Eli figured the Mexican government could stand the loss; it was already an old hand at skinning, and would understand. A lot of the older outfits coming in from Missouri cached a part of their goods that way, but it surprised him a little that McClure had thought of it. Generally a man didn't, his first time out.

Eli emptied his cup and stood. "It's been a long trip," he said. "This coon's ready for his robes."

"You'll be around tomorrow?"

"Yeah. I'll make a quick *paseo* through town to see who's in. I'd still like to have a bigger outfit, but we're set now with who we've got if we have to. I'll also want to have a look at the stock, and know exactly what you've got cached on the Cimarron, but that can all wait until tomorrow." He paused, studying the man before him, the short, thickset body and the weathered face already showing signs of a fondness for brandy, but firm yet, and confident. He decided he was going to like Silas McClure. He was green to the mountains, but it was a greenness balanced by his experience on the frontier with the Dragoons. And if McClure had his weaknesses, he appeared to be a man capable of handling them.

Eli went outside and gathered the sorrel's reins. McClure followed as far as the door. "Do you have a place to stay?" he asked.

"Maybe," Eli said, stepping into the saddle. He'd been asking himself that same question ever since he'd left St. Louis. He gave McClure a small wave and rode out of the yard, the pack animals following reluctantly, snorting their displeasure at leaving the horses and mules inside the corral.

He skirted the plaza and rode south out of town. On his left the foothills of the Sangre de Cristos rose abruptly, appearing, in the deceptive moonlight, smoothly rounded and unblemished. Just above the base of the nearest foothill a single adobe shack squatted on a niche of flat ground. Its small windows were dark, the stubby chimney without smoke. A footpath linked the trail he was on now to the solitary house, like a pale ribbon snaking through the sage. Eli halted at the foot of the path and studied the house contemplatively. He listened for the muted tinkling of a goat's bell, the soft clucking of chickens as they settled in their roosts, but the night was silent; not even a breeze whispered in the sage.

He wondered idly if she had moved on, or found another man. A lot of things could have happened in the months he'd been gone. He remembered the look on her face as he'd ridden out the last time, the discontented angle of her mouth and the flat, silent reproach in her eyes. He supposed he couldn't blame her for her feelings. Lord knew he wasn't much of a husband, not even by the slack standards of common-law marriage that they'd adopted. Always putting out for the mountains, gone for weeks and, increasingly as the streams closer to the Mexican settlements became trapped out, months at a time. He told himself it didn't matter, that there were plenty of others who would be glad to be courted by a handsome American rich in furs and traps and fine horses. He could damn near have his pick around the settlements, if he didn't decide to find himself some willing squaw up in the mountains. But somehow, without having actually thought it all the way through, he knew he didn't want anyone else. He wasn't sure just what it was that attracted him to Consuelo Aragon, but he did know that whatever it was, it suited him just fine.

He reined onto the footpath. "*Vamonos, Poco Rojo,*" he told the sorrel. "Let's go see if anyone's home."

CHAPTER FOUR

The brassy light of the midday sun distorted the shape of the remuda grazing on the flat plain, slimming and stretching into impossible heights the torsos of the three vaqueros who lazily circled the herd. Beyond the herd, the dusty green line of cottonwoods bordering the Pecos River seemed to shimmer in the searing heat. A ribbon of smoke curled from among the paling autumn leaves like a shallow channel gouged into the surface of a washed-out blue china plate.

Just below the crest of a rocky ridge nearly a half mile away, Mateo Chavez studied the loosely bunched remuda thoughtfully. He was hunkered in the shade of a sloping boulder, a misshapen corn-husk cigarillo canted from a corner of his mouth. He knew the others were impatient to get on with it, to either go on down and do what they had come to do, or return to the little brush jacal they had constructed in the hills behind them, where the jug of pulque that made the hours pass quicker waited. Mateo knew they didn't truly understand the consequences of what they were about to do. For them, it was still a lark, an adventure in which they saw no real danger, and only enough excitement to make it interesting. They didn't understand the unbending pride that guided their uncle's— Mateo's father's—life. But Mateo did, and he knew that for what they were about to do, Don Julio Chavez would never forgive them.

"Mateo. What do we wait for?" Tomas Ortiz asked his cousin. "Those lazy sons of whores who watch your father's horses have not even seen us, and we sit here in plain sight."

A smile cracked the hard countenance of Mateo's face, and his black, mestizo eyes narrowed.

Jorge Rodolso echoed his cousin's complaint. "We bake our asses in the sun while those fools sleep in their saddles."

Like the others—Tomas and Jorge's brother, Antonio—Jorge spoke only Spanish. They had never bothered to learn the language of the Americans. Only Mateo understood the importance of learning to speak English; only he, among all the clans of the Chavezes and Ortizes and Rodolsos who lived south of the village of San Miguel, sensed both the dangers and the advantages of the foreign traders who passed regularly along the Santa Fe Trail. And Mateo knew that if a man wanted to avoid those dangers while reaping the benefits, he would have to learn the language.

"Mateo!"

"You are fools if you think we have not been spotted," Mateo replied. "My father would not hire such men, and the Apaches would not allow them to keep their scalps if he had. They see us. They only wait to see what we will do."

"What will we do?" Tomas asked in exasperation.

"We should wait for darkness," Jorge said. He pushed away from the shade of a piñon and scooted down to Mateo's side. "What do you say, Mateo? In darkness we will slip down like the puma and take what we want."

While Mateo could appreciate the simplicity of Jorge's plan, an unaccountable stubbornness prevented him from acknowledging it. "No. That is what they will expect. Tonight not even a puma could slip down there."

"Then what?" Antonio asked, his patience wearing thin in the blasting heat.

An idea flashed through Mateo's mind; he grasped it before it could flit away, shaped it even as he spoke. "We will stampede the remuda now, in daylight. They will not expect that. We will take only a few head, no more than twenty or thirty, and the vaqueros will not follow. They will be too busy chasing after the rest of the remuda to worry about us."

"*Carajo,*" Tomas growled. "By tomorrow night we will be in Santa Fe, lying drunk between the thighs of a whore, eh?" He laughed. "Yes. I like that. A chance to drink and fuck before Don Julio puts a noose around our necks."

Worry flickered across Antonio's face. "He would not hang us, Mateo? Your father. We are family."

"No," Mateo conceded bitterly. "Don Julio would not hang his son, or the sons of his sisters. Probably he will only brand us as thieves."

"Like Jesus?" Antonio whispered.

"Yes. Like Jesus. On the cheek, so that everyone can see." Silence greeted his words, and Mateo's anger flared. "You knew this," he accused, swinging around to face his cousins. "You know what my father is like."

"Yes," Tomas said. "But it is as Antonio says. We are family."

"We steal his horses," Mateo replied bluntly. "He will brand us if he catches us."

"Then, Mother of God, why do we do this?" Tomas asked.

"Because we are tired of being treated as less than men," Mateo said. He lifted his *escopeta*—the bell-mouthed, smooth-bored long gun his father had given him—and shook it for emphasis. "Because we are tired of being treated like fools and slaves, and given our fathers' worn-out trash as our own, while they ride silver-mounted saddles and carry fine British muskets." His voice lowered without softening. "We will take these horses that should be ours anyway, and buy goods that we will trade to the Comanches, and when we return we will be rich. We will have pesos and buy more goods and go back to the Comanche to become even richer." Mateo swiveled on the balls of his feet, staring once more at the grazing remuda. "We do it to become men."

Jorge licked nervously at his lips. "Mateo is right," he said. "If we do not do this thing now, we will always be our fathers' sons, and never true men."

Tomas was less enthusiastic. "All right," he said simply. "We have come this far."

Mateo glanced at Antonio. At fifteen, he was the youngest of the four, but not by much. Antonio gulped once, then nodded.

"Good." Mateo turned back to study the plain below them. "I have been thinking. They know we are after the herd. If we leave now, they will think we will return tonight, and maybe relax their guard this afternoon." He pointed with his chin. "To the north. See, where the ridge comes out from this one? We will approach the herd from the other side. Tomas and I will stampede the remuda. We will wave our serapes and scream like souls lost in hell. Jorge, you and Antonio will cut out as many head as you can and drive them up the arroyo below us. Take them to Santa Fe as if the Apaches were after you. Tomas and I will make sure the herd is truly stampeded, then we will catch up. But do not wait for us, or worry about strays. Just ride hard for Santa Fe. Understand?"

"Yes," Tomas said.

"Yes," Jorge and Antonio echoed.

Mateo smiled grimly. "By the time they regather the remuda, we will be far away. They will send a rider to the rancho and that will take at least a day. There will be time." He stood, flinging the cigarillo away. "Let's go," he said tightly.

He had been christened Mateo Estevan Phillipe Rodolso Chavez eighteen summers before, birthed on a shaggy buffalo robe somewhere along the Canadian River, where his parents, along with most of the others from the rancho below San Miguel, had gone in search of buffalo. Eighteen years ago his father had not been the man he was today—neither as rich nor as politically powerful. But he had been well on his way.

They were *ciboleros,* his family and the families of the Rodolsos and the Ortizes—the mestizo buffalo hunters of *Nuevo Mexico,* who each year ventured boldly into the heartland of the *Comancheria* in search of the great herds. It could be said that they traversed the Comanche's hunting grounds boldly because there was no other way they could take their squawking, creaking, dry-axled *carretas* into the land of their enemies. Their heavy-horned oxen plodded at a snail's pace beneath tawny clouds of dust that could be seen for miles, while their slabbed, cottonwood wheels cut trails into the sod that could be followed through the blackest night. They traveled together for protection, flanked by lancers—the young, hot-blooded *cazadores* who actually hunted the buffalo—and others of their rancho and other ranchos and pueblos, adding their own lances and bows, rusty *escopetas* and muskets, to the caravan's skimpy defense.

They hunted for robes that they traded to the American traders, and dried meat and tongues that went to Mexico City. But mostly they hunted for the glory and thrill of the chase. Among their own, at least, they were a proud and arrogant people, a rung above even the Comanche traders, the *Comancheros,* whom Don Julio despised. There was no dignity in a trader's life, according to Don Julio, no test of courage or skill. Only the *cibolero* dared challenge the frenzied herds, driving his mount among the stampeding buffalo, dodging and thrusting with his lance until his clothing was spotted with blood and his curved iron lance head glistened with it. A man, a true man, rode among the herds. Only women—even those who dressed like men and shaved like men and called themselves men—walked beside their carts with the dogs and children. Such was Don Julio's opinion, and such was his influence in that part of Mexico that few men openly disagreed.

Such, also, was the environment in which Mateo had been raised. His father's word was law. Not just within the family, but throughout the unnamed settlement where the Chavezes and the Rodolsos and Ortizes lived. Even in San Miguel and Santa Fe, the word of Don Julio Chavez was known and respected. And Mateo Estevan Phillipe Rodolso Chavez? Ah, he was Don Julio's son. Always, he was Don Julio's son. That had been title enough for Mateo's brothers, but it wasn't enough for Mateo. Not anymore. Since he was ten he had longed to be free of his father's shadow, to be his own man, respected for his own accomplishments. At fourteen he had discovered another desire, to be called *Don* Mateo, and to have the peons sweep their hats off in respect when he rode past, as they did for his father.

At seventeen he had raised his *escopeta* to his shoulder, sighting down its long, rust-pitted barrel at Don Julio's advancing form. It had been dusk then, and Mateo had just come in from the sage-covered plain behind the rancho with a pair of rabbits dangling from his hand. His father, crossing the courtyard, had been unaware of Mateo's presence in the shadows beside the corn bin. Mateo's finger had caressed the weapon's trigger, stroking it as he might have stroked the velvety muzzle of a favorite horse. But he hadn't pulled the trigger, and his father soon disappeared into the shadows of the family portico.

The ease with which the long, awkward gun had come up had been shocking to Mateo, but it was the desire to pull the trigger that truly frightened him. For days afterward his feelings had spun in turmoil. Then, perhaps a week later, Don Julio had discovered him in one of the back corrals, grooming a yearling filly out of his father's big gray stud. For some reason perhaps not even Don Julio could explain, the sight inflamed the elder man. Enraged, he vaulted the railing with a bullish roar. Mateo knew what to expect; it wasn't the first time he had heard that sound. He dropped his brush and sprinted for the far side of the corral, the safety of the empty plains beyond. His father raced after him, bellowing for him to stop, his quirt slashing the still air.

Mateo leaped for the fence but his moccasins slipped on the bottom rail and shot through, and the momentum jerked his hands from the top rail. He landed on his back with a loud *woof,* the air driven from his lungs, the scud of rosy evening clouds spinning crazily. His father's blurred form appeared above him. There was a whistle of air, and then Mateo's cheek exploded with pain. White lances darted across his vision, blinding him. His cheek went numb, but he could feel the warm trickle of blood across his neck.

Mateo tried to roll beneath the bottom rail, but his father was too quick. He jumped Mateo's body, blocking his escape and laughing harshly at so easily outfoxing his son. His quirt was a blur as it cut the air, welting the flesh of Mateo's arms, shoulders, and back. Crying in fury and shame, half blinded by pain, Mateo tried again to reach the fence and the tall sage beyond, where he knew his father wouldn't follow. He grasped the lower rail, and the quirt sliced the thin flesh of his knuckles. Mateo screamed and jerked his hand back. His father was breathing hard now, winded by his rage. He stepped back to catch his breath, and Mateo made a final, desperate lunge for the fence. He rolled beneath the lower rail and kept on rolling until he was safely out of his father's reach. His father stood leaning against the fence, laughing softly, his hard, glittering eyes boring into his son, forcing Mateo's gaze toward the ground. Bruised and bloodied, Mateo rose to his feet and stumbled into the sage. From the courtyard, the silent, frozen stares of the others—the Rodolsos and Ortizes, even his own family—followed woodenly.

After that, Mateo's hatred of his father didn't surprise him anymore. But neither did the urge to kill him return. Mateo wanted more than just his father's life now. He wanted a revenge that could be savored, to inflict a wound that would never heal. Stealing a part of his father's remuda would be only the first step.

"Maybe we will go to Mexico City with our money, eh?" Tomas said. He was tightening his cinch, laughing and joking nervously, revealing the tension they all felt.

Mateo unrolled his serape from behind his saddle and shook it out. Had there been time, he would have preferred a puma's hide to wave in the faces of the remuda. Fresh-skinned, its scent would have stricken the horses and mules with terror. But they would have to make do with their serapes. Already Mateo had the uneasy feeling that time was running out.

Tomas mounted, and Mateo looked at each of his cousins in turn. They nodded their readiness as his gaze touched each one. He gathered the reins of his *grullo*. "Let's ride, my friends," he said.

They trotted their horses single-file down the arroyo that would take them to the edge of the plain where the remuda grazed. The sun hammered them. Sweat darkened their shirts and beaded their foreheads beneath the broad brims of their sombreros. Mateo's *escopeta* rested butt down in a leather cup hanging in front of his right stirrup, the muzzle pointed skyward and tied to the saddle's pommel. Of them all, only Mateo owned a gun. Jorge had brought along one of his father's buffalo lances, carrying it in the same fashion Mateo carried his *escopeta*. Jorge also had his bow and a quiver of arrows slanted across his back, as did Tomas and Antonio. Mateo carried a shortened cutlass in a scabbard off his left hip, and they all had their long, heavy-bladed *belduques;* they would as soon have gone naked as without their knives.

They rounded a bend in the arroyo and the plain opened before them. From this lower angle Mateo could see a flat-roofed adobe cabin among the trees along the Pecos. A column of smoke rose from the fire pit in front of it. Between the cabin and the remuda were five or six vaqueros, sitting their horses in a close group. Mateo smiled without humor. He knew the vaqueros were discussing them, and what they should do to protect the herd come nightfall. He wanted to laugh for his own cunning. He hadn't expected his plan to work this smoothly, to actually draw the horsemen away from the herd.

Mateo led the way at a trot. His cousins fanned out to ride at his side. On the near edge of the remuda, a horse lifted its head and whickered questioningly. It was the signal Mateo had been waiting for, the acknowledgment that they had been spotted, the herd alerted. Mateo yelled and slammed his spurs into the *grullo*'s flanks. His cousins followed his lead, screaming and flapping their serapes in the air; within seconds the remuda was in flight.

It was a large herd, probably three or four hundred head, and Mateo and his cousins used it as a shield between themselves and the vaqueros for as long as possible. Jorge and Antonio drove into the rear of the herd like a wedge, splitting off a fair-sized bunch and turning it toward the hills to the west. Mateo and Tomas continued to ride with the remuda, waving their serapes and yelling. Dust whorled in thick, suffocating clouds that turned their sweat to mud. The pounding of hooves was thunderous, drowning out Tomas' yells, muting even Mateo's voice. Bits of dirt torn from the hard earth peppered his face and chest. After a while he jerked his bandanna up to cover his mouth and gave up trying to yell. His eyes teared and stung, and Tomas disappeared in the thickening dust clouds. Mateo rode alone then, a castaway in a flowing, bobbing sea of horses and mules.

A shallow boom, faint but unmistakable, broke the spell of the stampede. Mateo threw a glance over his shoulder. A vaquero was worming his way deeper into the running herd, an old miguelet pistol held aloft like a torch. Mateo thought there might be others following, but the dust was too thick to tell for sure. It didn't matter. He and Tomas had accomplished what they had set out to do. It was time to abandon the herd.

Mateo began to work his way toward the edge of the remuda. He spotted Tomas and shouted, then had to shout a second time before Tomas heard him. Mateo motioned toward the west, and Tomas nodded his understanding. Together they began to ease free of the running herd. A second shot boomed from behind them, and Mateo thought he felt the whiffling passage of the ball past his cheek. He swore and bent lower along the *grullo*'s stretched neck. He could see the edge of the herd now, and the steep, rocky hills beyond. He gave a little shout of relief when they finally broke free.

In the distance, Jorge and Antonio were driving forty or fifty head of horses toward the crest of the ridge from where they'd first watched the herd. Tomas shouted triumphantly as he reined his horse alongside Mateo. Then he flinched, and an oddly startled expression passed over his face. Leaning slowly forward, he let his reins go slack as he wrapped his arms around the knobby horn of his saddle.

"Tomas!" Mateo screamed. He swung his horse after Tomas's mount, raking the *grullo*'s flanks with his spurs. Without a firm hand on the reins, Tomas's horse bolted. Tomas lurched drunkenly in the saddle, barely hanging on. Forcing his *grullo* close to Tomas's mount, Mateo leaned from his saddle to pull the reins from his cousin's loose grip.

"Hold on," Mateo shouted. Tomas didn't look up. The lower left side of his shirt was soaked with blood that was already creeping past his belt and into the waistband of his leather trousers. Cursing his helplessness, Mateo dug his spurs into the *grullo*'s flanks. A vaquero shouted for them to stop, but Mateo didn't even glance around. There was another shot, and a puff of dust far ahead of them.

The plain began to tilt upward, the terrain changing abruptly. A piñon branch slapped Mateo's knee; the iron-shod hooves of their mounts rang against stone. Mateo put his hand on Tomas' shoulder to help steady him. "Sonofabitch," Mateo cried in frustration. "Sonofabitch!" He pounded the sides of his heavy wooden stirrups against the *grullo*'s ribs. There was another command from behind for them to stop, then a third, severed in midsentence by a high-pitched yelp. Looking ahead into the westering sun, Mateo spotted a hazy form standing tall above the horizon, a bow drawn, an arrow notched. Jorge yelled encouragement even as he lifted his bow for another shot.

Antonio caught Tomas's horse at the top of the ridge. Mateo jerked the *grullo* to a stop and jumped from the saddle, tugging at the knot that held his *escopeta* to the pommel. But the vaqueros had already given up. Three of them sat their mounts at the base of the ridge, well out of range. One clutched his thigh, where Jorge's arrow had embedded itself. Another shook his pistol at them, shouting, "Your fathers will hear of this! I promise you!"

"Tell him," Mateo whispered fiercely, scrambling back to Jorge's side. He held the *escopeta* against his chest to keep his hands from trembling. "Tell him everything."

Jorge looked shaken. "That was very close, Mateo. I did not think they would fight."

"They do not fight," Mateo sneered. He nodded toward the base of the ridge, where the vaqueros were retreating. "See, a few shots, some curses and threats, and they are satisfied."

"Mateo! Jorge! Come! Tomas is hurt!"

"Watch them," Mateo instructed Jorge. "They are bravest when someone runs."

He went to Antonio's side. Tomas still clung to his saddle, and they had to pry his hands from the saddle horn to pull him off his horse. They laid him in the shade of a piñon, and Mateo slit his shirt with his *belduque*. He sucked his breath in sharply at the sight. There was a small, puckered hole just below the ribs, the flesh around it bruised in a swirl of yellow, black, and blue, glistening with bright red blood. There was no exit wound.

"Mother of God," Antonio whispered. He looked at Mateo, tears welling in his eyes. "Do something, Mateo. Do something."

Jorge came up behind them. "*Carajo,*" he breathed.

"Mateo! He is dying!"

Tomas's leg twitched, and there was a frightening rattle in his chest, like something small and dark and vastly sinister awaiting its chance to escape.

"*Mateo!*" Tears streaked Antonio's cheeks, and his face was twisted.

Mateo jerked his dingy, battered gray sombrero off his head and slapped Antonio across the face and shoulders with it. "What did you expect?" he shouted. He slapped Antonio a second time, then flung his sombrero away. "What did you expect?" His voice shook with rage and helplessness.

"Not this," Jorge said soberly. He knelt to stare at his cousin's pallid face. A pinkish froth had appeared at the corners of Tomas's mouth earlier; now it seemed to withdraw, and the rattling in his chest suddenly stopped. No one spoke, and for a moment there was only the deep silence of a huge and empty land.

"Not this," Jorge repeated, his chin dipping toward his chest.

Mateo took a deep breath, then stooped to retrieve his sombrero. He walked stiffly to the *grullo,* catching the reins and swinging into the saddle. The stolen horses were spread across the hillside below them, walleyed and jumpy. They would be hard to handle in this rough country, and more than likely several would escape into the arroyos and canyons that split the earth between here and Santa Fe. Well, there was nothing they could do about that, Mateo reasoned. There wouldn't be time to take an easier route, one better suited to driving livestock.

"Mateo." Jorge stood and came toward him. "What about Tomas?"

Mateo glanced at the body. "We will have to leave him. There is no time—"

"No!" Jorge's voice was sharper than Mateo had ever heard it. He grabbed the *grullo*'s bit, glaring into the shade of Mateo's sombrero. "He is our cousin, and our friend. We will bury him beneath a cross, and light a candle for his soul in the first church we come to."

Mateo leaned forward, the muscles along his jaw knotting. "It is too late," he spat. "Too late for all of us now. Don't you understand that?"

"No, Mateo. The Lord will forgive us for stealing horses, but He would never forgive us for leaving Tomas like this. We will bury him. You know we must."

Mateo jerked savagely on the *grullo*'s reins, pulling the bit free of Jorge's grip. "Do as you wish, then. But we cannot bury him here. We will have to take him with us."

Jorge nodded, but his shoulders remained rigid. "Good. Then only the three of us will know where he lies." He turned away, his voice softening. "Antonio. Bring Tomas's horse."

Mateo guided the *grullo* down the slope toward the stolen horses. He felt confused and angry, more shaken by Jorge's sudden defiance than Tomas's death. He told himself that it didn't matter whether they buried Tomas or not, or where. It would all mean nothing once Don Julio learned of their betrayal. Yet there was within him a sense of something passing, something good and warm that had died on this sun-scorched ridge even as Tomas died. They would go forward now. There was no turning back.

Chapter Five

A twig snapped, scraping away the thin veneer of Travis Ketchum's sleep. He came awake with a start, then lay unmoving beneath a canopy of twinkling stars, straining to hear above the rushing of the river and the rapid pounding of his pulse.

Moonlight flooded the tiny, brush-rimmed clearing along the Rio Grande del Norte. It glimmered off the splashing waters like dull silver, and washed away the tarnished shades of black and rust that streaked the boulders cleaving the rushing river. On the opposite bank, the towering, chalk-colored cliffs were bathed in shadow, but they were too sheer and crumbling to hide anyone's approach. Whatever had awakened him had to be on this side of the river, and not very far away.

Lying on his back, staring at the white oval of the moon, Travis could envision the Mexican soldiers in their gaudy blue uniforms making their way cautiously through the brush. Their muskets were cocked and ready to fire, their bayonets locked in place to finish what the musket balls left. They were smiling as they crept forward, chuckling at how they had so easily outwitted this rawboned and foolish young gringo. The image filled him with a sense of doom that was like steel bands tightening across his chest.

He slid his hand along the cool iron of the long-barreled Kentucky rifle tucked alongside him under his blankets. He knew he should give himself up. He had only one shot with his rifle, and his imagination had already placed at least a dozen soldiers in the brush surrounding the little clearing. But he would rather die than go back to that stinking hole within the Governor's Palace in Santa Fe they called a prison.

Perhaps he could have beaten the original charges. They were trumped up anyway. Too many complaints against the American intruders swarming into Mexico, and not enough being done to atone for it, according to the fat-bellied old corporal who'd brought him his food twice each day and escorted him to the privy to empty his waste bucket every evening at dusk. Travis, alone and unknown, had been nothing more than a scapegoat to appease some distant government official.

The old corporal had seemed truly saddened by the injustice of Travis's arrest, but Travis reasoned that sympathy wasn't going to unlock any doors. After nearly twelve weeks lodged inside the minuscule cell with only a straw pallet on the floor for sleeping and a leaky thunder bucket for waste, he had become desperate. Then last night, on their way back from the privy, a sound had distracted the corporal's attention, causing him to stop and turn. It was the opportunity Travis had been waiting for. He slammed his emptied waste bucket down on top of the corporal's head, and the old soldier crumpled with a grunt, a dark blue splotch in the gathering dusk.

Travis found his rifle and gear where he had been told they would be, and stole a horse from an adobe corral on the outskirts of town. The Sangre de Cristos, rising abruptly in the east, seemed the likeliest route of escape, so Travis turned west instead, driving straight into the sterile wastelands of the desert.

It had all gone as smoothly as planned up until that point, but then luck abandoned him. Less than ten miles from Santa Fe, the horse stepped in a badger's hole and sprained its leg so bad it was unable to go on. Travis turned the animal loose and pushed forward on foot, carrying the saddle over his shoulder. He traveled all night and most of the next day, swinging in a wide loop to the north, toward Taos and the American trappers who often outfitted there. He'd come west to be a mountain man, and his encounter with Mexican politics hadn't changed that.

Travis reached the del Norte at sundown, flopping onto a gravel bar to drink until his gaunt belly swelled into a tight, hard ball. He vomited it all up afterward, heaving until his arms trembled and his face was beaded with perspiration. Weak and chilled, his stomach cramping, his feet blistered inside his square-toed boots, he fell into his bedroll. All he wanted was sleep, but even that luxury was denied him at first. His calves knotted as he tried to relax, and his shoulders ached from the pull of his saddle and rifle. Every time he started to drift off, he would find himself back in the desert, trudging resolutely through the blazing heat. He dozed in time, but it was a fragile sleep, filled with jerking, twitching muscles and haunting dreams.

And it had all been for nothing, he thought bitterly. He wondered if they'd waited for him at the river all along, lounging in the shade, knowing that he'd have to come to it sooner or later. He flexed his fingers around the wrist of the Kentucky that had once belonged to his grandfather. Lord, he hated the thought of some damned Mexican getting it.

Another twig snapped, no more than fifteen or twenty feet away. The sound came from the bushes upriver, above his head, loud as a pistol shot. Travis eased the flint back to full cock. His heart still pounded, but he felt suddenly calm otherwise. He had made his decision; he wasn't going back.

There was hollow thud from above, followed by an almost familiar exhalation of breath. Travis put his free hand on the edge of the blanket and braced his heel into the sandy soil. There wouldn't be much time. Maybe none at all.

"Now," he breathed, and swung the blanket back and the rifle around, rolling to his stomach in one smooth motion. "Right there!" he bellowed. "You just stop right there, or I swear I'll blow a hole in your belly big enough for a possum to crawl through!"

His assailant snorted and lifted its head, its huge ears flopping comically forward.

Travis stared incredulously, his hands trembling, then slowly tipped his face forward until his forehead rested on the Kentucky's comb. "Oh, goddamn," he muttered shakily.

The mule snorted and stomped its hoof. Travis lifted his head, then laid the rifle aside and climbed slowly to his feet.

"Whoa, boy," Travis cooed. "Easy, big fella." He eased forward a step, and the mule's head snapped up, its nostrils flaring. Travis froze, knowing the mule was on the verge of bolting. He tried a different approach then, edging over to his saddle and kneeling beside it. Fiddling with the tie strings that held his canvas jacket to the cantle, he said conversationally, "Where'd you come from, big fella? You break outta somebody's corral?"

One of the mule's ears twitched. "Bet you're lonely, huh?" He slipped his arms into the jacket and buttoned it. "Kinda cold, ain't it? Funny the way the temperature drops after sundown out here. Back in Arkansas it stays hot all night. During the summer, at least. It gets cold during the winter, though. Last winter we got eight inches of snow in January. That's a heap for Arkansas. Mostly it rains, and sometimes the rain freezes so you can barely walk from the house to the barn. I'll bet you ain't never been to Arkansas, have you?"

The mule listened attentively, its big ears cocked forward. Travis turned slowly to face it. It was a jack, he saw, and had the lines of a fine animal, tall and well put together. It was a blue-tipped bay, its muzzle banded by the dark strip of a halter.

"Reckon you're mine if you let me catch you," he told the mule. "One thing I learned coming out here is that finders is keepers. Bought me a little gray mare back in Fort Smith and joined up with a wagon train heading for Santa Fe, a freight outfit for Mr. B. J. Skinner, of Little Rock, who I don't guess you'd know. On the near side of Cross Timbers some Osages run off with some horses, and my little gray was amongst 'em. Well, sir—" Travis stood and tugged the hem of his jacket down over his belt, then, casually, eased forward a couple of steps; the mule listened raptly—"some of the boys who worked for Mr. Skinner went after 'em and caught up a couple days later. Was some blood spilt, and Harvey Toon, who was kinda like the wagon boss of the train, comes back with a couple fresh scalps. Some of the others had scalps, too, but only Mr. Toon had two of 'em. Well, they had my gray, too, but when I went over to fetch 'er, Toon says to me, 'What're you aiming to do there, boy?' and I says 'I aim to saddle this here gray of mine and get on to the mountains.' Well, Mr. Toon, he laughs and so does some of the others, and that's when Mr. Skinner comes up and says the gray belongs to Mr. Toon now. Says a man loses his horse, that horse belongs to him who's got it. An Osage stolt it from me, and Mr. Toon stolt it from the Osage, and I'm just outta luck all the way around."

The mule whiffled softly, and Travis edged closer. He raised his hand to let the mule stretch its neck for a tentative sniff, then moved his hand back to scratch the animal's neck. The mule's ears flicked back and forth, and Travis grinned. "Like that, big fella? Feels good, huh?"

The mule nuzzled his chest, taking a big whiff this time, then stepped forward and put its head flat against Travis's chest.

"Lord Almighty," Travis said, blinking in surprise.

At dawn Travis rode upriver until the cliffs on the opposite bank petered out, then splashed the mule across the del Norte and clambered up the opposite bank. He climbed a steep, sage-covered slope to the top of the nearest hill and drew rein. Straight ahead, the Sangre de Cristos rose into a sky so deep and blue it looked almost violet. A fresh dusting of snow mantled the gray peaks above timberline, as white and delicate as a fine lace shawl. Between the mountains and the river the land was a tumbled maze of red-dirt hills dotted with piñon and juniper; deep, twisting arroyos; and narrow, grassy valleys shaded with small groves of cottonwood and box elder. Somewhere near the foothills lay the High Road, the main route between Taos and Santa Fe. But it wasn't the only route, Travis knew. There was an older trail between the High Road and the river, a winding, rocky path, rarely used anymore if what he'd heard was true. For a man on the dodge, it seemed the way to go.

He lifted his reins and the mule started off without prodding, picking its way nimbly down the hill. At the bottom they followed a valley eastward, coming to the old trail within a half hour.

"Looks like our luck is changing," Travis told the mule. He leaned forward to study the path. Fresh hoofprints marred the dust, heading north toward Taos, but he couldn't tell how many or when they'd passed. If they had been made yesterday, they could belong to soldiers combing the hills for him. But if they were older than that, then whoever made them probably hadn't even heard of his escape. He studied the tracks for several minutes, then shrugged and turned onto the trail.

"It ain't what's ahead that worries me so much, anyhow," he confided. "It's what's behind us we got to look sharp for."

Travis kept a steady pace throughout the morning. The trail wound through the hills, rising and falling with a monotonous regularity. From time to time his belly would rumble ominously. Although he hadn't eaten anything in more than thirty-six hours, it was the months he'd spent in prison that were beginning to sap his strength. As the sun glided past midday and his shadow slowly switched from left to right, he began to feel the effects of his captivity. His vision wavered, and from time to time he would squeeze his eyes shut against a wave of dizziness. He thought he heard his brother's voice as if from a long way off, the words too faint to understand, but the tone recognizable—pleading.

"Sorry, Chet," Travis mumbled. "I'm sorry." A choking sob hiccuped its way through his consciousness, and he jerked and blinked, pulling the mule to a halt.

"Goddamnit, are you deaf? I said drop that rifle and put your hands up."

Travis squinted into the brassy sunlight at the top of the nearest hill. Among the darker shadows of a piñon he spotted a splash of color and the vague outline of shoulders and a broad-brimmed hat.

"I said, let it drop!" the voice commanded.

Travis's anger flared unexpectedly. He pulled the rifle closer and shook his head. "No!"

There was a moment of silence from the top of the hill, then the man under the broad-brimmed hat said "Jesus" and stepped away from the tree. Travis could see him clearly then, a tall, slim, well-built man, maybe two or three years his elder, but no more than twenty or twenty-one. He wore striped wool trousers tucked inside his nearly knee-high boots and a red cotton shirt with a black silk bandanna. "Keep a bead on him, Clint," the man ordered. "I'm going down."

From somewhere to the left of the first man, another answered, "I'm watching him."

The first man started down the hill, his boots skidding in the talus, raising a reddish dust that clouded his ankles. Coming up at the bottom, he leveled his rifle on Travis's belly. "My name's Jake Orr," he said, "and that's my mule you're riding."

"Uh-uh," Travis replied. "It's my mule."

Jake looked momentarily exasperated. "Listen, I'm the one holding the gun."

Travis didn't reply.

Jake's voice rose a notch. "I'm going to put a hole in you in about two seconds if you don't get off that mule."

"You do what you think best, but I ain't getting off this mule until suppertime."

"Jake, he looks about done in," Clint called down. "Maybe we ought to give him something to eat."

"Just shut up, Clint," Jake hollered in return. Under his breath, so that only Travis heard, he added, "I'm not feeding a thief."

"I ain't a thief," Travis clarified. "This here is my mule."

Jake's rifle sagged a little. "You can't be that dumb," he said uncertainly.

"No, but I'm feeling almighty stubborn. I got hooked out of a good gray mare by a man named Harvey Toon, back in the Cross Timbers, and I ain't gettin' hooked outta this one."

Jake snorted contemptuously. "I could just plug you where you stand, and nobody would ever know."

"Maybe," Travis said.

"You think I won't?"

"I think you better make your first shot count, because I won't miss."

"My brother would kill you before you could touch your trigger."

"Maybe. Maybe not."

A smile wormed across Jake's face. "You're the one who broke out of the *calabozo* in Santa Fe, aren't you? Do you know there are soldiers looking for you? I'd be a hero if I brought you back."

"Aw, Jake, there's no sense in that," Clint called. "He's an American."

"That cuts no ice with me," Jake snapped. "We know he's a mule thief. Hard telling what else he's done."

"That mule pulled loose on its own," Clint answered. "We'd already given up looking for him."

Jake's face reddened. "God*damn*! Maybe you did, but I didn't." He leveled his rifle again. "Get off that mule!"

"Uh-uh."

Jake's thumb stretched for the flintlock's cock, but Travis beat him to it. He carried the Kentucky across his saddle, and it didn't take but a second to cock it and let the muzzle swing toward Jake's chest. Jake's eyes widened, and his thumb froze on the hammer.

"You're a little slow, Jake."

"Sonafabitch," Jake said.

"This is my mule," Travis repeated wearily. "I've had just about everything I owned taken away from me, one way or another. I don't figure to let it happen again."

Jake licked his lips. "Clint could—"

"Not before I pulled this trigger, he couldn't."

Jake took his thumb away from the cock. "Looks like you win this one," he said tautly. "But this isn't over between us, skinny. Not by a long chalk." He turned to the hill, shouting, "Clint, get your ass down here. And bring the stock."

Jake started along the base of the hill to meet his brother, and Travis let his grip on the Kentucky relax. When Jake had stalked out of sight among the trees, Travis let the hammer down to half-cock. "Well, big fella," he said to the mule. "Maybe our luck ain't changed that much after all."

They rode at a plodding walk toward the little grove of cottonwood on the far side of the valley. Jake led, his head swiveling constantly as they drew near the trees. Clint and Travis brought up the rear, hazing a trio of pack mules in front of them. To the east the upper spires of the Sangre de Cristos were wrapped in the delicate golden light of a dying day, but the valley and the surrounding hills were already immersed in early twilight.

Among the trees Travis could see the ruins of an adobe shack, and behind it the remnants of an old picket corral. The grass beneath the trees and around the dilapidated fencing was tall and still faintly green, hinting of a spring or seep. They halted at the edge of the grove and let the pack mules wander off to graze. Jake eyed the ruins critically for several minutes, then announced, "The water must've dried up. Otherwise they wouldn't have abandoned it."

"Maybe Indians drove them off," Clint remarked. "Remember what they said in Santa Fe."

A grimace passed over Jake's face. "They said you were simple, but I've kept you anyway." He nudged his horse into the trees without looking back.

"I'd shoot that sonofabitch before I'd let him talk to me like that," Travis said to Clint. He dismounted and began unsaddling the mule.

"You don't know everything," Clint replied. "It's not just because he's my brother."

Travis shrugged. "Makes no nevermind to me."

Jake made a quick pass through the trees and returned. "This will do. You two picket the stock and start a fire. I'll see if I can find something to eat." He leered at Travis. "Considering one of us has already eaten our supper on the trail, and the other"—he gave Clint a withering glance—"offered it to him."

"You want me to pay for what I ate, sing out," Travis said.

"You can pay for the meat *and* the mule when we get to Taos, if I decide to sell it."

"A mule found is free to the finder," Travis returned. He'd dropped his saddle in the grass and was squatted beside it, loosening his picket rope. He stood then to face Jake straight on, and said, "This mule is mine."

Jake laughed and turned away, spurring his horse to a gallop.

"You and Jake would have liked each other once," Clint said glumly.

"I sorely doubt that," Travis answered. He picketed his mule close to the trees and went to inspect what must have been a well at one time. He dropped a stone into the yawning black pit, but stirred up only the dusty whir of a rattlesnake. He thought Jake was probably right about the water drying up, although considering the richness of the grass and the size of the trees, it was doubtless a seasonal thing.

"Would you give me a hand with these packs?" Clint asked. He was standing beside one of the mules, the hitches half loosened, the packs sagging.

Travis shook his head. "Nope," he answered, turning away from the well.

Clint blinked. "No?"

"Uh-uh. I'm going to see if I can scare us up some meat."

"But Jake's already hunting. He told us to make camp."

Travis didn't bother with a reply. He checked the Kentucky's priming and tightened the flint. It was nearly dark, but he figured there was a half hour's worth of shooting light left. Cradling the rifle in his arm, he struck out toward the del Norte, a mile or so to the west, leaving Clint to struggle with the packs alone.

The lingering russet glow of daylight was beginning to dim as Travis made his way into the hills bordering the valley, as if the earth itself were sucking the light down some vast hole beyond the western edge of the horizon. Among the trees and at the bottoms of the deeper arroyos, the shadows were already thickening to ebony.

Travis wound deeper into the mass of hills, moving quickly but with a hunter's stealth. Twenty minutes later he inexplicably stopped and brought his rifle up. Something moved near the ridge to his left, and he twisted slowly at the waist, keeping his head turned away to watch with his peripheral vision what would have been invisible if stared at directly. A deer was making its way toward the top of the ridge. It was too dark to fire into the hill itself, but if the deer didn't alter its course it would top out about eighty yards away, silhouetting itself briefly against the paler sky to the west.

Travis sank carefully to one knee and took a deep, steadying breath. He tucked the rifle to his shoulder and silently thanked his grandfather for the silver-bladed front sight. A time or two, on his journey across the plains, he'd cursed the silver for catching the sun's brilliant rays and exploding the sight to three times its normal size. But he swore now, as the doe's form broke the smooth line of the horizon and he brought the slim front sight into line with the deer's shoulder, that he'd never replace it.

He stroked the trigger and the rifle cracked sharply, spewing a cloud of gray powder smoke that momentarily obliterated his view. He stood and began to reload without taking his eyes off the ridge. When the smoke cleared, it revealed a flat, motionless mass, a lump on the horizon with a single rear leg canted up and back like a skillet's handle. Travis's hand slowed on the ramrod as he stared soberly at the doe, feeling the familiar mix of delight and regret at the taking of a life.

As he finished reloading, the last of the light drained out of the sky, and silence settled over the land. It occurred to Travis that he hadn't yet heard the sound of Jake's rifle, and he smiled grimly as he started toward the ridge and the dead deer.

CHAPTER SIX

It was late when Eli awoke. Gray light was already filtering in through the shuttered windows, and from the rear of the house Consuelo's calico nanny was bleating to be milked.

He stretched languidly atop the husk-filled tick, then pulled the blankets up to his ears, burrowing deeper into the bed's warmth. Frosty mornings never bothered him on the trail, not even when he had to shake a foot of wind-driven snow off his blankets before arising. But it was different when he slept indoors. He seldom got up before Consuelo had the fire going, and even then it was only to stumble over to the corner fireplace with the blankets wrapped tight around his nakedness, standing hunched and shivering until the room warmed up.

It was a thing she liked to tease him about, most days. "Wagh," she'd say, mocking the short grunt of exclamation that was common among mountain men. Then, lowering her voice to a man's grumble, she'd add something like "Let's go wade in an icy river, boys," or "Cold doin's don't bother this *hiveranno* none." And more often than not, Eli would play along, saying "Uh-uh. Water's too cold. I'm going back to bed," or some similar foolishness.

He smiled sleepily, remembering the warmth he always felt on the *inside,* standing before the fireplace watching her prepare breakfast. But it was a sad smile, too. He knew they wouldn't tease one another that way this morning. They had been together off and on for a good many years now, but it seemed like they always had to start over again whenever he came back from a long trek.

Consuelo stirred, rolling over in her sleep to face him. Her warm breath, still slightly tinged from last night's supper of goat's cheese and tortillas, washed softly over his face. He watched her as she slept. Her expression was calm, her dark face smooth save for the track of the pillow along one cheek. In the gentle, diffused light, she looked young and innocent, giving Eli an impression of what she must have been like as a girl.

She had been sitting on the stoop when he rode up last night, her cigarillo glowing red in the darkness. She hadn't seemed at all surprised to see him, and he wondered if word had already drifted up from town that he was back. He greeted her cautiously, pushing his hat back so that she might see his face better in the moonlight. She nodded in return, saying "Hello, Eli," in that smoke-husky voice he always forgot when he was away any length of time. She regarded him thoughtfully for a couple of minutes, as if searching for some kind of change, then said, "I see you didn't get what you expected."

She was talking about his father's plantation back in Virginia, he knew. He shook his head. "Jason got everything except a gold-handled walking cane, a broadcloth suit, and a thousand dollars. I sold the cane in St. Louis."

"Life can be a sonofabitch sometimes." She took the cigarillo from her mouth and flipped it into the yard. "So?"

"I came back, didn't I?"

She seemed to consider that a moment, then shrugged and stood with a little grunt of stiffness, and went inside. Eli dismounted and put the horses in the corral behind the house. He stacked his gear under the lean-to, then followed her inside. He'd been gone nearly five months this time.

Consuelo sniffed and rolled onto her back, pulling the blankets with her and allowing a draft of cold air to brush Eli's naked flank. He grabbed the blankets and jerked them back, and Consuelo came awake with a little start. She smiled when she realized what she'd done, but didn't laugh. "The sun is already up," she said, glancing toward a window. "I am lazy this morning."

"You worked hard last night."

"You work best when hard, but you don't work so long anymore."

Eli chuckled. "I didn't hear you complaining."

"You wouldn't hear the roof fall on your head when you make love." She raised up on one elbow and ran her fingers through the hair on his chest, stopping at the base of his throat. *"Mío hombre,"* she said tenderly.

He patted her hand, then ran the ball of his thumb over the angry flesh of an old scar encircling her wrist.

"Don't," she said, pulling her hand away.

"Does it still hurt?"

"Yes. Inside. It reminds me of my children."

Eli lay back, staring at the ceiling. He never knew what to say when she spoke of her past that way, especially of her children, stolen by the Navajos.

He had been drawn to her from the first time he'd met her, at an informal *baile* here in Taos. She wasn't a beautiful woman, not by the standards of the day, but there was a quiet competence about her that appealed to his own sense of independence, an unassuming dignity in the way she moved and spoke. She was tough as bull's meat, no doubt about that, hardened by a life few women could have survived. She was emotionally calloused and physically scarred, though she had her soft side, too, which she revealed to him from time to time. She rarely mentioned her years of captivity among the Navajo, or her first husband, who was killed in the raid that had resulted in her capture. Only occasionally did she bring up her children, and then it was in such a cold and distracted voice it often brought a chill to Eli's spine. He had long ago decided that the loss of her children was a raw and festering wound buried deep within her soul, scabbed over now with bitterness and anger. Eli never picked at the scab. Some wounds, he thought, were best left alone.

Consuelo threw the blankets back and rolled out of bed. She padded naked across the room to squat in front of the corner fireplace, raking away last night's ashes to reveal a handful of coals glowing dully beneath a film of ash. Tossing in a few twigs and some kindling, she quickly fanned the coals into flame.

When the fire was blazing, Eli got up to stand in front of it, spreading his blanket wide to catch the heat. Consuelo pulled on her dress and sandals, and draped a mantilla over her shoulders against the morning chill. Taking a reed basket and a little tin kettle, she went outside to gather eggs and milk the goat. By the time she returned, Eli was dressed and hunkered in front of the fire, smoking a short Durango cigar while waiting for his coffee to boil.

Consuelo set the milk and eggs on the table. "Not so much anymore," she said, watching him intently.

"You need another goat." He frowned, remembering. "You used to have five or six. What happened to them?"

"I sold all the goats except the old nanny, and all the chickens except some laying hens that are old and should be eaten. With the money I bought an ass and a sawbuck packsaddle."

He shifted around, cocking a brow questioningly.

"Take me with you, Eli." She said it so softly, with her eyes lowered self-consciously to the table, that he barely heard her.

Eli turned back to the fire, feeling an inexplicable wariness at her unexpected request, as if some brownskin he was trading with had asked to hold his rifle. He knew it had been hard for Consuelo to ask. In her mind, asking for anything was little more than begging, and she'd begged only once in her life—for her children. Eli knew she would rather die than suffer that humiliation again. So he understood the hesitation of her words. He wasn't as sure about his own feelings.

He took the cigar from his mouth and examined the frayed, soggy tip. "It'd be a rough trip," he began uncertainly.

"I can take care of myself. I can take care of you, too, as your wife."

"The way things are shaping up, you'd be the only woman along. That could cause trouble."

Consuelo's voice hardened. "You think I don't get my share of man trouble around here?"

"It'd be different in the mountains. Here there's whores and such. Out there, a man ain't got that option."

"I would be with you. No one would bother Eli Cutler's woman."

"Maybe you'd be with me, but there's never any knowing what might come up in a season. It would be a long walk back if something happened."

"It was a long walk back from Navajo country, too," she said bluntly. She threw her shawl on the table and went to a wooden chest set against the wall. Flipping the lid open, she pulled out a long, hooded blanket coat, what the French-Canadians called a capote. She tossed it across the bed and bent again to scoop up several pairs of moccasins, dumping those beside the capote. Eli watched silently as she emptied the chest, piling more moccasins and maybe half a dozen heavy wool skirts and leggings, and twice that many shirts—men's shirts—on top of the capote. She added a couple of pairs of heavy buffalo mittens with the hair side out, moccasins to match, needles, thread, soap, awls, a belt ax and extra knives, plus spices for cooking. There was coffee and chocolate and a full carrot of tobacco, with *hojas* already cut and pressed for her cigarillos. She pulled out a heavy leather belt with an iron buckle that carried a sheathed butcher knife and pouches he knew contained a whetstone and her fire-making gear—flint and steel, and some punk to catch the spark. She went across the room and got her shotgun, shot, and powder flasks from the corner, bringing them back and laying them on top of everything else.

"Looks like you're ready to go," Eli conceded.

"I sold my skillets and the big kettle. I have left only a couple of smaller kettles and a new griddle." She caught her lower lip between her teeth, her gaze taking in the tiny one-roomed house. "I am tired of this place, Eli. All the memories here are bad. You are the only good memory, but you're gone too much. I can't live this way any longer. I had family in El Paso, many years ago. My father's brothers. If I do not go with you, I will go there to see if any still live."

Eli let her words settle. She'd given him an ultimatum, and one not without a certain amount of justification. It wasn't much of a life he'd created for her here. He recognized her loneliness, the lack of security and continuity which he knew she craved but would never ask for. Yet as strong as his feelings for her were, he found himself reluctant to make the commitment allowing her to accompany him would imply. In the back of his mind was Girardin's innuendo of a partnership somewhere down the road, and all that that could eventually mean for him.

His thoughts shifted briefly back to Seven Oaks, and the pampered life he had led on his father's big plantation just outside of Richmond, Virginia, along the James River. How well he remembered that white-columned, two-storied mansion, with its broad, well-manicured lawn that separated the house from the river, and the vast array of barns, stables, and sheds built behind it. Even now he could smell the sweet aroma of lilacs and the scent of fresh-mown grass on hot summer nights. His father had owned fifteen hundred acres of sprawling fields planted in tobacco, sorghum, and corn, and the deep, virgin forests, where Eli had spent countless hours hunting deer, elk, and wild boar. There had been more than a score of slaves to toil in those sweltering fields, and half a dozen more to care for the house and outbuildings. His had been a life of luxury, a status he hadn't fully realized until he'd left home. It seemed a long time ago now, that day just three weeks shy of his twenty-first birthday, when his father made the blunt announcement that it would be Eli's brother, Jason, who inherited Seven Oaks in its entirety.

There had been nothing personal in his father's decision, Eli knew. Perhaps that was what made it so hard to stomach at first, that cold, brittle efficiency that so marked his father's every move. Certainly it shouldn't have hit him as hard as it did. It was, as his father saw it, nothing more than a matter of birthright, that Old World practice of the eldest son inheriting everything, while his mother and siblings were left with only the family name and a modest inheritance. It was a tradition still in vogue in England, where Eli's great-grandfather had originally hailed from, and had Eli lived there instead of in America, he probably would have used the thousand dollars his father left him to purchase a commission in the King's Army, serving out his time in faraway India or Africa. But this was America, and Eli could admit now that he had secretly hoped his father might abandon that old-fashioned practice in favor of dividing Seven Oaks between both his sons.

Eli had been stunned at first, barely able to comprehend the hundreds of ways his life had been shattered, his hopes and dreams stripped away. He felt little bitterness toward his father. Having grown up on Seven Oaks, in the heart of what had once been a staunch British colony, he knew what a burden tradition could sometimes become. But his resentment toward Jason had grown almost overnight. By a simple act of fate, Jason had become one of the wealthiest men in Virginia; by that same fickle hand, Eli had lost everything.

He left home two days later, rejecting his father's suggestion that he go to sea as he rejected Jason's passionless condolences. On the far western frontier, men were making their fortunes in the Indian trade, and despite his father's sharp criticism, Eli declared his intention of going to St. Louis and becoming a part of that trade. Yet even as he packed his bags, he swore to himself that someday he would return. Someday, when he had carved his own destiny in a hard and cruel world, when he had achieved a position of power and wealth equal to that of his brother, he would return. To what end, he had had no idea at the time, and as the years passed, his desire to go back had lessened. But had the old dreams faded, too? he wondered.

Eli's father died in March, passing away quietly in his sleep. Jason immediately sent a letter to Taos, where Eli picked it up at the end of the season. He had been saddened by his father's death, but not overwhelmed by it. He had saddled his horse and set out across the plains, arriving at Seven Oaks in July. A peculiar feeling enveloped him as he stepped off the gangplank of the small packet at Seven Oaks landing. He wasn't sure what he had expected after more than six years away, but it certainly wasn't this curious lethargy, this sense of detachment. He was glad to see his mother and sisters, of course, as they were him. Jason had been somewhat standoffish at first, but relaxed when he realized Eli didn't intend to challenge his position as the new master of Seven Oaks. Although Eli recognized most of the slaves, he felt no particular gladness to see them again. His entire visit, in fact, had been overwhelmed with a sense of nagging impatience, a feeling that he had returned too soon . . . or too late.

He had planned to stay the summer, and perhaps the winter, but within three weeks his desire to return to the mountains, to get on with his own life, had gotten the better of him. He finished up what business remained of settling his father's will, then collected his suit of clothes, the gold-handled walking cane his father had never used, and a voucher for one thousand dollars, said his good-byes, and left.

Depression gripped him before he reached Pittsburgh, and he spent his days traveling down the Ohio, then up the Mississippi to St.

Louis, locked in his cabin. It was all lost, he thought, his dreams, his ambitions, everything.

And then Sylvester Girardin had invited him to a small dinner party one night, and suddenly everything seemed possible again.

Eli shook those thoughts away, looking across the small room of the tiny adobe house on the side of the hill above Taos. Consuelo's eyes had narrowed in the time he had spent ruminating, her anger building steadily. He knew it hid the hurt she felt from his long silence. Guilt gnawed at him as he weighed the pros and cons of her request. He tried to tell himself that having a woman along would only create problems for the brigade, igniting jealousy among the men, especially during winter quarters when they were likely to be laid up by deep snows. She would be a burden, too, always needing to be looked after and cared for and worried about, all without adding anything to the brigade's efficiency. Being Eli's woman, she wouldn't be expected to help with the pack string or stretching and fleshing the pelts, and the boys would likely quit if she tried to trap. No, Eli thought, taking a woman along meant nothing but trouble.

Yet even as all this flashed through his mind, he knew he was lying to himself. Men packed squaws along all the time. Nearly any large brigade, and most of the smaller ones, included a few Indian women and their children, and there was seldom any trouble. Nor would Consuelo be a burden. Likely it would be just the opposite; she would be there, doing what needed to be done without complaint, seeing that the fires were kept burning and his gear kept dry and repaired, pitching in wherever she was needed, even framing and fleshing the skins he brought in, if it came to that. True, if she tried to trap, the men would probably quit, claiming a woman's scent would jinx a stream from mouth to head, but there would be plenty of ways she could help.

There would be other advantages as well. Having a woman along would be a comfort that could make the long months easier to endure. It would be nice having someone close to talk to and be with. It would be unusual to take a Mexican woman into the mountains rather than a squaw, but not unheard of.

Shrugging, he said, "Hell, if that's the way your stick floats, I won't cut it loose. Come along, if you want."

He looked at her, expecting gratitude, perhaps even excitement. He received, instead, the quick blast of her anger.

"Do not do me any favors, Eli Cutler," she flared. "I am not some dumb Indian squaw that can be kicked around and treated like a dog. If you do not want me, then I will go to El Paso. It does not matter. You are only a man, and there are many more in Mexico."

Eli looked back at the fire without answering. He worked the cigar from one side of his mouth to the other, and pulled the coffee back from the flames. It was ready now; he could hear it bubbling inside the blackened tin pot.

"Eli?" Her voice was softer, the anger already waning.

"Yeah?"

"Do you love me?"

Once again he felt caught off balance, trapped, torn between his feelings for her and his dreams for the future. "Hell, Connie, I ain't sure I know what love is. I like you, I know that. I'd rather be with you than any other woman I know of. But I don't know if that's love or not."

"I think," she said gently, "that it must be. *Sí*. It is love if you do not wish to be with another. I love you, too, Eli. There is no one else I would rather be with." She was quiet a moment, thinking. Then she said, "I think maybe I will go with you, instead of to El Paso. I will look after your lodge and your skins, and care for your animals as a woman should." She smiled. "I am truly Eli Cutler's woman now, am I not?"

Eli took the half-smoked cigar from his mouth and dropped it into the flames. Watching the hard brown outer leaves start to curl, he said, "Yeah, I reckon you are."

Eli had to duck to enter the low door of the little hole-in-the-wall cantina on the south side of the plaza. He paused to let his eyes adjust to the dimness. The room was narrow but deep, with a short bar backed up against the rear wall. There were no customers yet, but jackknifed over the business side of the bar was a long, spare-framed man with a curly mane of jet-black hair. He looked up blearily as Eli entered, squinting without recognition.

"You wanna step away from the door there, hoss," the barkeep growled hoarsely. "That sun's fair blindin', this away."

"Bill, are you still drinking all the profit out of this establishment?"

The barkeep was silent a moment. Then he straightened cautiously and said, "Wagh! This coon knows that voice, he surely do.

But you still ain't nothin' but a blur. Come on in, hoss, and have a bite of Lightning."

"Or the other way around," Eli responded dryly. He headed toward the bar, and as he came closer, the barkeep suddenly grinned.

"Well, hell, it's Eli Cutler. This child didn't expect to see ol' Eli before greenup time next spring."

"How, Bill," Eli said, leaning into the bar.

"How yourself, by God, and see how ye like it." Bill Wolfskill slapped his hand into Eli's palm, his grip like contracting iron. "Well, hell, ol' Eli's back in the mountains. Say, amigo, I was sorry as hell to hear about your pappy goin'. That was damp powder, sure. But ye be back with ye hair, and that's what counts as far as this child's concerned." He reached under the bar and brought out a clay jug stoppered with a corn cob. "This calls for a drink, or I'm a flea-bit b'ar." He grinned broadly, revealing a broken row of yellowing teeth. "Course, there's them that say I ain't nothin' but already, but we'll drink us a toast or two anyhow, what do ye say?"

Eli didn't say anything. He slipped a finger through the jug's handle and, balancing it on his elbow, tipped the jug to his mouth. The alcohol hit the back of his throat like liquid fire, causing him to gag and sputter. He jerked the jug away, spilling a little whiskey down the front of his shirt.

"Hyar, now," Wolfskill said loudly, concern rounding his eyes. "Have a care there, hoss. That's my best stuff."

Coughing, Eli shoved the jug back across the bar. His eyes watered and his nose ran, but he laughed in spite of it, and croaked, "That's a mite raw yet, ain't it, Bill?"

"Well, some maybe," Wolfskill allowed. "But she's been aged near a week, which is about five days more'n most I serve."

"Whee oh my," Eli said, his voice still scratchy. It was Taos pure, all right, and it made a fire in the gullet that took a long time to burn out. He watched in awe as Wolfskill lifted the jug, his Adam's apple bobbing eight, ten, a dozen times. On twelve he slapped the jug back to the bar, gasping and red-faced.

"It'll cut the varnish, by God," Wolfskill wheezed. "Wagh! Raw as fresh-kilt meat and hotter'n the center o' hell."

"Lemme try that jug again," Eli said. "It snuck up on me the first whack."

Wolfskill scooted it back and Eli got his elbow under it once more.

He started with a smaller swallow this time, and although the bite was the same, it wasn't as unexpected. He made sure of thirteen swallows, took a fourteenth for good measure, and lowered the jug to the bar. He belched, grabbed a hurried breath, and belched again. For a while then he just stood there while the whiskey slammed through his system and the room danced. When he thought he could speak without choking, he said, "Didn't figure to see you still cooped up behind a bar. You give up on trapping?"

"This coon is about half froze to put out for a season or two, Eli. By God if he ain't."

Wolfskill was a Kentuckian by birth, a trapper and mountaineer by choice and profession. He was a sometime partner of Ewing Young, and a good hand by all accounts. Eli had trapped with him a couple of seasons back, and liked him fine. He'd never asked what persuaded the gangling mountain man to give up the high lonesome to peddle whiskey in Taos; he half-suspected Bill couldn't have answered him anyway.

"Town seems empty," Eli said, swinging around to look out the door.

"Well, it is, by God. But hell, it's closing in on October right quick. Most of the boys put out a couple, three weeks ago." He eyed Eli speculatively. "Where's your stick float this year, Eli? And don't go tellin' me it ain't nary business o' mine. Hell, I already *know* that."

Eli chuckled. "I've got more'n one wiping stick to my rifle this year," he admitted. He told Wolfskill a little about himself and Mc-Clure, leaving out any reference to Sylvester Girardin and the GS& T. "McClure's signed on Cal Underwood, Remi LeBlanc, Johnny Two-Dogs, and Cork-Eye Weathers."

"Cork-Eye! Lordy, Eli, you don't want Cork-Eye."

Eli shrugged. "It was McClure who hired him."

Wolfskill shook his head. "By God, ye was along the time he got treed by a black bear, down on the Heely, weren't ye?"

"I reckon," Eli said, laughing. "His rifle didn't fire and he got run up a cottonwood. Stuck up there all night."

Wolfskill laughed and choked and rubbed his nose with the sleeve of his shirt. "Funnier'n hell," he snorted. "Never seen such a mad bear. 'Bout had all the bark peeled off'n that tree, but too crippled by a brownskin's arrer to make the climb hisself."

As Eli remembered it, Cork-Eye had been pretty upset, too. By the time they found him the next morning, he was so angry he was shaking. He had climbed down from the tree after they killed the bear and walked off in a huff, refusing to talk to anyone for days.

But Wolfskill had called his shot accurately in claiming they didn't want Cork-Eye riding with the brigade. *Eli* didn't want Cork-Eye riding with the brigade. He was a slacker, lazy and incompetent, and something of a coward, to boot. If the brigade hadn't been so small to begin with, Eli might have told Cork-Eye to cut his pin and find a different outfit. But even a coward could fight if the odds were desperate enough, and even a slacker could take some of the load off the others. Eli would have to keep an eye on Cork-Eye, make sure he pulled his share, that was all.

The others—Remi LeBlanc, Johnny Two-Dogs, and Old Cal Underwood—were good men all, and McClure had been smart to take them on. Remi was a French-Canadian by birth, and he'd been in Taos longer than any of them. He was loud and given to boasting, but always cheerful. He was steady as a rock in a fight, and could make the beaver come by anyone's standards.

Johnny Two-Dogs was a half-breed Iroquois, a man truly caught between two worlds. His father had been a post factor with the old North-West Company who had returned to Canada after his retirement. He had left his wife and two daughters in the wilderness, but took his son with him, eventually sending him to England to finish his education. When the North-West Company succumbed by merger in its long-running feud with Hudson's Bay Company, Johnny had declined a lucrative position with HBC. He'd come south, into American territory, to join his mother's people, who were even then venturing onto the plains and into the mountains as trappers. But Johnny's education had taken its toll, and he had been as unable to adjust to an Indian lifestyle as he had to the fur-trading combine of Canada. He came to Taos four or five years ago, an outcast from two cultures, but determined to make it on his own.

Old Caleb Underwood was as strange a bird as any Eli had ever met. He was a tall, gangling, weather-beaten old man who had spent his life as a hunter and trapper, first in the woods of northern Wisconsin and Minnesota, then farther south, among the Osages and the Sac and Fox tribes. He had trapped the Upper Missouri for Manuel Lisa, back in 1807 and 1808, and lived with the Pawnees during the

War of 1812, when the fur trade had almost perished. Some said Old Cal was more Indian than most Indians, and that he would sell his partner's soul to save his own hide. He was guided by superstition and fear, and no one trusted him, but unlike Cork-Eye, Cal wasn't a coward. And his skills and knowledge of the mountains were unsurpassed. Old Cal would be an asset to the brigade, though probably hard to get along with.

"Them others is good men," Wolfskill said reflectively, as if he had been following along the trail of Eli's thoughts. "McClure did a good job pickin' his crew, him bein' such a greenhorn."

"It's a small outfit, though," Eli said.

"Sometimes small is best. Means you can move fast, and not leave much sign for brownskins to pick up."

They talked of other things then. Eli related what he'd learned back in the States, and Wolfskill filled him in on what had been happening in the mountains since Eli had left last spring. They spoke of Big Tom Reed and the massacre, and Wolfskill mentioned that there was talk, he didn't know the source, that Reed had twisted his story around some, and maybe wasn't as innocent as he'd let on.

"Ain't nothin' that'll convict him, mind ye, but the boys has all shied away from him this season. He went down to Chihuahua and picked hisself up some hardcases. Weren't no one else wanted to put out with him."

"The truth will come out sooner or later," Eli observed.

"That's what the boys figure. They'll spread out over the mountains this fall and start nosin' around some of the tribes, they'll l'arn what happened."

They passed the jug again, and when Eli could speak, he said, "Where'd everybody put out for, Bill?"

"Well, hell, I know what they told the gov'nor to get their licenses, but you know as well as me that don't mean squat." He tapped the side of the jug with his finger. "Not even a healthy dose of Lightning will loosen a man's tongue enough to spill where he aims to set his traps."

"You seen Old Cal or Remi or Johnny this morning?"

"Nope, but they'll be cached somewheres along the river, I figure. That Cal don't shine to walls and a ceiling when he shuts his eyes. 'Fraid he'll suffocate in his sleep. He's as loco as a Digger, Eli, or this child wouldn't say so."

"If you see them, pass the word that I'm looking for them, will you?"

"*Bueno*. Will do. If I wasn't hog-tied to this damn bar, I'd put out with ye myself."

"A knot's an easy thing to fix," Eli said, grinning. He laid a coin on the counter and turned to leave, but as he did, the room suddenly changed shape and he stumbled back into the bar.

Wolfskill laughed uproariously, pounding the top of the bar with his hand. "Shotgunned on ye, didn't she?"

At the far end of the room the oblong patch of light that was the door looked like a tiny, slanting opening several hundred yards distant.

"It's 'cause this place is so damn narrow and dark," Wolfskill explained with sudden sobriety. "I've paced 'er off, and it's forty feet from the door to the bar, but it's a good bit farther goin' back, dependin' on how much ye've drank."

"Christ," Eli muttered, passing a hand over his face. He pushed away from the bar to try it again, keeping his eyes on the expanding opening of the door this time, and ignoring, as much as possible, the sudden waywardness of his feet. It wasn't until he was almost there that things started to slip back into perspective. He exited with Wolfskill's laughter ringing in his ears, and Wolfskill's whiskey churning threateningly in his belly.

CHAPTER SEVEN

Thunderheads pushed up in the west, craggy white cliffs that rose to enormous heights above the gray, snow-streaked peaks of the northern Sangre de Cristo range. The black-bellied clouds filled the sky, blotting out the afternoon sun and casting a chill shadow over the pine-covered slopes that flanked the western leg of the La Veta Pass Trail. Darting tongues of lightning flicked along the dark ridges, and the air felt charged with electricity, laden with a heavy, sulfurous smell. The wind picked up as the storm slid down the Sangres and across the valley; it whistled through the pines with a low, mournful wail, thrashing the tops of the trees as if in rage. Rain began to fall, slowly at first, then faster, becoming a deluge that quickly hid the rolling hills behind slanting gray veils of precipitation.

Crossing a high, open meadow about halfway down from La Veta, a party of Mexican traders began whipping its remuda toward a sheltering grove of pines at the lower end of the clearing. Their shouts and curses came faintly through the hammering rain—condemnations of the weather, the mules, and the *segundo* for pushing on when they could have taken refuge at the upper end of the clearing and avoided this icy soaking. Lying on his stomach beneath the sprawling, twisted limbs of an ancient Ponderosa pine about two hundred yards away, Pete Meyers sympathized with the plight of the *arrieros*, the Mexican mule skinners. The storm had come on faster than he had expected, too.

Wedged between lichen-covered boulders some yards to Pete's left, his shoulders hunched to the driving rain, Charlie shouted, "Looks like they're gonna cache."

"Be my guess," Pete acknowledged. He climbed stiffly to his feet, hidden from the *arrieros'* view by the driving sheets of rain. The wind buffeted him, molding the back of his serape to his shoulders, whipping the frayed hem around his knees, but the thick, coarse weave easily shed the raindrops that slipped through the Ponderosa's limbs, and cut the frigid blast of the wind to a tolerable level. It was his feet that suffered. His moccasins, worn thin and ungreased after their long trek out of the plains where the Pawnees had accosted them, quickly sucked up the cold water, making the soles of his feet throb and burn.

They could have ridden, of course. They had saved Pete's buckskin, Charlie's appaloosa, Annie's paint, and two of the mules, but riding would have meant leaving most of their property behind, not just the packs of buckskin they had worked so hard for all summer, but their traps and plunder, as well. It was a sacrifice none of them had been willing to make, although the rugged rock- and cactus-scarred country between the Arkansas and the Front Range of the Rockies had taken its toll on their bodies, the long climb over La Veta Pass taxing them even more.

It was Charlie who first spotted the *arrieros* coming up behind them yesterday morning, near the eastern base of La Veta.

"We got company," Charlie called to the others, hauling up to eye the distant remuda suspiciously.

Instant dread passed through the group. The threat of being caught afoot by Indians had gnawed at them all for days. Without saddle stock, they felt exposed and vulnerable, edgy. But it was only a party of *mercaders*—Mexican traders—on their way back to the settlements after a summer trading expedition among the Plains tribes. Annie, Red-Winged Woman, and the kids quickly disappeared into the brush with the livestock, while Pete and Charlie waited at the edge of the trail for the *arrieros* to catch up. Their leader was a tall, broad-shouldered man in his mid-forties, handsomely built but with an arrogant demeanor. He wore leather trousers that buttoned from ankle to hip, the buttons left fashionably open to the knee to reveal dusty *calzoncillos* above his sturdy moccasins. His shirt was linen, his buckskin jacket snug-fitting, ending just above the waist; his hat was flat-crowned and flat-brimmed, with a decorative sweatband of copper pesos. He carried a British-made musket across the bows of his saddle, and a sword at his waist.

The others, eight more in all, were dressed as common peons— cotton shirts and trousers, sandals or moccasins on their feet, battered straw or oilcloth hats on their heads—and lacked the tall man's haughtiness. They carried bows and arrows, and an occasional lance; a couple had well-worn machetes strapped to their saddles. Pete stepped into the middle of the trail when the Mexicans were still a hundred yards away, and lifted the muzzle of his rifle into the air, pulling the trigger. The rifle's flat report boomed, signaling an unloaded weapon, friendly intentions, although he still had his pistol in his belt, and Charlie had both his pistols and his fusil loaded and primed.

The Mexicans drew up nervously. Several of them notched their bows, and the *segundo* lifted his musket to the cradle of his left arm. After several minutes of quiet scrutiny, the segundo spurred his horse forward alone.

Pete let the butt of his rifle rest in the dust between his moccasins, grasping the barrel just below the muzzle and resting the wrist of his free hand across the forearm of the other. His eyes narrowed as the segundo loped toward them, an uneasy feeling crowding his chest. The segundo slowed as he drew near, bringing a powerfully built blood-bay stallion to a shuffling halt. He viewed the two dusty, disheveled trappers with a look of disdain, and Pete felt his anger start to boil.

"Here's a coon lookin' to get his topknot lifted," Charlie murmured out the side of his mouth.

"Buenos dias, señors," the segundo said, stilling the bay with a steady rein. "What brings two such fine-looking gringos to my country?" He laughed sarcastically.

"I think I know you," Charlie said. "Didn't my dog used to fuck your mama?"

The segundo's face darkened abruptly. "You are trespassers, and you block my path. I would suggest that you move, or I shall be forced to run my mules over you."

"I would surely hate to waste powder killing every little pissant mule in your remuda," Pete returned easily. "Now, it'd be a different matter if it was just you and your boys. You might call that a public service, like pickin' nits off a whore's snatch."

The segundo whirled his mount, curtly motioning the others forward. "Let's go," he shouted. "We do not have all of autumn to waste here." He reined back to face the trappers. "May your prosperity continue," he jeered, and spurred his horse past them.

Pete and Charlie stepped out of the way as the *arrieros* drove their mules forward. They met the nervous glances of the peons with challenging stares, but no one spoke, and after a minute the dust of the passing herd settled, the Mexicans soon disappearing around a bend in the trail.

"Well, it wasn't what you'd call a profitable exchange," Charlie observed.

"No, it wasn't, but I'm thinkin' they're gonna make camp in another hour or so. If we was to hump it a little, we could be waiting for them somewhere down the trail tomorrow."

Charlie fingered the hilt of his knife. "I reckon," he growled softly, "we could at that."

Pete hadn't counted on the sudden appearance of the storm when he and Charlie chose this place to await the Mexicans' arrival, but he was quick to note its advantages. The rain would mask their approach on the remuda, muffle the sounds of their theft, then wipe away the traces of their escape. Furthermore, it would keep the *ar-*

rieros huddled beneath their serapes, making their job that much easier.

The rain's benefit wasn't lost upon Charlie, either, although he worried about his weapons. His blanket coat wasn't as tightly woven as Pete's serape, and his pistols were getting wet. "We're gonna have us a time if we have to fight our way outta this," Charlie said as he and Pete started across the clearing in the pounding rain.

They slogged steadily through the falling torrent, crossing the meadow on a blind path. The remuda remained invisible until they were almost upon it. With the mules in sight they stopped once more, and Charlie leaned close. "How many ye want?"

"Six," Pete immediately replied, although he had half a notion to take the whole damn bunch.

Charlie slipped his reata off his shoulder and shook out a loop. The nearest mules had already spotted them, but didn't bray or raise a fuss. They stood with their heads down, cold and miserable, muddy water sluicing off their hides. Pete could see the trees on the other side of the herd where the Mexicans had sought shelter, although the *arrieros* themselves were hidden from sight by the mules.

Charlie glanced at the sky, his expression worried. "Rain's gonna let up any minute now," he said. Although it still fell steadily, blindingly, the storm had lost some of its fury. The light seemed brighter, and the wind had calmed. It was cold, though. Their breath fogged the air in front of their faces, and Charlie's nose dripped steadily.

"Let's get to it," Pete said. He pulled his own rawhide reata from beneath his serape and started toward the mules. Charlie veered off to the left, while Pete took a more direct approach. He made his picks as he closed on the herd, knowing there wouldn't be time to examine each animal individually. He singled out a roan with a long head, a black with a white snip along its nose, and a short-coupled bay. He kept one eye on the trees as he eased into the herd.

It was a small bunch—thirty-five or forty animals—but only about half carried packs of buckskins and robes, traded from the Cheyennes for gourds, maize, *jerga,* blankets, and square sheets of tin, silver, or copper from which the Indians would fashion small trinkets or arrowheads. Pete chose animals without packs, not from any moral restraint, but because even during the brunt of the storm the Mexicans had been prudent enough to keep the laden animals closest to the trees. He worked quickly, lining the three mules out on the reata before cutting their hobbles. It took less than two minutes to snake his catch free of the remuda and start them back across the meadow. Charlie caught up with him a hundred yards out, a grin plastered across his wet face. "Slick as shootin', by God, or this coon wouldn't say so," he enthused.

Pete felt the same heady rush of excitement, but was unable to share his feelings. His emotions—excitement and tension in particular—always seemed to sink inside of him, bottling in his guts like steam in a closed kettle. In situations like this, when others were ready to laugh with nervous energy, he would grow cold and distant.

They stopped and Pete quickly fashioned a jawline bridle to the roan. The rain was slackening quickly. To the west the foothills of the Sangre de Cristos were beginning to emerge from the mist, glistening in sunlight. The storm had been typical for the mountains, quick and hard-hitting, but passing swiftly. They would have to hurry now, and he was about to say as much when a shout rose from the trees. Pete snapped his head around, cursing under his breath. He saw an *arriero* standing among the mules, pointing toward them.

"Damn!" Pete muttered under his breath. "Here's damp powder in more ways than one." He grabbed a handful of the roan's skimpy mane and swung himself astride.

Charlie bellied across the withers of a sorrel and swung his leg over the animal's back. "Yeow!" he cried, straightening aboard his mount. "Do we run, or fight?"

Common sense told Pete they should run. Their pistols were wet and probably useless; the mules, strung together as they were, were sure to slow them down; they were outnumbered at better than four-to-one odds; and while they might be without working weapons because of the rain, the Mexicans, armed with bows and lances, were far from handicapped. He reached under his serape and pulled the big .54-caliber pistol from its sheath at his waist. "Let's see how bad they want to fight, at least," he told Charlie.

"Wagh!" Charlie jerked his mule around to face the trees where the *arrieros* were swarming like ants. "This coon was half feared ye'd want to run, Pedro, *mí amigo*. He is damn glad to see ye don't."

Pete's heart hammered in his chest as the Mexicans came rushing out of the trees, loosening their bows as they fought their way through the remuda. He heard the segundo shouting angrily at the peons, warning them to be careful with their aim, to kill the gringos but to not harm the mules. Charlie laughed. "There be a man who has his priorities straight in his noggin."

"I noticed," Pete replied grimly, "that the bastard ain't makin' near as much effort to show himself as the others."

"That's a *rico* for you," Charlie agreed.

One of the *arrieros* finally worked himself clear of the remuda and dropped to his knee to notch an arrow. Charlie lifted a pistol and gently squeezed the trigger. The flint snapped downward with a shower of sparks, but the priming only fizzled, the main charge in the barrel refusing to catch. "Sonofabitch," Charlie said, the laughter suddenly gone from his voice.

There was movement in the trees. Pete caught a glimpse of a mounted rider weaving his horse through the dark trunks in an effort to flank the now-agitated remuda.

"Jump in here anytime," Charlie snapped, pulling his second pistol.

"Oh, you're doin' just fine," Pete replied calmly, keeping his eyes on the mounted rider. "Ain't no way I could do 'er any better."

"I ain't fixin' to take on the whole goddamn bunch by myself!" Charlie exploded. "Get your pistol out!"

The horseman broke free of the trees to the west of the remuda and spurred his mount to a gallop. It was the segundo, brandishing his musket as he raced toward the trappers. Pete heard the click of Charlie's second pistol, the slow hiss of the priming, then, seconds later, the shallow boom of a damp charge, like a cork pulled from a bottle of expensive wine—a hangfire, and no telling where the ball flew.

"*Sonofabitch!*" Charlie shouted, jerking on the sorrel's single rein, fastened out of his *reata*. "Let's get outta here, Pete."

But Pete held his mule steady. He licked his lips, his eyes bright and fixed. The segundo swept forward, his musket held high.

"Meyers! Goddamnit, come on!"

"You go ahead," Pete said. "I think I'll wait for the segundo."

"Forget that sonofabitch. Let's go!"

"You go on! Get the mules packed and get the women outta here. I'll be along."

"Goddamn bullheaded Dutchman," Charlie said angrily, reining his mule back and pulling his knife. "All right, you shoot him, and I'll get his scalp."

Pete laughed. "Hell, I don't *want* his scalp. What I want is to wipe that arrogant look off his face."

"Just do it quick-like, then," Charlie said. He gave the peons a worried glance, "We're runnin' outta time."

The segundo was less than thirty yards away when Pete cocked his pistol and pulled it from the protection of his serape. The segundo jerked his mount to a sliding halt and threw the musket to his shoulder, jerking the trigger in his haste. Pete had no idea where the ball flew, but it wasn't close enough for him to hear. The segundo stared at the two trappers in disbelief, then quickly jammed the musket between his knee and stirrup strap and yanked the sword from its scabbard. He waved the blade menacingly above his head and shouted, "You will surrender immediately. Lay down your weapons."

Charlie guffawed as Pete lifted his pistol.

The segundo's eyes widened. "If you fire at me you will—"

The pistol bucked in Pete's hand, and the segundo was slammed from his saddle. The peons suddenly stopped, their cries of outrage sheered into a stunned silence.

"Wagh," Charlie said softly. "That's makin' 'em come. Good shooting, Pete."

The segundo sat up, clutching his shoulder. His hat had been knocked off his head, and his lank, black hair fell across his forehead. The front of his jacket was crimson with blood, his face pale, his expression dazed.

"You want me to scalp anything?" Charlie asked.

Pete drew in a deep, shaky breath, lowering the pistol. "Naw. I believe I'm satisfied."

"*Bueno,*" Charlie said, sheathing his knife.

The rain began to flag. Toward the Sangres, a double rainbow had appeared, arching high above the valley floor. Pete's thoughts went to Annie and Red-Winged Woman, waiting in a shallow canyon behind them. They would have the packs off the saddle stock, and the saddles in place. The packs would be resting on dry ground beneath the trees, and the women would be anxiously scanning the hills, watching for the mules their men would bring, watching for their men. Pulling the roan around, Pete said, "Let's go to Taos."

CHAPTER EIGHT

They reined up at the edge of the plaza, and Travis let his gaze roam curiously over the milling humanity before him. Men and women moved through the dusty square in a manner that seemed both hurried and relaxed, while children darted among them, laughing, calling to one another in play. From one of the narrow streets that wound into the plaza from the north trudged a burro train—seven shaggy, sleepy-eyed animals made twice as tall in silhouette by their towering loads of piñon wood. The train was preceded by a middle-aged man on a bony mule, followed by a boy afoot, dressed in ragged, knee-length cotton trousers and a baggy shirt that had been repeatedly patched and repaired; the boy carried a willow switch that he used against the burros' flanks whenever one of the animals slowed its pace. Despite the crowd, there were no soldiers in sight, and Travis breathed a shallow sigh of relief. The smell of *chili colorado* and *refritos* filled the early evening air with a rich, spicy fragrance, and his stomach rumbled noisily.

Jake gave him a scornful glance. "Is that belly of yours ever going to shut up?"

Travis grinned and said, "Hell, Jake, that's supper I smell. Why'n you come along and I'll let you feed me for a change?"

Jake's face flushed, but he didn't reply. He jabbed his spurs into his mount's ribs and rode into the plaza, forcing a number of pedestrians out of his way. Travis chuckled to himself; he knew the deer he'd shot last night, the only meat taken, rubbed at Jake like a burr caught in the seat of his pants.

"You shouldn't push him like that," Clint said. "You think you understand him, but you don't."

"Aw, Jake ain't so bad," Travis replied. "He's kinda like a dead horse. Once you've been around him a while, you don't hardly notice the smell."

"Jake's killed three people, Travis," Clint said softly.

Travis's grin faded. "Are you telling me that straight up? Jake's killed three men?"

"Just don't push him too far. Or turn your back on him." Clint nudged his horse after Jake's. The pack mules followed on a lead, the second and third hitched to the tail of the animal in front of it. Jake had dismounted in front of a cantina across the plaza, and Clint pulled up beside him, straightening the mules out at the hitching rail while Jake went inside.

Travis glanced around the plaza once more. Nothing he saw looked familiar. Conversation flowed around him like warm honey, but he understood none of it. Glances touched him and moved on. The burro train had halted in a cluster in front of a cobbler's shop on the west side of the plaza, and the boy had run inside. He reappeared a moment later with the shop's proprietor, who inspected the various loads critically for several minutes before making his choice. At last he pointed to one of the burros, and the boy ducked in and separated the animal from the rest of the train and drove it around back. The proprietor and the man on the mule talked until the boy returned with the bare-backed burro, carrying a saddle blanket and a rawhide rope over his shoulder. Their transaction finished, the cobbler went back inside his shop while the wood-cutters drove their burros on to the next place of business.

A wave of loneliness washed over Travis, worse even than what he'd experienced locked inside the Governor's Palace, where he'd at least had the marginal company of the crusty old corporal. For the first time since leaving home last spring, he missed Arkansas. Even the grudging acceptance of his neighbors had to be better than this, he told himself.

Angrily, he shook that thought away. He knew better. Hanging Creek Falls, the little dirt-water mountain community northeast of Fort Smith that he'd once called home, had had no sympathy for a coward, especially one who had allowed his brother to be killed by river pirates.

Travis guided his mule around the burro-train and rode across the plaza. He dismounted beside Clint's horse and entered the cantina. It was too early to be rowdy, but there was still a fair-sized crowd inside. Jake and Clint stood at the bar, and Jake's spine was rigid; his jaw, seen from the angle of the door, looked like a lump of iron thrust above the bar. Clint's head was lowered, his shoulders slumped in resignation. Travis slouched into a chair beside the door and leaned the Kentucky against the wall, wondering what he'd missed. A platter of greasy mutton sat on a nearby table. Travis eyed it hungrily, but the soldiers in Santa Fe had taken his money, and he had only the doe's untanned hide for trade; he didn't want to waste it on cold meat.

"What does a man have to do around here to get a drink?" Jake shouted, startling the room into silence.

Clint glanced nervously over his shoulder, and Travis saw the desperation in his eyes as they touched on him. At the end of the bar a Mexican inside a dirty apron walked slowly toward the two brothers. He said something in Spanish that Travis didn't understand.

"I want some service," Jake said loudly. His fists, Travis noticed, were clenched on top of the bar.

The Mexican shrugged and looked at the men he had been talking with. He said something in Spanish, and the room laughed.

Jake's body seemed to convulse. He jerked upright, shoving away from the bar. Clint said, "Take it easy, Jake."

"Who are you laughing at?" Jake demanded. He turned to face the room, his eyes blazing. "Who are you laughing at?" he shouted, showering spittle.

A pint-size Mexican at a table close to the bar snorted laughter, and Jake seemed to explode. He flung the table aside and grabbed the Mexican by his shirt, hauling him to his feet. "Are you laughing at me?" Jake screeched. "Is that what you're doing, you goddamn fucking greaser? You think this is funny now?" He flung the little Mexican into his chair so hard it crashed backward.

No one moved, but the silence changed. A Mexican stood and tossed his cards on the table. Others began to stand also, drifting almost mechanically toward the bar. A few edged toward Travis, and he swore under his breath and straightened. Jake was grinning maniacally as the crowd began to close on him. "Are you in on this, Ketchum?" he called.

Eyeing the approaching Mexicans, Travis reluctantly stood. He picked up the Kentucky and held it in both hands. That momentarily stopped the advancing line of Mexicans, but then several others stood, and a couple drew their knives. Those who had hesitated suddenly grinned and began to move forward again. Then Jake pulled his pistol and everything ground to a halt once more. Laughing, Jake said, "How about that, Ketchum? These men aren't as tough as they thought they were."

"Goddamnit, Jake," Travis said.

"Come on, Jake," Clint said, putting a hand on his brother's shoulder. "Let's go."

Jake shook the hand away. "I haven't had my drink yet," he said. He edged down the bar until he stood opposite the barkeeper. "Have you got any bourbon?"

"They won't serve bourbon in a place like this," Clint said.

"What would you know about a place like this?" Jake sneered. He spun to face Travis. "Little Clint here hasn't even been with a woman, have you, Clint?"

"Jake, don't do this," Clint pleaded.

"Let it go, Jake."

"Shut up, Ketchum," Jake said pleasantly. Swinging his pistol around to cover Travis, he suddenly grinned. "Looks like you're the slow one this time, doesn't it?"

Clint said, "Jake, let's go."

Jake glared at his brother. "For Christ's sake, are you going to be the baby of the family until you die?"

"We don't have to do this."

Jake's face started to redden. "Shut up, will you! Just shut the fuck up!" He faced the bartender again, straightening his arm until the pistol's muzzle was less than a foot from the barkeep's chest. "I want some brandy, then," he rasped. "Do you understand that, you sonofabitch?"

"*Sí,*" the barkeep said. He made a cautioning gesture with his hands as he backed down the bar. There was a jug on the rear shelf. He lifted it down and pulled the cork, pouring the dark amber liquid into a lopsided clay glass. He brought the drink back and set it on the bar in front of Jake. "*Beberse,*" he said.

Jake took the glass and drank slowly, his gaze never leaving the bartender's face, the pistol never wavering. When he finished, he dropped the glass to the floor and grinned wetly. "That wasn't so hard, was it?"

The barkeep shrugged and shook his head. "No."

Jake laughed. "It is truly amazing how a pistol can educate a man, isn't it? Five minutes ago you didn't even understand English. Now you're speaking it like an American. You ought to thank me for that."

The barkeep didn't reply.

"Well, it doesn't matter," Jake said cockily. Glancing at Clint, he added, "How about a woman before we leave, little brother?"

"Christ, Jake, no. Let's just get out of here."

Laughing, Jake sauntered toward the door. Travis moved to flank him, and Clint stepped in on the other side. They backed toward the door together. A few of the Mexicans followed. Clint and Travis shouldered through the door first. The rapidly cooling air of early evening hit the back of Travis's neck like a specter's icy caress. He shuddered involuntarily as he backed toward his mule. Jerking the reins loose, he swung into the saddle. Clint handed him the reins of Jake's horse, then mounted his own and lined the pack mules out behind him. When he was ready, he hollered, "Come on, Jake."

But Jake wasn't in any hurry. He stood in the door, leaning against the jamb. At his brother's words, he let the pistol's hammer down to half-cock and slid it into a leather sheath at his belt. He stood there a moment longer, then turned his back contemptuously on the crowd. "Hell, that wasn't so bad," he said, walking over to accept the reins Travis offered him. He pulled himself into the saddle and backed his horse free of the mules. "I feel like having a woman. How about it, Ketchum? Clint's too chickenshit to dip his wick. Are you?"

"I reckon not, Jake."

"You reckon you ain't afraid, or you reckon you don't want a woman?"

"I don't want a woman right now."

"Well, I guess that fits. Come on, Clint, let's go see what Taos has to offer."

Jake jogged toward a side street, but Clint held back, uneasily watching the Mexicans who crowded the cantina's door.

Travis's pulse pounded loudly in his ears. "Your brother's crazy," he said tautly.

"I know," Clint replied miserably. "Sometimes he just gets like that, and I never know what he'll do."

"Then why are you still with him?"

Clint looked at him. "He's my brother, Travis. I can't just abandon him."

Travis nodded. He'd felt the same way toward his own brother, Chet, who was always going off half-cocked and devil-may-care. But Jake wasn't kin, and that made all the difference in the world to

Travis. "I'm cuttin' my pin, Clint. I'm in enough trouble with Mexico as it is. I don't need to go looking for more."

"Just stay out of his way," Clint said, tugging on the mules' lead. He swiveled in the saddle. "And watch yourself. Jake hasn't forgotten that mule, or the deer."

Travis eyed the Mexicans who still crowded the cantina's door, their gazes as cold and hard as a winter's storm. Several still had their knives in their hands. Sighing, Travis reined his mule away from the cantina, careful to avoid the street where Jake and Clint had disappeared. Loneliness engulfed him. He wanted to go home, to go back in time to a place where he had been liked and respected, where he had friends and family and purpose.

But there was no going back now. No possibility of ever recapturing what had been lost after his brother's death. Lifting his shoulders resolutely, Travis turned down a side street.

Chapter Nine

Consuelo wasn't around when Eli returned to her little house on the side of the hill. It was late, but he waited until the sun dropped below the horizon before leading the packhorses out of the corral and tying them to the posts supporting the lean-to. He rigged the sawbucks in place and lashed his gear to the frames. He didn't hurry, but Consuelo still hadn't shown up by the time he pulled the last knot tight. He knew he should wait, but there was no telling when she might return. He went inside and dropped a goatskin poke filled with coins on the table. She would understand, he told himself. It was what he always did when putting out for a season, and she would know that he meant for her to remain behind this time, too. The money would help her get through the winter, or to her relatives in El Paso, if that was what she wanted.

He went outside and mounted the sorrel. An achromatic light filled the western sky, turning the fields of wheat and maize into a patchwork of tarnished gold, purpling the long stretch of sage that

ran into the wild distance. From up here the lights of Taos glowed
warmly, reminding him of the pleasure he'd felt his first night back,
the way it had almost been like coming home. The memory brought
a pang of sadness, and he rode away from the house without looking
back.

Eli didn't fully understand why he was leaving the money. He
tried to tell himself that it was all for Consuelo, what was best for
her, whether she saw it that way or not, but he'd always had trouble
lying to himself. The decision had come to him that afternoon. He
had been leaning against the wall outside Wolfskill's saloon, waiting
out the lingering tendrils of dizziness, when a couple of women approached under the portico, gliding effortlessly beneath their flared,
stiffly rustling skirts. The woman on the inside was young and at-
tractive, her narrow waist accentuated by the sharp flaring of her hips
and breasts; she had a smooth, aristocratic face, a slim nose, and
bold, seductive eyes—a señorita from one of the wealthier families
of Taos, those whose homes were built just off the plaza.

Her companion was heavier, without the constraint of a whale-
bone corset, and quite a bit older—an aunt, perhaps, brought to Taos
to serve as the younger woman's duenna. Behind them followed a
huge, apple-cheeked Mexican carrying a brace of pistols in his belt
and a saber over one hip, no doubt the women's bodyguard.

The sight had amused Eli for some reason. Maybe it was the girl's
candid stare that appealed to him; or the snappish scorn of the
duenna, and the way she moved protectively closer to her young
charge when she spotted Eli. He grinned hugely at them both, and
doffed his hat as they drew even.

"*Buenos días, señor,*" the girl murmured, smiling just enough to
reveal the pearly tips of her teeth.

"*Buenos días,*" Eli returned.

The duenna grabbed the girl's arm and gave it a sharp tug, hurrying her past. Eli laughed, and the girl glanced over her shoulder with
a startled expression, stumbling on the hard-packed, corrugated dirt
beneath the portico. Eli winked, and the girl smiled again, but hesitantly, confused.

"*Adios, señorita,*" Eli called, and she had time to nod once before
her duenna gave her another tug, pulling her off balance.

The bodyguard slowed uncertainly, and Eli let the smile slide off
his face. "*Qué pasa, gordo?*"

The Mexican flushed at the insult, but then went on as if he hadn't heard. Eli watched until they disappeared into one of the shops circling the plaza. It was then that his thoughts turned to Consuelo—plump, settled Consuelo, her ponderous, vein-tracked breasts as soft as warm butter, her thighs fleshy. It occurred to him that she had probably never been beautiful in the way this girl who'd just flirted with him was, nor as refined. Consuelo had never sat at elegantly served dinners, or drunk wine from fine crystal. She didn't play the piano or recite poetry or read novels. It made Eli remember Girardin's veiled promise of partnership, the opportunity to grow with a growing firm. He envisioned a house and grounds in proportion to Girardin's mansion, or even that of Seven Oaks, and shining carriages with matching teams to take him to his office every morning. There were monthly visits to a barber, and baths taken on a regular basis, with maybe a few slaves to tend to the more mundane chores. It was a dream that had been with him for a long time now, but Eli knew the life he craved would never tolerate a coarse, mix-blooded woman who smoked cigarillos and cursed like a bull-whacker. He had told her that morning that she could come with him if she wanted, but he knew now that that had been a mistake. Consuelo would be an anchor that forever held him back, and there was no sense in stringing her along, letting her think he was wanting more with her, when he knew he wanted much less.

So he left her the money, and the opportunity to do with it as she saw fit. Maybe she would keep it and stay in Taos. Or maybe she would go to El Paso, as she'd threatened. He told himself that it didn't matter, and knew that was also a lie.

He took his gear to the warehouse and stored it inside. McClure and the Mexican boy, Pedro, were going over the pack saddles, checking the rigging and the rust-colored oilcloth panniers for tears or defects. Pierre Turpin, the cook, sorted his kettles beside the fireplace. Remi LeBlanc, Johnny Two-Dogs and Old Cal Underwood sat cross-legged to one side, playing cards. They had a jug of Bill Wolfskill's Taos Lightning sitting on the Navajo blanket that served as a table, and twigs they were using as stakes—cottonwood, willow, and piñon, representing a good-sized chunk of their next season's catch. McClure came over as Eli dumped his gear inside the door, a troubled expression clouding his face.

"Everything appears to be in shape. We'll leave at first light, and should return within the week. I anticipate no more than five or six days."

Eli nodded. "*Bueno*. We'll put out as soon as you get back."

McClure was taking Remi, Johnny, and Old Cal over the mountains to pick up the supplies he'd cached there last summer. Eli would remain in Taos with Pedro and Turpin, taking care of the last-minute chores and hopefully signing on a few more hands.

"I made arrangements at Cobos to pick up extra shoes for the mules. The new mules will need to be shod before we leave, and they'll all need to be checked."

Eli squinted down at McClure's short, roly-poly form, and told himself to go easy. McClure was a worrier, fussing around like a nervous mother; it was irritating at times, but maybe not all bad.

McClure's gaze went to the trappers sitting by the fire, and his brows furrowed. "I suppose they would mutiny if someone suggested they help with the chores," he said quietly.

"They might," Eli acknowledged. He squatted to dig a dented tin cup from his saddlebags. The mountain men's lack of discipline rubbed at McClure's army training, but that was something he was going to have to bend to, Eli reasoned. Sure as hell, the boys weren't going to change. Standing, his cup dangling from a finger, he said, "Old Cal and Remi and Johnny figure mucking around like this is a swamper's job. They'll be doing their share and more when we get to beaver country."

"Yes, of course," McClure said curtly. He looked at Eli. "You'll pick up the shoes while I'm gone."

"I'll see what I can do," Eli replied. He moved away, leaving Mc-Clure to his fretting. Old Cal looked up as he approached, blinking morosely. He was a tall, gangling splinter of a man, with skin like scorched leather shrunk over a crude framework of bones. His long, iron-gray hair hung lank and greasy over skinny, sloping shoulders, and his cheeks, beneath smoky eyes, were sunken around missing teeth.

"How, Eli," Old Cal said in his scratchy, whining voice.

"*Qué es?*" Eli replied, spiraling down to sit cross-legged between Cal and Remi. Cal passed him the jug, and Eli took a pull. Lowering the jug to his knee, he wiped the burn from his lips with the back of his sleeve. "Lord, that's hot," he said. Then, slipping Remi a wink, he added, "I wish ol' Wolfskill would water his whiskey down a mite."

Old Cal's head snapped up with a horrified expression. "Water it down?" he croaked. "Hoss, ye can't water down good whiskey. That be blasphemy ye're talkin' of, and h'it won't shine with this chile. Not by a long chalk, h'it won't."

Keeping his face deadpan, Remi said solemnly, *"Non,* Cal, Eli is right. Wolfskill, his whiskey has too much fire." He shifted his rump on the blanket, a short, broad-framed French-Canadian of indeterminate age, with thick black hair that only came down past his collar— short, by mountain standards—and a broad, swarthy face. His eyes were a washed-out blue, twinkling with devilment. *"Oui,"* he added, refusing to even glance at Old Cal. "It would not hurt to add a little water, no?"

"But how's it gonna *help*?" Old Cal wailed. He looked at Eli and shook his head. "Hoss, ye done spent too much time back in the States. Ye have, now, and I've seed it happen afore." He looked at the others, his tone pleading. "Do ye hyar, boys? Ol' Cal's seed it. Coon gets hisself some kinda title like booshway, and the next thing ye know he's wearin' underwear and smokin' fancy seegars like some kinda grandee." He slewed his gaze back to Eli. "Hoss, them doin's won't wash with this crowd. Won't wash atall." He sniffed self-righteously.

Eli laughed, pouring a shot of whiskey into his cup, then passing the jug on.

Johnny Two-Dogs had been studying his cards quietly while Eli and Remi baited Cal. Now he folded them and laid them carefully aside. Stretching his feet toward the fire, he said, "Hell, Cal, you're just afraid a little civilization's going to rub off on you." Johnny was a tall, handsomely built man of thirty or thirty-five, with long, raven-colored hair and a dusky complexion. He grinned impishly at the look of indignation on Old Cal's face.

"Danged right I am!" Cal cried. "Knowed a man once took to wearin' underwear, and lost all interest in womens, he did. Started drinkin' tea, too, 'stead of whiskey. Craziest goddamn thing this coon's ever seed." He shook his head sadly, staring at the dark designs woven into the blanket.

Before anyone could reply, boots scuffed the hard-packed dirt floor behind Eli, and the laughter quickly died. Eli looked over his shoulder. A kid stood just inside the door, dusty-faced, stoop-shouldered, as sober as a cloudy day. He wore run-down boots, shabby trousers, a ragged canvas jacket streaked with dirt, and a cloth cap with a creased leather visor pulled over his long, tangled blond hair. His chin bristled with a fine but unkempt beard. He looked like a bum, Eli thought, except for the long elegantly carved Kentucky rifle he carried in the crook of his left arm.

"Scrawny little runt, ain't he?" Old Cal observed loudly.

"I'm looking for Eli Cutler," the kid said.

"You've found him." Eli stood and hitched at his trousers. McClure came up to stand beside him, but didn't speak.

"My name's Travis Ketchum. I'm looking for a job, and I heard you might be hiring."

"Might be," Eli acknowledged, taking in the kid's bedraggled appearance once more. "Ever trap beaver?"

"Some, back in Arkansas. Mostly muskrat and coon and such. Hunted deer and bear for their hides, too."

McClure cleared his throat, a nonverbal appeal for Eli to hire the kid on the spot, but something held Eli back. He studied Travis's face. The boy stared back silently, obviously needing a job, but too proud to say more than he already had. It was a good sign, Eli decided.

"Got a horse and traps?" Eli asked.

"I've got a mule and a good rifle, though some might call it light. I was hoping to get the rest on credit."

Eli was silent a moment, eyes narrowed as he continued to study the kid. "*Bueno*," he said at last, coming to a decision. "You can spread your bedroll here tonight, if you want. Tomorrow you'll go with McClure." He jerked a thumb toward the clerk. "He's got some business to take care of on the other side of the mountains and can use an extra hand. If you work out, we'll hire you for the season, supply you ourselves on company credit, and take it out of your pay when we get back. Sound fair?"

A look of relief crossed Travis's face. "Yes, sir, I reckon it does."

Eli nodded, shoving down the feeling of uncertainty that still plagued at him. "Take your mule to the corral, Travis, and welcome to the brigade."

CHAPTER TEN

Boots thudded in the hall outside the cubicle where Mateo Chavez lay, and the coarse, ripped blanket that served as a door swayed inward. Mateo sat up, grabbing his cutlass from the floor beside his stained corn-shuck mattress, but before he could pull the weapon from its scabbard, the blanket swung back and the boots clopped on.

Mateo lay back as the voices receded down the hall. He forced himself to relax. Beside him, her massive, flabby breasts sagging deflatedly to either side of her humped stomach, Rosa studied him curiously.

"You are *bandito* maybe?" she asked.

"No," Mateo replied. He was a horse thief, perhaps an accomplice to murder—by Don Julio's standards, at least—but he wasn't a bandit; so far he'd avoided that.

"Ah, *mío tigre*," Rosa muttered, rolling onto her side to face him. The heat that radiated from her body reminded Mateo of a large, smoldering log; sweat plastered her greasy hair to her forehead and dampened her pimpled chest. Clear-headed after his nap, if not entirely sober yet, Mateo became aware of her smell—the stale, musky odor of sex mingled with the stench of unwashed flesh and cheap, cloying perfume. He sidled toward the edge of the mattress, but Rosa followed, stroking his chest, trailing her fingers down over the hard, flat plain of his stomach. "My tiger man," Rosa purred. "You are the best Rosa has ever lain with. Better even than the governor and all his soldiers."

Mateo didn't know whether he wanted to laugh or cry. He pictured the Governor's Palace on the north side of Santa Fe's plaza, and recalled the soldiers he'd seen there and elsewhere around Santa Fe. Had she ever washed between them? he wondered.

"Too soon?" Rosa asked, drawing her hand back from his groin in disappointment. "We will wait. Rosa needs her rest, too. *Hijo de puta,* there is a crowd tonight, and everyone is horny." She rolled onto her back and rubbed her forehead, sighing dramatically. "In the winter there is hardly any business at all. Too cold to come to Rosa then. Better to snuggle in with their fat wives, even if they do not let them slip their skinny horns into the fold." She laughed. "Asses. Do they not know Rosa can make them forget the cold as she does the heat."

Mateo jerked his knees up and jackknifed around until he was sitting on the pallet with his ankles crossed on the hard-packed dirt floor. His clothes lay in a heap beside him. He rummaged through them, dressing from the head down as he had learned to do as a boy on cold winter mornings when he didn't want to leave the warmth of his robes—shirt and sombrero first, then his dingy cotton drawers and leather trousers, and finally his moccasins and *botas,* the knee-high, scarlet-trimmed leather leggings he wore as decoration and protection against the thorny mesquite and cactus.

Rosa watched silently as he dressed, but he could sense her growing displeasure. She would be expected to follow when he returned to the main room of the cantina, to circulate among the customers while urging them to drink and gamble and, eventually, come with her to this tiny, foul-smelling crib lit by a single tallow candle. Mateo knew she had hoped to entice him into a second round, but his desire was sated now. He thought only of escape.

"Such hurry." She mocked a hurtful tone. "You do not like Rosa?"

Mateo didn't reply. From the pouch on his belt he withdrew a pair of coins and dropped them on the mattress beside her fat, scarred belly. "*Dos pesos,*" he said flatly.

Rosa picked up the coins and examined them in the candle's smoky light. "*Sí,*" she said. "*Dos pesos.*" Looking up hopefully, she added, "Most men like Rosa. They give her more *pesos* that she does not have to share with the pig who owns the cantina. You like Rosa, eh?"

Mateo smiled bitterly. "Only when I'm drunk, and I'm not drunk now."

Rosa's face crumbled like hardened clay struck from behind. Then it tightened abruptly, and she snarled, "You are like all men, eh? Big, tough, macho. But Rosa does not think you are so big or tough. Your penis is like a worm. I could not even feel it. You are like a little boy, and just as stupid. It was not good for Rosa. It would not even be good for a sheep. Go. Go back to your flocks. Do not bother Rosa. She likes only real men. True *hombres*."

Mateo picked up the cutlass and Rosa's face blanched, but he only belted it around his waist and turned to the blanketed door.

"Wait," Rosa called after him. "Rosa did not mean that. You come back later, huh? You ask for Rosa. She treat you good."

"*Sí*," Mateo said wearily. "Rosa is a first-class whore."

Her face brightened at the compliment, and Mateo pushed the blanket aside and stepped into the darkened hallway. To his right, the clamor of the cantina—the drunken shouts and laughter, the call of bets being made at the monte and faro tables, the screech of a violin and the erratic blats of a trumpet that passed for the cantina's orchestra—assaulted him. Through the narrow opening at the end of the hall he could see a corner of the main room, the splashy blues of a soldier's uniform, the white linen shirt and slicked-back ebony hair of a professional gambler, the crimson and black swirl of a whore's skirt. Mateo paused, reluctant to return to the blast of noise and stench, to stand at the gaming tables foolishly tossing his money away, to pound Jorge or Antonio on the back, and to be pounded in return, grinning like an idiot when he only wished to hide. But there was no back door here, and the windows were too small to crawl through. He was trapped.

He made his way down the hall, slowing as he neared its end. The main room was big and low-ceiling, crammed with men and a handful of women. A long, ornately carved bar against the rear wall was packed with drinkers, maybe half of them foreigners—teamsters, adventurers, investors who had come to milk Mexico of its wealth, speaking Spanish tinged with French, German, British, and American accents. Candle chandeliers hung suspended from the ceiling, and a huge potbellied stove freighted in from some distant Missouri settlement sat in the middle of the room, its cold iron rusted with tobacco spit. An emerald green parrot from far to the south was tethered to a small swing that hung behind the bar, nearly obscured by a fog of tobacco smoke.

Mateo halted in the arched entry to the main room, and his heart lurched toward his throat. Across the cantina, his back to the wall and his thumbs hooked behind a broad leather belt, stood Gregorio el Toro, his father's foreman. Their eyes met and locked, and Gregorio smiled sardonically without moving. Two men Mateo had never seen before appeared suddenly at his side. Both carried pistols in their belts. The man on Mateo's right gripped his arm and said, "Do not fight us, amigo. It would do you no good, and only make matters worse." He lifted the *belduque* from Mateo's belt, while the other man withdrew the cutlass.

Gregorio ambled across the room with a puma's lazy stride. The mocking grin never wavered. He was tall and broad-shouldered, with a heavy gut and an ugly face scarred by smallpox. His eyes were small, glittering with triumph beneath the swayed brim of a peaked, oilcloth sombrero. He stopped in front of Mateo and returned his thumbs to his belt. Leering down the broken slope of his nose, his voice rumbling like distant thunder, Gregorio said, "So, the cock has flown the coop, eh?"

The man on Mateo's left chuckled harshly.

"What's the matter, boy? Some whore pinch your tongue off back there?"

Again, the man on Mateo's left laughed.

Gregorio took a deep breath and let it go. The powerful odor of onions and pulque washed over Mateo's face, but he couldn't look away; he felt immobilized by Gregorio's opaque stare, hypnotized. Fear gripped him like a spike driven through his brain. Mateo knew it wasn't Gregorio's skill with the herds that had induced his father to hire him as foreman of his growing hacienda. On the Pecos it was more important to know how to handle men and fight Indians than raise sheep and cattle and horses. Gregorio's skill in fighting the Apaches on their own terms, in matching their savageness with his own special brand of cruelty, was almost legendary. Death and torture were old friends to Gregorio el Toro, fear his stock in trade. Mateo hoped desperately that his father had also come, and that he had only sent his foreman inside to retrieve his son. He still believed his father might brand him as a thief, but even that was better than what he knew Gregorio was capable of.

"Come with me, little cock," Gregorio growled. "You'll talk soon enough, or I'll cut your lips off."

Gregorio turned away, and the men gripping Mateo's arms forced him to follow. Gregorio's sullen expression and brutish reputation cut a broad swath through the crowd. Several turned to watch them leave. No one spoke or attempted to interfere.

In the bright moonlight outside, clustered in the middle of the street, sat a group of horsemen. Mateo recognized Jorge and Antonio in the middle of the group. Antonio sat hunched in pain, his nose hovering just above his broad saddle horn, and Jorge's face was bruised and swollen. A vaquero came forward, leading Mateo's *grullo*. His bedroll and the *escopeta* were tied behind the cantle.

"Get on your horse," Gregorio ordered.

Mateo eyed the *escopeta* as he checked the cinch, but he knew Gregorio would have pulled the charge before making it so accessible. His knife and cutlass were still with the men who had escorted him from the cantina.

They mounted, and Gregorio led them away from the center of town. Mateo fell in beside Jorge, glancing at him once, then looking away, repelled more by the hopelessness of his expression than by the puffed and discolored flesh. Jorge looked like a man on his way to the gallows.

They followed the Santa Fe Road out of town, then turned onto a narrow *carreta* track that led into the foothills. Before them the Sangre de Cristos were a solid, humped mass, without feature. Mateo knew where they were headed. They had sold most of the horses they had stolen from his father's remuda to a trader on this road, and Gregorio would want to retrieve as many of the mounts as possible before returning to Don Julio's rancho. Mateo thought it was a good sign that they were going after the remuda. It suggested that they might be taken home to be punished.

It was only a short ride to the trader's corrals. They turned off the main trail and descended into a little hollow surrounded by piñons. The house was dark, but there was a fire burning near the entrance to the barn, with several men standing beside it. Mateo spotted his father's broad tan sombrero and silver-buttoned vaquero trousers among the tightest cluster of men, and felt a rush of relief. Gregorio led his band of riders to the edge of the light and halted.

Don Julio stepped away from the crowd, the rigid line of his jaw revealing the anger that boiled inside. "Where?" Don Julio spat.

"The Green Parrot," Gregorio replied. Jerking a thumb toward Mateo, he added. "We waited while this one visited a whore. A last fling for the condemned."

The curled brim of Don Julio's sombrero lifted as he stepped past Gregorio. His lips looked thin and bloodless, and his eyes glinted as if lit from within. "To a whore? You shame me this way to visit a whore."

Mateo forced himself to meet his father's gaze. "Just for tonight—" he began, but before he could finish his explanation, Don Julio's arm flashed up, then down. Mateo never saw the quirt, but he felt its cut through his leather trousers. The *grullo* jumped at the loud pop, but Mateo brought it under control, reining back to face his father. In the stable's entryway he could see the trader's stern approval, could sense the silent laughter of the others. Humiliation engulfed him, but he wouldn't look away or lower his eyes.

"I do not know you," Don Julio hissed. "You are not of my blood."

"I am the son of your wife," Mateo whispered.

Don Julio's face paled. "You dare speak that way to me?" he breathed, his voice shaky. "You corrupt her honor by calling her your mother." He stepped back and slapped his quirt against his leg. A fist slammed into Mateo's spine between the shoulder blades, spilling him from the saddle. Others moved in quickly to grab his arms and drag him to his feet. Gregorio appeared before him, blocking the light from the stables. He patted Mateo's sides roughly, tugging at his belt, his shirt. Then he stepped back and dropped Mateo's money pouch into Don Julio's hand. Don Julio tossed it to the trader without looking at it. Jorge and Antonio were each in turn knocked from their mounts, their clothing raided, their money passed back to the trader without being counted or acknowledged. When he was finished, Gregorio moved aside and Don Julio stepped forward once more, facing the three of them.

"Hear me well," Don Julio said in a voice that still quavered. "No longer do you belong to the rancho of Don Julio Chavez. You!" He poked the tip of his quirt into Mateo's chest. "You are no longer Chavez." His gaze raked Jorge and Antonio. "Nor will you claim the name of Rodolso. For your mothers I will spare your worthless lives, but you are no longer of our families, and if you are caught on Rancho de Chavez again, you will be hung as thieves and murderers, your bodies left as carrion to feed the vultures. Is that understood?"

Numbly, Mateo nodded. A sadistic smile crossed Don Julio's face then. He looked at Gregorio and said, "The iron."

Fear flooded Mateo. He felt lightheaded, and his legs began to tremble. He stared into his father's face and read the madness there. For the first time that evening, Don Julio actually smiled.

"The others first," Don Julio whispered to his son. "Then you, twice." He touched Mateo's left cheek gently, almost lovingly, then the right. "Both sides, so that you may know the consequences of your actions."

Behind Mateo, Antonio whimpered like a frightened child. Gregorio stepped away from the fire, a hot branding iron held away from his massive body in one gloved fist. The end of the iron glowed cherry red. He fixed Antonio with a look of disgust and growled, "Bring him."

At Gregorio's command, the two men holding Antonio hauled him forward. Antonio screamed. He kicked at the dirt, strained backward against the forward pull of the men holding him, struggled, and screamed again. But he was no match for the burly strength of the two men gripping his arms. They dragged him to the fire and halted, and Gregorio calmly backhanded Antonio across the face, severing another terrified scream. "You will be silent," Gregorio instructed, holding the hot end of the iron near his own cheek so that it cast a reddish hue across his face. "You will take this like a man, and not add further embarrassment to the name of Rodolso." He nodded to a third man, who came around behind Antonio and gripped the youth's head in an armlock, twisting it so that the left cheek was exposed. Scowling in concentration, Gregorio lowered the iron toward Antonio's face. "Do not squirm, little cock. I do not want to botch this job."

Mateo glanced wildly at his father, but Don Julio was staring transfixed at the scene before the fire. His eyes were bright with anticipation, his lips peeled back in a skeletal grin. Antonio gasped as the heat of the iron touched his cheek, but was strangely silent as the glowing metal seared his flesh.

Mateo straightened, lifting his head, squaring his shoulders. His shame and humiliation fell away, replaced by a cold, numbing rage. He lifted his foot and brought it down sharply against the instep of the man on his left. The man howled in pain, and Mateo jerked away from his grip, twisting toward the man on his right and slamming his fist into his stomach. The second man grunted as he jackknifed over Mateo's fist. Mateo pulled free of his captors, snatching the pistol from the man's belt as he dropped to his knees. Stepping clear,

Mateo cocked the pistol as he raised it, staring through the weapon's sights into his father's startled eyes.

"Let them go," Mateo said tonelessly.

Don Julio's jaw trembled in restrained fury. He lifted his quirt and brought it down savagely against his own leg. "You dare threaten your father," Don Julio said. "You dare lift a weapon against your own blood. What kind of animal have I raised?"

The absurdity of his father's indignation shook Mateo to his core. For the first time, Mateo recognized the true depth of his father's insanity, and he felt, oddly, a momentary pang of sympathy, a sense of loss, and waste.

Gregorio dropped the iron back into the fire and hooked his thumbs in his belt. "So, the *niño* has found his spine at last. I wonder if he will know what to do with it?"

Mateo swung the pistol to cover the beefy foreman. There was no sign of fear on Gregorio's face. There was only a mocking disdain, and Mateo realized that while the pistol might stop his father, it would never stop Gregorio el Toro.

"Drop the pistol, boy," Gregorio said.

"Let them go."

Gregorio's brows knitted in irritation. "I have not yet finished the branding. Drop the pistol."

Mateo brought the pistol back to cover his father. "Tell your men to let them go."

"I will kill the first man that releases a prisoner," Gregorio announced loudly.

"Do you still control Rancho de Chavez?" Mateo asked his father. "Or have you given that over to Gregorio, too?"

Don Julio's eyes flitted uncertainly toward his foreman. Then his nostrils flared. "I control the rancho."

"Then if you want to live, you will tell your men to let Jorge and Antonio go."

"You do this thing, Mateo, if you resist my authority, I will hunt you down," Don Julio said. "Mexico will not be large enough for you to hide in."

"I know."

"I will not rest until your head hangs from my gatepost."

Mateo's stomach lurched queasily. He knew Don Julio would

exhaust every means possible to fulfill that promise. Nor would Mateo's head be the first head to hang at his father's gatepost.

"Release them!" Don Julio barked, his voice ringing through the dark hollow.

"Stand your ground," Gregorio countered. He spun belligerently on Don Julio, his face dark. "My orders are to brand these thieves," he said defiantly. "They cannot be dismissed because of some little cock with a pistol. I have my reputation."

"Your reputation will not be harmed. I promise you your revenge."

"My name is Gregorio el Toro," the foreman said evenly. "I will not cower before a boy with a gun."

"You have your orders," Don Julio returned curtly. His voice rose with the harsh authority Mateo had associated with his father since boyhood. "Release the two boys. Give them back their weapons."

"You will regret this," Gregorio said softly.

"If you wish to keep to your position at Rancho de Chavez, you will remember who pays your salary," Don Julio replied.

The men holding Jorge and Antonio dropped their hands and stepped back. Antonio fell to his knees, his hand going to his cheek, hovering over flesh too painful to touch.

"Jorge, get my *belduque* and cutlass. Then help Antonio onto his horse."

"*Sí*, Mateo."

"Gregorio," Don Julio said loudly. "You will take as many men as you need and hound these three until you recapture them. You will brand Jorge, then turn him and his brother loose. Mateo you are to bring to me."

"I will capture them as I wish?"

"You will capture them as you wish," Don Julio confirmed. "Just be certain that Mateo is still in one piece when you return him to Rancho de Chavez."

Gregorio gave Mateo a searching, almost sensuous look. "*Sí*, Don Julio. The boy will be returned in one piece. I do not guarantee that you will recognize him, though. There are some things I have learned recently from the Comanches that I am anxious to experiment with."

"Just make sure he recognizes me," Don Julio breathed, staring at his son. "And that he can still feel pain. Do not make him numb to pain."

"Shut up," Mateo whispered. "Both of you, shut up."

Jorge helped Antonio into the saddle, then mounted his own horse. Mateo backed to the *grullo,* mounting without taking his eyes off the men clustered at the fire, or lowering the pistol. Seated, he glanced at Jorge. "Stampede their horses."

Jorge nodded and reined over to the corral. He pulled the gate open without dismounting and guided his horse inside. Yelling, waving his sombrero, he drove the horses out of the corral and scattered them into the piñons. Returning to Antonio's side, he said, "We are ready, Mateo. Let's get out of here."

Mateo took a deep breath and swung the pistol to Gregorio. The foreman merely laughed.

"Aim carefully, little cock. It will take a well-placed shot to bring down this bull."

"If you follow me, I will kill you." Mateo spun the *grullo* and raced after Jorge and Antonio, swallowed by darkness before his father's men could fire their first shot.

They didn't haul up until they reached Santa Fe. Jorge, still in the lead, slowed his mount to a walk. He glanced over his shoulder, his face sick with fear, although it was far too soon to expect pursuit. It would take Don Julio's men at least an hour to round up their horses. With luck, they wouldn't come after them until dawn.

They stopped in the middle of the street, and Jorge said, "What now, Mateo? We have no money, no place to go. What do we do now?"

"We go north," Mateo said. "Into beaver country."

"We are not trappers. We are *ciboleros,* buffalo hunters."

Mateo shook his head. "I am going north to become lost in the mountains. Not even Gregorio would follow us there."

"Can we believe that? I think Gregorio would follow us into hell, and fight the devil himself for our souls."

"We cannot not believe it," Antonio whispered, lifting his face from the shadows of his sombrero. It was only with effort that Mateo did not turn away from his cousin. Centered on Antonio's cheek surrounded by black and horribly swollen flesh, was the perfect letter T.

"We will go into the mountains, where there is no law, and where Don Julio's influence cannot reach us," Antonio said. "And where no one will ever again see my face."

CHAPTER ELEVEN

Eli added another limb to the fire, then sat back to idly watch the flames begin their slow consumption of the wood. Birds chirped in the trees around him, and the rushing sound of the river from somewhere beyond the alders to his left added a melodic placidness to the tiny clearing just east of town. It was early yet. The sun was still hidden by the mountains that towered behind him, and the air, especially along the river, was chilly enough to cloud his breath. Eli drew a bent Durango cigar from a pouch at his belt and straightened it along his thigh. Lighting the cigar with a twig from the fire, he inhaled with satisfaction. It was coming together, he reflected with a mixture of pride and surprise. Cork-Eye was still up at the village of Río Colorado with Vidales, and McClure was due back from the Cimarron today or tomorrow. Their gear was in order, and most of the stock was shod and ready to go. They would finish shoeing the last of the mules this afternoon and be ready to put out as soon as McClure returned.

Across the fire a humped buffalo robe stirred, and Eli smiled. A moccasined foot slid free of the robe's warmth and gouged a shallow trough through the loose, sandy soil, then went limp again. Eli drew patiently on his cigar. A mule brayed from the direction of town, and from the river, shielded by alders, he could hear the sharp, playful squeals of Charlie Williams's daughters as they splashed in the icy waters, and fainter, the voice of their mother, Red-Winged Woman, cajoling caution.

Charlie and Pete Meyers had roared into Taos like a dry blue norther three days before, running their ponies neck and neck through the narrow, winding streets, whooping and hollering to let the world know they'd arrived. An aggregation of squaws, kids, dogs, and unruly mules had followed in their wake, scattering chickens and burros and village curs like weeds. Barefooted children had skipped nimbly out of their path, while older citizens, somewhat less agile and considerably less tolerant, leaped awkwardly aside, flinging curses and obscene gestures into the fog of dust left in their passage.

Eli had been standing in front of Wolfskill's when the two trappers pounded into the plaza, and he'd bought them drinks for old time's sake, and listened and laughed as they related their escape from the Pawnees below the Arkansas, and Annie's exploded fowler. They had other tales as well; what man could spend a season in the mountains without collecting a few? Pete told them about the grizzly that had cornered Charlie behind the Flat Irons, and Charlie expounded on Pete's encounter with a *carcagieu,* or wolverine, that had tried to steal some meat drying on a willow-frame stage. Toward sundown the squaws had taken the kids and most of the stock upriver to find a place to camp, but Charlie and Pete remained at Wolfskill's until late in the night, working into Bill's stock of whiskey.

Eli had known both men for a long time now. They were old hands to the mountains, and as good beaver men as any Taos had ever produced. They were mountain men to the core, kin to the wolf and the eagle and the blowing wind, young enough to revel in the freedom and hardships of the mountains, yet old enough to have a little common sense about them, too. It was something Eli admired in them, and others like them—Old Cal and Remi and Johnny, for instance. They'd found their niches early in life, and never searched for anything more. Likely they'd die among these peaks, with a companion at their side if they were lucky, or alone, one of many who simply disappeared and was never heard from again, if they weren't. But they would never trade their lives here for what they'd left behind in the States, never feel the spurs of ambition, or want for something more. In a way, Eli envied them for that.

After a couple of minutes a hand appeared at the top of the robe and slowly peeled the shaggy pelt back, revealing, by degrees, thinning brown hair, a broad, high forehead, and red-rimmed hazel eyes set in a deeply tanned face; a full mustache hid the upper lip and curved down both sides of the mouth. The robe slid back even more, exposing broad shoulders, muscular arms, and, under the twisted collar of a faded red shirt, a mat of graying chest hair. An old, puckered wound cratered the flesh close to the thickset neck.

"*Qué pasa,* Pete?" Eli inquired.

Pete Meyers sat up with exaggerated carefulness, wincing gingerly at the assault of daylight. He squinted in Eli's direction and cocked an eyebrow in greeting.

"Want some jerky?" Eli asked, nudging a rawhide parfleche with his toe.

Pete growled something unintelligible, cleared his throat, and said, "Annie's around. She'll fix something soon as she sees I'm up."

"Your squaws took the horses down to the river to drink, but they had some goat on earlier."

"Goat'll do just fine," Pete said, cupping his face in his hands and noticing, perhaps for the first time, the puffy bruise under his right eye. He probed the cheek gently with his fingers, scowling. Glancing at Eli, he said, "Did I kill anyone?"

"Not that I've heard of."

"*Bueno.*" He looked relieved as he pushed the robe all the way back and crabbed closer to the fire. "Whew. It's been a spell since this coon's spreed like he done last night."

"Man's gotta cut loose once in a while, especially if he plans to put out again in a few days."

"I reckon," Pete replied. He glanced at another low, robe-covered mound several feet away. "That Charlie?"

"Be my guess, although I ain't checked."

"Well, we put away a heap of rotgut last night, or this child wouldn't say so."

"You were playing monte at Salazar's when I came through around ten o'clock."

Pete seemed to perk up. "Salazar's, huh?" He loosened the thong holding down the flap of a belt pouch and poked around inside. His expression dulled then, and he let the flap fall back. "Well, it don't surprise me none. A man's gotta keep his wits about him when he plays for money at Salazar's."

A horseshoe pinged off a stone from the direction of the river, and a moment later Annie hove into view, riding her paint bareback and leading Pete's buckskin and one of the mules. A couple of Annie's curs followed, belly hair dripping. Annie's face didn't alter when she saw Pete sitting by the fire, but Eli thought he detected a flicker of disapproval in her eyes as she rode to a reata stretched between a couple of aspens and tied the ponies to it. She went to the packs stored under a brush and hide arbor and brought out an *appola*—a fresh-cut stick sharpened at both ends—and a couple of hams cut from the carcass of a goat, and brought them to the fire. She stabbed one end of the *appola* into the dirt at an angle over the fire, then fixed the hams to the other end. The weight of the hams bent the *appola* until the meat was hanging just above the flames. With breakfast on, she went back to the arbor and started rummaging through her packs.

Pete fumbled his pipe from a tobacco pouch around his neck and began to fill the bowl. "This coon is feelin' frazzled of town doin's, Eli," he said deliberately.

"I've been waiting to hear that."

Pete looked up, grinning. "Shoot, I knew that. Otherwise you'd have put out with McClure and them for the eastern slopes."

Eli laughed. "Have you and Charlie given much thought to the fall season?"

"Well, we just got in. I reckon I'm about ready to head on out again, but Charlie ain't said yet what he's got in mind."

"Know which way you'd head?"

"Naw. I'd just as soon tag along with you as any, but we ain't sold all our 'skins yet, and I ain't certain sure Charlie's washed all the dust off his tonsils. He seems to collect a wee mite more'n I do over a summer."

"What kind of skins have you got?"

"Whatever's left, I reckon. Was four, five packs of tanned elk we brought in, but likely we've drunk into considerable of that. I ain't figured yet what we lost at Salazar's."

"Maybe I could help you with what's left."

Pete eyed him thoughtfully. "You goin' trader on us, too, Eli?"

"Some, I guess. Mostly I'm wanting you and Charlie to come along, if you're of a mind to. We could use the extra guns."

"*Señors,* you would not move, please."

The voice came from the alders along the river. Pete swore and reached for his rifle, then froze as a vaquero stepped from behind a tree with a musket leveled.

Eli stood as half a dozen armed men moved out of the bushes. One of them had a hand clamped over Red-Winged Woman's mouth; others carried Blossom and Magpie and Little Pete.

"You hurt that woman or those kids and I'll cut your goddamn heart out and eat it raw for breakfast," Pete said.

"I do not wish to harm women or children," an older man with a trimmed gray beard replied. "I only seek my mules."

"Mules?"

"Please, *señor*, do not risk angering me with denials." The old Mexican snapped his fingers, and a vaquero led several mules into the clearing. Eli recognized them as the animals Pete and Charlie had brought into town with them.

Pete grinned broadly. "Those your mules? Hell, we thought they was broken-down sheep some leg-pissin' *pelado* throwed away as useless."

"You must know, *señor*, that I try to overlook the rudeness of foreigners in my country. I remind myself that perhaps they could not be tolerated by their own, and were thus banished to the solitude of the mountains and the kindness of strangers. But when they steal from me, when they wound my segundo so that he cannot work, I must question the wisdom of that struggle. Where, as you Americans say, do you draw the line?"

"Any goddamn place you're of a mind to," Pete replied.

The Mexican sighed as if troubled almost beyond endurance. "I should hang you, of course. That is the customary treatment of horse thieves in my country. But I am reluctant to do so with foreigners. I do not wish to deepen the unrest that already exists between our nations."

"Why, you goddamned goose-quilled sonofa—"

"Hold on, Pete," Eli interrupted. "He's got the guns."

"I'll shove them goddamn guns—"

Eli grabbed Pete's arm and squeezed it lightly.

"Goddamnit, Eli, I ain't gonna take this. If this nigger wants him a fight, I'll accommodate him. I'll wade straight into his liver with my knife."

"They're his mules, Pete."

"I ain't said they weren't. But just 'cause we stole his mules don't mean I'm gonna sit here and let him—"

"*Señor*, perhaps I could explain. As you see, it is us who hold the weapons. It is—"

Pete laughed, cutting off the older man's words. "*Seenoir*," he said, mangling the word. "You might have the weapons, but I can still come over there and kick your ass up between your shoulder blades if I take a notion to. You got your goddamn mules, now get outta here."

"I do not think you understand," the Mexican blustered.

"No," Eli said, stepping between the two men. "Pete's right. Take your mules and go, before someone gets hurt."

"I could kill you both with impunity," the Mexican snapped, his voice rising a notch.

"You can sure as hell try," Pete said.

Before the Mexican could reply, a rifle cracked from the trees downriver, and a bullet kicked dust and gravel onto the Mexican's boots. Charlie's robe flew back at the same moment, and he sat up with a cocked pistol in each hand. While the Mexicans were staring dumbfounded at Charlie, Pete picked up his rifle and Eli drew his pistol.

"Let 'em go," Charlie said.

The Mexican's nostrils flared, but that was the only trace of emotion Eli saw. "Very well," the Mexican said. He made a quick motion with his hand, and the vaqueros holding Red-Winged Woman and the kids released their grips. Red-Winged Woman grabbed the kids and hustled them to the arbor, where Annie stood with a knife clenched in her fist.

"Reckon you'd best head on back," Eli said calmly.

The Mexican nodded. "*Sí.* But next time, my friend, I will not be so generous. Nor so careless." Watching the old man's face, Eli knew he wasn't bluffing. This was no barefoot peon armed with a hoe or machete. Turning, the Mexican shouted "*Vamonos, mí amigos,*" and walked off with his back as straight as a hickory ramrod. His vaqueros followed, leading the stolen mules.

"I got me half a notion to raise some hair off'n that one," Charlie said, standing and belting his pistols. Red-Winged Woman herded the girls to his side, and Annie followed with Little Pete in her arms. They waited together until the Mexicans were out of range, then turned to the trees from where the shot had come. No one spoke until a couple of men—boys, really—stepped into the open, leading their horses and several pack mules. They looked like they had just come off the trail. Both wore striped wool trousers and linen shirts that were starting to show some wear. Silk bandannas were knotted around their necks, and their boots were scuffed and hazed with dust. Their hats had been new not long before, but were scuffed and dusty now, the brims already starting to sag.

"Looked like you folks was having some trouble," the taller of the two said.

"Nothing we couldn't handle," Charlie said gruffly, still simmering over the Mexican's treatment of Red-Winged Woman and the children.

The taller kid glanced at him, then away. "I'm looking for Eli Cutler," he said.

"That would be me," Eli replied.

"I'm Jake Orr, and this is my little brother, Clint. Bill Wolfskill, back in town, said you were looking for trappers. My brother and I'd like to sign on with you."

Eli glanced at Clint. The younger Orr's gaze held his for only a moment, then slid off. Eli's gaze swung back to Jake, noting the pistol at the young man's waist and the heavy-barreled rifle butted between his boots. The rifle was plain but well-made, of heavy bore; the reddish brown finish was dinged and scratched, as if it had seen plenty of use, the browning around the touch hole burned to a dull, tarnished gray.

Jake was watching him arrogantly, almost challengingly, and a voice whispered in the back of Eli's mind, *Here's trouble*. Then he smiled. When couldn't Eli Cutler handle a couple of teenagers? he asked himself. "Have you got outfits?"

Jake nodded. "Two dozen Bobtail traps between us, plenty of powder and ball and winter clothes." He grinned cockily at Charlie. "Our own horses and mules, too."

Eli rushed in before Charlie could respond. "How about moccasins and mittens?"

"We've got mittens."

"You'll need moccasins, too. A dozen pair apiece, at least. You can buy them around town, or you can make your own. You can't wade an icy stream in boots unless you want to lose your toes to frostbite."

"Sure, we'll buy whatever we need."

Eli nodded thoughtfully, then, on impulse, added, "I don't want you as freetrappers. If you come, you hire on for the season, which starts now and ends when we get back. That means you take orders from me. Straight down the line."

"Like fool greenhorn boys is supposed to," Charlie said pointedly.

But Jake just laughed. "Sure," he said, bobbing his head. "Sure, that's fair."

Eli glanced at Clint. "How about you? I ain't heard your opinion yet."

"We'll be ready," Clint said quietly.

Sometimes, Eli thought as he walked across the clearing to shake hands and welcome them on, a man just had to ignore his doubts and take his best shot.

CHAPTER TWELVE

They hired the last of their hands that afternoon. Eli had just dropped the rear hoof of a cranky black mule and was straightening slowly to arch the kink from his lower back. Although the day was cool, sweat rolled freely off his face and dripped into the dust beside the warehouse. A pile of moldy straw dumped against the warehouse nearby irritated his sinuses and made his eyes tear. He wiped the sweat from his forehead with the rolled-up sleeve of his shirt and moved out of the way as Pedro led the mule to the corral.

"This one does not like his new shoes," Pedro said, watching the animal lift its hooves prissily.

"He'll get used to 'em," Eli said. He tossed hammer and rasp into a leather sack that carried the shoeing tools they'd take with them into the mountains, and turned at the sound of clopping hooves coming up the hardpanned dirt street behind them. A trio of Mexicans guided their horses into the yard and halted. The one in the center carried an ancient *escopeta* across his saddle, a knife and a stubby cutlass at his waist. The other two riders carried only knives and short bows, although one of them also carried a lance, its tip curved slightly. *Ciboleros,* Eli realized, taking in their short-waisted jackets, their buffalo-leather moccasins, and their long, shaggy hair bound behind their necks in leather queues. Suddenly the almost haughty way they sat their saddles didn't seem nearly so absurd.

"*Buenos días,*" the rider in the center said.

"*Buenos días,*" Eli returned.

"I speak English," the Mexican said, as if Eli had already dismissed the possibility. "You are Eli Cutler, yes?"

Eli nodded, and replied in Spanish, "Yes. Why are you looking for me?"

The three exchanged glances, and the one in the center said, "You speak like a Mexican. It is good that one who comes to our country learns our language."

"I asked why you were looking for me."

"I am Mateo Chavez, of the village of Don Julio Chavez, south of the bend of the Missouri Road. These are my cousins, Jorge and Antonio Rodolso. We are hunters, and we wish to accompany your brigade into the mountains."

"Trappers?" Eli asked.

"Buffalo hunters," Mateo replied with a hint of curtness. "We have fought the Comanche and the Arapaho and the Kiowa, and for many generations our families have also fought the Apaches, who now know our strength and do not raid our village."

"I'm not going out to fight Indians," Eli said.

"This is true, but sometimes it is necessary to fight. You know this yourself."

A grudging smile crossed Eli's face. "Yes, I won't take a man who doesn't know how to fight, and I am aware of the reputation of the *ciboleros*. But I need trappers, or muleteers. Do you know how to pack a mule?"

"Yes. It is a thing every boy knows. If you need *arrieros* we will do that for you."

"I'm paying twenty dollars a month for swampers, or its equivalent in pesos. I'll advance credit for gear, if you need it."

Mateo glanced at the one called Jorge, who shrugged and nodded. Antonio, his cheek bandaged and swollen, said, "It is why we came, Mateo. Let's do it."

"It is settled, then," Mateo said to Eli. "We will go."

"Good. Put your ponies in the corral, and we'll check their hooves as soon as we finish the mules."

Consuelo arrived at the warehouse that evening, leading a burro packed awkwardly with her belongings. A willow crate on top of the load held several laying hens, and a calico goat followed behind, bleating furiously. Eli watched in stunned silence as she led the burro to a *carreta* beside the corral and began to unlash the chickens. At Charlie's soft laughter, he pushed to his feet and strode angrily across the yard.

"What the goddamned hell," he grated.

Consuelo glared at him. "We agreed," she said tautly.

"We ain't taking a goddamn goat and a bunch of chickens into the mountains," Eli said.

"Who's ridin' that goat, Eli?" Pete called innocently from the fire Pierre Turpin had kindled in the warehouse's yard. "Do you use goat spurs to make it go, or do you use a quirt?" Charlie and Pierre hooted laughter, and Mateo, grinning hugely, translated for Jorge and Antonio. Eli's face reddened.

Consuelo turned back to the burro and jerked a knot free. "We will eat the goat and the chickens here, and I will tan the goat's hide for a water bag. It will be useful for the trip."

"Christ," Eli breathed so that only Consuelo heard him. "Did you have to bring them here to butcher?"

Her eyes flashed. "I will butcher them where I please."

Eli ran a hand over his face without answering.

"You command the brigade, Eli, but you do not command me. I sold my home and all my furniture, and tomorrow I will buy a horse so that I do not have to walk. Wherever you go, I will be there, and there will be a fire and food and dry moccasins, and at night, if we are not too tired, I will be your woman and we will make love and the robes will be warm even in the snow. But I am not a squaw. I will not be beaten or ordered around like one, told what to butcher or when to butcher or where to butcher." She thrust her scarred wrists toward him. "I was a slave once. I will not be one again."

"Nobody's talking about beating you or treating you like a slave. Any man does, I'll cut him."

"No," Consuelo said flatly. "*I* will cut him. His balls first, then his throat." She reached into a pannier and pulled out the goatskin poke of coins he'd left on her table several nights before. "Maybe I will cut your throat first," she said, slapping the poke against his chest.

Eli took the money wordlessly and turned away. At the fire, several of the men were still grinning, but Pete was strangely silent, studying Eli thoughtfully. "A woman is an unpredictable critter," Pete observed quietly.

Eli was saved from making a reply by a commotion in the street, a party of riders moving toward them from the direction of town, their identities masked by the deepening dusk. In the corral several of the horses raised their heads and nickered. Eli moved casually toward the fire as Pete and Charlie faded into the shadows beside the warehouse. Jake and Clint stood uncertainly, Jake cradling his rifle so that it was handy. Mateo dragged his *escopeta* across his lap, but didn't stand. Neither did the Rodolso brothers, although they also slid their bows close.

It wasn't until the horsemen were within fifty yards of the warehouse that Eli relaxed. "It's McClure," he told the others, and walked out to meet him.

McClure halted a big chestnut gelding at the yard's entrance and slid from the saddle. A rare smile crossed the man's face. "A most productive tour," he announced enthusiastically.

"Trouble?"

"Not a moment's. The supplies were all intact and undamaged. We ran into some fresh snow crossing the Sangres, but not enough to slow us down."

Old Cal rode into the yard, touching the brim of his hat as he passed Eli on his way to the corral. The others followed single-file, the mules stretched out on leads, looking somehow smaller under their bulging packs.

"*Bueno*," Eli said, counting the packs. "Looks like we're ready." He watched McClure's men ride into the yard, noting the look of recognition that passed between Travis and the Orr brothers, and the quiet scrutiny of the others.

"You've found more men," McClure observed.

"Four, plus Charlie Williams and Pete Meyers. That's seventeen, and a bigger party than I expected a week ago."

McClure took a deep, satisfying breath. "Then I would say you are right, Eli. We are ready."

CHAPTER THIRTEEN

McClure returned from town early the next morning, clutching a crumpled piece of paper that he shook above his head as he strode into camp. His short legs seem to pump with indignation. Eli, seeing the livid expression on McClure's face, moved to intercept him.

"Crooks!" McClure thundered, coming to a halt. "Thieves, every one of them!"

"What happened?" Eli asked.

"A government courier just delivered this," McClure replied, shoving the paper toward Eli. "He's waiting in town now to escort me back to Santa Fe."

Eli glanced at the single sheet of foolscap. It looked like an official document of some kind, written in Spanish. Although Eli spoke the language fluently, he had never learned how to read or write it. "What's it say?" he asked.

"I don't know," McClure admitted brusquely. "The courier couldn't read, either. But he did say there was a sergeant and five soldiers available to take me back if I refused to cooperate."

Eli turned to where Consuelo was tending the fire. "Connie."

"*Sí,* Eli?" She came to his side, and he gave her the paper.

"What does it say?"

She scrutinized the document for several minutes, then looked up uncertainly. "I don't know all the words, but I think it says your license to trap must be reissued."

"Reissued?" McClure looked confused. "What does that mean?"

"It means," Eli explained wearily, "that you're to go back to Santa Fe and bribe the bastard all over again. It means that more than likely you won't get a reissue, but even if you do it'll probably take several weeks."

"Weeks! By God, I won't stand for this, Eli. We're already late as it is, and this pompous ass of a governor wants to delay us even further! This is an outrage, and I won't allow it. I won't!"

"We pull out now, it's gonna cost us when we get back."

"A fine?"

"At the minimum."

Pete had been squatting next to the fire with a tin cup of coffee in his hand, following the conversation. Scratching his jaw reflectively, he said, "Hell, Eli, ain't no sense in puttin' out early. Five *soldados* ain't hardly enough to work up a good sweat."

Eli shook his head. "Naw, it ain't worth it for the trouble it'd cost others, Pete." He crushed the paper into a ball and tossed it in the fire. "*Bueno*. We'll pull out now. Pack your traps and saddle up."

McClure blinked. "Just like that?"

"Yeah, just like that." Eli turned to Two-Dogs. "Johnny, take the Orrs and empty the warehouse. There are some robes and summer plews inside. Take them to Wolfskill's and see if he'll hide them for us. Tell him we'll settle up at the end of the season. Remi, you and Chavez fetch the mules Pedro's grazing out west of town. Run them in and get them packed, pronto. I'll get the Rodolsos busy wrapping everything into the panniers." He glanced at Consuelo, but she was already rolling up their sleeping robes. The squaws, too, were beginning to break camp.

"I suppose you're right," McClure said dubiously, eyeing the sudden scurry of activity.

"We were going to put out tomorrow, anyway," Eli reminded him gently.

Although McClure nodded agreement, Eli could see he was still doubtful. It must have cut cross-grain to the soldier in McClure to ignore an order, even one issued by a foreign military.

"Go on back to town," Eli suggested. "Find your courier and tell him you'll go back to Santa Fe with him in the morning. Then hump it back here." He thought for a minute, then said, "I'm going to buy that little dun mare off the company for Connie. She's not going to have time to find her own mount now. Maybe one of the mules, too. That burro would only slow us up."

McClure nodded absently, his mind elsewhere. "There's something else you should know, Eli. The soldiers who are to accompany me back to Santa Fe originally came to Taos looking for an escaped American spy. From the description floating around town, I'd say he'd bear a striking resemblance to young Ketchum there."

"Travis?" Eli glanced at the youth, who was helping Pierre Turpin pack his kettles.

"Oh, I doubt it, too. Nevertheless, someone is bound to talk, and as soon as the soldiers get wind that we might be harboring a fugitive, it could make our own exit a little more difficult."

"The hell with 'em," Eli snapped. "The kid rides with us."

"All right. I'll stand behind that." McClure started to turn away, then paused, a smile flickering across his face. "There was another rumor I heard this morning that I thought you might be interested in. It seems a trio of horse thieves came to Taos recently, seeking employment. Mexican buffalo hunters, they say."

"Chavez and the Rodolsos?"

"It may prove prudent to know. I would give a prime beaver pelt to know what young Antonio is hiding under his bandage, and how it happened."

Shrugging, Eli replied, "I ain't much concerned with Antonio's face. Whatever it is, it hasn't stopped him from doing his share of the work. As far as their being horse thieves, I couldn't say I was overly worried about that, either. It's a handy talent to have, sometimes. Especially where we're going."

"I understand Jake Orr has accused Travis Ketchum of stealing the mule he's riding, as well. It would seem we are overrun with shady characters."

Eli laughed, and Pete, standing and tossing his dregs onto the ground, said, "You know, Eli. If this outfit traps half as good as it steals horses, we oughta have us a right profitable season."

Pete kneed his buckskin over beside Charlie and settled down to wait while Eli and the Chavez kid made a last-minute check of the packs. Annie and Red-Winged Woman sat their ponies to one side, the pack mules he and Charlie had bought in town yesterday standing snorty and high-headed behind them. Blossom glanced at Pete, and Pete winked, causing the girl to look shyly away.

"This don't shine atall," Charlie grumbled.

"Aw, one trail's as good as the next," Pete replied.

"I ain't doin' it, by God. I ain't tippy-toein' through town like some goddamn chicken thief."

"I ain't never known a chicken thief to steal less'n he was hungry. Eli's just hungry, is all. Got hisself a taste for booshwayin'."

"Mebbeso, but I ain't slippin' outta town the back way because of some little pissant of a governor. I say we mosey down to Santa Fe and kick ol' Armijo's ass up 'twix his shoulder blades, by damn."

Pete leaned forward to prop an elbow on his saddle horn, looking at his shadow. It was a wonder and a worry the way he and Charlie got along sometimes, he mused. He could never decide whether they had partnered together for so many years because of their similarities or because they were so different their weaknesses and strengths fit together like hand and glove. They had seen a passel of country together, no doubt about that, sharing the lean times as well as the good. Which wasn't to say they didn't have their arguments now and again, or that they didn't, from time to time, maybe even want to kill one another, or at the very least bounce the blunt end of a hand ax off the other's head just to see which was harder. A season or two they had even gone their separate ways, and like as not sworn as they did that never would be too soon to see that son of a bitch again. But it always blew over, and more and more of late, especially since taking wives, they just rode out the stormy weather between them by ignoring one another.

Charlie was a great one for getting his feathers ruffled, standing on principles that, as far as Pete was concerned, often didn't even warrant notice. Like now, worrying that Eli might want to slip out of town the back way rather than ride out the way they had come in— flat out and loud, whooping and hollering and firing their rifles in the air, leaving in a style that told the world who they were and what they thought. Or at least that part of the world huddled along the Taos River. Truth to tell, Pete had never much cared for such grandiose displays. He sure couldn't see fretting over it now. Eli hadn't even said which way they would go, or how, and here Charlie was stewing and steaming over something as like to happen as not.

Charlie looked at the animals milling nervously behind Red-Winged Woman and Annie, and shifted aim. "Galls my ass to pay what we did for those hammerheads."

Pete grinned at the sudden switch, but glanced at the animals out of politeness. Taken as a whole, he supposed they were a pretty sorry lot. Most were ribby and dull-eyed, their backs scarred by old saddle sores and bot wounds. But he had seen worse. Time and a little care would get this bunch back in shape again. He watched a little crop-eared gray packing in Charlie's string that stood alone and to one side, its eyes rolling malevolently. "This coon's thinkin' you did somebody a favor by buyin' that little gray over there," he observed.

"That gray'll shape up or I'll take a lodgepole to it," Charlie replied sullenly.

"You oughta name it something," Pete said, needling a little. "Maybe Devil-Eye, or Short-Ear."

"I ain't namin' something I might have to eat before winter's gone."

"You named War-Heels," Pete pointed out, meaning Charlie's short-tempered appaloosa.

"War-Heels named herself, by God. Go stand behind her and count the spots on her ass, you don't believe it."

Pete laughed. "I reckon I'll pass on that," he replied.

Eli and Mateo finished their inspection, and Eli walked over to his sorrel and swung into the saddle, sitting quietly a minute while he looked over the waiting trappers and the remuda.

"Look at that," Pete whispered, grinning. "Feelin' like a cock in a henhouse."

"Is, for a fact," Charlie agreed. "Well, it sits all right on him. Ol' Eli don't take it to his head, the way some others would."

Eli took a deep breath. "*Bueno,*" he said loudly, speaking to them all. "We're ready. Johnny, you and Remi take the lead. Let 'em know we're coming."

"Yeow," Charlie cried happily. "This hoss knew ol' Eli wouldn't slink outta town like a whipped-ass pup. *Owgh, owgh, owgh, owgh!*"

Johnny yipped shrilly as he pulled his mare around, laughing and matching Charlie's war cry with his own. He rode out of the yard at a hard gallop, Remi following on a red and white paint, howling and yipping to match the others. Charlie and Old Cal took it up, too, and Pedro, sitting out of the way on the top rail of the corral, laughed and joined the ruckus. Eli gave Johnny and Remi a fifty-yard head start, then shouted "*Vamonos*" and touched the sorrel with his spurs. Chavez and his cousins swung their reatas behind the pack string, crowding the mules after Eli and Consuelo with cries and the stinging pops of their rawhide hondos. The rest fell into the flow of loose mules and horses and running, barking dogs. In less than half a minute the whole bunch was riding pell-mell toward the plaza—fifteen men, three women, and three kids, with more than fifty head of horses and mules, and probably a dozen curs now, some of them new.

Pete and Charlie rode stirrup to stirrup, bent low over their saddle horns with their ponies' manes popping like tiny whips in their faces. The brim of Pete's hat flopped up against the crown, and the warm noon air, thick with rising dust, brushed his face. They rode near the front of the thundering whirlwind, laughing and yelling like lunatics. Just before hitting the plaza, Pete glanced over his shoulder. Annie was close behind them, her dark hair floating on the wind from beneath a new, stiff black hat, her coppery face split in wide grin, her quirt rising and falling. Seeing her, sharing for that one brief instant some of the wild exuberance he felt, Pete yipped louder and tickled the buckskin's flanks with his spurs.

They swept through town like a flood channeled by the narrow, winding streets. Pete howled and *owghed* and laughed until his throat felt raw and his eyes stung with tears. Taosans leaped out of their way, and village dogs bolted for cover. But the trappers didn't slow their pace for anyone or anything. They veered across the north side of the plaza in a thunder of pounding hooves and hoarse cries, and curved onto the road at its northwest corner. Pete's heavy wooden stirrup bounced off an adobe wall at the street's mouth with a little explosion of dust and grit. A mule scraped the same wall with its pack and stumbled and nearly fell before catching its footing and lunging forward with an angry squeal. A few others bottlenecked there as well, but made it through without injury. The trappers whooped even louder a couple of minutes later when the town at last fell behind them.

They settled down to a lope after that, spreading out some, though trying to keep the pack animals toward the center. It was a fine, warm day, the air tangy with the taste of fall. Cottonwoods and willows were turning yellow along the streams, and the aspens on the higher slopes of the Sangre de Cristos were like pockets of gold scattered among the darker pines. They passed the pueblo of San Geronimo de Taos several miles north of town, the tall, sprawling structure looking almost deserted save for the curl of smoke above several of its multileveled flat roofs. A couple of squaws drawing water from a nearby stream barely looked up as the brigade passed, going about their business as if the centuries of isolation and solitude had granted them an immunity to the raucous invasion from Europe.

Eli slowed the brigade to a jog shortly after passing the pueblo. The fields of wheat and maize had fallen behind them now, and to the north the valley stretched away from them like a broad, empty sea. To their left the canyon of the del Norte was a shallow scar, its true size masked by the flatness of the land that hid its immense depth and sheer rock walls until a man was almost at its rim. Pete kept a wary eye on the mules, but the pack animals seemed satisfied with the slower gait, the impulse to bolt or cause trouble driven out of them by the hard run.

Charlie reined his appaloosa closer, eyes twinkling as he sniffed the thin, high desert air. "Smell that sage. By God, this hoss was ready to put out, Pete. A mountain man weren't made to eat *chili* and *refritos* every goddamn meal. He needs buffler and beaver tail and painter meat ever so often. Town grub sets a mite heavy after a while."

Pete didn't reply. He was looking behind him, and after a minute, Charlie also looked.

"Something?" Charlie asked.

"Maybe. Maybe only a feeling."

"Maybe's good enough," Charlie replied. "Let's pull out for a spell."

They pulled their ponies to the side, motioning to the women to stay with the brigade. Those coming from behind looked at them curiously, but only Silas McClure and Travis Ketchum pulled out to stop.

"What is it?" McClure asked.

Pete pointed with his chin toward the distant pueblo. "Dust, looks like."

"Cattle?"

"I reckon not."

"Soldiers," McClure said heavily. "Travis, go get Eli. On the double."

Travis whipped his mule around and loped after the brigade. Pete checked the priming on his rifle and pistol. Charlie and McClure did the same. Eli joined them a few minutes later, bringing with him, besides Travis, Old Cal Underwood and Remi LeBlanc.

"*Qué es?*" Eli asked, pulling his horse to a stop beside McClure and eyeing the growing funnel of dust to the south.

"Soljers," Old Cal whined in his high-pitched voice. "Do 'ee hyar, boys? Soljers, with they fur up, too."

"Could be," Eli acknowledged thoughtfully.

"We gonna fit 'em, Eli?" Old Cal asked. "Gonna burn powder

agin 'em like they was brownskins out to lift our'n topknots? This nigger'd a sight druther jus' cache."

"Aw, you're just gettin' old," Pete told him. "There ain't but a handful of 'em."

"Old, I be, and old I aim to die, too," Old Cal shrilled loudly. "Ye be too hot-blooded for ye own good, Pete Meyers, and it'll git ye kilt, come some fine day. This nigger says cache, *muy pronto*."

"No," Eli said quietly. "We ain't hiding."

"Reckon it's me they want," Travis said suddenly, his voice tight and oddly drawn. He swallowed, and nudged his mule forward. "I can't ask you to fight my battles for me, Mr. Cutler. I'll take care of this myself."

Eli gave him an amused look. "Just what the hell do you intend to do?"

Travis shrugged. "Guess I don't rightly know for sure. But I ain't gonna drag you all into it."

"Hell, Eli, could be this kid's got more pluck than we figured him for," Pete said.

"You signed on for the season," Eli told Travis flatly. "You're a Cutler man now. You stay where you are."

The soldiers began to take shape beneath the dust, half a dozen horsemen in soiled blue uniforms. The soldiers slackened their pace as they drew closer, finally stopping about a hundred yards away. Pete spotted an assortment of lances, bows and arrows, and a couple of ancient firelocks among them, but nothing a man would take seriously. A heavyset sergeant in a deep blue jacket trimmed with gold braid rode forward alone, stopping again about thirty yards away. "*Señors*, I am afraid you have left Taos prematurely. As was explained to your clerk, there is a problem with your license to trap here in Mexico. You would please follow me back to Santa Fe, and we will straighten this matter out."

Eli said "No" and let it go at that.

The sergeant's face twitched uncomfortably. "Please. It would be so much easier if you returned voluntarily."

Eli shook his head. Charlie said, "I do admire that scalp of your'n. It would decorate a saddle up real fine."

The sergeant glanced at Charlie, then let his gaze move among the others. It stopped on Travis, and his brows lifted in surprise. "Ah, you have found our poor runaway. The *niño* on the mule—"

"No," Eli said, sharper this time.

Gently, the sergeant replied, "*Sí*. I am afraid it must be."

Eli cocked his rifle, the crisp, metallic ratcheting carrying all the way to the watching soldiers in the suddenly quiet air. The soldiers exchanged uneasy glances, keenly aware of how underarmed they were against the trappers. Pete lifted his rifle to the crook of his arm and curled his thumb over the cock.

The sergeant sighed and looked behind him, studying his men silently for a moment. Then he looked at Eli again and said, "Before the revolution our army was a thing to be proud of, with men of bravery and determination. Now it is a haven for fools and thieves and those who cannot make their way through the world without guidance. In the old days, I would not have turned away."

"Tell your commanding officer I'll talk to him next spring, when I get back."

"You must understand that you will be reported as spies and insurgents against Mexico, and arrested upon your return."

"No," Eli repeated.

The sergeant's face hardened. "It must be easy to be an American, eh? Everything yes or no, and always as you wish it. Maybe it will be so this time, too. Or maybe by spring I will have real men to command again. Then it will not be so simple."

Eli didn't offer a reply, nor did the sergeant wait for one. He reined his horse around and rode back to where his men waited. As far as Pete could tell, he didn't say anything to them; he just rode on through, and his men slowly fell into a ragged line behind him.

"I would like to have that sergeant riding with us," Eli said when the soldiers were on their way. "He's got the makings, I'm thinking."

"I doubt if he would give up the uniform," McClure countered almost wistfully.

"Well, it doesn't matter now," Eli said. "Let's go pick up Cork-Eye and Vidales, and get on to the mountains."

They pulled their horses around and rode after the brigade. Far ahead, the mountains beckoned. No one looked back.

Chapter Fourteen

They camped that night along a tiny runnel flowing out of the Sangre de Cristos, and just before noon the next day spotted the village of Río Colorado, squatted in the shade of a sprawling cottonwood grove. Smoke drifted lazily into an azure sky, while the burnished gold of the cottonwoods provided a brilliant cap to the quiet village. Toward the Sangre foothills a mixed herd of oxen and horses grazed on the tall, summer-cured grass. Closer, a man drove a plodding ox ahead of a *carreta* filled with firewood. Seen from a distance, the village looked placid, almost idyllic, but Eli had lived on the frontier too many years to be deceived by first impressions.

McClure trotted up beside him. "Do you know these people?" he asked.

"Not really. I've passed through here several times, but that's about it. They're *ciboleros,* mostly—cut from the same bolt of cloth as Chavez and the Rodolsos. If pushed, they won't back down like those soldiers."

Scowling, McClure asked, "Do you anticipate trouble?"

"I always anticipate trouble, but I don't expect any. Cork-Eye's already told 'em we were coming. If he hasn't done anything to upset them, we'll be welcomed."

McClure nodded thoughtfully, and they rode the rest of the way in silence. Río Colorado was a collection of perhaps a dozen flat-roofed adobe homes. There was no central plaza, nor even a recognizable street. The earth around a walled-in spring near the center of the village was packed hard as concrete, but weeds and bunchgrass grew elsewhere, laced with paths that radiated outward like crooked spokes. The trail from Taos, little more than a path itself, ended abruptly at the southern edge of town.

The man driving the ox stopped and pulled a lance from the *carreta*'s bed as the brigade rode into town. He stood calmly beside the bullock, letting Eli come to him. He was old, with long gray hair and a thin mustache. His clothing was made of buffalo leather and coarsely woven *jerga*. He wore hard-soled moccasins of Pima design, and a flat-crowned, flat-brimmed straw hat.

"Good day," Eli said in Spanish. He introduced himself and McClure. "We're looking for a one-eyed man named Cork-Eye Weathers, and a muleteer named Juan Vidales."

"Yes," the man replied. "They are housed there." He pointed with his chin toward a shack on the northern skirt of the village.

"*Gracias,*" Eli said.

"You will stay?" the man asked.

"Tonight only. We wish to buy pemmican for the winter. Does the village have enough to sell?"

The man smiled condescendingly. "We have some, yes. I am José Silva. You see me this afternoon, after siesta, and I will sell you some good pemmican, seasoned with berries."

"*Bueno,*" Eli said. "I will." He pulled away and rode toward the shack Silva had pointed out. Its walls were no more than four feet high, made of untrimmed, sun-whitened cottonwood logs, with jutting corners. A flat roof of crudely thatched saplings was rainproofed with several stiff deer hides, already curled at the edges and alive with scavenger bugs and blowflies. A litter of old hides, hooves, antlers, and bones cluttered the yard. Broken snores drifted from between the unchinked logs to claw at the putrid air surrounding the shack.

Eli reined up about twenty feet away and leaned forward to rest an elbow on his saddle horn, the forearm of his other arm across that. He studied the unorganized camp for several minutes and felt a vague stirring of disgust and anger.

"Cork-Eye's a poor choice, I'm thinking," he told McClure bluntly.

McClure's lips thinned at the criticism. "He was available," he retorted. "Others weren't. Not then."

Eli bit back his reply. He knew Cork-Eye was available because no one else wanted him, but McClure couldn't have known that. It was too bad, but McClure had done the best he could under the circumstances.

The others had fanned out in a large crescent fronting the door, and Pete remarked acidly, "You couldn't throw a cat through any of the cracks in that shack, but I do believe you might squeeze one through in a couple of places."

The others laughed, and the snores from the shack broke off with a startled sputtering. A moment later a single, protuberant eye appeared at one of the larger cracks, blinked once, then vanished. A second later Cork-Eye stooped through the door, knuckling his good eye. He was a stumpy, potbellied man with long gray hair fringing a bald pate. His buckskin trousers were grease-blackened, and he wore a rumpled calico shirt that was faded nearly colorless and badly stained, the cuffs frayed and the elbows nearly worn through. A long, pink-ridged scar ran down his forehead, jumped the puckered socket of his left eye, and disappeared into the stiff bristle of a two-week-old beard. The wound was the work of a Blackfoot's tomahawk, Cork-Eye claimed, and had severed most of the muscles in his cheek, causing it to sag like a wrinkled dug; the socket was a watery, purplish hole, crudded at the edges. For a while after losing the eye, he had kept it covered with a bandanna, protected from dust and cold with a shallow cork, but for as long as Eli had known him he had left it exposed in all but the bitterest weather, laughing off anyone's attempt to shame him into covering it again.

"Hello, Mr. McClure, Eli." He looked around at the others, nodding to those he knew. "Boys," he greeted. "Looks like you caught me napping."

Charlie snorted laughter, but no one else responded. Coolly, McClure said, "Where's Vidales?"

"Oh, he's safe. Don't you fret none about that. I sent him out with the stock so's they could get 'em a bite of grass."

Eli's patience snapped abruptly. He straightened and made a circular motion with his hand. "We'll camp here tonight. Cork-Eye, go get Vidales. Tell him the booshway wants to talk with him."

Cork-Eye seemed to perk up. "You booshwayin' this here shitaree, Eli?"

"I wouldn't be telling you to get off your ass if I wasn't." Eli saw the flash of hurt on Cork-Eye's face, and wheeled the sorrel away before he said any more. Consuelo was standing beside her dun near the rear of the brigade. Eli rode to her side and swung down, handing her his reins. "Find a place upwind of Cork-Eye's shack for our camp," he instructed her curtly.

"Eli, he is not worth your anger," Consuelo said softly, indicating Weathers with a nod. "Send him back to Taos. He is useless."

"I know, but he's hired and he can shoot, if it comes to that. And it will, sooner or later."

"He is lazy and a coward. He will only get someone killed."

Irritably, Eli said, "Weathers is my worry. Go set up camp."

Consuelo shrugged and gathered the dun's reins. "*Sí*, Eli. As you wish." She turned away, leading the sorrel and her own dun with the same hand, and flipping her quirt at the mule that carried their personal gear. Eli watched her with a feeling of resentment. He knew he had angered her with the sharpness of his words, but he told himself that she was just going to have to get used to it. They weren't in Taos now, and he had a brigade to run; he wasn't going to debate every decision with her.

"Eli. Cork-Eye's coming with Vidales."

Eli swung around to face McClure. Beyond the clerk's shoulder he saw Cork-Eye coming into camp with a lean, solemn-faced Mexican in tow. Brusquely, he said, "Let's go see what he has to say."

They met Cork-Eye and Vidales behind the shack. McClure said, "Juan, this is Eli Cutler."

"*Sí*. I know Eli. He has wintered in Taos many times."

McClure paused, staring pointedly at Cork-Eye until the latter moved off self-consciously. When Cork-Eye was out of earshot, McClure went on. "Eli is booshwaying the brigade this season, Juan. He wants to talk to you about what happened last year with the Reed party." -

"I will tell what I know," Vidales replied gravely.

"This way," Eli said, jerking his head toward the sage plain that separated the village from the del Norte, several miles to the west. Vidales and McClure fell in beside him. Eli wondered how to broach the subject of the massacre, but Vidales surprised him by starting the conversation without prodding.

"For a long time I did not know whether I wanted to speak of this thing," he began quietly. "My wife urged me not to tell anyone. She said that what the Americans do is not our concern. I know also that she feared what might happen if Reed found out I was alive. So for a long time I did not say anything. But I knew my silence was wrong. Too many men died, men who were my friends. Finally, I told Mr. Young—"

"Ewing Young?"

"Yes. It was he who sent to St. Louis the papers I saved."

Eli's pace slowed. He stared across the broad valley to the distant hills, their flanks looking as soft as velvet, their crowns darkened with stands of pine. A knot had formed in his belly as soon as Vidales began to speak; it drew tighter now, like a fist clenching his intestines. "What happened in the mountains, Juan? Did Tom Reed sacrifice his men for a cache of furs?"

Juan hesitated only a moment. "This I cannot answer. Only Reed can speak of what lies in his heart. But it was foolish. We all knew that. There was an Indian camp along the White River, south of the Uinta Mountains, and we went in to trade. They were Shoshones, they said, but some of the trappers did not believe them. Myself, I don't know. They had plews and buckskins for trade, and a few buffalo robes. And women. Many of the men wanted to lie with their women, but the chief said there could be no trade, no women, with metal objects in his camp. He said his religion, what he called his medicine, was weakened by the white men's metal."

A chill ran down Eli's spine, and his scalp crawled, but he didn't interrupt.

"This chief said there would be a feast that night," Vidales continued. "He said there would be music and dancing, and that afterward they would trade. Reed ordered his men to leave their weapons in the lodges that had been provided for us, but the trappers refused. They did not believe this chief. They said his heart was black. It was then that the Indians attacked. They had been hiding their weapons, their tomahawks and knives, under their blankets and shirts, and they fell upon the trappers and slaughtered them. Not all at once. Some of the trappers fought and hid in the sage, but within a morning they were all dead."

"And Reed?" Eli asked tonelessly.

"He lived," Juan said simply. "I saw him later, talking to the chief, but I could not tell if he was a prisoner. He called this chief Bad Gocha."

Eli's muscles felt taut as a bowstring. "Well, that's some, by God," he breathed. "That's some. I reckon Reed's guilty now, for sure."

McClure shook his head. "It seems that way, Eli. It does. But we can't be certain. Not certain enough to warrant taking the law into our own hands."

"By God, Silas, it's the only law we've got out here."

"And all the more reason to remain cautious. Reed put out for the Gila country. We can't be sure he's after the cached furs."

"He wouldn't just let them rot. Reed signaled his intentions when he didn't inform Girardin of the cached furs, Silas. There ain't no other way to read it. I don't doubt he'll work the Gila some. He'd have to set a trap or two if he wants to show up next spring with a bunch of plews. But it's an easy ride from there to the Salt Lake country. Down the Gila and up the Colorado, the Virgin, the Ashley." He traced the route in his mind, the chill that had coursed his spine earlier growing until he felt as cold and hard as steel. "It's the long way around, but it'll still get him there," he finished grimly.

"That's a lot of miles just to fool the authorities."

"It wouldn't be the authorities he'd want to fool. It'd be the mountain men—you, me, the boys. He's pushing his luck already."

"Then how do we catch him at it? It's too late to follow him."

"Following wouldn't do any good, anyway. Reed's no greenhorn. He'd catch us at it sooner or later." Eli looked at Vidales. "What about it? Think you can backtrack to where Reed cached his fall furs?"

"*Sí.* Behind the front range of the Wasatch Mountains there is a valley with three rivers that converge near the mouth of a canyon. It was there that Reed and Antoine Girardin buried the furs. I will know the valley when I see it."

"*Bueno,*" Eli said abruptly, facing McClure. "We trap through the fall months, then, same as Reed. Come time for winter quarters, we'll settle close to the cache and see who shows up. That fair enough for you?"

"It's risky. What if they head straight up there without taking time to trap?"

"It's a gamble," Eli conceded. "But it ain't likely. Reed wouldn't want to seem too eager, and there're other outfits trapping between here and the Wasatch. He'll go around by way of the Gila, I figure, and set his traps along the way, too. Besides, we can't afford not to trap. What we recover from the cache will help defray the costs of last year's expedition, but we have to make this one pay for itself as well. It's going to take a heap of skins to do that."

McClure nodded, satisfied. "All right. We'll do it your way."

"There's one more thing, Silas. I want Bad Gocha, too."

McClure frowned. "That wasn't part of the instructions. Mr. Girardin wanted only the man responsible for his son's death. That's Reed. If he shows up at the cache."

"Four years ago, along the Provost River that separates the Salt Lake from Utah Lake, Bad Gocha pulled the same trick on Etienne Provost," Eli said. "He killed nearly a dozen men, all of them friends of mine."

"I won't let personal feelings interfere with the running of this brigade, Eli. Reed is a white man, and a traitor. He needs to answer for his crimes. But Bad Gocha is a renegade, shunned by his own people. Killing is as natural to him as breathing."

"Bad Gocha is a madman," Eli replied bluntly. "That's why we have to stop him. Because if we don't, then the next time he kills, we'll be as guilty as Reed."

CHAPTER FIFTEEN

It was still dark when Eli awoke. His hand moved instinctively to the polished, curly maple stock of his rifle as he listened to the sounds of the night. Beside him, Consuelo snored lightly, a solid ball of warmth beneath the shaggy buffalo robe that served as their blanket. A fire crackled in front of Cork-Eye's crude shack, and in its light Eli saw Old Cal Underwood, Jorge Rodolso, Pierre Turpin, and Silas McClure talking quietly among themselves. Something about the way the men stood, the way they moved, alerted Eli to trouble even before McClure detached himself from the group to approach his bed.

"Eli?"

"I'm up," Eli replied softly. He stood, shrugging into his jacket, pulling his hat on over tousled hair. Glancing at the stars, he judged dawn to be no more than half an hour away. As he moved away from his robes to meet McClure, he noticed that the grass under his moccasins was brittle with frost and that the air had a sharper bite to it than he had felt all fall.

"We have a problem," McClure said heavily, stepping close to Eli's side and speaking quietly so as not to awaken the others. "Rodolso says three of the mules have been hamstrung."

"Hamstrung!"

"This way," McClure said. Eli followed the clerk toward the pasture where the brigade's remuda grazed. Old Cal and Jorge left the fire to intercept them before reaching the herd.

"What happened?" Eli asked in Spanish.

"I do not know," Jorge replied guardedly. "I was on the far side of the herd, keeping my watch. Perhaps an hour ago I saw a man enter the remuda from the camp, but I did not think anything of it. I did not see him leave, but later I noticed the horses were becoming upset. When I entered the herd to investigate, I smelled blood. That is when I found the crippled mules."

Eli felt a sudden surge of energy, as if even the brisk pace he had already set wasn't fast enough. "Who was it?" he asked tightly.

"I could not tell. I was too far away, and it was dark. I saw a silhouette only, but did not recognize the man."

"But you said he entered the herd from our camp?"

"Yes."

"Who was watching the near side of the herd?" Eli asked, switching to English.

"I was, Eli," Old Cal whined. "I didn't see ary a thing, either. First I knowed somethin' was afoul was when this greaser hyar came a humpin' it int' camp."

"Where were you standing?"

"North o' the shack, but I didn't see or hyar a thing."

"Silas?"

"I'd just gotten up and roused Pierre to get breakfast started. I'm afraid I didn't know anything was amiss, either, until young Rodolso came running into camp."

Eli sighed as they reached the wounded mules. The animals were standing apart from the rest of the remuda, isolated by the odor of blood. Jorge slipped a noose around one of the mules, although it was basically a wasted gesture. With the tendons in their rear legs severed, none of the animals was capable of walking off. Eli patted the mule's neck sympathetically, then ran his hand over the flank and down the hip until he came to the hock. The damage was obvious, even in the predawn darkness. The mule snorted in pain and seemed to shudder as Eli's fingers explored the blood-soaked cut, but it didn't attempt to move away. Eli wondered if the animal had already sensed its fate, the uselessness of trying to fight or flee. Straightening, Eli wiped his bloody fingers clean on the mule's hip. "Have you examined all three animals?" he asked Jorge.

"Yes. They are all the same."

"Just these three?"

"Yes."

"By God," Eli grated in English, clenching his fist in helpless anger, "when I find out who did this, I'll break his goddamned neck."

McClure looked stunned. "Who would want to sabotage his own outfit?"

"I don't know, Silas. I don't know."

" 'Twas some other outfit's doin's, that be what this coon's thinkin'," Old Cal exclaimed. "T'ain't no other answer. This hyar be American Fur's doin's, or I wouldn't say so!"

"It's possible," Eli agreed. "Someone signed on with us, but working for another outfit. No way of knowing who's behind it, though. Could be Astor, or it could be Smith, Jackson, and Sublette, or even old Ashley himself, wanting to get back into the trade." Eli shook his head in exasperation. "Or it might've been one of the villagers. For all we know, Cork-Eye could've rubbed someone the wrong way, or tried to get friendly with someone's wife or daughter."

"Hell's fire, ye danged fool!" Old Cal cried. "This 'ere ain't no Mescan doin's. These critters woulda raised too much of a fuss if some stranger tried crawlin' amongst 'em in the dark!"

Eli glanced toward the camp where Pierre was going ahead with breakfast. "So, we've got a turncoat riding with us."

"Ain't ary other way t' read it, Eli. Sign's as plain as tracks in the mud."

"What do we do?" McClure asked.

"There's not much we can do except double the horse guard and keep our eyes peeled. One thing is certain, though. If it's not a villager, it'll happen again." Eli started back to camp, feeling a weariness settle on his shoulders. He had contracted with Girardin to lead a brigade into the mountains and, if possible, to find his son's killer and retrieve a cache of stolen furs. That in itself would have been a formidable task, already rife with the inherent dangers of mountain life—fickle Indian tribes, starvation, frigid weather, treacherous rivers, and burning, waterless deserts, not to mention the hundreds of small mistakes that could so easily escalate into disaster. A loose shoe on a horse, a narrow, rain-slick mountain path, and the next thing you knew a man was dead at the bottom of a chasm. A cinch pulled too tight on a pack mule could cause the mule to drown crossing a river, taking most of their gunpowder with it. A sunny day could entice them over a mountain pass where a fast-moving storm could trap them in six feet of fresh powder. It was enough to turn a young man's hair gray, Eli thought, even without the possibility of a traitor among them.

"*Jefe?*"

Eli stopped, turned, grateful for the darkness that hid the uncertainty mirrored in his eyes.

"What about the mules?"

"The mules are crippled, Jorge. They'll never walk again. If you don't cut their throats, they'll just starve."

"*Sí, jefe.*" Jorge hesitated, then said, "*Jefe.*"

"*Qué?*"

"This will not happen again while I am on guard duty."

Eli nodded. "*Bueno.* See that it doesn't."

Thunder rumbled through the valley, low, drawn-out, fading gradually to the south. A gust of wind swooped after it, skittering dust and sand that stung Travis's face and snapped the frayed collar of his jacket against his cheeks. The sky was a tattered gray canopy, now and again dropping a misty rain that cloaked the sage-covered plain with an unnatural sheen. The hills flanking the valley were hidden by the clouds, their nearness assured only by the slight upward tilt of land to either side, the slopes striped with dark ranks of pines that fingered down from the flowing nimbus like claws.

Travis faced the stinging wind miserably, chilled all the way through. His feet, jammed inside stiff cowhide boots, felt numb and useless. His nose was sore and blistered, rubbed nearly raw from constantly dragging his sleeve across it. They had left the village of Río Colorado hours ago—the last fragile toehold of civilization. Ahead lay the woolly unknown, a challenge as much mental as physical, its conquest, assuming he survived, a kind of badge to be worn with honor. Still, he had to fight the urge to look back periodically as they left the village, to watch it grow steadily smaller in the sunless gray light, knowing that as it did, the option of turning back diminished at an equal rate. He had wondered then if this was what a sailor felt putting out to sea for the first time, this mingling of anxiety and excitement, dread and anticipation.

The brigade was strung out over several hundred yards, plowing stubbornly into the wind in a way that reminded Travis of his pa, and the way he had attacked the hard-rock country of northwestern Arkansas where they had settled while Travis was still on the tit. Those riders closest to him—Charlie Williams, Remi LeBlanc, Old Cal Underwood—rode in a stony silence that seemed to rebuff intrusion, their features set in the same enduring obstinance that had driven his pa from spring planting to fall harvest. Only, as Travis saw it, the wind was a hell of a lot easier to cope with than the rocks in his pa's cornfield.

Thinking of Arkansas brought a lump of homesickness to Travis's throat. He missed his family—his ma and pa and sisters. He even missed the perpetually run-down collection of buildings—the squatty, one-room log cabin his pa had built with just his ma's help, the corncrib and tobacco shed, the smokehouse and barn—that had been his home until last spring. But mostly he missed his older brother, Chet, who had died last fall on the Mississippi River just above Natchez.

Grief struck Travis as the memory of his brother swam into his mind. He dropped his head to hide the hot welling of tears, to be alone with the shame and guilt. Rain pattered his shoulders, and he remembered that it had rained the day Chet died, too, a day of gloomy overcast and intermittent showers, not unlike today, although warmer and more humid.

They had been on their way to New Orleans when it happened. Travis and Chet and Chet's friend Homer Drew had built a flatboat that summer, contracting with several of the farmers around Hanging Creek Falls to float their harvests down the Arkansas and Mississippi rivers to market. For a first attempt at self-sufficiency, they hadn't done too bad. It was a small cargo they freighted—some tobacco and cotton, about twenty kegs of honey, plus a couple of bales of furs—but they figured to net around eighty dollars apiece out of it, and see a little of New Orleans in the process. They made it down the Arkansas without a hitch and thought they were home free after that, despite the heavier traffic on the Mississippi. They hugged the western shore to stay out of the way of the bigger steamboats and keelboats, tying up at night in some out-of-the-way eddy, then pushing on through the daylight hours. One of them would man the big walnut sweep by which they guided the craft, while another stood in the bow to watch for sandbars and sawyers. Travis had been the off man the morning the pirates struck.

It was Homer who first spotted the pirogues, gliding out of a bayou behind them. "Company," Homer sang out cheerfully. He eased off the sweep to drag a forearm across his brow, the sleeve of his cotton shirt coming away dark with perspiration.

Travis had been reclining on a bale of furs, experimenting with the clay pipe he had purchased in Fort Smith. He sat up at Homer's shout. Chet walked back from the bow, and Travis knocked the pipe's dottle into the river and followed. There were only two pirogues, about a hundred yards behind them yet. There was a man in the stern of each, handling a paddle, and in the nearest a third man stood in the bow, a foot braced against the gunwale, an arm draped across the knee. Low, canvas-covered loads were humped like small gray mountains in the center of each pirogue.

Watching them, Travis felt a prickle of fear ripple down his spine. "Best they keep their distance," he blurted to Chet. "Pa says not to trust no one."

Homer laughed. "Aw, what's the matter? Travis afraid?"

"They're just trappers," Chet said. "Or maybe 'gator hunters, on their way to New Orleans, same as us."

"We oughta let 'em tie up to us," Homer said. "They could take a spell on this oar."

Chet's laugh revealed a flash of white teeth. "They ain't likely to volunteer for extra work, but maybe they've got fresh meat to trade. I've had a bellyful of catfish."

Travis nervously slipped the stem of his pipe through his hatband. He felt a sudden restlessness, as if the flatboat, with its crawling pace and clumsy maneuverability, had become a cage. The pirogues were gaining rapidly on them, skimming the choppy water with a gracefulness that reminded Travis of a running deer. Beyond the two pirogues the river stretched away like a broad, unbroken plain, deserted. "I don't think we oughta let 'em come aboard," Travis said.

"Aw, quit being such a sissy," Homer chided him. "Even if they tried to cause trouble it'd be three against three, and we've got shot-guns."

Travis glanced at his brother for reassurance, but Chet was watching the closing pirogues with an intensity that only increased Travis's anxiety. "What is it?" he asked.

Chet shook his head.

"Oh, for crying out loud," Homer exclaimed. "You, too? I swear you Ketchums are the spookiest bunch of 'fraidy cats I've ever seen."

"Shut up, Homer," Chet said in a quiet, fluttery voice. He hadn't moved, but his muscles were tensed, his nostrils flaring.

"What is it?" Travis repeated quietly.

"I think I saw the canvas move on that near pirogue," Chet replied.

Travis felt rooted, unable to move or speak. Only his thoughts possessed the gift of motion now, racing in illogical circles that made him half dizzy. Homer scampered away from the sweep as if it had turned into a snake, stumbling in his haste to reach Chet's side. "Aw, you're just shittin' me," Homer said hopefully.

Chet shook his head once more. "No, I ain't."

"Are you sure?" Homer asked.

Chet nodded dumbly. The pirogues were less than thirty yards away now. The man in the lead craft had straightened, and Travis could see the butt of a large horse pistol tucked into a crimson sash wrapped around his waist. He was grinning hugely, his mouth like an open wound within the shag of his beard and mustache, but without amiability. He looked, Travis thought sickly, like a half-starved man who had just discovered a succulent fruit waiting to be picked from its vine. Travis glanced at the Louisiana shoreline, no more than fifty feet away, but knew they would never make it in the flat-boat; the raft was too slow and cumbersome, the Mississippi's current too strong.

"We could swim for it," Travis offered weakly. "It's the boat they want."

"We don't know that," Chet argued.

"Oh, hell, Chet, they're river pirates. You know that as well as I do," Homer said. "The kid's right. This ain't our cargo."

"There," Chet said thinly. "Did you see that?"

"No," Homer moaned. "Oh, Christ. Come on, Chet."

"I saw it," Travis breathed so softly he wasn't even sure the others had heard. His eyes were riveted to the canvas on the near pirogue, the corner that had seemed to lift up an inch or so, then lower slowly, as if held from within.

"Get the shotguns," Chet ordered.

Travis ran to the front of the flatboat, where they had built a sandbox for their fire and rigged a lean-to to sleep under. They had three single-barreled shotguns and Chet's pistol. Travis tucked the shotguns under one arm and used his free hand to gather up the pistol and the shooting bags and powder horns. But before he could duck out of the lean-to, there was a shout, followed by the crack of a pistol. The bullet passed overhead with a thumping whine.

"Chet!" Travis shouted. He scrambled out of the lean-to and raced along the side of the flatboat between the cargo and the gunwales. He stopped abruptly when he saw the pirogues, his throat constricting. The pirates had closed to within thirty feet, veering now to flank the flatboat. Oddly, it was the nearness of the pirogues that surprised Travis more than the sudden appearance of several additional men where the humped canvases had been. The man with the crimson sash was still standing at the bow, but now the pistol hung loose in his hand, its muzzle dribbling smoke. Travis swallowed as half a dozen long guns swung to cover him, but didn't move.

"*Bonjour, mes* travelers," the man with the pistol shouted. "Stand where you are. We come aboard."

"Keep your distance," Chet called back.

Several of the men laughed, and the man with the pistol grinned. "Or you will do what, my young pup?"

"We've gotta swim for it," Travis said just loud enough for Chet and Homer to hear. "Chet, we can't fight them. There're too many."

"Get ready," Chet whispered. He walked to the sweep and calmly swung it toward the main channel. The flatboat seemed to shudder as the current caught it and pivoted it broadside. A corner of the bow dipped and bobbed, throwing them off balance. "Now," Chet cried sharply, and while the men in the pirogues shouted and cursed and cocked their long guns, Travis dropped the shotguns and sprinted toward the western rail.

Homer was right behind him, and they hit the water with a splash that sounded almost as one. Travis dove toward the muddy bottom, toeing his shoes off for greater speed. He could feel the river pulling at him, its undertow trying to suck him back toward the main channel. He fought the current, knowing that if he surfaced too soon he would die, half suspecting he would anyway.

Dead men tell no tales.

Where had he heard that expression, and why did it come to him now?

It was dark under the water; not black, but murky and, save for the pull of the current, without direction. Travis's fingers scraped mud and he jackknifed with a newfound strength, going deeper to pull himself along the bottom, and making better time because of it. But his chest was beginning to burn, and he knew he couldn't stay down much longer. A roaring that was like a distant storm filled his ears, and red spots danced before his eyes. A burst of air broke past his lips, and he began to claw at the riverbottom, fighting it more than using it. The fire in his lungs grew almost unbearable, and he began to battle the water as he had the mud, but rising now, the foggy light above him brightening as he neared the surface.

Even then, he almost didn't make it. He flailed weakly at the water, sucking air across his tortured throat. He tried to shout for help, but managed only a raspy croak. Then a sawyer snagged him by the collar, jerking him back and down. He came up coughing water, suddenly mad. "Sonofabitch," he gasped, swinging his fist blindly. Sputtering, choking, he fought the sawyer's grasp until his collar ripped and the current pulled him free. But his strength was gone now, and his anger, too, and when the river pulled him under again, he went without struggle.

It was dark when he awoke, but clear, the sky blue-black and cloudless, flaked with starlight. The night was alive with sounds—tree frogs, cicadas, squawking night birds he couldn't name, and the deep, booming roars of bull alligators. Travis lay without moving for a long time, just looking at the black latticework of tree limbs overhead, watching the slow swing of Spanish moss in a torpid breeze. After a while he became aware of a soft sobbing, and letting his head loll to the side, he saw Homer Drew sitting barefoot next to a cypress tree, his head in his arms. It all came back to him then, and he forced himself to sit up and look around. The river lapped close by, rippling pewter in the faint light, but empty. They were surrounded on the other three sides by a black wall of trees. He almost asked about Chet then, but Homer sobbed once more, and suddenly Travis didn't want to know. Not then, when he felt so weak and vulnerable. He lay back while the tears came and went and came again, and in the morning they walked downriver together until they found Chet's bullet-riddled body wedged against the bank. They buried him there, on the Mississippi's shore. Afterward, Homer went on to New Orleans and Travis went back to Arkansas and tried to put his life together again.

Someone cried out in Spanish, jerking Travis back to the raw, windy mountains. Looking over his shoulder, he saw Antonio Rodolso spurring after a pack mule that had shied away from the main bunch. Travis swung back into the icy blast of the wind, letting the fragmented memories of that day slowly fade. He had failed his brother there on the Mississippi, he knew, causing his death as surely as if he had pulled the triggers himself. He had tried to deny it at first, arguing that he couldn't have known Chet would stay behind and try to fight the pirates alone to give him and Homer the edge they needed to escape, but it was no use. Nor could he continue to buck the entire population of Hanging Creek Falls. He was a coward in their eyes, something less than a man, and in time he had come to believe they were right. Wasn't Chet the ultimate proof of that?

Something wet touched Travis's cheek and he blinked and looked up, noticing for the first time the drifting fall of snow, flakes no bigger than gnats and barely enough to call attention to. But there, nonetheless, and like a door of sorts, slamming down behind him with all the finality of the real thing. He was on his way now, hell or high water, and come spring he intended to either be a full-up, sure-enough man again, or dead.

CHAPTER SIXTEEN

They crossed the Trinchera late on their third day out of Taos, and soon afterward swung to the northwest, still following the del Norte on their left. To their right Blanca Peak looked like a timber-skirted mesa, made flat and stubby by an unbroken line of clouds.

The clouds were beginning to worry Eli. He knew the high country was getting snow. The question was, how much? Would they be able to force their way over Buffalo Pass, still two long days ahead of them, or would they have to backtrack to find another route over the mountains? He wasn't worried about reaching the valley behind the Wasatch Range where Big Tom Reed had cached his stolen furs. There were plenty of other passes they could use. But it could make a difference with the fall season, cutting deeply into the brigade's profits. With such a late start they were already pushing their luck; they couldn't afford the wasted days that backtracking would entail.

It had continued to snow off and on down below, too, although the ground was too warm yet for it to stick. Sometimes it rained or sleeted, the dampness penetrating the protective layers of clothing they wore with a bone-numbing chill. And the wind never let up. It pounded them hourly, sapping their patience as much as it did their strength. The days were miserable, and the nights not much better, yet despite the adverse weather their spirits remained relatively high. There was an almost contagious excitement in putting out for a season that not even the weather could completely quell.

Coming to a low rise, the sorrel's ears suddenly perked forward. Eli's chin lifted, and his hand moved almost imperceptibly on his rifle. He glanced quickly over his shoulder. Silas McClure rode directly behind him, bundled tightly in a long blue wool coat, his Dragoon's cap pulled low. The rest of the brigade was strung out over several acres, the pack mules bunched loosely in the center. A number of the old hands caught Eli's eye questioningly, but no one spoke. Swinging back to the quartering wind, Eli made his way cautiously to the top of the rise. He hauled up as he neared the top, and made a slashing motion with his hand that would bring the brigade to a halt. Silas McClure rode up beside him, stretching his pudgy body to peer past the rise.

Perhaps a mile away a herd of antelope was drifting with the wind, a slow-rippling, pale-rust blanket, at least three thousand strong. Even over the soughing of the wind Eli could hear the low clatter of dewclaws and the short, snorty warning whistles of those animals on the fringe of the great herd that had immediately spotted Eli and McClure. The herd froze as one, heads high, the hair around their tails ruffling to reveal the characteristic white rump that signaled danger. Beside Eli, McClure laughed softly. "Like a thousand eyes opening at once," he said.

"Quite a bit more than that," Eli replied. He twisted in the saddle to motion Pete Meyers, Charlie Williams, and Remi LeBlanc forward. He would have preferred Johnny Two-Dogs, but he had sent the Iroquois half-breed and Jake Orr into the hills along the del Norte earlier that day to hunt. Now it looked like supper had found them, instead.

Pete came up first, drawing rein close enough to Eli for their stirrups to bump. He whistled quietly as he studied the herd. "There be fresh meat, boys, and this coon is half froze for fresh meat." He looked at Eli. "You want me'n Charlie to make a little raid on this herd?"

"You and Charlie and Remi."

The others had come up beside Pete, and Remi smacked his lips appreciatively. "It has been too long since Remi has eaten of *cabbri*," he said hungrily. "*Le bison,* elk, *oui,* but not antelope." He grinned at Eli. "We make the meat, eh?"

"You make the meat," Eli agreed.

"*Oui.*"

"Remi and Charlie are both carrying smoothbores," McClure pointed out. "Those aren't weapons I'd choose for antelope."

Charlie laughed. "You just ain't learned to shoot yet, McClure. This coon can make a fusil shine, and ol' Remi is almost as good."

"*Oui,*" Remi said solemnly. "Almost."

McClure's lips thinned, but he refrained from further comment. Eli said, "Take as many antelope as you can get. We'll wait here a spell and give the horses a breather."

He dismounted and led the sorrel back below the rise of ground, out of sight of the antelope. While Pete, Charlie, and Remi hobbled their ponies and checked their long guns, Eli spiraled down out of the wind, crossing his ankles under him and putting his back to a clump of sage.

"I'll go check the packs," McClure said stiffly, kneeing his chestnut toward the brigade.

"That hoss is tighter'n a fiddle string," Pete observed when McClure had ridden out of earshot.

"He's a good man," Eli said, pulling a cigar from the pouch at his belt. "Give him time to work the army out of his system and he'll shine, for a fact."

"I gave Bill Wolfskill a dollar apiece for seegars, back in Taos,"

Charlie said, eyeing Eli's cigar. "By God if I wouldn't give you two dollars for the one you're holding in your hand right now."

Eli smiled ruefully, then reluctantly returned the cigar to his pouch. Cigars were rare in the mountains, and he had less than a dozen left, and not yet a week out. "I reckon not, Charlie."

"Well, that figures," Charlie said with fake hurt. He started for the rise, dropping to his hands and knees before reaching the top, and quickly disappeared from sight. Pete and Remi did the same, though taking different paths. The trappers would stay below the line of sage for as long as possible, but even crawling, Eli knew it would take all their skill just to slip up close enough for a shot apiece.

From where he was sitting, Eli could just make out the brigade, stopped on the flats about two hundred yards away. McClure had already caught Mateo and the two Rodolsos, and was leading them into the remuda. Most of the others had dismounted to get out of the wind. Eli's gaze strayed toward the distant line of trees that marked the del Norte, but there was no sight of Johnny or Jake.

He leaned back after a while, bunching the collar of his jacket up around his ears and tucking his hands into the pits of his arms. It felt warmer out of the wind, and Eli gradually began to relax. He closed his eyes, breathing in the crisp scent of sage and the moist odor of rain, feeling a comfort in his solitude that was new to him. He had sensed for some time now a gradual changing within himself, a shifting of perspective that he didn't fully understand. He knew it was somehow tied to his new job and its responsibilities, but he hadn't yet decided how, nor had he taken time yet to analyze it.

"Eli."

The voice startled him, and he surged to his feet with his hand on his pistol before he recognized Consuelo's voice. "Connie," he breathed. "What are you doing here?"

"Maybe the same as you. I sought privacy. Then I saw—"

"Privacy? Damn it, Connie, this ain't Taos. You can't go wandering off alone like some . . ."

"Squaw?"

There was a tautness in her voice Eli knew he should heed, but he rammed on anyway. "They're Indians," he said flatly. "They can take care of themselves."

"Bullshit." She came closer, putting her hands behind his head and pulling him down roughly until their lips met. She arched provocatively into him, grinding her hips against his, mashing her breasts against his chest. Her tongue pushed past his lips, darting and stroking. He resisted passively at first, aware that they were still within sight of the brigade, but then his arms came up as if of their own will and tightened around her waist. As his irritation evaporated in the heat of desire, Consuelo pulled back, breaking the kiss and laughing mockingly. "*Carajo*, Eli, I think a Ute war party just stole the remuda."

Stung, he pushed her away.

"I am not some frail *señorita*, Eli, who must always be pampered. Do not treat me that way. Do not tell me where I can go, either. I don't need your permission."

"Damnit, Annie and Red-Winged Woman were born out here. They—"

She stepped back, her eyes flashing. "Is it me you truly worry about, Eli? Or your future?"

Her question brought him up short. Consuelo went on before he could sort out a reply.

"What will happen to me when you go to live in St. Louis?" she asked. "When you become a company man and leave the mountains forever. Will you leave me, too?"

Eli took a deep breath and looked away, his expression betraying the confusion he felt, the division of his desires. What did he want? What did he really want?

"Are you afraid I'll ask to go with you to St. Louis, Eli? Is that what frightens you? Or are you more afraid you'll want to stay here, with me?"

"No one's said anything about St. Louis," he replied lamely, but deep down he knew she had struck the core of his uncertainty. She had a way of surprising him with her insight, and shaming him a little, too, by making him realize how often he dismissed her opinion because she was a Mexican and a woman.

"It doesn't matter," she said then, and he thought he heard scorn in her voice. "See, I am like you. Nothing matters."

"I didn't say it didn't matter."

"Yes, I think you did. We say so much by what we do not say. You and I are alike in that manner as well. We often speak with our silences." She turned toward camp, stiff-backed, but holding her head up proudly, and he realized how hard it had been for her to approach him on this subject, how much it had taken out of her emotionally. For a moment he wanted to call after her. But he didn't. There was nothing he could say that wouldn't be a lie, and he knew she would see through it instantly. So he stood watching helplessly as she threaded her way through the sage, feeling cold and empty inside, and sorrowful, too, as if something he loved dearly had just died.

Chapter Seventeen

Eli stopped his sorrel on the rim of the bench overlooking the Saguache and let the brigade drift up around him. Far below, the river twisted luminously through a belt of cottonwoods and alders, flowing eastward toward the larger San Luis Valley. Tall grass grew on the shelves of bottomland between the snaking oxbows of the river, bending and rising with the breeze. A herd of elk was moving slowly through the timber, their autumn-dun hides so nearly blending into the shadows among the trees that only the yellowish patches of their rumps showed clearly in the fading light; there must have been thirty or forty head, Eli thought, although it was hard to tell for sure.

To the west the La Garitas were bunched solidly against the darkening sky, their humped black slopes blotting out the sunset. Ahead and to the east, other mountain ranges rose up to fence them in, smaller and more clearly defined in the distance, and less intimidating.

Eli brought his gaze back to the basin. He breathed deeply of the clean mountain air and wondered, for a brief, foolish moment, if it was possible for a man to become intoxicated by the sweet, pure tranquillity of the wilderness, to lose himself in its splendor the way an alcoholic might lose himself in a bottle of whiskey. He entertained the notion for only a moment, then straightened his shoulders and shook it away, embarrassed by the emotion, his momentary lapse of practicality. "Charlie," he said brusquely, "you and Travis ride on down and see if you can get an elk for supper."

Charlie nodded and kicked his appaloosa over the edge of the rim. Travis tagged after him on his mule, following at an angle that would take them well downwind of the elk. After they were gone, Old Cal Underwood pulled his horse out of the line and came over beside Eli. He leaned from the saddle to spit past his stirrup, then wiped his lips with the sleeve of his capote and said, "They ain't gonna git 'em no elk thata way. We oughter jus' go on down and git up a fire afore full dark, is what we oughter do. Hell, we got us a little pronghorn yet, what Pete and the boys shot yesterday."

"We'll give 'em a few minutes," Eli replied curtly, wishing Old Cal had found someone else's ear to chew on.

"Ain't sayin' Charlie ain't the man who couldn't," Old Cal countered. "But this coon says we be wastin' time. Oughter been settin' our traps now, 'stead of dickerin' with greasers for pemmican we likely won't need. Oughter been out a month now, if'n we be wanting to cross Buffler Pass before she closes. Do ye hyar, Eli? Gonna be cold doin's ahead, and no sense in it that this hoss can see. A man'd go under quick-like up thyar, he ain't keerful."

"Cal, you and Charlie are a pair," Pete chimed in from down the line. "Neither one's happy unless he's unhappy."

"Don't listen to Ol' Cal, then," the trapper flared. "Be no hair off'n his arse if ye don't." He sniffed as if insulted, and stared moodily across the valley.

Pete chuckled, which only made Cal madder yet. Eli leaned forward to watch as Charlie and Travis reached the valley's floor and rode into the alders a quarter mile downstream from the elk. A gust of wind blew across the bench, slipping under his bandanna to brush his neck with icy fingers. Glancing again at the La Garitas, he knew Old Cal was right. Autumn was about finished now for sure, and winter was coming on fast. Still, they had done the best they could under the circumstances, and they hadn't lost more than a few hours dickering for the pemmican that would be their insurance against the deep snows of winter, when hunting would be difficult at best, if not impossible. It made him a little angry to have to stomach Old Cal's remarks, but he thought Pete was right, too; some men, and Old Cal was one of them, just had to complain; if it hadn't been the pemmican and the late start, it would have been something else.

A spit of muzzle flash lanced the darkness below, followed by the rolling thunder of Charlie's fusil. The sharper crack of Travis's rifle quickly followed, but the elk were already bolting, scattering like yellow billiard balls across a black felt table.

"*Bueno,*" Eli said. "They've got all they're gonna get. Let's go." He touched his spurs to the sorrel's flanks and went over the edge, leaning back to hang on to the crupper strap until the steep grade leveled out about a third of the way down. It was full dark by the time they reached the trees, but the sky was clear after the long spell of rain and snow, and there was enough starlight to see by. Eli led the brigade into a clearing he had used in the past and swung his arm in a circular motion that didn't need verbal explanation. Dismounting, he unsaddled the sorrel and lugged his rig toward the river side of the clearing, where Pierre Turpin was already unloading the mule that carried his kettles.

The brigade quickly fell into the evening ritual of chores—watering and picketing the saddle stock, gathering firewood, kindling fires. Charlie and Travis returned with the skinned and gutted carcass of an elk draped across Travis's saddle, and Red-Winged Woman immediately came forward to help Pierre with the butchering. On the far side of the clearing Pete was helping Annie with their mules, pulling the packs off without hurry, talking, joking, now and again brushing against one another in a way that seemed both sexual and innocent. Watching surreptitiously, Eli felt a pang of regret for the words that had passed between Consuelo and him the day before. His eyes sought her out across the clearing, where she was piling their own gear around the camp's perimeter, adding it to the packs of the others as a sort of low fortification against attack. She worked with a quiet, almost angry efficiency, and when she was finished she took her dun and Eli's sorrel out to picket in the tall grass away from the trees, never once glancing in his direction.

Pierre was sloping *appolas* above the fire by the time Mateo, Jorge, and Antonio drove the remuda out to grass, skewering the willow rods with chunks of elk meat that dripped and sizzled in the flames. He fussed with them in a motherly fashion, keeping them close to the heat but out of the flames, and all the while muttering under his breath, scolding them the way Annie sometimes scolded her mules. Eli went to squat beside the fire, holding his hands out to the warmth. His fingers were numb from the cold, and even hunkered close to the blaze, his breath came out in quick, visible clouds of vapor. There would be frost before midnight, he knew, heavy as a week's growth of whiskers by first light.

Charlie sat cross-legged to one side, staring sleepily into the fire. Little Pete balanced on one of his knees, his black eyes bright, curious, one chubby fist clenched around the drawstring of Charlie's hat. Little Pete was watching Remi across the fire, and Remi, aware of the child's interest, was filling his pipe with a comical elaborateness, screwing his face into nonsensical expressions of concentration. Eli watched them silently, smiling a little at Remi's antics, and laughing softly when the baby did.

Finally satisfied with the slant of his *appolas*, Pierre stood and brushed his hands against the seat of his wool trousers. "Is supper soon," he said. "Coffee and biscuits, too, while dem last."

"Which won't be long," Charlie grumbled without looking up. Charlie liked his coffee, Eli remembered, and always packed along more at put-out than anyone else he knew. But he always ran out before the season was half over, too. A man couldn't pack enough town grub to last him through the winter without stringing along half a dozen extra head of pack mules and hiring someone to care for them so he could run his traps.

"*Oui,*" Pierre was saying in response to Charlie's glum prediction. "Maybe a month yet, then, *poof,* no more. Red meat and river water then."

"Cheery bastard, ain't he?" Pete Meyers said to no one in particular.

Pierre laughed and headed toward the Saguache with a copper kettle. Mateo came in from the remuda and said, "Riders coming."

"How many?" Eli asked, looking up.

Squatting on the balls of his feet, Mateo replied, "Two. Johnny and Jake, no?"

Probably, Eli thought, but he shoved to his feet anyway and strode out to the edge of the trees. The three antelope that Charlie, Pete, and Remi had shot were already nearly gone, and Eli kept Johnny and Jake, and sometimes Old Cal or Remi, out every day hunting for fresh game.

Eli waited at the edge of the trees until he spotted the two men coming in, riding single-file with an empty packhorse trailing them. Johnny hauled up as he came even with Eli, and said to Jake, "Go on and grab yourself some supper."

Jake nodded sullenly and rode past Eli without acknowledgment. Sensing trouble, Eli asked, "What's up, Johnny?"

"Let's step away from the trees," Johnny replied, dropping from the saddle to walk beside Eli.

They made their way toward the base of the bench. Eli walked slowly, feeling the pressure of the wind on his face and the moist give of the earth beneath his moccasins. The fringe on his buckskin trousers swished softly through the tall grass, but other than that and the gentle clop of Johnny's horse, there was no sound, not even the familiar yipping of coyotes or the distant howl of a wolf. They stopped about a hundred yards out, and Eli pulled a cigar from the pouch at his belt, running his fingers impatiently along the crinkly brown leaves. "What's up?" he repeated.

"I thought you might want to keep this to yourself, considering what happened back at Río Colorado."

A nugget of dread had formed in Eli's bowels when Johnny asked him to move away from the trees. It hardened now into a solid lump, swelling outward until even his limbs felt heavy and awkward. He put the cigar away with an abrupt movement, and his voice hardened. "What is it?"

"I think we're being followed. Jake and I split up in the foothills and I rode south a ways, just moseying along, looking for sign. I ran across tracks on top of a hill—three men riding shod horses. They must have seen me coming and cleared out before I got there. I caught a glimpse of them disappearing into the pines above me, but they were too far away to recognize. I could see the brigade from where they were standing."

"Who were they?"

"Mexicans, looked like. They were wearing sombreros, at least, and their tracks were made by Mexican moccasins. One of them was a big man. The other two looked average-sized."

"And you're sure they're following us?"

"Not certain sure, no. Call it a hunch."

Eli stared into the darkness beyond Johnny's shoulder. "Could they have been soldiers?" he asked.

"I doubt it. I followed them for a while and they were hiding their tracks pretty good. These men, whoever they are, are experienced. They know what they're doing."

"What do you make of it, then?"

"Hard to say, Eli. They could be connected somehow to whoever hamstrung our mules, or they could be someone else entirely." He hesitated, then said, "I could make a little *paseo* back that way tomorrow, if you wanted. They're good, but they aren't that good. Give me a day or two, and I could run them down."

Eli considered Johnny's offer for several minutes, then shook his head. "No, not yet. Let's get over Buffalo Pass first. If they're still following us then, we'll hunt them down and find out what they're up to. Just to be safe, though, I want you and Jake to hang back tomorrow, see if they show up again."

"Sure, Eli."

"And, Johnny, thanks for keeping this to yourself. Let's keep it that way for a while longer yet."

"Sure." Johnny gathered his reins, pulling the mare closer. "You know," he said thoughtfully, "this is shaping up to be a real interesting season."

"It could get that way," Eli acknowledged. He was thinking of Big Tom Reed and wondering if there was any connection between the stolen furs and the incidents that had plagued them since Taos—the governor's order for McClure to return to Santa Fe and reapply for a license, the crippled mules, and now these strangers following them for who knew what reason. It seemed like too much bad luck to be chance, but if there was a link between it all, Eli failed to see it yet.

A hoarse cry from camp interrupted Eli's thoughts. There was a commotion at the fire, then a woman screamed, and Eli's blood went cold. Swearing savagely, he grabbed the reins from Johnny's hand and swung into the saddle. "Gotta borrow your horse, Johnny!" he called, pulling the mare around and racing toward camp.

He jerked the horse to a stop at the edge of the trees and leaped from the saddle. The trappers were standing around the main fire, rifles at the ready. In the center of the knot of men Pierre Turpin was holding his hand up, staring dumbly at his fingers. Eli met Consuelo's gaze as he pushed through the crowd, and his heart hammered with relief to find her unharmed; he was sure it was her scream he had heard. He went to Pierre's side and took the cook's wrist in his hand, turning the palm to the light of the fire. At first he thought Pierre had cut himself with a butcher knife, and it took a moment to realize that the blood wasn't his.

"*Sacre,*" Pierre whispered, staring hypnotically at the slick shine on his fingers.

"Tell it," Eli ordered bluntly.

"There," Pierre said, pointing to the path that led to the river. "The Mexican, me thinks."

Eli glanced around the fire. Mateo Chavez and the Rodolsos were standing uncertainly at the rear of the crowd. Vidales wasn't anywhere in sight.

"Sonofabitch," Eli muttered as he spun toward the river. The others crowded after him like a pack of hounds. They found Vidales close to the water's edge, curled on his side in the half-frozen mud as if asleep. Eli knelt beside him and pulled him onto his back. The front of Vidales' shirt was sodden with blood, shining faintly in the starlight.

"Yeow," Charlie murmured.

"What happened?" McClure demanded.

Eli stood, breathing heavily. "Knifed, it looks like. Someone drag him into camp. It's too dark to see anything here."

There was a moment's hesitation among the men, then Travis Ketchum and Mateo Chavez shouldered forward to grab Vidales by the arms. They dragged him to the fire, the heels of his moccasins gouging shallow troughs in the sandy riverbank that filled slowly with water. Eli looked questioningly at Charlie, the first of the brigade to reach the trees, and the only experienced man among them who had arrived while there was still some light left to see by.

"Not a thing, Eli. Not even a track, although it was already pretty dark, and we were concentrating on the elk."

Eli's voice sounded weary. "All right, some of you spread out and see what you can find. Jake, grab Jorge and Antonio and get out to the remuda, and stay sharp. If there're brownskins around they'll likely make a try for the stock."

"He wasn't scalped, Eli," Pete pointed out quietly.

"I saw that."

"Ain't really no place closer'n fifteen, twenty feet that would've hid a brownskin, either," Charlie added.

"What are you saying, Charlie? That one of us killed Vidales?"

Charlie shrugged. "I ain't sayin' nothing, Eli. It just don't wash, is all, callin' this brownskins' work. Especially after what happened back at—"

"Just spread out," Eli cut in sharply. He turned up the path toward camp, McClure and the women dogging his heels. Travis and Mateo had laid Vidales out beside the fire, folding his arms over his stomach. They stood back soberly as Eli knelt once more at the muleteer's side. He looked at the rawhide-wrapped handle of a large-bladed knife jutting obscenely from Vidales' chest, angling downward as if whoever had stabbed him had done so with an underhanded thrust, then grimly took the handle and jerked the knife free. He tossed the blade on the grass beside the fire and looked at Pierre. "What happened?"

"I went for more water," Pierre replied bleakly. "I stumbled over . . ." He let the words trail off.

"Did you see anything? Hear anything?"

"*Non*, Eli! Nothing!"

Eli glanced at Travis, Mateo, McClure, and the women. "How about the rest of you? Did anyone see or hear anything out of the norm?"

Mutely, they shook their heads. Mateo, nodding toward the blade, said, "That is his knife, isn't it?"

Eli picked up the blade, examined it closely, then looked at the rawhide sheath at Vidales' waist. It was empty. "Goddamn," he said, tossing it back to the grass.

McClure's eyes flashed in indignation. "This has gone too far, Eli. We have to stop it. Now."

"You go ahead," Eli said harshly, standing and glaring at the stubby clerk. "You just go ahead and march the killer out here, and I'll by God put a stop to it right now."

McClure met Eli's anger without flinching, but he had no answers, either. Finally, shaking his head in helplessness, he stalked into the darkness just as Johnny arrived on foot. Johnny gave Vidales a considering look, then lifted his gaze to Eli's stony stare. "Yes, sir, a real interesting season."

CHAPTER EIGHTEEN

They were three days crossing Buffalo Pass and dropping into the valley of the Grand River, on the western slopes of the Continental Divide. It had been rough going all the way, the snow on top chest-deep to the horses in a couple of places, although soft and powdery yet, so that they had been able to plow through without crippling any of the stock. It had been cold, though, frigidly so, with a battering wind that howled day and night. By the time they reached the relatively barren slopes of the foothills the horses were gaunt and glassy-eyed, the mountain men not much better.

Eli drew up beside an outcropping of crumbling red rocks to let the sorrel blow. Far below and to his left, he could see the brigade winding slowly down from the piney ridges, a snaking line of color against the brown hills, etched clearly despite the distance.

To the north, and uncoiling beyond sight into the west, lay the Grand Valley, its broad flats rippling as the wind passed over the sage. Beaver streams ribboned the vast basin, and groves of cotton-wood and aspen rose like yellow atolls in a dusty green sea. Great herds of elk and antelope dotted the valley's floor, and overhead eagles soared in slow spirals, floating gracefully on gentle updrafts. Rolling hills encircled the valley, looking—from a distance, at least—as smooth and round and perfect as a woman's breast. To the south, east, and north towered the rugged mountain ranges that were the heart of the Southern Rockies—the San Juans, the Sawatch, the Crested Buttes—but to the west there were only broken hills running away toward a pale, cloudy horizon. It was through those lacerated ridges to the west that the Grand eventually flowed, angling north-west through the Black Canyon of the Grand before emptying into the Colorado River.

Eli stared at the valley for a long time, dissecting it into chunks and quarters, and studying each piece carefully until he was satisfied it was uninhabited by men. When he was finished, he settled back and let a smile play across his face. He had gambled highly that none of the bigger outfits would swing this way first, beating them to the streams and leaving in their wake only empty beaver lodges and skinned carcasses rotting in the alders. There was an overwhelming sense of relief in knowing that he had gambled successfully, but no real lifting of his spirits. Vidales' death prevented that.

He glanced again at the crawling line of trappers, swampers, women, and children, and felt once more the dark, brooding sense of betrayal that had never quite left him since discovering Vidales' body along the Saguache. There seemed to be little doubt anymore that whoever had killed Vidales, whoever had hamstrung the three mules back at Río Colorado, rode within his view even now. Anger boiled within him at the thought. He remembered Vidales' quiet dignity around the campfires at night, his humble intelligence, and the fondness with which he had referred to his wife and only son, a boy of thirteen this summer. They had not been close, he and Vidales, but the *arriero* had been a Cutler man, and Eli swore he would see justice done, that this senseless death would not go unpunished.

The brigade was nearing the valley's floor when Eli finally nudged the sorrel away from the rocks and descended the hill on an intercepting course. As he came close, McClure pulled away from the main party to meet him.

"Is this it?" McClure asked, nodding toward the basin.

"It is. The Valley of the Grand. It's a rich country, Silas. Not like it was a few years ago, but we ought to do all right here. I saw plenty of game from up above that I doubt would be around if anyone else was. I'll have some of the boys take a look-see to be sure, but I think we're the first ones here this season."

"How long will we stay?"

"As long as it takes, I reckon. A couple of weeks, maybe, no more than three."

McClure pursed his lips, staring across the flats as Eli had done a few minutes before. "It is a grand country, is it not?" he said reflectively.

It was some, all right, Eli thought, and maybe grand was as good a way to describe it as any. There was something about this country that made a man want to stand tall and proud, to fill his lungs and bellow like a bull buffalo during the rut, or to race with the elk. It was something a man couldn't describe without feeling a little foolish, yet he knew inexplicably that his wasn't a solitary reaction, and that the others felt it, too. A man would have to be dead inside not to.

Pete Meyers pulled away from the brigade and loped his buckskin toward them. Stopping beside them, he said, "How, Eli, McClure."

"Pete," Eli responded; McClure merely nodded.

"I've been listenin' to the magpies, Eli, and they tell me ye be fixin' to hunker down here a spell."

"Is that what they're saying?"

"Uh-huh. 'Course, you know magpies. You can't believe no more'n half of what they say, and then you never know which half to believe."

Smiling, Eli said, "Are you and Charlie wanting to cut your pins?"

"Well, we've trapped this hole before, and we've got us an idea or two about where we want to set our traps, if you're aimin' to set a spell."

"I do, and you and Charlie are welcome to put out in any direction you want. I probably won't split the rest of the boys up until tomorrow."

"Wagh! That'll shine, Eli. It will, now." Turning away, he called over his shoulder, "We'll mosey on back in a week or so and find ye."

Eli nodded. "*Bueno*. Luck to you."

"Won't need it where we're going," Pete replied, grinning broadly.

"Is that wise?" McClure asked when Pete had ridden out of hearing. "I would imagine some of the men will complain."

Only Old Cal, Eli thought, and a man just had to learn to let Underwood's pessimistic whining slide off like the rain. "Pete and Charlie will probably bring in a third of the plews the outfit takes this year," Eli explained carefully. "Since they're riding with us, they'll offer us first chance to buy their catch, mountain style. It's just good business to give them a little extra rein when you can. Snub 'em too tight and they'll put out on their own hook. We'd lose their plews and two extra rifles." He grinned fleetingly. "Three, if you want to count the Pawnee Killer."

McClure snorted. "I don't believe that story for an instant, that she killed ten Pawnees with a single shot. It's absurd."

"Well, that's a possibility I wouldn't discount, either, but when you get to know Annie a little better you might reconsider."

"How long have you known them?" McClure asked thoughtfully.

"Pete and Charlie?" Eli shook his head as if reading the direction of McClure's thoughts. "I reckon not, Silas. I'd sooner suspect you as either one of them."

"I don't know any of the men very well, but perhaps that's to our advantage."

Eli glanced at Annie and Red-Winged Woman, cutting their pack string out of the remuda. Pete and Charlie sat their ponies to one side, going back and forth in animated conversation. Eli gave McClure's statement a moment, then shook his head. "I reckon not," he said. "Not those two."

"It had to be someone with the brigade."

"I know. But not Pete or Charlie."

"Or Caleb Underwood or Remi LeBlanc or Johnny Two-Dogs?"

"No. Not them, either."

"Then one of the greenhorns?"

"Maybe."

"Maybe?" McClure sounded faintly sarcastic. "There is hardly a question of a murder, Eli."

"Maybe Chavez, or one of the Rodolsos. Jorge seems all right, but Mateo has a chip on his shoulder the size of an adobe brick, and Antonio is hiding something under that bandage of his that's riding him like a curse."

"What about the Orrs, or Travis Ketchum?"

"Maybe." Those three were still unknown elements, as yet unproven.

McClure shifted in the saddle, hunching his shoulders forward as if priming for a fight. Eli resigned himself to what he knew was coming.

"We have to put the question before the men," McClure said stiffly. "Who was accountable at the time of Vidales' murder, and who is without alibi?"

"No. We've already been over that. I won't accuse the whole bunch, and that's what it would amount to if we started poking them with questions like that."

"An inquiry is the only logical approach. Damnit, man, we can't allow this traitor to continue to sabotage our efforts."

"That's exactly what you'd be doing if you tried to interrogate these men," Eli retorted. "They aren't soldiers, McClure; they wouldn't stand for it. Hell, the whole bunch'd quit on us."

"They've signed contracts," McClure snapped. "And I'd see to it personally that each and every man was fined or punished for any breach of it."

"You'd just as easy saddle the wind as try to enforce your contract out here. What they signed in your ledger don't amount to a handful of beaver scat to them. What counts, what is truly binding, is their word. And yours. Question them on this and you'll be breaking the *spirit* of your word, Silas. Do that, and you might as well call it quits here and now, cut your losses and go on back to Taos. Just back off a spell, and let me handle it."

"I would like to see some evidence of your handling it," McClure replied stoutly. He pulled his mount around and rode back to the brigade, a solid, inflexible weight in the cradle of his Dragoon saddle, stiff-backed with anger.

Watching him ride off, Eli wished he knew if he was right or not in holding the clerk back. All he had to go on was his intuition, and that told him that the old hands, at least, would quit as soon as McClure raised any suspicions toward them. Yet McClure had made a valid point, too; they hadn't done anything to ferret out Vidales' murderer, had just pushed on as if nothing had happened, knowing full well that if left unchecked, the culprit was bound to strike again.

Sighing, Eli looked across the valley, remembering the first time he had seen it with old Provost back in '24. Lord, the beaver had been thick then, like furry dollars ripe for the plucking, and the deer and elk so swarming a blind man could have made meat. Those had been some good days, he reflected, some of the best of his life, possibly, before Bad Gocha's treachery on the Provost River, and Etienne's unbelievable stupidity in ordering his men to leave their weapons behind. That Eli was able to look back upon them with such clarity and pleasure came as something of a surprise to him. For the first time it occurred to him that if he was to gain something from Girardin's offer, it would not be without its price.

"Leveeee!"

McClure's voice cracked the fragile shell of the morning, and Travis groaned and huddled deeper into his blankets. He could feel the cold seepage of air even through the layers of wool, nipping at the tops of his ears, his fingers, and his toes.

"*Levee*," McClure bawled once more. "Come on! We're wasting daylight!"

"Daylight!" Travis grunted, fingering his blankets down just enough to peer over the edge. "What daylight?"

"Come on, *mon ami*," Pierre said, grinning crookedly at him from beside a crackling fire. "This day you become the trapper. Brrr." He shook himself like a dog coming out of water. "Soon you will stick your feet into *le rivière*, and then you will know why it is better to cook than to trap."

"The sonofabitch is right," Jake Orr said, his voice thick and nasal from congestion. He squatted before the fire, almost leaning over the crackling flames.

Remi LeBlanc laughed sarcastically. "Someday soon, Remi thinks, you will remember this morning with fondness," he said, standing inside the fire's circle of light, but outside its warmth.

Travis threw his blankets back and sat up, hurriedly pulling on his boots, coat, and cap. The others were drawing up to the fire now, too, and Travis sensed an air of expectancy among them, an excitement he hadn't noticed before.

"Do ye hyar, boys," Old Cal was exclaiming. "The Frenchman's right. They be cold doin's to come, or this nigger wouldn't say it."

"Can't be no colder than the time me and Milt Sublette and Charlie Williams holed up south of here," Cork-Eye said, standing opposite the fire with his hands tucked beneath his armpits for warmth. "That was three, maybe four seasons back, on the south slopes of the San Juans, but higher'n this. It got colder than a witch's tit, for a fact. Ol' Solomon Dreyer was along that trip, too. You remember Solomon, don't you, Cal?"

"Well, I reckon," Old Cal replied. "He was the slickest coon with a knife this nigger's ever seed. Better'n a Mescan, he was."

"He was some with a blade, for a fact," Cork-Eye agreed. "But the season I'm talking about, ol' Solomon had him a Mexican squaw, little sprite of a gal not much bigger than Charlie's oldest daughter. She was some punkins though, and a hell of a cook. She brought along a whole damn sack of chilis, and could whip up a stew that would wake the dead with an appetite.

"Well, we were hauling in the plews, or I wouldn't say so. Filling our traps nearly every day, and hard put to keep 'em stretched and grained before the next bunch come along. Then damned if it didn't turn cold. Froze so hard and fast it froze our traps in the streams. Couldn't chop 'em out with an ax. That was the hardest ice I ever saw, and we ruined three axes proving it.

"But hell, it was early—the shakies had barely started changing color—and we figured we was bound to get an Injun summer yet, so we decided to just ride it out. It was tough, boys, and no other word to call it. It was too cold to hunt. Hell, it was snuffing the gunpowder before it could explode, it was that cold. We liked to starve until it started freezing the clouds right outta the sky. They'd ice up and get heavy, and the next thing you'd know they'd come streaking to the ground like frozen sheep. Well, our medicine was good that year, I guess, 'cause one of those clouds dropped on a elk and killed it right outside our camp. We scooted out and managed to get it skinned and butchered before it froze, although it was a close one even with four of us working on it. But anyway, we got it inside, and Solomon's woman decided she'd whip us up a big stew, using all her chilis, on account of us needing the warmth. Well, wasn't anyone going to argue with that.

"Boys, that was some eating or I wouldn't say so, and right then me and Charlie and Milt knew why ol' Solomon had packed her along. That stew set in our bellies like a coal fire, and it wasn't no time a-tall before we were shucking our coats and shirts and sitting there all but bare-arsed, sweatin' like darkies and not three feet away the shakies were freezing and bursting. But along toward robe time that fire she'd kindled in our bellies started looking for a way out, and we were a miserable bunch, I'm here to tell you. We laid there all night, farting and belching and plain damn sick, feeling worse than I ever got from ol' Wolfskill's whiskey. But the funny thing was, those farts didn't break, and they didn't smell. They just came rolling out like pebbles and drifted off into the air, and by and by we forgot all about 'em.

"Well, it was about a week later that the freeze finally broke, and it was then the trouble started for fair. Those farts started thawing and popping like gunfire, going off every which way until a man didn't know where to duck. Must've been three or four hundred go off in the time it takes to saddle a horse, and the next thing you know ol' Solomon comes barrelin' outta his shanty like the devil himself was after him, hollerin', 'Fort up, boys, the brownskins are shooting at us!'"

Travis had seen it coming, but he laughed along with the rest anyway. Pierre had been slicing chunks of meat from the hindquarters of an elk that Johnny had brought in the night before, sliding them onto his *appolas*. "It is true that a man must be careful with his wind," he said gravely. "*Sacre,* I remember a man my first winter in *les montagnes.* A Creole, he was, from Quebec. He got into the trade whiskee and drank nearly the whole keg without sharing. *Oui,* it is a small-minded man who will not share his whiskee, no? But he paid for it. He came into camp and sat on a twenty-five-pound keg of gunpowder. Then he farted, and *poof,* no more Creole."

They laughed again, and Remi deadpanned. "I always heard Creole cooking was hot, no?"

They were still chuckling when Eli rode in on his sorrel. "It looks clear," he said to Mateo. "Run 'em down to the river for a drink while the boys eat their breakfast."

Mateo nodded and walked off, his cousins following quietly.

"Punch up that fire, Pierre," Eli ordered curtly. "Be daylight soon."

"*Oui,* Eli," Pierre replied obediently, bending to the task. An uneasy silence settled over the camp in the face of Cutler's trenchant disposition. Eli remained mounted, staring pensively into the flames while his horse shifted nervously under him.

"I ain't takin' me no pilgrims," Old Cal said suddenly. He spat and shook his head. "No, sir, I ain't, so you can jus' git that notion outta yer head right now, if that be what ye were thinkin'."

Eli looked up, his eyes glinting coldly. "Nobody said you had to pair with one of the new men," he told Cal. "Remi, do you want to take the Orrs?"

"*Oui,*" Remi replied, winking at Jake and Clint. "Remi will make first-class trappers of them, you will see."

"*Bueno,* Jake, Clint, you go with Remi, and listen to what he tells you. He was pulling beaver out of these streams when you two were still pups. Travis, I want you to pair up with Johnny, and the same deal applies. Keep your eyes open, watch, listen, do what he says.

"Cal, that leaves you and Cork-Eye."

Old Cal's head shot up, and his mouth gaped. "I ain't takin' *him,*" he shrilled. "No, sir. I'll go with Johnny."

"I reckon not," Eli replied, meeting Cal's stare evenly. Old Cal's mouth began working loosely, but no words came forth. "Remi," Eli went on, shifting his gaze. "I want you to take the south side of the valley. Work those streams that look the best and don't bother with the smaller ones. Johnny, you and Travis take the north side. Cal and Cork-Eye can take the east. The rest of us will trap the middle of the valley and hold down the fort. Pete and Charlie are up there somewhere. If you run into them, leave 'em be. They're the same as Cutler men as long as they ride with us."

"You want us to stay out until we're finished?" Johnny asked.

"No. No use in that. Swing back here every four or five days and bring in your catch. The swampers'll take care of your plews, and you can spend more time running your lines." He paused, staring at a spot just above the fire, then said, "Hell, I guess that's it, boys. Good luck, and watch your topknots." He reined away, jogging toward the river to help Mateo and the Rodolsos with the remuda.

Travis rolled up his bedroll and tied it behind the cantle of his saddle. The rest of his gear—his extra powder and lead and a little leather bag of flints for his rifle, a tin kettle and cup, a razor, extra socks, and a small bottle of castoreum he would use to bait his traps—he packed into his saddlebags. He'd gone into debt to McClure for most of the extras, plus a belt ax and four good beaver traps he carried in a burlap bag hung from the off side of his saddle horn.

Breakfast was ready by the time he finished. He ate lightly, and washed his cup out afterward in the river. He came up from the creek just as Mateo and the Rodolsos brought in the remuda. Most of the men went after their mounts with stiff rawhide reatas or hemp ropes, but Travis took only his bridle, and met the mule halfway.

"Hello, Blue," he said, scratching the mule behind a flopping ear. He pried the mule's mouth open with his thumb and slid the bit past the big, yellowing teeth. By the time Johnny came in with his bay and a couple of pack animals, Travis had Blue saddled. He cinched the sawbucks onto the pack mules and rigged the light panniers while Johnny readied his pony, then climbed into the saddle. But Johnny held back, a teasing smile working at the corners of his mouth. He said loudly, *"Bueno.* This hoss is ready to put out first, and he reckons he'll be first back, too, and with the most beaver. I have a fine, four-point Hudson's Bay blanket to wager against anyone who wants to disagree."

His challenge brought an instant clamor from the others. *"Oui,"* Remi cried, letting go of a breaching strap and coming partway toward them. "Remi will bet two new calico shirts that he will be first in, with the most beaver."

"I'll take 'em if'n they fit," Old Cal crowed. "And match ye both with a carrot of 'baccy, good Virginia leaf."

"And I'll throw in a buffler robe, though I do doubt I'll be givin' it up," Cork-Eye said.

"I'll meet you all with a tomahawk that's never been used," Jake called, and in the wake of his utterance there came a long, cold silence.

"Best be makin' wagers amongst yer own kind," Old Cal growled at last. "And keep ye distance from the old masters."

Jake looked crestfallen. His eyes traveled from one man to the next, but when they reached Travis, the dismay vanished and his gaze hardened. "How's that mule, Ketchum?"

"Let's go," Johnny said to Travis. He swung into the saddle and booted his pony in the ribs. Travis grabbed the leads of the two pack animals and followed him out of camp, threading past the crude breastworks of logs and unneeded panniers that Eli had had them construct the day before. He was aware of Jake's angry glare fixed between his shoulders, and looked over his shoulder at the last minute, grinning broadly just for the hell of it. Jake's face flushed to the color of an early beet.

The sky was shaded to a rich pearl as they crossed the river, the sun still far below the jagged rim of the Continental Divide. There was a thin film of ice covering the shallow pools close to the bank, and frost clung thickly to the alders, shattering into a sparkling crystal shower as they forced their animals onto the north bank. Away from the camp and the lure of the remuda, Travis looped the lead ropes of the pack mules over the jutting pickets of the sawbucks. They set off at a lope toward a shallow canyon with a scattering of cottonwood at its mouth, about a mile's distance from the camp. Johnny slowed when they reached the trees, and let Travis come up alongside.

"Pete and Charlie are probably somewhere to the east of us," he said. "We'll go due north now, then angle back to the west, make a loop and clear out most of the streams." Travis nodded but didn't reply, and Johnny grunted as if in approval. "Jake Orr is a hard one to take. I don't envy Remi a bit, although he set his own foot in this trap, and not the first time, either." They rode in silence for a ways, then Johnny said, "You got the makings, Travis. Maybe as good as any I've seen in a while. I'm not sure Eli's seen it yet, but the others have."

Johnny's compliment caught Travis by surprise, and for a moment he didn't know what to say or how much he wanted to reveal. Uncertainly he ventured, "I ain't decided yet whether I want to stay. I, ah, I came out here for a reason."

Johnny laughed. "Most men do, running away from something or the other—the law or a woman, or maybe just responsibility. What you were back in the States doesn't matter. You get a whole new start out here." He hesitated, his thin brows furrowed in thought, then said, "I'm not following my own advice here, but I'll say it anyway. Keep your peace and don't go horning in on what doesn't include you, like Jake did. If you see a plug come off a powder horn and good DuPont spilling on the ground, don't say anything. If a man's pony runs off, don't offer to fetch it back for him, or loan him a spare of yours. Let him get it back himself, or walk. Don't offer anything a man doesn't ask for, but give him the shirt off your back if he does. Do your share around camp, like you been doing, but no more. You do that and you'll get along. Time'll tell which way your stick will float, but I'm betting you'll stay. I'm betting come green-up time next spring, you'll be a mountain man sure, and never look back to the States, or miss them, either."

"Is that the way you feel?"

"Mostly. I had it easier than others, I guess, especially for a mixed-blood. My father was a trader for the Upper Mississippi Company, but he came from a wealthy family with English connections. He sent me to England for an education, and I spent a year at Oxford. I didn't like it, though." He chuckled. "The girls who lived around the school were all right. They were drawn to me because of my mother's blood, and that was good. But their fathers always wanted to hang me or have me whipped, whichever it took to keep me out of their daughters' skirts. Seemed like the older I got, the more I felt like a dirty siwash, so I said the hell with it and came on back. It's better out here. Some, anyway."

"How come your last name is Two-Dogs?"

There was a trace of sadness in Johnny's smile. "It was my uncle's name, on my mother's side. When I returned from England

I discovered that my parents had both died on the prairie, caught by a blizzard and froze to death. I'd had my fill of my father's family, and the white world didn't want a half-breed, no matter what his education was, so after the Old North-West Company folded back in '21 I joined my uncle's band, and every year we'd come west to hunt buffalo and trap. After a while, I just stayed." He fell silent then, his face clouded with memories, and Travis, feeling suddenly like an intruder, let Blue drift back until they were riding single-file.

They followed the canyon for several hours before it petered out, then climbed a ridge and started down the other side. Thick stands of pine covered the lofty, north-facing slopes now, and groves of aspens grew in the smaller side canyons they passed. The country became rougher, sharper, and more hostile. Crumbling ledges of sandstone jutted from the sides of the ridges, with scrub cedar and sagebrush clinging to the scanty soil in the crevices. They passed a few small seeps, the grass around them greener than elsewhere, but nothing big enough to set a trap in. It was afternoon before they came to a small valley with a twisting stream that ran down from the north. The east bank of the creek was low and flat, covered with good forage for the stock, but the west bank rose sharply toward a timbered ridge. There was a grove of aspen at the upper end of the valley, its golden leaves shimmering in the breeze.

"This'll do," Johnny said, drawing up to stare at the valley. "See the way she runs?" he pointed to the creek with his chin. "There's beaver working this creek."

Travis saw only water, dark and rippling and, even from here, faintly musical. But he didn't doubt Johnny's claim. Blue snorted suddenly, and threw up his head. Johnny's mare turned skittish at the same instant, dancing back with her nostrils flaring. Travis tightened his grip on the Kentucky, scanning the dark ranks of pines that climbed upward from the creek's western bank. He didn't see anything, but knew that with the trees growing so close together an army could have hidden among them without effort. Johnny's mare had quit dancing, but all four animals were watching the forest closely, their muscles taut, necks arched, ears perked forward.

"Painter, likely," Johnny said, forcing his pony forward again. "We'll have to watch close to see it doesn't spook the stock. This isn't a country to be put afoot in."

"Painter?"

"Panther, cougar, mountain lion. Call it what you want."

"Would it kill a mule?"

"Yep, but they aren't likely to, not with all the deer sign we've passed."

They rode down to the aspens at the head of the valley and dismounted. Travis gathered wood for the evening's fire while Johnny built a crude lean-to at the edge of the trees that they would cover with blankets until they could get some deerskins to shingle it with. In an hour they were finished.

"All right," Johnny said, stepping back from the shelter. "It'll do for no longer than we'll be here." He pulled his hip-length buckskin jacket tighter, glancing at the sky, the litter of fleecy clouds skimming rapidly eastward. "We might as well split up now. I'll go upstream and take one of the mules with me. No sense taking a chance if there is a painter nearby." He stepped into the saddle and, without so much as a nod, threaded a path through the aspens.

Travis watched until Johnny disappeared from view, then glanced at the tiny shelter, the pile of firewood stacked nearby. The camp looked lifeless and forlorn. A fire would have helped, he reasoned; a fire, or even the clutter of ashes inside a circle of soot-blackened stones, gave a place a feeling of belonging, of home. This was merely a collection of limbs and a few abandoned blankets, no more inviting than a deadfall. A quiver of panic ran through him that he had to consciously fight back by reassuring himself that he wasn't really alone. Johnny would be back by sundown, and even if he wasn't, the main camp was little more than half a day's ride to the south. Breathing deeply, Travis tightened Blue's cinch, then headed downcreek with the pack mule.

The valley narrowed at its southern extremity, the slopes on either side steepening into a sharp V, with only a game trail hugging the creek's left bank. Travis kept to that and made good time. A couple of miles below camp, the valley widened once more, with a beaver dam at the lower end and the creek above it swelling like an engorged tick. There was a thick growth of aspens on the western shore, dotted with the gnawed stumps of a beaver's work, and a trio of mud and branch lodges that rose like bristled caps from the deep, still water.

Travis dismounted next to the aspens and freed a pair of traps from the tangle of chains inside his burlap sack. He dropped them on

the grass and laid his rifle beside them, then walked through the trees
to select a couple of straight, slim aspens, maybe half as round as his
forearm. He chopped them down and trimmed them into stakes
about four feet long, then went back to collect his rifle and traps. The
marshy ground close to the pond was overgrown with sedge grass,
the moist soil printed with the tracks of elk, deer, and bighorn sheep,
scratched with the lighter markings of birds and mice. He spotted the
winding trail of a snake and followed it until it turned back into the
sedge. He walked on, forgetting his traps as he read the stories written in the mud. The snake had been after a mouse, and farther on he
came to the trail of a coyote, bouncing high over the sedge, also after
a mouse. Here a badger had come to drink, and over there a beaver
had dragged a heavy limb into the water, its webbed rear feet leaving a deeper print right at the shoreline where it had pushed off. Scat
was as thick along the bank as tracks, and just as revealing. The elk
and deer were fat, ready for the winter, and the mice were thick, food
for coyotes, owls, and other birds of prey. Near the southern tip of
the pond, close to the dam, Travis came to an abrupt halt. He reared
back in quiet awe, only half believing what was plain before his
eyes. "Gawddamn," he murmured, squatting to trace the outline of
the huge print with his fingers. "Jesus," he added.

He stood then, his heart quickening as he dropped his traps and
stakes and curled his thumb around the flintlock's hammer. He had
heard of grizzlies all his life, but he hadn't expected anything like
this. Not even the exaggerated tales told around the trappers' fires at
night had prepared him for something this large.

He glanced toward the aspens. The tracks were no more than a
few hours old, but Blue and the extra mule stood quietly among the
trees, their heads drooped. Travis turned a slow circle, but the valley
appeared empty. He glanced again at Blue and the pack mule, and
forced himself to relax a little. "I reckon that bear's long gone, or ol'
Blue would be raisin' a fuss," he said to himself.

He made his sets on the west bank, in the afternoon shade of the
aspen grove. The first he set near the dam, the other close to the
pond's upper end. He set both traps in six to eight inches of water,
about a foot from the bank, then played out the five feet of chain toward the middle of the pond. In thigh-deep water he slipped a stake
through the chain ring as far as the notch he had whittled at the
halfway point, then hammered the stake into the pond's muddy bot-

tom until it stood firm. Next he sloped a twig above each trap and carefully uncapped the horn container he used to carry his castoreum, dipping the tip of the twig into thick, oily liquid the mountain men called "bait." Finished, he stood back to survey his work. If he had done everything correctly, the beaver would come out of their lodges after he left. Drawn by the powerful scent of his bait, they would cautiously approach the twig, their webbed feet thrusting their chunky bodies forward by slow degrees, their flat, paddlelike tails floating just beneath the surface. With luck, when they stopped to sniff the tip of the twig, they would place a foot in the trap, tripping the pan. Then, in pain, fear, and surprise, the beaver would dive toward the illusive safety of deeper water, where the trap's chain would prevent his escape, and the trap's weight would hold him under until he drowned. It was a cruel death, but quick, and Travis consoled himself with the rationalization that death was a part of life; he thought fleetingly of the nearly barren streams of western Arkansas, trapped out a generation before, then quickly banned the thought from his mind. A man doesn't tame the wilderness, his grandfather had proclaimed upon handing him the long-barreled Kentucky rifle on the day Travis left home, he conquers it. Civilization demanded no less. It was, in some ways, a frightening thought, far too weighty to tackle on the wild frontier. Such thoughts were best left to more idle minds, Travis had long ago reasoned.

Streaming water, Travis climbed out of the pond and flopped in the grass. He caught the heel of his left boot between the ground and the heel of his right boot and tried to pull it off, but the wet leather clung tightly to his foot and refused to budge. He lifted his legs to drain as much of the water from his boots as he could, the cool air already penetrating his soaked clothing.

Mounting Blue, he pushed on and made another set about half a mile below the first two, and his fourth just beyond that, in ponds quite a bit smaller than the first one, with only a single beaver lodge in each. The sun was already hidden behind the steep ridge to the west when he turned back, the air turning sharp. He could see his breath when he exhaled, and his wet boots felt like ice around his feet. He was shivering violently by the time he came in sight of their camp, his feet aching with a slow-throbbing pain, and he had to keep flexing his legs to fight the cramps that threatened the muscles of his calves.

There was a small fire burning in front of the lean-to, and behind it the figure of a man turning a skewer of roasting meat above the flames, the scene a yellow globe of warmth and humanity surrounded by the cold blackness of the night. It made Travis feel suddenly small and insignificant, as if his own presence here at this tiny, isolated spot on the earth had no more meaning than that of the coyote, mouse, and the snake that had fought and died along the beaver ponds.

"Gawddamn," Travis muttered, as he had on seeing the huge print of the grizzly beside the pond, "Jesus." Only this time he spoke through thin, bloodless lips and chattering teeth. He rode to the edge of the fire's light and slid from the saddle, hanging onto the horn until his legs felt strong enough to support him.

"You look half froze," Johnny said nonchalantly from the fire.

"About that," Travis replied shortly. He unsaddled the mules and led them into the trees, tying them off with a short lead. Then he came back to the fire and sank beside its warmth, huddled and shivering.

Johnny studied him quietly for a moment, then looked down at the knife he was honing on a piece of stone. "There's a haunch of deer hanging in a tree behind the lean-to, if you're hungry."

"I can wait a while," Travis said. He eyed the meat roasting over the flames, his mouth watering, but he was too cold to relish the idea of leaving the fire.

"I was hunting the Salt River country about three or four years ago," Johnny said, drawing his knife across the stone in long, even strokes. "Below the Snake River, where she comes out below the Tetons. That's pretty country, or I wouldn't say so. Except it's almost trapped out now. That's Ashley's old stomping ground, and Sublette and Jackson and ol' Bible-thumping Jed Smith, now that they bought out Ashley. Anyway, I was riding with a greenhorn that year who'd just come to the mountains. His name was Larson, but we called him Lars. He used to set his traps wearing brogan shoes, but froze all the toes off his right foot before November. He walked mighty queersome after that, though we still called him Lars, instead of Stumpy or Gimp."

Travis stared into the fire for a long time. Eli had ordered him to round up half a dozen or so pairs of moccasins back in Taos, as well as gloves and a better coat, but he hadn't pushed it, and in the day-

to-day bustle of getting the outfit ready to put out, Travis had neglected to round up those things he would need for himself. Money
had been a part of it, he supposed; he was already into debt for his
traps and such, but he knew now that he had made a mistake in ignoring Cutler's warning. A smile wormed across his face. "Yeah, I
reckon I oughta make some moccasins. I still have that deer hide I
got south of Taos."

"Wagh! Now that's a good idea you had there, Travis. You see
what I mean about savvying mountain doings? I doubt if Jake
would've thought of that. Moccasins'll dry faster than those boots
you're wearing, and be easier on your feet, too. They wear out quick,
but hell, the mountains are full of deer, and it isn't any trouble to
make a new pair."

"You wouldn't happen to have a pattern, would you?"

"Well, not rightly a pattern, but it isn't any trouble to sketch out
what you need on a tanned hide. Plenty of charcoal in the fire to trace
an outline of your foot. *Bueno.* I'll show you how as soon as you get
a hide tanned." He pointed the tip of his knife at the meat roasting
over the flames. "Just so happens I thought to bring along this buck's
head. You can use his brains to tan your hide."

"Well, I guess that's some good luck on my part," Travis replied
dryly.

Johnny chuckled. "Help yourself to some meat there, *amigo.* I
don't mind sharing with a partner."

CHAPTER NINETEEN

Remi LeBlanc eyed the two boys with distaste as he sipped at his
morning coffee. He was glad they were going back to the main camp
today. It would be good to be among friends again. He would have
to suffer the brunt of their ridicule for a while, but that was to be expected; he would have been just as unmerciful had the moccasin been
on the other foot. In four days they had taken only sixteen
beaver and two otter, all but two from his own traps.

The thought brought a grimace to Remi's face. He had let the others down by not pulling in his share, and although there was some excuse for the poor showing, it gave him little solace. *Sacre,* he thought as he glanced once more at the brothers; he had been foolish to accept such a challenge, to think that he could teach these two how to become mountain men. Yet he knew it was more than just the challenge. He was like the antelope, whose worst enemy was its own curiosity. Jake and Clint Orr had intrigued him from the first, and he had wanted to learn more, to see what mettle they were made of. Now he wished only to wash his hands of them, to trap and fight and live and love as a mountain man was meant to. *Hijo de puta,* he thought, switching to Spanish, *a man was not meant to nurse fools.*

Remi lowered his tin cup and brushed the droplets of coffee from his mustache with the sleeve of his capote. Well, it was done now, and he could see it through the season—he had given Eli his word on that—but in the future he would be more careful. He would learn from this mistake that a wise man did not volunteer impulsively, even if it meant passing up an opportunity to needle Old Cal.

He glanced at Clint, nibbling morosely on an ashcake, and Jake, sitting across from him and sulking as he scowled at the blinking embers of their breakfast fire. The brothers had argued again that morning while bringing the horses in from their picket lines. Remi had no idea what the disagreement had been about, but it had marked them both, as it always did. They would be silent all morning now—Jake moody and impossible to get along with, and Clint cowed by his brother's anger—until by noon Remi's own temper would fray like rotten rope.

"Ah! *Mon Dieu,* it is time we go," Remi announced bluntly. He stood, tossing his coffee aside. "You two pack the mules, and we will take our fine catch back and ask Eli if we can become swampers, like Pierre, eh? You two would like that, no?"

Jake glared at him, but then rose without speaking and stalked toward the mules. Only once had Jake argued, and Remi had explained to him without words, with only his hands and the sudden glint of his knife, why Jake would argue no more. But he knew he had made an enemy for life; Jake wasn't the kind of man to forget an insult, or to shrug it off with time.

Clint had come up to Remi afterward and said miserably, "You shouldn't push Jake like that. He can't take it."

"Listen to Remi, little one," Remi had snarled, grabbing a handful of Clint's shirt and jerking him roughly forward. "Remi will push who he likes, and cut the throat of any man who does not like it. You understand this thing that Remi tells you, eh?"

Clint had blanched but nodded, and that had ended that, too—for a while, at least. But Remi didn't trust either of them anymore. They reminded him of the *caragieu*—the wolverine—that often destroyed for the sheer joy of destruction, slipping into a trapper's camp and shredding his packs, his gear, his furs. They were like that, Remi knew, both of them in their own way, and he growled his displeasure as he knocked the dregs from his cup.

He brought his horse in, a little red and white paint he had traded from a Crow up in the Big Horn country a couple of seasons back, and saddled it while Jake and Clint struggled with the mules. They were fighting a jug-headed roan with an ugly disposition. They had managed to get a bandanna over its eyes to blindfold it, but couldn't get the cloth tied to the halter. The mule was snorting, dancing, tossing its head, and the bandanna kept slipping off. Every time it did, the mule would strike at one of the boys with a front hoof, or snap at them with its big yellow teeth. Both Jake and the mule were getting madder by the minute, while Clint just became more flustered in his attempts to anticipate Jake's commands. Shaking his head in disgust, Remi left them to their clashing wills and rode out of camp alone, taking what he had come to call the ridge trail, which led him through a small gap in the hills west of camp toward a high ridge that overlooked the surrounding country. It was a ride he made every morning, to be alone and away from the steady bickering of the Orrs. But there was practical reason behind it, too. He liked to know what went on around him, to watch the wildlife and read what they told him by their actions, and to scan the horizon for sign of smoke that would indicate the presence of others. Remi had lived a long time in the wilderness by such cautions, and he planned to die an old man, warm and snug, and not by some brownskin's arrow. He smiled to himself then, and amended aloud, "*Oui*, an old man warm and snug in the arms of a beautiful woman. That is the way Remi will die, making love." He was whistling by the time he rode through the gap.

He dismounted before reaching the top of the ridge and hobbled the paint, hanging the bridle from the saddle horn so she could graze. The ridge rose sharply above him, running south into the distant foothills of the San Juans, but terminating abruptly, mesalike, to the north, overlooking the valley of the Grand; the mesa's tip was crowned with a pile of stones, a man-made cairn that had stood for no telling how many generations. Sometimes, crawling toward it on his hands and knees, Remi would wonder who had made it, and when, and what life had been like back then, before the Europeans came. He never wondered why it was made. That was obvious. It was a lookout, a place of concealment atop the treeless knob where a man could lie and watch all day without discovery; the mountains, plains, and deserts of the West were spotted with such cairns, as timeless as the stones they were made of. It was their familiarity that made them so unobtrusive, Remi knew. A man could not worry about every pile of rocks he saw in his travels, not and take much beaver.

Near the cairn, Remi got down to crawl the rest of the way. He stretched out comfortably on the frosty grass before peering around the rocks. He felt a distinct pleasure in the view, in the sweeping vistas that rose from the autumnal valley of the Grand to the far, snow-capped mountains heaped beneath a deep blue sky. Cloud shadows rode the far hills, dipping and rising with the contours of the land. He thought he could see a ribbon of smoke that marked the location of the main camp, but he wasn't sure; it was a long way off, and maybe only wishful thinking.

With his first look out of the way, he settled down for a closer scrutiny. He wished he had a spyglass like McClure's, or even the small one Charlie Williams carried in his shooting bag, but every time he managed to latch on to one he soon lost it gambling at monte or euchre. Hitching himself forward on his elbows, he peered past the base of the cairn to scan the near side of the valley, catching his breath as the sight unfolded.

"*Enfant de garce,*" he muttered with a stricken expression. He counted slowly, his gaze roving among the smaller hills, stopping when he reached forty. Scrambling backward off the skyline, he stood and made his way quickly to the paint. They would have to hurry, Remi told himself, if they wanted to warn the others of the approaching Arapahos.

Eli dismounted and handed the sorrel's reins to McClure. A brisk early morning breeze soughed through the valley, rattling the red-barked alders that banked the Grand, whispering through the silver-hued sage. Beyond the alders, Eli could hear the murmur of the river as it slid swiftly past. A dead cottonwood on the opposite bank creaked threateningly in the wind, its smooth, barkless trunk as white as an unsmoked hide.

"We have to assume it will happen again, Eli."

Eli sighed. McClure went on, speaking earnestly.

"I don't have to tell you who the next logical target would be. You, my good friend, and then myself. It would create chaos within the brigade, and Girardin Shipping and Transport would be finished. The men would scatter, taking GS&T supplies with them."

"You seem to be more worried about the trade goods than your own hide, Silas," Eli said, jobbing the stocky clerk a little.

"I doubt I would care much what happened to the trade goods if I were killed," McClure replied stiffly. "But I am alive now, and those goods are my responsibility. That's a position I take to heart. But it isn't you or me this traitor wants. It's the company's collapse in the mountain trade that he's after."

"I ain't arguing against what you're saying, it's just that I'm tired of arguing about it at all. It's not getting us anywhere."

"Precisely my point. Nothing has changed. We still don't know who the killer is, or how he'll strike next. And we aren't doing anything to find out, either."

Eli shook his head in resignation. He had known when McClure asked to accompany him as he ran his traps this morning that the ex-sergeant would bring up the subject of Vidales' death. Although Eli had dreaded the confrontation, he hadn't turned the man away. He knew McClure worried about the brigade as a whole; that was his job, and he deserved a chance to air his views, no matter that Eli still disagreed with them. "Let it slide, I say. The killer will turn up sooner or later."

"I don't believe that anymore," McClure replied. "This man is too clever. I wouldn't put it past him to masquerade behind a show of ignorance. Cork-Eye, for instance, or Underwood."

"Cork-Eye or Old Cal?" Eli laughed. "Hell, Silas, I've known those men for years. They aren't working for anyone except us, and Cork-Eye's barely doing that."

"Then you still maintain it's one of the new men?"

"I don't see how it could be anyone else."

"What about Pierre?"

Eli was quiet a moment, remembering the blood on Pierre's fingers. "Well, it's true I haven't known Turpin as long as some of the others, but I'm not sure he had enough time to kill Vidales."

"It takes only a second to plunge a knife into a man's chest or draw it across a mule's tendons."

Eli sighed, staring across his saddle toward the rolling, dun-colored hills. He had to admit that McClure's constant insistence that they interrogate the men individually was gnawing steadily at his own self-doubt. A tiny voice in the back of his mind kept whispering that it was McClure who had the military training, the long years of experience in leading men. Only Eli's familiarity with the mountain men upheld his own conviction that such a move would ultimately prove more disastrous to the brigade than McClure's questioning. Men like Old Cal, Remi, Pete, and Charlie were a different breed than the soldiers McClure was used to dealing with. For the time being, at least, McClure was just going to have to accept that. "Let it slide, Silas," Eli said at last, with more vehemence than he had intended.

McClure looked away, his jaw rigid, his eyes smoldering. Eli took the opportunity to slip into the alders, following his old path through the brush. He came out on the bank above the purling waters behind a sandbar and stared down at the icy depths. There was no beaver lodge in the river—the current was too fast for that—but he had discovered a burrow in the side of the bank, and had made his set downstream from the beavers' underwater entrance. It looked like he had taken a skin, too; the stake he had driven into the shoal's gravelly bottom was slanted toward the center of the stream, with only a few inches bobbing above the river's surface.

Eli leaned his rifle against the alders and stepped into the current. The numbing shock of the frigid water around his naked ankles caused him to suck in his breath. Gooseflesh rippled his arms and legs as he made his way to the trap stake. In hip-deep water he pulled the stake toward him, running his hand beneath the surface to the chain. He drew the trap and its catch up from the murky bottom, grunting softly as he held aloft the nearly eighty pounds of steel and flesh. It was a buck that he had taken, sleek and fat, its rich chestnut pelt glistening with droplets of water that caught the rays of the just-rising sun like tiny, oblong beads. Eli hauled the carcass onto dry land and dropped it on the bank. It took only a few moments to free the beaver's webbed rear foot from the trap and skin it. In addition to the pelt, he took the castoreum glands from near its anus, and the broad, scaly tail for Pierre's kettles. The rest he tossed into the alders. Before he could reset his trap, McClure bulled his pony through the brush, dragging the sorrel after it.

"Indians," McClure said in a hoarse whisper, sliding from his saddle.

Alarm ran through Eli. "Where?" he asked, grabbing his rifle and the sorrel's reins in the same motion. He flipped the frizzen forward. The priming pan was full, the flint keen-edged and clamped tightly in its leather blanket within the lock's jaw. He snapped the frizzen closed and raised his eyes to McClure.

"To the south," McClure said, straining now to peer over the alders on the opposite bank. "Damnit, I can't see anything from here."

"How far away were they?"

"A couple of miles. Just coming out of the hills."

Eli swore softly. They were quite a ways off yet, but he knew they weren't likely to miss the smoke from Pierre's fire, or the remuda Mateo and the Rodolsos were grazing along the river. "Well, it was bound to happen," he said. "I just wish some of the others were back. We're pretty short-handed, even for Utes."

"Eli, I don't think they were Utes."

Eli had been sliding his toes into the heavy wooden stirrup of his saddle. He stopped at McClure's words, standing beside his horse with one leg raised. "What do you mean?"

"There were maybe forty or fifty warriors, but no dust, like there'd be if they were dragging travois, and they were riding single file. I've seen some of the plains tribes do that when they're on the warpath."

Eli let his foot drop back to the ground, his mind calculating rapidly. If the Indians were Utes, it was possible they were heading for the Bayou Salade, on the eastern slopes of the Divide, to hunt buffalo; or they could be on their way to Taos to trade their furs and buckskins and maybe a few Paiute slaves. But neither possibility seemed likely. It was too late in the year to be hunting or trading, and if they were just moving their village before the icy clutches of winter snared the high country, they would be heading west, toward the lower elevations.

Eli pulled the sorrel close and swung into the saddle, straightening slowly until he was able to see above the alders. The Indians were still a long way off, but in the clear air he could see them plainly. The scene was as McClure described it—forty-plus warriors, several of them leading extra ponies in addition to a small remuda being hazed from behind. Ducking from sight, Eli said, "I was hoping they'd be Utes. This is their country, and I was hoping to find some to trade with."

"Then this bunch is hostile?"

"Arapahos, likely. Coming back from a raid with a lot of horses and maybe some prisoners."

McClure bit his lower lip. He was new in the mountains, but even a greenhorn understood that the sighting of Arapahos was bad news.

"They're riding in the open," Eli said thoughtfully, "I reckon they haven't spotted our camp yet, or they would've already ducked into the hills."

"Then we should return as quickly as possible and deploy the men into defensive positions."

Eli didn't remind him that they had only six men in camp to deploy, and most of those pitifully armed. It wasn't the time to dwell on what they didn't have. "*Bueno,*" he said tautly, reining the sorrel downriver. "Let's ride."

CHAPTER TWENTY

Only four of the Arapaho braves approached the camp. They came across the broad plain from the south on ponies that showed a lot of rib from hard riding. They wore breechcloths, fringed buckskin leggings, and brightly decorated moccasins. Slanted across their backs were bows and full quivers of arrows. Three of the warriors wore small buffalo robes pulled over their naked bronze shoulders; the fourth wore a buckskin shirt and carried a lance across the withers of his horse. They halted their ponies just out of effective rifle range, and the warrior with the lance asked in sign, the common language of the plains, if they might approach. From behind the waist-high barricade of logs and packs, Eli signed in return, stating that only one man could come forward, unarmed and without a robe.

"What are they saying?" McClure asked as the Arapahos conferred among themselves.

"They're just wanting to talk right now, check us out. Likely they'll ask to come into camp to trade, but we won't let them."

"And the others?"

"Hard to say. They might be in the hills yet, or cached somewhere along the river. Keep the boys on their toes, Silas. I expect there'll be powder burned before this day is over."

The brave without a buffalo robe handed his lance and bow to the man next to him, then started forward alone. Leaving his rifle behind but carrying his pistol in his belt hidden by his buckskin jacket, Eli climbed over the breastworks to meet him. He paused for a moment outside the compound, his fingers resting lightly on the knotty logs. McClure watched in grim silence, his saber drawn, the little pepperbox pistol he normally carried in a sheath at his waist clutched in his other hand, its five muzzles pointing toward the ground. Behind McClure the remuda stood motionless among the scattered aspens of the camp, their heads tied low to their hobbles. Jorge and Mateo manned the east wall of the compound, while Antonio, solemn-faced behind his grimy bandage, and Pierre Turpin stood at the west wall. Alone at the north wall, facing the river and scrutinizing the opposite bank against treachery, was Consuelo. Eli's gaze swept the compound, taking in at a glance its limited strengths, its many weaknesses. He had made a mistake in not insisting that the swampers be better armed, he knew, then exacerbated the problem by sending all his trappers out at once. Such simple oversights, yet experience had taught him long ago that it was the simplest mistakes that brought a man down the swiftest. He should have kept at least a couple of the old hands in camp; he should have furnished rifles or trade guns to those who didn't have their own; he should have been more selective in choosing their camp, making it where the alders and aspens didn't grow quite so close, even if it meant dragging their firewood in from a distance; he should have made the compound smaller and better fortified, more easily defensible; and he should have made allowances for the size of the remuda, so openly exposed to any stray bullet or arrow. All this he should have done, but hadn't.

As if reading his thoughts, McClure said, "It's my fault, Eli. I knew better, but I was so obsessed with Vidales' murderer I let it cloud my judgment."

"No. I'm the brigade leader. I'll take responsibility."

"We shall both take responsibility," McClure said, then added wryly, "For whatever good that will do us now."

Taking a long breath, Eli faced the plain.

The warrior riding toward him looked to be about fifty years old, slim to the point of gauntness, with graying hair and wrinkled flesh the color of burnt umber. He wore a bearclaw necklace around his throat, and a bone-handled knife above his right hip. A single eagle feather was fastened to his hair, a sign of courage and leadership. His face was blackened with war paint beneath his eyes, one cheek dotted with a trio of vermillion spots the size of copper pennies. He drew rein on his pony when Eli was about twenty yards away, and regarded the mountain man with haughty contempt.

"Do you speak English?" Eli asked, watching the old man's face closely for any sign of comprehension. He doubted if the warrior would openly acknowledge understanding, but it would tell Eli a lot about the man he faced if he knew what kind of past contact he had had with the white race.

In sign, the warrior responded: *You speak the tongue of the hair-faces. These are not the words of the People—the Arapaho.*

Reading nothing in the warrior's lined face, Eli switched to Spanish. "Do you speak Spanish?"

Again, the warrior signed that he did not understand Eli's words, reiterating that he spoke only Arapaho. Yet this time Eli thought he detected a flicker of recognition in the Indian's eyes. Eli wasn't surprised. Mexican traders had been roving the Front Range of the Rockies—the Arapahos' homeland—for close to seventy-five years now. That this warrior understood a smattering of the language, yet refused to admit it, told Eli what he wanted to know. In sign, Eli said: *I do not speak the language of the People, but I speak the language of the plains—the hand talk.*

I am Wolf That Runs, the Indian said. *I have been with the Utes, trading. Now I return to my own people. Would the Long Knives like to trade?*

Eli gave the brave a considering look. *Yes. The Long Knives would like to trade. What does Wolf That Runs have?*

Horses.

We do not need horses, Eli told him. *The Long Knives want beaver or otter. We will also trade for buffalo robes or buckskins, if they are tanned well, but we do not want much of these. Buffalo robes are hard to pack, and take up too much room. Give us beaver and we will trade.*

The Arapaho said, *I have some beaver and some otter, some robes and buckskins. These I will trade with the Long Knives, who are my friends. But first we must come into your camp and receive tobacco and coffee and sugar, as is the way of trading. Do you have the water that makes the young men crazy?*

No, Eli replied. *We do not have the firewater that causes the young men to become crazy. And the People cannot come into our camp. We do not have coffee and sugar, but I will give you some tobacco and some beads for your squaws. I will give each man a mirror, too. But you cannot come into camp. We will trade here, away from camp.*

The Arapaho's face showed sudden anger. *Why do the hair-faces hide behind logs like Utah women? Are they afraid of Wolf That Runs?*

Eli allowed a deliberate smile to cross his face. *This morning,* he told the Arapaho, *a hawk came into our camp. This hawk told me that many warriors approached. This hawk told me that these men have been to the land of the Utahs and taken scalps and prisoners they will turn over to their squaws to torment. This hawk warned me not to trust these warriors, for their hearts were bad and their tongues were split so that they can speak out of both sides of their mouth. Is this true?* Eli asked. *Is your tongue split, so that it speaks both truth and lies?*

The Arapaho's nostrils flared, and his hands became faster, choppier, slashing the air to emphasize his anger. *The hair-faces are enemies of the People. They bring death and disease to our children, and the sickness to our women so that they are no good to lie with. They bring the water that builds a fire in the throat and makes men crazy, so that they give away their robes and ponies for more of the crazy water. All this the hair-faces have done. It is their hearts that are bad, and they must pay for what they have done now. The People do not want a woman's trash. We want long guns, and powder and lead and molds to make bullets. And knives and swords and the short guns, too, that we can carry at our waist. The hair-faces must do this now, or the People will kill them all.*

It is true, then, what the hawk told me, Eli responded. *The Peo-*

ple's tongues are split and their hearts are bad. They did not come to trade, or they would not have left so many in hiding in the hills like squaws. They would not wear robes over their shoulders to hide their war clubs. No, the People will not be allowed into the camp of the Long Knives. The Long Knives will trade and remain friendly if the People wish, but not for rifles or powder or lead. These things the Long Knives will not trade to split tongues.

The Arapaho's face became like stone. *Then the People will not trade with the dog-faces,* he signed tautly. *The People will rub out their enemies, and take what they please. Wolf That Runs has spoken.* Without further comment, the Indian turned away.

Eli watched the warrior's rigid spine with regret, yet he knew the confrontation had been unavoidable. Wolf That Runs hadn't come to trade. He had come seeking knowledge, to probe the brigade's strengths. While he had talked of trade, his eyes had freely roamed the compound behind Eli, taking in its skimpy defenses, it wealth of horses and mules and trade goods. The odds were too much in favor of the Arapahos, the animosity between them and the whites too ingrained. Now it would be war, with blood spilled and death on both sides. There was no way around it, no way to escape what instinct told him they could never win.

The Arapahos came like true warriors. They didn't charge foolishly across the open plain to the south, exposing themselves to the deadly rifle fire of the mountain men. Nor did they rend the air with their war whoops or fling their arrows uselessly against the thick breastworks of the whites. Such scenes were more often the fabrication of overactive imaginations, tales of the uninformed and uninitiated related around glowing hearths in the midst of civilization. Indians loved life as deeply as their white counterparts, and in the reality of mountain warfare, they seldom conducted such reckless, headlong assaults. In the reality of the Battle of Grand River, in the fall of 1828, the Arapaho came afoot, flitting among the alders like copper ghosts, brief flashes of darting color that rarely offered the beleaguered mountain men a decent target.

Eli knelt behind the breastworks on the east side of the compound, where the alders grew closest. They had cleared out some of the scrub their first day in camp, and wedged it into the gaps between the cottonwood logs Cork-Eye and Old Cal had dragged up from a jam on the river, but even with that, they only had about fifty yards of cleared space between the compound and the nearest clump of brush where the Arapaho might hide. It wasn't much, although Eli allowed he had fought from worse positions.

"Here they come," McClure called from the west wall, where the alders were just as thick but not quite as close.

"Make 'em count," Eli shouted back. He glanced at Mateo and Jorge, and added in Spanish, "Do not fire until I tell you to. We only want one weapon empty at a time."

"Do you forget that I can use my bow three times as fast as you can your rifle?" Jorge asked, notching an arrow.

It was a point well taken, Eli thought. "Good. See that you do, but not until I give the word." He faced the alders again, cocking his rifle. The Arapahos were still a hundred yards away, in no apparent hurry to advance.

The sun had climbed to its zenith in the time it had taken the Arapahos to prepare for battle. Now it burned steadily through Eli's shirt, and beads of sweat rode his brow. Blowflies buzzed torpidly over the stretched plews, and deerflies drove the remuda half crazy with their bites. The waiting had grated on them all, but it was behind them now. A fusil boomed from the scrub across the river, the bullet whining overhead. Two other fusils sang out from the alders to the west, and McClure answered them with his rifle. Eli spotted a brown hip and thigh jutting from behind an alder about seventy yards away, caught it in his sights, and fired. Through the rolling cloud of powder smoke he saw the hip spin from sight and heard a distant cry of pain. Eli pulled his rifle back and quickly reloaded. Pierre's fusil boomed, and McClure shouted angrily, "Save your powder until they charge, man."

But Eli knew they wouldn't charge, not in the way McClure expected. They would continue to edge closer, sniping and taunting, picking at them the way a finger picks absently at a scab, scraping them off one by one with wounds or death until there wouldn't be enough men left to defend the four walls. It was then that they would attack, swarming over the undefended walls, falling on the wounded and outnumbered with their 'hawks and knives . . . hacking, slicing. Eli's fingers tightened around his rifle, remembering the sickening wet thunk of those killed along the Provost River with Etienne Provost, the smell of death, and the taste of fear. He glanced over his shoulder at Consuelo, hunkering behind the breastworks, peering through a crack between the logs. *I should kill her if it looks like the Arapaho might overrun the compound,* he thought. *Better death than a return to the slavery she's already escaped from once in her life.* Yet the thought sickened him almost physically, and he knew he could never do it.

An arrow arched high against the deep blue of the sky, whistling softly as it fell toward the compound. A mule grunted as if in surprise, its hindquarters staggering; then all four legs gave as if the animal had been poleaxed, and Eli swore savagely.

Another arrow slid across the sky and struck the ground inside the compound with a harmless thud. McClure's rifle cracked flatly, and Pierre hooted laughter.

"Him got one, by *Dieu,*" Pierre shouted.

"Mateo!" Eli called tersely. "Grab one of your cousins and saddle the stock."

Mateo nodded without hesitation and laid his *escopeta* aside. "Antonio, come on. We must put the saddles and *aparejos* on the remuda before any more are killed."

Eli turned back to the alders with a sense of satisfaction in Mateo's instant comprehension of what he wanted, and why. The saddles would help; so would the Arapahos' desire to capture the remuda unharmed. But they were still in a tight spot. Even being careful, the Indians were bound to kill some of the herd.

The arrows came quicker for a while then, sometimes two and three at a time flashing across the blue lid of the sky. Their flint and iron arrowheads struck the breastworks with quivering *thunk*s that could be felt from inside, and the ground among the aspens was soon feathered with the slanting shafts. Within an hour half a dozen additional animals had been wounded, but only the first mule had died. The saddles and *aparejos* Mateo and Antonio had put on the stock were festooned with arrows that might have proved fatal if not for the protection of leather and wood.

It was a waiting game, mostly, a war of nerves. Eli fired seven or eight times within the first couple of hours, but as far as he knew he only struck three braves, none of them seriously. The afternoon passed slowly, as if time had lost its motivation in the unexpected warmth of the day. The firing from the Arapahos began to slacken, and the taunting ceased. Eli tensed at the growing silence. His head throbbed from the heat and the banging of his big rifle, and pain stabbed his eyes. The golden leaves of the quakies hung motionless in the still air, and the odor of blood from the wounded stock seemed to grow stronger and more nauseating.

"*Hijo de puta,*" Jorge murmured. "This waiting, it—"

"Keep your eyes peeled!" Eli snapped. Even his muscles ached now, as if they had been drawn taut too long. And then McClure's voice cracked like the bark of a rifle.

"*Smoke!* Eli, they're going to burn us out!"

CHAPTER TWENTY-ONE

Travis paused in his work to listen to the music of the high-country valley—the faint rushing of the wind in the pines across the creek, the occasional clatter of a fallen aspen leaf, the distant tear of grass from where Blue and the extra mule were grazing on the flat below camp—and marveled again at the feeling of serenity that had enveloped him since arriving here with Johnny four days before. Alone most of the time now, he had experienced an unexpected metamorphosis in his solitude. After that first day of almost overwhelming loneliness, he had grown used to the long silences of the valley and began to find pleasure in the natural quiet. He came to value his time alone and would pause often in his work to drink in the beauty that surrounded him, scanning the hills and ridges for herds of elk or bighorn sheep, lying on his back to watch the fleecy clouds that dominated the blue bowl of the sky. Sometimes he would walk along the splashing creek, searching for the tiny rainbow trout that idled in its deeper pools. He still thought about his brother, and the events that had led to Chet's death on the Mississippi and his own exile from Hanging Creek Falls, but the memories came with less pain here, as if the high, thin air, the rim of snowcapped peaks, and the autumnal splendor of the little valley were a soothing balm.

He settled easily into the routine of a trapper, rising each day before dawn to run his line, then returning to camp late in the morning to scrape the fat and clinging flesh from the skins he had taken overnight, lacing them into circular willow frames to dry. In the evenings he worked on the deer hide, soaking it with the brains Johnny had given him, then stretching it in a pole frame and working on it with a staker until the skin was soft and supple, a creamy shade of white. He had decided that morning that he would smoke it with sage tomorrow, and maybe cut out a pattern for moccasins with Johnny's help. He had shot a second deer while running his line yesterday, and in addition to the extra hide he was also drying some sinew to use as thread.

Travis was sitting in front of the lean-to graining a beaver plew, guiding the porous, loaf-shaped stone slightly larger than the palm of his hand lightly over the flesh side of the skin, removing the last vestiges of fat from the hide's epidermis. Johnny was still running his traps. With eight, it took him twice as long as Travis to oversee his line, and he often didn't return to camp until late in the afternoon. They had taken nearly thirty beavers since arriving in the valley; the stretched plews were scattered around the camp and throughout the aspen grove, the reddish flesh sides turned to the sun like pale, oversized pennies. The afternoon had turned off warm, an appreciated switch from the long, chilly days since leaving the Mexican settlements, and he was contemplating a nap when Blue snorted a warning. Travis looked up, his hand slowing on the skin. Blue and the pack mule were facing the lower end of the valley, their muscles taut and quivering. Dropping his graining stone and the half-finished skin, Travis grabbed the Kentucky and surged to his feet. Following the direction of Blue's gaze, he found himself staring at the finger of timber that pinched itself out close to the veed notch at the end of the valley. Although he saw nothing out of the ordinary along the base of the pines, he knew the mules had, or had at least scented something.

Travis stood uncertainly in front of the lean-to, his hands suddenly sweating around the Kentucky's polished stock. The track he had seen in the mud his first day in the valley immediately came to mind. He had looked for additional sign of the giant bear as he ran his traps through the followings days, but except for that single print embedded deeply at the pond's edge, he hadn't seen anything.

Almost reluctantly, Travis started across the meadow. He spoke soothingly to the mules as he passed them. Blue flicked an ear, but neither animal took its eyes off the lower end of the meadow. Travis crossed the creek well above the line of the mules' sight and paused at the base of the slope to stare up into the shadowy timber. The pines grew close here, the ground beneath them a barren carpet of dead needles and spindly shrubs. It looked dark and ominous under the trees, but he knew there would be downed timber deep within the cool recesses of pines, and beneath those fallen trunks, fat grubs that a bear would relish. Taking a fresh, resolute grip on his rifle, Travis began the arduous climb into the trees.

It was colder under the pines, quiet save for the sound of the wind moving through the boughs far above. Travis moved cautiously upward, his eyes probing the deeper shadows. He climbed at an angle toward the lower end of the timber, and stopped every couple of minutes to look and listen. He was several hundred yards into the trees when a limb cracked from somewhere above him and he snapped the Kentucky's muzzle up.

"Easy," he whispered to himself. "It's just the wind."

His heart pounding, Travis moved on. Through the dark bars of the forest he could see a spot of sunlight not far ahead, a translucent column of light spearing a hillside clearing. Something moved within the bleaching light, something reddish tan and big, and Travis stopped again and thought, *Oh, hell.* He stared for a long time, gradually making out the humped shoulders, the sloping rump, a single front leg. Even sitting on its haunches, the bear looked massive. It faced away from him, its head hidden from sight, no doubt buried in some tender morsel of food. Travis breathed deeply, licking at lips gone suddenly dry. It took every ounce of his will to start climbing the steep slope toward the little clearing.

When he was fifty yards away he paused and cocked the Kentucky. He debated a shot from here, but decided the distance was too great for such a light weapon, the standing timber too thick. He studied the grizzly thoughtfully. Its fur seemed to ripple in the sunlight, yet something didn't quite look right. Travis had hunted plenty of black bear in Arkansas. He knew them, knew their ways, and this bear wasn't acting anything at all like the blacks he had hunted in the past. It wasn't moving or lifting its head to sniff the air. It just sat there like a stone, its head dipped from view, its . . .

Travis's shoulders slumped. Relief flooded through him. He

moved the Kentucky's hammer to half-cock and walked into the clearing, laughing weakly as the wind swooped down to stir the reddish tan patch of autumn-dried bushes that his imagination had turned into a monster. He turned to look out over the hills on the opposite side of the valley, and his heart seemed to leap into his throat. He had been looking for a giant grizzly; he hadn't expected Indians at all.

Remi clenched his fists in helplessness as he watched the smoke building to the west of the main camp. He was crouched behind a sagebrush less than a mile from the center of the battle. From here he could see the scurry of Indians moving among the alders, the occasional puff of gun smoke from the compound's walls. The sounds of gunfire came like hollow booms, barely audible.

He glanced behind him to the mouth of the draw where Jake and Clint waited with the horses, and debated again the merits of sending them after the others—Johnny and Travis, Old Cal and Cork-Eye, maybe even Charlie and Pete, if they weren't holed up too far back—and once again he decided against it. No one knew where the others were, and it could take days to root them out. Remi knew the handful of men and the lone woman inside the compound didn't have that much time. It would be better to keep Jake and Clint here, Remi thought, than have them wandering lost among the hills.

The smoke continued to climb into the sky. Remi could see the tiny yellow blazes dancing among the alders, and the Arapahos creeping forward under the cover of billowing smoke.

"*Sacre,*" Remi muttered. "*Non!* Remi will not stand for this. He will not sit here on his ass while his friends are rubbed out." He scooted back from the sage and quickly made his way to the mouth of the draw where Jake and Clint waited on their ponies. Remi jerked the paint's reins from Clint's grasp and swung into the saddle.

"What's going on?" Jake asked.

"They have set fire to the prairie," Remi replied. "They are in a hurry and will try to overrun the camp now, before nightfall."

"Where are you going?" Clint asked.

"*Sacre bleu,* Remi goes to help his friends. You stay here with your brother so that you may hold one another like little girls." He jerked the paint around, but Jake suddenly forced his horse forward, cutting off Remi's mount.

"Are you calling us cowards?" Jake demanded.

"Jake," Clint said. He looked pale and frightened, his voice fluttery. Remi laughed aloud at him, then looked at Jake as if daring him to repeat his question.

"I'm going with you," Jake said. "By God, don't try to stop me."

Remi looked at Clint. "So you will stay here alone, eh, and fight the Arapahos when they come after your scalp?"

Clint's eyes dulled in dread. "We could hide. It's silly to go out there just to die with the others. We should get help."

"*Non!*" Remi said sharply. He forced the paint past Jake's horse. "Remi has already wasted too much time. Jake, let's go."

They spurred down the draw and hit the edge of the flat at a run, neck and neck. Remi glanced over his shoulder as the paint flattened out through the sage, smiling grimly when he saw Clint pounding after his brother, the pack mules racing behind with their ears laid flat. Then he faced the plain again and felt an excitement as old as his first love, as fresh as the fragrance of spring, rise up within him. His little paint streaked through the sage, nimbly dodging those bushes she couldn't jump. The smoke had thickened in the short time he had been in the draw, and now it unfurled upward like a huge gray stain against the blue sky. The Arapahos spotted them before they were halfway across the long plain. Perhaps a dozen warriors were sprinting back through the alders toward their ponies, and Remi knew there was no turning back now, no changing of plans. They had to make it to the compound before the Arapahos cut them off or they would be wolf bait for certain.

He bent low over the paint's neck. Her white mane gently slapped his face. His heels pounded her flanks. They were still a hundred yards off when an Arapaho came out of the alders and dropped to one knee, drawing his bowstring. Remi swore and shouted an insult. He saw the arrow loosened and watched its flight—a blurred streak across the smoky sky—until it passed from sight behind him. A rifle roared then, kicking up a chunk of soft loam several yards to the Arapaho's side, and Remi glanced back to see Jake bursting through a tattered cloud of powder smoke.

"*Carajo, tonto,*" Remi shouted furiously in Spanish. He mentally chided himself for not teaching the boy better. He should have told him never to waste powder and lead from the back of a running horse unless the target was big enough or close enough to be sure of a hit.

Jake had thrown away a thing he might need desperately in the next few minutes, and had only a piece of worthless, torn sod to show for his effort.

They swung close to the alders, racing along the outer edge of scrub. Another Arapaho jumped out of the brush just ahead of them. Remi swerved the paint toward him, forcing him to leap back into the alders before he could fire. Others began to emerge from the alders, darting out and loosening an arrow or touching off a trade fusil, then quickly leaping back again. But there was a price for their hurried firing—inaccuracy. Twice Remi felt the tug of an arrow at his clothing, but he raced on unhurt, and suddenly the breastworks appeared before them like a tangled *embarras* left after spring floods. Remi reined the paint toward a low spot in the wall and slammed his heels into the mare's flanks. He saw Eli's hat bob up, followed by a quick, mushrooming cloud of powder smoke, but the rifle's report was lost in the rush of wind and the angry howls of the Arapahos. Arrows whizzed past him, embedding themselves in the breastworks. He screamed as the paint gathered herself for the jump, felt the thud of an arrow in the saddle's cantle as her rear legs pushed upward. The paint stumbled as she hit the ground inside the compound, her front legs folding. Remi cried out and kicked free of the stirrups, pushing himself out of the saddle as the mare fell. He lit on his feet but the momentum tumbled him forward. His ankle twisted suddenly, turning him so that he fell on his back, and his head rapped solidly against the hard-packed ground.

Blackness swirled at the edges of Remi's vision. White-hot lances pierced his skull. He lay sprawled on his back, aware only of a pale, dancing light before his eyes, the dull strumming of pain that coursed through his body like a slow wave curling toward his toes. Then the sharp but distinct crack of a rifle pierced the black haze of his mind; he groped for it mentally, hanging on to it the way a drowning man hangs on to a rope, letting it pull him back from unconsciousness.

He sat up slowly, weak but functioning. The paint stood nearby with an arrow canted from the saddle, another protruding from her hip; blood traced an ugly crimson path down her snowy leg. Eli's voice came as if from a long way off, flowing on the same current of sound that brought him the Arapahos' discordant howls. He saw his fusil lying in the dirt beside him and carefully picked it up. His fingers felt stiff and clumsy, his arms as limp as warm tortillas, and he knew, instinctively, that if he moved too fast or tried to rise too soon he would pass out. So he took his time, repriming the fusil and checking the flint, and when he finished he felt better, stronger and clear-headed. But when he tried to stand, his ankle buckled in an explosion of pain.

"*Remi!*" Eli called desperately. He was reloading, ramming an un-patched ball down the barrel of his rifle. Jake knelt at a corner, aiming a pistol through a crack between two logs. Remi watched Jake squeeze the trigger and saw the pistol buck in his hands. Slowly then, babying his throbbing ankle, Remi forced himself to his hands and knees and crawled to the breastworks.

Smoke swirled among the alders like a low-lying fog. Through it he could see the Arapahos advancing steadily through the scrub. There must have been a score of braves hugging the closest alders. Fusils boomed, splintering the logs of the breastworks. Arrows thudded into the logs or whisked overhead. A warrior darted out from the alders with only a tomahawk and ran a twisting path toward the breastworks. Remi pulled the big lock of his fusil back to full cock. The warrior came on, dodging back and forth. Jake cried a warning, but he was busy reloading. Mateo and Eli were also reloading. Clint fired, but missed.

"*Sacre bleu,*" Remi murmured, shouldering his fusil. "So it comes to this, eh? But Remi will not . . ." The fusil roared, slamming his shoulder. Through the mushrooming cloud of powder smoke he saw the warrior jerk back from the slug's impact, the quick, red puncture of the wound centered in his chest.

Remi pulled back and closed his eyes, resting his head against the logs. He waited for the dizziness to pass before opening them again. When he did, he saw Eli kneeling next to him, peering anxiously into his face.

"Are you all right?" Eli asked.

"*Oui*. Remi is fine."

Eli peeked over the breastworks. "They're pulling back," he said. He grinned weakly. "I reckon if you hadn't gotten that brave he would've made it through the wall. If he had, I don't think we could have stopped the rest."

"Then we taught them a lesson, no?"

Eli shrugged, still staring toward the alders. "Oh, I ain't so sure about that, Remi. I ain't so sure about that at all."

CHAPTER TWENTY-TWO

Travis booted Blue over the ridge and down the far side. Johnny was already near the bottom, descending the last few yards in a shower of dust. Travis piled up behind him and they turned south, down canyon, at a steady jog. Travis kept looking over his shoulder. He knew it was unlikely that the four Indians he had seen earlier that afternoon were following. They had been a long way off when he spotted them from the tiny clearing among the pines, and riding in the opposite direction. But he couldn't deny the little sliver of dread that made his scalp crawl every time he looked back.

They came around a bend in the canyon and Johnny jerked his mare to a stop. Over the half-breed's shoulder Travis saw a distant line of riders, and he swore and pulled Blue around. They rode back around the bend and Johnny dismounted, handing his reins to Travis without a word. He disappeared back around the bend, but returned within minutes.

"Arapahos," Johnny informed him gravely. "I don't think they saw us."

Travis let his breath go in a heavy rush of wind. "Well, Arapahos ain't as bad as Comanches or Blackfeet, right?"

"All it takes is one arrow, Travis," Johnny said, mounting. "Doesn't matter whose it is."

Travis took a deep breath, knowing Johnny was right. "How many was there?" he asked. "These ain't the same Injuns I saw."

"No. There's eight or nine in this bunch. Heading back across the Divide, I'd wager. They claim the country around the forks of the Platte and down the Front Range of the Rockies. Sometimes, coming back from a raid, they'll split up when they get close to home. A big war party will scare the game away, but a bunch of smaller parties will fare better. If this is a big war party, these hills are probably swarming with scattered little bands."

"What are we gonna do?"

Johnny stared pensively at the canyon's bend. "Same as we've been doing, I reckon," he said at last. "Head on back. If there's a passel of them, Eli will probably need all the help he can get."

"How are we gonna get back to the base camp with Arapahos around every bend?"

"There won't be Arapahos around every bend. We'll just have to watch close and take our time." He flashed a grin. "Hell, dodging Indians is as much a part of the business as trapping. Come on, I'll show you a few tricks."

They were in a rough, rolling country, but there was a pattern to it. From the Grand the ridges and hills ran back north and south, those ridges cut with valleys or shallow canyons of their own, running east and west, and these, likewise, were scarred by even smaller canyons, some hardly more than coulees, again running north and south. A lot of the canyons had trees growing along the bottoms, a few surrounding seeps or hidden springs, but many just growing on the little flats that dotted every canyon. It was to the smaller, third-line canyons that Johnny clung, scampering his mare from one shallow coulee to the next, his head swiveling rapidly as they hurried over the tops, his long, black tresses flapping beneath an otter-skin cap.

Travis imitated him as best he could, trying to take in as much as he could during those few seconds they were exposed against the skyline, but he could only stare dumbly when Johnny hauled rein an hour or so later and said, "Looks like more trouble than I'd anticipated." At Travis's blank stare, he nodded toward the south. "Smoke coming from the direction of the base camp."

"A cookfire?"

"No. My guess is that the Arapahos are trying to burn them out."

Travis's stomach curled into a knot. "What are we gonna do?"

"I'm not sure there's anything we can do now," Johnny replied quietly.

"We gonna fight 'em?"

Johnny gave him a considering look. "Is that what you want to do?"

Travis was quiet a moment, staring south toward the faint smudge of smoke rising in the thin air. Although fear gnawed steadily at his intestines, he felt a strange sense of anticipation, too, an eagerness to prove his mettle, as his grandfather had once proved his against the Shawnee back in Kentucky in the old days. Travis had waited a long time for an opportunity such as this, a chance to redeem himself in his own eyes, if not in the eyes of the citizens of Hanging Creek Falls. Swallowing back his fear, Travis nodded. "Yeah, I reckon that's what I want to do."

"*Bueno,*" Johnny said. "Let's go take a look."

Eli glanced over his shoulder to where the sun had just sunk below the serrated line of hills, streaking the sky with pale ribbons of yellow, gold, and rust. Smoke from the Arapahos' fires still palled the aspens, but the fires themselves had never amounted to much. In the end it had turned out to be too damp along the river. Once the fire had passed the last line of alders, it couldn't be reset without exposing the Arapahos to the unerring rifle fire of the brigade. The last flame had died out at sunset, still several yards short of the walls, and as the smoke cleared, the Indians pulled back. So maybe Remi had been right after all, Eli mused; maybe they had taught the brownskins a lesson.

Exhausted by the day-long battle, Eli tried to relax. He leaned into a cottonwood log where he could rest and still keep an eye on the alders. His sinuses were clogged and aching from the smoke that had whirled through the aspens all afternoon, and his throat felt raw enough to bleed. When a fly lit on his cheek, he allowed it to cross the smooth plane to his brow before summoning up enough strength to wave it away.

In the middle of the compound the wounded stock stood in hobble-frozen misery, suffering from thirst, bleeding wounds, biting flies they couldn't escape, and the strain of being all but hog-tied for nearly ten straight hours. From time to time one of the horses would whinny pitifully or give an experimental tug on the rope holding its head close to its fetlock, but the mules stood in quiet endurance, only their hides occasionally twitching in an effort to shake loose the arrows that jutted from their hips, shoulders, and necks. Eli stared gloomily at the remuda. Three of the mules and McClure's chestnut lay crumpled in death, bristling with arrows and already beginning to bloat. Almost half of them had been wounded. They needed water

hat a purty sight? Hide'd be about prime now, too."
to look. On a ridge across the creek a black bear had
f some scrub. Pete watched as the bear ambled toward
seberries on the dry, open slope above them, pausing
ime-to sniff the frosty air, switching directions capri-
norning's subdued light gleamed off the bruin's shiny
the rolls of fat along its ribs and haunches. Feeling the
as thought, the pull of hibernation. "He'll be caching
on absently.

Ciled his stirrup down and said, "He can cache in my
elly, what he's aimin' to do. This coon's half froze for b'a
meat.

Pet back to his saddling, drawing the latigo tight and knotting it ngers were numb on the cold leather, and his breath exploded ttle vaporous clouds that half-shaded his work. They
mount hout speaking, without needing to, and forded the creek
shed partway into the patch of gooseberries, its
ump like a black tunnel against the scarlet foliage.
a sign with his hand and angled to the right, intending
d on the bear from the opposite side. Pete dismounted
of the trees flanking the little creek and tied the buck-
bleached cottonwood log with a single, thigh-thick
ward like a cock-eyed hitching rail. He checked the
g on his rifle, then started across the meadow. The
grass gave out at the base of the ridge, the slope
bare save for several patches of berries, a few bar-
bushes, and sprawling tracts of prickly pear. The
from sight now, although Pete could still see the
berry patch. He moved cautiously upslope, his
igging at the flinty soil. When his line of vision
r of the hill, he stopped and settled back on his
arlie's move.

bove the early-morning trilling of a pair of gros-
the voices of the women as they fussed with the
was too far away to make out the words, Pete
arguing about the bear. Red-Winged Woman
ue packing the mules, as the men had com
ver practical, always independent, would no
the packing, but would likely insist they un

and grass and care; he felt a deep-seated sympathy for the animals,
knowing their agony wasn't likely to end anytime soon.

Remi was slumped against the breastworks nearby, his injured
ankle stretched before him. Despite the cooling breezes, sweat
beaded the French-Canadian's swarthy face. He looked pale and
drawn, his ankle, between the ragged hem of his buckskin trousers
and the top of his pucker-toed moccasins, swollen, bruised. On the
other side of Remi, Mateo Chavez rolled a cigarillo. He looked as
worn as any of them, his shaggy black hair falling across his face, his
hands trembling. His cheek, where the ancient *escopeta* had
slammed against it in recoil, was also puffed and bruised.

Grinning amiably at the Mexican, Remi said, "Not so bad today,
eh?"

Mateo glanced up, his dark eyes smoldering. For a moment Eli
wondered whether he would answer Remi's question or not, but then
Mateo managed a curt nod and said, "Not so bad." He finished
rolling his cigarillo, lit it with a piece of char, then shoved to his feet
and made his way to the remuda.

"He is touchy, that one, no?" Remi said to Eli.

"Some," Eli allowed quietly.

"He and Jake, *sacre bleu,* they would make a pair."

"Chavez is a good hand," Eli said, watching Mateo move among
the stock, inspecting the wounded. "What about Jake?"

Remi chuckled. "Maybe a little more time."

Jake was rumped down close to his brother on the far side of the
compound now, his head drooped as if asleep. "If he gives you any
trouble, let me know," Eli said.

Remi's voice hardened. "That one will not give Remi trouble, Eli.
Sacre, I would cut his throat myself."

"*Bueno,*" Eli replied, satisfied that Remi could handle the problem. He gathered his energy and forced himself to a crouch. "Keep
your eyes open, Remi. I want to take a look at the stock."

He went to the sorrel first, stooping to cut the rope that had held
the gelding's head down all day. The sorrel raised its head slowly,
nickering softly. An arrow was slanted from the flesh between the
sorrel's neck and shoulder, another jutted from the saddle. Eli
clutched the arrow in the sorrel's neck and tugged at it experimentally, feeling the sudden give and slide, cursing to himself as he
pulled it free. There was no head. The Arapahos had wrapped the

flint arrowheads to the shafts of their war arrows with sinew that the sorrel's blood quickly softened. When the shaft was pulled free, it left behind a keen-edged stone that would continue to saw at the muscle surrounding it.

"Bastards," Eli said. He flung the shaft aside.

"They will have to be cut out," Mateo said, coming over with a headless shaft of his own. "It will be hard, and it will take a long time for the wounds to heal."

"No way around it, I guess," Eli said in resignation. "But no sense in starting now, either. It'll take several men to hold an animal down while someone digs for the head. We can't afford the men or the time."

"Then we should leave the shafts where they are, so that we will know how deep they are, and in what direction to cut."

Eli stared bitterly toward the alders, as if the day's encounter had been a personal affront rather than a chance meeting. "We're going to have to find some more ponies somewhere," he said. "We can't hole up here waiting for all these wounds to heal."

Mateo shrugged indifferently and moved off. Eli patted the sorrel lovingly, then went back to his place by the east wall. The day was fading rapidly now, the valley bathed in soft lavender hues that seemed to compress what light was left, so that what lay close at hand seemed brighter and more vivid, while the hills and distant mountains appeared to lose their individual shapes, flowing into a solid mass that looked as soft as velvet. "We'll have to set a heavy watch tonight," he told Remi. "At least half the men on at a time."

"Good, although Remi does not think the Arapahos will attack during the night. It is not the way of the savage, no?"

"It ain't, but it wouldn't be unheard of, either."

Antonio Rodolso got up to leave the north wall, where he had moved after Remi and the Orrs' return. The bandage on his cheek seemed to glow dimly in the fading light, a tiny beacon among the thickening shadows. He joined Mateo in the aspens, flopping beside him in the grass.

"The stock, they are too injured to ride?" Remi asked thoughtfully.

Eli nodded. "I'd already thought about that, but we'd never outrun 'em now. Not even in the dark."

Remi was silent a minute, then said, "It is just as well, maybe. The

others, Johnny, Cal, Charlie, Pete, th...
come. Soon now we will not be so ou...

Maybe, Eli thought, but it was a big...
telling how far back the others had gone...
but it wasn't something he was going to ...
rose suddenly in anger, drawing Eli's attenti...

"You act like you don't care," Antonio accu...
are above everything. You did not even mourn ...
as if he were a stranger, and not your cousin."

Eli didn't hear Mateo's response, but he saw th...
tensed up and flung his half-smoked cigarillo away...

"You think you are better than we are," Antoni...
think we are all fools, and only you, Mateo Chavez, fat...
always followed, are worthy of life or happiness."

Mateo's head jerked around, and Eli saw the qui... of...
prise that crossed his face. But when he spoke, his w...ere o...
a low, harsh rumble, inaudible.

Antonio listened for almost a full minute, then s...s h...
disgust and stood up. "I wish I'd never come," he ...kil...
gave up our homes and families for you. We—"...ever...
ished his sentence. Eli heard the wet, fleshy thu...rr...
fore he actually saw it, buried to the fletchin...
ribs. The youth's eyes widened and he gra...
hands. Mateo leaped to his feet, catching ...
to the ground. Eli swore and ran to th...
looked up as he arrived, his eyes sw...
his knee beside the pair, Eli put ...
all he could do. Antonio was ...

The morning's light ...
snowy blades of the C...
ded with rosy cloud...
dropped leisurely i...
squeezing out the ...
up against the ti...
and Charlie W...
heavy on the t...
trappers' wake. Pet...
the cinch ring, and it too...

pack what was already in the panniers. She would want to be ready to butcher the bear as soon as her man and Red-Winged Woman's man killed it. She would want her brass kettle sitting by the fire ready to render the bear's fat into oil, and wood enough for the fire, and stages built for drying the meat, and a frame constructed for tanning the hide. And likely she would have her way about it, too, and they would hold over here an extra day while the women processed the bear into food, grease for their moccasins and gun patches, and a fine warm robe.

Had they been in a hurry, Pete might have told them to pack the meat on top of the panniers and let it dry on the way, but he didn't see where an extra day would make any difference. He doubted if Charlie would, either.

Resting comfortably, Pete felt the faint, rippling vibration of a running horse through his moccasins long before he heard it. He jumped to his feet and ran back to the buckskin, jerking the reins loose and vaulting into the saddle just as Charlie came pounding over the ridge.

"Brownskins," Charlie shouted, pulling his appaloosa to a plunging, head-tossing stop.

"Whereabouts?"

"Couple ridges over. 'Rapahos."

"Arapahos?" Pete looked doubtful.

"By God, that's what I said. I reckon I know a damn 'Rapaho when I see one, even if he is a long ways off."

"Did they see you?" Pete asked.

Charlie looked suddenly disgusted. "Hell, yeah. I skylined myself like some damn fool pilgrim never seen a mountain afore."

"Wagh," Pete grunted. "That's damp powder, amigo, but no way around it now. Get the women movin', and I'll find us a place to cache."

"Yeow," Charlie cried, spurring his mare toward the creek.

Pete took off up valley at a lope. Before him, the mountains humped up solidly against the sky, spotted with groves of golden aspens among the darker shades of pine, thick-timbered, impenetrable. The valley twisted and turned, and within two hundred yards he had lost sight of the camp. He rode alone then, with only the beating of the buckskin's hooves to keep him company. His eyes shifted constantly, searching for some break in the mountains ahead that might offer them a passage through. This was all new country to him. He and Charlie had been trapping farther south, and had only come up here yesterday to look for fresh beaver ponds.

The valley climbed steadily. From time to time a smaller valley or shallow canyon would open up on one side or the other, but Pete dismissed them with only a glance. Ahead he had spotted what looked like a gap leading deeper into the mountains. He wanted to get into the high country if he could. The Arapahos were still a long way from home, and they wouldn't want to tarry too long ferreting out a couple of trappers and their women. At least that was his hope.

The valley narrowed in time, becoming a canyon pinched in between sheer rock walls. Pete slowed as he entered it. Shelves of sandy soil grown over with rushes and slim saplings pushed into the creek. Aspens and a few stray pines grew along the bank, and in the deeper pockets of shade, where the sun never touched, there were patches of fresh snow. Pete rode on doggedly with no discernible trail to guide him. The lack of a trail bothered him, but he didn't turn back. It was as if some unseen force were drawing him forward. The canyon's stone walls towered above him, streaked with crimson and yellow and gray, shutting out the sun and creating a perpetual twilight along the narrow, winding floor. After a while the ground disappeared altogether and he was forced into the creek, the cold, tumbling water splashing his moccasins and lower legs. Rounding a bend in the canyon, he came to a sudden stop. Pictographs dotted the dark rock walls far above him—strangely drawn figures of winged men and serpents with hands and cloven feet—their locations high on the sheer stone walls defying explanation.

Lower down, within reasonable reach of mortal men, were more familiar designs—deer, bear, bison, bighorn sheep. He saw a stick-figure of a man with a humongous head and oval eyes, carrying a spear and followed by a pack of dogs or wolves. Another depicted a woman being carried away by an eagle. A chill ran down Pete's spine as he studied these ageless drawings, whether from the icy touch of the river or the ominous spiritual powers of the ancient religion that had put them there, he couldn't say.

Pushing on to the next bend, Pete once again jerked the buckskin to a halt. High on a cliff face before him was a single pictograph—a huge winged serpent painted in red and topaz, staring down in silent vigilance as it had for hundreds, perhaps thousands of years. Pete sensed in its raptorial stare an expression of disapproval, of violation. He felt like a trespasser, and in some vague sense, a desecrater. His scalp crawled as he stared up into the fierce yellow eyes of the serpent, and he had to forcibly pull his gaze away.

He pushed on through the narrow chasm, not feeling easy again until he had put the pictograph behind him. He rounded another bend and rode into a patch of sparkling sunshine. On his left was a wide shelf of land covered with frost-killed ferns and dead grass. Above the shelf was a cleft in the canyon's wall, a slender, V-shaped notch linked to the canyon's floor by a fanning, bush-studded talus. Pete studied the slope carefully for several minutes. There was no sign of a trail anywhere on the nearly vertical incline, but his eyes had picked out several shallow ledges gouged into the shifting, treacherous soil, places where a horse or mule might gain a momentary purchase before scrambling on to the next one. It would be rough and dangerous as hell, but he was fairly certain it could be done. More important, he didn't think the Arapahos would follow them past the pictographs on the canyon's walls, especially the winged serpent behind the last bend. It was a gamble, sure, and at best it might only slow the Indians down until they found a way around, but if it worked it would buy the trappers some time. And sometimes that was all a man needed, Pete thought as he reined the buckskin around to fetch the others.

CHAPTER TWENTY-THREE

Pete saw Annie coming out of the trees along the creek and pulled the gelding to a stop. He stood in the stirrups and waved her forward. Annie thumped her heels against her pony's ribs and galloped across the grassy meadow. The mules followed, hazed by Red-Winged Woman and the girls. Annie's face showed worry as she came up, but no fear. They were in a bad spot, no doubt about that, but they had been in bad spots before and come through all right. Pete saw that she felt the same way now. He hooked his thumb over his shoulder and said, "About a rifle shot upcanyon you'll come to a break in the south wall. That's where we'll climb out. The Arapahos won't follow."

Annie eyed the canyon's mouth suspiciously. "This is not a good place," she said in Spanish.

"Just don't go past the break and we won't upset any spirits."

"You do not know what upsets spirits," Annie retorted. "It is not for us to guess about such things." She eyed the canyon's mouth, the broken country surrounding it. "This was a holy place for the ancient ones, the Ones Who Were Before. It is not good that we come here."

"Look, there are some drawings on the canyon's walls, but that's all they are. Just drawings, made a long time ago."

"Yes, there will be drawings . . . warnings. It is not wise to ignore the messages the Ones Who Were Before left. We must find another way."

"There ain't no other way," Pete snapped. "Goddamnit, there's 'Rapahos on our tails, woman. Get on upcanyon and wait for us at the break. Me'n Charlie will be along directly."

Annie shot him a dark look, but said no more. Red-Winged Woman came up, her eyes wide with fright. "My husband not follow," she said in broken English. "He stay behind, slow Arapaho."

"Your husband has fought the Arapaho before," Pete said. "I reckon he can take care of himself well enough." He repeated his instructions to go as far as the break in the canyon's wall and wait for them there. "I'll go find Charlie," he said.

Red-Winged Woman flashed him a look of gratitude and nodded.

Pete waited until the women had waded their ponies into the creek before touching his spurs to the buckskin's flanks. He gave the gelding its head, loping downstream in a smooth, ground-eating gait. Twenty minutes later he came to a long, sloping meadow and halted. In its center Charlie stood behind the appaloosa, his fusil balanced across the saddle, pointed toward a war party of Arapaho who had stopped just out of range. Warily, Pete lifted his rifle to the cradle of his left arm, keeping his right hand near the trigger. "Charlie," he shouted. "You have a man backing you."

The Arapahos were arguing among themselves, gesticulating wildly as if they suspected a trap. They probably hadn't had time to examine the site of the trappers' camp, Pete reasoned, and they didn't know how many men they faced yet. That much, at least, was good luck.

"Get the women outta here," Charlie shouted without looking around. "There ain't but a dozen bucks in this pile."

"Spirits are watching the women," Pete shouted in Spanish. "I offered these spirits tobacco, and these spirits have promised to protect us all. These spirits say they are angry with the Arapaho, who are in a country that is not their own, and that these spirits will destroy these Arapahos if they try to harm us."

At this, Charlie looked around. Even from a distance Pete could see the stretch of his grin. "It is good that the spirits are our friends, and that they hate the Arapahos like everyone else," Charlie called loudly, for the Arapahos' benefit. "*Bueno.*" He lifted the fusil and mounted carelessly, turning his back on the angry warriors and walking his appaloosa to Pete's side as if he had all the time in the world. "I hope," he said casually as he drew closer, "that one of those brownskins understands Mex."

"They ought to. The Spaniards have been trading amongst 'em a good little bit now."

"I am also hopin' you've got something more up your sleeve than a bluff," Charlie said.

"Well, some, now, or this child wouldn't say so. Found us a canyon with a bunch of old drawings on the walls. Spooky damn place, all right. Like to made my own scalp start crawlin'. I don't reckon these 'Rapahos'll follow us too far into it."

"Be some hot doin's, they decide to."

Pete nodded gravely. He had already considered that. If the Arapahos followed, or if they got up on the rim above them, the canyon could prove to be their graves. "We could go back to St. Louis and sell apples on a street corner," Pete suggested. "It wouldn't be as profitable, but it'd be close, and I don't reckon we'd have to worry 'bout losin' our scalps."

Charlie laughed. "We could take in laundry."

"Or bake pies and sell 'em on the levee."

Charlie's laughter faded. Still grinning, he said, "Well, it ain't come to that yet." He glanced over his shoulder to where the Arapahos were edging deeper into the meadow. "Soon as we make our break, them coons is gonna be on our tails like gnats on a buffalo's ass. How far is this magical canyon you found?"

"About a mile back. We'll be riding in water just after we reach the canyon's mouth."

"Wagh," Charlie grunted, gathering his reins. "You ready?"

"Let's ride!"

Charlie drove his spurs into the appaloosa's flanks, and Pete whipped his buckskin after him. The Arapahos followed immediately, howling, yipping, brandishing their weapons above their heads. One of them touched off his fusil, but the ball sailed harmlessly overhead. The Arapahos were well mounted, but Pete's buckskin and Charlie's appaloosa were just as good, and better cared for. They didn't lose them, but the Arapahos didn't gain any, either. There was still about seventy or eighty yards between them when the trappers reached the canyon's mouth.

Charlie screamed as soon as they entered the canyon, his voice echoing chillingly through the dark fissure, seeming to climb partway up the dank rock walls before crashing back like thunder, louder and more powerful than any human voice had a right to be. Pete howled, too, a weird, yodeling cry that seemed to crackle between the narrow walls. He risked a backward glance just before they rounded the first bend, and saw the Arapahos hauling up in a tangle at the canyon's mouth, some of them shouting angrily and shaking their weapons after the retreating mountain men, while others pulled their ponies to the side, round-eyed and silent.

Pete took the lead, jogging his horse through the tumbling, knee-deep water and making an effort not to look at the winged serpent as he passed. The woman hadn't waited at the bottom of the cleft as Pete had instructed, and he figured that was probably Annie's doings, too. Her paint and a couple of mules were already on top, and they had Red-Winged Woman's horse about halfway up. Red-Winged Woman was tugging at the reins while Annie urged it on from behind. Blossom and Magpie held the loose stock in the middle of the creek, the dogs standing with them in water up to their chests. The women stopped when they saw their men, and Annie shouted, "This is not a good place to leave the canyon," in an accusatory tone.

Charlie whistled softly, eyeing the distant notch. "She's got a point, amigo."

"They've got three of 'em up already," Pete pointed out. He rode over and grabbed the lead rope of one of the mules. Riding to the edge of the talus, he paused, looking up. Annie and Red-Winged Woman must have sensed what he intended to do, because they suddenly began hauling and shoving at Red-Winged Woman's horse, urging it up the slope at a quicker pace.

"Just keep ridin'," Charlie told Pete. "I'll be right behind you." He took the second mule, then began speaking to the girls in a low voice. When Pete judged the women were close enough to the top, he took a hitch around his saddle horn with the mule's lead and drove his spurs into the buckskin's flanks.

The going was rougher than he had imagined, the soil broken by the animals that had gone before them. The mule lost its footing about halfway up, and Pete felt the lead rope tighten just as the buckskin was about to take another plunging drive. He quickly unwound the rope and tossed it free before the mule could pull them back. It went faster after that, without the added weight of the mule. The buckskin was puffing by the time it gained the top, its legs trembling. The mule scrambled up behind them, squealing angrily and baring its huge yellow teeth. Annie grabbed the lead rope before the mule could find a target and quickly wrapped it around the animal's nose.

"Do not make so much noise," she scolded. "Do you want to become an Arapaho mule?"

Blossom and Magpie came next, their dark eyes wide with a mixture of fright and excitement, and a minute later Charlie guided his appaloosa over the top, dragging the last mule after him. They paused a moment to let the animals blow, eyeing one another questioningly. Then Charlie said, "Best we push on. Just in case."

Charlie took the lead, the women, kids, pack animals, and dogs coming after him. Pete brought up the rear, keeping a sharp watch over his shoulder until they reached the pines. Just before plunging into the dark ocean of conifers he pulled up to stare back the way they had come. The canyon was on his left, cutting boldly though craggy, juniper-studded hills. Hugging the opposite rim like the shadow of a cloud passing over the land was a group of horsemen. Pete leaned forward in his saddle, resting an elbow on the horn. He studied the war party thoughtfully, absently counting the number of riders. Charlie came back beside him, chuckling when he spotted the Arapahos.

"That bunch ain't likely to cause trouble anymore. They'll be all day figuring out how we lost 'em, and on the wrong damn side of the canyon when they do."

"They've been gelded, for a fact."

"Yeow, let's cache, amigo."

"Hang on, Charlie. I been thinkin'."

Charlie gave him a wary look. "Ain't no sense in thinkin' what you're thinkin'. Luck has dealt us a decent hand for a change. I say we play it out."

"It just sours my milk to hell and gone to get chased outta a country by a passel of brownskins. It does now. 'Sides that, it'll give 'em a big notion about themselves if we let this slide, make 'em that much harder to deal with the next time a white man crosses swords with 'em."

"There are twelve Injuns in that bunch. I reckon if they want some big notions about themselves they can have 'em."

"Now, see, that's the difference between you and me," Pete said. "You see twelve Injuns, but danged if I don't see twelve ponies. Some of 'em right pretty, too."

"Well, hell," Charlie sighed. He sniffed and looked away, his expression one of thorough disgust. Then he said, "I did see a little steel-dust gray in that bunch that Blossom would surely take a shine to."

"Wagh!" Pete exclaimed, grinning broadly. "Now you're talkin'. Let's go get us some 'Rapaho ponies."

Dawn had come slowly to the valley of the Grand, its pearly light descending over the embattled compound like a fine gray mist. Eli waited on his stomach for the shadows to dissipate, the hostilities to resume. His rifle was poked through a gap between a couple of logs, his pistol lay at his side. He wore his buckskin jacket against the chill but had shed his blanket coat as soon as it began to turn light. In spite of the tension, the cold was taking its toll. His fingers felt stiff around the heavy stock of his rifle, and his teeth threatened to chatter every time he tried to relax. He wished he had draped the capote over his shoulders instead of tossing it aside, but he refused to take his eyes off the emerging alders to do it now. Things would warm up soon enough, he assured himself.

Yet the light grew and the hills began to take on the clarity of full day. A magpie *cawed* from the rushes across the river, and a giant blue heron glided silently overhead. Puzzled, Eli let the rifle's buttplate drop from his shoulder. He peered through the gap at the frost-furred alders, but there was no sign of the Arapahos.

"*Sacre bleu,*" Remi groused. "Why do they not come? This waiting puts gray in Remi's hair."

No one answered, and after a moment Remi muttered another curse and climbed stiffly to his feet, thrusting his head cautiously above the top of the breastworks. An arrow sliced the cold morning air, stirring the long hair that flowed past the French-Canadian's collar before disappearing into the aspens behind them. Remi ducked, grimacing. "*Mon Deiu.* I thought maybe they had tired of this game and gone away in the night."

"Sons of bitches," Eli murmured.

"Maybe they do not wish to waste so many arrows today, eh?" Remi surmised. "*Oui,* Remi thinks that must be it. They will try to pick us off one by one, as they did young Rodolso last night."

"We'll just have to watch closer," Eli replied. They had all been a little careless last night, punch-drunk with weariness, numbed by the steady, day-long battle. "We're damn lucky only one of us got rubbed out yesterday," he added.

"This outfit is death on Mexicans," Remi said solemnly, eyeing Chavez at the northeast corner of the compound. "First Vidales, then Antonio. Who next, eh?"

"That's the question, ain't it?" Eli replied flatly.

A fusil boomed in the distance, its echo rattling the stillness. Another followed, farther away. Eli glanced at McClure, then let his gaze run past the others. They were all watching him in turn, as puzzled as he was. Then came the crack of a lighter rifle that was like the pop of a mule skinner's whip, and a muscle in Eli's shoulder twitched.

"*Sacre,*" Remi said, perking up. "That is Travis's rifle, no?"

"Sounds like it," Eli agreed. He scrambled to his knees, peeking warily over the top of the breastworks, but no arrow flagged the morning air this time, and the chatter of gunfire in the east increased. Far back among the alders, he spotted several warriors racing away from the compound. "They're going to need some help," he told Remi. Spinning to face the compound, he barked, "McClure, I want you, Remi, Connie, and Clint to stay put. Watch that west wall, goddamnit. The rest of you come with me."

Eli vaulted the breastworks and raced toward the alders, deliberately not giving himself time to consider the consequences. He expected at any moment to feel the cold punch of an arrow or the slam of a fusil's ball, and was more than a little surprised when he made it to the nearest clump of alders without drawing either. He fell to his knees with a breathlessness that came more from fear than exertion, and tried to calm his racing heart while the others gathered nervously around him, hunkering down in a tight cluster that reminded Eli of chicks huddling beneath the protection of a hen's wings in a storm.

"All right, we'll spread out from here," Eli said. "Mateo, I want you on the left, then Jorge, me, Jake, and Pierre on the right. Got it?"

Jake and Pierre bobbed their heads; Mateo quickly translated Eli's instructions to Jorge, who nodded curtly and said, "*Sí.*"

"Stay in sight of the man flanking you," Eli ordered as they started forward through the alders. "I want a solid front."

He might as well have been whistling into the wind. Within a hundred yards he found himself alone deep within the alders, ankle-deep in slough water capped with a film of clear ice. He paused and swore under his breath. The sounds of fighting in the east intensified, and he wondered if Travis and Johnny were being forced back by the Arapahos' numbers. Had they realized how big a tiger they were grabbing by the tail? he wondered. The urge to hurry was strong in him, but he forced himself to go slow, to ease along from one clump of alders to the next.

The imprint of the Arapahos was everywhere. He saw flattened grass and moccasin prints in the half-frozen soil, and now and again a patch of dry, bare earth where an Indian had settled for a while, sitting or kneeling. He saw broken and spent arrows, the black ashes of a dead fire, and, once, the smear of dried blood on the grass, like flakes of rust scraped off iron. Most of the sign he saw had been left from the day before, but a lot of it was fresh, too, no more than ten or fifteen minutes old.

There was a low, sharp hiss from Eli's left, and he froze, dropping to a crouch. But it was only Mateo, motioning for him to come over.

"Horses," Mateo whispered as Eli joined him, nodding toward a gap that opened onto the flats along the river. Through the arching, frost-whitened limbs, Eli saw a spotted fabric of dun, sorrel, gray, black, and bay.

"The pony herd," Eli breathed.

"*Sí.*" Mateo gave him a considering look. "It would upset the Arapahos plenty if they thought someone was trying to steal their horses."

"A diversion?"

"*Sí*, a diversion."

"*Bueno*," Eli said, coming to a swift decision. "Let's take a closer look."

Mateo led the way, slipping through the alders like a cat, head swiveling, eyes alert, a different person entirely from the anger-filled young *arriero* Eli had come to know. He moved swiftly over the spongy ground, quick, sure, no move wasted, no sound made. They came to a shallow arroyo and dropped to their bellies, crawling to the edge of the sage plain that stretched along the river. Stopping behind a low clump of sage, Eli took his first good look at the pony herd. It was a fair-sized bunch, maybe fifty head of horses and three or four mules that had probably been stolen in a raid; he had never known an Indian to ride a mule, although they occasionally used them to pull their travois. There were two guards watching the remuda—boys no more than fourteen and fifteen years old—sitting astride wiry mustangs. A third guard, only slightly older than the first two, stood watch over a cluster of Ute captives held beneath a nearby tree. Eli counted four prisoners—a small boy and girl, and two older women, still in their teens. The guards' attention, Eli noticed, was drawn toward the sounds of the battle to the east.

"Only three," Mateo observed. "I have seen worse odds."

"Do you think you can slip up on the boy on the bay?"

Mateo studied the ground separating them. "No," he replied matter-of-factly. "But I can get close."

"How about the other one?"

"*Sí*. That one would be easy."

Eli was silent for a minute, his resolve suddenly weakened by the guards' tender years.

As if reading his thoughts, Mateo gave Eli a scornful look. "They are men, *jefe*. As Antonio was a man. Do you think the Arapahos hesitated because of Antonio's age, before driving an arrow between his ribs? Do you think they would hesitate to do the same to you or me? They would not. Nor will I."

Eli took a long breath. Mateo was right; it was the way of the land, the way of war—kill or be killed. "Rub him out," he ordered flatly. "Be quick about it, too. I'll slip up as close to the other one as I can. As soon as you're spotted I'll kill him, then rush the buck watching the prisoners. You grab as many of the ponies as you can and hightail it back to camp. We'll need what we can catch to replace the wounded stock."

Mateo nodded. "It is done," he said, and ghosted back from the clump of sage.

The decision made, Eli glanced regretfully at the three boys. He had killed maybe a dozen Indians since coming West, but he never found enjoyment in it the way some did, and he liked it even less when the person he had to kill was a youngster or a woman. Yet death was a way of life out here beyond the laws of civilization, a part of what made the living so sweet. It was too bad these three had to die so young, but he knew they wouldn't see it that way, the way a man or a woman brought up by European standards would see it. For these three youths, and their families, there would be honor in a warrior's death, a glory that would make them even greater on the Other Side. That didn't mean they wanted to die or that their deaths wouldn't be grieved by those who survived, but they understood— maybe better than a lot of the "civilized" men Eli knew—what dying meant to a free people, and how it was a part of that freedom.

Eli checked the flint and priming on his rifle and pistol, then settled down to wait. All three boys were looking to the east now, where the sound of gunfire had intensified once more. Eli wondered if they could see the battle from where they were, and how the mountain men were faring against such overwhelming odds. Time seemed to advance with an agonizing slowness. Only minutes had passed since Mateo slipped back into the alders to approach the remuda from downwind, but it seemed like hours, and each desperate shot from a trapper's rifle increased Eli's sense of impotence. At last, with his patience stretched to the breaking point, a gray gelding on the edge of the remuda lifted its head, its tiny ears perked toward the alders. Eli cocked his rifle, bringing it to his shoulder. Although he couldn't see Mateo, he could follow the *arriero*'s progress by the reactions of the gray. He held his breath, praying the horse wouldn't nicker and reveal Mateo's approach to the distracted guards. He lined his sights on the Arapaho on the bay and waited. Several more ponies were watching Mateo now, high-headed, snorty, but it was the gray's shrill whinny that finally caught the guard's attention.

The Arapaho on the bay whipped his mount around just as Eli squeezed the trigger. The rifle roared and bucked, and the Arapaho pitched backward off his horse with a surprised look on his face. Eli leaped to his feet just as Mateo's *escopeta* blossomed smoke and fire, slamming the second youth from his horse. The third guard was racing toward Eli on foot, an iron-tipped lance cocked above his shoulder. Eli jerked his pistol up, cocking the big, stiff-springed hammer with the forearm of the hand that held his rifle, thrusting the muzzle forward and firing just as the Arapaho began his throw. The pistol's heavy slug took the Indian in the shoulder, jerking him off his feet as if he'd hit the end of an anchored line. A bright, crimson stain appeared on the Arapaho's fringed antelope leather shirt, and his lance skidded harmlessly across the frost-slickened grass. The boy writhed in agony, and Eli called himself a fool for turning away without finishing the job with his knife, but he had no stomach for killing or scalp-taking, not against one so young.

He headed toward the bay, intending to help Mateo with the remuda. From the corner of his eye he saw the two Ute women scoop up the children and run toward them, crying loudly in their native tongue. Eli cursed and tried to wave them back, but hope of rescue overrode their common sense. Eli watched helplessly as the remuda spooked, scattering like a covey of quail over the open plain. Mateo, mounted on a dun he had taken from the second guard, pounded after it.

Eli ran to the bay, tethered to the end of the long, single rein of a jawline bridle that was still attached to the Arapaho's wrist. He cut the pony loose and swung onto the padded leather Indian saddle, jamming his moccasins into the rawhide-wrapped wooden stirrups. He pulled the animal around and raced after Mateo and the fleeing remuda. He heard the desperate pleading of the women as he passed, but didn't look around. The remuda was fanning out toward the distant brown hills, too sundered now to gather completely, but there was a little bunch of ten or twelve animals toward its center that Mateo was closing in on, and Eli reined the bay after them. He thumped his heels rhythmically against the bay's rib cage, and whacked the pony's hip with the coiled-up rein. Mateo was swinging wide around the little band, bending it slowly back toward the river. Eli raced to intercept the horses, to guide them back to the compound. The horses slackened their pace as they were turned back, dropping to a gallop, then a trot. With the little band under control, Eli straightened and relaxed. He felt like whooping his joy. Then

Mateo shouted and drew his attention to a rising cloud of dust in the west.

"It is the Arapahos from McClure's side," Mateo yelled.

Eli swore. At least a dozen warriors rode toward them, yipping their war cries. He kicked the bay's flanks and bellowed, "Let's go, Mateo! Let's get 'em back to the river, pronto!"

He rode into the bunch, swinging his rein, forcing the horses into a run. The nearest alders were at least a quarter of a mile away yet, the Arapahos a little more than that, but coming on fast, and without a band of loose stock to drive before them. Mateo rode low over the dun's neck, his empty *escopeta* held across the animal's withers. Eli's own weapons were empty, too, but there wasn't time to reload. He swung the coiled rein viciously at the rumps of the horses nearest him and shouted hoarsely. The Arapahos were closing rapidly. He could see the blue glint of fusil barrels, the cold black nibs of iron lance heads. The warriors were yelling louder now, already sensing victory. When they were less than a hundred yards away, he screamed "*Now, Mateo! Now!*" and pounded up hard on the remuda's flank, turning them once more while Mateo, on the opposite side, dropped back. The stampeding horses veered sharply toward the attacking Arapahos, and Eli and Mateo forced their own mounts toward the center of the tiny bunch, howling and cursing wildly.

They hit the Arapahos like a battering ram of flesh and flashing hooves. Eli heard a scream and saw several horses go down, taking two or three of the Indians with them. He tucked the loose end of the long rein between his thigh and the saddle and lifted his rifle, using it as a club to ward off the probing lances, to slash back in retaliation. He smashed the brass buttplate into a coppery face and heard, even above the thunder of pounding hooves and inflamed shouting, the startled grunt as the Indian tumbled backward off his mount. A lance sliced through the layers of leather and cloth covering Eli's ribs. He felt the sudden chill of morning air against his exposed flesh, the quick, spilling flow of blood, then promptly forgot it.

They burst through the other side of the Arapahos and reined toward the alders, forcing as many of the running horses as they could before them. Mateo, racing at his side, laughed harshly. "They follow, but they will never catch us now."

Eli risked a backward glance. The Arapahos had pulled their horses around and were pounding after them, but Mateo was right, the alders were too close, the Indians would never catch up before they reached the compound.

They had lost most of the horses when they swerved into the Arapahos, but still had three head running before them, plus the bay and the dun. McClure and Consuelo came out of the compound to help them stop the running horses and haze them through a narrow gap in the breastworks. Remi and Clint stood ready at the wall, but the Arapahos pulled up well out of range. Eli slid from the bay's back and tossed the rein over the pony's neck. He quickly reloaded his rifle and pistol. McClure caught Eli's arm, spinning him around just as he slid the reloaded pistol into his belt.

"Where are the others?" the clerk asked angrily.

Eli didn't reply immediately. He was watching the Arapahos who had chased him and Mateo into the compound; the Indians were riding swiftly toward the hills after the stampeded stock, apparently abandoning the battle that still rang out in the east.

"My God, man! You didn't leave them out there?"

Eli pulled away from McClure's grip and ran toward the east wall, where Mateo was dodging through the gap Consuelo was hurriedly refilling with packs and light logs. "Chavez!"

Mateo jerked to a halt.

"Stay put," Eli ordered. "We're not going to run back and forth looking for one another."

"I go to find Jorge."

"Your cousin is with the others. Your being out there ain't going to make a damn bit of difference. Best thing to do now is just sit tight and wait."

"Go to hell," Mateo replied emotionlessly. He turned and loped into the alders.

McClure came up behind him. "I hope those ponies were worth it," he told Eli darkly. "Because if those men don't come back, I'll see you released from the GS&T, and personally press charges of manslaughter against you."

CHAPTER TWENTY-FOUR

The firing tapered off and the smoke began to clear. Travis lay on his stomach behind the sun-bleached trunk of a fallen cottonwood tree, still a quarter mile from the compound. The trunk's knotted surface was ripped and splintered, limbed with arrows. To the southwest he could see several Arapahos rounding up the horses Cutler and Chavez had stampeded, herding them back toward the river, but before them and to the side the alders seemed deserted, as if the Indians had drifted away on the same breeze that was even now raking away the last vestiges of gray powder smoke.

"What's going on?" Travis asked Johnny.

"Hard to say, but I'm for getting out of here if we can. We've tangled with a hornet's nest, Travis, and we've been damn lucky one of us hasn't been stung yet."

Their attack on the Arapahos' eastern flank had been more accidental than planned. They had dodged little bands of roaming Indians all day yesterday, finally holing up in a narrow side canyon where they found Old Cal and Cork-Eye cached within the deep brush. After dark they had circled around to the east and tied their horses and mules well back from the Arapahos' position. "They're going to need our help," Johnny told them last night. "Something that'll surprise the Arapahos, and maybe spook them off."

Old Cal had gone wall-eyed at the notion. "Ye be a fool, Johnny Two-Dogs! Do ye hyar? A moon-teched fool. Best we cache and wait 'em out. Ol' Eli kin handle them 'Rapyhos."

But Johnny had remained adamant. "We'll jump them from behind first thing in the morning. Between the four of us and Eli's men, we ought to be able to rout them."

" 'Rapyhos don't spook, boy. Listen to Ol' Cal here, and larn ye-self somepin."

Johnny ignored the old man's admonitions. "Let's go," he said, and Travis followed without question, never once looking back to see if Old Cal or Cork-Eye was coming or not. They slipped close enough to the Arapahos' camp to see the wavering light of a tiny fire, then settled down to wait out the darkness. As the first light of the new day dropped over the valley, Travis looked for Old Cal and Cork-Eye, but neither man was in sight.

"Best not count on those two," Johnny whispered. "Old Cal's as superstitious as a Papago, and Cork-Eye's little better than a coward."

"Then why the hell are we letting them travel with us?" Travis asked.

"Hush," Johnny breathed. Ahead, Travis saw an Arapaho come out of the alders and begin to loosen his breechcloth. Chuckling, Johnny said, "Here, now, Travis. Someday you'll get to tell your grandkids how you saw an Indian take a shit."

Travis watched the Arapaho lower himself, then looked away in embarrassment, freezing when he found himself staring down the bore of a battered Northwest fusil. He squawked weakly and felt Johnny's elbow slam into his shoulder. He stumbled to the side just as the fusil roared. Johnny yelled and rushed the Arapaho, his knife flashing. Travis whirled. The Indian they had been watching was on his feet now, sprinting for cover. Travis shouldered his rifle and pulled the trigger instinctively. The Kentucky cracked flatly in the still air, and the Indian spun limply into a clump of alders before bouncing off and sprawling in the grass.

"That's it," Johnny said tersely, climbing to his feet and wiping his blooded blade against his trousers. "The grease is in the skillet now."

He had been right, too. For half an hour they fought desperately while the Arapahos pushed forward. They fell back as far as the little stand of timber where they were holed up now, and dug in behind the fallen cottonwood. It all seemed like hours ago, but there was still frost on the grass close to the river, and the morning sun hadn't even crested the snowy peaks of the Divide.

"Come on," Johnny said, slapping Travis's shoulder lightly with the back of his hand. "Let's see what happens."

He stood and made a run for the alders, skidding to a stop once and wheeling in a new direction, but making it without drawing fire. Travis lunged to his feet and followed, and soon both men lay panting among the alders.

"Bueno," Johnny murmured. "Lady Luck's going to give us a second chance this time."

"What are we going to do?"

"We're going to get our ponies, then we're going to hightail back into the hills and find Underwood and Weathers."

"We're going to run?" Travis asked incredulously.

"We're going to save our necks if we can."

Travis shook his head. "You go on. I'll stay."

"What! Don't be a fool, Travis. Come on."

"I ain't running no more, Johnny. I'd rather die than do that."

Johnny stared at him in disbelief, then his dark eyes turned hard. "You goddamn dumb greenhorn. I thought you had more sense than that."

Travis looked away and refused to answer.

"All right," Johnny said with resignation. "It's your neck."

"I ain't runnin' no more," Travis murmured, still unable to meet Johnny's probing gaze.

"I didn't say you had to, kid." He clamped a hand over Travis's shoulder. "Luck to you, then, and if they don't put me under, I'll see you get a decent burial."

Travis gulped and nodded, suddenly incapable of speech. His throat closed off and tears welled in his eyes, not out of fear, but out of the hopelessness of his emotions, the pain of Chet's death that had become his own private hell. He wouldn't run anymore, not even if he had to die by staying.

Johnny scrambled deeper into the alders and was gone. Travis stared dumbly after him, then turned and started toward the compound where Eli and the others waited. He hadn't gone twenty yards when he heard the scuff of a moccasin behind him. He turned, bringing up the Kentucky, but the Arapaho was close enough that he simply pushed the barrel aside. Travis saw the warrior's victorious smile, saw his arm rise, then fall, saw the dark, blood-stained wood of the war club. Then the world was lost in an explosion of pain and blackness.

Eli and Remi stood at the north wall of the compound and watched the snaking line of horsemen disappear into the tawny hills across the river. "Eight," Remi said after the last rider had dropped from sight. He gave Eli a gauging look. "Thirty-nine, altogether."

Eli nodded thoughtfully, having already come to the same count. The Arapahos were pulling out; not in one big party, as they had come, but in smaller bunches of six to a dozen, each riding in a different direction, although with a general easterly bent.

From the shade of an aspen, Pierre Turpin said, "By *Dieu*, dem Indian, they give up, no?"

Pierre, Jake, Jorge, and Mateo had returned to the compound soon after Eli and Mateo brought in the Arapaho ponies. None of them had gotten close enough to spot their allies, a fact that worried Eli immensely. A foreboding silence had spread through the alders after their return, and he couldn't help wondering if the Arapahos' thirst for revenge had been slaked against those unidentified individuals who had attempted to come to their aid.

"Remi thinks Pierre is right, Eli," Remi said. "If the Utes follow, the Arapahos will run."

Eli glanced at the two young squaws and the children who had come slinking into camp shortly after Mateo returned to the alders to find his cousin. It was the oldest squaw who had told them that many Ute warriors were on the way, and that the trappers would be rewarded handsomely when their fathers and uncles learned of the trappers' bravery in rescuing them. Eli had some reservations about the girl's assurances, but he admired her audacity. She was short and broad-framed, and despite the half-starved appearance that was the earmark of Indian captivity, she was already showing the signs of plumpness that would mark her later years.

"Then where the hell are they?" Jake said, glowering at the squaws. Jake was holding his right hand across his stomach, protected by a hastily wrapped bandage. An Arapaho's arrow had nicked the flesh between the thumb and forefinger, a piddling affair, at best, but one which seemed to cause him unlimited despair.

Pierre had also been wounded during his reconnaissance outside the compound walls. An arrow had pierced the fleshy part of his thigh, although its damage had been minimal. It would probably hurt like hell for a few days, but it was a clean wound and would heal quickly.

As if Jake hadn't spoken, Remi said, "*Sacre bleu*, Remi tires of waiting."

"I'm tired of it, too," Eli growled. He hefted his rifle, as if the decision he had to make might be reached in its balance. Finally, he said, "I'm going to make a quick *paseo* out there, see if they've cleared out or not."

"Remi will go with you," Remi said.

"Remi will stay put," Eli countered. He glanced at the French-Canadian and grinned to take the sting out of his words. "Someone has to pull this outfit through the winter if I don't come back."

Remi didn't smile. "Maybe you should wait a while, eh?"

"Maybe," Eli conceded, then clambered over the breastworks and started toward the alders.

He reached the edge of the brush and paused, cocking his rifle, then pushed on, following the path he had taken that morning. Little had changed except that the frost had long since burned off and he couldn't see his breath anymore. The grass was still pocked by the prints of unshod ponies, laced with the paths of comings and goings. A red-winged blackbird settled on a limb some distance before him, a sign he took as encouraging. He'd gone maybe two hundred yards when he heard the clop of a pony's hoof and stopped again, bringing his rifle up instinctively. The slow thud of approaching horses came on steadily, but without hurry, and Eli held his ground. A minute later Old Cal Underwood and Cork-Eye Weathers rode into view. They spotted Eli and reined toward him. Old Cal rode slumped in the saddle as usual, as if half-asleep, although Eli knew he missed nothing. Cork-Eye sat his mount rigidly, his head swiveling back and forth as if he expected an Arapaho behind every bush. Their pack animals lumbered behind, nearly dwarfed by plews still stretched in their willow frames. Then another rider came out of the alders, and Eli started to grin when he recognized Johnny Two-Dogs, but the smile froze when he realized Johnny was leading Travis's mule, with Travis's limp form draped across the saddle.

A gust of wind swept through the aspen grove, loosening a shower of leaves that clattered to the ground with a dry, papery sound. Several skittered into the open grave to rest against the gravelly bottom like gold coins tossed in for luck. Mateo shivered at the image and looked away. His serape flapped in the wind, and in his hand his sombrero fluttered and bucked. To the west the sky was black with an approaching storm front, the hills veiled in driving sheets of rain. It had been warm earlier, but as the storm grew closer, the temperature plummeted.

Mateo stood at the head of the grave, shivering again as the sweat dried on his brow and along his spine. Jorge stood at his side, his face hard and cold in the dimming light, aged beyond his years. With a touch of shock Mateo realized his cousin did not look like the boy who had ridden with him from his father's rancho just a few short weeks before. Tragedy had marked him with its own special brand, stripping away the last vestiges of his youth.

Maybe it had marked them both, he thought suddenly, lifting his eyes to the flat line of hills, their summits lost behind a purple tapestry of rain. Maybe it was tragedy that had deadened his own feelings, making him feel like a vacuum inside, empty and waiting.

Mateo had never understood the complexity of his emotions, the seething anger, the dissatisfaction that oppressed his every accomplishment. And over it all the hollowness, as if he somehow stood outside his body, observing the empty shell of his life with indifference. He had thought getting out from under his father's control and making his way as a man would fill the emptiness inside, but even that hope had been dashed. If anything, the emptiness had only increased.

Johnny Two-Dogs and Cork-Eye Weathers came forward, lifting the ropes that were looped under Antonio's buffalo-robe-wrapped body and lowering it into the grave. Eli Cutler removed his hat, the weariness of the last two day showing more strongly in his face than any other, Mateo thought.

"Lord," Eli began. "This here is Antonio Rodolso. He was a good hand. We'd appreciate it if You'd outfit him proper on the other side. Amen."

"Amen," Jake and Clint Orr echoed.

"Adios," Johnny added.

"Fittin' service, Eli," Old Cal crackled. "Fittin', by God." He leaned over the grave and called, "Watch yer topknot, Rodolso. I aims to send ye a 'Rapyho, next chance I get. Send 'im to ye with his hair on, I will."

"Eli."

Mateo looked up at the warning in Remi LeBlanc's voice. He followed the French-Canadian's gaze south, across the plain, and felt his blood go cold.

"Son of a whore," Jorge said softly.

A trio of riders were crossing the plain, coming on slowly as if out for an afternoon jaunt. Mateo didn't recognize the two men riding flank, but the big man in the center was as familiar to him as the sound of running buffalo. Jorge edged closer, speaking for Mateo's ears only. "He has come, as he said he would."

"Yes," Mateo replied, feeling the old hardness, the anger, return. "He has come."

"It's them," Johnny said to Eli.

"Them?" Old Cal snorted. "Who be them?" He was looking from Johnny to Eli.

McClure had been standing near the rear of the group with the Ute women, sheepish after his confrontation with Eli earlier that morning. But all his old bluster seemed to come flying back. He pushed through the men to stand at Eli's side. "Who are they?" he asked crisply.

"I don't know," Eli said. "But I reckon they've been dogging our trail for some time now. Johnny spotted them almost two weeks ago, on the other side of Buffalo Pass."

"Two weeks! Why wasn't I told?"

Eli gave McClure a scorching look and stepped away from the grave. The others followed as far as the edge of the breastworks, where they spread out in loose formation. No one spoke again until Gregorio el Toro stopped his horse about a dozen yards away.

"*Buenos dias,*" Gregorio called. His gaze settled on Mateo, and a contemptuous smile crossed his face. "So, we meet again, *niño*. Have you expected me?"

"Who are you?" Eli interjected bluntly.

"I am Gregorio el Toro, of the Rancho de Chavez, on the Pecos River. I have ridden far to collect these two little birds who have flown their father's coop." He might have laughed then, or cleared his throat; Mateo wasn't sure. "Flown their father's coop with their father's horses, eh, little cock?"

"My father's horses were returned to him," Mateo replied in a voice that sounded small and childlike, even to his own ears.

"I've heard of you," Eli said. "Gregory the Bull, in English."

Gregorio looked uncharacteristically pleased by the recognition. "*Sí,* I am well-known, even among the *Americanos.*"

Eli laughed harshly. "I didn't say I was impressed."

Gregorio's smile vanished. "I, likewise, have heard of you, Eli Cutler. I was told that you were a little man, but then, it was a whore that told me this thing. Perhaps I misunderstood." His gaze flitted to Consuelo, and his mirthless smile returned.

Eli's eyes narrowed, but he refused to rise to Gregorio's bait. He said, "You've come a long way for nothing, *gordo*."

Gregorio chuckled at the insult. "Ah, but I disagree, *Señor* Cutler. It has been a long journey, true, but I will have my way." He flicked his quirt toward Mateo. "This one is to be returned to Rancho de Chavez. The other is to be branded, like his brother."

"*Branded!*" Old Cal exclaimed. "So that be what young Antonio was hidin' under them bandages."

"My brother hid nothing!" Jorge blazed. He glared at Gregorio. "The wound would not heal, but he was not ashamed."

"I think all thieves must be ashamed, little one. It is a part of the price they must pay, especially those who steal from their own families."

"Mateo and Jorge are working for me now," Eli said evenly. "You'll have to bide your time. Maybe when we get back, next spring . . ."

Gregorio glanced deliberately over one massive shoulder, scanning the hills to the south. Then he looked at the approaching storm. "Soon the passes will be closed. My patience grows short, *Señor* Cutler, but I will have my way."

"Go home, *gordo*. You've bit off more than you can chew this time."

Gregorio smiled. "We will see, eh?" He jerked his horse around. "Hector, Salvador, *vamonos*." The three men rode off at a gallop, the dust their horses kicked up blown away by the wind.

CHAPTER TWENTY-FIVE

Dawn came wet and gray, with four inches of slushy snow on top of the sleet that had emerged from the rain at dusk last night. It had been a cold, miserable night all the way around, and although the snow had stopped around midnight, the skies remained damp and overcast.

Eli saddled one of the uninjured horses and made a short ride through the alders close to camp, but found no sign of either the Arapahos or Gregorio el Toro and his men. He sent Johnny and Old Cal out on a wider sweep after he returned, but he suspected at least the Arapahos had vacated the valley for good. They had been looking for a quick victory, something to cap an already successful raid against the Utes; they weren't likely to be interested in a long siege, especially with a new storm and fresh snow approaching, threatening to choke the high passes that still separated them from their homelands.

Gregorio el Toro was another matter. Eli had talked with Mateo and Jorge last night, and knew that the heavyset vaquero wasn't an antagonist to be taken lightly. Nor would he be apt to back down. Still, he had only two men with him, and no matter how tough they were, Eli doubted if they were any tougher than the men he had riding with him. Gregorio might be a thorn in Eli's side personally, but he was no threat to the GS&T.

Mateo, Jorge, and the Orrs were tending to the wounded stock, under Silas McClure's supervision. In the end they had lost five mules, and although they had gained five Indian ponies in the raid he and Mateo had made on the Arapahos' remuda, those ponies wouldn't be enough to compensate for the wounded animals, a few of which would be incapable of carrying packs for several weeks.

Consuelo came out of a hastily rigged lean-to they had constructed last night and walked to Eli's side. She looked tired, her shoulders sloped with fatigue, the flesh under her eyes baggy. "*Qué pasa?*" she said, stopping and wiping her hands on a rag.

"How's Ketchum?"

"Hungry, but quiet. Very quiet."

"Can he ride?"

"Would you stay here if he couldn't?"

"I'd rig a stretcher for him, if he needed it," Eli responded stiffly.

Her voice softening, Consuelo said, "I gave him some meat and broth. I think once he has eaten he will be stronger."

"*Bueno.*" Eli started to turn away, but Consuelo's voice stopped him.

"Eli?"

"Yes."

She stepped closer, her voice lowering. "How long has it been since we made love?"

"I . . ." He stopped, confused.

"Once we loved one another with a passion I did not fully trust . . . it was so good, like a farrier's fire, so hot and bright. Now we grow apart, and the fire has cooled. I do not know how to fight this thing you want, this St. Louis. I do not understand it. If it were another woman . . . but not ambition, not like yours. My ambitions have always been smaller, a house, a husband, children to carry on, grandchildren. These are the things I long for, Eli. Once I thought you wanted them as well."

"I don't reckon I ever really thought about what I wanted. Not before this. Hell, I was just living, not really looking past the next season. But I'm getting older, Connie. When I look at men like Old Cal—"

She smiled gently. "You are not like Old Cal. You are not like any man. It is what I always admired about you. But now I fear it. What will you do, Eli? Where do I fit in?"

He sighed, looking away. "I don't know," he admitted.

"I know you are torn," she said mildly. She put a hand on his arm, giving it a light squeeze. "But soon I think you must decide. I will not share my bed forever with a man who does not love me."

Roughly, he said, "It's too late to go back, if that's what you're thinking."

"True, it is too late to return to Taos. But it is not too late to make my own bed, to sleep alone. That is my decision, as St. Louis is yours."

He sighed. "I . . . I can't answer your question right now. And I don't know when I will."

"*Sí.* I understand. But now you understand also, how it is with me? How it must be." She looked past his shoulder and smiled. "Duty calls," she murmured, and moved away.

Eli turned as McClure approached. The little clerk nodded, watching Consuelo walk away. "Did I interrupt anything?" he asked almost apologetically.

"We were finished."

McClure hesitated, pulling his wool Dragoon's cap off and scratching his bald head. "It isn't good, but with the ponies you and Mateo brought in yesterday, I think we'll manage."

"*Bueno.* I want to shift camp to the west end of the valley today."

"Have we trapped this upper end sufficiently?"

"Not as well as I would've liked, but maybe as good as we'll have time to if we want to get up into the Salt Lake country before freeze-up. No reason we can't swing through here on our way back to Taos next spring, either." He didn't add that he wanted to put what had happened here behind them, or that he thought the men would feel easier, and thereby work harder, in a new place.

"The plews won't be winter prime next spring."

"Plews won't be prime anywhere in the spring, but we'll take what the valley offers, and leave the rest for later."

McClure nodded thoughtfully, although Eli wasn't sure he agreed with the decision. McClure had seemed distant and subdued all morning, and Eli didn't know whether it was from their confrontation the day before or if something else was bothering him.

"I'll see to the packs, then," McClure said.

"Johnny and Cal should be in soon. If the Arapahos have put out for the Front Range like I figure they have, we'll move out before noon."

McClure nodded, looking away to study the white hills. "I'm . . . maybe I was wrong . . . yesterday, I mean. All things considered, we did admirably. Only one man dead, a few minor wounds. I'm not sure the Dragoons could've done it any better. I was premature in my assessment of the situation regarding the horses you and Mateo brought in. I made a threat that I now regret. I apologize for that."

"It's done," Eli said gently. "Put it out of your mind."

McClure paused a moment, then went on. "Do you believe in premonitions, Eli?"

"You mean spooks and ha'nts?"

"No, I mean a sense of things to come, a feeling that something isn't right."

Eli shrugged soberly, considering. "Yeah, I guess I do," he admitted. "You live out here long enough, your perspective changes. Riding alone in the mountains, especially at night, I've often felt a sense of . . . I don't know, a presence, maybe. I felt it the first time I came out here, but I never felt it back East, not even under similar circumstances."

"I have an ominous feeling, something that's been bothering me ever since leaving Río Colorado. I don't know how to describe it other than as a sense of foreboding. Whether it is toward the brigade or myself personally, I haven't been able to decide."

"Hell, it ain't likely something you need to fret about. Feelings come and go, and we've had our share of problems this trip, no doubt about that. More than most, and that's a fact."

McClure finally drew his gaze away from the hills, nodding self-consciously. "Of course. I didn't mean to burden you. I just wanted to bring it up."

"It's a big country," Eli said. He shrugged uncertainly. "Hell, it wasn't any bother. . . ."

McClure smiled without reassurance. "Well, I had best see to the packs."

Eli watched him walked away. It occurred to him that he was starting to feel the same way.

They rode steadily through the deepening cold. Gray clouds capped the valley, and the snow that had been slushy at dawn was starting to freeze as the temperature dropped. Two days before, during the height of the Arapahos' attack, sweat had tracked Eli's face freely, but he suspected it would be a long time before he felt that kind of heat again.

Remi and Jake Orr rode in the vanguard, perhaps half a mile ahead, looking small and insubstantial in the cheerless light. Old Cal and Cork-Eye flanked the brigade to the north, where the alders grew thick along the river. Old Cal had grumbled, of course, arguing that he didn't want to take a bullet meant for a greaser, but Eli had remained firm. "Mateo and Jorge have their hands full with the remuda. They can't be tending that and watching over you at the same time."

Old Cal had bristled at the insult, but took the flank without further protest. Eli wasn't overly worried about Arapahos anymore, although he knew there could be a few lingering around the valley. Most, though, were probably bucking deep snows as they fought their way over the Divide, wishing they hadn't tarried in their futile efforts to rout the mountain men.

Even keeping a steady pace, the brigade's progress was slow. The wounded stock in particular suffered from the frigid temperatures, and the *arrieros* had to push them unrelentingly to keep them mov-

ing through the crusting snow. Pierre, Remi, Jake and Travis, all
wounded during the battle with the Arapahos, coped in their own
fashion, but it was young Ketchum who caused Eli his greatest concern. Travis had appeared more dead than alive when Johnny
brought him in yesterday. His scalp had been split open by an Arapaho's war club, the hair caked with drying blood, and the side of his
face was swollen and discolored. He rode near the front of the
brigade now, but was still slack-limbed and silent, his face ashen.

Johnny's attitude toward his partner's injury seemed a little
starched, but maybe understandable. Johnny had risked his life going
back in after Travis, arriving just in time to prevent his scalping, but
he was still angered by it.

"That kid's got a death wish, Eli," Johnny had told him that morning, shaking his head with the wonder of it. "He's damn near as dangerous as a she-grizz with cubs."

"Do you want a new partner?"

Johnny had thought about it for a moment, but then shook his
head. "No. I'll stay with Travis. I still say he's got the makings, if
that Arapaho clubbed any sense into his head."

The others—Pierre, Remi, Jake—had suffered only minor
wounds that would heal with time. Consuelo had tried to talk Remi
into splinting his ankle, fearing that it might be broken, but the
French-Canadian had downplayed her concern. "It is only a sprain,"
he assured her. "Remi has suffered much worse at the monte tables
in Taos and Santa Fe."

Pierre, his thigh ripped by a flint-tipped arrow, benefited from the
unexpected aid of the two Utah squaws. They had, without instructions, taken over the cooking and the caring of the plews that still
needed to be grained and smoked against moisture and bugs. Even
before they were certain that the Arapahos had left the valley, the two
women had slipped down to the river and gathered an armful of
alders that they used to stretch the most recently trapped pelts of
beaver and otter. They had worked hard to prove their worth, and
kept the children busy, too, gathering wood and tending fires. Their
fears were obvious. Freed of the uncertainty of their fate among the
Arapahos, they now feared the trappers.

Eli glanced over his shoulder at the two squaws walking beside
the packhorse that carried Pierre's kettles and skillets. The two children rode a mule led by one of the women, nearly lost beneath a

shaggy blond buffalo robe. Behind the Utes came the remuda, herded by Mateo and Jorge. Clint Orr rode with them, helping where he could, staying out of the way when he couldn't, and hopefully learning the ropes. Eli had decided to split the two brothers after learning of Remi's dismal catch. Perhaps they would get along better if they were kept apart, and Mateo needed an extra hand.

Eli's gaze lingered longest on Jorge. The young *arriero* drove the remuda with a grim anger, the sound of his quirt against the hides of balking animals floating over the brigade like the pop of distant rifle fire. Jorge, always quiet but never withdrawn, had turned abruptly morose after Antonio's death, and Eli made a mental note to seek him out that night and give him a chance to talk, to work through some of his grief. He would talk to Consuelo, as well. Perhaps a woman's voice, a woman's ear, would help ease the burden of his loss, especially a Mexican woman, who could converse with him in his native tongue.

It was growing dark by the time they reached a big grove of cottonwoods near the lower end of the valley and Eli gave the order to make camp. He studied the irregular bellies of the clouds nervously. They seemed to hang lower than they had earlier, as if weighed by the moisture trapped within them. Already a few light flakes were feathering down on a lazy breeze.

Mateo, Jorge, and Clint circled the remuda and brought it in. Mateo loosened a reata from his saddle and roped a mule, dragging it to the edge of the trees where he and Jorge blindfolded it and began pulling the packs off. Eli hooked an arm under the fork of his saddle and dragged that and the saddle blanket off with one motion. Consuelo led the animal away, while Eli helped Mateo, Jorge, and Clint with the mules.

The two Utah squaws were helping Pierre with his pots and kettles by the time they finished. Someone had kindled a fire and the kids were sitting close to its warmth, watching the women. Consuelo had lashed a straight limb between a couple of trees, framed a lean-to with other limbs, and was shingling it with bark peeled off the trunks of fallen cottonwoods. When she finished, she shoveled the snow out and gathered grass along the river for a floor that she covered with an old robe.

McClure was setting up the brigade's only wall tent with the help of Cork-Eye and Jake Orr. He looked up gloomily as Eli approached.

"Everything under control?" Eli asked.

"Yes. We'll have the trade goods inside shortly."

"*Bueno.*" He glanced up to where the limbs were thrashing in the strengthening wind. Inside the cottonwoods, though, the air was strangely still, the snow floating downward as big and soft as dandelion fluff. It would snow heavily tonight, he thought, and maybe into tomorrow, too.

"We should've brought tents for the men, as well," McClure said.

Eli shrugged. "I'd just as soon use a lean-to or a shanty, myself. Build a fire out front, and it's a hell of a lot warmer than a tent. Doesn't take up any room in the packs, either."

McClure nodded distractedly. Jake straightened from where he was hammering an iron tent stake into the ground. "By God, what I'd like is a tipi. It'd be like living in a chimney."

"It's a pleasure, all right," Eli said. "I've spent a winter or two in a lodge, and it's cozy. But a man can't pack lodgepoles along everywhere he goes. A tipi is fine for winter doin's, but a man on the move's gotta make do with less."

Cork-Eye came around the green and white striped canvas, hitching at his trousers. "Now, I say Jake's right," he announced loudly. "A lodge shines, 'specially if a man's got him a female to tend to it."

Jake laughed crudely, while McClure snorted. Cork-Eye gave the clerk a baleful look and moved off. "I can't stand a coward," McClure said, "and I have pegged both Cork-Eye and Cal Underwood as prime examples of cowardice. Hiring either of them was a mistake I deeply regret."

"Those are the chances you take. Quit railing yourself over it. We've got a pretty good outfit, taken as a whole."

"Perhaps," McClure agreed reluctantly. "Jake, go bring Weathers back here, then the two of you get these trade goods inside."

A mule brayed, its wheezing *haw* cutting through the still air. In the light of a smaller fire set off from Pierre's bigger blaze, Mateo was examining a wounded horse. Eli watched as Clint led the pony several stiff, hobbling steps away, then turned it back to the light. Mateo studied the pony's stride critically, arms akimbo beneath his serape.

Following Eli's gaze, McClure spoke softly. "What are we going to do, Eli? The day's journey nearly killed a couple of mules, and it weakened numerous others. Another day like today and we stand to lose a dozen or more animals. We can't afford that kind of loss."

"We'll stay here awhile, let the storm blow out, give the boys a chance to trap, give the wounded stock some time to heal."

"Time will help," McClure agreed. "But some of those animals will need months to recuperate completely."

Eli glanced at the two Ute squaws fussing over supper. "I have an idea. Excuse me, Silas."

Eli went to the fire and hunkered down, smiling at the children. "Warm, huh?" He held his hands out to the flame, rubbing them together vigorously, pantomiming his meaning. "Feels good, a day like today."

The children remained mute, staring at him with round, questioning eyes. He sniffed the stew. It was beaver tail, rich and full of fat; it would set well on a cold night such as this. He sniffed again, loudly, then rubbed his stomach, exaggerating every movement until the little girl flashed a bright smile of understanding. Eli's smile broadened. "Beaver tail. Good, huh? Makes the belly warm."

Pierre, munching on a slice of liver on the far side of the fire, said, "By *Dieu*, dis is the life, Eli. Couple pretty womens, no work, eh? Man just sit on his butt, let *les* squaws do all the damn work, *non*?" He reached over to pat one of the squaws on her buttocks, laughing when she moved away. "Make a man hungry for more than just food, no?" He grinned lewdly.

"Enjoy it while you can," Eli replied absently. He studied the two women thoughtfully. They were maybe seventeen or eighteen, short like any Ute, pretty beneath the burns and bruises of captivity. They wore buckskin dresses decorated with elk teeth and a row of dyed porcupine quills, and silver earrings that dragged at their lobes. One, a little taller and a little slimmer than the other, had a small white scar canted downward from the corner of her mouth, across her dusky chin. Both were watching Eli solemnly, a little fearfully, he thought. Aware of the Utes' long association with Mexican traders, he spoke in Spanish. "My name is Eli Cutler," he said. "What are you called?"

They both ducked their heads, and Pierre chuckled. "By *Dieu*, they think you be one mean chief. That is what they tell me. Like the *caragieu*, the wolverine. You, Mateo, both, when you save them from Arapaho."

"We will not harm you," Eli told them. "We want to take you back to your families. We want to trade with your village—horses, mules, furs. Trade." He made the sign for trade with his hands, pushing his left out and opening it, pulling the right back and closing it into a fist. "Trade," he repeated. "Where is your village?"

The tallest woman, with the scar on her chin, met his eyes. "I am Falls on the Rocks, daughter of Lean Bull. This is Grass That Burns, my uncle's daughter."

"Who is your chief?"

"Frog That Walks Like a Man, who you call Bowlegs."

Eli grinned at the mention of the name. "Wagh! I have traded with Bowlegs in the past. He is a good man. I remember your father, too. A brave warrior."

"Yes," Falls on the Rocks said, becoming bolder as they spoke. "I remember you, too, Eli Cutler. You shot at the mark with the men of my village, and won many furs from them."

"Yes," said Eli, still grinning. "It was a good day."

"Our village is camped on the River of the Black Canyon," Falls on the Rocks continued. "At the forks."

"Yes," Eli said, putting together in his mind a map of the country to the west of them. "Not far from here. Four, maybe five days. But we cannot push the wounded horses that far. Not now. Too many would die. We will have to go slowly, and trap along the way. Do you understand? We will take you back to your village, but we must go slowly."

"Yes. I understand. Grass That Burns and I will stay with you until you return us to our village."

"Yes. Good. Will your father come after you?" He remembered Grass That Burns' nearly frantic promises of the day before, when she claimed that many Ute warriors were already following and that they would help the trappers if the mountain men protected them from the Arapahos.

But Falls on the Rocks lacked yesterday's desperation. "I do not know," she confided shyly. "Maybe. The Arapahos attacked our village seven suns ago. I and Grass That Burns were downriver. I did not see the battle. I do not know how many of our men were killed. I saw many scalps, but I think some of them were old and belonged to the Navajos. The Arapahos took us as we ran back toward the village. They already had the children."

Eli's brows knitted in contemplation. "Then maybe, if the Arapahos were running when they took you and Grass That Burns, they did not greatly harm your village. Maybe it was a brief fight, a running fight." He made a quick, cutting motion with his hand. "We will know more when we get there. For now, help Pierre with the cooking and gathering wood. Help stretch and grain the plews. You will be back with your family in a few weeks."

Falls on the Rocks smiled, her eyes suddenly twinkling. "Thank you, Eli Cutler," she said. "My family will remember you."

From the shadows behind him, Consuelo snorted laughter. "Be careful, mighty warrior, this one wants you in her robes." She came into the light, smiling maliciously. "It would be a shame to end up living in some hide tipi eating bugs, instead of that fancy St. Louis mansion you have your heart set on."

Eli surged to his feet, his temper flaring. "But maybe that's what I want, too," he blurted.

Consuelo jerked to a stop, her face paling. Falls on the Rocks glanced fearfully between them.

"Then go to her," Consuelo whispered. "I will not stand in your way."

"Goddamnit," Eli grated.

"She will make you a fine wife," Consuelo said in a barely audible voice. "She will cook and mend and cater to your every whim." Her voice trembled, and her eyes welled sudden tears. "She will never tell you to go to hell, or threaten your *cojones* with knife or tongue. She will be the perfect wife, never—"

"Stop it," Eli said harshly. "Goddamnit, just stop it."

She shut up, gasping for breath, struggling for control.

"I don't want her," Eli said.

"But you do not want me, either."

He spread his hands in a helpless gesture. "Maybe not. I don't know. I have my job, my responsibilities . . ."

"Yes, of course. Your job." She backed up a step. "I will remove my robes from—"

"Leave your robes. Just leave everything."

"No, Eli. It has gone too far for that. I will sleep elsewhere from now on, alone."

"Connie . . ."

"I will not be a burden. I will earn my keep, and when we return to the settlements, I will go to El Paso." She turned, plunging into the darkness, tears of hurt running down her cheeks.

"Son of a bitch," Eli breathed. He glanced at Pierre, who watched him with a maddening soberness. "Something troubling you?" he asked sharply.

Pierre shook his head. "*Non,* Eli." He limped over to the fire and tapped Falls on the Rocks on the shoulder, causing the girl to flinch. "You," he said, motioning toward a kettle, "stir that, before we give you back to the Arapahos."

CHAPTER TWENTY-SIX

Remi drew rein at the mouth of the canyon and studied the grove of cottonwoods where Eli had ordered camp made the week before. A thread of smoke curled into the glassy blue sky, and to the east of the trees the remuda grazed peacefully, looking like a mottled stain against the old, churned snow. He could see the figures of several men moving among the trees, the Ute women in their buckskin dresses, and Mateo Chavez in his flowing serape. There was no sign of trouble anywhere, and Remi grunted his satisfaction and booted the paint with the heel of his sound leg.

Jake followed silently, leading the pack animals with their bulky, angular loads of stretched plews. They had done all right for themselves this time. With Clint remaining behind to help Mateo and Jorge with the remuda, Jake had settled into a kind of surly competence. He didn't speak much, not even around the fire at night, but he did his chores without dispute, and saw to his lines like an old hand.

The upset of balance between the two brothers amused Remi to no end. He spotted Clint sitting his mount close to the pony herd, hat cocked back, a cigarillo dangling from a corner of his mouth. The sight made Remi want to laugh, but he didn't. Although he wasn't actually afraid of either Jake and Clint, there was something about the two young men that intimidated him.

Eli and McClure and Jorge were constructing a fur press when Remi and Jake rode into camp. Eli left the careful fitting of the cottonwood poles to McClure's supervision and came over, grinning broadly when he saw the plews fastened to their pack mules.

"*Qué pasa,* Remi?"

"The days pass, my friend. That is what passes." He dismounted and limped over to the fire, where a pot of coffee sat brewing at the edge of the coals.

"Looks like you and Jake took a fair catch."

"*Oui.* Did not Remi say he would make a trapper out of this one?"

Jake swung down from his pony and started pulling the willow framed pelts off the mules; he grunted at Remi's assessment, but kept on with his work. Remi poured himself a cup of coffee, nodding gratefully as Grass That Burns came forward with some meat.

"*Sacre bleu,*" Remi murmured, accepting the food with a grin and a nod. "Remi thinks he should maybe consider a woman again, eh, Eli?"

"I believe Pierre has his eye on this one," Eli replied.

Remi chuckled. "Ah, that Pierre. He is a horny bastard, no?"

Eli hunkered down nearby. "Any trouble?"

"*Non,* none. The beaver, they are fat and sleek. Twenty-two plews we take this time, plus some otter."

"You're going to make Johnny and the others eat their words, Remi."

"*Oui,*" Remi acknowledged immodestly. He glanced at the plews decorating the camp, the crude press taking shape nearby. "The others have taken much beaver, too, eh?"

"Almost a pack. Not bad for a couple of weeks work."

Remi raised a brow. "And of Pete and Charlie, you have heard . . . ?"

"Nothing," Eli answered, and Remi thought he detected a trace of worry in his voice. It had been over a week now since the Arapahos' attack, and nearly twice that long since anyone had heard from the two freetrappers.

"Maybe soon you will send someone to look?" Remi suggested.

Eli hesitated, then shook his head. "I wouldn't know where to tell 'em to begin. Besides, Pete and Charlie know how to get by on their own hooks. They'll come in when they're ready."

Remi shrugged, but he knew Eli was right. His first year in the mountains, he had partnered with an old hand. The booshway had sent them both out on a scout, and they'd split up to follow the two forks of a river. But only Remi returned. The next day he had gone in search of his partner, but hadn't found a trace, and by the time he got back, the others were ready to pull out. Sometimes the mountains could swallow a man whole, leaving only his memory.

"You make the press?" Remi said.

"I'm thinking it's time to move on. Falls on the Rocks says her people were camped at the forks of the Grand. I want to catch them there if I can, before they move for the winter."

"You will stay long, among the Utes?"

"Three, four days, maybe. Do some trading, then push on."

"Remi has wintered with the Utes before, and they are a good people."

"Figured we'd winter in the Salt Lake country," Eli replied offhandedly. "There ought to be some St. Louis boys up there or on the Snake. Some company will make the winter seem shorter."

Remi shrugged and sipped noisily at his coffee, grimacing as he lowered his cup. "*Sacre bleu!* Pierre! What is this that is watered down like trade whiskey? Surely we do not run out so soon?"

"By *Dieu*, we do," Pierre called from the other side of the camp, where he and Mateo were cutting beaver pelts from their frames in anticipation of pressing them into bales. "Tell Eli, you. Him know."

Eli smiled, sadly, Remi thought. "Figured we'd save the last sack for winter quarters, when everyone can have a share."

"Blah! Remi must have better. This is like mule piss."

"Harder to pack, though," Eli replied mildly.

Remi chuckled grudgingly. "True, but, *enfant de garce*, such hardship. Remi should have stayed in Montreal, no? With the women and the fine wine."

"By *Dieu*, in Montreal they would have hang Remi," Pierre called, laughing.

"But with a silk rope, my friend. Only the finest silk."

Eli laughed and stood. Remi looked up expectantly. "Remi will go back out tomorrow, no?"

"It's up to you," Eli said. "I'll want to put out in a couple of days, but you can catch up."

Remi was silent a moment, considering. Then he said, "*Oui*, I think so, then. Remi will circle wide, trap *beaucoup* beaver, then to *le* forks of *le* Grand? We will meet you there, Jake and Remi."

"*Bueno,*" Eli said. "Sounds good to this child. Just watch your topknot."

"*Oui.* This Remi will do." He took another sip of coffee, then made a face and poured it back in the pot. He would go tell Jake, and they would draw what supplies they would need. They would be out a week this time, maybe longer, traveling through country that was unfamiliar to him, and without the base of a permanent camp to come back to in case of trouble. They would take plenty of supplies this time, he thought, just in case.

The brigade rode northwest along the Grand, picking their way through the sage and greasewood that brushed the stirrups of the mountain men. To their right and far off, Travis could see the dark smudge of pines covering a low mountain range, but nearer there was only scrub piñon and juniper and the harsh red of the land—*colorado,* Mateo called it; red-dirt land.

Although the sun was shining, it was cold, and the wind had a keen edge to it, causing the still-healing flesh of his scalp to throb painfully. They had left the worst of the snow behind when they broke free of the hills that formed the western rim of the Grand Valley, and they had been dropping in elevation ever since—two days now—although there were still patches of it beneath the sage, crusted over and littered with tiny sage needles, shaded with red dust that was like a film of rust.

On their left the Black Canyon was a gash in the piñoned hills, narrow and sheer and coolly dark. Travis had ridden over to see it last night with Clint, Jorge, Old Cal, Johnny, and Consuelo. From its rim the Grand had looked like a purling black and white ribbon, seen only in snatches from above. They had tied their mounts well back from the edge and gone forward on foot, staring into the canyon's depths with something like awe. Travis had been impressed not so much by its size but by its almost foreboding presence. Here, he thought, Satan might dwell. No one spoke as they peered into the canyon, and Old Cal had seemed actually cowed, his expression like that of a frightened child.

Travis was the first to turn away from the canyon. He didn't intend to go back.

Eli was pushing rapidly through the rolling hills. The pace suited Travis just fine, but Old Cal had predictably grumbled. "Gonna kill them ponies, he is," he whined to Travis that morning, jogging alongside on his slat-ribbed mustang, his bare ankles exposed between the tops of his grease-blackened moccasins and the ragged, muddy hems of his leather trousers, swaying in huge Mexican stirrups, apparently immune to the cold. "Do ye hyar, boy? Man's got no sense, pushing like he does."

Travis didn't answer, and pretty soon the old trapper had drifted up to Cork-Eye's side, his reedy, complaining voice carrying back to him on the gusting breeze. The trouble with Old Cal, Travis decided as he watched the old man's hunched, bobbing shoulders, was that his protests were too often rooted in a degree of truth, or at least close enough to make a man worry. Eli *was* pushing the wounded stock hard, as if fretting he wouldn't get all that he wanted to accomplish finished before the deep cold of winter set in. He was a man driven, all right, but Travis was still inclined to put his faith in Eli above Old Cal, whom he suspected would have found fault in Utopia.

By nightfall the depression that hid the Black Canyon had dropped from sight in the southwest. Eli was cutting cross-country now, following a faintly definable trail that had seemed to appear from nowhere; a shortcut, Travis surmised. They hauled up in a shallow bowl and set about making camp. Travis unsaddled Blue and turned him over to Jorge, then went to help Clint construct a breastworks from the packs. Afterward, while Pierre and the two squaws set meat to roasting over a greasewood fire, Travis climbed a nearby hill to watch the light drain out of the sky. The size of the country and the unbelievable distances that could be seen in the thin evening air humbled him even more than the Black Canyon. He stared at the far rim of the horizon and wondered how many days, or weeks, it would take just to reach that one point. How many deep canyons slashed that arid land? How many jagged peaks and rocky mesas blocked the way? Coming West, he had never imagined anything like this.

Clint came up behind him, his rifle held across his chest. He squatted nearby and let his breath out gustily. "Big, isn't it?" he said, as if reading Travis's thoughts.

"Looks like you could just about drop Arkansas in the middle of it and never know it was there," Travis agreed.

Clint laughed softly and made himself more comfortable. "When

I was small I sailed from New Orleans to Tampa Bay, in Florida. This reminds me of the Gulf of Mexico. It's as if there's no end to it."

"You've been to New Orleans?"

"Yes, several times."

Travis shook his head. "I headed there once, but never made it. Is it true they got dancing girls there that don't hardly wear a stitch of clothing?"

"There's just about any kind of perversity a person might crave in New Orleans," Clint said. "It's a strange and wonderful city."

Travis mulled the word *perversity* over in his mind for a few minutes and decided he liked the implications, even if he didn't fully understand the meaning. He couldn't think of anything in Hanging Creek Falls that might qualify as an actual perversity, unless it was the tales they used to tell about New Orleans, down at Mitchell's Mercantile.

"You and I have first watch tonight," Clint told him. "As soon as it's fully dark."

Travis glanced at Clint. There was a difference in him of late, a strengthening that would be hard to describe, yet was as obvious as the red dirt under his feet. It had started sometime during the battle with the Arapahos and had been growing steadily ever since, as if being shut off from Jake's constant bickering had allowed him to find something new within himself. It made Travis smile to see it.

"How's your head?" Clint asked.

Travis winced unconsciously. The war club's blow had knocked him senseless for a couple of days, but he felt all right now except for an occasional headache and a persistent itching where his flesh was starting to heal. He reached up to touch the scab, then shrugged. "It's fine. I don't hardly notice it anymore."

Clint shook his head, looking back the way they had come that day. "I never would have expected this. It's still hard to believe sometimes. My father wanted me to be an attorney, you know. Instead I ended up out here, fighting Indians and sleeping in the snow."

"So why did you come?"

"You know the answer to that. I came to take care of Jake, try to keep him out of trouble." He shook his head. "Chances are I threw my life away because of him."

"What's to keep you from going back?"

"Jake killed a man back in Louisiana. It wasn't the first time Jake's killed, but this guy was unarmed. It was pure murder, Travis, but my family didn't want to see him hang. It was Jake's idea to come out here. I would have preferred the East Coast, where I could pursue my schooling, but . . . I don't know. No one in our family ever had much luck arguing with Jake."

"No," Travis said thoughtfully. "I reckon I can see that." Then he gave Clint a considering look. "But I noticed you ain't had as much trouble of late."

"Times change," Clint said. He stood as if to leave, then paused with his gaze on the fading horizon. "Jake doesn't like you. I guess you know that."

"Jake doesn't like anyone that I noticed."

"No, but he says he's going to kill you."

"Huh!"

"Jake is like a steam engine. Every so often he has to blow off some anger, otherwise he'd explode. He's getting that way now. I saw it the last time he and Remi came in. And he's been simmering over that mule ever since the del Norte. It's none of my business anymore, but if I were you, I'd watch my back. Jake is mean, right down to the core. Sooner or later he'll challenge you over that mule. When he does, you'd best be ready to kill. It's the only thing that'll stop him."

"Jesus, Clint."

"Yeah," Clint responded dryly. "It's a hell of a note." He hefted his rifle to the crook of his arm. "It's getting dark. I'll take the south side of camp, and you can have this side." He walked off, disappearing in the deepening shadows. Travis remained where he was, facing the west where the sun had long since sunk, its afterglow staining the horizon like a splash of fresh blood.

Remi gave the paint her head as she navigated the twisting, rocky path. Perhaps a hundred feet below his left stirrup he could see the stream that was his destination, slow-moving at this late season, but deep in its pools, with yellowing grass and a handful of bastard maples lining its banks. Overhead, the sky was a deep violet-blue band capping the canyon's walls, unmarked save for the tiny speck of a hawk wheeling on an updraft. A few stunted piñon leaned out from the canyon's rims, looking more black than green against the bright sky.

It was a strange country in which to look for beaver, but, *sacre,* who would have guessed? In the middle of barrenness they had found paradise.

Remi wasn't sure exactly where he and Jake were, but that was all right. He had found his way into this maze of canyons and mesas, and he would find his way out when the time came. What mattered was the brown gold they had discovered in these sluggish waters, never before trapped. *Enfant de garce,* but they were taking the plews—six and eight a day, mostly, and no end in sight.

The paint's left foreleg slipped suddenly, and she jerked back with a frightened whinny. Remi's heart slammed into his throat as his shoulder and knee slammed into the side of the canyon's wall.

"Sacre bleu," he murmured, but let it go at that. Far below, the stones the paint had kicked loose were just splashing into a shallow pond.

They reached the bottom and Remi stopped at the stream's edge, lifting his gaze to the snaking ribbon of trail that had brought him down from the canyon's rim. He felt a nagging dread at the thought of going back up, but shoved it aside.

He turned downcanyon, whistling now, his eyes twinkling in the cool breeze. He was happy to be alone again, free of Jake's moodiness, his smoldering anger. *Hijo de puta,* he thought in Spanish; had he known Jake would react so violently to such a small prank he would have saved it for another—Travis, perhaps, who was quiet but not so touchy. But Remi had been as lonesome for laughter as he had been for conversation, and when he spotted Jake shivering in the cold wind last night he had been unable to resist.

"You should find a stone to take to your blankets," Remi offered.

Jake immediately looked up, face pinched with suspicion.

"Oui," Remi went on innocently. "Remi has done this many times. Warm *le roche* in the fire and take it to your robes. It is like a little stove, no?"

"It'd burn," Jake said doubtfully.

"Non! Do not let it get so hot. Warm, yes. Very warm, so that it lasts, but not hot."

"How come you haven't done it yet?"

Remi grinned sarcastically. "Because Remi is tougher than you, young one."

Remi feared he had lost him then, but Jake lacked the stubbornness of someone like Travis, and after several minutes of silence, Jake said, "Just warm it up in the fire, huh?"

"At the edge of the fire," Remi corrected. And then he set his hook. "Use a stone from the river, one that has been underwater."

"Why?"

Simplicity, Remi warned himself. "This Remi does not know. It will . . ." he spread his hands, "radiate. That is the word, no?" He had to bite the inside of his lip to hold back his grin. "Radiate. *Oui,* that is the word Remi seeks."

So Jake fetched his stone from the river, an oblong, porous black rock about the size of a loaf of bread, and placed it on the coals. Remi watched the stone soberly while Jake fixed himself a second cup of coffee from his private stores. When he judged that the time was close, he stood and announced that he was going to bed. "You let *le roche* warm up good," he told Jake. "It will be cold from the water, and will take a long time the first time. Like a woman, no?" When Jake nodded his understanding, Remi went to his robes, cocooning himself within its thick, shaggy protection. He pulled the robe over his head, leaving only a narrow gap through which to view the outcome of his ruse.

It took a little longer than he had anticipated, but after half an hour or so the stone popped once, sharply, and Jake's head jerked up. Before he could react further, the stone exploded like a bomb, showering the camp with chips of rock. Jake squawked and fell backward, legs flapping. His coffee cup soared into the air, showering him with the dark, hot liquid as he flailed like a turtle on its back. Remi laughed so hard tears came to his eyes, but then Jake came up like a wolf gone mad, clawing for his pistol.

Sacre, he thought, that had been close. He had scrambled free of his robes at the last second, grabbing a piece of firewood as he came up and knocking the pistol away just as it belched its lethal charge. The ball ricocheted harmlessly down canyon, and for a moment they had stood unmoving, hunched and glaring, breathing hard in their anger. "You should go to your blankets now," he told the trembling youth. "Before Remi forgets that he is the professor, and cuts your throat."

"I'm going to kill you for that," Jake rasped.

"Remi does not think so. Remi thinks you are a coward. It takes bravery to kill another."

"You can go to hell," Jake shouted, but he had jabbed his pistol back in his belt, then grabbed his blankets and stalked into the darkness, his face a mask of fiery hatred.

Remi slept with one eye open last night, and saddled his horse before dawn, leaving camp before Jake returned. He sighed now, guiding the paint downstream. "Remi will have to watch that one closely," he said aloud.

He made his first set a quarter mile downstream, in a still pool rimmed with soggy yellow leaves, then moved on leisurely, making three more sets within the next couple of hours. Finished, he rode on out of curiosity. The canyon was narrow but flat-bottomed, stippled with small, dark pools that were like opaque jewels. Coarse river grass grew along the shelves of sandy loam, and from time to time he passed meager groves of cottonwood or box elder. It was quiet in the canyon. No breeze stirred, and the sound of the stream was a bare murmur. It was a peaceful setting, yet unaccountably, Remi began to glance over his shoulder. A feeling of uneasiness came over him. He scanned the canyon's rims, seeing nothing but sky and piñon and sloping rock. Yet the feeling persisted, and after a time he gave it up and turned back, suddenly anxious to get out of the canyon, to see horizons that a man couldn't hit with a rock.

He had returned nearly to his last set when the paint stopped suddenly and threw her head up. She whinnied nervously, nostrils flaring wide. Remi lifted his fusil, curling his thumb around the hammer. His dark eyes darted along the canyon's rims, then probed the shadows along the steep, crumbling walls, but nothing stirred.

"What is it, *mon cheri?*" he asked the paint gently. He touched her with his heels, and they moved forward again, but the mare was spooked, and she kept pulling at the reins, constantly wanting to trot. Remi's uneasiness grew. He told himself that it was only a critter—a bear or a catamount—but his fear argued that it wasn't bear country and that he had seen precious little sign of deer, vital to a mountain lion's diet.

"So what does that leave?" he asked himself.

Jake, his mind answered.

"*Non,* this Remi does not believe." But deep down, he wasn't so certain. Jake was violent; he was angry; and he was a coward. It was a dangerous combination.

Remi was in sight of the trail leading out of the canyon when the paint spooked again, jumping so violently he nearly lost his seat. "*Bastard!*" he shrieked, jerking the mare back harshly. "*Hijo de puta.*"

The paint was trembling now, and Remi muttered grimly, "No, this cannot be Jake."

They started up the narrow trail, the muzzle of Remi's smoothbore pointing the way. The paint was still skittish, bringing her hooves up high and setting them down daintily, swinging her hips nervously on the narrow path. Remi cursed her and told her to mind the trail. They were maybe thirty feet above the canyon's floor when he saw a piece of the cliff above him detach itself, streaking like a tawny comet across the blue sky, screaming shrilly—a mountain lion after all, Remi saw. He should have known, but by then it was too late. The paint reared and threw herself away from the lion. Remi saw the emptiness beneath him, the canyon floor rushing upward, and then there was an explosion of sand and water and pain. . . .

He came awake once, in the early shadows of sundown, and saw Jake standing silently atop the canyon's rim, peering down. He tried to raise his arm, to shout, but it was as if he were paralyzed, capable only of staring until the scene finally blurred and darkness returned.

CHAPTER TWENTY-SEVEN

They spotted the smoke first, a dozen twisting gray threads that appeared to hang motionless in the pale winter sky. Climbing a low rise, Eli saw the forks of the Grand and Uncompahgre rivers perhaps a mile below, coming together in a swampy bottomland grown over with rushes and alders. Situated between the two rivers was a sprawling grove of cottonwoods, their arching limbs stripped by the season. Brown leather tipis dotted the landscape like smoky thumbprints. Tiny figures in buckskins and bright trade cloths tracked between the lodges. To the north of the village a pony herd of several hundred animals grazed under the watchful eyes of young guards.

Grass That Burns was jabbering excitedly to Pierre as they came up the rise, her white teeth flashing like moonlight in her round, coppery face. Falls on the Rocks, Eli noticed, seemed considerably more subdued, and he couldn't help noticing the way she kept glancing at him with almost wistful resignation. She had kept her distance since the flare-up between him and Consuelo, as he had to her, but the young Indian woman's interest had been plain to them all.

Eli halted the brigade on top of the rise so that they were skylined to the tribe below, easily recognized. After the Arapahos' surprise raid, he figured the Utes would be jumpy at best, and he didn't want the brigade mistaken for skulking renegades. Even though he was certain their visit would be welcomed by the Utes, and especially so with the women and children they were returning, such an error in protocol could lead to hard feelings among the Utes and affect the outcome of their trade.

There was a commotion at the village, a sudden quickening of activity. Like a pond emptying through a ruptured levee, the pony herd began to flow toward the river and the protection of the bottoms close to the village.

"We've been spotted," Johnny said.

"So it appears," Eli observed laconically. He glanced at Johnny, then the others, lifting a brow in inquiry.

"This hoss ain't fer lettin' an Injun out-Injun a white man," Old Cal replied to Eli's unspoken question. "Lead out. This chile'll set to with ye."

"*Bueno!*" Johnny exclaimed, grinning broadly. On the flats just below the village, thirty or forty Indians rode out of the trees and formed a defensive line.

Eli spoke to Mateo in rapid-fire Spanish, and Mateo whipped his little mouse-colored gelding back toward the remuda, shouting for Clint and Jorge to tighten the gather. Eli trotted his sorrel down off the rise to the flat, sage-furred plain that separated them from the Utes. The others followed, fanning out to either side. The Indians were coming toward them now, trotting their ponies, and Eli whooped and slapped his stirrups against the sorrel's barrel. The brigade broke into a run, yelling, shouting, charging toward the on-coming Utes in a pounding wave. And the Utes, their distant howls barely audible above the thunder of hooves, also lifted their ponies into a run. Like a pair of blunt battering rams, the two groups converged.

It was a traditional form of rendezvous, long established among the western tribes—mock warfare designed to show strength and courage, and through that, peaceful intentions. Like crude, rough-housing children, they came together in a swirl of red dust and hoarse shouts—whirling and ebbing and pulling apart again, calling back and forth in an polyglot of Spanish, Ute, and English as they turned toward the village, slowing now, laughing, exchanging greet-ings, expressing joy over the return of the women and children. Eli brought his mount close to a patchy red and white mustang and reached out to shake the hand of the stocky, bowlegged chief who rode it. Old Bowlegs was laughing and joking, but he was telling Eli also that it was good that they were here, that the Utes were glad to see the white trappers. They had furs to trade, and yes, horses and mules, if the mountain men wanted them. But first they would feast and catch up on the news of the mountains. There would be dancing and singing, and the trappers would be welcomed by their friends, the Utes.

Drums beat a steady, mesmerizing cadence outside the thinly-scraped hide walls of Bowlegs' tipi, a primitive pulse that reached into a man's gut and pulled out the things he foolishly thought civi-lization had long since buried. Its rhythmic throbbing strummed an-cient chords, stirred primal feelings. Like the heady rush of Taos Lightning, or the mind-fogging sensation of peyote, used by some of the southern tribes in their religious ceremonies, it made a man feel stronger and more alive than anything he might experience in the day-to-day monotony of business and responsibility. It could, Eli de-cided, almost make a man forget St. Louis and the trappings of pros-perity a partnership in the GS&T might bring him.

Unexpectedly, his thoughts swung to Falls on the Rocks, her lithe, dusky beauty, her willing smile. It had been a long time since he had taken an Indian woman to his robes, not since before Consuelo had come into his life with her brassy, smoke-husky voice, and her straightforward approach to life. The unintentional comparison gave Eli a start, and he blinked and brought his mind back to the business at hand.

He was sitting near the rear of Bowlegs's lodge, on the old chief's right. On his own right and continuing around to the oval door opposite him sat Silas McClure, Old Cal, Johnny, and Pierre. On Bowlegs's left sat a number of subchiefs—Horses Running, and Sees Tomorrow, the village shaman, whom Eli remembered from earlier visits—as well as some new faces. There was a potbellied old man with gaping teeth called Yellowfoot; a young, hot-eyed warrior named Breaks Their Necks; and a sober-faced middle-aged Shoshone, Sad Smiling Man.

Bowlegs's lodge was small. With twelve men crowded inside the tiny, ten-hide tipi, it was hot and close, the air pungent with the odor of grease and smoke and sweat. Despite Bowlegs's offer to share the lodges of the Utes, Eli had ordered the trappers to set up a separate camp at the eastern edge of the village. He had them put up the tent for the trade goods, but let the young men of the village take their stock out with the main pony herd. They kept only a couple of saddle horses and some of the wounded stock close by, where Mateo could watch them personally. Bowlegs had sent his invitation to eat and smoke the pipe that afternoon, as Eli expected, a ritual both religious and social, and one that he had sat through many times in the past.

It was Sees Tomorrow, keeper of the pipe and tribal medicine man, who led them through the ceremony. He withdrew a wine-colored pipestone bowl and a long cherrywood stem from an otter-skin case and carefully, lovingly, fit the two pieces together. From a quilled buckskin pouch he took a pinch of kinnikinnick—a mixture of tobacco, willow bark, sage, and other ingredients, depending on Sees Tomorrow's medicine—and dribbled it into the bowl. He repeated the procedure several times until the bowl was filled and packed to his satisfaction, then with a pair of silver tongs likely traded from the Spanish, he lit the pipe with a coal from the fire.

It was quiet inside the lodge. All eyes were fixed intently upon Sees Tomorrow's broad, lined face as he laboriously pulled the kinnikinnick's smoke through the long stem. Eli wasn't a religious man himself, but he was often moved by the native rituals he observed, and occasionally disturbed by the many similarities between the tenets of the various Indian tribes and the Old World Christianity he had grown up with. Were there that many differences between the Virgin Mary and White-Painted Lady, of the Apache, or the parables of the Old Testament and the oral legends of the trickster, Coyote? Had the world once been destroyed by flood, as related not only in the King James Bible, but in so many Native American stories as well? Eli found such parallels humbling, yet they also infused him with a certain amount of assurance. He had long ago turned away from the Protestant church and its restricting dogma, preferring to believe as the Indians did, that God dwelled everywhere.

Sees Tomorrow lowered the pipe. A thin curl of smoke still dribbled from the mouthpiece as he pointed it away from him, toward the lodge door but canted slightly upward. In a soft, intoning voice, he began his prayer. He offered the pipe first to the East, where the Sun arose each day bringing new life. He offered it to the South, the source of warmth, of gentle summer breezes, and of life-giving rains. Then to the West, where the Sun sank each night, older and wiser, after imparting those blessings on all it left behind. He offered the mouthpiece to the North, where the cold winds of winter originated, creating strength and endurance, and bringing with it death, which was part of life. Then he lifted the pipe above his head, offering it to the Sky and the Creator who lived there, and Who made all things beautiful. And finally, he lowered the stem, offering smoke to the Mother that was Earth, who nourished all things and gave them life—the plants and animals, and even the rocks and soil and water, for these were all a part of life's cycle. He gave thanks for these things, and asked that the Four Directions and Sky and Mother Earth receive them on the sacred smoke he offered.

Finished, Sees Tomorrow carefully cradled the pipe in his lap, and with a pick fashioned from the leg bone of a turkey, scraped the dottle from the bowl. He refilled it without hurry and relit it, then passed it on to Bowlegs, who would repeat the process, though substituting his own prayer toward the four directions and earth and sky. After Bowlegs the pipe would be passed to Eli, who would follow the example of Bowlegs and Sees Tomorrow, reciting his prayer in English, though, so that McClure, who had never sat through a pipe ceremony before, might repeat it without offense. After McClure the pipe would be passed back to Horses Running, and from there to Yellowfoot, Breaks Their Necks, and Sad Smiling Man, before returning to Old Cal, Johnny, and Pierre. Eli glanced through the smoke hole overhead, noting the softening of the day's light. It would be an hour or two before full dark enveloped the land, but that long at least before the smoking was completed. Then one of Bowlegs's wives would enter with food she was preparing even now, and they would eat, and afterward Bowlegs would want to talk. He would be curious about their battle with the Arapahos, and the rescue (as it had become known) of the squaws and two children. He would want to know what news Eli brought with him from the Spanish settlements, and of rumor, too. What had the Arapahos, the Pawnees, the Cheyennes, and the Comanches been up to this year? How had the buffalo hunters fared on the *llano estacado,* and what traders had come out from the Missouri settlements? He would want to know it all, everything that had happened in the lands to the east and south that might somehow, someday, affect his people.

And Eli would tell him. It was understood. He would relate not the long hours of fear and waiting under the hot sun, holed up like rabbits by the Arapahos, but of how, even outnumbered, they had attacked the Arapahos, saving the lives of four members of Bowlegs's village and driving their enemies over the mountains. He would tell him how they had done this for their friends, the Utes, so that they might come and trade in peace. He would also tell the old chief what he knew of the activities of the Arapahos, the Cheyennes, and the Comanches. He would recount Pete and Charlie's battle with the Pawnees, and of Annie's exploding fowler, anticipating broad smiles at the Pawnee Killer's good fortune in rubbing out so many shaved-heads with one shot. He would tell him that the buffalo hunters—the *ciboleros,* Mateo's own kin, perhaps—had made a successful hunt along the Canadian and Palo Duro. He would tell him also of the buyout between Alexander Henry and William Ashley and the new firm of Smith, Jackson, and Sublette. He would add what he knew of the new outfits, and new men, penetrating the rugged mountains surrounding the Utes' homeland. And through it all, he would emphasize trade—the furs and buckskins they wanted, and the horses they needed. It was why they had come. It was understood.

And still the amenities wouldn't be finished, although by that time the hour would be late and the white trappers' knees would be cramped and screaming from sitting cross-legged for so many hours. Yet there were things Eli wanted to know, too, and despite the long, dragging hours yet to come, he would be eager to learn what the old chief knew. It would be Eli's way of discovering what faced them yet, what the Shoshones and Bannocks and Blackfeet had been up to, and where the St. Louis trappers—Smith, Jackson, and Sublette— had sent their brigades. And maybe, if he were lucky, he would learn what Bowlegs knew of the Reed Massacre, and discover if Big Tom Reed had passed this way. Was he ahead of them now, or had he gone around as Eli had gambled he would, working his way up the Colorado, the Virgin, and the Ashley rivers?

It would be a long night, but hopefully a fruitful one. Resolutely, Eli accepted the pipe from Sees Tomorrow and set to it.

It was snowing. At first Remi thought it was his eyes—that the white, bobbing flakes were some configuration of his pain—but as time passed he became aware of the growing numbness in his fingers and cheeks, the unfamiliar wetness on his eyelashes. Only his leg was truly warm, burning with an inner fire that reminded him of clamps pulled from a blacksmith's forge and fastened around his ankle. Sharp, driving bolts of agony throbbed up his right leg to explode in his groin.

He dragged a hand to his face and rubbed weakly at his eyes. He felt confused, his senses scrambled. Only fragments of memory remained—the fall, and the scream that might have been his own or the mountain lion's, then the eruption of blackness that had swallowed him like a bottomless maw. He vaguely remembered calling for Jake, and turned his gaze on the canyon's rim. It was empty, blurred by his own tearing eyes and the jittery passage of snow. Yet the image persisted, and Remi felt a deep, faint stirring of anger. Had Jake stood there, staring callously down at him, or was that only a figment of his muddled imagination? Remi stared at the canyon's periphery for a long time, his features as cold as the wind that whipped his cheeks with tiny grains of sand. "*Sacre bleu,*" he said at last. "Remi thinks maybe he will have to kill that one."

He chuckled then, a dry, raspy sound, like a dull file drawn over a horse's hoof. He suspected he would not kill anyone for a while, and that maybe he would die himself. He was in a bad spot, and if Jake had really abandoned him here, then maybe he was in the worst spot he had ever been in.

He twisted to his side, sucking his breath in at the quick, white-hot stab of pain that racked his leg. In spite of the cold, sweat popped out across his forehead. His leg throbbed steadily. *Enfant de garce,* he thought, then shifted to English; *son of a bitch.* He blinked away the sweat that ran into his eyes, gritting his teeth. He knew he could die easily here, without dignity, and shook his head fiercely. *"Non,"* he said. "Remi will not go under like this, like some turtle flipped onto its back."

He pulled himself into a sitting position, leaning back on his hands and tipping his face to the falling snow until the pain abated a little. It was when he looked down the length of his body that true fear finally pierced his consciousness. His right leg, the one he had injured jumping his paint over the breastworks during the battle with the Arapahos, was swollen to at least twice its normal size, stretching the old buckskin of his trousers leg tautly. His ankle, visible between the trousers' hem and the top of his moccasin, looked black.

"Ah," he breathed softly, turning his face to the sky, to the prodding flakes of snow and the intruding cold. "Gangrene, eh? Maybe so." He took a moment to absorb the full implications of his injury, to let the fear come surging through his mind, to feel weak and helpless and alone, and then, with a Herculean effort of will, he pushed it all aside. Suddenly, the ankle didn't matter anymore. A single thought penetrated his brain, and he grasped for it in desperation. He would kill Jake Orr.

"Oui," he whispered into the deep, cold silence. "That one Remi owes."

It was after dark before Eli returned to camp. Most of the mountain men were still visiting among the Utes, talking with old friends, doing a little trading on their own; not a few were busy courting the unattached women of the village. Silas McClure and Pierre Turpin were inside the trade goods tent, taking inventory after three long days of trading. Their shadows, illuminated by the light of a tin candle lantern, were etched sharply against the green and white panels of canvas as they progressed methodically through the bundles and crates. Travis and Mateo were standing guard between the wounded remuda, tied among the trees along the river, and the tent. At the fire only Consuelo was up, sitting with a robe drawn over her shoulders and staring pensively into the crackling flames. Eli flopped down opposite her, yawning. He felt tired after the day's trading, but satisfied;

it was his contentment that allowed him to relax, to let his muscles go limp and his lids to droop.

Consuelo eyed him through the dancing flames. "You are late. Have you eaten yet?"

"Yes, at Bowlegs's lodge."

"How goes the trading?"

"Almost finished," he answered. Over the past few days he and McClure had garnered nearly three packs of prime furs—beaver, otter, fisher, mink, and marten. They had also bartered for thirty beautifully tanned deer and bighorn sheep skins, plus several tanned pelts of badger and wolf. They had been lucky to find old Bowlegs's village, luckier still that no other traders had visited the Utah camp this season. The Utes were eager to trade, willing to spend a little more for a little less this time around. Despite the calamities that had befallen the outfit since putting out, Eli felt a sense of hope for the success of the brigade that he hadn't experienced since arriving in Taos from St. Louis.

"When do we leave?" Consuelo asked.

"Soon, I reckon. A few more days at the most. The biggest part of the trading is finished, but they'll have held their best skins back until the last, waiting until the prices have been established. They'll start bringing their good stuff out tomorrow, wanting even more."

"Will you give it?"

"Yes. It's the way it's been done for countless generations." He shook his head in wonder. "People like Old Cal, Pete, Charlie, they think we're the first. I guess I was like that for a while, myself. But look around, Connie, the old ruins, the irrigation systems west of Sante Fe. The first piece of New Mexican turquoise I ever saw was dug up from an Indian burial mound back in Ohio. You see abalone shells all over the plains. Hell, the pipe we smoked out of our first night here, old Sees Tomorrow's medicine pipe, came from the Great Lakes region. You ever wonder how it got here? Or what kind of trade routes existed before the Europeans arrived, so that that piece of turquoise could get to Ohio? I was just a kid when Lewis and Clark got back from the Pacific, but I remember my father and his friends talking about it, and the thing that stuck in my mind was that, all the way out, they kept running into trade goods from other lands." He laughed then, shaking his head. "Anyway, yeah, I've kept the prices low so far in anticipation of the Utes holding back their best skins. That's a little trick I learned the hard way."

Consuelo leaned forward, lifting the back of her hand for emphasis. "See, Eli. You *are* different. Only you would think of such things, or wonder about them, and want to know more. Who else but you would give more than a passing thought to turquoise or pipestone?"

"Oh, I reckon most of the boys have wondered about those things at one time or another."

"Wondered about it, yes, but not like you, Eli. They look, but they do not see or question. You are different, yet you are afraid to acknowledge that difference, afraid to see yourself as you truly are. You want to be one of the boys, but you know you will never be like them. You will never be content to live the life of a mountain man or a—" Consuelo's mouth snapped shut, severing her appraisal of him in midsentence. She leaned back with something like shock on her face, and her hand dropped like a bird shot out of the sky. There had been, Eli thought, a trace of pride in her voice as she spoke of the differences that separated him from the others, a hint of tenderness in her expression, but that changed completely in the time it took her hand to fall to her lap.

"Pierre has taken the squaw, Grass That Burns, as his wife," Consuelo said, changing the subject so completely it took Eli a moment to catch up. "Once I would have said she was foolish to marry a cook," she continued, "but now I am not so sure. I hear them in their robes at night, and I can tell you that she is happy."

"That will wear out in time."

"Maybe sooner than she realizes," she replied, her voice hardening. "Clint Orr has also taken a squaw, a young one who is yet skinny and climbs in trees like a little girl."

"I know," Eli replied. "He came to me for an advance on his wages so he could buy some blankets and such."

"Her name is White Feather, and she has never been with a man before. Especially a white man, a trapper. She does not know what they are like. She does not know that when Clint tires of her he will probably discard her like a worn-out moccasin. Or trade her off to another."

Eli shrugged uncomfortably. "I don't know. I'm beginning to think Clint might be cut from a different bolt of cloth than his brother."

"He is an American," Consuelo said flatly, "and a male."

Eli's eyes narrowed in anger. "I was beginning to think you might appreciate being discarded, or traded off, you being so dissatisfied with the way things are now."

"It is not me who is dissatisfied, Eli. Once you were proud of this brigade and what it meant to you. But now your pride withers, and I have not decided yet whether it is failure that you fear most, or success."

She was like a buffalo, Eli decided out of the blue, quick and sure-footed, able to change directions in the blink of an eye. Only a few moments before she had praised his intelligence, his probing curiosity; now her words lashed him like the sting of a whip. Yet at the same time it occurred to him that there was some truth in what she said. Once he had felt a brightness for the future that had shimmered before him like sheets of gold, but time and a traitor's sabotage had dulled that vision to tarnished brass. Was it possible to fear success as much as he did failure? It was new thought, and he turned it over curiously in his mind. Failure, he mused, even a failure caused by events beyond his control, would potentially wipe away many of the doubts that now clouded his future. It could destroy his hopes for a partnership with the GS&T, thus allowing him the freedom to ignore ambition if that was what he wanted to do, and settle down to the uncomplicated life of a hunter. For the first time he began to see the allure of defeat, to wonder if it would be as bad as he had once imagined . . . or as simple as he now thought.

Consuelo laughed softly at the concentrated look on Eli's face. She said, "You ought to smoke that cigar before it falls apart from your constant handling."

Eli looked at the crumbling cigar, and a smile twitched at the corners of his mouth. The tension around the fire seemed to evaporate, like a summer's dew sucked from the land by a thirsty sun. Putting the cigar back in its pouch, he said, "I've only got a few left. I reckon I'll save them for later." He lifted his face to the mantle of limbs overhead, reflected in the yellow-gold light of the fire. The sprinkling of stars above the trees reminded him of bits of frost, and the cold weather yet to come. There was a storm approaching from the south. He had watched it build that afternoon, the deep, slate-colored clouds rolling slowly forward, blotting out the horizon by sundown. Sniffing the southerly breeze, he thought he could detect its moist fragrance even now, an ominous presence still lurking far to the south, but coming, inevitably coming.

"You can feel it," Consuelo said softly, watching Eli's face. "More cold, more snow. This time I think that winter will come for good."

"*Jefe.*"

Eli looked up. Mateo's voice came from just beyond the circle of firelight, edged with warning. "Someone approaches."

Picking up his rifle, Eli walked out to Mateo's side. "Where?" he asked.

"There." Mateo pointed south with his chin. "He comes slow, like the wolf that fears the trap. Travis has gone for a closer look."

They walked down to the river, stepping behind a clump of alders where they couldn't be silhouetted by firelight. Eli couldn't see anything in the darkness, but he trusted Mateo's judgment. Footsteps sounded behind them, and McClure appeared at their side, his ruddy cheeks stubbled, eyes narrowed. "Now what?" he asked brusquely.

"That's what we're about to find out," Eli replied.

At that moment Travis's voice rang out from downstream. "It's Jake. Jake's come in."

"Jake?" Mateo echoed.

"Just Jake?" McClure asked, puzzled.

Travis came into view, leading a string of pack animals. Behind him, sitting small and hunched in the saddle, came Jake. His face was reddened by the wind, and a fever blister oozed pus from his upper lip. He gave Eli a surly look as he rode up, but didn't speak.

"Hello, Jake. Where's Remi?" Eli asked.

"He ain't comin'," Jake replied sullenly, his gaze shifting challengingly between Eli and McClure.

"He is hungry and cold, Eli," Consuelo said from behind him. "Bring him to the fire. There is coffee left, and some stew left over from supper. You can talk to him after he has eaten."

Jake's eyes flitted past Eli, and he licked his lower lip hungrily. Eli's anger flared suddenly. "He ain't a kid, Consuelo. I don't reckon he needs a mother."

Consuelo's voice held a bitter note as she replied. "Half of this brigade are children. Look around you, Eli. Mateo, Travis, Jake. All barely old enough to shave. They should be home, with their own mothers, their own families."

Mateo gave a short snort of laughter, but the others remained silent. Eli studied Jake closely. The youth appeared subdued, beaten down by cold and fear and loneliness. It occurred to Eli that Jake was slowly crumbling with the passing weeks, even as his brother grew stronger and more confident. He wouldn't last long in the mountains. His kind might thrive in cities, or more civilized lands, but they lacked the fortitude to brave the unpopulated wilderness. Jake, Eli realized, was used to feeding off others, like a scavenger. Forced by the independence of the mountain men to rely only upon himself, he was slowly starving.

"The hell with it," Eli said abruptly. "Come on up to the fire."

Jake gigged his horse toward the camp, while Mateo led the pack animals to the remuda. The mules, Eli noted, were well-laden with plews. McClure had also observed the full packs, and he gave Eli a searching glance before the two men walked away from the river.

Pierre had built up the fire, and Jake slid from his horse and flopped beside it. Consuelo draped a buffalo robe over his shoulders, then stood back as Pierre dished up a plate of stew. "Food first, no?" Pierre announced, studying Jake's slumped form. "Then *le* coffee, with maybe whiskey a little, no?" He glanced questioningly at Eli.

"No," Eli said. "Food and coffee, but we ain't flashing whiskey around an Indian camp." He squatted on the balls of his feet, resting his elbows across his knees. His gaze was hard as he looked at Jake, filled with impatience. "Tell it," he ordered bluntly. "Where's Remi?"

Jake shrugged without taking his eyes off the stew as it was spooned into a plate. "Nothing to tell. Remi fell off a ledge and was killed. I came on by myself."

"Remi fell?" Eli felt a twinge of doubt, but held it in.

"That's what I said," Jake snapped, glaring suddenly at Eli across the dancing flames of the fire.

"Where?"

"I don't know. Not for sure. Somewhere southwest of the Black Canyon. There's a lot of canyons back there, and we found some beaver in a couple of them. LeBlanc wanted to trap them out before we came on. One night he didn't come back, so I went to hunt for him. I found him at the bottom of a ledge. He was dead, so I buried him and came on."

"Goddamn!" Travis said softly.

The others had fallen silent, and for a couple of minutes there was only the popping and cracking of the fire as Eli weighed Jake's story. Something about it bothered him, something about *Jake* bothered him, but he supposed that had been true since their second day on the trail. Jake was an odd fish, no doubt about that, but Eli found it hard to believe that he was capable of theft. Nor could he envision him striking out on his own through such a desolate country unless he was forced to. And Remi was reckless, Eli cautioned himself, always taking chances, pushing his luck. It was only a matter of time before such behavior caught up with him. "*Bueno,*" he said finally, heavily. "I reckon you did all you could. Welcome back."

Jake's voice took on a sulking quality. "It's been snowing all the way. I'd ride out of it for a while, then it would catch up again. It's been hell, but I didn't stop or abandon the furs. They're mine, Cutler. I didn't trap all of them, but I brought them in." The self-pity disappeared behind a look of angry defiance. He glowered at Eli, refusing to acknowledge the stew Pierre held out for him.

"I never said they weren't," Eli replied. He looked at McClure. "It's fair. They were partners. Credit whatever Jake brought in this trip to his account."

McClure nodded without reply, but he was obviously uneasy, as if Jake's story had struck him as a little too abrupt, too. Jake took the plate Pierre offered him and dug into it greedily. Broth ran freely down his wind-burned chin, but he didn't bother to wipe it away. Eli stood, the heaviness of Remi's death coming over him in a slow-moving wave. "Well," he said, staring over Jake's head to where the lodges of the Utes glowed warmly. "For every man who gets rubbed out by a brownskin, another falls off a ledge or drowns crossing a river. Remi LeBlanc was a good man, and a good friend. I hate to hear of him going under like that."

"What do we do now?" McClure asked.

"We go on, Silas. Same as always."

"To the Salt Lake country?"

"Yeah," he said quietly. "To the Salt Lake country."

CHAPTER TWENTY-EIGHT

Remi's death affected them all in subtle ways. The old hands, those who had already trapped a season or two with the tough little French-Canadian, took it hardest, although it would have been difficult to tell by an outsider. Death was a constant companion in the mountains, a lady they had all courted on many occasions. They weren't immune to grief, but in the harsh environs of the wilderness they had learned to keep it in check. Sure, they mourned the loss of Remi, and not a man there would forget him. But they wouldn't wail and gnash their teeth, cut off their hair or a finger, or slice their arms with a knife, the way a squaw would when she lost a husband or son. They were men, and manlike, they held their feelings in.

The younger hands seemed more confused by the old-timers' stoicism than anything else. The brigade had already lost two men— Juan Vidales and Antonio Rodolso—so death wasn't new. But they had been new men themselves, Vidales virtually unknown, having died so soon after putting out, and Antonio keeping to himself, with the dark secret of his branded cheek always turned away from the fire at night. But Remi was different, and it seemed to the younger men, Travis and Clint in particular, that there should have been more feeling involved, more pain for the loss of a good friend and trusted comrade. They seemed unsettled by the quiet acceptance of the older hands, and perhaps more aware of their own vulnerability. Who would mourn them if they died? Travis wondered. Who would feel for him as he felt for Chet?

At night, around the fire, the men talked about Remi, reliving old stories, past antics. A few pestered Jake with questions that he answered in a clipped, uninviting tone. But invariably, the conversation would turn in other directions, reliving other old stories, the antics of other men. Laughter would peal through the dark sky, and decks of cards would appear as the men turned to games of chance, or wandered back to the Ute village to spend some time with a squaw. Life went on, the trading continued, the stock wounded in the Arapahos' siege began to heal; the sun shone and the stars glittered, and to the south the storm crept forward, a shroud they all watched in fearful anticipation.

A gust of icy wind swept through the branches above Cork-Eye's head, rattling the limbs like dried bones shaken in a basket, then moving on with a mournful howl. Cork-Eye stirred and sat up, pulling a tattered buffalo robe tighter around his shoulders. He glanced around him, then sniffed, spat, and rubbed his empty, draining socket with a grimy knuckle. Lifting his eye to the stars, he made a quick calculation of the time and judged that it wasn't yet past eight o'clock in the evening—two hours yet from the time when Travis would return from the Ute village to relieve him.

Cork-Eye lifted a meaty haunch to fart his displeasure at the injustice of his standing guard. He was an old hand, and to his way of thinking such duty, especially on a night like tonight, was so far beneath him as to seem inconceivable. He had told Eli that, of course, and Old Cal had seconded the opinion, but Cutler, the bastard, had naturally refused to listen. But by God if it didn't sour his milk to sit here watching over a pile of pissant trade goods while the rest of the boys were out having a whoop-up.

His continued abuse by the older hands was the consequence of his handicap. Cork-Eye had come to that realization a long time ago. A man without a limb—be it leg, hand, or eye—was just plain damn taken advantage of, although Cork-Eye had to admit he seemed to have it worse than others. It puzzled him that the boys could misjudge him so, and made him feel downright weepy at times. It was a curse few could have borne, and he just thanked the Lord he had had the foresight to blame his robbed eye on a Blackfoot's blade, rather than the St. Louis whore who had been the real culprit. Had Cutler known the truth, he probably would have made it even harder on him. Chances were he wouldn't have understood why it had been necessary for Cork-Eye to go ahead and cut the bitch's throat, either. But that was the way of it for a man with a handicap, Cork-Eye knew. By God, it was all hardship and bad luck, no matter which way he pointed his nose, and being forced to stand guard while the rest of the boys were off in the bushes with willing squaws was just further proof of that.

Cork-Eye listened for a moment to the pounding drums, the brittle clatter of deer-hoof rattles, and the tinkling of tin cones sewn to the costumes of Indian dancers. The mellow intonations of a flute as some randy buck tried to lure a squaw into the darkness just added to the insult. He rubbed the heel of his palm over his crotch as he peered toward the village. By God, he was feeling horny, and if he didn't get a chance to dip his wick soon he would just tell Eli to go to hell and find someone else to watch over his precious trade goods. He had, Cork-Eye decided, just about reached the end of his good-natured patience.

A shadow flitted through the darkness under the trees and disappeared behind the tent where the trade goods were stored. Cork-Eye started, his eye widening. Had he not happened to glance that way at just the right moment, he knew he would have missed it entirely. He sat quietly for several minutes, wondering what to do. It was probably an Indian, he told himself, some goddamn thieving buck come to do a little after-hours shopping. The thought made him angry. Why the hell did this kind of thing always happen to him? He glanced at the fire. He should build it up, he supposed, let whoever was nosing around the trade goods know the camp wasn't entirely deserted. The trouble was, he had let the flames die down to embers, and it would take too long to stoke up a really good blaze. By that time, whoever was slipping up on the tent would have already wormed his way under the wall and helped himself to whatever struck his fancy.

Cursing gruffly, Cork-Eye heaved to his feet and let his robe drop. The wind smacked his exposed flesh, and he shivered and swore anew. By God if he didn't have half a notion to go over there and kick some brownskin ass. He picked up his rifle, then paused and licked his lips. He glanced toward the Ute village, hoping to see some of the boys returning. He had only seen the one shadow, but it occurred to him now that perhaps there had been more. Hell, there was no telling how many Indians were over there right now, just waiting to lift his scalp.

"It ain't right," he murmured, his fingers flexing around his rifle. "Goddamnit, it ain't right."

It didn't surprise him that Cutler had left him here alone after making such a big fuss about doubling the guard ever since some greaser hamstrung the mules back at Río Colorado. It was just one more example of how he was always being taken advantage of.

"Cutler, you goddamn knife-in-the-back sonofabitch," Cork-Eye said loudly enough for anyone skulking around the tent to hear. He listened for some sound of the intruder's retreat, swearing again when it didn't come. Then, incredibly, a light seemed to blossom behind the tent. Cork-Eye blinked, then laughed. "Well, of all the goddamn gall," he said, staring toward the tent. "Hey! Are you so goddamn cocksure of yourself you'd light a—"

Cork-Eye came around the tent and stopped, his eye widening in surprise. "You!" he said. He glanced at the tent, where a tiny blaze was already eating into the green and white canvas. "Hey, you're gonna—" He grunted and stepped back at the sudden pain in his chest. Looking down, he saw the knife slipping free, followed by a quick spurting of blood. "No," he croaked. "Oh, God, no . . ." He fell to his knees, watching the blood pump from his chest in thin, arcing streams, slowing gradually until it stopped altogether. There was a slight pull then, and he found himself floating through the dry limbs over the burning tent and his own crumpled posture, turning finally to a brighter light, a warmer place. Strangely, he could see from both eyes now. . . .

Wearily, Eli surveyed the tent's wreckage in the dawn's bleak light. The charred canvas, scorched furs, and still-smoking bundles of trade goods were scattered around the camp. He fished a cigar from his belt pouch and nervously ran his fingers along it, peeling away tiny flakes of leaf. Shock and disbelief sagged his shoulders; weariness permeated his every muscle. Defeat clawed at him and made him want to turn away, but that was a luxury he knew he couldn't afford with the eyes of the brigade upon him. He took a long breath and let it go, lifting his gaze to McClure's hostile stare.

"Go ahead and say it," Eli said sharply.

"We should have kept the guard doubled. Even here. Especially here."

"Yes," Eli answered bluntly. "We should have kept the guard doubled. Anything else?"

McClure's face was pinched with anger. He flung an arm out to encompass the ruined trade goods. "Another man dead, the plews damaged, and half our merchandise destroyed!"

At least half, Eli thought dejectedly. The tent was gone. The trade blankets, the bolts of blue and scarlet cloth, the packages of vermillion, and maybe a pack of furs were gone as well. But they had salvaged a lot, too. Most of the furs had already been pressed into bales, so that while the upper layers were ruined, those pelts toward the center were untouched. The knives, tomahawks, and camp axes were scorched, but could be polished up, the handles replaced. Packets of needles, awls, arrowheads, and fishhooks had been dragged from the ashes largely undamaged. Most of the beads were melted beyond recovery, but the jewelry and trinkets made from brass, copper, pewter, and silver had been retrieved, warped, slightly melted, but repairable. The brigade's bartering power had taken a serious blow, but it could have been worse. He felt little remorse for Cork-Eye's death, and couldn't help wondering if things might have been different if someone more competent had been on guard.

McClure's gaze swept the camp. "It's time we got to the bottom of this," he stated coolly.

Johnny Two-Dogs looked up, his eyes narrowing in suspicion. "Just what are you driving at, McClure?"

"You know what I'm driving at," McClure blustered, his darting gaze taking in the entire brigade. "You all know what I'm driving at."

"I God, boys, he be accusing *us!*" Old Cal exclaimed.

An angry murmur stirred through the group, and Old Cal put his hand on his knife.

"No one's accusing anyone," Eli said. He pegged McClure with a warning look. "We're just tired and short tempered—"

"Is what he says true, Eli?" Johnny cut in.

"By *Dieu*, me think it is," Pierre added.

"Shut up, Frenchy," Old Cal growled, elbowing the cook aside. He glared at Eli, his face dark. "Ye tell it straight, Eli. Are ye accusin' anyone here?"

Eli sighed, putting his cigar away. "No," he said, then repeated it in sign for emphasis. "No. We all know someone with the brigade is doing this, and when I find out who it is, I'll hang him myself. I'll swear to that. But we aren't accusing anyone."

Pierre shoved Old Cal back. "By *Dieu*, you shove me again, I cut you throat."

"Like you knifed Vidales?" McClure said.

"Jesus *Christ*, Silas," Eli exploded, knocking Pierre's hand aside as it reached for the knife in his belt. "Quit that, Pierre."

"Enfant de garce," Pierre breathed heavily. "Him no talk that way. I cut him goddamn throat."

"No one's cutting anyone's throat," Eli pronounced. "Now by God, let this drop."

"Ain't!" Old Cal countered in his reedy voice. "Ain't gonna let no puffed up pork-eater call Cal Underwood a traitor."

"Cal speaks for me, too, Eli," Johnny said quietly.

Eli turned on McClure. "Apologize," he snapped.

"No." McClure's voice sounded almost squeaky at Eli's request. "These men are under contract. I have a right to question them. Every one of them."

"Apologize, McClure."

The clerk's face darkened. "I won't."

Old Cal pulled his knife. "Let me worm it outta him, Eli," he whined. "I calculate I'll find me an apology somewheres 'twix his hump-ribs."

Eli stepped between Old Cal and McClure, his gaze raking both men. Silence dropped over the trappers. Finally, Old Cal's breath exploded. "Wagh! Ye takin' the pilgrim's side on this, Eli? Blackin' ye face agin those o' us what nursed ye through ye greenhorn years?"

"I'm asking you to save it until the season's over, Cal. I don't care how you settle your differences then. Just don't let it interfere with your trapping."

"You're asking for a lot," Johnny said tightly.

"I've got a lot at stake, Johnny."

"Sacre bleu," Pierre breathed. "All right, Eli. For you I do this thing. But not for this one." He jerked his thumb toward McClure.

Johnny nodded. *"Bueno.* I reckon I'll side with Pierre on this."

Eli looked at Old Cal. "What about you, Cal? Think you can let it ride until the season's over?"

Old Cal shook his head. "I ain't so sure I can, Eli, but by damn, this ol' nigger'll a give it a try." He resheathed his knife and eased back a step. "But you keep that pork-eater away from me. I be warnin' ye, hoss, I'll not be toleratin' a man what calls me a scoundrel."

"I won't ask you to, Cal." He looked at the others. "I won't ask any of you to stay if you've got a mind to leave. But that's where I draw the line. If you stay, you trap beaver and save your fighting until the season's over."

There was a long silence after that, and then Pierre and Johnny nodded together, and Pierre said, "*Oui*, I will stay, Eli."

"Aye," Old Cal grumbled at last. "Reckon I will. Won't make ye no guarantees, though. No, sir, I won't do ye that." He turned and stalked away, mumbling to himself.

Eli glanced at the new hands—Travis, Mateo, Jorge, Clint—and made them the same offer. All four youths shook their heads. "We'll stay," Travis said.

"*Bueno*. Grab yourself some breakfast, then. I want everything here separated and repacked. Pitch what's ruined, but save anything that might catch a brownskin's fancy. Pierre will give you a hand." He looked at Cork-Eye's body, lying to the side wrapped in his ratty buffalo robe. "Travis, first you and Clint get some shovels and dig a grave."

"Eli."

Eli glanced at McClure.

"I want a word with you."

"Lead off," Eli responded flatly. He followed the clerk to the river, where McClure stopped but refused to meet his gaze.

"I am reaching the limits of my patience," McClure said. "I haven't forgotten the responsibility Sylvester Girardin entrusted in me—"

"Oh, for God's sake, knock it off, McClure," Eli cut in angrily. "You're doing more to hurt this venture than whoever it is who killed Vidales and Cork-Eye."

McClure's face was livid as he turned to Eli. "Action, Mr. Cutler. Action, rather than inertia. By God, sir, will you sit on your duff and allow this traitor to destroy us?"

"You sonofabitch," Eli exploded, his patience snapping at last. "You nearly cost us every experienced hand we have today! Now back off!"

"It's time we quit skirting this problem. It isn't going to go away otherwise."

"Let me handle it, Silas," Eli said wearily. "Just let me handle it." He felt ragged and torn, ready to shatter into a thousand pieces.

McClure started to reply, then broke off as his attention was caught elsewhere. Following the line of his vision, Eli saw old Bowlegs and a delegation of Utes approaching from the village. "We have company," McClure said softly.

Bowlegs stopped before them, glancing briefly at the ashes where the tent had stood. His eyes sought out Eli then, revealing a sadness that wasn't just for the plunder that was lost and would never reach Ute hands. "It is a bad thing to have one among you who cannot be trusted," Bowlegs said in Spanish, his voice betraying an empathy that caught Eli by surprise. "You have had bad medicine this year, my friend."

"Sometimes bad medicine is part of life," Eli replied carefully, remembering Sees Tomorrow's prayer their first night with the Utes. "It is like the north wind that is cold and angry, but it gives a man strength and endurance. Sometimes even bad medicine is good."

Bowlegs smiled. "It is good to see that it has been such with you." His expression took on a sly cast then, and he glanced once more at the destroyed tent. "There is uneasiness among the lodges. Our men say that you do not have the trade goods that you promised for our ponies. Is this true? Have the blankets and cloth that our men wished to trade for been burned by the wolverine among you?"

"It is true," Eli admitted. "But there is still much to trade. Knives and tomahawks, bracelets for the women to wear on their wrists, rings to wear on their fingers. Perhaps mirrors, to decorate a pony's mane or a warrior's hair."

"Bracelets and mirrors do not shield the body from the north wind, my friend. We had desired blankets and cloth. We have furs and many ponies, but our men do not wish to trade these things for a woman's trinkets."

"What's he saying?" McClure asked.

"He's dickering," Eli replied in English. "He figures he's got us over a barrel with the horses because we lost so much of our trade goods."

"Does he?"

"Somewhat," Eli admitted nonchalantly, careful not to give anything away with his expression. "Just take it easy and don't look worried."

"Can we afford both the horses and the furs they have left? You said they were saving the best for last."

"Old Bowlegs is sharp as a fox when it comes to trading, but he knows there ain't likely to be another outfit up this way this year, either. That's our ace."

"Does the man who makes the marks know of the value of a Ute pony trained for war?" Bowlegs asked, referring to McClure.

"Yes, but we do not wish to trade for war ponies. We want pack animals, as I have said."

Bowlegs smiled indulgently. "It is a sad thing that you do not have enough ponies," he said. "Perhaps we will have to wait for Mexican traders, who always bring many blankets and much cloth."

It was Eli's turn to smile. He did it graciously. "That is true, old friend. Maybe it would be best to wait until next year, when the Mexicans come. You will have many fine furs and 'skins to trade then."

Bowlegs's smile widened knowingly. "We will talk later, Eli Cutler. I think it will be a fine thing to see, this trade we will do this year."

"Good," Eli said. "I hope we can trade many more goods here. I would not like to have to take it all up to the land of the Shoshone to trade."

"We will talk later," Bowlegs repeated, and walked off without further comment.

"Well?" McClure asked.

Eli shrugged. "They have us over a barrel, Silas. I reckon old Bowlegs knows that as well as we do."

CHAPTER TWENTY-NINE

Shortly after noon, McClure looked up from where he was sorting copper bracelets. His brows furrowed as he stared toward the village. "Something's up," he told Eli, motioning toward the widely spaced lodges where warriors were hurrying toward their horses.

"Riders," Johnny said, looking south over the same path the brigade had taken nearly a week before. Eli stood, spotting a thin, billowing cloud of dust climbing into the thin air, churned up by at least a score of horses.

"Arapahos?" Jake asked, a trace of panic in his voice.

"I reckon not," Eli replied easily. "Not traveling like that."

One by one, the trappers and their women stood and stared south-ward. McClure went to his bedroll and came back with the leather case that held his telescope. He leaned a shoulder into a tree and lifted the glass to his eye. After studying the approaching horses for several minutes, he finally shook his head. "I can't make out a damn thing."

"Let's see that far-looker," Johnny said. He extended the scope all the way out, then slowly brought it back until it was in focus. He was quiet for several minutes, then he laughed delightedly. "Hell, that's Pete and Charlie, and damn if they don't have a bunch of ponies with them."

"Wagh!" Old Cal cried, perking up. "This coon figured they'd gone under this time, certain."

"By *Dieu*, you no rub them two out so easy," Pierre observed, grinning broadly.

Johnny lowered the spyglass and handed it to Eli. "Maybe your luck's changing," he said. "It looks like Pete and Charlie have latched on to someone's ponies, and if I know those two, they'll be looking to trade."

Eli lifted the glass, focusing intently on the approaching horse-men. Then a strange grin came over his face as he closed the tele-scope and returned it to its case. "You know, Johnny, you just may be right."

Pete sat on the bank beside the river, listening to the slide of the water, the faint gurgle of tiny waves breaking against the rocky shore. Reeds and scrub willow rustled softly in the still air, as if wanting to pull up roots and follow. Downriver, the Utah village was going about its daily routine—squaws busy gathering wood for the night, or fixing an evening meal; men talking, gambling, working on their weapons or with their favorite ponies; children laughing and running, the boys playing at games of war and boasting of the glory days to come, while the girls helped their mothers and learned the skills they would eventually need as women. Dogs lolled about, or trotted like slinking coyotes among the brown leather tipis and brush wickiups. On the plain north of the village the pony herd grazed. Taken as a whole it was a scene of riotous placidity, of hurried ac-tivity and lazy contentment, of love and harmony and war and worry and all the thousand little idiosyncrasies that made up any commu-

nity, white or brown, and Pete smiled a little, watching it with appreciation, yet glad he wasn't a permanent part of it.

Spurs jingled familiarly behind him, and Charlie flopped in the
grass nearby and pulled a bent cigar from a dark brown pouch at his
belt. "You figuring on selling Eli them 'Rapaho ponies?" he asked,
fishing his flint and steel and a little piece of char from another
pouch.

"They're your ponies, too."

"Yeow, that they be, but this hoss ain't as particular toward money
doin's as you are. Besides, ol' Eli and that McClure fella are headin'
this way. I figure we'd best be makin' up our mind."

Pete glanced downstream to where the two mountain men were
splashing their horses across the Grand. The Mex, Chavez, rode with
them. Eli and the boys had ridden over earlier to exchange greetings
and news, and Eli had mentioned then that they might be interested
in trading for some of the ponies Pete and Charlie had brought in. He
hadn't pushed it, though, and Pete had told him to come back later,
after the women had a chance to set up a proper camp.

"Wagh," Pete grunted softly, accepting the cigar Charlie casually
handed him. "It might be easier to get rid of 'em here, rather than
drive the whole bunch up into the Rio Verde country lookin' for Sublette's outfit."

"That's kinda what I was thinkin'," Charlie said, drawing on his
own cigar. "This coon's tired of wranglin' *cayuses*. 'Sides, ol' Eli
ain't a bad cuss, and I reckon they'll be needing some extry ponies.
Ol' Bowlegs'd skin him good, considering Eli's predicament."

Eli, McClure, and Mateo came splashing out of the river, spurring
their horses up the steep bank. Pete glanced across the river to the
black scab of the trade tent, and drew thoughtfully on his cigar. In
the weeks that he and Charlie had been out on their own, he had
started to forget the problems afflicting the brigade, and he wondered
if he was ready to throw in with such a strife-riddled outfit again.

Eli drew rein a short distance away, with McClure and Mateo riding up on either side of him. "Hello, Pete, Charlie. You boys ready?"

Pete smiled. "Fall off, gents, and sit a spell."

They dismounted, and Charlie bawled for Blossom to come and
fetch their mounts, but the girl was already there, leading them away.
McClure, squatting awkwardly nearby, said, "You said those were
Arapaho horses?"

"I didn't stutter," Charlie shot back.

"Would you mind telling us how you acquired them?"

"Jesus Christ, McClure, how do you think we *a-quired* 'em?"

"The Arapahos ran us into the timber, back in the Valley," Pete said. "We took offense."

Eli was squinting toward the band, grazing on rawhide hobbles. "I believe I recognize a couple of those ponies from the bunch Mateo and I tried to steal. That little strawberry roan for sure."

"Could be you ain't got a knack for stealin' horses," Pete offered solemnly. "Now, me and Charlie have filched us a pony or two over the years, and it is an art, or I wouldn't say so. I recollect a time up in the Wind Rivers we stole a couple of good buffalo runners off a party of Crows, which ain't quite as hard as pickin' berries outta a bear's mouth, but is likely close."

"They stole 'em back," Charlie grumbled, an imposition he'd never quite forgiven, Pete knew.

"Well, they did for a fact," Pete acknowledged. "But it was a high ol' time for a while there." Noticing Eli's thinly veiled impatience for a story, and reckoning that a little agitation might help when they got down to the dickering, Pete decided to go ahead with it. Besides, he reasoned, a good yarn never hurt anyone.

"Wagh! This was, what, two summers back, I reckon. We was up high, tryin' to stay cool and waitin' for beaver to come into prime when a party of *Absaroke* come into the valley below us and began running some little bunches of mountain buff. Well, Crows bein' notionable and there bein' only the two of us, we decided to stay holed up and not let on we was close by. We watched 'em a couple of days, and pretty soon we started to take a shine to some of their ponies. Crows have got some of the finest horseflesh in the mountains, bein' fair to middlin' thieves themselves, so we figured we'd be gettin' the cream.

"Now, ol' Silas here might not know, bein' a pilgrim and all, but an Injun don't let his buffalo horse run loose with the rest of the cavvy. No, sir. Take yourself a look around this here Ute camp and you'll see what I mean. They keep 'em picketed close, and sometimes at night they'll run the picket line right into their lodge and tie it around their wrist, or so I've heard. I ain't actually ever seen that done, but I know a few ol' boys who'll swear to it. So we had our work cut out for us if we wanted a couple of those runners. First thing we did was shag the women back into the high country, on account of a mule, which any farm boy knows, ain't much for cooperatin'. Told Annie and Red-Wing to head on over the top and we'd catch up before they hit the Bighorns. Well, we were serious or I wouldn't say so. Told the women to take our saddle horses, too. We was gonna ride outta there on buffer horses, or by God, we wasn't gonna ride."

"Kept our saddles, though," Charlie interjected. "Crows generally ride pad saddles, and they're hell to stay on, especially in the mountains."

"We wouldn't've had time to steal saddles anyway," Pete argued.

"Decided to, by God, I would've."

"Well, it ain't no matter anyway, because we kept our Mexican hulks. Waited, what, two, three days?"

"Three," Charlie said.

"Three, then, just sittin' up there watchin' and waitin'. Then on the third day a storm blew up outta the south, clouds black as pitch, and I says, 'Wagh! It ain't gonna get no easier'n this.' So as soon as the sun went down we slipped outta the pines where we'd been cached and made a beeline for them ponies.

"Well, I'll tell you, boys, it was easy as fallin' down and only about half as painful. The night was blacker'n a Blackfoot's heart; the wind blowin' hard and mournful, and all them Crows had taken to their lodges on account of all the evil spirits that was about. We already knew which runners we wanted. Hell, we'd studied that camp for so long we knew where every stick of firewood lay. So we just walked in in the middle of the storm and cut their picket ropes and led them ponies outta there easy like and had 'em saddled in no time.

"But then damn if them Crows' medicine didn't start to shine for 'em. We was maybe ten miles outta the village and makin' tracks for the Bighorns when a fork of lightning came down no more'n forty feet away. Splintered a pine that must've been older than God and Old Cal put together. Damnit, Eli, I've sit a lotta ponies over a lotta rough country without being throwed, and you know it. Ol' Charlie has, too, or I wouldn't say so. But we was *both* throwed that time, and them ponies lit out for the Crow camp like they was colts runnin' home to their mamas."

"*Yeow!*" Charlie said, taking up the story. "We didn't know what to do. Wasn't just the ponies then. They had our saddles and bridles and bedrolls, too. We figured we was gone beaver, sure, once them *Absaroke* figured out what happened. T'weren't nothin' for it but we had to go back."

"Only thing is, the night's near gone by now," Pete took over. "But like Charlie says, t'weren't no dodgin' it, so we hoofed it back there fast as we could, but it was too damn late. Them ponies must've caused a ruckus comin' in, because we could see Crows all over the place."

"Swarmin', they was," Charlie added.

"Well, I'll swear they were. They'd just startin' to figure out what had happened when we got there. Me'n Charlie hunkered down nervous-like in the rocks and tried to get our rifles ready, though it was still drizzling and we both knew they weren't gonna fire, no matter how tight the locks were wrapped.

"Well, about that time a bunch of Crows lit out, followin' the trail the buffalo runners left comin' in, and that was our first bit of luck, 'cause it meant they was gonna be several hours backtrackin' just to where we'd been throwed, the rain fallin' like it was. Meanwhile, damn if the rest of 'em don't dump our gear right there in the middle of camp, in plain sight, then go back inside their lodges to get outta the rain."

"Didn't all go back," Charlie corrected.

"Didn't say they all went back. Said most of 'em did."

"You said they all went back. Makes 'em think that camp was plumb empty, which it wasn't. Was some kids runnin' around, and squaws fetchin' water and wood and such."

"Well, hell yeah, there was kids and squaws. Anybody ever seen a brownskin village knows there's gonna be kids and squaws, and dogs, too. Dogs are the worse. They got better sniffers."

"Just sayin' the village wasn't empty, is all," Charlie mumbled, scowling.

"Well, *shit,* then. So there's our saddles sittin' in the middle of the camp, and *most* of them Crows is goin' back inside their lodges to get outta the rain, *except* maybe six or seven hundred squaws filin' down to the river for breakfast water, and a couple of thousand kids and dogs, and maybe a dozen giraffes, but even with all that, we figured we could slip through 'em."

Charlie mumbled a curse, but let it go without further comment.

"Now, here's the funny part," Pete went on as if he hadn't heard. "On account of them buffler runners bein' rode during the night, they were left behind, too, picketed no more than twenty yards from our saddles. The only question is, how are we gonna get there? Squaws and kids aside, it's them Crow dogs this child was frettin' over. We might slip in during the night and in the middle of a storm, but they ain't likely to let us pass in daylight, which it damn near was by then."

"More light than dark," Charlie amended.

"I reckon," Pete agreed. "Time was runnin' out, certain sure. So we did the only thing we could think to do, and hoped for the best. We slung our rifles over our shoulders and stood up and walked right into that camp."

"You walked openly into an enemy camp?" McClure asked dubiously.

"It was the only thing we *could* do," Charlie replied. "Hell, we hadn't taken time to hide our tracks, assumin' we even could've in the dark like that. And it wasn't gonna be no time a-tall before them *Absaroke* started stirrin' outta their lodges again."

"Charlie's tellin' it straight. Our goose was about cooked, no two ways about it. So instead of slinkin' through camp like a couple of coyotes lookin' for bones, we just stood up and walked in like we owned the place."

"Yeow," Charlie said gently, his eyes taking on a faraway look as he remembered that long trek to the center of the village.

"Well, I reckon," Pete echoed.

"Were you spotted?" McClure asked, leaning forward eagerly.

"Well, hell, yeah, we were spotted!" Charlie exploded. "Who in hell thinks they're gonna walk into an *Absaroke* camp in the middle of the day without bein' spotted? Christ!"

"It wasn't the middle of the day," Pete corrected. "But we were spotted, all right. Kids, squaws, dogs. Hell, we must've had twenty, thirty dogs sniffin' at our heels and growlin' like they meant to eat us alive, though I reckon it ain't much of a man that lets a brownskin's cur worry him. Anyhow, one of them kids, or maybe it was a squaw from down by the crik, finally lets out a shout, and them lodges started spillin' bucks. Me'n Charlie didn't slow down a lick, though, or try to run. We'd already talked it through, and decided what we'd do if we were spotted, so we just kept walkin', expectin' to feel an arrer in our gizzards any minute, but none come, although that camp was swarmin' again.

"Well, we walked up and fetched our saddles, then took 'em over and threw 'em on those buffalo runners like we did this ever day of the week and twice on Christmas. Well, them Crows didn't know what to think. Ain't likely nobody's ever showed 'em that much gumption before. They stood around with their hands over their mouths like we was spirits. Surprised hell outta 'em, I'll say that."

"And you just rode out?" McClure asked incredulously.

"Oh, hell no. Them Crows was surprised, but they weren't stupid. They grabbed us before we could get in the saddle and bundled us up like we were a couple of bales of robes and left us in a pile with our saddles. Then damn if they didn't go back to their lodges until those fellers trackin' us came back." Pete laughed softly at the memory. "I figured we was gone beaver for sure that time," he admitted reflectively.

"So'd this hoss," Charlie added. "It was a touchy situation, all right, but I reckon they admired our pluck, and as it turned out, me'n Pete knew a couple of them ol' boys, so they let us keep our hair and our plunder, but told us to git before some of the younger bucks changed their minds. Did it, too. Hoofed it outta there totin' our saddles over our shoulders."

"And you walked all the way to the Bighorns?" McClure asked. "Were Annie and Red-Winged Woman waiting there for you?"

"Well, we didn't exactly walk," Charlie hedged. "Come dark, we made us another raid. Only this time we took some ponies outta the remuda. T'weren't no runners, but it was better'n wearin' out good moccasins hikin' after our womenfolk."

Eli and Mateo were grinning, recognizing the truth of Pete's tale, but also recognizing the stretch of it, too. Only McClure swallowed it whole. "But what I don't understand is, why?" McClure asked. "Did you intend to sell them?"

"Nope."

"Were they better horses than the ones you owned?"

"Not so's you'd notice."

"Then . . ." McClure spread his hands in confusion. "Why?"

Mateo laughed openly, and Pete scowled. It seemed like the dumbest question he'd heard in his life, and it just went to show how much of a greenhorn McClure really was.

Eli said, "You two took up the wrong profession, trapping beaver."

"Well, we've been contemplatin' a *paseo* out Californy way," Charlie admitted. "I've heard they've got 'em a passel of horseflesh out there, just ripe for the pickin'."

"What would you do with them?" Eli asked.

Pete gave him a sidelong look. "Why, sell 'em to horse-shy trappers, I figure."

"Such as us?"

"If you're in the market."

"I might be, depending."

"Oh, Lord, here it comes," Charlie moaned.

"Well, it may not be all that bad," Eli allowed. "We're talking credit, payable in Taos, St. Louis, or at next summer's rendezvous, whichever you boys would prefer."

"Credit shines," Pete said. "*Depending,* of course."

Eli glanced again at the nearby herd. "I figured five dollars a head, providing they're sound, of course."

"We was figurin' on sellin' the whole horse, Eli," Pete said dryly. "Not just the head."

Eli chuckled without offense. "Tell you what, I might go six."

Charlie shook his head sadly. "That hurts, Eli. Me'n Pete always thought higher of you than that."

"I reckon we'd want to sell the whole remuda," Pete said. "Maybe keep a couple for our own string, but get rid of all the rest. If you're willing to go that route we could likely cut you a better deal."

Flushing with impatience, McClure said, "Name your price, then."

"Well, if we're dickerin' in insults rather than horseflesh, I was thinkin' fifty dollars a head," Charlie said. "Mountain prices, ye understand."

"Fifty dollars!" McClure's cheeks puffed with indignation. "By God, that's robbery, and nothing more. "

"Take it easy, Silas," Eli said amiably. "We can get closer than that." He glanced at Mateo with a twinkle in his eye. "Did you bring that jug, Mateo?"

Mateo nodded.

"Why don't you go fetch it. I'm getting dry."

Mateo went to his horse and came back with a brown half-gallon crock jug. He handed it to Eli, then rumped down nearby.

"Yeow," Charlie murmured, eyeing the slope-shouldered jug thirstily.

"Have a sip," Eli offered, pulling the cork and pushing the jug toward Charlie.

Pete cocked a brow toward Mateo. "Coon's tryin' to get us drunk," he said.

"*Si*." Mateo agreed, watching Charlie lift the jug to his lips.

Pete sighed. "Hell, I can see where this is going. Set your price, Eli, and let's see if it's close."

"Ten bucks a head. No more."

Pete chewed reflectively at his lower lip for a moment, then shook his head. "Nope. Won't do it. Not for that price."

"Then make a counteroffer," McClure huffed.

Charlie lowered the jug with a great expulsion of air. "Whooowee," he breathed. "This is the hair of the bear, Pete! Figure it as part of the trade."

"*Aguardiente*," Eli said. "Pure Lightning. Have another try."

"Don't mind if I do."

"You are a hard man, Cutler," Pete said woefully. "Twenty dollars a head."

Eli smiled. "Let's mosey on over and take a look at them."

They all went, Charlie dangling the jug from a finger. Pete pointed out the ponies they wanted to keep, and Mateo cut the rest out, hazing them to one side. There were eleven head, wiry little mustangs, but stout and sharp-eyed.

"These are war ponies," Pete explained. "The pick of the crop. Ol' Bowlegs won't trade you ponies of this quality."

"I won't argue that, but Bowlegs has some mules in his herd, too. I'd prefer mules anyway, to tell you the truth."

"I know that, but so does Bowlegs. He'll charge you a pretty penny for 'em, and won't take credit, either. A deal like that cuts into your fur trading."

"That's true, but I won't pay twenty dollars a head." Eli eased through the little band, studying each animal critically, the way it stood and the way it walked, taking his time. When he came back he nodded agreeably. "That's good horseflesh, all the way around. Twelve bucks a head, Pete, and I'll want all of them."

"Take it," Charlie insisted.

"No." Pete shook his head stubbornly. "I won't take a rubbin'. Fifteen is as low as I'll go."

"Where would you sell them if we don't buy them?" McClure asked manipulatively.

"Ol' Bowlegs'll take a bunch, and if they don't want 'em all, Sublette's boys'll take the rest."

McClure's face flushed darkly, but Eli barely stirred. He stared thoughtfully at the strawberry roan, then sighed. "It's a fair price, considering the circumstances. Write them out a letter of credit, Silas."

"This is outrageous," McClure stuttered. "I saw ponies as good as these selling for six dollars a head in Santa Fe."

"These are better," Eli replied. "And we aren't in Santa Fe right now."

McClure glared. "And you want to buy their beaver at the end of the season? My God, man!"

"Maybe," Eli said, then looked at Pete and laughed. "Depending, of course."

CHAPTER THIRTY

Remi found the paint downcanyon, in a grove of aspens growing in a little cul-de-sac. The mare lifted her head at his slow, hitching approach, then whinnied loudly and burst out of the trees toward him. The gashes and cuts on her legs and chest, the saddle half turned under her belly, attested to her terror and the wild flight she had put herself through after the mountain lion's attack.

"You are *l'enfant*, no," Remi scolded lovingly as he took the broken reins in his hand. He patted the mare's neck and scratched her gently behind the ears. She put her forelock against his chest and pressed lightly into him, and Remi closed his eyes against the welling tears. With the paint, he knew there was a chance—slim yet, but still a chance. Without the horse, his situation would have been hopeless. "*Oui,* you are glad to see Remi. Well, little one, Remi is glad to see you, too. *Mon Dieu,* so glad."

He cut new reins from his reata, then straightened the saddle, but the effort left him so winded and trembling that he had to lean against the mare's shoulder until he caught his breath. The horse swung her head around and tried to nuzzle him. He smiled weakly and said, "A moment, *cherie,* but no more, eh? There is much distance to be traveled. This Remi does not forget."

There was a sense of urgency in everything he did now, a gnawing fear that time was running out. He had no idea how long he had lain on the canyon's floor, drifting in and out of consciousness. It seemed like days, although he doubted if even he could have survived that long, exposed to the elements as he had been. Although Remi was proud of his ability to withstand the cold—he had twice paddled a birch-bark canoe from Lake Winnipeg to the Athabasca country, near the Arctic Circle, for Hudson's Bay—he knew the circumstances were markedly different now. Then he had been younger and stronger, with two good legs and a dozen hearty companions. Now he was weak and injured and alone. Now, there was no room for mistakes.

Taking a deep breath, he slowly put his weight on his injured ankle. Pain stabbed upward like tiny bolts of lightning, lancing into his groin. The dark wings of unconsciousness fluttered around his head. Gritting his teeth, he grabbed the saddle horn and pulled himself up. Once in the saddle, he leaned forward and squeezed his eyes shut until the threat of passing out faded. Then he lifted his head and wiped the beads of perspiration from his brow. Fear jabbed at his gut like iron-knuckled fists, forcing a small, shaming whimper from his throat. In all his years he had never felt so small and helpless, so totally vulnerable, and it took all his will not to give in to it now, not to tumble from the saddle and lie with his head buried in his arms like a frightened child.

Shoving the feelings down as best he could, Remi turned the paint upstream. They came to the trail that led out of the canyon and stopped. The sloping ledge was covered with six inches of fresh snow, unmarred by prints, but the scent of the big cat must have lingered, because when Remi tried to force the paint forward again, she threw her head up and whinnied shrilly, dancing back several paces.

Remi jerked hard on the reins, pulling her to a stop. *"Non, non, ma cherie,"* he told the mare angrily. "This we cannot have."

He booted her with his good heel and tapped her hip with his fusil, but she refused to move closer. Remi closed his eyes as a wave of dizziness washed over him. When it passed, he lifted his gaze to the gray band of sky and said, "Maybe Remi tries too soon, no? Maybe he should wait awhile."

He suddenly remembered the traps, left downcanyon, and in that split instant the gloom and anxiety left him and he smiled. He pictured the beavers they had probably drowned for him at the bottom of the ponds, and could almost smell the rich, fatty meat, dripping over a fire, could almost feel the strength flowing back into his limbs, sharpening his senses, lifting his courage. He had come close to making a terrible mistake, he realized then, a mistake that might have easily proven fatal. He needed food and warmth and rest, and it all waited for him down here, in the canyon. On top there would be nothing except the cold, empty miles, forging his way blindly through a blasting wind that would quickly sap what little strength remained. But down here there was hope, and a chance of salvation. Feeling a small measure of relief, he turned his back on the trail. As he did, a new thought came to him, and he laughed. "Jake," he called loudly, his voice echoing between the narrow walls. "This is Remi's gift to you. Another few days, my friend. Enjoy them well."

Mateo pulled the noose from the dappled jenny's neck and stepped back as the mule scampered toward the remuda, kicking up a cloud of powdery snow as it joined the growing band of animals already packed and ready to move out. He recoiled the well-greased reata mechanically, brushing the snow from its tightly woven braids with numb fingers. Ten inches of fresh powder lay over the land, sparkling like fresh-cut diamonds in the dazzling, early morning light. In the crisp, clean air beneath a cloudless, winter-pale sky, the snorts and whinnies of the agitated remuda carried sharp as tin whistles.

Mateo's glance strayed toward the camp while he waited for Travis to drag up another mule. Pierre and Grass That Burns were packing their kettles away, while Consuelo and Clint's squaw, White Feather, stripped the deer hides from Consuelo's willow-framed shanty and rolled them into tight bundles. Old Cal, Johnny, Pete, and

Charlie Williams lounged near the fire, smoking and talking. Their horses were saddled and stood hip-shot nearby, but the mountain men did nothing while waiting for the wranglers to finish packing the remuda, and for Eli and McClure to return from Bowlegs's lodge, where the *jefes* had gone after breakfast to say their good-byes to the old chief. After eight days of trade and rest, the brigade was moving out once more.

"Lazy bastards," Mateo said, eyeing the relaxing trappers. It irked him that they could sit by so casually while he and Clint and Travis wrestled with the cantankerous remuda.

Clint gave him an amused look. "You worry too much, amigo," he said, tucking his fingers into the relative warmth of his armpits. "They don't pack mules, and we don't trap beaver. It evens out."

Mateo was silent for a moment, struggling for a reply that would convey his contempt for the gringo trappers without offending Clint. "They think they are gods," he said finally. He wanted to say more, but his grudging respect for the young *Americano* forestalled a more scathing remark.

"Well, I won't argue with that," Clint admitted, grinning. "But I don't see any point in belaboring it. Sure, they act like lords now, but in a couple of days they'll be wading in water up to their waist, so cold it'll shrivel their balls." He chuckled as he wiped his dripping nose with a sleeve of his capote. "Compared to that, packing mules sounds almost pleasant."

Irritation rose in Mateo at Clint's lack of affront, but he didn't say anything. Travis rode in on his mule, dragging a pack animal after him. He was grinning as he came up. "Whoowee, boys," he cried, his voice crackling through the calm, frosty air. "Two more critters to go, then we're done."

"Then let's get at them," Mateo said, handing his reata to Travis and taking Travis's in turn. "I want to stand by the fire awhile before Cutler comes back."

Travis laughed. "Comes back huffin' and puffin', you mean." He changed the tone of his voice in a rough imitation of Eli's voice. "Burnin' daylight, boys. Let's go. Let's ride. Gotta get to that next stream, set that next trap."

Mateo smiled in spite of his irritation, but the smile faded when Clint nudged his arm and nodded toward the rolling hills to the east. "Isn't that Jorge?" Clint asked. "Coming out of that draw?"

Mateo squinted against the snow's glare, feeling his heart sink a little. "*Sí*, that is Jorge."

"It don't look like he found that stray," Travis remarked.

"No," Mateo agreed. The numbness he had felt earlier in his fingers now seemed to spread throughout his body. He waited quietly as Jorge loped his horse across the white plain. When he was within a couple of hundred yards, Clint said, "I think he's hurt."

"*Sí*," Mateo replied heavily. "He is hurt."

Jorge was riding hunched in the saddle, his face tipped downward and hidden by the brim of his sombrero. It was a posture Mateo remembered well with Antonio, in the days after Gregorio's branding. He handed his reata to Travis and turned toward the camp, arriving just as Jorge pulled his winded mount to a stop and slid from the saddle. Mateo reached out to grasp his cousin's shoulder, but Jorge shook the hand away. "Leave me alone," he said, keeping his face hidden by the brim of his sombrero.

The trappers stirred at Jorge's unusual entrance into camp, and his peculiar behavior. Pete and Johnny got to their feet and came over, looking concerned. "What happened?" Pete asked.

Jorge drew in a deep, ragged breath, then stepped away from his horse and lifted his face. The curled brim of his sombrero slid up like a window shade to reveal a charred and horribly swollen cheek, centered by a crude T. Clint gasped, and his face went white. Pete swore in a savage voice.

"Clint, go fetch Eli," Johnny ordered curtly.

Old Cal stood next to the fire, owl-eyed at the damage done to Jorge's face. "God*damn,* boy, ye've been marked fair."

"Get him over to the fire," Pete said. "We're gonna have to tend that burn quick."

"*Tend it!*" Cal shrieked. "Meyers, ye damn fool, they ain't no tendin' somethin' like that. I'm a-tellin' ye, the boy be marked for life, and ugly as sin, to boot. Ain't airy a damn thing ye can do about that."

"Shut up, Cal," Charlie said roughly.

"Leave me alone," Jorge said, turning away.

"By God, the boy be learnin' hisself some 'Merican, 'pears like," Old Cal said in amazement. "'Bout damn time, too, to this coon's way o' thinkin'."

"Leave him be," Consuelo said, hurrying forward. She put a hand on Jorge's shoulder, and he allowed it to stay. "You are hurt," she said in Spanish. "You must allow me to take care of it, before it becomes infected."

"It is nothing," Jorge replied in his native tongue. He looked at Mateo, his expression suddenly bitter. "The handiwork of an old friend."

"Gregorio el Toro?" Consuelo asked.

"Yes."

Consuelo glanced at Mateo. "We must take care of your cousin's wound. A burn is quick to become infected. It could scar him even worse, if it does not kill him."

"There is salve in the packs."

"Get it."

"No," Mateo said, watching Jorge. "You get it. Jorge and I must talk."

For a moment Consuelo looked as if she might argue, but then she nodded and turned away. "Bring him to the fire when you are finished," she called over her shoulder. "We must not wait too long."

When Consuelo had moved out of earshot, Mateo squared himself before his cousin. His gaze went to the angry red flesh of Jorge's cheek, then rose to meet his eyes.

"Now I know how Antonio felt," Jorge said in a fractured, defeated voice meant only for Mateo's ears. "How ugly and scarred he must have thought himself. And he was right. Look at it well, Mateo. It will be with me the rest of my life." He lowered his head, fighting back the hot tears of shame. "That son of a whore. That son of a whore, Mateo. He will not give up."

"You are alive," Mateo said flatly.

"Yes, you would say that," Jorge responded with bitterness. "Mateo Chavez, the great survivor."

"There is nothing else," Mateo replied angrily. "To survive is everything." Jorge shook his head but refused an answer. "Where did this happen?" Mateo asked.

"About two leagues east of here. They caught me as I rode past a little outcropping of rock."

"How many?"

"Just the three of them. Gregorio and Hector and Salvador." He glanced toward the Ute village, where Eli was jogging toward them with McClure and Clint in tow. He smiled thinly, without humor.

"The big boss comes. Now maybe he will want to go after Gregorio."

"No," Mateo breathed, his nostrils slightly flaring. "Gregorio is mine."

"Gregorio would chew you up like a piece of bread, then spit you out onto the rocks. Let Eli handle it. He will know what to do."

"I do not need an American to handle what is my responsibility. It is me that Gregorio wants. I will handle it my way."

Jorge shrugged without comment. Eli slowed to a walk as he approached the two cousins. Like Pete, he swore when he saw the ugliness of Jorge's wound. "The Bull?" he asked bluntly, in Spanish.

"Yes. It was one of Gregorio's men who took the mule I thought had strayed. Gregorio sends you a message."

Eli's eyes narrowed dangerously. "Tell it."

"He wants Mateo. He asks that you send him to him; only then will he release the mule."

Eli laughed in wonder. "That simple, huh?"

"For Gregorio el Toro, yes."

The others had drifted up behind Eli, Consuelo among them. It was she who said, "I have heard of Gregorio el Toro for many years, Eli. His cruelty is said to be boundless."

"He is a rabid dog," Mateo added grimly. "I have seen him kill Apache women and children as coldly as he would dispatch a rattlesnake with a machete."

"What's he saying?" McClure interrupted, unable to follow the rapid flow of Spanish. "What are they all saying?"

"Hold your water," Eli replied in English, then switched back to Spanish. "Where does he propose this trade be made?"

"There is to be no trade. You are to send Mateo to him. He will turn the mule loose for you to find on your own."

Eli looked past Jorge's shoulder to the distant line of hills, as if unable to follow Gregorio's twisted logic. "I am going to cut that arrogant son of a whore's liver out and feed it to him personally," he said finally.

"No," Mateo said. "That is for me to do."

"Uh-uh," Eli replied absently, still staring at the snowy ridge of hills. "That is for me and some of the boys to handle. I want you here with the remuda."

Mateo's voice was calm as he replied to Eli's statement. "This is something I must do alone. I owe this to Jorge and Antonio both, as well as myself. If you do not let me do this, then I must ask for my wages."

Eli looked at the young *arriero,* his expression softening. "I know how you feel about this, Mateo, and I know it goes back to before you hired on with us. You've got a fair-sized bone to pick with that sonofabitch, but this is my outfit and I can't let—"

"Eli," Mateo said gently, cutting him off. "I will draw my wages now."

"Damnit, boy, it'll be three against one out there. Don't be a fool."

"I am aware of the odds, as I am of el Toro's reputation. But it is something I must do." He took a deep breath. "It is something that is worth the risk of dying for."

Eli was silent for a several minutes, turning his gaze back to the hills. Then he nodded. "All right. I guess I can understand that. Take what you need out of our supplies. If you make it, our trail will be easy enough to follow—"

"Eli!" Consuelo stumbled forward, a look of horror on her face. "You cannot mean this! You cannot send this boy out to his death!"

"Consuelo, he isn't a boy. I doubt if he has been for a long time."

"He is one young man against three hardened killers. If you allow him to ride out there alone, it will be the same as murder."

"Señora. Thank you for your words, and your concern, but I know Gregorio. I know what I face. This must be done my way."

"You fool!" Consuelo cried, stepping forward and slapping Mateo's face so hard he took a startled step backward. "You do not know what pain and suffering are. None of you do!" She whirled, facing the men gathered around her. Tears streamed down her face. "You do not know how precious life is. You are men . . ." She halted, then laughed sarcastically. "Of course, you are men. How stupid of me to forget." She pushed through the crowd and stalked back to camp, her shoulders rigid as an oak beam. Only those who spoke Spanish—Pete, Charlie, Johnny, Old Cal—understood her wrath; the others stood dumbfounded, too taken aback to react.

Mateo looked at Eli and grinned faintly. "She is hot-blooded, that one," he said, rubbing his cheek.

"She's telling you the truth," Eli said harshly. "You're throwing your life away if you go out there by yourself."

"Perhaps," Mateo conceded. "But to be a man, that is sometimes necessary."

Eli appeared to think that over, then shrugged his shoulders in resignation. "I'm not sure I believe that anymore, but there was a time when I did. When I was your age. Go with God, Mateo, but just in case, watch your back."

Chapter Thirty-one

Mateo stood alone under the cottonwoods as the brigade rode out. He was mounted on the *grullo,* with a roan packhorse at his side. The roan carried his bedding, a square canvas shelter about eight feet square, and enough food to last five days. It was a small pack, and under more normal circumstances he would have just strapped it all behind his cantle, but Eli had talked him into taking an extra mount. "You might have to do some hard riding," he had told Mateo as Clint led the roan forward. "Or your little gray there might come up lame. This ain't a time to be without a horse."

Glancing across the camp to where Consuelo was watching him with an intensity that might have equaled hatred, he finally nodded. "All right, but I will return the roan, and the mule, too."

Lowering his voice so that others wouldn't overhear, Eli said, "There ain't no shame in turning back, either. Don't forget that. Tell the boys you couldn't find Gregorio, or that the Utes got him. Tell 'em whatever the hell you want to, nobody'll question you."

"Thank you, Eli," Mateo said, turning to his horse. He toed a stirrup, then swung into the saddle. "But I will not turn back. This thing must be finished between us."

Eli reached inside his coat and came out with his pistol, a leather sack of gunpowder, another of round balls, and some flints. "I reckon you'll need this more than I will," he said, offering them up. "You know how to load it."

Mateo patted his *escopeta.* "This will be enough."

"Take it anyway," Eli said, lifting the pistol a little higher.

Mateo hesitated, momentarily torn between Eli's generosity as well as his own need of a better weapon, and the sudden return of his old animosity toward the *Americanos*—their arrogance and condescending ways. Then his face turned hard, and he shook his head. "I do not need your charity," he said in a clipped voice. "I will use my own weapons until I can afford better."

Eli lowered the pistol. "Have it your own way," he said, turning abruptly toward his sorrel and the waiting trappers. Clint and Travis wished him luck as they rode past. Old Cal shook his head in disgust and squirted a stream of tobacco juice into a patch of unblemished snow. Pete lifted his hand in a wave, but Consuelo refused to even glance in his direction. Only Jorge paused, drawing his pony up several yards away. His salved face was wrapped in a linen bandage, but the skin around it was swollen to an ugly red, his eye closed by the puffy flesh. Jorge watched him silently for the space of a dozen heartbeats, then nodded his message and reined back to the remuda.

Within seconds the brigade was moving out, flowing northward over the white land like a mottled river. The Utes came out to watch them ride off. Several young men rode after them at a run, yipping shrilly, brandishing their lances and tomahawks as if routing a hated enemy, hauling up only at the last minute to shout out their goodbyes and a few ribald jokes. Most of them rode back to the village then, but a few continued on with the mountain men. They would ride with them for a mile, or ten, before turning back to the monotony of village life.

Mateo reined away before the Utes turned their attention on him. He didn't want to talk to anyone now, and he wanted to escape the swarming crowd of men, women, and children as unnoticed as possible.

He rode toward the line of hills, following Jorge's tracks of that morning. His sombrero rode low over his eyes, but the glare of the morning sun reflected upward, half blinding him. He knew it wasn't by chance that Gregorio waited for him to the east, taking full advantage of the time as well as the country. The edge of the hills was perhaps a mile away. Mateo covered half the distance at a steady jog, his eyes never leaving the arroyo from which Jorge had emerged after being released by Gregorio el Toro. Yet he had no intention of riding straight into the arms of el Toro's men. When Mateo had covered half the distance to the hills his gaze flitted right, then left. The hills were cut by numerous arroyos, each nearly indistinguishable from the next. Mateo tried to plan his strategy as he rode. Which would be better? he wondered. Swing off to the north, or to the south? In the end he couldn't decide. He didn't know this country, or have any idea of what he would face when he got into the hills. Nor was there time to scout out the land, for he was certain that Gregorio had already spotted him and was waiting. The trick, he knew, was to get into the hills before Gregorio and his men could stop him, to somehow keep ahead of his pursuers until he could find their trail and have an idea of where they might be. For now he was the hunted, and they were the hunters. His only chance for success was to switch that, to put them before him, rather than behind.

At three-quarters of a mile he suddenly raked his heavy-roweled spurs along the *grullo*'s flanks. The horse leaped forward in surprise, neighing shrilly. Mateo spurred the horse again, angling south toward a different arroyo. The roan packhorse, snorting its displeasure, followed at a lope.

Mateo raced across the flat, snow-covered plain, watching the hills for any sign of pursuit. The *grullo* kicked up a fog of white powder, running flat-out with its neck stretched even with its withers and its nose pointed toward the arroyo like an elk's. Mateo worried about badger holes and prairie dog villages, or stones buried beneath the snow that might trip the horse, but the *grullo* had been born a mustang, raised in the rocky hill country along the front range of the Sangre de Cristos, dodging wolves, panthers, and the ever-increasing numbers of mustangers as markets in the United States opened up. It hadn't forgotten its upbringing. The horse streaked across the ground, as fleet and nimble as a buffalo. The arroyo opened up before him, twisting into the hills. The sides were steep enough that the snow had trouble clinging to them. Pieces of rusty earth showed through the white coverlet, like old scabs. The *grullo*'s hooves pounded loudly in the narrow cleft, the roan's a faint echo behind it. Mateo followed the winding path of the arroyo, his *escopeta* resting lightly across his left arm, eyes fixed to the skimming rim of the gully. About two hundred yards in, the arroyo suddenly fanned out into a little flat with the golden whiskers of bottom grass stubbling the snow's surface. The arroyo forked neatly before him, a lone piñon standing dark as slate at the top of the veed notch between the two gulches. Mateo aimed for the arroyo on the right, hoping to put even more distance between himself and Gregorio and his men, but at the last moment his attention was jerked back to the teardrop shape of the piñon. There was movement behind it, the flash of buckskin and oilcloth, and an instant later a vaquero stepped away from it, lifting a polished musket.

Mateo tried to pull the *grullo* up, to raise his *escopeta,* but he was too slow. The vaquero—Mateo recognized him as one of Gregorio's riders—snapped the musket to his shoulder and pulled the trigger. A gray-white cloud of gun smoke blossomed from the weapon's muzzle. Mateo felt the solid blow of the bullet slam him sideways in the saddle. Dancing black dots fluttered in his vision. Mateo reached for his saddle horn, but even as his hand descended toward it, the horn seemed to disappear into an inky mist.

It was good to be on the move again, Travis reflected. A week's rest had replenished his strength, allowing his body to shake off the last residual effects of the Arapaho's war club. The wound had closed completely now, with only a hard scab remaining, itching under his cloth cap as it began to heal. Recuperated, he felt a renewed enthusiasm for his decision to come to the mountains, to get on with his goal of becoming a trapper.

They rode north at a steady pace, cutting straight through the hills and making good time in spite of the snow. The Utes had already trapped out the nearby streams in anticipation of traders—either American trappers or the Mexican *mercaders*—so that Eli was inclined to keep the brigade moving along without interruption. By early afternoon of their second day after leaving the Utah camp, they came in sight of the timbered junction of the Grand and Colorado rivers.

The brigade halted on top of the bench overlooking the two rivers. Travis, nosing Blue out to the very edge, studied the terrain thoughtfully. He had to admit the Rockies had been something of a surprise to him. He had once pictured stately pines, lush, tall-grassed meadows, clear-running streams, and towering mountain peaks that pierced the belly of the sky like jagged knives. What he had discovered instead was a mostly barren country of rolling hills, clumps of bunchgrass and scrawny cedars. The valleys were often beautiful, with sprawling groves of giant cottonwoods and bastard maple growing along sparkling rivers; higher up and in some of the side canyons there was white-barked aspen, as delicate-looking as the porcelain angel that his mother had hung over the fireplace every year at Christmas. But for the most part they avoided steep, piney slopes and high meadows. He had never wondered why. Their four days of struggling over Buffalo Pass had answered that question.

Eli had sent Johnny and Old Cal ahead earlier to make a quick scout of the forks area. Travis could see Johnny now, sitting his pony just outside a belt of trees lining the Colorado, waving them in. Despite Johnny's assurances, Eli took a couple of minutes to scan the river upstream and down, before finally calling, "*Bueno,* let's go."

They rode down the steep slope of the bench, churning a broad path through the snow. Travis could hear the river a long time before he saw it—a kind of dull, liquid roar that seemed out of place for this time of year. From the expression on Johnny's face, he knew what they would find on the other side of the alders. Travis reined Blue close to Eli and halted.

"Must've been a heap of rain or melt-off somewhere upriver," Johnny told Eli. "She's running full, bank to bank."

"Where's Cal?" Eli asked.

Johnny gave a short, harsh bark of laughter. "Cached somewhere, I imagine. You didn't think he was really going to make a scout, did you?"

Eli's face darkened, but he didn't say anything. A couple of the older hands snorted their disapproval. "The old coot is probably holed up somewhere, burning bark and looking for sign in the smoke," Charlie said. "Hell, Eli, you can't count on that old fart."

Eli shook his head, as if Old Cal's dereliction was a problem he didn't want to deal with right now. "Let's go take a look," he said.

They threaded their way through the trees until they came to the Colorado's swollen banks. The river was running high and wide, filled with silt and debris. Travis watched an uprooted pine slide past, its still green boughs sodden, drooping. Up close, the river's sound was loud and angry. Eli stared morosely at the rushing waters for several minutes, then reined his horse away from the tumultuous noise, back through the trees to where they could speak without having to shout.

"All right," Eli said, speaking to them all. "We're going to have to make some boats. Johnny, you and Travis and Pete and Charlie spread out upriver and see if you can get some good deer or elk hides. I want enough to make at least two skin canoes if you can find 'em. Otherwise we'll make bullboats. The rest of you set up camp. We're gonna be here three or four days, so I want a breastworks thrown up."

To one side, Charlie murmured, "Boys, we are gonna have to shoot straight, 'cause this coon hates a goddamn bullboat. It's like riding a bobber, and there ain't nothin'll a tip faster."

Pete said, "Ol' Charlie here had him a bath three, four years ago. He ain't a man to overdo a good thing."

Grinning, shaking his head, Charlie said, "You goddamn peckerwood, you."

Pete laughed as he pulled his buckskin around and headed up the Colorado at a leisurely pace. Charlie and Johnny fell in behind him, and Travis brought up the rear, leading a trio of packhorses, their loads already spilled by Clint and Jorge. He looked back once, seeing Eli deep in conversation with McClure. Annie, Red-Winged Woman, Grass That Burns, and White Feather were leading their mules off to the side, while Jorge, Clint, and Jake drove the rest of the remuda closer. Jorge's cheek was still heavily bandaged, and he rode with his head tipped forward. Travis wondered what it felt like to have a white-hot iron bar sear into your cheek, to smell the stink of your own burning flesh and hear it sizzle to a blackened crisp right under your ear. He shuddered involuntarily and looked away.

It was early, and they took their time. It was a pretty country right here along the river. Eastward, the benches rose higher and started to pinch in, canyonlike. Above the benches Travis could see the beginnings of the mountains, black with pines at this distance, white with snow, streaked with cliffs of gray and red. The air turned cooler where the canyon's walls blocked out the sun, and the snow creaked loudly under the hooves of their mounts, announcing their presence far in advance. The noise bothered Travis, who was used to hunting silently. He was about to ask how they intended to get within rifle range of a deer or elk when Johnny abruptly veered away to study something close to the canyon's wall. He came back with a tight grin on his face. "Griz," he said simply.

Travis straightened in his saddle, suddenly interested. "Griz?"

"Grizzly bear," Charlie replied, swinging his fusil up and butting it to his thigh. "The devil's own spawn."

"I know what a grizzly is," Travis retorted.

"Then why the hell'd you ask?" Charlie shot back.

"Which way?" Pete asked, nudging his buckskin casually between the two men.

"Upcanyon, same as us. I'd say about noon yesterday, maybe a little later."

"Well hell," Pete said, his eyes taking on an almost childlike twinkle. "It's been a long time since this coon's suppered on bear meat. You reckon a griz's skin'd do for a boat, same as elk?"

"Wagh!" Johnny grunted.

"Yeow!" Charlie echoed softly.

Travis's excitement rose. He remembered the huge print he had seen back beside the pond where he had set his first beaver trap, and his breathing quickened. Something in his gut told him this was what he had been waiting for ever since he'd spotted that first track. Pete kicked his horse toward the grizzly's prints, and Travis urged his mule after him. The trail was easy enough to follow through the snow. It hugged the south wall of the canyon, skirting fallen boulders and tangles of dead timber. To their left the Colorado was a distant murmur, hidden by cottonwoods and alders. They kept an eye peeled in that direction for elk or deer, because not even a grizzly's hide would make a full canoe, but their attention was caught up in the chase, the excitement yet to come.

Two hours later the trail turned up a narrow side canyon, a twisting, rock-strewn path climbing steeply between sheer dark walls. Charlie cleared his throat and spat. "I ain't hankerin' to take a pony up that," he declared in a worried voice.

"Won't have to," Johnny replied. He sniffed the air and studied his mount's ears. "That bear isn't far ahead now, and it's probably already holed up for the winter."

Charlie scowled, and Pete said, "Seems a mite quick, Johnny. A griz don't hibernate the way a blackie does. Sleeps deep, sure, and ain't much for wanderin' during the freezing months, but this child ain't hankerin' to bet his traps that bear's asleep yet, 'specially if he was out just yesterday."

"Look at his tracks," Johnny countered. "The way they scruff the snow and kind of weave. That bear's heading for his robes. Besides, my mare isn't afraid. She'd be jumping all over the place if there was any danger from up there."

"Maybe you just got a dumb horse," Charlie offered.

"Maybe," Johnny acknowledged. "But at least it doesn't have spots on its ass for brains."

"Ohhh," Charlie replied, as if hurt. He kicked free of a stirrup and swung down. "There's only one way we're goin' to know for sure what's up there," he said. "Less'n you girls have changed your minds."

The others dismounted and tied their animals among some pines to one side of the canyon's mouth. Charlie led the way, easing upward from one precious toehold to the next. The canyon wasn't steep, but footing was always treacherous in greased, slick-soled moccasins, and snow offered little more traction than ice. Travis was wishing he had his boots, with the heavy heels and stiff soles that could jab easily into the slippery surface, but he had left them back in camp and was wearing three pairs of newly constructed moccasins, like the others, with a length of wool wrapped between the first and second pair, and wool socks on his feet.

A frosty breeze snaked down the canyon, and on it Travis thought he could catch the occasional musky odor of the bear, although he wasn't sure. Pete and Charlie had the lead, and Travis marveled at the way they worked together, the time-honed teamwork of the two old partners. Pete followed in Charlie's footsteps, watching when Charlie moved, moving only when Charlie watched. In this way the two men climbed quickly upcanyon, with Johnny and Travis following close behind. They were near the top when Charlie stopped and threw up a hand.

"Cave," Charlie whispered.

Travis saw it then, a small black opening drilled into the wall on their right, a single tall pine standing protectively above it. Even from here he could see the tracks of the grizzly climbing the short talus slope beneath the cave's entrance. The trappers halted about twenty yards away.

"*Bueno!*" Johnny breathed.

"It ain't that great," Charlie mumbled under his breath. "Someone's gonna have to go in there and call *levée* on that critter."

"I'll go," Travis said, pushing forward.

Charlie snorted. "You ain't never tangled with a griz, bud. Best you leave this fandango up to us as has the experience."

Travis felt Johnny's dark eyes upon him, like tiny drills that could penetrate his soul. "Let him go, Charlie. I imagine Travis is still spoiling for something to fight with."

"That's old Ephraim up there, Johnny," Charlie said, referring to the grizzly by mountain slang. "This kid ain't—" He clamped his mouth shut then and shook his head. "Hell, it ain't no nevermind to me," he finished.

Travis ignored Charlie's statement. He was watching Johnny, aware of the restrained animosity the mixed-blood had harbored toward him ever since the fight with the Arapahos, when Travis had refused to follow him in retreat. The rift pained Travis more than he wanted to admit. He had grown to respect the usually lighthearted trapper, and he had learned much from him, not only of the mountains and their ways, but of the East and Europe, as well. It was Johnny who had regaled him with the stories he had learned at Oxford, of Napoleon and Josephine; of Cleopatra and the mighty, unexplored Nile, the infamous River of Life; of Joan of Arc and King Arthur's Round Table, and the tales of Robin Hood; of Remus and Romulus; of the fall of Troy, and a hundred others. Combinations of history and fable, the dusky-skinned man had told him, but Travis had listened fascinated, aware that this was something special that they alone shared, for Johnny seldom revealed such insights while among the other brigade members. It had been a brief thing, those nights around the campfire while they grained skins and made moccasins for the coming winter, but Travis missed them greatly.

Finally Travis tore his eyes away from his partner. "I don't guess there's much to it," he told Charlie. "I'll just go on in and poke him in the nose and see what happens."

Charlie grunted. "You want us to bury you here? Or would you prefer we pick up the pieces and take them back to camp where the squaws can cry over your grave?"

"Here'll do," Travis replied, pushing past the trapper.

"Hold up there, Travis," Pete called quietly. He shrugged out of his dirty white capote and tossed it over a boulder. "I'll go with him," he told Charlie. "Make sure he gets it right."

They climbed the talus slope below the cave and stopped under the lone pine. Pete cut a limb from the tree and stripped the needles from it while Charlie gathered a handful of grass. They wrapped some dry tinder they carried in their shooting bags inside the grass, and tied the whole works around the head of the limb with a piece of leather.

"I hope he ain't too far back," Pete whispered, glancing at the cave's entrance. "This torch ain't gonna last long."

With the torch readied, they took a couple of minutes to see to their weapons, repriming and checking their flints. Pete loosened the knife in his sheath, then looked at Travis. "We're gonna go in there and spit in its eye, Travis. Then we're gonna hightail it outta there like the fires of hell were after us. Keep runnin' when you get outside and don't slow down until you're sure Charlie and Johnny have killed it."

"What if they don't?"

"If they don't, you'd best sprout wings."

Travis nodded soberly. "All right," he said with more calmness than he felt. "Let's do it."

"Goddamnit, boy, did you hear what he said?" Charlie exploded without raising his voice. "This ain't no picnic."

"I heard him," Travis replied.

Charlie's eyes narrowed. He grabbed Pete's arm, squeezing it tightly. "Listen, amigo, you watch yourself in there. If you've gotta feed this kid to the bear to save your own hump-ribs, by God, you do it."

"I'll see how hungry it is first," Pete said.

"Hell," Charlie grunted, dropping his arm.

Pete looked at Travis and winked. "Kinda like an old mother hen, ain't he?"

Travis shrugged, feeling suddenly alone again, vulnerable.

"Well, you boys watch your topknots," Johnny said nonchalantly. He backed off a step, glancing up slope for a place to sit and wait.

Pete scratched his whiskered cheek thoughtfully. "Well," he said with a heavy breath. "Let's go take us a peek at the elephant, huh, kid?"

They cautiously approached the cave's entrance. Travis wrinkled his nose as they paused a final time just inside the small dark opening. This time there was no denying the bear's odor. It rolled thickly from the cave, as if from something rotten. "Must be a nest of 'em," Travis said.

"You're gonna think there's a nest of 'em in a couple of minutes." Pete set his rifle aside and lit the torch with his flint and steel. The dry tinder burst into flame, and Pete hefted his rifle. Grinning weakly, he said, "Time to dance."

They went in together. The air inside the cave felt warm after so many days of frigid temperatures, moist and musty. A litter of brown pine needles and a few old cones created a dry clutter in a little nook about ten feet inside. The cave was low—both men had to stoop slightly—but about ten feet across, almost oval in shape. The floor was covered with a thick layer of dust, marked with prints. Travis, staring silently at the huge tracks of the grizzly, slowly lifted his eyes to Pete's.

"Big, ain't he," Pete said dryly.

"I saw tracks that big once," Travis replied with an odd hitch in his voice. "Back along the Grand, before the Arapahos came. I guess I knew then we was gonna tangle someday. I just didn't know when."

"Well, this ain't the same bear," Pete said.

"No, but I guess he'll do." Travis pressed on without waiting. The odor of the big bruin grew stronger as they moved deeper into the cave, filling his sinuses. The sounds of the outside world—the hum of the breeze moving between the canyon's walls and the gentle squeaks and creakings of the swaying pine—gradually faded. Travis could feel his blood pumping through his veins, sharpening his senses and tightening his gut. The cave's floor dipped downward, although continuing into the side of the mountain in an almost straight line. The flame of their torch flickered and danced, but the smoke seemed to hang close to the ceiling. Instinctively, Travis knew this wasn't a large cavern. It would be a straight, shallow shaft, created by nature—a natural home to who knew how many generations of bears, panthers, wolverines, and wolves, not to mention pack rats, mice, and snakes.

The floor steepened downward and the cave's entrance disappeared behind them. With it went a sense of comfort, of escape. The total darkness was like a door being slammed shut behind them. Travis slowed, allowing Pete to come up beside him. Just ahead was a dry, papery rattling, a sound so faint he hadn't even been able to hear it until they stopped. They paused for a couple of minutes, listening to the low breathing of the sleeping bear, then edged forward. Pete carried the torch in his left hand, the rifle cradled in his left forearm, right hand gripping the weapon's wrist. It was cocked, his finger steady on the trigger. Travis eased the Kentucky's hammer back to full cock. There was a snort, then what might have been an expulsion of air. Travis's scalp crawled. He stopped and hugged the wall. Pete put his back to the opposite wall. The minutes ticked past without another sound. The torch sputtered, a hank of burning grass peeling back from the branch. Bits of smoking grass dropped to the floor, and a dense cloud of smoke roiled turbulently from the torch until it caught flame again, brightening, throwing shadows. The sweet fragrance of burning grass floated past, and then the silence was shattered by a thunderous roar. Travis cried out in fright, and he heard Pete's startled yelp. Claws scratched stone somewhere just ahead of them. A grunt that might have been wrenched from a lunging animal seemed to explode on the musky air.

"Run!" Pete shouted, whirling toward the entrance. But there wasn't time anymore. Escape was too far away, and the bear too close. Travis whimpered as he lifted the Kentucky to his shoulder. The torchlight flickered, fading as Pete raced back the way they had come. The sound of claws continued to ring in Travis's ears. He remembered the size of the tracks they had followed, the long gap between the front pads of the bear's foot and the sharp impression of the curved claws. His rifle trembled; the Lord's prayer tumbled from his lips. Shadows moved, darkness against darkness. There was a sensation of an enormous bulk streaking forward, of wind being generated. Travis jerked the Kentucky up, firing blindly. Muzzle flash briefly illuminated the grizzly's shape, giving it size and dimension. There was another roar that seemed to drown out the thin, reedy pop of the Kentucky. The bear veered toward him, and he threw the rifle at it in a gesture of helplessness, without force, like a child throwing away a bad apple.

Then the light returned and Pete was skidding to a halt. His voice echoed through the cavern, incomprehensible in the snapping rush of impressions that flooded Travis's mind. He heard Pete's shout, saw his pa's run-down chicken house, felt the hot breath of the grizzly as it closed on him. Pete threw the torch in the bear's face, distracting it. The giant bear seemed to scream in its fury, its dripping, gleaming teeth flashing. It whirled toward Pete just as the trapper's rifle lanced the darkness with yellow flame. Sparks showered the charging grizzly, sizzling the thick, silver-tipped pelt. The torch rolled across the dusty floor, the light dipping almost to nothing before flaring up once more. Travis felt the percussion of Pete's shot against his cheek, like a slap from a ghost. The bear's flank caught him on the hip, momentarily crushing him against the wall. Then the bear moved on and Travis went spinning into darkness, the sharp sting of dust filling his nostrils, the breath knocked out of him.

He got his hands under him and rose shakily to his knees. Taking a deep, quivering breath, he leaned against the wall. Sweat tracked his face. In the dim light of the torch he saw Pete sprawled on his back on the floor, one knee cocked at an angle toward the low ceiling. From beyond the cave's mouth he heard the crack of Johnny's rifle, the boom of Charlie's fusil, a single triumphant shout, and then silence.

Travis sagged, feeling sick to his stomach. Pete groaned and stirred, then sat up. Blood sheened his forehead from a shallow cut below his scalp, and his face appeared ashen. He looked around bewilderedly, blinking against the blood that ran into his left eye.

"Pete?" Travis said.

"Sonofabitch," Pete breathed. He tried to climb to his feet, but the effort cost him too much. He sank back to the floor, lowering his head.

"Pete? Are you all right?"

"Yeah." His voice sounded small in the still air, as fragile as rim ice. Tears formed in Travis's eyes. He squeezed them shut, turning his face to the wall.

"Travis?"

Travis didn't answer.

"Boy, are you hurt?"

"No," Travis said into the wall, shame cracking his voice. "I . . . I think I peed my pants. Goddamnit, I peed my pants."

Pete's laughter rippled softly through the shadows. "I should've told you," he said. "Hell, I should've remembered. Always empty your bladder before you enter a grizzly's den, kid. Any old timer'll tell you that."

CHAPTER THIRTY-TWO

Mateo sat with his back to the crumbling dirt bank, his knees drawn up under his serape and the brim of his old gray felt sombrero tied over his ears with a bandanna. His face was drawn from lack of food and sleep, his eyes red-rimmed and gritty, narrowed with pain. His jaw trembled in the frigid air, although he kept his teeth clamped tightly together to prevent them from chattering and giving away his position. Above the black, serrated ridge of mountains to the east the dawn was like an arched, rose-colored door that led into another land, a land of warmth and plenty, without pain or fatigue or hunger . . . or memories.

Mateo kept his eyes on that glowing pastel opening, drawn by its promise of something better. His expression was as cold and emotionless as death, but inside something new reached out with longing for that final escape. Unconsciously, he slid his thumb along the razor's edge of his cutlass, parting the flesh over the ball without awareness of the pain or the quick dripping of blood. He felt strangely disassociated, like two separate entities that were only fragilely connected. In one there was loneliness and despair and a deep-seated but indeterminate pain. In the other there was nothing except the image of the door and the dream of what lay beyond it.

The cutlass moved in his hand. At that same instant a horse nickered somewhere to the north. Mateo jumped, the cutlass slicing deeper into his thumb. He swore under his breath, jerking the hand away from the blade and shoving the bleeding thumb instinctively into his mouth. He looked in the direction of the nickering horse, praying that his own didn't answer. He had left the *grullo* tied in a stand of saplings perhaps a quarter of a mile away late last night, then made his way back here in the frosty light of a haze-ringed moon to set this crude ambush. If the *grullo* whinnied now, it was all up. He didn't think he had the strength to race back to his pony, to begin the chase anew.

He was cradled in a washed-out flute along the side of a hill that was indistinguishable from a hundred other hills surrounding it, save for the odd-shaped indentation with its recessed perch about a dozen feet above his own trail. He had been half-asleep when he passed it late last night, glancing up and to his right only at the last minute, making his decision instantly. He continued on without pause, leaving no break in his trail that might arouse suspicion. When he came to the saplings he dropped weakly from the saddle and tied the *grullo* among them, then made his way back on foot, flanking his old trail well to the side so that no trace of his return would be visible.

The night was waning by the time he worked his way down the flute and found his perch. The clear predawn air was numbingly cold, but he made himself as comfortable as the tiny spot would allow, then sat back to wait.

Time had blurred since the gunshot from the lone piñon had nearly knocked him from his saddle. He had retained consciousness only by the narrowest margin, losing the roan Eli had loaned him, with its supply of food and blankets. The *escopeta* had tumbled unknowingly from suddenly numbed fingers. He vaguely remembered driving his spurs into the *grullo*'s flanks while trying to brush away the misty blackness that threatened to envelop him. The *grullo* had taken the bit in its teeth and run, and Mateo made no effort to check its flight. He rode as if drugged, aware only of the pounding gait of his horse and the fiery lance of the wound across his ribs. The *grullo* eventually grew tired. Its pace slowed. Mateo opened his eyes, unaware until then that they had been closed. He lifted his head, staring into the blazing whiteness of the snow-blanketed land. All around him the country looked the same—rolling hills spotted with twisted cedars, interlaced with winding arroyos. The sky was a deep blue bowl, ribboned with tiny wisps of clouds. He reined his pony to the top of a hill and drew up to look around. He found the sharp spine of the Divide to his left, and with that, reestablished his direction. When he glanced behind him he discovered three dark shapes moving rapidly over his back trail, no more than a mile away. It was no trouble at all to pick out the massive contours of Gregorio el Toro, riding in the rear.

Later, when his senses had fully recovered, el Toro's lagging position began to intrigue Mateo. The giant foreman had never struck him as the kind of man who would easily relinquish his lead-dog authority. That he did so now gave Mateo fresh insight into the kind of man he was chasing, or being chased by. It was a piece of information that might provide him an edge, if he could find a way to use it to his advantage.

They settled into something of a pattern over the next couple of days. Although Mateo's determination to face Gregorio and kill him never flagged, there wasn't any doubt as to who were the hunters and who was the hunted. Time and again Mateo tried to double back in order to shake his pursuers. He tried to outrun, then to outwit them. But always they were one step ahead of him, seemingly instilled with an uncanny ability to outguess his every move.

The snow was his biggest nemesis. With a solid blanket covering everything between the mountains and the Grand, there was no way to hide his tracks. The deep snow and freezing temperatures hampered him in other ways, too. Combined with the loss of blood from his wound, it sapped his strength and fogged his mind, so that at times he would ride for miles as if in a daze, before snapping out of it suddenly, and with no clear idea of where he was, or why. The musket's ball had ripped across his side, chipping one of his short ribs and exposing the bone. He had bandaged it with a strip of cloth torn from the bottom of his shirt, and poulticed it with a mixture of horse hair and chewed tobacco. Although shallow, it was sore as hell and constantly bothering him. His whole left side was stiff from the hip up to his shoulder, and any movement only aggravated the pain.

The weather was taking its toll on the *grullo,* too. Gregorio and his men were able to follow a trail already forged by the *grullo* through the deep, crusted snow. As tough as the little mouse-colored gelding was, he soon began to show the effects of the grueling pace. They both wore down fast and needed frequent rests.

Still, Mateo knew he had been lucky. By pushing himself and the *grullo* beyond what he thought either of them would have ever been capable of, he had managed to stay ahead of his pursuers, but time was running out. Gregorio was slowly closing in, forcing him toward the mountains, where the country was rougher, the snow deeper. Soon he would be trapped, weakened and unarmed—easy prey to the three hardened vultures who followed him. Yesterday afternoon, just before dusk, Mateo had again feigned to the north, then quickly switched directions, riding hard to the south in another attempt to get around Gregorio and back toward the more open country along the

Grand. And as he had twice in the past, Gregorio had split his forces, riding hard with one other man to intercept Mateo to the north, while sending his second man to the south. It was this man whom Mateo waited for now, whose horse had just whinnied, and who still approached.

Mateo slid the cutlass from beneath his serape. He could hear the squelch of dry snow as the horseman approached. It sounded like one man, and Mateo prayed that it was. He knew Gregorio had already discovered his ruse of doubling back, and was even now following his trail south. Soon the three men would join forces once more, increasing the odds beyond hope. But for now, for one brief opening in time . . .

The horse appeared suddenly, a high-headed sorrel with a crooked blaze and a broad snip down its velvety nose. Its rider wore a high-peaked oilcloth sombrero and an ankle-length leather riding coat, split up the back as far as his waist. He rode with his head down, following Mateo's tracks in the growing light, his face hidden by the broad, curled brim of his hat. A polished musket was balanced across the high pommel of his saddle, and Mateo smiled grimly. This was the man who had shot him from behind the piñon, and who would now pay for his attempt at murder.

Mateo remained as if frozen until the rider was directly below him, then he simply tipped forward, pushing off with the balls of his feet. The sorrel sensed his presence at the last moment and threw its head up, crushing the brim of the rider's sombrero. The rider cursed and tightened his grip on the reins, looking up just as Mateo's cutlass began its swing toward his neck.

The rider was Salvador. Mateo recognized him from the time Gregorio had ridden into the brigade's camp on the upper Grand. Salvador's face registered surprise, then fear. He started to lift his arm in defense, but Mateo's attack was too sudden, too vicious; it carried with it all the pent-up rage of the past—the beatings, the fear, the humiliation, the cruel brands seared into the young flesh of his cousins. The cutlass swept cleanly into the flesh between Salvador's neck and shoulder, parting tendon and muscle, severing nerves. He screamed as Mateo's balled body struck him, slamming him from the saddle. The sorrel whinnied shrilly, reared, then bolted. The muffled drumbeats of its hooves quickly faded.

Mateo landed face-first in the snow. He lay there, gasping from the effort, then staggered to his feet. The cutlass had been wrenched from his grasp, buried solidly in Salvador's shoulder. Mateo's hand snaked under his serape and the *belduque* appeared as if by magic, its cutting edge up. But Salvador remained where he had fallen, his face drained of color, his eyes rolled back in shock. He gasped for breath, his good arm flapping uselessly in the bloodied snow, his legs kicking spastically. Blood pumped from a sheared artery deep in the vaquero's chest, squirting in a thin, crimson arc across the snow. Cautiously, Mateo moved forward, but Salvador was already dying, the blood slowing, the eyes glazing. The killer's arm fell back in the snow, the fist closing once, then relaxing in death.

Slowly, Mateo straightened. His breath sent little puffs of vapor jetting into the thin air. He looked over his shoulder, back the way Salvador had come, and was surprised at the growing light, the quick flight of the night's shadows as the dawn spread, like the darting of a mouse before a coyote. He could trace the trail he and Salvador had made over the hills, and was relieved to see that it was empty. So far, at least, Gregorio and the other man, Hector, had not caught up.

Mateo jerked the cutlass free and wiped it clean with snow. The musket lay half buried nearby. He brushed the snow from it with the hem of his serape, then dug under Salvador's heavy coat for his shooting bag and a leather powder flask. Sheathed at the vaquero's belt was a pistol. Mateo grunted in satisfaction as he slid it free. It was a British-made Tower, a .70-caliber smoothbore. Mateo shoved it in his belt. He would retrieve the holster later. For now he was worried that snow had gotten into the powder in the musket and rendered the weapon useless. Quickly, keeping a close eye on his back trail, he pulled the old charge, field cleaned the musket, then reloaded it. Snapping the big frizzen closed, he breathed a sigh of relief. He was armed again, with more and better weapons than his old *escopeta* had ever been.

He went over Salvador's body with a quiet efficiency, looking for additional ammunition and food. He stripped the corpse of holster, knife, and fire-making kit, then rolled it into the middle of the trail where Gregorio would have to ride around it, acknowledging Mateo's intention.

With a final scrutiny of his back trail, he turned toward the saplings where his *grullo* was tied. After that he would find Salvador's sorrel, remembering the bulging saddlebags and the bedroll strapped behind the cantle, long-awaited food and warmth, both badly needed. In the east the rosy door that he had contemplated only minutes before had disappeared, replaced now by a flat, pale sky. Mateo regarded it silently, almost reverently, then nodded in understanding. The door had been closed, but that was all right. He knew of its existence now, knew what it offered and that if life on this earth ever became too hard again, it could be easily opened. Peace waited for him there like an old friend. There was nothing to fear.

On the eighth day after regaining consciousness in the bottom of the canyon, Remi saddled the paint in preparation for leaving. The beaver carcasses he had found in the grass beside the ponds where his traps had been set had added strength to his limbs, but the memory of their marbled, skinless carcasses raked at him like sharp-roweled spurs. "*Sacre,*" he murmured to himself, as he had a hundred times past. He owed that one. For stealing his traps and plews, for leaving him alone and injured, Jake would die. This Remi swore, despite his leg.

His leg. That was the problem. He did not know if it was gangrenous, but the color had changed little during his days of rest. The ankle was still swollen and hot to the touch, and he was unable to put much weight on it. For two days Remi had burned with a fever, remaining wrapped in his bedroll whenever he wasn't roasting meat or crawling to the pond for a drink. For a while he had feared the fever even more than the injured leg, for he knew that the fever could affect his mind in disastrous ways. He had seen men thrashing in delirium, kicking their robes aside, crawling away from food and warmth in a frantic search for something to slake their burning thirst. Such men, without others to care for them, to keep them in their bedrolls and bring them water when they reached blindly for it, would soon die of exposure. But on Remi's second day the fever had broken and his mind had cleared. He ate as much of the greasy beaver as he could stomach, and drank copious amounts of water. Slowly, he began to regain his strength. He was still weak-limbed and trembly, light-headed occasionally, and given to fits of nausea, but he knew this was likely to be as good as he got on his own. He needed help. For the first time since childhood. And he needed it desperately.

He hobbled around until he could pull himself into the saddle, then reined toward the ledge and the trail to the top. He wasn't sure how many days Jake had on him now, but he was gambling the youth wouldn't be able to travel fast. Jake didn't have the knowledge of the country that Remi did, or the skills to use it to his advantage. Remi was confident that if his leg allowed it, he could make up for the time he had remained in the canyon recuperating. He wouldn't even try to follow Jake at first. Eli had said he would take the brigade to the forks of the Grand, where he hoped to find a village of Utes. Remi would go there first. With luck he would find Jake already there, smug in whatever lies he had told. Grinning savagely, Remi reined the paint away from his old camp. In his mind he was picturing Jake's face when he rode up, the terror in his eyes as Remi squeezed the trigger.

Their voices came soft on the wind, a light murmuring mixed with the odor of woodsmoke, rising and ebbing. Mateo, barely daring to breathe, eased forward another cautious foot. It was full dark again, the night sky garnished with starlight, the moon not yet risen, although its light was already bathing the sky to the east with a milky, translucent glow, silhouetting the sharp peaks of the Divide. The cold was brutal, drilling into Mateo like a thousand knives.

He paused, listening, eyes straining, sniffing the wind. A horse snuffled on its tie rope. A man cleared his throat and spat. Gregorio's and Hector's conversation continued uninterrupted. Taking a shallow breath, Mateo crawled forward another couple of feet. Salvador's musket was balanced across his back, held there by a canvas sling. The pistol was sheathed at the small of his back where it was protected from the snow. His cutlass, *belduque,* and Salvador's *belduque* were also at his waist, ready to grab.

Gregorio and Hector had made their camp in a little stand of pines spread across the crest of a hill close to the mountains. A broken ridge of rocks extended to the north like the arthritic spine of some prehistoric beast, and a tumbling stream wound around the south and west sides of the hill. Aspens grew along the little creek, and farther down there had been signs of beaver and elk.

Despite Mateo's best efforts, he had not been able to elude the two men enough to make a break for the more open country flanking the Grand River. Slowly but inevitably he had been forced into the deeper snow close to the mountains, while Gregorio and Hector, using the trail Mateo had already broken through the knee-deep drifts, steadily closed the gap between them. Stopping at dusk, the *grullo* winded and sweating, and Salvador's sorrel equally played out, Mateo realized that by tomorrow it would all be over. His back was to the towering peaks that led up the Divide, the slopes ahead all but impassable. Short of abandoning his horses and trying to make his way across the mountains on foot—a feat he knew he was inadequately skilled to accomplish—Gregorio would run him down before the sun reached its next apex. Staring at the jumbled mountains before him, Mateo made his decision. If he could no longer flee, then it was time to fight, no matter what the odds.

Leaving the horses where they were, he made his way back on foot. Gregorio and Hector were less than an hour behind him, but it was already growing dark, the land robed in the deep purple of twilight. Mateo knew Gregorio would not push on without a break. It was the big man's policy to stop occasionally and fix a fire for some coffee and food. While he rested, he allowed his prey to gain time, but in Mateo's case it was a time usually spent in ferreting out new trails or backtracking out of box canyons. In this way, and although Gregorio still kept the pressure on himself and his men, he was also able to allow them an opportunity to replenish themselves both physically and mentally.

But Mateo knew they wouldn't rest long. The pines had been handy, offering relatively dry ground beneath their spreading boughs, wood for a quick fire, an opportunity for some food and maybe an hour's nap, taken in turns. When the moon came up they would be on his trail again, hounding him into the night.

The moon. Mateo glanced over his shoulder. Already its pale light was spilling down the western slopes, chasing the deeper shadows before it. A rounded shoulder was already visible between two peaks, gleaming like a sliver of polished bone. Soon the oblong disk would pull completely free of the mountains and Gregorio and Hector would break camp. Mateo, exposed on the long, bare slope below the pines, would be quickly spotted. After that there would be no question of the result. If he was lucky he would be killed instantly, by bullet or blade. If not, he would be captured, and tomorrow he would begin the long, tortuous ride back to his father's rancho, where he would face the brutal fury of Don Julio's revenge, of which death and decapitation would be the final insult.

Taking a deep breath, Mateo pushed on, inching his way toward the pines on his stomach. He was following a natural depression in the snow, a serpentine track that probably covered a shallow arroyo. Its shelter was minimal at best, but he was counting on the slope's lack of concealment to lower Gregorio's guard. Both vaqueros had been following him for weeks, living off their wits as much as the land, without packhorses to lighten the hardships of wilderness travel. Even Gregorio, despite his reputation, was human, Mateo reasoned. It would be difficult to outfox his father's trained killer, but not impossible.

Mateo was less than ten yards from the edge of the trees and their concealing shadows when Gregorio barked a command. Hector replied in a drowsy voice, complaining bitterly. Gregorio laughed and stood. Mateo froze where he lay. "You whine like a sick dog," Gregorio snarled to Hector, his voice brittlely clear in the cold air. "Come on, off your lazy ass. It will not be much longer now."

There was a stirring, then Mateo heard the splash of Hector's urination against a tree. "Don Julio's gold is not worth this," Hector said as Gregorio walked toward the horses with his heavy, silver-mounted saddle clutched lightly in one hand. "I wish now that I had stayed in Santa Fe."

Gregorio's voice lowered dangerously, a tone Mateo recognized well. "Your constant whining is beginning to annoy me, Hector. If it does not cease, I may be forced to return to Rancho de Chavez with the boy myself."

Hector muttered a curse, but was careful to keep the words muted and unintelligible. Gregorio chuckled mirthlessly as he flung his saddle over his mount's back, handling the heavy rig as if it were no more than a sack of straw. Mateo carefully slid Salvador's musket over his shoulders. Gregorio was hidden by the bulk of his horse, making a poor target, but Hector was silhouetted clearly against the starlit sky beyond the trees as he buttoned his fly, less than twenty yards away. Mateo's thumb caressed the musket's big lock, yet he hesitated to cock it, to warn the two vaqueros of his presence by the crisp ratcheting of sears as the musket was brought to full cock. He would get only one clear shot, and as dangerous as he knew Hector must be if he was riding with Gregorio, it was his father's foreman who chilled Mateo's heart like ice implanted inside his breast. He would kill el Toro first; then, with the big foreman out of the way, he could deal with Hector on more equal footing.

Hector finished buttoning his fly and hurried toward the pile of gear where his saddle rested. Mateo eased the musket's cock back. There was a slight click, then two more. Mateo tried to time the sounds of the musket with Hector's saddling, but nothing escaped Gregorio's pumalike hearing. The foreman stepped away from his horse as Hector lugged his saddle to his own mount. Putting out a meaty palm, Gregorio caught Hector's chest and stopped him in midstride. For a moment, neither man moved. Then Gregorio laughed. "So, the little cock has returned to the coop on his own, eh?"

In a flash of understanding, Hector dropped his saddle and started to lunge for his weapon, leaning against a nearby tree, but Gregorio's grip tightened on the smaller man's collar, and he jerked Hector back. Mateo swore as Gregorio pulled Hector in front of him. Gregorio's voice boomed across the chilly silence. "Mateo Chavez!" The words echoed over the hills, fading into the distance. "You must be cold and hungry and tired. There has not been much time for rest, even with what little food you might have found in Salvador's saddlebags. Why don't you come in, so that we can talk?"

Mateo let the musket's muzzle swing ever so slightly, the blunt front sight losing itself in the shadowy bulk of the two men.

"Come, Mateo. We are old friends, you and I. I have taught you well how to fight the Apache and the Comanche, have I not? Let's not let your father's insanity come between us." He paused, listening, then added, "I have a proposition, Mateo. It would benefit us both, and harm only your father, whom I know you hate as much as I do. Come in and listen to me. I will cause you no harm. I give you my word."

Mateo stroked the trigger gently, as he might the side of a woman's hardened nipple, yet his finger refused to tighten. Gregorio's words reached hypnotically through the night. Could they be true? Mateo wondered. He knew Gregorio chafed at taking orders from any man, yet he had stayed on at Rancho de Chavez for years, heeding Don Julio's every whim like a faithful dog. Had there been a reason for such devotion other than loyalty?

"We could be a team, Mateo, you and me. A power no man, no country, could intimidate."

Mateo's mind reeled with the possibilities. Fantasies that he had once considered impossible suddenly flickered back to life. At last he could have the authority and respect he craved. He could live in comfort, surrounded by material wealth and Indian slaves. Heads of state would seek his advice, while doe-eyed *señoritas* flirted for his attentions. He would trade with the Comanche, as he had always dreamed of doing, and increase his wealth tenfold in as many years. And when his dynasty had reached its peak, when his name was known throughout Mexico, when his power was unconquerable, then he would use his influence to drive the foreigners—the British, the Germans, and most of all, the Americans—out of his country.

Yet Mateo knew he could not accomplish so much alone. He would need help, men he could trust implicitly. Was Gregorio el Toro such a man?

Only Don Julio's expertise in matters of business surpassed Gregorio's skills at running the sprawling Rancho de Chavez. But Gregorio was more than just a cruel and cunning foreman. He was intelligent, and more important, he was greedy. Yet even Mexico, as corrupt as its power had become since its break with Spain, had laws. A man as politically influential as Don Julio couldn't just disappear. There would be too many questions, too much suspicion, and too many heirs. Such a coup as Gregorio el Toro suggested would have to be done carefully, and it would need cooperation from within the family itself.

A shiver ran down Mateo's spine as these thoughts flitted through his mind. Then Hector suddenly struggled, attempting to break Gregorio's ironlike grip, and the big foreman cuffed him as one would an unruly pup, growling, "Hold still, you little cock, before I slit your throat."

In their struggle the two men had partially turned, offering Mateo a side view. The front sight of his musket wavered, then something inside him snapped. A cold rage filled him. The musket steadied and his finger slowly tightened on the trigger. Even above the musket's roar, Mateo heard the solid *thump* of lead striking flesh. Hector squealed loudly and fell, his legs kicking. Gregorio jumped to the side, whipping out a long-barreled pistol. Its muzzle spit a yellow, sparking flame, the ball sailing no more than inches over Mateo's head. Mateo jerked Salvador's pistol from its sheath and lunged to his feet, darting for the ridge of broken rocks that snaked to the north. He ran as fast as the deep snow would allow, his knees pumping as he floundered through drifts. He carried the empty musket in his left hand, but doubted if there would be time now to reload. His

ruse to lure Mateo into camp ruined, Gregorio would press his op-
ponent unrelentingly, pushing the younger man into a mistake that
the vaquero would quickly turn to his own advantage. Mateo recognized this and was determined not to offer Gregorio that chance.

A shot rang out just as Mateo ducked into the rocks. The bullet
screamed off stone less than six inches from his ear. Mateo dove for
shelter, spitting snow as he crawled deeper into cover.

Silence drifted over the tall hill then. Mateo, still in a crouch,
pressed his back against a sloping boulder. He lifted the pistol beside
his shoulder and cocked it. He tried to control the harsh rasp of his
breathing so that he might better hear Gregorio's approach, but it
was like trying to stop the moon from rising. Fear racked him, made
him jumpy. Pine boughs, swaying gently in the growing moonlight,
created a dozen creeping shadows. Mateo swallowed and blinked.
He forced himself to relax, to think. It would be a game of skill and
stealth now, and although Mateo longed to reload the musket for the
security a second weapon would give him, he knew he dare not set
the pistol aside for even a moment.

Time passed with a painful slowness. The moon pulled free of the
Divide, a pale silver orb casting its cold light over the rocks. Gradually, Mateo calmed. The sounds of the night returned. From the trees
a horse's shod hoof stomped the frozen ground; the breeze murmured through the pines; even the snow seemed to whisper as it ad-
justed to the plummeting temperature. Then Mateo heard the subtle
scrape of leather against stone, easily distinguishing the source as the
hard rawhide sole of a moccasin. He shifted slightly to face the direction of the sound. He let the pistol's muzzle lower until it was leveled toward a gap in the rocks. Gray starlight filled the narrow
opening, giving him a clear field of fire. He waited silently, barely
daring to breathe. Within moments he heard another slow footfall.
Alarm rose in him. Surely Gregorio el Toro would not be so foolish
as to make the same mistake twice. Yet the sound was unmistakable.
Was it another ruse, or had Gregorio's reputation overshadowed the
man? Mateo glanced behind him, around him. The moonlit expanse
of the long slope was fully exposed now. Only the tracks of his own
passage disturbed the field of snow. Around him the rocks rose in a
tumbled heap. It would be possible for a man to approach through
them, but not a man of Gregorio's size. The gaps and fissures were
too narrow, too restricting. El Toro would never allow himself to be-

No, Mateo thought, *he isn't*. The genuine panic in Gregorio's voice convinced him at last that the man was truly injured. He reloaded the pistol; then, keeping his cutlass in his free hand, he stepped into the clear. The dark hulk of Gregorio's body was slumped to the ground beside the tree. Slowly, Mateo approached, the pistol thrust before him. "Throw your weapons away, Gregorio."

"I cannot move."

"Throw your weapons away, or I'll shoot!"

"Mateo, please, have mercy. Please."

The big man lifted his head slightly, but otherwise remained immobile. Circling to the side without lowering his pistol, Mateo came into full sight of Gregorio's collapsed form. "Gregorio, I have a pistol trained on the top of your head. If you move, I will shoot."

"I know."

"Where are you shot?"

"In the chest, the first time. Across my neck the last time."

"Can you feel your toes?"

"Yes. They burn. And my fingers. I can move them, but only a little."

"Then I do not think you are permanently crippled. You have been stunned, not paralyzed."

Gregorio lifted his head even higher, revealing for the first time the moisture in his eyes. The Bull, the fabled Bull, killer of men, women, children, torturer and scourge of the Pecos River country, was on the verge of tears. Mateo felt a surge of revulsion as he resheathed his pistol. "So the great terror has fallen like a babe from the cradle," he said without pity.

"Help me, Mateo."

Mateo squatted, reaching out. As he did, Gregorio moved, his left arm darting out from behind his body, a cocked pistol snapping forward like the strike of a rattlesnake. But before he could pull the trigger, Mateo's cutlass flashed. The blade cut into the flesh of Gregorio's wrist, embedding itself in the bone. Gregorio screamed and rolled away, the pistol falling from his grasp. Calmly, Mateo picked it up and stood. "Such a foolish ploy for one with a reputation such as yourself."

Gregorio's eyes widened. "Mateo, it was true. I swear it. For a while, after your bullet struck the back of my neck—"

Mateo lifted the pistol. "If I never do another thing for my people,

come trapped in a place where he couldn't maneuver. Mateo turned back to the star-dusted gap, lifting the pistol expectantly. He had only moments to wait.

A head appeared at the bottom of the gap, rising slowly. Moonlight glinted off a musket barrel, and a second later a man hove into sight, paused only a second, then started to drop into the deeper shadows. Mateo fired as the man kicked away from the gap, the pistol bucking in his hand. He heard a cry, the sound of a body tumbling awkwardly through the rocks, then three quick, gurgling gasps, followed by silence.

Mateo waited with his heart pounding until the clattering echo of the pistol shot faded. He pulled his cutlass and laid it across his lap, then hurriedly reloaded both the musket and the pistol. Finished, he resheathed cutlass and pistol, then started cautiously forward, worming his way through the rocks.

It was Hector, lying sprawled between the rocks, facedown in the snow with one moccasined foot caught in a tiny cleft in the stone. Blood stained the snow around him, and the back of his heavy wool coat was ripped where the pistol's ball had exited, the hole ragged and soggy. Mateo knelt at his side, but the vaquero was dead. Standing, puzzled, Mateo made his way through the rocks. He moved cautiously, like a hunter stalking a deer, but his mind was numb. He had heard the sound of lead striking flesh with his first shot and had been certain—absolutely certain—that Hector had been shot, seriously wounded if not killed. So who had taken that knuckle-sized sphere of lead, if not Hector?

Mateo paused at the edge of the trees, cocking the musket savagely, without regard to quietness. A few embers still glowed red from the site of the campfire, reflecting eerily off the lower boughs. A horse stomped a hoof against the cold, but there was no other sign of life. Mateo stepped under the trees. It felt strange to be walking on bare ground again, the soft passage of his heavy winter moccasins muffled by a thick, musty carpet of brown needles. He worked his way toward the fire, circling wide to come at it from the west. Yet he hadn't gone a dozen paces when Gregorio's hoarse chuckle stopped him cold.

"So, the little cock comes at last," Gregorio observed.

Mateo spun, bringing the musket up, but there was no target. He ducked behind a tree, listening to the sound of Gregorio's harsh, wet laughter.

"I could easily shoot you," Gregorio said. "But I promised—" His voice was choked off by a fit of coughing, tinged with a liquid rattling. Mateo smiled bitterly. So his aim had been true after all. Sniffing loudly, Gregorio went on, "I promised your father I would return you alive, and Gregorio el Toro is a man of his word. Besides, I will need a slave to care for the horses and see to the chores around the camp until I am healed. That will be your job, boy. To make my life easier. My job—" Again there was that quick, choking cough, the hurried gasps. "My job," he continued, fighting for breath, "will be to make your life a living hell. You will pay for the aggravation you have caused me, little cock. This I promise you."

"You do not sound like a man to be making such threats anymore," Mateo answered in a mocking tone. "Perhaps the bull has become a steer?"

Anger filled Gregorio's voice, booming through the dark grove. "Do not think el Toro has lost his balls, cock. I have been hurt worse than what your little musket ball has done to me. I have suffered pain at the hands of the Apaches and Comanches both. This is nothing compared—" He coughed, then spat, and when he went on, his voice was weaker, though no less determined. "This is nothing compared to an Apache's knife."

"I do not think you will live to return to my father's rancho," Mateo said. "Perhaps you should lie down now, and let me tend to your wound."

Gregorio laughed. "You have pride, and spirit. I like that in a man I am about to break. It makes the game more of a challenge. But trust me, boy, I *will* break you. Tougher men than you have learned to grovel and beg. I have had killers become women who jump at my slightest call. That awaits you, little cock. Think about it. Dream of it at night. It is a long way back to Rancho de Chavez. By the time you arrive, you will welcome your father's brutality for the peace and luxury it will afford you."

To Mateo's mind came the image of the rosy door he had witnessed only that morning, awaiting Salvador's approach through the cold dawn light. He knew Gregorio was wrong. He would never break like a castrated slave. Death no longer struck fear in him; he was a survivor, as he had told Jorge his last day in the Utah village. Suicide wasn't an end, it was merely another option.

"Drop your weapons, little cock," Gregorio ordered.

Mateo leaned the musket against a tree and stepped a
"*Throw it, damn you,*" Gregorio shouted.

Mateo smiled. "I do not wish to harm it, dead man. It weapon, and I will need it when I return to the brigade."

At last, Gregorio showed himself. He stepped from behind to Mateo's right, his long gun leveled in one hand. Bracing a der against the trunk for support, he said, "Your mouth wearie already, cock. You will learn to do as I—"

Mateo threw himself to the side, hitting the ground rolling. G gorio fired, his single bullet plowing into the carpet of needle showering Mateo's face with dust and mold. Yanking Salvador's pistol from its sheath, Mateo tried to find Gregorio with its front sight, but the big man had vanished like smoke in the wind. Mateo scuttled toward a tree, taking shelter behind its trunk.

"You will regret such foolish bravado," Gregorio called through clenched teeth. "I will have a finger for that wasted shot."

"Are you hungry, Gregorio?" Mateo taunted. "Or has your belly been filled with lead?"

Gregorio grunted in anger. "You will regret—" He coughed, bending forward at the waist and losing the protection of his tree. Mateo braced the pistol in both hands, sighting on Gregorio's bobbing form. He squeezed the trigger, hearing, even above the roar of the pistol, Gregorio's howl of pain. "You . . . you little . . . cock . . ." Gregorio gasped.

Mateo jerked his cutlass free. "What has happened to the great Toro, who once inspired fear by his mere presence?" Mateo got his feet, careful to keep the tree between them. "Perhaps he sho change his name. Gregorio de Vaca, eh? Gregorio the cow."

There was fear in Gregorio's words when he spoke again. "I not move. Your shot . . . mother of God, Mateo . . . I ca move . . ."

Mateo remained hidden. If he had lost his fear of death, he ha lost his respect for the big man's treachery.

"Mateo, I will make you a deal. A real one this time. We v partners, you and I. Mateo?"

"I don't think I would be interested in becoming a partner crippled man," Mateo called. "Perhaps it would be best if I l for the—"

"*Mateo!* Son of a whore, Mateo, I am not faking."

I have done this," he whispered, punctuating his words with the blast of the pistol.

Chapter Thirty-Three

Travis ducked his head into the frayed collar of his canvas jacket as hard-grained pellets of wind-driven snow stung his cheeks and the backs of his hands. His exposed ears ached in the gripping cold, and his fingers felt like frozen nubs at the end of useless clubs. He had finally broken down and purchased a heavy, four-point Hudson's Bay blanket on credit from Eli, and Pete's woman, Annie, had helped him cut out a pattern for a hooded capote, with enough material left over for a couple of pairs of mittens, but the garment was only half finished. As the brigade wound higher through the swaying pines, Travis tried to warm himself with the promise of the capote's warmth. Another evening of sewing, two at the most, and the knee-length coat would be ready.

Blue stumbled over a fallen tree trunk, breaking the flow of Travis's thoughts. He lifted his face miserably to the trail ahead. The brigade was strung out single-file through a dense pine forest, climbing steadily. The pack animals had been placed on lead ropes as they entered the trees, with each man handling two to three animals apiece to prevent them from scattering or becoming lost; when the brigade reached open country again, the mules would be turned back over to the care of the *arrieros*. Travis could see the rumps of the three mules ahead of him, rocking easily, and beyond those the sloped, raillike spine of Old Cal Underwood. Through the snow-mantled boughs he could see pieces of the others, splashes of color flashing briefly through the limbs as the trail switched back and forth.

They had been four days crossing the swollen Colorado River. When the brigade reached the far shore, Eli ordered a skin canoe left on the south bank, in the unlikely event that Mateo Chavez might actually survive his encounter with Gregorio el Toro and his men, and come after them. Without any real hope that he would, the brigade pushed on. They had left the river behind them yesterday, after following it downstream for twenty miles or so, and reached this low range of mountains running east and west at dusk. They had started their slow ascent just after dawn, but Travis, his concept of time numbed by the cold, had no idea how long ago that had been, or how far back. It seemed as if he had spent a lifetime passing through these towering pines, climbing steadily along a snow-slickened trail that he was barely able to make out.

He heard a shout from somewhere above him, followed by laughter. Pete Meyers's voice drifted down on the wind, eliciting more laughter. The brigade continued without pause, but Pete's voice lingered in Travis's mind. It had surprised him when none of the men mentioned his accident in the cave to the rest of the outfit. The dark evidence of his urination after the grizzly's charge had been too obvious to miss against his rust-colored trousers when he and Pete finally emerged from the cavern's darkness, but except for a quick exchange of glances, neither Johnny nor Charlie had acknowledged it.

The giant grizzly had lain crumpled near the mouth of the cave, a gaping bullet wound at the base of the skull the obvious cause of death. When both Johnny and Charlie claimed credit for the killing shot, Pete announced that the two men could blame well skin the thing themselves. "This coon's needin' a pipe, anyway," Pete had said. "My nerves is plumb frazzled."

So while Johnny and Charlie skinned and butchered the bear, Pete and Travis sat in the sunlight and talked. Afterward, they continued upriver until just before dusk, when they ran into a herd of elk. The men scattered through the trees, slipping to within a hundred yards of the grazing beasts. At a signal from Johnny, they fired their weapons simultaneously, dropping four big bulls in their first volley. Pete, reloading faster than Travis would have thought possible, managed to drop another before the herd disappeared into the timber of a side canyon.

It was dark by the time they skinned and butchered the elk, so they spent the night at the kill site, and Travis washed his jeans in the river and let them dry beside the fire overnight. They killed two more elk and a deer the following morning, and returned to the camp by early afternoon, the pack mules heavily loaded. Old Cal, Jake, and Clint had also gone out to hunt, so they had plenty of skins, and more meat than they could ever carry with them.

Travis had been fascinated by the construction of the canoes and the ingenuity of the mountain men. The framework had been made from the sturdy green limbs of willow trees. The ends that would eventually support the gunwales had been bored into the frozen ground in parallel rows that came to a point at each end. The upper ends of each limb had then been lashed together, the sharp points and stray splinters shaved off with a knife, then smoothed down even more with a rasp. The gunwales were tied in place, and then the green elk and deer hides were lashed over the frames of the canoes with the epidermis facing outward, sewn together with sinew. Next the mountain men had built small fires near the crafts, occasionally shoveling glowing coals underneath to hasten the drying process. With time, the hides had shrunk to an ironlike tightness, like flesh over the ribs of a starving man. The canoes had then been uprighted and rawhide stretched between the gunwales at the third and two-thirds marks in each vessel for extra strength. After the canoes were dragged to the Colorado's banks, Pierre, Clint, and Jorge coated the outside of each craft with a mixture of animal fat and ashes, paying particular attention to the seams. Finally, the canoes had been launched, the tough yet flexible crafts riding the choppy waters of the Colorado with surprising stability.

Johnny had cut the claws off the grizzly's hide and given five to each of the men involved in the bear's death. He strung his own on a piece of leather that he hung around his neck; Charlie attached his to his appaloosa's headstall, while Pete gave his to Annie, who said she would work them into a new buckskin jacket she wanted to make for him when they went into winter quarters. Travis had shoved his five into his jacket pocket, uncertain as to what to do with them. He was too embarrassed to display them in any way, although Pete had been more than generous in relating their exploits to the rest of the brigade, even embellishing it in places. Travis, Pete declared, had shown the hair of the bear, standing firm in the grizzly's charge and being the first to strike coup against the shaggy brute. Travis had barely been able to hold his head up during Pete's telling of the tale. Didn't he know, Travis wondered, that he hadn't run because he had been too petrified by fear? It had been Pete who returned to face the grizzly's charge, probably saving Travis's life in the process. Yet when Travis tried to give Pete his five claws, the trapper had laughed. "Hell, no," he exclaimed. "You earned 'em. Keep 'em."

But the memory of his soaked trousers and the numbing terror prevented any pride in ownership. So, clinging to the flexing gunwales of the skin canoe as it cut through the dirty gray waves of the Colorado, Travis had pulled the claws from his pocket and dropped them one by one into the river's depth.

The trees thinned, and Travis lifted his eyes past the line of animals strung out in front of him and spotted a notch of blue sky above the swirling ground blizzard, a sense of emptiness beyond. A shout of triumph floated down from above, and twenty minutes later Travis crowded up with the rest of the brigade atop the wind-scoured pass, staring north across a frozen world.

"Halfway there," Eli shouted, his words nearly whipped away by the keening wind.

"There be the White," Old Cal crowed, pointing to a break in the country far below and maybe twenty miles away. "Wagh, this coon's took hisself a heap o' beaver outta them waters."

Johnny, sitting his mare beside Travis, said, "Old Cal's right. I've trapped the Río Blanco many a time, and it's good country. Maybe some of the best I've ever trapped."

"If Sublette, Jackson, and Smith's boys ain't already there," Pete said.

Old Cal jerked upright, his eyes going wide as an owl's. "So what if they be, Pete Meyers?" he squeaked in indignation. "T'ain't no nigger, red nor white, gonna keep Ol' Cal off'n the White. Do ye hyar?" He swiveled his head at the others. "White River, that be Ol' Cal's country, and ain't no moss-eatin' St. Louy pilgrim gonna run him off'n it either, by God."

"Hell, nobody's tryin' to run you off," Charlie said disgustedly. "Pete's just sayin' maybe it's already been skimmed. It's a hell of a lot closer from here to where them boys rendezvous than it is from here to Taos."

Old Cal grumbled and looked away. Grinning at the trapper's discomfort, Pete needled, "Now, that's the truth, Cal. Could be since we set our traps in the Grand first, we'll have to play second fiddle here."

"There's only one way to find out," Eli said, lifting the sorrel's reins. "Come on, boys. Let's get outta this wind before it blows us back to the Colorado."

Old Cal gave Pete a dark look. "Them be Old Cal's waters, ye hyar, Pete Meyers? Ain't no moss-eatin' pilgrim gonna—"

"Aw, shut up," Charlie said, putting an end to the old trapper's words, but not his surly glare.

There was what might have been a trail dropping off the bare ridge and into the slash of pines about fifty yards below them. Eli led them toward it, his sorrel breaking a path through the crusted snow that came above the horse's knees. The others strung out single-file behind him, a long, colorful snake winding down into the trees. Jake, who had been riding near the front of the brigade, pulled his mount out of the line until Travis came alongside. His voice roughened by the cold, he growled, "How's that mule holding up, Ketchum?"

The question, delivered in Jake's usual sneering manner, took Travis by surprise. It was the first time in weeks that Jake had brought up the subject of the mule, and the first time since returning to the brigade alone after Remi LeBlanc's death that he had shown any of his old character.

Jake kicked his horse forward, forcing it to break through the hard snow at Travis's side. "You and me ain't finished, Ketchum."

"What the hell brought that on?" Travis asked, unable to shake his surprise.

"I'll be wanting that mule back pretty soon. I'll let you know when." He spurred his horse on ahead, obliging Travis to haul back on Blue's reins until Jake had slipped into the line of trappers behind Old Cal.

Weariness settled over Travis as he booted Blue into motion. He was reminded of Clint's warning, back near the Black Canyon: *Sooner or later he'll challenge you over that mule. When he does, you'd best be ready to kill. It's the only thing that'll stop him.*

Travis sighed and gave Blue a taste of his heel. "Come on, mule," he said. "Life ain't gonna get no easier waitin' for summer."

It was hell going down, too, the snow deeper on the north slope of the mountain range, and harder to buck. The shadows deepened and the air grew colder; the occasional laughter that had punctuated the trappers' ascent that morning gradually gave way to terse phrases and explosive curses as they dragged the pack animals through the belly-deep drifts. Yet for all that, they made good time. They camped that night in a canyon with prehistoric paintings on the yellow sandstone walls, and reached the White River around noon the next day, wind-whipped and beaten down, but intact. While the rest of the hands set up camp, Eli sent Johnny on a quick *paseo* upriver, while Eli himself went downriver to explore.

It seemed warmer along the White, although there was still several inches of snow on the ground. Moister, maybe, Eli thought, without the sharp dryness of the higher elevations; the wind had let up, too, and that always helped. He rode slowly, staying with the river for several miles, and turned back around midafternoon, making a wide swing to the south.

It was a beautiful day, the sky high and winter-pale, scudded with fluffy white clouds that sailed swiftly eastward. He made his way through a country similar to that which he had left on the lower Grand—low, rolling hills dotted with piñon and juniper, arroyos like raw gashes ripped through the earth, sage and bunchgrass poking up through the snow—but with subtle differences, too, signs that they had left the lower deserts behind for good and were edging into the more northern reaches. Patches of cactus were smaller and fewer, and the mesquite had disappeared entirely; the sagebrush was taller, the rocks and cliffs more broken, the soil less red. Aspens were more predominant along the waterways, indicating a higher altitude. They were small things, to be sure, but noting them gave Eli a sense of satisfaction. Progress was being made, the brigade was moving forward. They were three-quarters of the way to the Salt Lake country now, and despite the setbacks, they were making good time, and taking in a fair share of plews in the process.

Eli took his time, enjoying the rich bounty of the land as much as the solitude. He saw elk and deer, and the hills were queued with the dainty prints of pronghorns. Buffalo sign was less plentiful, but it was there, for the first time since leaving the plains east of the Sangre de Cristos, and it made Eli's mouth water for fresh hump and tongue. He saw the tracks of wolves and coyotes, martens, fox, and fishers. The widely spaced prints of loping jackrabbits twisted through the sage, and the thin, scurrying trails of mice and other rodents marked the snow in every direction. Twice he spotted the broad pad marks of a catamount, and once, far in the distance, he watched a band of wary, wild-maned mustangs flee over a hill. Excitement rose in him, and his hunter's blood pulsed a little quicker. He had to remind himself that there was still good hunting in Missouri, but somehow, the thought of stalking deer along some farmer's cornfield tempered his exhilaration.

It was still a couple of hours before sunset when Eli pulled up on a ridge overlooking the camp. He leaned forward with his elbow across his saddle horn, his other arm resting over the first. Pierre's fire made a thin, transparent column of smoke that rose up straight for about fifty feet before bending to the east. A couple of the women were gathering firewood inside the trees; others were setting up small hide lodges and shanties, while the men added the finishing touches to McClure's breastworks. The remuda was grazing on the hills south of camp, under the watchful eyes of Jorge and Clint. Far upstream, he saw Old Cal making his way alone, and although the distance was too great to tell for sure, he was certain the strange old mountain man had his trap sack draped over his mount's croup. Pete and Charlie had also put out to set a few traps. They had apparently found a ford nearby and were riding downstream, but along the White's north bank. Although they were probably two miles away, he could clearly see Pete pull off his hat and wave it in a friendly, acknowledging gesture. Eli took his own hat off and waved in return, garnering a wave from Jorge and McClure in the process. He smiled. It was good to know the camp was alert and that he had been spotted immediately.

He found a path leading off the ridge and rode down, but rather than turning toward the camp, he reined toward a low rise with a jagged escarpment of yellow-hued sandstone. Dismounting, he found a dry place among the rocks and sat with his back to a broken, sun-warmed cliff. He dug a well-worn cigar from his pouch, and on impulse, lit it with flint and steel.

He sat there for a long time, smoking, thinking, listening to the sorrel pick grass. With the responsibility of the brigade temporarily out of his hands, he turned his thoughts to the killer of Juan Vidales and Cork-Eye Weathers, the man, or woman, who had hamstrung the brigade's mules back at Río Colorado, and burned its trade tent. He tried to piece together the little he knew, to make sense of it all, and of course, to figure out who the culprit was. He had already dismissed all the old hands as suspects. With the exception of Pierre Turpin, he had known them all too long and trusted them implicitly;

Cork-Eye had been his only doubt among the old-timers, but Cork-Eye's innocence had been established by his own death. That left only the new men—Travis, Mateo, Jorge, the Orr brothers, and possibly Pierre.

So who? Eli asked himself, circling back to the same question that had haunted him for weeks. Who had the experience, the opportunity . . . the motive?

His jaw clamped down a little tighter around his cigar. The motive was always money or revenge, he thought. He drew on his cigar, staring at a spot just above the sorrel's head. Money or revenge? He pondered the possibilities. If the traitor was working for one of the bigger St. Louis outfits, as McClure believed, it would be for money. But no amount of money would compensate for experience, not where the old boys from St. Louis were concerned. Eli had realized a long time ago that the fur trade was often bloodiest in the boardrooms of St. Louis and New York; it wouldn't be their style to leave something like this in the hands of untried youngsters. He lifted his gaze to the distant camp. Pierre might have the experience, Eli thought, but Pierre had worked for Ewing Young's outfit last season, not returning to the Spanish settlements until late in the summer. Young wasn't big enough to worry about sabotaging the competition, and as far as Eli knew, none of the St. Louis outfits had representatives in Taos or Santa Fe. It had to have been someone who had been back East this year, and again, that left only the new men—Travis, Jake, Clint.

His thoughts jumped, taking another tack. That was the key, he decided. Not who had the motive. Hell, that could be anyone. But who had the opportunity, not just to knife Vidales and Cork-Eye, but to be coerced by one of the St. Louis outfits. Certainly not Mateo or Jorge. Travis hailed from Arkansas; Jake and Clint claimed Louisiana as their home, yet any one of them might have gone to St. Louis first. . . .

"But they're all too goddamn young!" Eli exclaimed, smacking a fist into the palm of his hand. He shook his head in exasperation. What was he missing? What was so plain before him that he was overlooking it entirely?

The sorrel had lifted its head and was watching him curiously. Eli shifted the cigar from one corner of his mouth to the other. If it wasn't one of the new men, then it had to be one of the old hands. Old Cal, perhaps, or even Johnny. But damnit, Eli thought, goddamnit, he didn't want to believe that. The thought sickened him to the core. The massive form of Gregorio el Toro took shape in his mind. El Toro had probably shadowed them since leaving Taos. Could he be the culprit? Or one of the Utes, who might have exchanged insults with Cork-Eye, back in old Bowlegs's village? Half a dozen notions flitted through his mind, yet in the end he was forced to dismiss them all. Whoever the traitor was, he, or she, was riding with the brigade. It was, he decided, the only thing he could be certain of.

Restless, Eli walked away from the camp. The snow under his moccasins crunched loudly as he made his way to the edge of the trees and stared south at the purple scar of their back trail, fading as the last of the daylight drained off to the west. He pulled his heavy greatcoat tighter, bringing the stiff wool collar up around his ears. He was aware of the sounds of the camp behind him—the rehashing of Pete's bear tale, the clatter of kettles and pans as Pierre and Grass That Burns cleared away supper's mess, the stomping and blowing of the remuda—yet he felt strangely isolated from it all, surrounded only by the demons in his mind.

Footsteps padded the snow behind him, and he turned as Consuelo came hesitantly toward him. She paused a few feet away, her gaze searching, until Eli smiled and held out his hands. She came to him then, slipping into the protection of his arms. They stood silently for several minutes, staring south together. It was Consuelo who spoke first.

"You will drive yourself *loco* if you do not quit worrying."

It didn't surprise him that she had sensed his mood. Sometimes he thought she understood him better than he did himself. "I've been thinking about this jasper who killed Vidales and Cork-Eye. I figured he would have tipped his hand by now. I reckon it's driving me a little crazy that he hasn't."

"I think it drives us all a little crazy," Consuelo replied. "Especially McClure. You must be patient, Eli. It will happen."

Eli shrugged. He had explained to her in the past how he felt—the responsibility, the worries. He remembered something she had told him once, just before he left for Missouri, then Virginia, in the wake of his father's death: "A shack is as grand as a *hacienda,* if there is happiness within." But he had been unable to accept her notion of happiness, of satisfaction through contentment. They seemed like two separate concepts to him, as unrelated as night and day. But she had argued even that, telling him that night and day were as intricately bound as a mother and child.

"There is no difference between winter and summer, Eli," she had told him. "And drought is the same as rain to the earth."

How was he to respond to such a statement? At the time he had dismissed it with a joke, but it had stayed with him, coming back when his own doubts were at their highest. He had never known Consuelo to speak foolishness, yet the logic of those words eluded him completely, making him feel somehow small and insignificant, like a child unable to comprehend the world of an adult.

"*Jefe!*" It was Jorge, standing first watch at the edge of the trees, about forty feet away. He stepped away from the scaly bark of a cottonwood that he had been leaning against and pointed along their back trail. In the dimming light, Eli spotted movement, a hint of shape. "*Caballeros,*" Jorge added.

"How many?" Eli asked in Spanish.

"Two, I think."

"Go get my rifle," Eli said to Consuelo. "And tell the others."

She disappeared, and Jorge came closer, the linen bandage still swathing his cheek gleaming softly. "The light is not so good, but they do not slink like wolves."

"No," Eli agreed. It wouldn't be like enemy scouts to so openly follow their back trail.

Consuelo returned with his rifle, horn, and bag, carrying her own shotgun as well. Most of the others came with her, rifles bristling. Behind them, Pierre was quickly dousing the fire. To the west the sky was a pale gray band, but overhead the stars were already twinkling. By staring to the side, using his peripheral vision, Eli was able to watch the riders' approach. The deep rasp of their ponies' hooves on the snow came to the trappers from a long way out.

"Mateo, maybe," Jorge whispered hopefully.

"Is no Mateo," Pierre said, coming up behind them.

"Are they white men?" Eli asked.

"No," Jorge replied, then switched to partial English. "Maybe so *el Indio.*" He leaned forward, squinting to see better. "Maybe so Mateo," he said, his voice quickening in excitement.

"Hell, I think he's right, Eli," Pete said. "Ain't that a sombrero I seen?"

Eli had also spotted the broad brim of a sombrero as the riders filed past a snow-covered bank, but he wasn't as quick to assume the *arriero*'s return against such overwhelming odds. "There's three of 'em, plus extra horses," he pointed out.

As the riders moved closer, the trappers faded into the trees. Only Eli, Jorge, and Silas McClure remained standing in the open. Eli moved his rifle to the crook of his left arm, detecting no danger in the riders' steady approach. Coming in to clearer view at about a hundred yards, Eli saw that the lead rider was indeed an Indian, looking huge inside a heavy buffalo robe drawn over his shoulders.

"A Snake," Charlie grunted from the timber. "A goddamn Shoshone."

"Snakes in the grass, be what they be," Old Cal whined petulantly. "Back stabbers! Do ye hyar, boys? Ol' Bad Gocha's a Sheep-eater. Man'll go under quick-like, he trusts a Snake."

Snake. Sheep-eater. They both meant the same to the mountain men, names given to the Shoshone, who ranged mainly along the Snake River, west of the Tetons. Eli held his peace. Although Cal was right when he claimed Bad Gocha was a Shoshone, Eli had never had any trouble with the tribe itself.

"Ol' Cal don't trust any brownskin," Pete observed with dry humor.

"He don't," Old Cal croaked in return. "And has got his hair for his efforts, he does, now. Laugh at Ol' Cal, ye want, but watch yer own topknots, or the Sheep-eaters'll have 'em."

"Eli," Johnny called softly. "Isn't that the Snake that was visiting old Bowlegs's village?"

"Damn if it ain't," Charlie said, stepping out of the trees. "And damn if that don't look like Mateo, coming up behind 'im."

"I believe you're right," Eli said, a smile coming unexpectedly to his face.

"Sonofabitch, that's Mateo," Clint echoed.

The mountain men started coming out of the trees as the three riders approached. Eli recognized the Shoshone, Sad Smiling Man, and Mateo. The third rider was a woman, slight of build, bundled up in a blanket coat, with a colorful Mexican shawl pulled over her head. Five spare head of horses followed, the mule Gregorio el Toro had stolen and the roan Eli had loaned Mateo among them. The little party drew up about twenty yards away, and the Shoshone called loudly: "Ho! I am Sad Smiling Man. I am a friend of the Long Knives."

"I am Cutler," Eli replied. "I remember Sad Smiling Man, and that he is a friend. Come, there is meat on the fire."

Sad Smiling Man dropped from his war pony and came the rest of the way on foot. He and Eli shook hands, then Eli looked past him to where Mateo still sat his little *grullo*. "*Qué pasa*, Mateo. I didn't think I'd see you again."

Jorge pushed forward, grinning broadly. "My cousin you do not yet well know," he shouted, stumbling over his English. "Welcome, Mateo," he added, switching back to Spanish. "I also thought you would be killed. I am glad I was wrong."

Mateo stepped down, and he and Jorge embraced. Stepping back, Mateo spoke to Eli: "I have brought you your stock, as I promised. The scalps of El Toro, Hector, and Salvador I left for the wolves."

"I hope they don't poison the wolves," Eli answered grinning. His gaze feathered over the younger man. "You look like you've been through hell, Mateo. Come on in. Pierre'll kick up the fire and put some coffee on. We still have a little left."

"This one," Sad Smiling Man said, indicating Mateo, "has taken a bullet in the ribs. When he returned to Frog That Walks Like a Man's village, he was fed and bandaged, and the cold taken out of his body. He is a strong man, but I thought it best that I come with him." He studied Eli quietly for a moment, then added, "We would smoke, my friend."

"Yes, we will smoke and talk. There is much I want to know."

Eli glanced at the third rider. He had assumed that she was Sad Smiling Man's woman, but as his gaze touched her, she drew back the shawl, letting it fall to her shoulders. Eli felt a jolt in the pit of his stomach, and from behind him, Grass That Burns squealed in delight. Consuelo snorted. "Well, well, isn't this interesting," she said sarcastically, then turned and stalked back to camp.

On her pony, Falls on the Rocks watched Eli nervously, her dark chokecherry-colored eyes pleading. Pete guffawed loudly. "Hot damn, Eli, if you ain't the bull elk of the woods."

"Shut up, Pete."

"Oh, sure, amigo. I'll shut up. But I'll tell you something first.

This ol' coon's thinkin' he'd rather go back into a grizzly's den than get 'twixt you'n Connie tonight. That gal's fixin' to lift your hair, sure as shootin'.''

Several of the men laughed, and Johnny added, "Eli is going to have to step careful for a while. He's got a scalping knife poised on two sides now."

Eli's face hardened, but his hands were tied. He hooked a thumb over his shoulder, saying, "Go on in. I ain't gonna turn you out."

CHAPTER THIRTY-FOUR

Sad Smiling Man spoke slowly, cautiously, aware that his mixture of Spanish, English, French, Ute, and Shoshone would be difficult for the white-eyes to follow. They had settled around the fire that the French cookman had rekindled—himself, Cutler, Mateo, the Iroquois half-breed, Two-Dogs, and the clerk, McClure—sharing the inner circle. But Sad Smiling Man was keenly aware of the gazes of the others, those that surrounded them, listening intently as he and Cutler spoke. Their eyes were like those of the eagle that misses nothing. In them, Sad Smiling Man saw caution, curiosity, distrust, acceptance, and, in the old one with the shrill, whiny voice in particular, outright hostility. They were the manifestations of the vigilance that such men lived by, and sometimes, despite their best efforts, died by. Sad Smiling Man had experienced such behavior many times before, and he understood the emotions that governed them. These white-eyes had come to the mountains—the lands of the Shoshone, the Ute, the Cheyenne, the Arapaho, the Sioux, the Nez Percé, the Flatheads, and the Blackfeet—few in number but strong in heart. They had forged their own way through cunning and bravery. He took no offense in their lack of trust in him. But he knew he would have to be careful. He would have to set his trap with the utmost care if he expected to lure these hated white-eyes into it, as he had done before, with the help of the man called Reed, and Sad Smiling Man's brother-in-law, Bad Gocha.

* * *

Mateo, Sad Smiling Man, and Falls on the Rocks ate first. Then Mateo recounted his ordeal in the mountains, telling his story in brief, terse sentences, as if he resented having to share even this much with the brigade. Eli knew there was much the young *arriero* left out, for he said nothing of the pain and suffering he must have endured, and barely acknowledged the bandaged wound around his ribs. When he finished, he stared quietly into the flames, as withdrawn as ever.

Neither did Falls on the Rocks have much to say, although her reticence could more easily be placed within the roots of shyness. Her eyes kept darting between her old friend, Grass That Burns, and Eli, filled with hope and uncertainty. She studiously avoided Consuelo's hard stare, although it was obvious she was aware of it. She had come because she missed her friend, Grass That Burns, Falls on the Rocks claimed. She would travel with the mountain men, if Eli permitted it, and not be a burden upon the brigade. She would earn her keep with work—caring for the skins the trappers brought in, keeping wood handy for the fire, butchering, helping with the packing and unpacking. These things were a woman's job, she said, and Eli would not be disappointed in her. Then she looked at him with a boldness he had never witnessed before and added, "Perhaps the heart of Cutler, that seems so cold, would warm to Falls on the Rocks if he knew her better."

Eli's quick, daggerlike glance stilled any hoots or jibes from the men, although it had little effect on Consuelo's quick snort of derision. Stiffly, he replied that Falls on the Rocks was welcome to stay with the brigade until they met another village of her people, perhaps along the shores of the Great Salt Lake, where Eli intended to winter. But that was all. Eli was not looking for another person to care for the plews or help with the remuda. If he was, then he would surely consider Falls on the Rocks, for she was a hard worker. But Eli was not looking for a swamper, and Falls on the Rocks would have to return to her people.

He let it go at that, ignoring the misty veil that came to the girl's eyes, as he did Consuelo's harsh bark of laughter. Turning to Sad Smiling Man, Eli said, "What brings my friend Sad Smiling Man to our camp?"

If Mateo and Falls on the Rocks had been sparing with their

words, Sad Smiling Man had no such difficulty. He spoke at length of his bravery and his many deeds. He related tales of warfare and coups counted against the Blackfeet, the Crow, and the Arapaho. He came, in time, to his decision to visit old Bowlegs's village with some spotted-rumped ponies he had stolen from the Nez Percé. He was hoping to trade them for Spanish silver, which he knew the Utes were likely to have, living closer to the Mexican settlements than the Shoshone did. Hoping to heighten the desire of the younger warriors for the colorful appaloosas, he had let the horses graze with the less spectacular sorrels, bays, buckskins, and grays of the Utes' herd. But he had postponed trading too long, he said with a rueful smile, for when the Arapahos attacked Bowlegs's village, they had run off with all four appaloosas, leaving him a poor man once more. He had been with the Utes for several moons, but now it was time to go home.

"Frog That Walks Like a Man has decided to move his village to the mouth of the Seedskadee, that the white-eyes call the Green, where the winters are milder," the Shoshone concluded. "But that country is not good for Sad Smiling Man. It is too dry, and there are no buffalo there. Sad Smiling Man is hungry for the meat of the humped ones, and has decided to return to his people on the Snake River. He asks that he might travel that way with his friend Cutler and the others, who are also his friends. Sad Smiling Man is a great warrior and will help the Long Knives fight the Blackfeet, whose country lies to the north."

Eli listened politely as Sad Smiling Man worked his way through his long-winded monologue. He had little difficulty following the Indian's polyglot of different tongues and knew that most of the old hands, at least, wouldn't, either; they had been around the mountains long enough to pick up a smattering of numerous languages, and those spoken by Sad Smiling Man were familiar to them all. But he didn't perk up until near the end. "Sad Smiling Man is welcome at Cutler's fire," Eli said. "And he is welcome to travel with the Long Knives. He is a great warrior and hunter, and Cutler's heart is glad that he will come with them to the mountains that border the Salt Lake. But Cutler is puzzled. He does not know why Sad Smiling Man is afraid of the Blackfeet in a land so far from their own."

Sad Smiling Man drew himself up. "Sad Smiling Man is not afraid of the Blackfeet, but he does not wish to die a wasted death. It is better to fight the Blackfeet with friends, so that the damage to my enemies might be greater."

Silence palled the camp for several seconds. Then Pierre breathed, "By *Dieu*, him say Blackfeet, dey here?"

"It would appear so," Johnny replied. Pierre looked at Eli, asking with a motion if he wanted him to kill the fire again.

Eli shook his head, watching the Shoshone carefully. "Has Sad Smiling Man seen these Blackfeet?" he asked.

"No," Sad Smiling Man admitted. "Runners came from the west with word that the Blackfeet approached. It was not known from where."

Eli breathed easier at that. It was possible there were Blackfeet nearby, but it was just as likely they were a hundred miles away, and maybe heading in the opposite direction, for all anyone knew. They would be vigilant, as they always were, but they wouldn't alter their plans.

"The Blackfeet are the enemies of the Long Knives, as they are the Shoshones," Eli said. "They are worse than even the Arapahos, who are their relatives. It is good that Sad Smiling Man has come to Cutler with the warning that the Blackfeet are restless. But the Long Knives will not hide like children. Pierre, put some more meat on the fire. Mateo has returned, and our friends, Sad Smiling Man and Falls on the Rocks, have come to visit."

Later that evening, Mateo drew Jorge aside. He led him to the gear he had brought back after his encounter with Gregorio el Toro, drawing back a blanket to reveal the foreman's silver-mounted saddle. He grinned. "We are rich, my friend."

Jorge gave him a curious look. "You are rich, Mateo, if such things are what makes a man wealthy."

Mateo's grin faded. "Such a saddle would be worth two hundred pesos in Santa Fe, perhaps more. Half of it is yours. And see." He bent over the pile of gear, withdrawing Hector's musket and pistol. "These are yours. You have earned them."

Jorge took a deep breath, looking into his cousin's eyes. "I do not want them, Mateo. Such things are unimportant to me now." He touched his breast, smiling sadly. "Many things have changed for me in here since I felt the touch of Gregorio's iron. It has been like a purging." He paused, as if searching for the words that would better explain these newfound feelings, but in the end, he could only shrug helplessly. "I have my bow and lance, and those are enough. These things, Mateo"—he motioned toward the musket—"they are just things. They will not make me any more of a man. They will not offer me peace. Someday I will have better weapons, because this is a dangerous land and a man needs to be armed well. But for now the bow and the lance are all that I desire."

Mateo felt his anger rise. He flung the musket back into the pile of gear he had taken from Gregorio and his men. "Damn you, Jorge! Where does such foolishness come from? The bow and the lance are for the old ones. They are the weapons of our fathers' fathers, and they served them well because their enemies were armed no better. But times change now, and we must change with them if we are to ever regain the pride that has been taken from us."

"I have my pride," Jorge replied simply. "And I have learned that it is not a thing that can be taken from us, or won back with muskets and swords."

Mateo's voice shook with rage. "All the way back, I thought of you, Jorge. It is what kept me alive when Gregorio ran me down in the mountains like a rabbit before the hounds. It is what made me warm when I had no fire, and full when I had no food. These things that you so stupidly dismiss are why we left our homes, why we came here, to work for the Americans. Now you will throw all that away?"

"I know you do not understand this, but . . . you speak of the British and the Americans as if you hate them, as if they are our enemies, yet it is a British musket that you try to give me, with powder and lead from the Missouri settlements. You are right, the times have changed." He shook his head in frustration. "Your anger, Mateo, it is like a poison that eats at you, destroying you from within. Once I shared that anger, but no more. I wish only to do my job, to make friends, and at the end of the season I will collect my pay and find another job." He paused, searching Mateo's face as if desperately seeking some sign of understanding. Finally he went on, his voice gentle. "It was different for me, Mateo. I did not grow up with a father who was a tyrant. My father was strict, yes, but . . . he did not beat me as your father beat you. He did not treat me as he did his dogs and his horses. Your father, Mateo, his spurs were always as bloody as his lance when he ran buffalo, and I know you felt his quirt many times as a boy. I think it is Don Julio's quirt that eats at you now, that makes you like a wounded bull."

"That is a lie," Mateo breathed. His vision hazed. He was aware of himself moving forward, of his fist lashing out without warning, but there was no sense of feeling, and only a faint jolt along his arm as Jorge flew backward. He stopped and drew a long shaky breath. Looking down, he saw the cutlass half drawn, and in confusion slid it back in its scabbard. "You are a liar, Jorge. My father punished me only when I was wrong or bad. But he taught me to be a leader, something your father would never be able to teach you."

"I know you do not believe that, Mateo. Your father was crazy. Look at your legs, your back. See the scars your father's quirt put there."

Jorge's words seemed to batter him. He stepped back, the image of the scars his father had carved into his flesh flashing before his eyes. When had his father beaten him so badly? As a child, surely, but when . . . how?

"Forget the past," Jorge cried. "Is that not why we left, to become our own men, free of our fathers?" He stood, shaking the snow out of his hair, and as he did his queue loosened. Reaching up, he yanked it from his hair and flung it aside. "The mark of a *cibolero,* Mateo. Get rid of it. Get rid of everything that reminds you of the past."

Mateo shook his head, dragging back a step. What Jorge asked was impossible. His past was as inextricably connected to his life as the scars now, and perhaps, in its own way, the past was a scar in itself. He looked away and down, turning his head in shame.

"I am sorry, Mateo. It was wrong of me to speak of your father in that manner."

Mateo shook his head. "Do not blame yourself, cousin. My temper is quick sometimes."

Laughing softly, Jorge said, "Ah, Chihuahua, that it is."

Mateo looked up, smiling until he noticed the swelling that was already discoloring Jorge's lip.

"It is nothing," Jorge said. "The others will think that a mule did it, fighting the halter. But there is something more I must say, and I have thought much about this since you left to fight Gregorio. Once I blamed you for the deaths of Tomas and Antonio. I thought it was your anger that forced us to come with you. But now I know you are not to blame. You did not force us to join you. It was our own decision. And for me, Mateo, it was the right decision. Someday I hope it will be the same for you."

"Maybe someday it will be," Mateo acknowledged quietly.

Jorge smiled. "Come back to the fire, Mateo. Join us."

Mateo shook his head. "Not yet."

"Then soon, my friend." He rested his hand on Mateo's shoulder, patting it a couple of times, then turned toward the camp. Mateo watched him return to the circle of firelight and make his way to Clint Orr's side. The younger Orr saw him and squirmed over on the log the mountain men had dragged up as a seat, making room for Jorge to sit beside him. Clint spoke. Jorge replied, nodding and smiling. Alone, Mateo turned away from the camp, heading for the river.

Remi LeBlanc stared at the cold fire rings and the churned, frozen snow where the Ute village had once stood. Discarded hides, old bones, and worn-out lodgepoles littered the site. The wind hummed forlornly through the leafless branches of the cottonwoods, and a wolf skulked into the alders downstream.

Remi didn't dismount, although he wanted to. His muscles screamed in agony, and hunger ate at his gut like a starving rat. But he was afraid to get down, afraid that if he did he wouldn't have the strength to get back into the saddle again. It was an unrealistic fear. He could tell by the wind-rounded edges of the broken snow that the camp had been abandoned for many days. By now its occupants were far away. He needed rest, food, and warmth. There were still a few piles of firewood stacked haphazardly beside some of the lodge sites. Perhaps he could find some food as well, or an old discarded robe that he could use as a bedroll—anything the wolves had left. But the grip of his fear was too strong, too overpowering. It was like a tremor centered in his soul, and all he could do was cling to his saddle horn and pray that it would soon pass.

He guided the paint slowly through the abandoned village, his eyes moving quickly over the ground, touching the scarred tree trunks and the empty frames where meat had once dried under slow fires. In these things he read the story of the village and its people; he saw its numbers, its wealth, its poverty, the laughter and tears. Loneliness flooded him, bringing tears to his own eyes, tears he angrily rubbed away, knowing he couldn't afford the luxury of melancholy.

The wolf—a long-bodied black lobo—came out of the alders again and sank to one hip, pink tongue lolling. Remi watched it dispassionately for several minutes before it came to him that here was the thing he searched for, food for his empty stomach, and a soft, heavily furred pelt to ward off the winter's cold. Slowly, he brought his fusil up, but the wolf proved too wise to the ways of the hunter and quickly darted back into the brush.

"Ahhh," Remi breathed, lowering the fusil to his saddle. "You have been shot at before, eh? Perhaps even stung by the bullet. You are smart to hide, *mon ami*, for Remi is hungry enough to savor even your stringy carcass."

He went on, coming to the site of the brigade's camp last and stopping once more. A frown creased his weathered face as he stared at the moccasin tracks littering the empty field. Which ones, he wondered, belonged to Jake Orr? The paint stretched for a single stem of grass that had escaped the trappers' stomping feet. Remi let the mare have a taste, then pulled her head up. "Come, *cheri*, there will be time for that later. Now we have far to go, and Remi does not have time to spare. *Sacre*, perhaps he has already used up too much of his time, eh?"

He rode north, following a trail that he thought was at least two weeks old, and wondered where the time had gone. He kept the paint to a plodding walk, his thoughts straying. It was several miles before a sense of danger infiltrated his consciousness, sending a prickle of fear down his spine. Without drawing rein, he let his gaze rove over the surrounding hills. Nothing out of the ordinary caught his eyes, but still the feeling persisted. As casually as possible, he looked behind him, then sharply drew the paint up, a curse slipping through his chapped lips. It was the black lobo he had seen back at the village, following at a distance. With it now were half a dozen other wolves, ranging from deep gray to almost white. The paint snorted when she caught sight of the pack, but Remi calmed her with a gentling hand. "Do not worry, *cherie*," he murmured soothingly. "Remi is not yet ready to feed these devils."

He went on, only occasionally looking back. Sometimes the pack of gray wolves were hidden from sight, and sometimes they weren't. But always, the black lobo shadowed them, like an omen.

Eli sent the trappers out in all directions, but with the instructions to remain within a day's ride of the base camp, and to come in at least every other day. With the possibility of Blackfeet in the vicinity, he didn't want to take any chances of repeating the mistakes he had made with the Arapahos along the upper Grand.

Meanwhile, he set Pierre, Clint, Jorge, and Mateo to fortifying the breastworks surrounding the camp. The women helped, and within two days they had the camp secured, with a separate area within the deeper cover of the trees for the remuda. He knew Indians weren't likely to deliberately shoot the horses or mules; although theft was a definite concern. The Blackfeet, Sad Smiling Man had confided, were rumored to be on foot, a common practice among the warfaring plains tribes, and a sure sign that ponies were high on their agenda.

Eli had hoped to stay on the White a week or more, but by the second day all the trappers were complaining. Even Pete Meyers, who normally took anything life offered with a grin and a shrug, seemed upset by the skimpy returns his traps netted. "This coon has ate poor bull before, and figured it was better than moccasin soles, but these waters don't shine for a man, Eli."

"They be trapped out, is what they be," Old Cal fumed. "Do ye hyar, boys? Old Cal says these waters be trapped out, and he's got hisself more'n half a notion who did 'er, too."

"We all know who did it," Charlie returned irritably, pegging Eli with a challenging glare. "Question is, how long are we gonna squat here taking what the St. Louis boys didn't figure was worth their time?"

Eli stared thoughtfully into the fire for several minutes. He knew the trapping would only get worse the farther north they traveled. He had been holding back the information that they were heading for the Salt Lake country in search of a cache of stolen furs. At first, back in Taos, he had kept the information from the others because he didn't want word of their venture to leak out in some cantina and perhaps reach the ears of Big Tom Reed. But after the hamstrung mules back in the village of Río Colorado, he had purposely withheld that information, hoping that if only he and McClure knew about it, or their ultimate destination, then perhaps the traitor would somehow tip his hand. But that hadn't happened, and he knew he was reaching a point when he would have to tell the others why they were heading straight into the heart of land the St. Louis outfits had been trapping for years. "We'll give it a few more days," he said finally. "If things don't pick up then, we'll move on."

With trapping so poor, Eli elected to stay in camp. He filled his time helping the *arrieros* check the shoes on the remuda and catching up in his own journal, which Girardin had asked him to keep. He was sitting alone on the bank of the river about a mile upstream from the camp on the fourth day after their arrival on the White, when he spotted Sad Smiling Man riding toward him. The Shoshone showed no surprise at finding him here, and Eli wondered if he had been looking for him.

Sad Smiling Man dismounted and came to sit beside Eli, the long fringe of his leggings dragging in the snow. Staring pensively at the hills across the river, Sad Smiling Man said, "It is good, this place. A leader should have quiet moments like this in which to think." Sad Smiling Man looked at him, his expression clearly reflecting the source of his name. "Does Cutler wish to be alone with his thoughts for a while longer?"

"No. My thoughts were running in circles anyway."

Sad Smiling Man nodded gravely. "That is a bad time in a man's life. It is like seeing buffalo in the sky, when he hears geese. Sad Smiling Man has known such confusion. It is good when it passes. It makes a man want to get on his fastest pony and race the wind. Or seek out his enemy, so that he might count coup against him."

Eli laughed. "It is good to know that a man does not always travel in circles. I'll look forward to racing the wind, although I may not go out of my way to find enemies."

"No. In these mountains a man's enemies are always nearby. He does not have to seek them out." Sad Smiling Man turned quiet for several minutes, deep in thought. Finally he said, "My friend Cutler is a wise leader, and he has chosen a good site for his camp. It will not be easy for Blackfeet to overrun this place. But Sad Smiling Man wonders why the Long Knives stay here, when there are no beaver to trap."

Eli remained silent, waiting for the Indian to get to his point.

"There is a place that I know of," Sad Smiling Man continued quietly, "where the beaver make this place appear to have none, where they are thick as the buffalo's dung in the grass along the Seedskadee. Sad Smiling Man knows of this place and would guide his friend Cutler to it. He would ask only for a few small gifts for this service. A rifle and powder and shot, a new ax, maybe a couple of ponies. These things Sad Smiling Man would ask for, so that he does not have to return to his village empty-handed."

Eli stared thoughtfully at the chill gray waters sliding past, weighing the value of Sad Smiling Man's words. It was possible, he knew. For all the beaver the trappers and traders had taken out of the mountains, there were thousands of square miles that had never seen the steel of a white man's trap yet, or felt the pressure of his moccasins. The Great Salt Lake itself had only been discovered four years before, by a young Ashley man named Jim Bridger. Eli had followed old Etienne Provost into the valley just a few months after that, in the fall of '24. But a grain of distrust gnawed at him. He had never allowed himself to be swayed by an Indian's logic, long ago recognizing its disparity from his own, the difference more cultural than moral. Would Sad Smiling Man lie about such a stream, just to get home faster?

And yet, Eli wondered, could he afford to distrust every Indian? Had it not been Bowlegs himself who told Eli of the route they had followed successfully over the mountains to the White, cutting perhaps a week off the time it would have taken them to get here following the old route? Legend said that Jim Bridger had discovered the Great Salt Lake, but how would the Utes, the Shoshones, the Bannacks, the Paiutes, and a dozen other tribes that had feasted and fought along its briny shores respond to such a claim? Surely they would laugh to hear that it was an American who had "discovered" their lake. Likely they would laugh even harder when they learned that at the time, Bridger had thought it a bay of the Pacific Ocean. The white men exploited the mountains for the European market, but it was often with the help of the indigenous peoples who already lived there, who knew the mountains and deserts intimately, who told the whites where to find the trails that led to the richest streams. And this was *his* brigade, by God. He wanted it to come out of the mountains a success, the mules and ponies laden with furs, the men—his men, Cutler men—proud and satisfied with what they had accomplished.

"There is a valley north and west of the Salt Lake where the beaver grow big as dogs, their pelts like the finest cloth, as many as the stars," Sad Smiling Man said. "This is the place Sad Smiling Man would take Cutler."

. And so it had come to this, Eli thought, the old doubts rushing
back in under a new guise. He glanced at the Shoshone, trying to
gauge the warrior's honesty, but Sad Smiling Man's face revealed
nothing. "I will think on this thing that Sad Smiling Man has told
Cutler," Eli said. "Tonight he will hear my answer."

The stars were just starting to appear overhead when Eli came
back from checking on the remuda. The evening meal was over, the
first watch already set. Pipe smoke mingled with the smoke of
Pierre's cook fire to create a thin blue pall that hung over the camp
like a cloud. The breeze had died, and in the vast, cold stillness the
camp was like a tiny bubble of motion and sound and warmth, a
speck of humanity surrounded by the huge emptiness of the high
desert. Everyone was in tonight, Johnny and Travis arriving just before supper with only three plews between them. It was that, as much
as anything, that clinched the decision for Eli.

Charlie had laid his *apishimore* out on the ground beside the fire,
and Johnny, Old Cal, and Clint were gathering around it. Charlie was
absently shuffling a worn deck of cards, laughing at some joke
Johnny was telling. Pierre was messing with his pots and kettles and
apollos, knowing that as the evening progressed the men would become bored or hungry and want more to eat. The rest of the brigade
was gathered around the fire in various activities—greasing or
mending moccasins, sharpening their knives, or just staring into the
flames, listening to Johnny's story. Only Silas McClure looked unhappy, sitting cross-legged on the far side of the fire, scowling at his
ledger. The others seemed almost cheerful, the poor catches of the
last few days forgotten in the camaraderie of the campfire. Jorge, Eli
noticed with a start, had finally removed the bandage from his cheek.
The flesh surrounding the wound itself was ridged with scar tissue,
a deep, ugly crimson that seemed to glow angrily in the firelight. Old
Cal had been right, Jorge was marked for life, yet the young man
seemed almost happy as he sat between Clint and Mateo, smoking a
corn-husk cigarillo and swapping stories with Travis. It was funny,
the way some men reacted to calamity. Others would have been ap-
palled at such a lifelong disfigurement, plunged into a well of depression and bitterness that might have marked them for life. Yet
Jorge had pulled himself out of his melancholy within a week or so,
had seemed, in fact, to rise even above what he had been before.

Eli stepped into the firelight. Several of the men looked up as he approached, judging from his expression whether all was well with the sentries and the remuda. Satisfied, they went back to what they were doing without comment. Charlie was speaking to Clint as he began to deal his cards. "On account you not bein' what we'd call a regular card shark," Charlie was saying, "we'll go easy on you tonight."

Old Cal cackled laughter.

"Never trust a horse thief, Clint," Johnny advised dryly.

"Now, you take ol' Johnny there," Charlie went on. "The man is a fair player. This coon's seen him clean up at Salazar's a time or two, for a fact. But he gets a mite jealous around masters like me and Ol' Cal here."

Johnny snorted and looked away as if insulted.

"Wagh!" Old Cal cried. "Git 'em out 'ere, Williams. This nigger's feelin' powerful lucky tonight, or he wouldn't say it."

"Yeow," Charlie howled, speeding up the deal. "A man who feels lucky is the easiest to fleece, this coon says."

Eli spoke up, stopping Charlie's deal in midair. "Best turn in early tonight, boys. We'll be putting out at first light tomorrow."

Silence greeted his words. All eyes turned toward him. Charlie slowly straightened and folded his cards; McClure closed his ledger and watched Eli speculatively.

"I've decided to push on. We'll be heading for the Salt Lake country. I want to try the mountains northwest of there."

"*Northwest!*" Old Cal shrilled. He looked around the camp in disbelief.

Johnny pulled thoughtfully on his lower lip until the murmur of surprise died down, then said, "I never heard of beaver northwest of the Salt Lake, Eli."

"It's never been explored, as far as I know."

"It ain't been explored because there's nothing out there," Charlie said quietly, as if his astonishment had taken the starch out of his normal abrasiveness. "Me'n Pete's tramped that country, and all we saw was Digger Injuns and flies."

"Northwest of the Lake?"

"Naw, it was them little pissant mountain ranges runnin' down south of the Lake. But we talked to some Diggers who said there wasn't anything out there. Just all flat and white with alkali."

Eli took a deep breath. "I never put much stock in what an Indian had to say, Charlie."

"You sure you ain't doin' it now?" Pete asked. The others glanced at him curiously. "I've talked to Sad Smiling Man, too, Eli, and this child believes those Diggers a heap more than he does that Shoshone."

Eli was aware of Sad Smiling Man stiffening, and felt a moment's doubt. He forced that away, too, saying, "You're a free trapper, Pete. I can't force you to come if you don't want to."

"Hyar now, what about the rest of us?" Old Cal put in. "By God, ye'll be draggin' us to our deaths, man."

"No one's going to die," Eli snapped. "But you're a Cutler man, Cal. You have a contract with the outfit."

Cal snorted. "Cutler man? Do ye hyar that, boys? Cutler men, we be." He stood, stretching his lanky frame to its full height. "By God, Eli, this coon says no. I come to trap the White and the Yampa, and to maybe winter in Brown's Hole."

McClure's head jerked up. "You were told we were wintering near the Salt Lake," he said coldly, his eyes glinting in the firelight.

"Tolt we'd set us a trap, now'n again, too, was what I was tolt," Old Cal began, but Eli cut him off, slashing the air with his hand.

"You want to settle up, do it now."

"Do ye think I won't? Do ye think Ol' Cal's not wintered by his lonesome afore?"

"What does Caleb Underwood owe the company?" Eli asked McClure.

"I would have to figure that out," McClure answered, "and charge what he still owes against what beaver's been marked to his credit."

Old Cal's eyes narrowed dangerously, and his fingers twitched above the knife in his belt. "Jus' what do ye be tryin' to pull on me, Eli?"

"You went into debt for your outfit when you signed on, Cal. You'll want to pay that off before you pull out."

Old Cal cocked his head back, and Eli braced himself, ready with either his fists or his knife. "You're cuttin' my throat, boy," Old Cal breathed. "Ye've turned on us, by God." He looked around him, and his voice rose and trembled. "Do ye hyar that, boys? Ol' Eli Cutler's—"

"Best cut yourself some slack, Cal," Johnny said, shoving to his feet. He looked at Eli, as if looking for some kind of answer in his face. "I signed up for the season, Eli, and I'll follow you to hell, if that's where your stick floats. But I kind of side with Pete, too. This hoss feels a little uneasy about this."

"It's poor bull, is what it be," Old Cal whined, but Eli heard the surrender in the words.

"Pierre has eat him poor bull before, by *Dieu*," Pierre said. "*Oui,* him go with Eli."

Eli began to breathe easier. With Johnny's affirmation, he knew the others would follow, even Pete and Charlie. But he hadn't realized until then how much he'd worried that they might not. They had been trapping all along, and doing all right, but not like they usually did. There had been too much ground to cover for such a late start, too much hard luck dogging their every step. It was time, Eli decided, that they knew what was going on, what eventually might be expected of them. He looked at McClure, and McClure's eyes widened. "No, Eli! Not yet."

"I reckon so, Silas. They've earned it." He took a long breath, then started. "Boys, there's more to this fandango than you've been told. . . ."

He told it all—Girardin and his massacred brigade, Bad Gocha and Big Tom Reed, the cache of stolen furs that they were out to retrieve. No one interrupted him, not even Old Cal or Charlie. When he finished, the silence continued. In the quiet, he added, "I'll make the offer one more time. Anyone who wants to cut his pin and go his own way, they'll be no hard feelings on my part. Silas will take care of the paperwork, but I'll see to it that you're outfitted with what you need to get back to Taos or go it on your own. I won't leave a man stranded."

"Hell, Eli," Pete said softly. "This coon's been wonderin' what kind of burr you had under your saddle. Now he knows, I reckon he'll stick." His voice turned husky with rare anger. "Wagh! I'd kinda like a chance to set things square with ol' Reed, tell you the truth. Never did take shine to that critter."

The others quickly added their consent, more anxious to avenge the outfit that had been nearly annihilated last year than to recover Girardin furs, Eli thought. "*Bueno,*" he said when the chatter of conversation ebbed. "McClure'll call *levée* on you before dawn."

CHAPTER THIRTY-FIVE

Remi stared hollowly at the story he read along the banks of the Colorado. Discarded willow limbs were strewn about, and an elk hide was draped over a cottonwood limb, unneeded and forgotten. He looked at the cold, dead ashes of the fire where the brigade had sat and eaten and smoked and talked, and the line of three smaller fires where they had dried the sinew-sewn hides to an iron tightness over the frame of their canoes. The canoes were gone, of course, probably somewhere downriver and on the far shore, as useless to him there as a steamboat on the Mississippi. He glanced again at the discarded willows and the single hide, and felt a glimmer of hope, although no smile appeared to accompany it. He had lost his smile somewhere between the Utes' abandoned camp at the forks of the Grand and the gray waters of the swollen Colorado.

Remi turned the paint toward the scattered willows. The horse gimped in her left foreleg, and he winced at her pain. She had pulled a muscle coming down a steep embankment, catching sight of the black lobo near the bottom and spooking wildly. Her limp had grown progressively worse ever since.

"*Oui,* you are lame, no?" he rasped absently to the paint. "So is Remi. But Remi is *l'homme,* the man, and you are the horse. So I ride you. That is the way. And maybe, you get too lame and we see no food, then Remi will have to eat you. That is the way, too. But, *sacre bleu,* maybe not. Maybe we will catch up with the others, and then Remi will give you some sugar from Pierre's packs, eh? You would like that, no? Remi thinks that—" He shut up abruptly, the willows and old hide somewhere behind them now, passed blindly as he talked to his horse. He chuckled without humor and reined her back, but there was a tightness in his chest that was a fear such as he had never known before. "Maybe Remi will not get out of this one, eh, *ma cherie*? Maybe this time Remi will go under."

The paint flicked her ear and came to a halt beside the willows.

Closer, he nodded in satisfaction. There would be enough to make a small, kettle-shaped bullboat from the willows the trappers had left behind and from the single elk hide. It would be small, but Remi himself was small, and there was little enough to be carried across with him. He had only his saddle and fusil; he had eaten the last of the beaver days before.

He steeled himself for the shock of dismounting, for the rippling explosions of pain that would travel from his ankle to his hip, to burst in his groin with a gut-tightening agony as soon as he swung his leg over the cantle. But there was no other way. The pain was like the fear, constant and unremitting, though not nearly so subtle.

He cursed in anticipation and slid awkwardly from the saddle, landing on his good leg and letting it give a little to cushion some of the shock. Even with that, he had to hang on to the saddle horn for a couple of minutes until the torment subsided to a bearable level.

"Ah, *sacre,*" he breathed, tipping his face away from the curly warmth of his buffalo robe saddle pad. Staring over the seat, he saw the black lobo sitting about a hundred yards away, waiting patiently. With it sat two others, both a smoky blue in color, smaller and obviously submissive to the larger wolf.

"But you wait, anyway, no?" Remi whispered to himself. "*Oui,* you wait because you know Remi will go under, and then you will help yourself to his body, and maybe to his horse, too, eh?"

The paint was watching the three wolves with her head high, snorty, rigid, her feet braced as if for flight. Remi jerked roughly on the reins, but she just swung back around, refusing to take her eyes away from the wolves. He pulled the saddle off and let it fall in the snow, then led the mare to a spot of grass and picketed her. Coming back, he sank wearily atop his saddle and pushed his foot out, pulling the fringed buckskin leg of his trousers up to reveal the still swollen and discolored ankle. He probed gently at the puffed flesh with blunt, dirt-encrusted fingers half numb with cold, wincing at each touch. But there was some relief in the pain, he had decided a few days back, and in the fading blackness. He had feared gangrene at first and had expected each morning and evening, when he examined his ankle, to find the first telltale sign of graying, lifeless flesh. But the darkness had gradually faded to a deep purple, swirled throughout with a pusy yellow and lingering threads of black, but changing nonetheless.

The thought came to him that even if he lived, he might be crippled for the rest of his life, so stoved up with rheumatism he might never again set another trap in an icy stream. Once upon a time the thought that he might have to give up his freewheeling life in the mountains would have sickened him, but now he accepted the possibility calmly, rationally. He had been so foolish, he knew, so reckless with life and limb, so convinced he was invincible, so certain danger was an aphrodisiac that made living itself sweet and pure. But that, too, had died. He lived now only to survive, to see another summer, another friend. The thought of revenge still glowed within him, but even that warmth had begun to fade.

His fusil leaned against the saddle beside him. He glanced at the wolves through the curly fall of his hair. They hadn't moved. They were sitting about a hundred yards away, rumped down in the snow at the edge of a clump of alders. It would be a far shot for a fusil, even under the best of circumstances, but hunger had made him desperate. He reached casually for the fusil, but the black wolf seemed to read his mind. It leaped to its feet and disappeared into the alders. The other two jumped after the black, but at the last instant one of the blue wolves paused, turning its head and eyeing Remi curiously, sniffing the air. Hope swelled in Remi's breast as he lifted his weapon. He brought the fusil slowly across his lap. The blue stood tautly, made wary by the black wolf's actions, but lacking the lobo's wisdom of weapons, or a hungry man's cunning. It stood unmoving at the edge of the alders, looking into Remi's eyes. Remi cautiously pulled the hammer back, afraid to break eye contact with the wolf, afraid of severing the fragile tie that held it there. He held his fusil in both hands now, cocked and ready to fire, but the smoothbore was still in his lap, and in order to get his shot off he was going to have to bring the fusil to his shoulder and swing partway around. It would have to be done quickly and smoothly, for he knew the wolf would dive for the alders' shelter as soon as he began his move. Remi would have only the briefest of moments to make his shot, a long shot at a small and probably streaking target.

Remi studied the wolf intently, gauging the distance, the likeliest point of the wolf's entry into the scrub. *Oui*, he told himself, his finger stroking the fusil's big trigger, *this time Remi will make meat*. He took a slow, steadying breath, closed his eyes, opened them, then snapped the weapon to his shoulder.

Remi twisted at the waist as he brought the fusil up, and pain erupted in his leg like a brand of fire. He cried out, and the fusil's muzzle wavered. The wolf bolted for cover. Remi jerked the muzzle back, squeezing the trigger as the small brass front sight touched the wolf's shoulder. But he knew even before the powder smoke mushroomed before him, blocking his view, that he had missed, that the sudden shock of pain had pulled his sight off target.

A breeze came and nudged the cloud of smoke aside. The alders where the wolves had disappeared swayed gently. Remi let the fusil's muzzle dip toward the snow. His shoulders were racked by a sudden and violent shivering, but it wasn't the cold he was reacting to. It was the loneliness, the hopelessness of his situation. "Mother of God," he whispered, his vision suddenly blurred by tears. "Not this way. Please, do not let me die this way."

It turned even colder after the brigade left the White River. The skies grayed over with a thin, high layer of clouds and the wind strengthened from the northwest. From time to time throughout the day it snowed, small, scattered squalls that they rode through within minutes, more a prelude of what was yet to come than any real problem in itself.

They followed a canyon running north from the river and topped out on a high mesa toward sundown, with neither wood nor water for a decent camp. They forted up behind their packs and endured the cold and darkness with only their pipes and *cigarillos* for comfort. Pierre passed out jerky and fist-sized balls of pemmican, then retreated to where Grass That Burns awaited in their robes. The others turned in early, too, and soon only low, snuffling snores and the mournful hum of the wind moving through the sage broke the silence of the camp. Not even the remuda stirred until daylight.

They ate breakfast on the trail, moving swiftly down off the high plateau, winding down another small, dry canyon to the Yampa. Eli sent Pete and Johnny ahead to make a quick scout, and Pete shot an elk. They feasted that evening around a big fire, gorging on the fresh meat and making up for what they had missed the night before. They spent a day on the Yampa, letting the remuda graze on the tall grass along the river. A few of the men set traps, but they made a poor showing of it.

"How far to the Salt Lake from here?" McClure asked Eli that night.

"A ways yet," Eli replied. "Ten days, maybe two weeks. Sooner, if it was summer, but it always takes longer this time of year." They stood apart from the others, shoulders hunched to the cold. Eli could smell snow on the gusting wind, and knew they would get more during the night.

McClure was silent, as he often was of late. Brooding had put its mark upon him. Where once he had been sober but optimistic, he was now most often gloomy, as thin-skinned as a minister. He had never repeated his premonition about his own death, but Eli couldn't help wondering if it still troubled him. On a whim, he asked, "Do you doubt Sad Smiling Man?"

"Yes," McClure replied instantly, his voice almost lost in the sounds of the river and the wind. "I doubt everyone now."

After a pause, Eli said, "Well, it'll be over soon, one way or the other."

"Yes," McClure said with a measure of relief in his voice. "Let's hope so."

They pushed on the following day, angling northwest, away from the Yampa. Two hard days through broken country blanketed with nearly twelve inches of fresh snow brought them to Vermillion Creek and the southern rim of Brown's Hole.

"Here it be, boys," Old Cal sang out as they rode down from the hills. "This coon has spent him a season or two in this Hole, or he wouldn't say it. Caught me a Shoshone's arrer here once." He looked hard at Sad Smiling Man, but the Indian refused to return the stare.

Eli filled his lungs with the clean high-country air. The skies had cleared off again, and the mountains—the Diamonds and the O-Wi-Yukuts and the Uintas, rose sharp and snowy around them. A hole, a park, a valley—they were all about the same to a greenhorn. It took a season or two in the mountains to come to understand them the way a mountain man did, to learn which ones a man could depend on for good hunting and feed for his horses, and for the richness of its rivers, the quality of the plews taken from its streams. Bayou Salade, just north of the Mexican settlements, was one such hole—a favorite of the mountain men, with a salt marsh at the southern end that attracted even the buffalo from the plains. Davey Jackson's

Hole, under the east face of the Tetons, was another. So, too, was Brown's Hole, an oblong valley of rolling, sage-covered hills laced with sparkling streams. Elk and antelope and mule deer ranged the narrow side valleys, and eagles soared the blue skies. Once Brown's Hole had teemed with beaver, but the years and Ashley's trappers had taken the cream of the crop. Still, it was a rich enough country, and because it ran roughly from the southeast, where the brigade had just entered it, to the northwest, in the direction of the Salt Lake, Eli decided to trap it as they went.

"We'll leapfrog it, two parties out and two parties with the remuda," he told the men. "Johnny and Travis will take the first stream, Old Cal and . . . Jake will take the second. Charlie and Pete the third." His eyes searched out Mateo. "You and I will take the fourth, amigo."

Mateo's eyes widened in surprise.

"Jorge and Clint can handle the remuda for a few days," Eli said. "The women can help, if they need it."

Mateo looked confused by Eli's offer, but he didn't balk. He nodded, and said, "*Sí*, Eli."

"No more than one setting on each stream," Eli told them. "I don't want to slow the brigade up too much."

"Wagh!" Old Cal cried. He jerked his pony around and rode into the remuda. "This nigger's half froze for beaver-gittin'," he hollered, cornering his pack animal and pulling the lead rope free. "And he still says he can out-trap any man jack o' ye."

Johnny laughed. "We haven't settled up from the Grand, yet, pard."

"The Grand or Brown's Hole, makes no nevermind to this coon," Old Cal responded shrilly. "I'll out-trap ye for the season, and add my bear-skin sleepin' robe to the wager, I will."

"I'll take a chance for that," Pete said.

Eli rode toward McClure, motioning for Mateo to follow. "We'll sign Chavez on as a skin trapper," Eli told the clerk. "Assign him three traps and whatever else he thinks he might need." He glanced at Mateo. "That shine with you?"

"Why are you doing this?" Mateo asked bluntly.

"We're a man short with Remi gone. Cork-Eye never was much, and neither is Jake."

"I am not a trapper."

"My hunch is that any man who can outfox Gregorio el Toro and a couple of his hardcases can trap with the best of them, given half a chance," Eli replied. "Do you want it?"

Mateo shrugged. "*Sí*, I will trap for you, Eli Cutler."

"*Bueno*. Go with McClure and get your stuff. Daylight's wasting."

Pushing, always pushing now, but making good time. And the beaver were in their prime at last. "Look at that!" Old Cal exulted their second night in the Hole, brushing the fur of a just-stretched plew with his fingers the way some men brushed their wife's cheek. "This here be gold, boys. Do ye hyar, brown gold."

But Eli knew it wasn't the money Old Cal was talking about. It went deeper than that, maybe all the way to a man's soul. Pete and Charlie and Johnny, perhaps even Pierre Turpin, knew what Old Cal was talking about. To a lesser degree, so did Mateo and Travis. But Eli could see it missed McClure and Jake Orr completely, that they looked at the willow-hooped plew Old Cal was holding and saw only a piece of fur worth four dollars a pound in Taos—a big brown coin to be traded off as soon as possible. Only Clint Orr still puzzled Eli, and he turned a wondering eye on the youth, marveling at the changes, yet distrustful of them, too, as if they were too great, too sudden, to be fully believed.

It was on Willow Creek, early the next day, that he and Mateo cut sign of others. Mateo had been riding ahead on his *grullo*, his gaze shifting constantly, like a true mountaineer. Suddenly he drew up, lifting the musket he had taken from Gregorio's man, Salvador, to the cradle of his arm. "*Caballos*," he whispered, eyes darting. Ponies.

Eli didn't have to dismount to examine the tracks. They were fresh and clean-cut in the snow, not more than an hour old. "Shod," he observed, lifting his gaze to a patch of dark pines blanketing the north slope of a side canyon. "Could be white men."

"Perhaps," Mateo agreed, but Eli knew what he was thinking, what they were both thinking. It could just as easy have been made by Blackfeet riding stolen ponies.

"Likely they saw us and skedaddled into the trees."

"*Sí*."

"Likely they're just waiting up there now to see what we aim to do about this sign."

Mateo gave him a pointed look. "What *will* we do?"

Heaving a sigh, Eli said, "Let's go see who's up there."

They hadn't gone a hundred yards before a voice stopped them again. "Reckon that'll do." In the narrowing canyon, the words seemed to float down to them from nowhere . . . everywhere.

Eli gave it a moment, then shouted back, "You don't sound like a Blackfoot."

"I ain't, and you don't look like one. Is that a greaser ridin' with you there?"

"I'm Eli Cutler, out of Taos. This is Mateo Chavez, one of my men."

"Cutler! Well, I reckon I know that name."

A head poked up into the skyline on the opposite side of the canyon from the trees, and Eli murmured, "Slick," and then louder, "It's been used in these parts."

"Hell, I'm Bill Byrum. You remember me, Eli?"

The name rang a bell, but Eli couldn't put a face to it immediately.

"North Park," Byrum continued. "We had us that fray with some 'Rapyhos."

"Wagh!" Eli shouted, grinning then. "Hell, yeah, Bill Byrum. Had a pony shot out from under you, as I remember it."

Byrum laughed. "Well, I did, now." He stood and started down the slope, sliding from one clump of sage to the next in his slick moccasins until he reached level ground. He was a man of average height and girth, dressed in grease-blackened buckskins and a blue capote. A mass of dark hair flowed from beneath a coyote-skin cap of crude construction. He was grinning broadly as Eli rode over and dismounted. "How, Eli," Byrum said, grabbing Eli's hand. He nodded to Mateo. "*Buenos dias,* there, amigo."

Mateo nodded stiffly, but didn't answer. Eli said, "You're not alone, are you?"

"Naw, I'm partnered with Curly Jamison this season, trapping for Smith, Jackson, and Sublette."

"I figured they'd be north of here," Eli said.

"Hell, I reckon. Most of 'em are headin' up to Flathead country this season. The high country's getting crowded anymore, Eli. Yours is the second outfit we've run across since rendezvous."

"So who's close by?"

"Just me and Curly, as far as I know. Had run into some Blackfeet about a week ago and cached for a few days, but we ain't seen hide nor hair of 'em since."

"Blackfeet?"

"Bunch of young bucks, looked like. Too goddamn young to know they ought to be holed up in a lodge somewheres up on the Three Forks, and not down here raiding for ponies with snow on the ground." He shook his head ruefully. "Man figures he's got a brown-skin figured out, then something like this happens. It keeps a coon off balance, for a fact."

"How many did you say there were?"

"I counted eighteen, all of 'em on foot yet, so they ain't had much luck to speak of. They were headin' south along the Seedskadee. Ought to be close to the Colorado by now."

"Where Bowlegs was going," Mateo said.

Eli shrugged at the irony of old Bowlegs taking his village away from the Grand to dodge the Blackfeet, only to settle right in their path. But Bowlegs was neither a fool nor a coward, and the Utes would handle themselves all right against such a small band of Blackfeet, especially if most of them were youngsters, as Byrum claimed. "We'll be camped at the mouth of Willow Creek tonight, Bill," Eli said. "Why don't you and Curly come on down and jabber a spell."

"Well, damn if we won't, Eli. Ol' Curly is a sour cuss, and I get about half-starved for conversation."

"*Bueno*," Eli said. "I'll make sure Pierre keeps some meat on the fire for you."

"Have you got any coffee?" Byrum asked hopefully.

Eli smiled, shaking his head.

"Well, we be outta it, too. Man surely can miss his coffee, or I wouldn't say so."

"We'll have meat and new stories, and I'll see if Pierre can't rustle up some cornmeal for a little bread."

"Bread! Wagh, this coon ain't had him any bread in near two years. Hell, yeah, Eli, you tell ol' Pierre that Bill Byrum'll be there with bells on."

Byrum turned away, hoofing it carefully back up the side of the little canyon. Mateo rode alongside Eli, watching Byrum's progress. "I do not trust that one," Mateo said quietly.

"Bill's all right. I don't know this Curly Jamison he's partnering with, so I couldn't say about him."

Mateo shrugged. "It does not matter to me, but if it was my bread, I would not share it with those two."

"It's just a little cornmeal and water and salt. I say that's a fair trade for whatever news we might get from them."

Mateo booted his horse, pulling away. "Whatever you wish, *jefe,*" he shot over his shoulder.

Eli watched Mateo ride away. He had seen men like him before, toting a chip on their shoulder the size of a small house, and had often wondered what made a person that way, so angry and distrustful, so quick to take offense. Most of the outfit had learned to ignore Mateo's anger, avoiding him as they did Jake. Not in the same way—the trappers had too much respect for Mateo's abilities to do that—but they didn't reach out to him much, either. Eli wondered what Mateo thought of such treatment from his peers. Did it eat at him? Offend him? Did it make him angry enough to strike back in subtle or not-so-subtle ways? It was a thing to consider, he mused as he watched Mateo's pride-rigid spine grow smaller in the distance. A man like Mateo, how much loyalty would he have to the brigade?

It was after sundown before Bill Byrum and Curly Jamison showed up. They were leading a string of packhorses laden with plews already taken, and enough supplies to last the winter. Eli went out to welcome both men. Curly was a lean, sharp-featured man, tall and weathered. He had shy eyes that always seemed to be looking elsewhere, and a quick smile that further revealed his uneasiness around strangers. He followed Byrum into camp after seeing to their horses, and hung close to his partner the rest of the evening.

Pete hooted when he came in, jumping off his horse and tossing the reins to Annie. "Byrum, you ol' coon, I heard you'd gone under to some Crow maiden's pappy."

Byrum laughed and they shook hands and slapped one another on the shoulders. "Hell's bells, Pete Meyers. If I'd have known you were with this bunch I'd have told Curly to hobble our ponies extra careful tonight."

Pete laughed and they squatted beside the fire. Charlie came up, settling awkwardly. "Hello, Bill," he said.

"Hell, boy, don't look so glum." Byrum glanced at Eli, grinning, but his words were directed at Charlie, needling a little. "Me'n Charlie had us a ruckus over somethin' or t'other at rendezvous a couple seasons back. I don't recollect exactly what it was, do you, Charlie?"

Charlie looked up, his eyes glittering dangerously. "It was my wife, Bill," he said quietly.

"Well, maybe it was at that, but I didn't know she was your squaw. I wouldn't have tried to lasso her if I did." He was still grinning, but Eli noticed the tautness in his words as he held his hand up to the light. "Ol' Charlie here is a bad man to rowl. Makes it plumb hard to scratch my ass."

Eli stared transfixed at the mutilated hand, with its two missing digits, then forcibly lifted his gaze. "Hell, Bill," he said weakly, trying to diffuse the tension between the two men. "I'd say you were lucky it was only your fingers Charlie cut off."

Byrum burst into laughter. "Now, that's the truth, Eli, it surely is." He sought out Pierre. "Say, Frenchy, where's that bread Eli promised?"

Pierre scowled and muttered under his breath, but refused to look up. He was sitting cross-legged beside the fire with a skillet in his lap, kneading some rough-ground Mexican cornmeal into a stiff dough.

Pete said, "Still trappin' for Ashley's old outfit, Bill?"

"Well, I am. Smith, Jackson, and Sublette now, though, which I reckon you Taos boys have already heard."

"So we did," Eli acknowledged.

"This Smith the Bible-thumper I've heard about?" McClure asked.

"He is, but he ain't so bad for a preacher type. Got the hair of the bear in him, or this coon wouldn't say it. Ol' 'Diah's been out here a good many years, and had him his share of troubles along the way, but they ain't dampened him any."

"We all been out here a good many years," Charlie said pointedly.

"The trouble with you, Charlie, is that your *spirit's* done been dampened," Byrum said. "'Course, maybe that's 'cause you been saddled with ol' Meyers here for so many years."

"I would trust Pete Meyers alone with my woman anywhere and for as long as needed, which is a hell of a lot more than I can say for you," Charlie replied.

Byrum laughed, shaking his head. To Pete he said, "Bullheaded, ain't he?"

Although there was some truth to Byrum's words, Eli could see that Pete wasn't going to turn on his partner to support them. "Charlie's got his reasons," Pete replied, shrugging. "And I ain't met a man I'd rather partner with, including 'Diah Smith, who this coon has met a time or two, and wasn't all that impressed with. Smith'll go under young, is my thinkin'. Daydreams too much, when he should be watchin' the skyline."

Pierre had fashioned his cornmeal into small cakes he tossed carelessly into the coals. Now he leaned forward with a stick to scoot them out of the heat. Byrum licked his lips, and even silent Curly was leaning forward in hungry anticipation. Pierre coaxed nearly a dozen fist-sized ashcakes into a pile, then fingered two aside and leaned back. "There, by *Dieu,* no more meal we got. These two Grass That Burns and me, we eat. All you fight over the rest."

The men fell into the ashcakes like hungry dogs, all except some of the greenhorns, who didn't yet realize how hungry they would become for bread after months of a steady diet of red meat and river water. Pete Meyers slipped a little chunk away inside his capote for Annie, but the rest of it was devoured by the men around the fire within minutes.

The talk shifted to the beaver trade after that. The annual rendezvous had been held at the southern end of Bear Lake last summer and was a poor doings, according to Byrum. Sublette and Jackson had carted the supplies out last fall, and the usual orgy had been made somewhat dismal by a short supply of alcohol. On top of that, Blackfeet had jumped Bob Campbell and his boys half a day's ride north of the lake, on his way into rendezvous, killing one man and wounding a couple others, further dampening the atmosphere.

Joshua Pilcher, an independent, but with ties to American Fur, had showed up at the rendezvous, Byrum went on. And 'Diah Smith was still somewhere in California, as far as anyone knew.

Eli stared thoughtfully into the fire as Byrum talked, egged on by Johnny and McClure, both of whom understood the importance of such information to a small outfit like the GS&T. It seemed that Byrum was right that afternoon when he claimed the high country was getting crowded with outfits, Eli mused, but so far as he knew, no one had made a move into the country northwest of the Salt Lake unless it was one of the Hudson's Bay outfits, down from Fort Vancouver. Eli weighed Byrum's information carefully and decided they would continue as planned, pick up Reed's cache, then make a push for the other side of the Salt Lake, providing the weather held. If not, they could winter somewhere along the Lake and make a *paseo* up that way in the spring. It would make them later getting back to Taos, but maybe richer, if Sad Smiling Man was telling the truth.

The talk began to deteriorate after a while, sinking into tales Eli suspected were heavily garnished with lies. The men kept the fire burning late, but Eli rose around nine o'clock and bid the storytellers good night. He checked the sentries, finding everything quiet, then made his way around the fire to his robes. He paused as he drew near, detecting another figure bedded down beside his spot. At first he thought it might be Falls on the Rocks, and he was wondering what he would do if it was, but then the top robe was peeled back and Consuelo came up on one elbow, her long hair loose, spilling over one heavy, naked breast. "Come," she said. "Tonight we will sleep as we once did."

Uncertainly, Eli peeled off his outer moccasins, his coat, and trousers, slipping into the double bedroll already made warm by Consuelo. "What changed your mind?" he asked, burrowing deep inside the robes.

Consuelo chuckled. "I noticed you didn't ask before you had your pants off."

Eli laughed softly as he snuggled against her. He wrapped his arms around her warm flesh and slipped his hands between her breasts. She jumped at their icy touch, sucking her breath in, but brought them tighter against her body. "Your hands are like icicles," she complained, rubbing his fingers.

"And you're warm as last night's coals," he murmured into her hair. "Damn if I hadn't forgotten how good it felt to sleep next to you."

Wrinkling her nose, Consuelo said, "That one is bad, Eli, like meat left too long in the sun."

"Who? Byrum?"

"*Sí.* He has eyes like a pick, always on the squaws. Red-Winged Woman told me he roped her on the Bear River and tried to drag her into the bushes, but that Williams saw what happened and saved her. She said Williams was like a madman and that there was a terrible fight. She said Williams would have killed Byrum if the others hadn't pulled him off."

Eli closed his eyes, remembering the tension he had sensed between the two men when Charlie came in to the fire, and the pale flesh of Byrum's mutilated hand as he thrust it toward the light. Finally he sighed. There was bad blood between those two yet, but neither of them was a Cutler man, and there was nothing he could do about it. If they wanted to finish their fight here tonight he would have to let them, although he doubted it would come to that. If it hadn't in the first half hour or so, it probably wouldn't at all now. He was thankful, though, that no one had brought out a jug. A little Taos Lightning could spark the smallest feeling into a roaring inferno.

"Byrum won't try anything here," he said. "This isn't a rendezvous, and the boys wouldn't tolerate any foolishness off him. Not even for Falls on the Rocks."

Consuelo stiffened. "It is good to know that you worry most about her," she said acidly.

"Oh, hell," Eli breathed, rolling onto his back. He wanted to laugh, but knew it would only make her angrier. He rolled his coat up as a pillow and slid his rifle, pouch, and horn under the robes beside him. He left his pistol and belt knife outside the robes, where he could easily reach them. Then he wiggled close to Consuelo once more, her body like a little furnace that he couldn't stay away from. "Why are you here, Connie?" he asked, enjoying her warmth, but careful not to actually touch her.

"Do you want me to leave?"

"I didn't say that, but you haven't shared my bed in weeks, and now all of a sudden you're back. I just wondered why."

She was quiet a long time before answering. "I came tonight to tell you about Byrum, so that you know of the bad feelings between him and Charlie. I do not think the time is right to come back for good. You are still too confused—about me, about Falls on the Rocks, about what you want to do with your life."

"Falls on the Rocks means nothing to me," he said flatly.

"Yet you brought her up first. And you do not send her away. She all but told you she wanted to come to your robes when she came in with Mateo and Sad Smiling Man, and all you said was that you did not want to hire her as a swamper. You have feelings for her, Eli. I can see that plainly enough."

"She's a kid. If I feel anything for her, and I ain't saying that I do, it's only that she's young and doesn't know what she wants."

Consuelo laughed. "Oh, Eli, that is a good one. Believe me, Falls on the Rocks knows exactly what she wants—you. And you want her. I see it in the way you look at her and the way you talk to her. You treat her like she is some green colt that needs a gentle hand. But she is not a colt, and she is not a child, either. She is a woman. All the men see that. *You* see that. I have seen you watching her, the way she looks in that buckskin dress with all the quillwork, the way she walks when she knows your eyes are following her, the way she is always there, watching you, waiting on your every whim. And you like it, Eli. Goddamnit, you *like* it!"

"Yes!" Eli flared. "By God, yes, I do like it! I like having somebody bring me my food and take care of my horse when I get in at night. It feels good to have someone so young and beautiful to wait on you the way she waits on me. And you're right, I've seen the way she fills out that dress of hers, and there ain't no doubt about what's under it. She's young and firm, and her nipples get hard when it's cold. You can see that easy enough, right through her dress. But dammit, Connie, I *ain't* interested in her. Get that through your head."

"I'll get that through my head when you get it through your pecker," she snapped. "You do not love me if you notice these things in another woman."

Eli grunted in exasperation and rolled away. Anger and frustration coursed through him, making his heart pound.

"I love you, Eli," Consuelo whispered. "But I do not think the time is right yet for us to make love. Do you understand?" She pushed the robe back and stood, hurrying naked through the darkness to her own bedroll.

Eli lay awake for a long time. Confusion swirled through him like the tumultuous waters of a river in spring flood. When he finally drifted off, it was into a shallow, restless sleep, marked by twitching muscles and much rolling. Dreams came, flickering images of a woman with reaching arms and firm, hard-nippled breasts. Her skin was a dusky copper, her teeth white as polished pearls. Her hair was long and dark and parted in the middle, the part painted with vermillion. Together they laughed and frolicked through a summer meadow; they made love on a carpet of wildflowers, and when they were finished they raced down out of the mountains hand in hand, racing across a lake he vaguely recognized as the Great Salt Lake.

There, the dream fragmented. The woman was gone, and a massive Indian was coming toward him, tomahawk lifted. Eli jerked his pistol free, pointing it at the Indian's broad chest, but when he tried to pull the trigger, it refused to budge. He struggled with the trigger, clasping the pistol in both hands. Panic overwhelmed him. The Indian drew closer, grinning with bloodstained teeth, and behind him Eli saw the remains of Etienne Provost's old brigade, which had been all but wiped out by Bad Gocha's band of renegades. He pulled mightily on the trigger then, and it finally began to move, creeping backward with an agonizing slowness as the Indian shrank in size to more realistic proportions. There was a click, and the hammer fell forward, but in his effort to squeeze the trigger he had pulled the front sight off. The pistol bucked and roared, while the ball sailed harmlessly past the advancing Indian's ear—

Eli awoke with a start, lying half out of his robes with one elbow digging a shallow pocket in the snow. Sweat beaded his forehead and ran down the side of his face, and his breathing was fast and ragged. He looked wildly about, but there was no Indian standing in front of him with a raised 'hawk, nor lifeless corpses sprawled in death. The camp slept quietly in the chill, predawn air, the silence broken only by the sawing snores of several men and the crunch of frozen snow beneath the sentries' moccasins.

The dream was still vivid in his mind, the latter part of it intimately familiar. For a long time after the Provost massacre, the dream had occurred nightly, always bringing him awake in a sweat, sometimes with a scream tearing hoarsely at his throat. But the first part of the dream had been new, and as his breathing slowed and became more regular, he lay back and pulled the robes up to his chin. In his mind he saw the face of the Indian woman he had run with and eventually made love to, recognizing it beyond any shadow of doubt.

It was the face of Falls on the Rocks.

CHAPTER THIRTY-SIX

Bill Byrum and Curly Jamison pulled out early. Eli walked with them to the edge of the camp.

"Well, this changes things," Byrum said, rechecking his cinch. "Me 'n Curly figured to winter here, but likely you and your boys'll trap it out in no time."

Eli didn't say anything.

"Likely you've already cleaned out the Yampa and the White on your way up, too," Byrum went on, giving Eli a searching look.

"That we did," Eli lied cheerfully.

Byrum laughed. "Hell, I don't know whether to believe you or not, but I reckon it don't matter none. Beaver enough for everyone." He heaved into the saddle and took a loop around his saddle horn with his packhorse's lead rope. "Well, Eli, I thank you for your kindness. Watch your topknot."

"Watch yours, Bill." He stepped back, nodding his good-bye to Curly. The two men rode out, making their way slowly toward the aspen-covered hills to the east.

McClure, who had been standing nearby, came over. "How do they do it?" he asked in wonder. "How do they stand the loneliness?"

"It takes a special breed," Eli acknowledged.

"Yes, I can see that. I've seen it among our own men. I respect it, to a degree, but I don't admire it, and I certainly don't envy it for myself."

"It's a lonely life," Eli replied vaguely. He turned back to the camp. "Let's be putting out, Silas. It's still a long way to the Salt Lake country."

The trapping was better than Eli had expected, and despite his anxiousness to push on, they spent two more days in Brown's Hole. At the northern end of the valley he kept Mateo in camp, and together they constructed another makeshift fur press, baling the plews already grained. They were doing all right, for all their travel, and Eli said as much to McClure.

"The pace will be worth it if we find Reed's cache in time," McClure agreed.

"Even more so if Sad Smiling Man is telling the truth." The Shoshone had taken to Charlie, who was always a little more Indian than Pete anyway, and was with them now, trapping somewhere in the O-Wi-Yukuts, to the east.

McClure shrugged dismissively. "I shall remain satisfied with beating Reed to the cache," he replied.

They left Brown's Hole the next day, following Red Creek north, then crossed a couple of low ridges to the Little Bitter and followed that back to the Green, or Seedskadee, above its deep, flaming red gorge. They were in the heart of what had once been some of the primest beaver country in the West now, moving steadily northward among the barren, orange-tinted hills. They kept to the valleys where the grass was lush and tall in the summer, and the streams like sparkling threads dropped carelessly from above, as if from some smiling god. It was a rich country still, except for beaver.

"Poor doin's," Old Cal grumbled as the brigade passed an abandoned beaver lodge, already half destroyed by floods. "By damn, I hate a bird that shits its own nest."

Eli also felt a certain sadness in the unchecked streams and crumbling lodges. He had been one of the first white men through this part of the country, and he remembered it when the beaver population had been opulent, their pelts thick and soft to the touch. It was hard to believe the land had been so devastated in such a brief span of years. It would come back in time, he knew, but it would never be the same, and he couldn't help wondering if perhaps the damage they were doing wasn't irreversible. It sobered him to think of the Seedskadee crowded with farms and towns, as grown-over as Missouri, or even Virginia. It was hard to imagine, but not impossible, if you looked back over the last few generations to see how far civilization had come since the Revolutionary War. Eli's own father, as a boy, could remember George Washington's presidency, and look how far the country had come since then.

They followed the Seedskadee for three days without setting a trap. Early on the morning of their fourth day, they came to the mouth of the Big Sandy River. Here, where the big St. Louis brigades and supply caravans normally crossed the Seedskadee, Eli called a halt. He had half hoped they might find a raft or boat of some kind pulled up on one of the beaches, but except for the litter of past camps, there was nothing here. They had passed several small herds of buffalo during the past couple of days, so he sent Charlie and Old Cal out to collect some hides for skin canoes. The rest he put to work constructing willow frames and setting up camp. It would take a couple of days at least to build the canoes, and most of another to ferry everything across the Seedskadee. After that it was a straight shot to the Wasatch Mountains and the valley where Reed's cache was hidden. Another week, perhaps, if the weather held and luck hung in there for them.

Remi stared dully at the old campsite. Several inches of new snow had fallen since the brigade had stopped here, but their sign was still visible beneath the fresh white blanket. Wearily, he leaned forward until he was curled over the saddle horn. A wave of nausea racked his body, but he didn't bother leaning to one side. There was nothing left inside to vomit anymore, not even the green bile that had come up yesterday.

Disappointment hammered him. He had counted on finding them here, scattered along the White River and its tributaries in search of beaver. But Eli had pushed on, goaded by whatever had driven him since arriving in Taos last fall. Remi wasn't sure it mattered anymore, not to him, at least. Eli's reckless pace was killing him, for without the others he knew he would soon die. He had begun to believe, since leaving the Colorado and climbing the treacherous trail over the mountains to the White, that he might even die with their help. But until today he hadn't considered giving up. The abandoned campsite on the banks of the White was like a last, frayed string snapping inside of him, hope withering, fate laughing.

But then something else snapped inside, and he looked up grimly, his cheeks streaked with tears. "Ah, Jake," he said hoarsely. "For you, Remi will go on."

He straightened, forcing his knotted, cramping muscles to obey. There was no sign of a skin canoe on either bank, and he decided they must have forded the river instead. It looked swift and broad, but not particularly deep. He nudged the paint forward. She gimped to the edge of the bank and halted, blowing softly. The mountains separating the Colorado from the White had been hard on the mare, and her leg had worsened. He wondered if she would have the strength to buck the river's powerful current. On a good pony and with his own health returned, he would never have hesitated, but now the paint's balking brought his own doubts rising to the surface. He stared fearfully at the gray sheet of water. Fingers of ice reached tentatively out from the still shoals close to the bank. He imagined the water swirling around his naked ankles as he forced the paint into the river, the thought of the pain it would cause him almost more than he could bear. He sat there for a long time, staring hypnotically at the flowing water. His mind numbed and began to wander as he watched the river, until he caught himself swaying in the saddle.

"*Sacre,*" he whispered, shaking his head weakly. He squared his shoulders and gathered his reins. "Come, *ma cherie,*" he told the mare. "It is time to quit this dreaming."

He kicked the paint with his good ankle, and they hit the water with a loud, icy splash. The paint lunged into the current, bucking chest-deep waters. Remi gasped at the pain and grabbed desperately for the saddle horn. His vision blurred, and another wave of nausea flooded him.

"*Non!*" he cried, leaning forward to curse the mare, the river, Eli, and Jake. Unconsciousness stained his brain like the dark seepage of a leaking quill pen. He fought it with every ounce of strength he had left, and was still in the saddle when they came dripping out the far side. The paint stopped on the sandy shore, her muscles trembling. Remi, still clutching the saddle horn, could barely raise his head. He sat hunched that way for a long time, his shoulders shaking with violent sobs. It was several minutes before he was able to stop his crying long enough to look back at the river, where his fusil had disappeared into the swift current.

Pete's eyes snapped open, and his hand closed instinctively around his rifle. He was curled on his side, a supple, buff-colored buffalo robe drawn over his head. Cautiously, he edged the robe back, his ears straining for the slightest sound. They were camped in a V-shaped cove on the west bank of the Seedskadee, having finished their crossing the day before. A crumbling sandstone bluff, its sage-crowned rim now silhouetted by the translucent glow of the setting moon, sheltered them from the westerly wind. Glancing at the stars,

Pete decided it was probably three o'clock in the morning, perhaps a little later.

Despite the waning light, he could clearly see the camp sprawled before him, the sleeping men and women like short, dark logs washed up in flood. They had formed their packs into a shallow breastworks, but there hadn't been time to rig a corral for the remuda. The horses and mules were tied to long rawhide ropes stretched between the trees along the river. It was the remuda that Pete watched closest, knowing that if something was amiss with the camp, the stock would warn him first.

He pushed the robe down and came up on one elbow, drawing his rifle closer. Something in his furtive movements must have awakened Annie. Her big brown eyes turned on him, forming a silent question. He shrugged in reply and quietly slid his body free of the heavy robe. He shivered in the cold, wearing only a cotton shirt, his buckskin trousers, and a dry pair of moccasins.

"What is it?" Annie asked in Spanish.

"Hush."

Annie sat up, quickly surveying the camp. She gave him a reproachful look. "There is nothing but sleeping men. Not even the dogs are awake at this hour."

Pete pulled his moccasins under his thighs, sitting cross-legged, shivering in the cold. "Something woke me up," he whispered. He tried to remember who was on the last guard. Jake, he thought, Jake and Pierre.

"Goddamnit, Eli," Pete grumbled softly.

"Eli cannot hear you," Annie scolded. "Come back to bed, you are letting—"

A sound of whistling air followed by a fleshy *thunk* stopped her in midsentence. She cried out, shattering the stillness of the night as she writhed around the arrow's bite.

"Injuns, goddamnit!" Pete howled, scrambling to his feet. "Brownskins, boys! Grab your rifles and get off your asses!" From the corner of his eye he caught the sight of a quick, flitting shadow racing toward the far end of the remuda. He snapped a shot in that direction, purposely holding high. He didn't want to hit a horse, not to mention Jake or Pierre.

The brigade came quickly to life. A rifle cracked on Pete's right as he reloaded. A fusil boomed, its report echoing back from the bluff.

Pete started toward the remuda at a run, then skidded to a stop. Charlie came alongside, stopping to touch his shoulder, then rushing on. Pete hesitated, torn between his concern for Annie and the fight that was just then swelling into a battle. Then he heard a shout from the river—a Blackfoot's war cry—and swore and hurried forward.

Lead buzzed the air around his ears; arrows sliced it with a cold *whish*ing. Horses whinnied in fright, mules brayed, and the dogs added their own incessant yammering to the confusion. Pete dodged forward in a crouch, coming to the edge of the trees where the remuda was tied. Mateo and Clint were already there, working frantically with the knots.

"Take 'em up to the bluff," Pete shouted as he ducked under a taut, vibrating rope and raced on. The trappers quickly formed a rough line above the riverbank and began to return the Blackfeet's fire. Pete snapped off two rounds from the protection of a cottonwood tree, then darted to his left. A bullet whistled close to his face, and he swore and dropped to his belly, crawling behind the shelter of a sun-bleached log. A few minutes later Johnny Two-Dogs and Silas McClure dove in beside him.

"We have a contingent penned down on a sandbar sheltered by those alders," McClure puffed, nodding toward a clump of scrub willows maybe forty yards away. "No more than five or six, but there's more fighting downriver."

"I think they got some of our ponies," Johnny added breathlessly. "Silas and I were trying to work our way to the river, but they drove us back. It looked like some of them were mounted."

A fusil boomed from the alders, striking the log above Pete's head. He tucked his face away from the shower of splinters and bark and swore. Johnny raised up, snapping a shot into the alders, signaling a rippling sound of gunfire that passed down the line of mountain men. The sound came back to them from the sandstone bluff like a second battle in progress, and both Pete and McClure turned their heads in that direction. "Our flanks are totally exposed to a rear attack," McClure said worriedly. "This is a complete fiasco." He shook his head. "We should have never left the protection of camp."

"Wasn't much to hide behind there," Johnny replied laconically. "Besides, these Indians are after horseflesh. It'd be a long walk to the Salt Lake without the remuda."

There was a warning shout from somewhere down the line, followed by the muted thunder of running horses. A rifle barked, and Pete heard Old Cal's voice swearing shrilly.

"Sonofabitch," Pete said.

The Blackfeet were stretched out along the river in small groups, caught with only the most meager of shelters for protection—low banks, flimsy alders, a few small, shallow depressions. Yet despite their poor position, they were keeping up a steady fire, preventing the mountain men from closing in.

McClure poked his head up, taking a quick survey of the ground between them and the river. A rifle banged from the river, the ball passing overhead with a thumping whine, and McClure ducked.

"You trying to play the turkey at a turkey shoot?" Pete asked tersely.

"If we could close off the northern end I believe we could bring the whole war party to an easy defeat," McClure replied.

"This child'll be satisfied with just routing the bunch we got cornered here," Pete replied.

"There's at least one man positioned in the grass to our left," McClure said. "If one of you were to join him and come downriver, perhaps we could squeeze this bunch off that sandbar at least. Drive them into the open. From there whoever stayed behind could swing in and join you. We'd have them like pecans in a nutcracker."

Johnny gave him an incredulous look. "That's a mighty big order," he said.

"Well, somebody's nuts would be in a nutcracker, all right," Pete added. "But I'd like to be a little more certain it was going to be them Blackfeet's nuts and not mine."

"Damnit man, do you want to sit here like bumps on a log? There's already one man over there. The least you'd be doing is reinforcing his position."

"You go squeeze those Blackfeet off their sandbar," Johnny retorted. "See if it's as easy as it sounds."

Firing broke out anew from downriver, intensified for several moments, then tapered off. McClure said, "Now is the time, if we're going to do it."

Johnny grunted. "I think I'll sit this one out, McClure."

"Pete?"

"Aw, hell, maybe I'll take a little *paseo* over that way. I'm curious now to see who's hunkered down in the grass there." He pushed back from the log, flashing a grin. "Watch your hair, amigos."

"Watch yours, Meyers," Johnny answered.

Bent low, Pete sprinted upriver. A fusil boomed from the sandbar. Johnny's rifle answered it. Pete bounded through the tall grass toward the dark smear of a trapper, barely visible in the dim light. A second later he dived into the snow at Clint Orr's side.

"Sonofabitch!" Clint exclaimed. "I'm glad to see you. I figured I've got at least a dozen of them cornered down on the river."

"That," Pete said, shifting around to a more comfortable position, "ain't likely." He poked his head above the rim of the shallow depression where Clint had taken shelter and studied the sandbar. The two men were about sixty yards away here, but at enough of an angle that Pete could see the silver purling of the river as it broke around the bar. He ducked back and glanced around him. "You picked a mighty poor place to hide," he observed.

"Pick, hell. This was the first hole I could find."

"Who's with the horses?"

"McClure told Mateo and Jorge to stay with them. He told me to come down from the north."

"That McClure, he's a fine one for passin' out orders, ain't he?"

Clint shrugged. "He's second in command. Besides, the fighting seemed to be shifting downriver anyway, away from the remuda. We decided to leave them tied up, rather than try to hobble everything in the dark."

"Well, I don't reckon it matters now, but I ain't hankering to stay here. I seem to remember a little arroyo closer to the river that'd offer more protection. Feel up to it?"

Clint lifted his head. "Is that that little notch I see over there?"

"I'd reckon so. It ain't much, but it'll sure as hell be better than this."

"Then let's try it."

Pete nodded. "Stay low," he said, and took off at a run with Clint close on his heels. He ran toward the broken bank and the faint, twisting line of the arroyo, extending back from the river's edge. An Indian yelled a warning in the Blackfoot tongue, and an arrow streaked past Pete's face like the flight of a hummingbird. Then he was sliding feet first into the arroyo, packing snow up his trousers legs as far as his calves. Clint jumped in behind him, half sprawling across the top on the opposite side. Pete grabbed a handful of the youth's shirt and pulled him back just as a fusil's ball whiffled overhead.

"Damn!" Clint breathed, his face buried in the snow.

"Hell, that wasn't close," Pete said. "I lost half my mustache to a Papago's arrer once. Now, that was a close shave."

Clint laughed stiffly and sat up. "What now?"

Pete studied the sandbar as best he could through the broken yellow stems of clump grass. He could see a good part of the bar from here, as well as the screen of alders that shielded it from McClure's position. But he didn't see any Indians. Either McClure and Johnny had overestimated their count, or the Blackfeet had found another way off the sandbar.

"Let's start firing into those alders," Pete said. "We can shoot right down the side of the bank with nothing to block our way."

Clint glanced to the west, where the domed glow of moonlight was sinking behind the bluff. The darkness was deepening rapidly now, gathering like pooled shadows along the river. Already the alders that had been clearly visible from the log where Pete had lain with McClure and Johnny were beginning to lose their distinctiveness.

"Buggers are awful quiet," Clint said, cocking his rifle.

"Too quiet," Pete agreed.

Clint lifted his rifle, leveling it on the alders. Pete readied his own rifle, waiting for Clint to flush a brave out into the open. Clint squeezed the trigger, his rifle roaring. The brightness of muzzle flash momentarily blinded Pete. He had to look away and blink several times before he could look back and see the sandbar. Nothing moved, nor had Johnny or McClure opened fire.

"What happened?" Clint asked, hitching his powder horn around to reload.

"Nothing that I saw. Try another one." When Clint was ready, Pete cupped his hand around his eyes to shield his vision, but even with that advantage he saw no sign of movement within the alders.

Clint looked at him, puzzled. "Are they still there?"

"Load up and try one more, close to the ground this time. Could be they're huggin' that sandbar." But Pete doubted it now. He glanced at the Seedskadee, flowing past like a broad, dark sheet of cloth. They had crossed it only yesterday afternoon, and he knew the current was swift and powerful, the water well over a man's head. It would be impossible for the Blackfeet to escape that way, and he was certain they hadn't slipped past him and Clint. That left only the south, downriver.

There was a shout from down the line, questioning in its tone. Someone else answered, and although Pete couldn't make out the words, he understood the implications well enough. "They've given us the slip," he said to Clint. "I'd bet my fall's catch on it."

"Can we catch them again?"

"I'm not sure I want to," Pete replied. He glanced toward the camp, thinking of Annie.

"Do you want me to try another shot?" Clint asked.

"Naw, the hell with 'em," Pete said suddenly. "I'm goin' back."

"Back?"

But Pete didn't take time to explain. He gathered his legs under him, took a deep breath, then lunged out of the arroyo. He raced across the flat ground until the river disappeared in the darkness behind him, then slowed and stopped. All seemed quiet toward the camp, but he made his way there with care, toeing his moccasins carefully into the frozen crust of snow to make as little noise as possible. He passed the remuda and could just make out the heaps of stacked gear when a fusil boomed from the center of the camp. He felt the gentle, almost childlike tug of the bullet as it passed through his shirtsleeve, then dropped to the ground, swearing loudly and viciously.

"*Sacre!* Do not shoot, *monsieur* Pete! Is Pierre! Pierre!"

"Pierre! You son of a cross-eyed coyote! I oughta peel your hide!"

"*Enfant de garce,* me think you Blackfoot. Accident, *oui,* an accident." Pete stood and came forward, brushing the snow off his trousers. Pierre scrambled over a pile of baled beaver plews, holding his hands high and nearly tripping. "Pete. *Sacre,* a close one that was, no?"

"A close one for you," Pete returned, jamming his rifle's muzzle against Pierre's chest and shoving him out of the way. "That was as damn fool an act as any greenhorn, Pierre. How long have you been out here? A couple of days?"

"Me think you Blackfoot," Pierre repeated, lowering his hands. He whispered softly. "Damn, me afraid you shoot Pierre."

"I ought to," Pete grumbled over his shoulder. "Get back on

watch, you damn pork-eater. But this time, be careful who you burn powder against."

"*Oui*, Pete. No more accident!"

Pete hurried to the bedroll where he and Annie had lain. Clint's squaw, White Feather, stood to one side, comforting Little Pete and Magpie. Red-Winged Woman, Consuelo, Grass That Burns, and Falls on the Rocks were hovering over Annie, working as best they could in the dim light. Blossom, Pete noted, was near Annie's head, holding her hand and chattering softly to take Annie's attention away from her wound. Pete's chest tightened at the sight, and he shoved into the knot of women and sank to his knees beside Annie's robes.

"Annie," he said gently, touching her cheek. "Annie, can you hear me?"

Annie's eyes rolled weakly toward his voice. "I told you we should not place our robes so close to bluff," she said in Spanish. "Now I have a Gros Ventre arrow in my leg and will have to limp while I keep your camp."

Pete sank back, a small laugh bubbling to his lips. "Hell," he said, his breathing coming easier as his muscles relaxed. "I thought you'd gone under, the way all these women were sitting over you like vultures."

"My friends protected me while my man went off to fight the Gros Ventre. Did you take a scalp to avenge this insult?"

"Not yet," Pete said. He started to pull the robe away from Annie's legs, but Consuelo slapped his hand away.

"It is too dark to see anything," she told him. "And too cold to have her uncovered. Red-Winged Woman and I stopped the flow of blood. I don't think the arrow hit a bone, but we'll have to wait until daylight to look at the wound."

"The arrow, deep it go, into thigh," Red-Winged Woman said in her broken English. "We push it through, add poultice." She leaned forward to draw the robe tighter around Annie's shoulders.

"*Bueno*," Pete conceded in the face of so much opposition. "We'll take a look at it in the morning, then." He stood, picking up his rifle. "I'm goin' to make a quick *paseo* around camp, make sure everything's all right."

"Gros Ventre," Red-Winged Woman said, holding out the arrow they had taken from Annie's leg. The Gros Ventre were the southernmost affiliation of the powerful Blackfoot tribe, ranging throughout the Three-Forks region and on east. Sometimes, especially in the spring and early summer, they would raid down this way, but it wasn't common to find them this far from home during the dead of winter. He couldn't help wondering if this was the same bunch Sad Smiling Man had warned them about, or if it was another band. He hoped it was the same bunch; he'd hate to think the whole Blackfoot Nation was so riled up it had taken to raiding all year long.

He took the arrow Red-Winged Woman handed him and brought it close to his face, studying the markings in the faint starlight. It was Gros Ventre, all right, but strangely, it was the sight of Annie's blood that caught his eye and made him feel queasy all of a sudden. He stared at the stained, flint-tipped head for a long time, then shoved it back to Red-Winged Woman. "Give that to Eli," he said gruffly. "He'll want to see it." He looked at Annie, tenderness welling up in him, and the knowledge that it would be so easy to lose her. But he didn't know how to voice such thoughts, and in the end the best he could do was order stiffly, "Don't go kickin' around and breaking that wound open."

He turned and hurried away, as if the air around Annie's bed had become thick and hard to breathe.

Pierre didn't kindle a fire until dawn. By the time he had breakfast ready, Johnny and Old Cal were circling down from the top of the bluff, while Charlie and Pete came in from the south.

"They've hightailed it," Charlie announced, pulling the black mule he'd saddled before dawn that morning to a rough stop.

"They got what they came after," Old Cal stated. "They came lookin' for ponies and got 'emselves well mounted, they did. Likely they'd got 'em all if ol' Pete hadn't sang out a warnin'." He glared at Jake Orr, causing the younger man to flush with anger.

Jake had been standing guard on the remuda when the Blackfeet struck last night, and Eli figured the brigade owed Pete for more than just the horses he'd saved. Had he not called out when he did, Jake would likely be dead by now, and probably several others as well. As it stood, the Blackfeet had stolen four horses off the mountain men. At least two of the Indians had been wounded in the brief battle along the Seedskadee, but except for the arrow that had pierced Annie's leg, the trappers had come out unscathed.

Pete said, "It looks like only a small bunch, maybe fifteen or sixteen warriors. They had about a dozen ponies cached in a little draw about a mile downriver."

"The war party Bill Byrum spoke of," McClure said knowingly. "They must have had some luck among the Utes if they had horses."

"Was a few of 'em riding' double coming in," Pete confirmed. "Sure as hell none of 'em were ridin' double going out."

Johnny said, "They went west when they left the draw, although my guess is they'll turn north the first chance they get. If they've had a successful raid, they'll want to get back home so they can strut in front of the women."

"I want to know why we're sitting here wastin' good daylight," Charlie interrupted loudly. Pete, Old Cal, and Johnny had all dismounted, but Charlie stayed in the saddle, the mule dancing nervously under him. He had been that way ever since he discovered his appaloosa had been one of the horses stolen last night.

"I'm not sure we should go after them," Eli said. "With the extra ponies we bought from you and Pete back at Bowlegs's village, I'm thinking we could make it to the Salt Lake country with what we have."

"By God, that's chickenshit talk," Charlie said hotly. "Them bastards run off with our ponies, Eli. Are you just gonna let 'em go?"

Sad Smiling Man had hung back while the old hands talked it out. Now he stepped forward, saying, "There is snow upon the ground, and that is a bad time to fight the Blackfoot. It is better to fight them in the spring, when there is grass to make the ponies strong."

Charlie snorted contemptuously.

"My friend, you are impatient," Sad Smiling Man intoned. "It is wise to remember that it is the vulture who eats."

"It's the goddamn eagle that gets first pickin's," Charlie shot back. He looked at Eli. "What about Annie? She ain't gonna be able to sit a pony for several days. What are you gonna do about her?"

Eli hesitated. Annie wasn't hurt badly, but she would need some time to recuperate. On the other hand, he knew time was running out if they wanted to beat Reed to the cached furs. The season was getting late, and if his calculations were correct, Reed and his men should be somewhere along the Ashley River by now, not much farther away from the Wasatch Mountains than Eli's outfit.

"Damnit, Eli, what's gotten into you?" Charlie demanded. "Have you gotten so coldhearted you'd leave me'n Pete behind just to get your fingers on another plew? By damn, if that's the way you feel—"

"No," Eli breathed heavily. "No, hell no." He looked at Pete, then Charlie, and finally McClure. "We'll stay put until Annie's feeling better," he told the clerk. Lifting his voice, he added, "If some of you boys want to go after the Blackfeet, I'll give you three days. After that, if Annie's up to it, we're pulling out."

"That's more like it," Charlie growled. "By God, grab your bedroll, Pete. We're gonna teach them Blackfoot bastards it ain't healthy to steal a pony from Charlie Williams."

With his saddlebags filled and strapped behind his cantle, Pete went to Annie's bed. She watched him reproachfully as he knelt at her side, and he smiled a little at the feistiness he saw in her eyes. "How are you feeling?" he asked in Spanish.

"I am good. I should go with you and keep you out of trouble."

"I've got Charlie to keep me out of trouble. You had best stay here and run the brigade. Eli would not know what to do if he did not have your advice."

Annie looked offended by his teasing. "My advice is always good," she replied testily. "It is your fault if you do not heed it and something bad happens."

Pete smiled. "Just see that you stay off your feet for a few days, and let Red-Winged Woman take care of things. I will be back as soon as I can."

Annie was silent a moment, then reached out to touch Pete's arm lightly. "It is cold to the north. Do you have the extra moccasins I made for you? The ones of buffalo leather, with the hair turned in?"

"I've got 'em," he said in English, taking her hand and squeezing it lightly. "Don't worry, we'll be fine." Then he gave her a devilish smile. "Maybe I'll steal you a good Blackfoot pony? Would you like that, a good buffalo runner?"

She glared at him. "*Qué? Me no sabe.*"

Pete laughed. "Too bad," he said, and turned away.

Charlie sat glumly atop his black mule, with Red-Winged Woman standing by his stirrup. She looked worried, Pete thought, but she hadn't made any attempt to dissuade Charlie from going after the appaloosa. Only Eli, McClure, Old Cal, and Jake had refused to vol-

unteer to ride with them, and in the end Eli had been forced to set a
limit of three men. Charlie had chosen three of the green hands to accompany them—Mateo, Jorge, and Clint. Pete had been surprised by
his partner's choices, although he understood the logic behind it. All
three were good men, two of them with extensive experience fighting Indians. At the same time, he had allowed Eli to keep some of
the best men with him. It was about as fair a split as a man could
have made under the circumstances, and Pete was glad that Charlie
wasn't so angry over the theft of his horse that he hadn't thought it
through. Mateo and Jorge were already mounted, and Clint stood
nearby with White Feather, leaning close and whispering in her ear.
Charlie had a scowl like a canyon across his brow as Pete strode up.
"Damnit, Pete, the sun's been up nearly an hour," he said. "What've
you been doin'?"

"Writin' my name in the snow, but I forgot how to spell it and ran
outta juice before I was finished."

Pete swung into the saddle, and Clint reluctantly let go of White
Feather and mounted. Eli came over and put a hand against the buckskin's shoulder. "If you're late, we'll take your women with us."

"I know you will, Eli."

"*Bueno*. Watch your topknot, amigo."

Pete grinned. "Watch your'n," he said. He gathered the buckskin's
reins and pulled away, calling over his shoulder, "Come *on*, Charlie.
Damn if I ain't always waitin' on you."

"Goddamnit!" Charlie exploded. He kicked his mule in the ribs,
loping out of camp behind his partner. Silently, Mateo, Jorge, and
Clint fell in behind.

Chapter Thirty-seven

He was lost in a vortex of darkness and wind, the trail he had been
following long since disappearing beneath the rapidly drifting snow.
Gone, too, was his sense of direction. At one point the wind had
blown steadily out of the northwest, driving before it a towering

black bank of clouds. But as the storm descended over the flat plains the wind had shifted capriciously, buffeting first one way and then another, like a woman bustling about her kitchen with company trudging up the lane. Now there was no north or south, east or west. There was only the deepening snow that pulled at his legs with each step, sapping his strength. The wet, clinging snow matted his capote on all sides. Ice had formed on his mustache and down his dark beard, making them appear white. Little pellets of ice had also formed in his nostrils, making his eyes tear painfully as he breathed in the frigid temperatures. From the darkness in front of him he could only faintly hear the musical tinkling of the lead dog's brass sleigh bells, a tiny, reassuring jingling, with no hint of the desperation he felt as the hours wore on.

His grip tightened on the fancy blue and green cariole he had borrowed from the factor at Fort Douglas. It occurred to him that a man could easily die out here and probably not be found until the spring thaw, if then. The thought worried him more than the impending danger of the blizzard. What would he look like after several months of being frozen in a snowbank? Would wolves or Indian dogs find his body before then? In his mind's eye he saw his ice-stiffened carcass, the skin beneath his ripped clothing only gnawed a little, far too frozen for any canine to devour. The picture made him shudder, and for a while he debated stopping, but then he had scolded himself for such a foolish notion. Where would he stop? Where would he find the wood or dried buffalo dung he would need for a fire if he was to survive the night on the open, empty plain? No, he must push on, for a while yet.

Not long after that, the shrieking of the wind seemed to change its pitch. It appeared to stretch, and then die, before rising again in another buffeting gust. But before it did, he heard a sound that brought a smile to his lips—the sound of a Red River jig. Within another hundred yards the music came to him clearly, and above the sawing of the fiddles and the wheezing pumps of the squeezeboxes and the mournful howling of the wind, he could hear the sharp, quick yelps of the dancers as they skipped across the worn puncheon floor of old Menard's cabin.

The yellow glow of a tallow lamp appeared like a beacon through the blowing snow, and the dogs picked up their pace, turning off the road that had been there all along and trotting swiftly, proudly, into the yard.

But then the yard disappeared, and so did the lamp. Remi's eyelids fluttered open. He found himself staring past the paint's gimping shoulder, his arms hanging limply on either side of her neck. His broken reins trailed in the snow. He had hooked his capote's sash over the saddle horn at some point, and now when he tried to straighten up, it pulled him back.

"*Enfant de . . .*" Remi began, then let the oath fade off. A small whimper escaped his split, bleeding lips; the dream had been so vivid, the promise of food and warmth so near . . . .

He fumbled at the knot binding him to the saddle, but his fingers were numb and awkward, and he finally gave it up. Gaunt, hollow-eyed, his calves aching from the cramps that jolted through them several times a day now, he rode on without any sense of direction. He was aware of the pain in his stomach, new and unfamiliar, like the desperate, sharp-nailed clawing of some beast trying to escape. He had lost track of the number of days since he had last eaten. His last substantial meal, such as it was, had been just before arriving at the Utes' abandoned camp at the forks of the Grand River—a couple of mouthfuls of dried beaver salvaged from the canyon where Jake had abandoned him. He had made do with odds and ends since then—a handful of berries stripped along the banks of the Río Colorado, some discarded bones at an old campsite of the trappers in a canyon south of the White, a piece of leather thrown away by one of the squaws. Last night he had punctured the paint's neck with the tip of his awl and feasted on a cup of warm, salty blood, although he hadn't been able to keep it down. It was last night, also, that he had begun to hallucinate, his mind drifting in and out. He saw men and women calling to him, villages with carts rattling down cobblestone streets; occasionally he saw demons with dripping fangs and cloven hooves, salivating as they waited for him to close his eyes.

At other times his thoughts became more rational, ranging far into the past to relive events he had all but forgotten over the years—such as the midwinter wedding of old Menard's daughter, Susette, to a young Hudson's Bay clerk named Oswald. *Sacre,* how many years ago had that been? he wondered.

He knew now that his time remaining on earth was short, but he didn't fear death as he once had; appearing inevitable, it had taken on an air of comfort, an escape from his worldly suffering. Remi had never been a religious man, despite his strong conviction in a just and kindly God, but now, during his more lucid moments, he sometimes prayed, not out of fear for salvation, but for the comfort it gave him. Soon he would know what only those who had gone before him knew, and he found himself oddly anticipating the journey, as he had once anticipated the fall hunt.

The paint stumbled on her bad leg, going to her knees and whinnying painfully as she lunged back to her feet. The sudden fall broke the sash holding Remi to the saddle, and he sensed himself tumbling without any real feeling of the fall. On his back, comfortable in the snow, he watched as the paint bolted awkwardly on her bad leg, holding her head to the side to avoid the trailing reins. Her flashing hooves kicked up a shower of powdery snow that twinkled in the sunlight. The paint disappeared over the rim of a hill, and Remi settled back to await death.

The sun and the blue sky surprised him after his dream of the blizzard that had caught him on his way to Menard's cabin. Thinking of Susette brought to his mind his own wife, a Cree he had married during his years trading for Hudson's Bay in the Qu Appellette country. He had called her Maltilda, for no reason he could remember, and had stayed with her for nearly four seasons. He'd fathered two children during those years, both girls, and therefore, in his mind, inconsequential. Being young and incredibly ignorant, he hadn't bothered to take them with him when he had been reassigned to the Hair Hills, south of Fort Douglas. It puzzled him that he should think of them now, after so many years. He wondered what had become of Maltilda and the girls. Gone back to the Cree, he supposed. But, *sacre*, he thought with a little start, they would be married now, those two girls, and maybe with children of their own.

"*Non*, it cannot be," he said conversationally. "Remi, a grandpapa?" He chuckled at the thought, warmed by it. "Ah, Remi should have stayed, no? To hold the little ones on his knees. That would have been a thing to know." He sighed and glanced to his side, feeling no surprise to discover the black lobo sitting patiently about fifty feet away.

"Where are your companions, *chien*?" Remi called, his voice barely a whisper. "Eh? They are not so hungry to have Remi's body, no? But you, my black-hearted friend, you do not give up so easy.

Well, Remi does not give up also. You come closer, eh, and Remi
will show you who has the longest fangs." His fingers fumbled with
the knife at his belt, and a sudden wild hope blossomed in his breast.
Had he the strength . . . the patience?

"We will play *le* game, eh?" Remi said, eyes misting at the
prospect of this one last chance to cheat death. Carefully pulling his
knife, he leaned back and closed his eyes to slits, slowing his breathing until his chest barely moved. At the far end of his blurred field of
vision the wolf was like a black smudge, a sooty thumbprint on the
window of his world. His knife lay in the low valley of his stomach,
his grimy-knuckled hand resting lightly atop the old walnut handle,
too weak to maintain a firm grip for more than a few minutes at a
time. And Remi knew this game would run far longer than that,
maybe into the night. He didn't know if he would last that long himself, but it was a gamble, and Remi LeBlanc had never walked away
from a wager in his life.

He dozed and woke and dozed again. The wolf remained as if
chained, sometimes standing or shifting from one hip to the other,
occasionally lying on its chest, its head alert above its paws. But it
never left or appeared to lose interest in its long-hunted prey. Remi
began to drift into a feeling of lassitude that made his own immobil-
ity easier. He could feel the sun shrinking as it sank toward the horizon. Its warmth retreated as the shadows grew longer and deeper.
Once, upon awakening, he saw a huge herd of elk moving slowly
over a ridge in the distance. The wolf, too, saw the elk; it stood and
whined low in its throat, but refused to be tempted by such formidable prey. Remi breathed a sigh of relief when he saw the wolf sink
back to a sitting position and return its attention to him. There was
still a chance.

He awoke to a tugging on his sleeve and cried out in panic. He
grabbed for his knife, but his cold fingers struck the scarred wooden
handle and sent it sliding off his stomach into the snow. He tipped
his head back, wanting to bawl at losing his one chance, knowing the
lobo wouldn't be fooled again by such deception. In such a despair-
ing state, it took him several minutes to realize that it was not the
black wolf that had tugged on his sleeve. He blinked, hearing a
human voice, and wondering if he was dreaming again. He forced
his gaze to one side, confused by the sight that greeted his eyes. The
voice went on, tinged with surprise.

"Hell, he's alive, Bill," the human said. He was a tall, lean man with a fall of curly auburn hair spilling from beneath a badger-skin cap. He smiled shyly when Remi looked at him, and bobbed his head in greeting. "I'm Curly Jamison," the man said, "and that's my partner, Bill Byrum. You hungry, old-timer?"

Remi gasped a little, and tears rolled down his hollowed cheeks, hot and stinging. "*Oui,*" he rasped. "*Oui,* Remi is hungry and cold and tired."

"Wagh," Curly grunted, bending closer to slip his arms beneath the Frenchman's emaciated body. "I guess we got the cures for those ailments back at camp." He stood, lifting Remi as if he were a child. Remi tipped his chin into the man's shoulder and blinked away the tears. In the distance he could see the black wolf, trotting off in the same direction the elk had taken earlier. Grinning weakly, Remi lifted the middle finger of his right hand toward the lobo's retreating form.

On the morning of the fourth day after the Blackfeet's attack, Eli gave the command to move out. Annie was feeling better, even hobbling around a little, against the advice of Red-Winged Woman and Consuelo. And the men were itching to go, growing cantankerous with too much free time. Jake and Travis had already come to sharp words over Travis's mule, and the altercation might have come to blows if Eli hadn't stepped in. The five men who had gone after the Blackfeet hadn't returned yet, but Eli was determined not to wait.

It took them three days to cross the high, windy desert between the Green and Bear rivers. Eli led them up the Muddy River until it petered out among barren, snow-dusted hills, then struck out due west. It was an empty, wind-scoured land that they rode through, full of rocky ledges and flat-topped buttes. There were no trees once they left the Seedskadee, no wood, and they were forced to make their fires with old buffalo chips dug up from beneath the snow. To make matters worse, it had clouded over the day they left, the sun little more than a pale orb that passed quickly overhead, as if ashamed of its puny efforts. A strong wind and scattered snow flurries added to their misery.

It was still early when Eli brought the brigade to a halt on a ridge overlooking the Bear. McClure and the others formed a group around him, sitting hunched in their saddles, their faces all but hid-

den behind their mufflers and bandannas. Far below, the Bear wound
crookedly through a U-shaped valley, glinting with silver ruffles
where it passed over rocky shoals. White-barked aspens and the red-
skinned alders lined its banks. On the side of the hill opposite the
river ranged a small herd of buffalo, their dark coats standing in
sharp contrast to the various shades of gray that dominated the landscape. A little thrill of anticipation ran through Eli when he spotted
the buffalo. Although they had passed several small bands along the
Seedskadee, those animals had all been bulls, their meat tough as
rawhide. This was the first herd of cows they had come across, and
his belly rumbled pleasantly at the thought of a supper of fresh
tongue and good hump meat.

"Wagh!" Old Cal grunted. "There be meat to be made, boys, and
cow meat, at that."

Johnny urged his horse forward. "How about it, Eli? It's been a
while since we've run buffalo together."

Eli hesitated. They needed the meat, and he had every intention of
sending a couple of the men out to shoot a few cows, but he hadn't
considered going out himself. Yet Johnny's invitation stirred up some
fond memories. There were few things quite as exciting as running
buffalo with a good horse. It was a feeling hard to describe, yet once
experienced, it somehow changed a man forever. The power and freedom . . . the exhilaration. It was, he thought, probably as close as a
human would ever come to understanding the things an eagle must
feel, diving out of a high blue sky for nothing more than the sheer joy
of feeling the wind through its wings. "What the hell," Eli said.

"Wagh! Now that shines," Old Cal said excitedly, reminding Eli
of a small boy at Christmastime. Old Cal and Johnny slid off their
horses to check their cinches. Sad Smiling Man quietly strung his
bow. Clearing his throat, Travis said, "I'd like to run 'em, too, if
that's all right."

"As a matter of fact, so would I," McClure added. He looked almost embarrassed by his admission, then grinned self-consciously.
"I ran buffalo several times during my service with the Dragoons. I
must say I found it stimulating."

Eli laughed. "Sure, why not? How about you, Jake?"

Jake shrugged. "Yeah, I'll go with you," he said.

"Pierre?"

Pierre shook his head. "*Non,* Eli. Pierre, him don' shoot the meat.
Him cook it good, but no skin, no butcher."

"I will go," Falls on the Rocks said quickly. "It is a woman's job to butcher buffalo."

White Feather also volunteered to accompany the hunters, much to the amusement of Consuelo, who said, "I'll go with Pierre. I don't have as much to prove as Falls on her Face."

Red-Winged Woman remained silent, but it was clear by her expression that she would go with Pierre. Annie's wound had proved too tender to take the long hours in a saddle, so Eli and Johnny had rigged a litter between two of the horses, bundling the woman tightly inside several buffalo robes. Red-Winged Woman had taken charge of the ponies immediately, seeing after Annie's every need and refusing to let her friend out of her robes until they camped each night.

Eli said, "Pierre, I reckon you and Connie can handle the remuda easy enough. The rest of us will be back in an hour or so and give you a hand with the chores."

"*Oui.*" He looked at the women who would accompany him. "Now Pierre, him be the booshway, eh?" He laughed at his own joke, and circled around to collect the remuda. Consuelo and Blossom went to help.

While Pierre led the remuda off the ridge, Eli slid from the sorrel's back and quickly checked his cinch. The hunters would be riding flat-out for a while, pushing their mounts recklessly over the rough terrain, and he didn't want his saddle slipping in the middle of a buffalo stampede. Mounting again, he quickly brushed the old priming from his rifle's pan and replaced it with fresh. He did the same for his pistol, then stuck it back in his belt. By the time he was finished, the other men had also checked their saddles and reprimed their weapons. "*Bueno,*" he said. "Let's go make some meat."

Chapter Thirty-eight

As they started down the slope toward the Bear, Travis guided his mule alongside Johnny. Just ahead, Old Cal was lecturing Jake. "Ye ever run buffler afore?" Old Cal asked. When Jake silently shook his head, Old Cal said, "Well, jus' keep outta the way, then, and let them of us what knows what we're doin' be doin' it." His long, skinny legs flopped against his horse's flanks, and he trotted on ahead to join Eli and McClure.

Johnny laughed softly as he watched Cal's gangling form descending the ridge. "That old fart can puff up like a prairie cock sometimes," he said. "But it's all wind. Look at the way he's holding his head so straight, and the way his shoulders are thrown back. Rocky Mountain College is in session, and Professor Caleb Underwood is chair of the department."

Travis smiled. He was glad he was paired with Johnny and not Old Cal. Johnny's coolness toward him after the Arapahos' attack had waned considerably since their encounter with the grizzly. He was more like his old self again, laughing, joking, telling stories.

"A buffalo is a big animal, and its heart rides lower than it does in other game animals," Johnny went on. "A buffalo is a hard animal to bring down if your aim isn't true. A deer or an elk will go down from shock, but I've never seen a buff do that. I killed a cow over on the North Platte a few seasons back that had three arrows in her ribs and a collapsed lung, but you wouldn't have known it from the way she ran. It took five balls before I brought her down.

"They're fast, too. They don't look like it when they're grazing like this bunch is doing, but it takes a good, deep-bottomed horse to keep up with a buffalo. The trick to running buff is to get in the herd quick and make your kills right away. Otherwise, you'll lose them. I remember an ol' boy I used to hunt with before I came south. Thought he was going to kill buffalo with a scattergun, because it was so damn hard to drop one with a rifle. Man never did make meat that hunt, but he learned. After that he got right in there, up close and pointed his rifle right at the heart. Of course, he didn't use his sights. I've never met anyone who could use his sights from a running horse. Get up close, I say. If your muzzle is more than a yard from your target, you're probably going to miss."

Travis listened intently, absorbing everything Johnny told him. He knew the Kentucky would be light for buffalo, but he also knew that his grandfather had killed his share of shaggies with it, back when the giant beasts had still roamed the eastern woodlands of Kentucky and Ohio. It would just take a little more concentration, was all. He was counting on Blue to bring him close enough that velocity wouldn't matter.

Eli led them down a shallow side canyon, using the ridge to shield them from the grazing herd. Near the bottom of the arroyo they halted again, and Old Cal edged forward on his pony until he could stand in his stirrups to peer over the top of the sage at the buffalo. Johnny dug half a dozen lead balls from his shooting bag and popped them in his mouth, tucking them in his cheeks until they bulged out like a squirrel's with a mouthful of nuts. He hitched his powder horn around until it rode in front of his chest, where it would be easy to reach. Uncertainly, Travis did the same. Old Cal rode back, his eyes bright with excitement. "Gonna be amongst 'em afore they know we be about, boys," he said in a low voice wound high with anticipation. "'Bout fifty, sixty head, to this coon's figurin', and the nearest no more'n a hundred yards away."

"Best we get on with it, then," Johnny mumbled around the lead balls in his mouth.

Travis felt foolish and a little disobedient to have the lead in his mouth. His mother had often warned him about chewing on lead, claiming it led to simplemindedness, and Travis had taken it for granted that she knew what she was talking about. By the same token, he didn't want to stand out among the mountain men and maybe draw Old Cal's sarcasm. He had already figured out the purpose of filling their mouths with extra bullets. From the back of a flying horse, it was going to be hard enough to reload their single-shot, muzzle-loading weapons. Having his horn on his chest and extra bullets in his mouth would make the chore that much simpler and quicker. He just hoped he didn't swallow any. He would hate like hell to choke to death on a rifle ball after coming through so much.

Eli glanced around the small party. "Ready?" he asked. Cal grunted an affirmative, and everyone else nodded. Looking at Jake and Travis, Eli said, "Keep close to the old hands until the buffalo start to run, then lay into your mounts with whip and spur."

"An' be watchin' where ye put ye balls," Old Cal mumbled, popping another ball into his mouth like it was candy. "I'll scalp the first greenhorn what puts a shot close to my old carcass. Do ye hyar, boys!"

"Let's go," Eli said.

They rode out of the arroyo in a tight group, stirrup to stirrup.

Blue's head came up as soon as he spotted the buffalo, his nostrils flaring to bray. Travis started to reach forward to grab a long ear and twist it, but suddenly it didn't matter. The buffalo caught sight of them immediately. Wheeling to put their noses to the wind, the buffalo stampeded toward the river. Yelling, slamming their jingling spurs against the flanks of their mounts, the mountain men took off.

The buffalo's speed amazed Travis, even after Johnny's brief words of counsel. Coming across the plains with B. J. Skinner's wagon train, they had often ridden through immense herds of the woolly beasts. But Skinner had refused to let his men hunt the animals, threatening to flog any man who disobeyed his orders and risked a stampede near his wagons. The two battle-scarred old plainsmen whom he had hired on as scouts and meat hunters had ridden far away from the creaking caravan to earn their dollar a day, and Travis had been left with an impression of slow, lumbering beasts, stupid and inattentive. That image was quickly destroyed now as Blue bolted across the frozen valley.

Blue quickly caught his stride, and the ground seemed to streak backward beneath his flashing hooves. It was the first time Travis had ever let the mule out all the way, and he was almost as surprised by Blue's speed as he was by the buffalo's. Within fifty yards he began to leave the others behind. He gave the mule its head and dropped the reins loosely over his neck. The buffalo hit the river like a boulder dropped from high above, kicking up a spray that glittered like jewels. They crossed the river in a flash and lit out for the horizon, startling a tawny herd of antelopes before them. Blue leaped off the river's bank, splashed through the knee-deep water, and scrambled up the far bank without pause. Travis yelled around the lead pocketed in his cheeks, caught up in the momentum of the chase. He began to close in on the rear of the herd that had been slowed by the density of the animals before it. Snow kicked up by the thundering hooves flew back in his face, and the wild, musky odor of the buffalo was strong in his nose.

The buffalo ran across a wide bottoms covered by a sparse grove of cottonwood and box elder, leaping sun-bleached logs with the nimbleness of deer. Travis hammered the mule's ribs with his heels. Blue seemed to sense the animal he wanted, and when Travis nudged him with his knee, he was both surprised and thrilled at the mule's quick response. Travis decided he had underestimated his find along the del Norte, and suspected that Jake had also.

The cow Blue began to close with was a large, shaggy brute with old, splintered horns. Travis could see a single wild eye rolling back toward him. The cow tried to veer away, but Blue stuck with her like a burr. Travis cocked the Kentucky and slid it forward. Remembering Johnny's instructions, he held his fire until he could almost touch the cow's pumping shoulder with the Kentucky's muzzle. The rifle cracked sharply in the cold air, spitting flame and smoke against the buffalo's light blond hair. She grunted and swung away, stumbling over an unseen rock. Blood gushed suddenly from her nostrils, and her front knees buckled.

Travis screamed in sheer delight, pounding Blue's ribs all the harder as he threaded his way cautiously into the rear of the herd. Buffalo ran on either side of him, and his view to the fore was limited to sloping hindquarters and flat saucers of snow that skimmed past his face and peppered his chest. He reloaded quickly and skated the ramrod back into its channel beneath the Kentucky's slim octagon barrel. Bringing the rifle up the curve of his arm, he sprinkled powder into the pan and snapped the frizzen closed before the wind could blow it away. By the time he was finished they were already starting up the far incline, and the buffalo's better endurance began to show. Blue leaned into the steepening grade, hooves digging at the treacherous footing. Travis leaned over the mule's neck and shouted into his flopping ears. Rifle fire crackled from behind him and to his right, but he couldn't see anyone from where he was riding.

Blue's gait slowed on the steep slope. Travis looked around for another cow. The animals were all around him, but there was nothing close now. The buffalo were beginning to pull apart on the grade, pulling ahead. Travis yelled for Blue to go faster, but the mule was giving him everything it had. Buffalo began to pass, and Travis swore and kicked harder. He felt driven now, wanting one more shot, one more chance to recapture the freedom and joy he had experienced at the beginning of the run. But Blue couldn't do it. They reached the top of the far ridge and the herd scattered, racing effortlessly across the rolling hills in their peculiar rocking gallop. Straightening, Travis pulled Blue to a trot, then a walk. Sweat darkened the mule's hide around the cinch, and he was breathing hard. Travis swung in a wide circle, wanting to cool the mule out slowly, but he hadn'd gone a dozen yards before Blue jerked and fell. Dimly, kicking free of the saddle, Travis heard the faint report of a rifle.

He fell hard, the wind driven from his lungs, the Kentucky's balls spraying from his mouth like broken teeth. He lay on his back, blinking up at the gray sky until he remembered the sound of the shot as Blue fell. He scrambled to his hands and knees and found the Kentucky lying in the snow nearby. He grabbed it and pulled it tight against his chest, his head jerking right and left. He expected to see Indians coming at him from every direction, but the ridge was empty, silent now save for the blowing wind that rustled the sage and yellow stalks of bunchgrass poking up from the snow. The thunder of the fleeing herd had faded, and the world seemed empty.

Slowly, Travis's gaze dropped to Blue. The mule lay on his side, his head thrown back, his eyes already starting to glaze. "Blue?" Travis said.

The mule didn't move. Travis crabbed forward on his knees. He put a hand along the mule's neck, but the long, floppy ears refused to twitch. A tear formed at the corner of Travis's eye, and he angrily scrubbed it away with the back of his hand. "I guess it was all bad luck, after all," he said shakily.

The sounds of approaching horses intruded. Travis glanced over his shoulder. Johnny Two-Dogs and Silas McClure were loping toward him, and behind them came Eli, riding hard. Travis looked around and spotted Jake trotting his horse along the ridge with a grin clearly visible even from here.

"Jake," Travis breathed. His right hand slid down to the Kentucky's lock. He flipped the frizzen open, gave the powder in the pan a quick glance, then gently closed it.

Johnny and McClure reached him first. Johnny jumped from his horse and ran forward, putting a hand on Travis's shoulder. "You all right, pard?" When Travis refused to look at him, Johnny gave his shoulder a little shake. "Travis?"

"That sonofabitch Jake Orr shot Blue," Travis told him in a voice dripping with hatred. "I'm gonna kill the sonofabitch, Johnny. I swear, I'm gonna kill him."

"Like hell you are," McClure piped in. He kicked his horse forward a couple of steps. "Johnny, take that rifle away from him until we get this straightened out."

But Johnny just shook his head. "It's not my place to take a man's rifle away from him."

"That's an order," McClure said sharply.

Johnny looked up. "Eli's here. Let's see what he has to say."

Travis heard Eli's sorrel pound up, then come to a sliding stop, but he never took his eyes off Jake. "What happened?" Eli asked.

"Travis says Jake Orr shot his mule," Johnny explained. "Travis is fixing to kill Jake."

Saddle leather creaked as Eli dismounted. Travis sensed the man coming up behind him, and quickly cocked the Kentucky. But before he could do anything more, Eli's arm snaked down over his shoulder and plucked the rifle neatly from his hands.

"Hey!" Travis said, spinning to his feet.

"Back off," Eli said, putting a hand against Travis's chest. "Let's talk to Jake before we start shooting."

"Gimme my rifle, Cutler," Travis shouted into Eli's face. His fists were clenched, his face as red as a beet. Anger made his voice shaky, but lurking just beneath the anger were tears, hot and shaming, and he fought the tears with more anger. "Gimme that goddamn rifle, you sonofabitch!"

"Travis!" Johnny said. He put a hand on Travis's shoulder, pushing him around to face him. "Just simmer down, pard. If Jake killed Blue, we'll take care of it. But let's see what he has to say first."

Jake had ridden up by that time, taking the scene in at a glance. The smile on his face quickly vanished. "What's wrong?" he asked.

"You been pushin' me about that mule ever since we run into each other on the del Norte," Travis said harshly. "But you didn't have balls enough to face me directly, so you shot him, you sonofabitch."

"What happened, Jake?" Eli asked coldly.

"How the hell would I know? I was running buffalo, the same as the rest of you. Then I saw you riding over here and thought that was where you wanted to regroup. I didn't even see Ketchum until I started this way."

"You were running buffalo way over there?" Eli asked.

Jake got a wary look on his face. "Yeah. Three or four split off from the main bunch after they got on top here. I went after them, but couldn't catch up."

"He's telling the truth," McClure interjected. "I saw him veer off after several head."

"Did you see who shot Travis's mule?" Eli asked.

"If I had, I can assure you I would have spoken up long before this," McClure replied testily. "Besides, how can we be sure it wasn't an accident? We were all shooting."

"The goddamn herd was half a mile away!" Travis shouted. "This weren't no accident!"

"Settle down, Travis," Eli said. "Do you know where the shot came from?"

"Hell, yeah, I know where it came from. It came from that yellowed-livered sonofabitch over there!" He flung his arm toward Jake, his finger trembling.

"That's a lie," Jake replied hotly. "Hell, it was my mule to begin with. I wouldn't shoot my own animal."

"The mule was mine," Travis grated, starting toward Jake.

"Damnit!" Eli shouted. He put his hand against Travis's chest once more, and Johnny grabbed him from behind. "Jake, that's a fifty-caliber you're shooting, right?"

"Yeah."

"What are you getting at, Eli?" McClure asked. "Surely you're not considering digging the ball out of young Ketchum's mule?"

"That's exactly what I'm considering."

"Hell, I don't reckon that would do any good," Johnny said. "I shoot a fifty-caliber, and so does Old Cal, if I'm not mistaken."

"As do I," McClure added.

Eli sighed, then looked hard at Jake. "I'm going to ask you this once," Eli said. "Did you deliberately shoot Travis's mule?"

Jake flashed a grin. "Why, no, I didn't deliberately shoot *my* mule. For all I know, Ketchum might have done it. I've seen him shoot."

Travis tried to lunge forward, but Johnny's grip tightened on his shoulders, pulling him back. Eli stepped between the two men, glaring at Travis. "Not here," he snapped. "Do you understand? If you want a piece of Jake Orr, you save it until the season's over."

"Goddamnit," Travis choked. "Goddamnit, I know Jake shot Blue. It ain't fair that he gets away with it."

"It would be even more unfair if you were accusing an innocent man," McClure said. "I have yet to meet a mountain man who would admit to ever missing his target, but it's absurd to think they don't. Johnny could have killed your mule, Travis. Or I might have myself.

You had best shelve your thoughts of revenge until you have more proof."

Travis shook Johnny's hands away. He took a deep, steadying breath. "I reckon we all know who kilt ol' Blue," he said. "But I'll save it. Sure, you bet. I'll save it until winter quarters. Then you'n me'll finish this thing up for good, Jake."

Jake sneered. "Are you going to cry, Travis. By damn if I don't think you are."

Tears had indeed appeared in Travis's eyes. He tried to knuckle them away, but they were coming too fast now, running down his cheeks and dripping onto his new capote. "Maybe I am cryin'," he said. "Maybe I'm cryin' cause ol' Blue was the best damn animal I've ever owned. So maybe you'd best remember these tears, 'cause I'm sure as hell gonna remember 'em. Winter quarters, Jake. You and me."

"And you'd better hope Travis isn't accidentally shot, too," Johnny added, looking hard at Jake. "Because if he is, and I don't know for certain who it was that shot him, or what happened, then I'm going to see this through for him."

Jake got a surprised look on his face at Johnny's words. "That ain't fair," he said. He looked at Eli. "That ain't fair. This whole damn brigade is against me."

"You fell asleep on guard duty and allowed a Blackfeet war party to infiltrate the remuda," McClure said icily. "Do you actually expect empathy from these men after nearly costing them their lives?"

Jake's face turned red. "I didn't fall asleep, goddamnit. I told you, I'd just gone down to the river to check on things."

"Yes," McClure said coldly. "You did tell us that, didn't you?"

Jake's jaw dropped a little. He looked at McClure, then Eli and Johnny. All three men returned his stare. "You sonofabitches," he breathed. "You bastards. All right, if that's the way you want it, that's the way you'll get it. I don't need any of you."

"What are you saying, Jake?" Eli asked.

But Jake just shook his head. "I ain't sayin' nothing. Not anymore." He jerked his horse around and spurred toward the ridge.

"Wagh," Johnny grunted softly when Jake had dropped from sight. "There's a man who'll bear watching for a while."

"Better make it longer than a while," Travis said. "He holds a grudge harder than anyone I ever met."

"I'm not worrying about Jake," Eli said flatly. He heaved into the saddle as if the encounter had drained him of energy. "Johnny, go find Cal and get his ass back here. We've got buffalo to skin."

"Sure, Eli," Johnny said, and swung on to his horse.

McClure said, "I'm going back to camp. I don't trust Pierre to pick a good defensive spot, and I have a feeling we'll be here awhile."

"Just tomorrow," Eli said. "Just long enough for the women to cut up the meat and do what they want with the hides. Then we're pulling out. We won't rest again until we reach Reed's cache."

Travis turned his back on the conversation. He walked to the top of the ridge and looked back the way they had come. He could already see a thread of smoke rising from the trees where Pierre had started the evening meal. Closer, he could see Jake spurring his horse toward the camp, pushing his mount recklessly down the steep slope toward the valley. Near the river, made small by the distance, Falls on the Rocks and White Feather had already started skinning the first buffalo. Travis lifted his eyes to the far ridge, from where they had first spotted the herd, surprised at how far away it looked. It seemed like only minutes had passed since they had started the hunt, but dusk was already approaching. It would be dark long before they finished skinning all the cows they had shot. He watched a couple of wolves slink out of the alders along the Bear and circle wide around the two young Indian women. Soon their mournful howls would bring others. The scavengers would eat well tonight, he thought, and likely ruin what meat nightfall would force the mountain men to leave. Suddenly, the waste seemed tremendous. Not just the meat, but the life itself that had been sacrificed for the thrill of the chase. Tears started afresh, rolling swiftly down his cheeks. This time, he let them come unchecked.

CHAPTER THIRTY-NINE

Sleep was elusive that night. Alone in his robes, Eli tossed and turned into the early hours of morning. At first he blamed the wolves for his problem. They were making such an ungodly racket up on the ridge that he thought it would be a miracle if anything within twenty miles slept that night. Their savage snarling as they fought over the meat the mountain men had left behind drifted over the camp like a soft, misty rain, causing the remuda to stir uneasily. But by midnight, buffeted on one side by the plaintive howls of the wolves and on the other by the clattering snores of the brigade, Eli was forced to admit the problem was his.

In frustration, he sat up and pulled the curly buffalo robe over his shoulders. He drew his belt close and felt for his tobacco pouch. There were only two cigars left from the stash he had brought with him from Taos. He had intended to save them both until winter quarters, when he might feel more inclined to relax and enjoy them, but he suddenly craved the soothing effect a good cigar often had.

He lit the cigar with flint and steel, then leaned back on his saddle. The night was totally black outside the tiny glow of embers from the campfire, the heavy cloud cover blotting out both the stars and the moon. He puffed for several minutes, drawing the smoke partway into his lungs before expelling it with a long sigh. When he finally began to relax, he tipped his head back and closed his eyes. Almost immediately the old doubts flooded back. There were so many now he hardly knew which one to concentrate on first. Where were Charlie and Pete and the three young men who had gone with them? Had they recovered the stolen horses, or had the Blackfeet ambushed them somewhere along the Seedskadee, leaving them dead or so badly shot up they were unable to return? Did they really need the horses the Blackfeet had stolen, or was he just so anxious to push on to Reed's cache that he had convinced himself that they weren't needed? And where was Reed? Eli had thought the brigade was making good time, but lately he had begun to worry that they had tarried too long here and there. What if Reed hadn't trapped along the way? What if his only intention had been to recover the furs and get out of the mountains for good? For all Eli knew, Reed might be well on his way to St. Louis by now, his mules packed with stolen furs, leaving behind only the empty cache. If that was the case, then Eli had in all likelihood jeopardized the success of the brigade by pushing too hard and not taking as much beaver as they might have at a slower pace.

Of course, Sad Smiling Man's claim of untapped beaver streams northwest of the Salt Lake could make up for all of that, yet Eli couldn't deny his misgivings toward the Shoshone, either. In the weeks since Sad Smiling Man had traveled with them, Eli had begun to detect an undercurrent of deceit in the man's manner. They were small things, mostly—slipping an extra piece of meat off the fire when he thought no one was looking, rather than just helping himself openly; using a *chispa,* or Mexican fire steel, to light his pipe one night, a week after Travis announced he must have lost his; trying to claim more than his share of the beaver taken in a week's catch, then feigning confusion and offering an apology when Pete caught him at it. Nothing a man would think twice about separately, but it had begun to add up as something to worry about.

Eli heard movement to his left and opened his eyes. Someone was rising and moving toward him, walking softly so as not to disturb the others. Eli put his hand on the pistol that lay beside him, but didn't pick it up. As the person moved past the dying embers of the fire, he recognized the lithe silhouette of Falls on the Rocks.

The woman came toward him without pause, kneeling at the foot of his bed. "Cutler does not sleep," Falls on the Rocks murmured. "Is there trouble?"

"Just thinking," Eli replied.

Falls on the Rocks stood and moved around behind him, sliding her hand under his robe to touch his shoulder. "You are tense," she said.

"Yes, a little."

Falls on the Rocks's fingers probed the muscles at the base of his neck, sliding expertly over the taut flesh. *I should stop her,* Eli thought, *put an end to this before she gets the wrong idea.* But despite his better judgment, he let her continue. His head lolled as Falls on the Rocks's massage became more vigorous. She dropped to her knees behind him, humming softly as her fingers worked magically at his neck. A small, pleasurable moan slid past Eli's lips, and his shoulders began to relax.

"You think too much, Cutler," Falls on the Rocks said. "A warrior must not waste his sleep on thoughts."

"Sometimes the thoughts don't go away at night," Eli replied. "There are too many, and they do not always receive the attention they demand during the day." They were speaking in Spanish, both at ease in a foreign tongue. "Tell me, what does Falls on the Rocks think about during the day?"

"She thinks about Cutler, most of the time, and wonders why he does not come to Falls on the Rocks's robes, when the Mexican woman so plainly does not want him."

Eli smiled. He had expected such a response; had, in fact, partially baited her for it. "Maybe he is afraid Falls on the Rocks would turn him away if he asked," Eli said.

"But he never asks," Falls on the Rocks teased, leaning close to breathe in his ear. "How is a man to know these things if he does not ask? Does Cutler not see the way Falls on the Rocks cares for him? Does he not know what is in her heart for him?"

"But I am a married man," Eli told her. "Consuelo is my wife—in practice, if not in the eyes of the law."

Falls on the Rocks's fingers slowed momentarily. "I do not understand this custom, then," she said in puzzlement. "The Mexican woman does not care for your horse. She does not prepare your meals or grain your skins before all others. Nor does she share your robes at night. She is like a stranger to you, who always looks at you with contempt. How is she your wife, then?"

"Sometimes . . . " Eli said. He struggled for the words to explain the rift that had grown between Consuelo and himself—the complexity of ambition combined with the arbitrary rules of European society that was so prevalent in old St. Louis. But the words wouldn't come. Even thought of, they sounded small and petty and underhanded. He took a drag on the cigar, then set it aside to free his hands.

"Have you asked the Mexican woman to come back to your robes?" Falls on the Rocks asked.

"Yes, many times." But not in so many words, he had to acknowledge to himself, not openly. Rather, he had hinted at it, stepped all around it, but he had never expressed his wishes candidly. But damnit, she had known what he wanted, he told himself. She knew how torn he felt. Suddenly the smiling contempt Consuelo had shown him on those occasions when he tried to talk to her brought anger. Damn her, he thought, what right did she have to act so smug all the time, when it had been her that had all but begged to come along?

"My man is angry," Falls on the Rocks whispered in his ear. Her breath stirred his hair, causing a shiver to run down his spine. "Sometimes to rub a man's neck is not enough," she said. "Sometimes a man needs to expel his anger through his seed." She crawled around to face him, taking his face in her hands. "A man is not made to sleep alone except when he needs all his energy for war, Cutler. If he does not lie with a woman occasionally, he will become confused and angry, and his judgment will be clouded."

Eli caught his breath as Falls on the Rocks loosened the leather thong at her shoulders. She shrugged, and her buckskin dress slid down to reveal her bare shoulders, the little hollows at the base of her neck. Her skin, Eli noticed, looked taut and supple, as soft as a newborn's. Falls on the Rocks shrugged again, and the dress slid off her shoulders and fell, dragging slightly at her naked breasts, then dropping to her waist. Eli's breath quickened as she leaned close. Her breasts hovered inches from his face, the nipples puckered taut in the cold air. Her long black tresses brushed his cheek like tiny strands of fire. She was kneeling astraddle his thighs, on her knees with her fingers laced behind his head, drawing him steadily toward her. He could feel her own breath on top of his head, could hear the pounding of her heart, only inches away. Desire washed over him. He put his hands on her ribs, rubbing the balls of his thumbs under her small breasts.

"For God's sake, Eli, go ahead and fuck her," Consuelo said. Eli jumped, spilling Falls on the Rocks back over his legs. Consuelo was propped up on one elbow several yards away. Her face, only partially revealed by the campfire's dying glow, looked hard as chiseled stone.

Eli's anger seemed to explode inside his head. He had to struggle to keep from shouting and awakening the others. "How long have you been spying on us?"

"Jesus Christ, the slut is sitting half-naked in your lap right beside the fire. That is not exactly spying."

Falls on the Rocks sat up, pulling her dress over her shoulders. "What is it this Mexican woman wants, Eli?" she asked. She leaned forward and put a hand possessively on his shoulder.

Eli sighed deeply. "Go back to your robes, Falls on the Rocks. It is time we all slept."

Falls on the Rocks gave him a startled look. "Is this what my man wishes, to sleep alone?"

"Yes," Eli said. He shifted his legs under her, forcing her off.

Consuelo laughed. "You are throwing away a very pretty prize, Eli. I could not help but notice that her tits do not sag like mine. She is much younger and would be much more playful under the blankets."

"Shut up, Connie."

Angrily, Falls on the Rocks stood and stalked off to her bed, flouncing as she passed Consuelo's robes. Shaking her head, Consuelo said, "Christ, Eli, you cannot decide what you want, can you?"

"Go to sleep," he said gruffly.

"Oh, I will sleep tonight. I will sleep well. But I am not so sure about you." She chuckled. "Damn, and your warrior's seed is still unspent." She laughed and lay back, draping her arm over her forehead. "That girl is as full of shit as most men."

Eli grabbed his cigar, but the coal had gone dead. He puffed on it vigorously a time or two, but the taste was cold and sour. Cursing under his breath, he shoved the half-smoked cigar back in his pouch. He thought he heard one or two of the men laughing under their robes, but he couldn't be sure. "Goddamn her," he breathed to himself. "Goddamn her to hell." He pulled his robe over his head and closed his eyes, but it was a long time before he finally drifted off.

It was almost daylight before Sad Smiling Man dared slip free of his robes. He eased to his knees and shrugged into his capote, then readjusted the coyote-skin cap he wore. Working as quietly as he could in the dark, he rolled up his bedroll and gathered the parfleche saddlebags that he had stolen from the Utes the night he left their village with Falls on the Rocks. He had removed the several pounds of pemmican and jerky he'd managed to hide away from the brigade over the last several weeks and replaced it with fresh buffalo meat salvaged from yesterday's run. He kept only a handful of pemmican that he would eat as he rode. When he was ready, he slid his quiver and lion-skin bow case over his shoulder, then rose and looked around.

The camp rested in slumber, the coals of last night's fire covered with a fine gray ash. Letting his gaze linger on Eli's bedroll, he smiled derisively. This man was a fool who had lost his way, Sad Smiling Man decided. He did not know what he wanted, and therefore he would soon end up with nothing. Sad Smiling Man wanted to laugh at Cutler's dilemma. He, Sad Smiling Man, would have taken both women—the young Ute for his robes, and the Mexican with the sharp tongue to keep his lodge. A scolding tongue was an easy thing to fix, Sad Smiling Man knew; it required only a stout piece of firewood and a willingness to work up a good sweat using it on a woman. But these were Cutler's problems and not his own. Not now, at least. Perhaps if he could find Bad Gocha in time, he could make them his problem. Bad Gocha was a hard and greedy man, but he was also fair. If Sad Smiling Man asked for only a few hours with each woman in exchange for the information he was about to bring the renegade leader, he thought his brother-in-law would agree.

Sad Smiling Man was certain Bad Gocha would be interested in the news he brought. Not just for a chance to murder and plunder another camp of hated white-eyes, but to learn that Reed had betrayed him by not revealing the presence of a cache of furs. Of course, Reed had already betrayed them by murdering Bad Gocha's sister and fleeing the mountains that gave birth to the Owyhee River, where the renegades often retreated to avoid the tribes that roamed the Snake River Valley and the rich valleys east of the Salt Lake—land claimed by the Shoshone and the Bannocks and the Utes. Bad Gocha's band was made up of many of the castaways of these tribes, as well as a smattering of Blackfeet, Arapaho, and Navajos, and although they were feared as one might fear a rabid dog, they were not tolerated long by the more powerful and honorable tribes. Sometimes a band of Shoshone would wander into the Duck Mountains, and the renegades would be forced to travel southward to avoid conflict. Even if they had been able to overwhelm the smaller band, Bad Gocha knew that news of such transgressions would eventually reach the ears of the elders among the Shoshone and Utes, and that both tribes would blacken their faces against the renegades. As it stood now, Bad Gocha's band was considered more of a nuisance and an embarrassment than something to waste time worrying about. While Bad Gocha simmered at such treatment by the larger tribes, he was wise enough to take his anger out on the pitiful Digger Indians who inhabited the country west of the Salt Lake, and the occasional band of white men or Mexicans whom he chanced upon. Bad Gocha's alliance with Big Tom Reed had been his only deviation from that policy, and Reed had repaid him by stealing all the letters of credit taken in the raid on the white-eyes the previous summer, killing his wife to silence her, then stealing three of the best horses the band owned to make his escape.

Yes, Sad Smiling Man thought, Bad Gocha would be particularly receptive to news that Reed was returning to the Salt Lake country.

Quietly, Sad Smiling Man made his way to the remuda. He had considered stealing many of the fine items the brigade had in its possession—rifles and muskets, kegs of powder, good English-made knives, and fancy tomahawks just waiting to be decorated with beads and soft, downy feathers. But he knew too many of the white-eyes had never trusted his presence among them. Even now, although no one moved or spoke, he was sure there were several pairs of eyes upon him. So Sad Smiling Man had decided to make this parting as unobtrusive as possible. He would get up in the middle of the night and retrieve his pony. Then he would mount and ride out without a word. Such behavior would be expected, he knew, and as long as he didn't steal anything, the white-eyes would consider it normal—for an Indian, at least. Had it not been for the importance of his message to Bad Gocha, he might have stayed with the brigade and tried to entice it into following him up the Owyhee. But that had changed when Cutler revealed the trappers' true agenda. White man's plunder and fresh women were a mouthwatering temptation in themselves, but the news that Big Tom Reed approached from the south would draw Bad Gocha out of his winter lair faster than all else. It was for that reason that Sad Smiling Man had decided to risk bringing even more suspicion upon himself by leaving this way. Had he not attempted to warn Bad Gocha, and his brother-in-law learned of his omission, his own life would have been worthless if he was ever caught by the renegade band again.

The trappers had brought their horses in at dusk to tether them to ropes stretched between aspen trees. Sad Smiling Man walked slowly down the line of horses and mules, speaking softly so that he didn't frighten them. He had almost reached his own horse when an unexpected sight greeted his eyes and he stopped and ducked, putting a hand on the 'hawk shoved in his belt. At first he thought someone was trying to steal some more ponies, but then he caught the scent of the young hothead called Jake Orr. Sad Smiling Man smiled grimly at this strange turn of events. He had picked a bad night to decide to leave the white-eyes, he decided. First Cutler had been caught in his own robes with the Ute girl by his Mexican woman, and now the little boy in the man's body had decided to run away from those who despised him so much. It made Sad Smiling Man want to laugh at the antics of the white race. He had thought them odd when they had first appeared in his land, but as he got to know them better, he found many of their ways comical. Suppressing a chuckle, he stood and softly cleared his throat.

Jake Orr whirled, dropping the saddle he was carrying toward his horse. His rifle was leaning against a nearby tree, but in the predawn darkness the boy couldn't see it. His eyes searched frantically as Sad Smiling Man walked forward. When the Indian drew close enough for Jake to recognize him, the fear in his eyes abated.

"What the hell are you up to?" Jake hissed.

Sad Smiling Man translated the boy's words carefully in his mind. His command of English was tenuous at best. He had been able to communicate with most of the old hands through a polyglot of several different tongues—English, Spanish, Ute, and Shoshone—with occasional need for hand sign, but he knew this one had never bothered to try to learn any language other than his own. Sad Smiling Man's disdain for Jake Orr ran deeper than even his feelings for the Diggers, who lived on beetles and ants and a few rabbits from time to time. The Diggers lived in the desert where they were seldom challenged, half-naked winter and summer, half-starved, full of lice they sometimes hunted off their own bodies for food, living in miserable brush huts with only the barest and most primitive utensils and tools needed for their questionable survival. Yet survive they did, despite hardships even many Indians wouldn't have been able to endure. For that reason, Sad Smiling Man granted them a marginal amount of respect. In Sad Smiling Man's estimation, Jake Orr didn't even rate that. Still, this was not the time to cause a row, for either of them, it seemed. Sad Smiling Man's mind worked swiftly, formulating a plan even as he approached the youth. It would be risky, he thought, and maybe foolish, but maybe it would work, too. There was no time to think this thing through. He would have to play it by instinct.

"It is time I left to return to my people," Sad Smiling Man said slowly, stumbling awkwardly over the English words he barely understood. "Now I see you have decided to leave."

"That ain't hard to see," Jake sneered.

"Where would you ride?" Sad Smiling Man inquired. "Perhaps we could go there partway together."

"I don't guess I'd be interested in riding with a mountain nigger," Jake shot back.

Sad Smiling Man was puzzled by Jake's remark. He had said it as though it was meant to be an insult, but Sad Smiling Man knew the term *nigger* was common among the mountain men and not taken as an insult. He had never heard it used the way Jake just did, but he decided the intent had been clear. Sad Smiling Man's hand itched to jerk his tomahawk out and split this silly young man's head open, but of course, that would be out of the question. Here, at least, where the others could witness his murder.

Jake picked up the saddle he'd dropped and carried it to his horse. Sad Smiling Man went on past and readied his own mount. It took only moments, and for a while he was torn between his need to get as far away from the trappers' camp as he could before the mountain men started to stir, and his desire to lure Jake Orr into following him. It was only when he saw that Jake's pack mule was already saddled and ready to go that Sad Smiling Man decided to risk tarrying a few more minutes.

Jake quickly saddled his horse and found his rifle. But then, like an idiot, he turned back toward the camp.

"Where would you go?" Sad Smiling Man asked quickly.

"It ain't none of your business, but I'm going to slit Travis Ketchum's throat. Then I'm going to piss in the wound."

Sweet waters of the Yellowstone, Sad Smiling Man thought. The mountain men would blame him for such a murder and hunt him down like a Blackfoot dog. He jumped off his horse and ran toward Jake, pulling him back into the trees. "Such a thing would be very foolish," Sad Smiling Man panted. "Cutler would put a rope around your neck and strangle you from a tree. Such a death is bad, for it prevents the spirit from leaving through the mouth so that it may begin its journey to the Other Side."

"What the hell are you talking about?" Jake said, too loudly.

"This is bad," Sad Smiling Man said, mostly to himself. Yet he realized he had forgotten many of the English words he had tried to remember when he approached Jake, and that the young man hadn't understood more than a word or two of what he had tried to tell him. Taking a deep breath, he started over. "If you kill the young warrior named Ketchum, Cutler and the others would kill you. They are already angry that you killed Ketchum's mule. Surely for killing Ketchum, they would put a rope around your neck and tie you in a tree."

Jake had been struggling halfheartedly against Sad Smiling Man's grip, but suddenly he relaxed.

"It would be better," Sad Smiling Man continued, thinking fast, "if you waited until Cutler thought you were far away. Then you could kill Ketchum and blame it on the Blackfeet."

Jake shook free of Sad Smiling Man's grip, but he nodded in agreement. "That might be a good idea," he said. "But the trouble is, I wasn't planning on following this outfit just to kill Ketchum. I'm going back to Taos."

"It is a long way to Taos," Sad Smiling Man said. He glanced frantically to the east, where a faint band of light had appeared. He realized that he could clearly see Jake's face now, and that in another couple of minutes the camp would start to stir. "Come," he said urgently. "The sun arrives, and soon the camp will be awake, too."

Jake glanced toward the eastern ridge. "Damn," he said. "I must've overslept."

"I am going," Sad Smiling Man said, letting go of Jake. "If you wish to accompany me to my people, you are welcome. From there you can return to the Mexican villages. Or you can stay until the great gathering of white-eyes in the summer, that is called a rendezvous. If you stay, I will see that you are given a good lodge and a woman to keep it for you."

Jake brightened noticeably. "You mean that? A woman?"

"Come. We must go now."

Still, Jake held back. It was obvious he was torn, and Sad Smiling Man wondered if he was remembering his long journey alone from the canyons where the Frenchman, Remi LeBlanc, had died.

Speaking slowly, so that he didn't garble the words, Sad Smiling Man said, "The Mexican town, it is a long way to travel alone. The snow and the cold, the loneliness. Such things would be hard to bear without the company of others."

Jake licked his lips nervously. He looked back to the camp, then south, toward the land of the Spaniards, with a trace of wistfulness.

"The woman I have in mind," Sad Smiling Man continued shrewdly, "is very young, very beautiful. Her breasts"—he held his cupped hands about six inches in front of his chest—"are very firm. The lodge that she kept for you would be very warm. That would be a good way to spend the winter, I think. With a woman who would do anything you wanted of her. Myself, I would like to spend the winter with such a woman, in a warm lodge, than to try to find my way back to the Mexicans by myself."

Jake swallowed, then slammed his fist against the hard seat of his saddle. "I could do it, if I wanted to," he declared hotly, as if Sad Smiling Man had said he couldn't. "That ain't the question."

Nodding, Sad Smiling Man replied in a low voice, "I know this thing you say is true. Perhaps I am an old man, too horny for my own good. Perhaps my heart is weak, to face so many moons alone in the cold and the deep snow, always afraid I would get lost and never find my way back. You may come if you wish, but it is your own journey." He shut up then, having said all he could think of, all he had time for. He went to his horse and swung aboard. He could hear Pierre and Grass That Burns talking softly in their robes. They would rise soon and start the morning's fire. There was not a second to lose.

Sad Smiling Man trotted his horse downstream, following the Bear. After a hundred yards, he looked behind him, chuckling when he saw that the coward, Jake Orr, was following.

CHAPTER FORTY

"Good riddance, I say," Old Cal sawed. He came up beside Eli, pulling the hood of his capote over his ears and tying the frayed sashes beneath his bony jaw. He watched the two deserters as they made their way casually north along the Bear, riding as if they had all the time in the world. "This nigger was half froze for Orr's scalp, anyhow. Do ye hyar, Eli? That coon was plain bad luck. A jinx, or Ol' Cal wouldn't say so. So was that sorry Injun, for that matter." He hawked and spat, then wiped his mouth with his sleeve.

Although Eli didn't reply, he was inclined to agree. This was the second time within a week that Jake, standing a night watch, had let the brigade down. The first time had nearly cost them their lives, and he figured they were better off without testing their luck a third time.

McClure came puffing up behind them, his normally ruddy cheeks a few shades deeper this morning. He stopped at Eli's side and glared after the two riders. "It appears nothing was taken," he said. "Still, I want to bring Jake back, at least. I won't tolerate desertion in an outfit."

"Go after 'em!" Old Cal exclaimed. He laughed suddenly. "By God, that be rich, McClure. Go on, waste prime trampin' time draggin' that worthless skunk back. Then ye can send someone after me, 'cause this coon be tired of such foolishness. He is, now, do ye—"

"No one's going after Jake," Eli broke in. He looked at McClure. "I know it galls you to let a man just walk out after he's signed a contract, but Old Cal's right this time."

"You damn right Old Cal's right this time. He be right ever'—"

"Hush, Cal," Eli admonished gently. He watched McClure's face, seeing the instant disapproval of Eli's decision, followed almost immediately by a grudging recognition of the logic behind it. "Jake's become a liability to the outfit, Silas," he went on. "If he didn't steal anything, that means he's taken only his own gear and maybe a few furs that weren't baled. I'd say we were money ahead on this deal."

"The man signed a contract," McClure replied without conviction.

"It's better this way. Let it go."

McClure's lips thinned, but then he nodded. "I suppose you're right, although if the circumstances were different, I'd shape that little man-child up . . . make a soldier of him, whether he liked it or not." Shaking his head in futility, McClure turned back to the camp, where Pierre was fixing a breakfast of buffalo meat and bone marrow.

Eli looked at Old Cal, bracing himself for what he knew would come. "You got something to say?"

His voice shaking with rage, Old Cal whispered, "Ye ever tell Ol' Cal to hush 'isself agin, Eli, I reckon he'll be obliged to cut ye throat. I'll let ye get away with it this once. But never agin. Do ye hyar?"

"I hear you."

Slowly, Old Cal backed away a couple of steps, then abruptly spun on his heels and stalked toward the remuda and his horse. He would saddle up and ride out alone for a while, and when he had cooled off he would come back as querulous as ever. Eli wasn't worried about Old Cal, but as he turned to watch the two deserters riding steadily away from them, he couldn't help a feeling of foreboding. Something told him they hadn't seen the last of Sad Smiling Man and Jake Orr.

They cut up the meat they had taken yesterday and packed it on the remuda. Annie and Grass That Burns wanted to dry it here, along the Bear, but Eli felt goaded to move on, driven by a premonition he didn't question. "It's too cold for meat to spoil," he told the women impatiently. "You can dry it tonight, over a fire."

Annie hobbled over to him, her dark eyes blazing. "It is always better to dry meat on a stage," she told him in Spanish. "Why does the white man always think he knows more than a woman in these things?"

"We're in a hurry, Annie," Eli replied gently. "I know you're worried about Pete, but he'll be all right. You wait and see. He'll be catching up any day now, bringing the horses the Blackfeet stole with him, and probably a few more besides."

"They did not get the horses," Annie snapped. "Do you not think a woman knows these things? Do you think I have not listened to the wind, and the eagles? Did you not hear the wolves and coyotes last night tell of their return? How is it that a white man can be so dumb in matters of importance, and still not lose his hair to some stinking Pawnee?" She turned away, muttering under her breath and kicking at one of the dogs that had followed her across the camp, nearly losing her balance on her injured leg.

Red-Winged Woman watched her friend from where she was changing the moss in Little Pete's cradleboard, but she didn't go to her aid or attempt to interfere.

From his place beside the fire, Pierre was chuckling. "That Annie one good squaw."

"She's feisty," Eli acknowledged. "But I doubt if Pete would trade her off for all the ponies in Santa Fe."

"No, by *Dieu,* that Pete, him no dummy."

They saddled up and rode out, crossing the low divide that separated the Bear from the Weber River watershed, named after old John Weber himself less than half a dozen years before, and reached the head of Echo Canyon shortly after midday. They made camp that night in a little grove of aspen about a third of the way down the canyon, and awoke the next morning to three inches of new-fallen snow. Conversation was kept to a minimum during breakfast. The fresh powder and gloomy skies put the whole brigade in a sour mood. The snow continued to fall, big, wet flakes drifting down from a windless sky, piling up quickly.

The canyon deepened as the day wore on, its wall rising high and porous on their right—red-rock cliffs towering a couple of hundred feet into the air, their time-worn crowns masked by clouds and falling snow. To their left the land rose steeply, scarred with side canyons. Despite the pace Eli set for them, the going was rough and slow. The old snow had a thick, frozen crust that the lead horses had to break through. Although Eli kept a continuous rotation of new riders up front, the sharp-edged ice soon took its toll. By the time they reached the mouth of the canyon, where Echo Creek spilled into the Weber River, the men had had enough. Eli ordered camp made in a cottonwood grove on the banks of the Weber.

Pierre built up a roaring blaze while the women constructed brush wickiups for everyone. Johnny and Old Cal drove the remuda out onto the bottom land bordering the river, but the stock were exhausted after the grueling day and had little energy left to paw down to the buried grass. Travis set to work laying in a supply of firewood, his ax ringing dully in the oppressive air until well after dark. Although McClure had made him a good deal on a little steeldust gray from the remuda, selling the animal to him on credit, the youth had remained pensive since the death of his mule, barely speaking to anyone during the day and sitting and staring glumly into the fire at night. Travis hadn't said anything about Jake's leaving, but Eli knew the unfinished business between the two young men remained heavy in his thoughts.

The snow refused to let up through the second night, and by morning it was over knee-deep to Old Cal, easily the tallest man in the outfit. It was beginning to look desperate, and Eli was aware of the worried glances the men and women gave him during breakfast. It was McClure who finally broached the subject that was on all their minds.

"I doubt if we would make ten miles today, Eli, if we tried. Perhaps we should stay here until this storm passes."

Eli stared quietly into the flames. Although indecision ripped at him, his outward expression remained calm and thoughtful. It was all up to him, he realized. The success or failure of the brigade might be determined within the next couple of minutes. If Big Tom Reed and his men were still coming up from the south, they would be following a route that was considerably lower in elevation than the trail the GS&T outfit had taken. They would have missed the brunt of the winter's storms. They would be fresher, stronger, more willing to endure this final hurdle thrown in their path. Some of the old Indians told stories of how the snow could bury the land beneath a blanket of white so deep it covered the backs of buffalo, but Eli had never seen more than a foot in those valleys, and seldom that much. Reed wouldn't be stopped by snow and cold. He was still coming, while Girardin's brigade—no, by God, *Eli's* brigade—were cowed here less than three days from the valley where a fortune in furs awaited.

But could they make it even if they tried? Eli wondered. His thoughts shifted rapidly, sorting out the pros and cons. They had been descending in elevation ever since crossing the divide between the Bear River and Echo Canyon, but had they dropped fast enough? Or would the snows continue uninterrupted, trapping them in the rolling mountains they had yet to cross—barren, sage-covered hills with only scattered aspen groves for shelter. Here, at the forks of the Weber and Echo, they had wood enough to last them the winter if they needed it. There was water at hand, and good rich grass in the meadows along the river. It would be a hell of a note, he thought, if he had led the brigade this far only to trap them in the mountains without enough shelter to survive. An outfit could starve to death easily in this country, or freeze if it couldn't find enough wood. It could lose its horses to the same fates and be left destitute and hopeless. Did he want to risk the lives of those who trusted and believed in him because of his obsession in beating Reed to the cache? Did he want to jeopardize the success of the whole outfit, and risk ruining his own reputation in the mountains, by recklessly challenging a Rocky Mountain winter?

And is failure all that bad? a tiny voice in his head asked. Did he, in some dark recess of his mind, want to fail? Consuelo had asked him that once, her question taking him by surprise. But in all the miles and all the weeks since then, he still wasn't sure of the answer. He glanced around the circle of faces watching him. No one spoke or offered an opinion. They knew the dilemma he was in; their expressions clearly reflected their reluctance to push on through the deepening snow. Not even Johnny showed much willingness to leave camp today.

"It might be prudent if we waited for the return of Pete and Charlie and the others," McClure added, glancing at Annie as if for support. "We're short-handed on the remuda, and short on fighting men, if we run into Reed at the cache."

Old Cal looked up, scowling. "Ye figure this bunch can't handle three men, McClure?" he asked.

"Not if they've joined Bad Gocha's bunch. From what Vidales told me, he commands a force of nearly thirty men. Even if the brigade were at full strength, those odds would be formidable."

Old Cal and Johnny exchanged glances. Eli poked at the fire with a long stick, thinking hard.

"If this snow doesn't let up soon, we won't get through at all," McClure persisted.

Eli gave him a long look. "You don't seem to be in as much of a hurry as you were when we left Taos," he remarked.

"I'm tired, Eli. We're all tired. We've pushed hard these last few months, through some pretty rough country and some pretty harsh weather. I guess my enthusiasm has waned somewhat."

"We aren't more than a few days away, Silas. If we stop now, we might not make it through for another month, maybe not until spring. I know it's hard on the men and horses, but we're pretty high right here. Another three, four more days, and we could be out of this."

McClure shuddered involuntarily, looking at the gray land surrounding them. "Is there an end to this anywhere?" he asked softly. He looked at Eli, his eyes moist. "We could all die out here. It's a brutal, brutal land . . . unforgiving. It could swallow this outfit up without a trace."

Old Cal snorted. Johnny was watching McClure worriedly, knowing, Eli thought, the way the dark, cold winters could work on a man, depressing his spirits to the point of making him give up entirely. "Hell, Silas, this isn't so bad," Johnny said. "Now, the Wind River Mountains, the Beartooths, up around the Three Forks country, it gets cold up there. I remember—"

"Please!" McClure interrupted, throwing his hands up. "No more." His gaze took in the circle of men with their wind-burned faces, their chapped and bleeding lips. "For the love of God, no more stories." He looked at Eli. "We're beaten, my friend. It's time to face up to that truth. I'll let Girardin know you did all you could. You couldn't predict this. My God, no man could've predicted this." He looked again at the thickening curtain of snow and swallowed audibly. "This is hell in reverse," he said softly. "Fit only for savages and animals."

Suddenly Old Cal laughed harshly. "By God, Eli, ol' McClure be right for a change. This land ain't fit for man nor beast." Then his eyes gleamed and his voice rose a shrill notch. "But this hoss ain't met a mountain man yet what didn't stand 'bout two feet taller'n the tallest pilgrim what ever pushed a plow or pen. He ain't, by God." Glaring at Eli, he added, "Boy, if ye be wantin' to make the Salt Lake country afore ye settle these young'uns in for their winter naps, why, then, I reckon we just gotta take 'em through. Either that or quit callin' ourselves mountain men."

"Wagh," Johnny said, grinning. "Old Cal's right, Eli. I've wintered on the Popo Agie and the Yellowstone. I've chipped ice off a campfire just to let out a little heat. Hell, this isn't so rough. Now, like I was saying, the Wind Rivers, they can get—"

Eli laughed loudly, lifting his head and straightening his shoulders. "Tell it when we get to the Salt Lake, Johnny. By God, somewhere up there, there's daylight wasting. *Bueno!* Let's ride, boys." He looked across the fire, meeting Consuelo's eyes, and was surprised by the sudden warmth he saw in them, the pride. It was a brief thing, like the flicker of lightning from a distant summer storm, then she rose and went about her packing; but in that one quick flash there passed between them a feeling of love that was unlike anything Eli had ever experienced before. He sat there a moment, while the others climbed to their feet in preparation for leaving, savoring the feeling of it. Then Johnny clamped a hand to his shoulder, squeezing lightly. "Best get on your feet, amigo, before Annie decides to pack you up on one of the mules."

They pushed on, fighting the snow with a new vigor, a fresh determination. They made ten miles that day, and ten more the next, staying with the river when they could, fighting their way through the steep tangle of hills when the trail along the Weber disappeared. There was no grass for the remuda, and precious little wood for fires. Frozen chunks of pemmican, thawed in their mouths, gave the trappers what nourishment they got. The snow eventually stopped, and the heavy clouds finally lifted at last, breaking up and scattering like a congregation after the last amen. The sun blazed down on a white world, but there was little warmth in the huge globe's rays, and the threat of snowblindness in its bright, searing reflection off sparkling powder. On the fourth day they edged past the shoulder of a cliff that forced them almost into the Weber, and came out into the last valley before the Salt Lake. Ahead of them loomed the eastern slopes of the mighty Wasatches, their jagged peaks like a serrated blade cutting into the belly of the sky.

The brigade drew up wearily, gaunt and thin-hipped, cheeks hollowed, eyes red-rimmed. The arduous trek through the low mountain range separating the upper and lower Weber valleys had sapped everyone, but the remuda was in the worst shape. Horses and mules alike were worn down to hide and bone, flanks caved in, ribs showing like washboards. The stock stood with heads lowered, a few pawing at the snow for the rich grass underneath.

"Well, thar she be," Old Cal said. He rubbed a greasy sleeve across his lips, scraping away a couple of scabs in the process and cursing when they started to bleed. Dabbing at his split lips with a grimy finger, he said, "By God, this coon's 'bout ready for his winter robe, Eli, damn if he ain't."

"Soon," Eli replied, booting his horse toward a sprawling grove of cottonwoods where a tumbling creek flowed in from the south. His excitement rose, remembering the map in his possibles bag that had started at a fork in a river in a valley just behind the front range of the Wasatches—the map Vidales had saved after last year's massacre.

McClure spurred his stumbling mount up beside him. They exchanged knowing glances, but neither man spoke. The brigade rode into the trees and dismounted. Eli handed the sorrel's reins soundlessly to Falls on the Rocks, then turned with McClure toward the river while the rest of the outfit set up camp. They came to the forks and stopped, and still neither man broke the long silence between them. They stared at the dark, turbulent waters where the two streams met, at the banks shrouded with snow, and the quiet, ice-filmed eddies beneath them. Finally, McClure sighed. Eli left the map in his pouch, knowing without looking at it that this wasn't the place. "We'll go north from here," he told McClure. "Ogden's Hole is the next park over. If I remember correctly, there's three rivers draining that valley." A thin smile creased Eli's face. "Cheer up, Silas. Three rivers means two forks. We'll be doubling our chances in Ogden's Hole."

CHAPTER FORTY-ONE

It was six hours later when Pete finally led his small party past the crumbling ledge hugging the north bank of the Weber River and spotted the campfires of the brigade. He glanced back at the others, but didn't smile. No one did. They were a starved-down bunch, all right, honed nearly to gristle by the long days of wind and cold, the scarcity of game in the brigade's wake. They had held over two days along the upper Seedskadee, waiting out the fever Charlie had taken as a result of his wound. On the third day he had announced himself fit enough to travel, and they started back downriver, hoping to find the outfit still camped along the Green, but not at all surprised when they didn't.

Pete and Clint hunted a little, while Charlie rested under the bluff along the Seedskadee, but the buffalo and pronghorns had cleared out, leaving only sign that was several days old. Not even an old bull could be found foraging by himself.

They followed the brigade's trail to the Bear, where they discovered Travis Ketchum's wolf-torn mule, a number of already scavenged buffalo, and sign of two men leaving on their own. Pete recognized the tracks immediately, but kept the information to himself. If Jake had indeed left the outfit with Sad Smiling Man, then Clint would find out about it soon enough. In the meantime, Pete wasn't inclined to interpret more than the tracks told him—that Jake's horse and mule and Sad Smiling Man's horse had left the brigade.

Despite the handiwork of the wolves, they managed to salvage a couple of meals from the buffalo and Travis's mule. They took what they could find and rode on. It was snowing by then, the wind hammering down from the northwest until they dropped into Echo. After that the wind left them alone, but the snow was a nightmare, even with the trail the brigade had broken several days before. But they were gaining, and that was the main thing.

They ran out of meat along the upper Weber and were in for starving times then. The trail of the brigade kept getting fresher, but their stomachs became more empty. Charlie, still feeling the effects of the Blackfoot's arrow that had pierced his shoulder, seemed to grow weaker as the miles dropped behind them. The fever returned by sundown of their last day, and sweat beaded his forehead. Pete debated giving up then, and finding a place to wait out Charlie's fever, but there was no wood or game, no grass for the horses, and only snow to melt down and drink. Grimly, he made the decision to push on. There was a quarter moon that night, and plenty of starlight. Charlie had agreed.

"Don't fret yourself none over this hoss," he told Pete. "Just tie me to the saddle if I fall asleep."

Fortunately, they hadn't had to resort to that. He drew up, letting Charlie come up beside him. "Just about there," he said. "Reckon you can hang on another mile or so?"

Charlie squinted ahead. "Yeow," he grunted. "If they ain't got meat on the fire, I'm gonna take a chunk outta this mule's damn butt."

Pete laughed. "I'm guessing' ol' Pierre has something on the fire," he said, booting the buckskin's ribs.

Travis challenged them when they were still a hundred yards away.

"It's Pete," Pete called in return. "Rustle Turpin outta his robes and tell him he's got five starvin' mouths that need feedin'."

The others were up when they rode in. Charlie dismounted stiffly and handed his reins to Blossom without a word, then sank wearily beside the fire. Red-Winged Woman dropped to her knees beside him, pulling his capote back with a little murmur of concern. Pete saw Annie limping about, and grinned. "Wagh," he grunted. "Can't keep a good filly down, can you?"

Annie took his buckskin, smiling up at him. "*Qué?*"

Pete laughed.

"Looks like you boys caught up with them," Eli observed, eyeing Charlie's bloodstained capote. "How bad are you hurt?"

"Just a scratch," Charlie replied.

"He's got a fever," Clint told Eli. He was looking around the camp, a puzzled expression on his face. "Where's Jake?"

Eli cleared his throat. "Jake decided to go out on his own, Clint. Him and Sad Smiling Man left us at the Bear."

"Huh?" Clint looked stunned. "Jake and that Indian? What happened?"

"He shot my mule," Travis said.

Clint turned to him in confusion.

"*Bueno*," Eli said. "We've all got a lot of catching up to do. But let's get these boys fed first; they look about done in to me."

It took a while to sort it all out, exchanging stories and anecdotes—what they had seen and what the sign told them. Before they were finished Clint, Mateo, and Jorge went to their robes, exhausted. Charlie remained by the fire, dozing off and on, but appearing stronger already, with meat and broth in his belly. Red-Winged Woman had changed Charlie's bandage while he ate, and added a poultice she said would take the fever down. Annie helped, scolding Charlie for allowing a Blackfoot to put an arrow in him, and Pete for not watching closer. "I should have come with you," she said. "A woman can smell a Blackfoot faster than a Pawnee."

"You could've," Charlie grumbled as he tried to lift a piece of meat to his mouth. "Except you'd already been stung by a Blackfoot's arrer. What was the matter with your sniffer that night?" Annie gave his bandage a tug, and Charlie said "Ow!" and dropped his meat.

"I would not have been wounded if you and Pete had listened to the warnings of the winged serpent," Annie said. "Did not the drawings of the Ones Who Came Before warn you that we should not hide from the Arapahos in their canyon? Did you not see the way the winged serpent looked at us?"

"Christ," Charlie said, shaking his head.

"Where did you catch up with the Blackfeet?" Eli asked.

"Up near the headwaters of the Seedskadee," Pete said. "Among the pines. The Blackfeet left the river and were making for the Hoback. They ambushed us just as we forded the Seedskadee. Charlie took an arrer in the shoulder, but the rest of us managed to duck into the willows along the river there. They kept us pinned down for an hour or so, then skedaddled. I reckon they just wanted to slow us up a little. By the time they quit, Charlie was passed out, so we decided to come back."

"You decided," Charlie grumbled. "Was me, I'd've followed those coons to hell."

"Well, I reckon. You'n Annie both. But I ain't that all-fired in love with my horse."

Charlie shook his head. "I just hope ol' War-Heels teaches them brownskins how she got her name," he said morosely. "I'd like to make a little *paseo* up there next spring and find a couple of Blackfoot skulls caved in."

One more range of mountains to cross.

Eli had the brigade moving before first light, and by the time the sun peeked over the hills behind them, they were nearing the lower end of Weber Valley.

"How far?" McClure asked skeptically as he eyed the rugged country before them.

"Not far, but the snow will be deeper up there. Maybe as deep as what we came through yesterday. It'll take us most of the day to get through."

"What if the cache isn't there? What if it's in another valley?"

"It'll be there," Eli replied. "There aren't that many valleys behind the Wasatch Mountains and opposite the Salt Lake. If Vidales' story was correct, the cache will be in Ogden's Hole."

McClure glanced at the vee'd notch on their left. "Does that trail take you through to the Great Salt Lake?"

"Uh-huh. It's a treacherous bastard, though, even in good weather. There's another trail, a pass, leading out of Ogden's Hole. If the snow isn't too deep, that's the one we'll take when we get ready to set up winter quarters." He gave McClure a reassuring glance. "Maybe even make it over tomorrow night, if we don't have trouble."

McClure smiled self-consciously. "It will be a welcome relief to stay in one place for a while. I must admit I am tired of this constant riding."

"Wagh," Eli grunted. "I reckon we'll all look forward to some robe time." He gave the signal to move out, feeling an immense relief as they started into the snowy hills. Tomorrow, he thought, he would know once and for all how much their efforts had been worth. Tomorrow, it would all be over. He could feel it in his bones.

Mostly they wintered along the upper Owyhee, in that borderland between the Snake River Valley and the flat, alkali deserts west of the Great Salt Lake. But occasionally they moved out of those lonely mountains to range farther east, like young cougars searching for their own home. Sometimes they wintered in the milder climates along the Wasatch Front; or in Willow Valley, which the white men had renamed Cache Valley; on rarer occasions they would pitch their lodges—their small hide tipis and brush wickiups—near Bear Lake, where the mountain men often rendezvoused in the summer.

It was more dangerous in those places. They were a hated band, even among their own people. As the dregs of their tribal societies, they had found some small sense of family among others of their own violent temperament. Theirs was a tribe based on need rather than morality, and their lifestyle reflected that selfishness. Adultery was common; so was murder. Fights broke out regularly, frequently resulting in death or disfigurement. Theft was accepted. At times they thought the other tribes feared them and went out of their way to avoid them, and that was good. But at other times the tribes would come against them in war, forcing them to flee into their distant retreats among the Duck and Grouse Creek mountains. Less angry men might not have ventured out at all. But then, less angry men wouldn't have discovered that the traitor, Reed, was returning to the Wasatch Mountains. They wouldn't have known about the furs he had hidden from them. And they wouldn't have had the opportunity to avenge the death of Bad Gocha's sister, whom Reed had beaten to death before running off to the Mexican settlements of Taos and Santa Fe.

Nor would they be riding hard to the south even now, less than a day away from the valley where Bad Gocha suspected Reed had cached his fortune in furs.

CHAPTER FORTY-TWO

As it turned out, Eli didn't need Vidales' map after all. As the brigade wound slowly down from the snowy hills separating the Weber from the Ogden rivers, they spotted a thin column of smoke rising from the trees far below.

Eli ordered the brigade off the ridge they were following, where the wind had blown the worst of the snow off and made traveling relatively easier. With McClure, Old Cal, Johnny, Pete, and Travis Ketchum at his side, he forged ahead, leaving Charlie Williams, who was still nursing his injured shoulder, to bring the rest of the remuda on at its slower pace.

The five men rode down out of the hills in single file, not stopping again until they reached a long, sage-covered slope that led to the low bluffs overlooking the river. The smoke was on their left now, between them and the mouth of the Ogden Canyon, lifting in a sinuous queue from the trees between the North and Middle forks of the river.

"It appears that we have reached our destination just in time," McClure said tautly. He had a double-barreled shotgun riding across the saddle in front of him and his pepperbox thrust into a sheath on his right hip. In addition to those two weapons, he had a pair of .60-caliber horse pistols holstered on either side of his saddle horn and his heavy saber strapped to his left hip.

"Looks that way," Eli agreed softly. His gaze flitted over the landscape. "It isn't going to be too hard to reach the river from here," he said, indicating a slight depression in the ground ahead of them that quickly deepened into a steep-sided arroyo. "But I don't see how we're going to get around them if they try to run."

"How many ways are there out of this hole?" McClure asked.

"There's Ogden Pass," Eli said, pointing toward the upper western side of the east-west running valley. "The way we came in, or they can go north into Cache Valley, if they want. This time of year, those are about the only options open, and they wouldn't make good time no matter which way they ran."

"Then they'll fight," McClure declared. "They have no other choice."

"Maybe they'll try to bluff their way out," Johnny said quietly. "Hell, they aren't the only ones who have cached furs up here."

"They'll fight when they see who we are," Eli said, glancing at the men around him. "Someone in this outfit is taking money from Reed. I'd bet a year's pay on that."

Old Cal bristled. "Ye be accusin' one of us of killin' ol' Cork-Eye and that greaser, and burning ye tent and hamstringing ye mules, Eli? Is that what ye be doin' now?"

"Someone here did it," McClure said sharply. "And we'll know soon enough who he is."

"That's why I want him alive, boys," Eli said. "Dead men don't talk. I won't ask any of you to take a bullet when it can be avoided, but don't shoot if you don't have to."

"*Bueno*," Pete said. "But we're gonna kill him, Eli. If Reed led his outfit into a massacre last season, the bugger's gotta die. You know that."

"Yes, I do. And Reed will hang if we're sure he's guilty. But I want the man who killed Vidales and Cork-Eye first, and I'll tell you straight as a good hickory ramrod, boys, I want him worse than I do Reed."

"Wagh," Pete grunted. "Then we'll just have to take ol' Tommy Reed alive then, won't we?"

"Let's ride," Eli said brusquely.

They made their way quietly down to the river, then turned west, fanning out some. As they neared the North Fork, Eli ordered Pete and Johnny over to the other side of the river, where they could cut off Reed's escape if he or one of his men decided to make a run for it that way.

Their cautions proved unnecessary, however. As they entered the dense thicket of trees between the two streams, Eli spotted the men who had started the fire. There were two of them, about fifty yards ahead and standing with their backs to Eli's men, while a third man hefted heavy packs of furs out of a freshly dug hole on a knob of higher ground. An elk hide draped over a nearby limb, and freshly skinned haunches of meat showed that the outlaws expected the job to

take a while. Eli grinned in wolfish satisfaction as he pulled the hammer back on his rifle, but even that brittle ratcheting of sears failed to
penetrate the excitement of the two outlaws standing over the cache.

"Let's ease up a little closer," Eli whispered to the men on either
side of him. Across the river, Pete and Johnny followed his lead.
When they were within twenty yards, Eli stopped again. "All right,
boys," he called loudly. "Turn around slow."

"*Jesus!*" one of the outlaws exclaimed. They both spun, and one
of them yanked a pistol from his belt. Pete's rifle roared, and the man
whirled away, his pistol flying into the alders along the river.

"Put 'em down," Eli thundered, standing in his stirrups and shouldering his rifle.

The second man took his hand away from the pistol in his belt.
"Who the hell are you?" he asked, bewildered.

"Who's in the cache?" Eli demanded.

"Is that you, Eli?" a voice called from the dark, broad-mouthed
opening chiseled into the frozen sod.

"Come on out, Reed, but do it slowly, and let me see your hands
all the way."

"I ain't armed, Eli. I left everything up on top."

"Then there won't be any trouble, will there?"

Reed swore savagely, then poked his head from the hole. "What
the hell are you *doing* here? Can't nobody follow simple instructions?"

McClure pressed forward, his eyes blazing. "Who are you talking
about, Reed? Who was supposed to be following your instructions?"

A long silence followed, then Reed chuckled. "Hell, I don't know
what you're talkin' about, McClure. You sure you boys ain't been
dippin' into Billy Wolfskill's Lightning?"

"Who's your man with us, Reed?" Eli asked flatly. "Who did you
pay to sabotage the outfit?"

"Boys," Reed called to his own men. "You keep your mouths shut,
you hear? Either of you spill the beans on this, I'm gonna slit your
gawddamn throats and eat your livers raw. I mean that, now. I ain't
bluffin' on this."

"That'll be enough of that," McClure ordered. He kicked his horse
forward, and the others closed in on the trio at the cache.

Eli's gaze darted over the furs the three men had already hefted
into the sunlight. There were seven packs already brought up, none

of them damaged by high water or melting snow that he could see. Whoever had dug this cache for Reed had known what he was doing.

The man Pete had shot was sitting up when Eli dismounted. His face was ashen, pinched in pain, his shoulder spilling blood that leaked between the fingers of his good hand, clamped tightly over the wound. Travis and Johnny took their pistols and knives away, piling them next to the rifles beside the fire. The second man hauled Big Tom Reed out of the cache, then stepped back.

"Buenos dias, Eli," Reed said loudly, smirking. He was a big man, as his name implied, tall and broad through his shoulders, solid as granite. He had a massive head, with high cheekbones and eyes as dark as sin. His hair was long and full, falling down to his shoulders in back, with a neatly trimmed mustache above his upper lip.

The other two men came from a cheaper bolt, Eli decided, if looks were any indication. The first man, still sitting on the ground with his shoulder bleeding, looked to be of medium height, with a thin, hawkish face and cold, remorseless eyes. The second man was perhaps the same height as the first one, but slimmer, with thin, greasy hair splaying out from beneath a filthy, shapeless hat. He blinked a lot, looking from one man to the next, as if unable to comprehend the hostility directed toward him.

Reed look around, his weathered face streaked with dirt and mud. "Hello, Cal, Johnny, Pete," he called in greeting. "How the hell have you boys been?"

"By God, don't ye be talkin' to me that way," Old Cal huffed indignantly. "Like we'uns was your friends. Do ye hyar, you snake-bellied turncoat? Don't ye be doin' it, now, or Ol' Cal'll ram his rifle butt down ye throat for ye."

"Why, Cal," Reed said, feigning surprise. "You mean our friendship doesn't mean a thing anymore?"

"I be tellin' ye, Eli, I'm gonna bust this coon up somethin' fearful, he don't watch that mouth of his'n."

Eli looked around the camp a second time, taking in the horses and mules, the gear strewn about. "Where's your swamper?" he asked Reed. "You left Taos with three men."

"Oh, he's around, " Reed said, chuckling.

"No, he ain't, Tom," the man who hadn't been shot said. He blinked several times, adding, "Don't you remember, Carlos was killed way back—"

"Shut up, you dumb sonofabitch,"the wounded man growled.

"Carlos was killed when?" Eli prompted, but the second man clamped his mouth shut, looking guilty.

"We aren't going to get anything out of this bunch," McClure said disgustedly. He had given Old Cal a sharp glance when the exchange between the two men began, but it was obvious now that Reed was only baiting them, trying to plant splinters of distrust between the men who held him under their guns.

"Let's beat it out of 'em, Eli," Pete suggested. His eyes shone with a cold fury. "They're guilty, sure as hell, caught red-handed."

"Boys, you are mistaken," Reed said. "I'm here under contract with the Girardin Shipping and Transport Company to—"

McClure stepped forward, ramming the butt of his shotgun into Reed's face. The big man's eyes widened in disbelief, and he went down hard, blood spurting from his mashed lips. A shattered tooth slid from the corner of his mouth like a bloody pearl and dropped into his lap. A high, thin screech of pain escaped his battered lips as the cold mountain air lanced his broken tooth. He clutched his mouth with both hands to shield it from the bitter air, whimpering in agony.

Old Cal reared back in surprise. "By God, McClure," he said in wonder. "Mayhaps I misjudged ye a mite."

"That'll be enough," Eli said, pulling McClure away. He dropped to one knee beside Reed and gently pulled his hands away from his mouth. After a brief examination, he rocked back and stood. "You'll live," he announced gruffly.

"You won't," Reed hissed between his bloody fingers. "If it's the last thing I do, Cutler, I swear I'll make you pay for this."

"I doubt if you live long enough to carry out that threat," Eli replied. "The boys are set on putting a rope around your sorry neck and stretching you from a tree. Tell you the truth, I don't think I could force myself to stop them." Reed glowered but kept his mouth shut. Eli turned away, facing the other two men. "What are your names?"

"Fellas call me Worm," the man who hadn't been shot replied. He nodded toward his partner. "This here is Frank."

"Is it true you boys used to hunt scalps down around El Paso?" Johnny asked.

Worm grinned as if scalp-hunting were something to be proud of. "Sure did. Collected quite a few over the years, too. Greasers pay top dollar for a good 'Pache scalp, fair for women or kids. But then, you don't gotta tell 'im which is which, see? 'Course, a itty-bitty kid's scalp ain't—"

"Shut up, Worm," Frank said wearily. "Can't you see they're just makin' a fool outta you? They're gonna hang us. They ain't friends."

"Hang us! What for?" He looked at Eli, clearly puzzled. "Me'n Frank here, we just come along for the furs. It was Tom what set that outfit up for them renegades last year."

"*Shut up, Worm,*" Reed screamed.

"Worm isn't very bright," Frank explained.

"You, too," Reed ordered through his hands. "Both of you just keep your mouths shut."

"But what for you gonna hang us?" Worm wailed. "We didn't kill nobody! We was huntin' scalps down in Mexico last year."

Eli turned away, sickened. The sun was going down fast now, the day ending. They could finish this later, he decided. "Travis," he snapped.

"Yessir?"

"Charlie's probably holding the outfit back until he gets word from us. Go tell him to bring it in. We'll camp here tonight."

"Sure," Travis said. He trotted toward his horse, mounted, and rode out of the trees at a hard gallop.

"Johnny, you and Old Cal keep these men guarded. The rest of us will rustle up some firewood. It's going to be a long night."

Moccasins crunched the snow behind him, but Eli didn't look around. He was sitting on a rock beside the Ogden River, listening to the pleasing gurgling of its cold waters as it slid past. He held his last cigar in his hands, idly running his fingers down its length, unaware of the bits of leaf that dropped off with each passage and littered the snow around his feet. The moccasins came to a stop, but still he didn't turn around. He felt strangely melancholy, even in the wake of success, but couldn't figure out why. So he sat and stared at the water, deep in thoughts that had no direction, no purpose.

"It is cold here," Consuelo said at last.

"It's always a little colder in places like this," he said without turning around. "This close to such high peaks, not to mention the canyon."

"Do you wish to be alone, Eli?" Consuelo asked softly.

He sighed and straightened, smoothing the cigar one last time before dropping it in the empty pouch at his waist. "No. Truth is, I could probably use some company."

She came forward then, choosing a spot close to Eli's knees to sit down, tucking her heavy wool skirt under her legs. "I should get a man's hat, like Annie's," she said, pulling her *rebolso* tighter over her ears and wrapping the loose ends around her chin. She gave him a searching look, her eyes sympathetic. "You are sad, Eli. Why?"

"I'm not really sure," he admitted. "I was just sitting here trying to figure it all out."

"Will you hang all three men tomorrow?"

"I don't know. I honest to God don't know."

"The men want to hang all of them. But first they want to beat the name of the traitor out of Reed." She looked at him curiously. "Why did you stop them, Eli? Do you not also wish to know the name of the man who betrayed the outfit?"

"Yes. I want to know who it is, and I want to see him hang beside Reed. But I don't want this turning into a lynch mob, either, and that's what would happen if I turned the boys loose. I don't think either me or McClure could stop them then."

"Ahhh," Consuelo said softly. "So, you still wrestle with your conscience?"

Eli bobbed his head. "Yeah, some. We'll beat it out of Reed if we have to, but not like that, not like a bunch of wild animals. And to tell you the truth, I don't know what to do about Frank and Worm. Their worst crime is stealing furs, but I'm not sure that's a hanging offense."

"Is it not an offense that requires punishment, though?"

Eli sighed, tipping his head forward to stare at the broken snow between his moccasins. "Yes," he acknowledged quietly. "But maybe a flogging, something like that. Trouble is, I've seen men who have been flogged. It takes a long time to recover from that, and I'm not willing to cut these men up so bad they can't fend for themselves, then just abandon them here on their own. On the other hand, I'm sure as hell not going to take 'em with us."

"It's a tough decision, but you have faced many tough decisions this season."

He looked at her, wondering what she meant.

She stood, pulling her capote tight. "It is too cold down here," she said. "I'm going back to the fire."

"Connie."

She watched him silently, but her face was masked by the cowl of her *rebolso,* so that he couldn't read her expression.

"There's nothing between Falls on the Rocks and me. What happened that night, on the Bear, that was a mistake, something she did before I could stop her."

"Yes, I saw you struggling to free yourself from her overpowering arms," she said sardonically.

"I ain't denying it happened, or that I didn't enjoy it at the time, what there was to enjoy. But I don't care for Falls on the Rocks. I love you."

Consuelo reached out, her hand gentle along his cheek. "Do you, Eli? I am not so sure yet."

"I reckon I messed a lot of things up between us. I'm sorry for that."

Consuelo studied him quietly in the thin light. "Yes," she said finally. "I think you are."

"I still haven't decided what I want to do about St. Louis."

She smiled. "When you do," she said, "let me know." She turned away, starting up to the camp. "Good night, Eli."

The moon hung suspended just above the towering peaks of the Wasatch. Stars glittered brittlely against their velvet bed. Dawn was only a short time away now . . . just long enough for them to find their positions on the flat plain between the North and Middle forks of the Crippled-Elk River, which the white-eyes called the Ogden. Here, Bad Gocha would await the coming day, the light that would allow them the true aim they would need against the hated trappers now asleep in their camp. Here, in the time it took the moon to travel from the tip of one lodgepole to the next, Bad Gocha would attack with the ferociousness of a *caragieu.* And here, he would at last satisfy his rage against the traitor Reed.

Bad Gocha's lips curled back savagely as Sad Smiling Man and Blue Thunder squatted beside him in the snow. Without a fire, the cold was bone-numbing, and the breaths of both scouts flagged the bitter air before their faces. Wrapped in a heavy buffalo robe, Bad Gocha listened quietly to the reports of the two men he had sent to reconnoiter the white men's camp. He was aware of the fear the two scouts had of him. It was a fear Bad Gocha had cultivated with care, realizing the importance of intimidation among such a volatile band. But now he couldn't help his smile. The news that the two men brought pleased him greatly. Fourteen white-eyes to torture and kill, nearly half that many women to pleasure themselves with, before absorbing them into his band. And children—always a valuable commodity among the tribes to the south—who would eventually be sold into slavery in Mexico.

When the two men finished their reports, Bad Gocha dismissed Blue Thunder with a barely perceptible nod. When the warrior had left, Bad Gocha looked at Sad Smiling Man, reveling in the wary demeanor of his brother-in-law's face, the submissive way he finally looked down, rather than face the intensity of Bad Gocha's stare.

"You have done well," Bad Gocha finally said, his voice like gravel on rawhide. "You have brought me a great prize in the man called Reed. For this you shall be rewarded. I will take the Mexican woman first, because I have never horned one before, and I am curious to know what it is like, but when I am finished, you may have her for yourself."

Sad Smiling Man looked up, licking his lips nervously. "There is another," he said. "Her name is Falls on the Rocks, a Ute who—"

Bad Gocha's expression changed subtly, and Sad Smiling Man stopped. Nodding toward the rifle in Sad Smiling Man's hands, Bad Gocha said, "You have already profited from this band of white men, my friend. Your rifle and the pistol you have kept hidden in your robe that you thought I have not seen. The curly-haired scalp you took from the little white man who cried like a coyote in a trap when you went to take his life. These things are enough. The rest must be shared among the people, if they are to not feel jealousy toward you and slit your throat while you sleep. Do you not agree?"

Sad Smiling Man sighed. "Yes," he replied, knowing that any other answer would be futile. "I will keep the scalp and the rifle and pistol. You may have the youth's horse and mule, and the treasures it carried, to do with as you choose."

Bad Gocha chuckled harshly. "You will keep the scalp and the rifle, my friend. The pistol you will give to me."

Sad Smiling Man's eyes widened, but then he nodded and dropped his gaze. "Yes, I will bring it now."

"Good, see that you do. I wish to try it against the white-eyes as soon as Sun returns to our land. Now go and tell the others to ready their weapons. We will attack at dawn, with Sun at our backs to help blind the white trappers when we fall on them like a hawk, falling out of the sky on a mouse. Go, tell them that Bad Gocha is ready once more to kill."

The first streaks of dawn touched the sky to the east and quickly spread, like an opening fan painted in shades of pink and red and violet. The light flooded the heavens first, then began its gradual descent over the land—a gray blanket falling from above, settling comfortably over the hills, then drooping into the valleys, chasing the night's shadows into hiding.

In those brief, nebulous moments as night segued into day, Mateo stood silently among the remuda. The new light of a new day brought solace now—cooling, for a brief period, the smoldering anger, and soothing the ache of a childhood he had finally come to realize was no childhood at all, but was rather a lesson in survival.

He had Jorge to thank for that new insight. His cousin, who had managed to throw away the shackles of the past with the simple act of removing his leather-bound queue, had become a different man these last few months, more open and giving, and in the giving, better able to receive. Like a snake wiggling free of its old skin, he had emerged new and vividly colored, a survivor in ways Mateo could only wonder at. And in the evenings, as Mateo watched Jorge interact with the others, he mourned that part of himself that refused to let him join in, that kept him alone and isolated even when he longed to join. Something vital had died under his father's quirts and fists, the sticks of firewood and the welting staff of his lance. He had decided that for him there would be no peace in this life, no chance to retrieve what his father had so callously destroyed. There was only this, these few precious moments when the camp still slept that he was able to watch the beginning dawn and reassure himself that the pathway to escape still waited.

His eyes misted, but no tears came. The ache inside him tore at his very core, but no releasing sob shook his shoulders. He stood stiffly with his hand on the *grullo*'s withers, wondering how long he could hang on until the pain became unbearable and he finally ended it with a ball from Salvador's pistol. How long must he endure this suffering, when he wanted so much to escape along the sun's growing, rosy path, to pass through that arched door into a better land?

He took a deep, shuddering breath, and lowered his hand. Pierre was stirring last night's coals into a fresh fire, and McClure was moving through the camp, calling *levée* on the men, dragging them from their blankets and robes with muttered curses and low, arthritic groans. Mateo patted the *grullo*'s neck affectionately, then turned toward camp and breakfast. The flour was gone, the coffee and salt depleted. The treats—the hard candies and sugar cones and chunks of Mexican chocolate that many of the men had brought with them—had been consumed weeks ago. Today there would be only humpribs dripping with juice, eaten half raw, and water straight from the river, so cold it would make his teeth ache. And tonight there would be more of the same, unless one of the hunters shot something today. The diet had soon grown monotonous to the greenhorns—Clint and Travis and McClure—but Mateo was used to long periods of simple foods. As a child, accompanying his family onto the buffalo ranges of the *llano estacado,* he had learned how to add a little spice to his meals with dried berries plucked from bare, rattling branches, or marrow dug from the heavier bones of big game and spread over meat like gritty butter. Wild onion, cattails, rose hips, and camas roots all gave a man a little variation in his meals, and helped ease the maladies of a pure meat diet—the constipation and scurvy and weak blood that dragged a man down over the winter.

A sound came to him, faintly at first, but growing rapidly. He paused, cocking his head to the side to hear better. A frown wrinkled his forehead. The sound was familiar, the crunching of snow beneath hooves, and might have been made by a herd of elk or deer, or even a bighorn sheep, come down from the higher peaks. But there was something almost sinister in this sound, something that told him it wasn't being made by wildlife.

It was the steady, unbroken rhythm that bothered him, Mateo finally decided. It was too uniform, too controlled, to be the hesitant footsteps of a wild creature.

Mateo's heart pounded as he made his way to the edge of the remuda and stared across the broad plain between the two rivers. The flats were furred in silver-green sage, dotted with clumps of alders and a few spindly cedars. He strained his eyes to penetrate the hazy light that had still to win dominance over the night. At first he saw nothing, and the sound of hooves undulated so much he wasn't sure if they were approaching or not. Then he spotted a line of movement, and his hand flew instinctively to the pistol thrust into his belt. He squinted as the line slowly emerged, becoming clearly drawn as it advanced across the plain. His eyes widened then, and a curse escaped his lips. He turned and raced back toward the camp, where his musket still lay within his robes, shouting, *"Indios! Indios!* Get on your feet!"

CHAPTER FORTY-THREE

Eli flew out of his robes at Mateo's first shout, grabbing his rifle and pistol, shooting bag and powder horns, in one fluid motion. Like all of the old hands, he had worn a pair of dry moccasins to bed, never knowing when he might have to scramble to his feet in the middle of the night. He left his capote behind in his rush to the remuda, but skidded to a stop less than ten feet away. He didn't have to go any farther to find out what Mateo was shouting about. He could see it plainly enough from right here.

"Bad Gocha's bunch?" Pete asked, coming up beside him while shouldering his own shooting bag and powder horns.

"Could be anyone," Eli replied. "No sense in going off half-cocked until we know for sure." But his mouth was dry, and his pulse pounded in his temples. He looked around the camp, assessing the brigade's position in a glance. In the aftermath of capturing Reed and his two hardcases the evening before, they had neglected to build a breastworks. The *arrieros* had placed their packs in a circle around the camp to give it some semblance of organization, but it was protection more psychological than real, Eli knew; they were flanked on two sides by the rolling foothills of the Wasatches, well within rifle range of snipers, and close enough, perhaps, for a good marksman to lob arrows into their midst.

McClure came huffing up just as Mateo ran into camp. While Mateo fetched his musket, Eli turned to McClure. "Grab the *arrieros* and get those mules packed on the double. Get Travis to help you. And the women. We might have to make a run for it."

McClure nodded and whirled to carry out Eli's orders.

Charlie, Old Cal, and Johnny Two-Dogs came up just as McClure raced away. "Saddle your horses," Eli told them. "We're going to ride out to see who they are."

The men nodded without comment and set off to retrieve their mounts. Eli stayed where he was, watching the Indians' slow approach through the tall sage. He estimated twenty-five or thirty warriors, perhaps a mile away yet—a ragged line of horsemen advancing eerily out of the predawn haze. He kept glancing at the hills behind the camp, but so far he saw no other sign of Indians. Still, he knew they couldn't afford a siege similar to the one the Arapahos had put them under back on the Grand. Not this close to the foothills—with their craggy rock cliffs and flaring sage, the trunks as thick as small trees.

Falls on the Rocks hurried forward, dragging his sorrel behind her. She handed him the reins, then touched his arm lightly, with a reassuring smile, before scurrying away to help with the remuda. Eli's capote and hat were draped over the saddle horn, and he shrugged into both as quickly as he could. Mounting, he rode toward the edge of the trees. Pete, Charlie, Old Cal, and Johnny loped in behind him. Charlie, who had been carrying his arm in a leather sling ever since his return from the Seedskadee, left the strap behind this morning. He sat beside Pete, flexing his arm experimentally.

"Let's go," Eli said quietly.

They rode out of the trees and brush, advancing perhaps fifty yards into the plain before stopping once more. The Indians drew up as well, and for several minutes neither group moved, the dawn's stillness broken only by the swirling of eagle feathers and the slow dance of nervous horses kept under tight rein. Eli pulled his telescope out of the case he kept tied to his saddle and studied the Indians carefully. Their ponies' tails were bobbed in preparation for war; lances and rifle barrels bristled the gray sky above their heads like quills from a porcupine's back. In the growing light he saw faces painted black and vermillion, yellow and white— each design as different as the man who wore it and the spirit helpers that guided him. He took a deep breath, lowering his eyeglass. "There's Utes and

Shoshones in that bunch, and maybe a couple of Navajos on one end there. It's Bad Gocha's bunch, all right. It has to be."

"This coon ain't never laid eyes on the child, personally," Charlie said. He looked at Eli. "Did you see him?"

"Not from here," Eli admitted. "Not with all that paint on their faces. But I'd wager he's there somewhere."

A horse pounded up from the camp, and McClure pulled his mount to a plunging stop among the mountain men. "They're packing the remuda in record time," he said, his gaze straying to the jagged line of renegades, less than a mile away now. "I have Connie and Annie guarding the prisoners with shotguns, but everyone else is packing mules. We'll be ready to pull out in half an hour or less."

Eli was quiet a minute, thinking. His gaze swept the broad plain, then strayed to the foothills, the passes to the north. Finally he said, "Keep Connie and Annie on the prisoners. As soon as you're ready to pull out, bring the rest of the men up here. Even Pierre. The only people I want back there are the women and Reed and his men. Tell Connie that as soon as the fighting breaks out, she's to get the outfit moving."

McClure looked at him in surprise. "Is that wise, Eli? Leaving everything in the hands of the women?"

"These bucks," Eli said, nodding toward the line of renegades, "are painted for war. We aren't going to parley our way out of this, Silas, but we might be able to bluff our way out with a show of force."

"But . . . women? What if they can't handle the remuda?"

Eli smiled. "This is Connie and Annie and Red-Winged Woman, Silas. Push comes to shove like this, they'll handle that remuda as good as any man.

"Look to the north of you, up North Fork. See that gap in the mountains to the left? That's Ogden's Pass. You tell Connie to make for that as quick as she can. Annie or any one of the Utes will know where the trail is." He smiled encouragingly. "Don't worry. They'll do just fine."

"I strongly disagree," McClure replied, his gaze returning to Bad Gocha's renegades, "but now isn't the time to debate the issue. I'll pass the word on to Connie and be back here with the rest of the men as soon as I can." He whipped his horse around and rode back to the camp at a gallop.

"Eli," Johnny said softly, pointing with his chin. "Looks like they're edging forward."

"Let's ride out a ways and meet them," Eli answered tightly. "Keep your eyes peeled. This could be a trap."

The mountain men rode deeper into the great plain, keeping their horses to a prancing, head-tossing walk. Eli's palm sweated around the forestock of his rifle, butted to his thigh. The light was full now, the sun's rays reaching high above the sprawling mountain range to their east. Yet the renegades continued to hold back, as if waiting for someone . . . or some thing. Looking again at the climbing bands of sunlight, the reason behind the Indians' reticence to attack suddenly became clear. They were waiting for the sun to rise above the mountains behind them, for its powerful rays to bounce off the snowy plain and into the eyes of the trappers, blinding them to the Indians' charge, making the front sights of their rifles swell and blur.

"Hell!" Eli exclaimed, pulling his horse to a stop and grinning broadly when the Indians did the same.

"Bastards gonna keep ol' Sol at their backs, ain't they?" Old Cal crabbed.

"That would be my guess," Eli agreed.

"I count twenty-nine," Pete added in a calm voice.

"Twenty-eight," Johnny corrected.

"Nope, I count twenty-nine," Pete replied firmly. He looked at Johnny, and both men grinned.

"Quit your damn yammerin'," Old Cal groused. "Be Jesus, what do it matter, twenty-eight or twenty-nine? There be too blame many of 'em, is what this coon sees, and we oughta be cachin', not ridin' straight into 'em." He shook his head, muttering under his breath at the foolishness of Eli's plan. Yet he wasn't looking behind him, Eli noticed, and when the time came, he knew Old Cal would fight as furiously as any of them.

They were all like that, he realized. Not a man among them appeared cowed, and Eli felt a sudden and joyous pride to be counted as one of them. These were his men, by damn—Cutler men. Riding calmly into a battle they all knew they could never win, and that some of them probably wouldn't survive, but riding nonetheless, doing what they had to do without complaint. It dawned on him finally that none of them would be here if they didn't feel the same trust and respect for him that he felt for them. He was an equal in the eyes of them all, else their fierce independence would have sent them in different directions long before. It was the thing that McClure didn't understand yet, with his bullying military ways and periodic strutting, a thing Eli himself only now truly grasped. And with that understanding there came a peace within himself that was new, a feeling of confidence unlike anything he had ever known before. His doubts began to fade, his uncertainty and confusion to ebb. No man had all the answers. They all did the best they could. And the only true image of a person came from within, yet had to be reflected through the eyes and actions of those around him. It was all life had to offer, but if a man did it right, he knew suddenly that it would be enough.

"Yeow," Charlie cried, pulling Eli back to the broad plain between the forks of the Ogden River. He was leaning forward to study the renegade band, scowling uncertainly. "Take a look at that coon in the middle there," he said hesitantly. "Ain't that . . . "

Eli's gut tightened as Charlie's words trailed off. It was the Shoshone, Sad Smiling Man. No doubt about that. He was sitting a good-looking chestnut horse, and carrying a rifle across the bows of a flat American saddle.

"Sonofabitch," Pete murmured, as Charlie eased back in his seat.

"I reckon that there's Jake Orr's rifle he's carryin'," Charlie said quietly. "Because that's sure as hell Jake Orr's horse."

Old Cal seemed to perk up at this new discovery. He cackled in jubilation. "By God, this ol' nigger tolt ye not to trust that red devil, didn't he? Didn't he? Do ye hyar, boys? Ol' Cal knows him a thing or two 'bout brownskins, and the smell of that'un never did shine for him. Mayhaps next time ol' Cal speaks up, ye'll be listenin' to him?"

There was a drumming of hooves from the rear. Eli twisted in his saddle to look behind him. McClure was riding toward them in the van of five men, and Eli grunted in satisfaction. "Wagh! I reckon this will whittle the odds down some," he said.

McClure forced his mount in beside Eli, while the others—Travis, Clint, Mateo, Jorge, and Pierre—spread out along the flanks.

"What's going on?" McClure asked, eyeing the still unmoving band of Indians. "Why haven't they charged?"

"They be waitin' for the sun, ye blamed fool," Old Cal crowed. He leaned from his saddle and spat, as if to rid his mouth of a bad taste.

"By damn if you ain't the dumbest goddamn pilgrim this coon's ever seen."

McClure gave Cal a hard look, then turned back to Eli. "So what do we do now? We're already outnumbered nearly three to one. It would be foolhardy to give these savages any more of an advantage."

"I agree," Eli said. "Are the women ready?"

"They are."

"Then let's go take the fight to them." Touching the sorrel lightly with his spurs, Eli started across the plain, letting the gelding pick its own path through the chest-high sage. The distance between the mountain men and the renegades seemed to close rapidly, although the Indians remained fixed where they were. Eli could see the nervous dancing of their mounts, the questioning glances the warriors began to throw at one of the men in the center of the line, sitting next to Sad Smiling Man. Eli gave him a closer look as the gap between the two groups narrowed. The Indian was riding a long-legged roan, painted with lightning bolts across its chest and down its forelegs. He wore a buckskin warshirt decorated with quills and fringe and scalps, and carried a long-gun in addition to the bow and quiver of arrows sloped across his shoulders. His face was completely masked in war paint, the bottom half black, the top in white, but Eli's breath quickened as he began to recognize the broad, powerfully built shoulders, the thick legs, the massive head framed by two long plaits of graying hair. The face itself, beneath the paint, would be ugly as a buzzard's, he remembered, the loose flesh canyoned by age and weather, the eyes slitted to a perpetual frown. It was the mein of a killer without conscience, Eli knew—a remorseless butcher in the purest sense of the word.

"That's Bad Gocha on the roan," Eli called out tersely. "The one in the fancy warshirt."

A couple of men grunted in acknowledgment, and Pete added a grim, "I see 'im."

At five hundred yards, several of the Indians started to pull back, the ragged line dissolving. Eli watched impassively as Bad Gocha harangued his men to hold their ground. He could almost hear the renegade's argument—that they faced an enemy far fewer in numbers than they, that there was much plunder to be gained, weapons, traps, horses, and women. But his warriors had counted on Sun's help this morning, and the benefits of a surprise attack; they had expected their presence to demoralize the white-eyes. Instead, far from demoralized, the mountain men were riding steadily, even fearlessly, toward them. That the fighting was about to take place while Sun still hid behind the mountains seemed like another bad omen. Perhaps now was not a good time to fight. Perhaps they would be better off waiting for another day, even another party of trappers.

But Eli knew there was a personal stake in this for Bad Gocha, more than the chance to kill the hated beaver trappers or to claim a fortune in furs and horses and captives. Last night Worm had let slip that Reed had killed Bad Gocha's sister in a fit of temper, and that the renegade had sworn to hang the traitor's scalp from his lance. Bad Gocha wasn't about to let this opportunity slip away. So as the line of warriors continued to disintegrate, Bad Gocha abruptly leveled his rifle at several of the braves. At this unexpected turn of events, the whole line ground to a halt, and the warriors who had been trying to turn away quickly brought their mounts back into place.

McClure chuckled. "Dissension within the ranks," he said brightly. "We might just do better than I thought if we can present a solid front and united fire."

The renegades quickly regrouped. Bad Gocha whirled his pony, starting it across the snow-blanketed plain to meet the trappers. Eli lowered his rifle to the crook of his left arm and tied his reins above the sorrel's neck in order to free both hands for when the fighting started. His pulse pounded, and his fingers and toes tingled with anticipation. At four hundred yards, he could see the Indians clearly— the raven hair, the shining gewgaws and coarse scalps tied along the outer fringe of their leggings or on their horses' bridles. He could even see the dark pits of Bad Gocha's eyes, circled in black against the white paint on his forehead, like twin entrances to hell. Eli was about to kick the sorrel into a lope when a woman's shout reached them from the rear. He looked behind him with a puzzled frown. Red-Winged Woman was racing her pony over their back trail, her quirt flailing against the pony's croup, her long, black tresses flying.

"Trouble," Charlie said tightly, hauling back on the black mule he had taken as a saddle mount.

"Keep in line," Eli ordered, but it was too late. The whole outfit came to an uncertain halt, some reining around to await Red-Winged

Woman's arrival, others still facing Bad Gocha's renegades, their attention divided. Eli swore and turned back. The renegades were urging their mounts on faster now, no doubt hoping to catch the mountain men in this moment of flux.

"Go back!" McClure bellowed. He stood in his stirrups and tried to wave the woman away, but Red-Winged Woman wouldn't be detoured. She came on at a dead run, her pony stretched low to the ground, kicking up saucers of hardened snow from beneath its pounding hooves. She didn't pull up until the last minute, then jerked her pony down so hard it almost fell, yelling broken English so marred by her excitement that it was nearly incomprehensible.

"Go, them!" she gasped, then shook her head in frustration. "Them go sumbitch mules!" She rolled her eyes angrily at the words that wouldn't come, and at those that appeared in their place. She slammed her fist against her thigh, shouting, "Shit, you, Charlie!"

"Damnit, woman, what are you doing here?" McClure demanded, his face livid. "Speak up!"

Pete spurred his buckskin in front of McClure. "Shut up, now, Silas. Give her a minute to think."

But Red-Winged Woman had given up on trying to deliver her message in English. She switched to rapid-fire Cheyenne, speaking directly to Charlie. Eli saw Charlie's face go slack in shock and knew her news was bad. Looking at Eli, he said, "Reed got away. Red-Winged Woman says he had him a little pop-gun hid away under his shirt, and when the women cut him loose to put him on his horse, he pulled it on them." Charlie licked his lips. "Eli, he took Connie with him. Red-Winged Woman says they were headed for Ogden Canyon when she lit out after us."

Eli's heart seemed to clutch in his chest, refusing, for a moment, to beat. A coldness that was unlike anything he had ever known before spread rapidly through his body. He looked from Charlie to Red-Winged Woman, then back again, unable to speak.

"Here they come," Johnny cried.

Numbly, Eli turned. The sun had finally appeared; its rays spilled over the horizon, filling the plain with its sparkling light, glittering brilliantly off the snow. Dimly, through the roaring in his ears, he heard the pounding of the Indians' mounts as they kicked their ponies into a run. Their shrill yips and war whoops crackled in the frosty air, raking at his nerves.

McClure booted his horse forward, forcing Pete's buckskin aside. "For God's sake, man, turn and fight! Lead your men! The renegades are attacking!"

Yet Eli couldn't seem to force his muscles into action. He remained frozen, his mind struck dumb by the news Red-Winged Woman had brought him.

"Form a line, men!" McClure shouted, waving his saber above his head. But the men refused to budge. Even in the face of the renegades' charge, they watched Eli wordlessly, awaiting his word, and his alone. "*Eli!*" McClure screamed, whacking his shoulder with the flat side of his saber. "Snap out of it! Do you hear me? Snap out of it!"

Eli licked his lips. He looked at McClure, then at the surging ranks of the renegades, and as he did, the numbness broke, shattering like rim ice under a bootheel. The Indians were closing rapidly. Three hundred yards, then two hundred and fifty—almost within rifle range now, almost upon them. Eli straightened, his face hardening. "Stay with McClure," he told the men. "I'm going after Reed and Connie."

McClure's eyes widened in disbelief. He leaned close, his face only inches from Eli's. "Damnit, man, we'll go after Connie when we're through here, but your responsibility is to this outfit. We need you." He waved his saber toward the screaming warriors. "We need every rifle—"

"I'm going after Connie," Eli interrupted bluntly. He looked at the others, the old hands in particular—Pete, Charlie, Old Cal, Johnny— and smiled warmly. "Give 'em hell, boys. Then fall back to cover the remuda's retreat. I'll find you on the Salt Lake, if I don't see you before."

Then he drove his spurs into the sorrel's flanks, bursting free of the little knot of trappers and racing back the way they had come. McClure's voice floated after him, filled with outrage. "Damnit, Cutler, don't you abandon your duty to this outfit! Don't you . . . "

The words faded, and Eli rode alone then, the sorrel's hooves beating a rapid tattoo as it carried him swiftly toward the yawning chasm of Ogden Canyon, and the trail of Big Tom Reed.

CHAPTER FORTY-FOUR

The renegades hit the mountain men like a rolling brown wave. Their shrill, bloodcurdling yells rived the morning sky like the ripping claws of a catamount. Gunfire roared at point-blank range; arrows and tomahawks and war clubs whisked the air with their own peculiar tenor. Horses whinnied in terror; men screamed in pain. Blood rained over the broken snow and dripped from the brittle, silver-gray boughs of sage. There was no order, no plan. Chaos reigned, and in those first frenetic seconds of the battle each man fought alone; like birth and death, they faced the unimaginable horror of the cold unknown bereft of guidance or reassurance of hope, pulled inevitably forward while wishing only to return to the comfort of what they had known before.

Mateo fought the *grullo* as the two groups met. The tip of a bow touched his shoulder—a coup counted. Rifles and smoothbores bellowed like angry bulls all around him. An Indian swerved toward him with a raised tomahawk. He leveled his musket and pulled the trigger, the blast of the huge .70-caliber ball tearing through the Indian's chest. There wasn't time to reload. He slung the musket over his shoulder and jerked the Tower pistol from his belt. Another Indian closed on his right. Two more swooped in from the left. He emptied the Tower's single, powerful round, then yanked hard on the reins. The *grullo* pivoted, its front legs momentarily pawing at the sky. A lance tore through the hem of Mateo's serape. He reversed the pistol and used it as a club, smashing the heavy brass stock cap into a warrior's face, feeling the sudden sag of the Indian's cheekbone, the warm shower of blood over his hand and wrist. The *grullo* jerked and screamed with an arrow buried deep in its neck, its hindquarters giving out first, the front legs buckling almost immediately afterward. Mateo jumped free of the falling mustang, tripped, fell, the pistol jarred from his hand. He lunged blindly to his feet just as an arrow *thunk*ed into his thigh. Shouting out in pain and anger, seized by a fury that hazed his vision in mists of red, he stumbled toward one of the warriors. His sombrero had rolled away in his fall. Now he lifted his arm under his serape and flung it aside as well. He slid the cutlass from his scabbard, clenching it tightly in his right hand, and drew his heavy-bladed *belduque* with his left. He shrieked the agony of his rage—a cry drawn from the blackest depths of his soul. Tears spilled down his face, flowing free at last, hot and purging. Three more Indians raced toward him, their ponies' hooves churning up clods of snow. Mateo lifted his cutlass and hobbled to meet them. A triumphant yell choked his throat. The cutlass whizzed through the hazy light and buried itself deep into the shaft of a lance, then tore free with a brittle crack of wood. He spun, slashing out with his *belduque,* and felt the warm spurt of blood against his face, the salty taste of it on his lips. The Indians swooped past, then jerked their ponies down and turned back. One held a severed lance. Another clutched at a deep gash just above his knee. The third lifted a trade rifle to his shoulder, yelling incoherently as he took aim and fired. Mateo saw the rifle buck, felt his feet lift at the ball's impact. There was no feeling at all then, just an incredible lightness as he floated upward toward the glowing, arched doorway . . . going home at last.

Travis saw Mateo go down, his body flung limply into the embracing branches of a sagebrush, and felt his bowels weaken. He jerked savagely on the gray's reins, spinning the horse in a tight circle, but Bad Gocha's warriors seemed to swarm everywhere. Their war cries rent the broad valley; their rifles and fusils created a demonic cacophony, some so close he could feel the warm passage of the muzzle blast on his cheeks. The heavy, rotten-egg smell of gunsmoke stung his nostrils, and the thick, roiling clouds caused his eyes to spring tears. He saw Johnny lurch in his saddle, the bloody shaft of an arrow sprouting from a bloody stain darkening his capote. He saw Old Cal's ashen face, hatless, the startling white forehead where the sun never reached streaming blood. He saw Silas McClure's horse shot out from under him, going down in an explosion of snow and sage. An Indian rode up beside him, swinging a tomahawk. Travis parried the blow with his rifle, but the Indian tried again, the bell-shaped head of the 'hawk striking sparks from the Kentucky's barrel, peeling a thin layer of browned iron from the top flat like a shaving of wood whittled from a stick. Travis yelled and kicked and pulled on the gray's reins, but the warrior wouldn't give up. He kept urging his pony close, hugging Travis's flank so tightly he couldn't get his rifle around to fire.

They danced that way for what seemed like hours, the 'hawk buzzing Travis's head like a deerfly while he blocked blow after blow by only the sheerest of margins. The Indian was screaming in his face, the rancid stench of his breath so strong Travis wanted to vomit. It was about all he wanted to do right then, just go away somewhere and heave his guts out, to empty himself of all the smells and sights and sounds, until only a shell remained, kneeling in the snow, smelling once more the clean fragrances of a winter's day. But the Indian wouldn't go away. He pressed closer and closer, until Travis was leaning from his saddle, his balance going by small degrees, his defenses become clumsier and more desperate.

Then the warrior's 'hawk finally slipped past Travis's rifle. He felt the cold, sharp bite of the blade under his arm, then a flowing warmth that he knew was blood. In panic, he pulled himself upright in the saddle, clutching for the horn. The gray turned unexpectedly under him, putting its hindquarters to the warrior's mount and lashing out with its rear legs. The warrior's pony screamed as the gray's iron-shod hooves snapped one of its knees. It fell, spilling the warrior over its head. Crazed with fear, the gray bolted back toward camp. At first Travis tried to stop it, to turn it back toward the violence and gore, but then he noticed the blood dripping from his fingers, and his courage failed him. He let the reins go slack. Tears stung his eyes. Shame and humiliation engulfed him at this final confirmation of his cowardice, but he was beyond caring now, beyond anything except mindless flight.

When Eli reached the camp with Red-Winged Woman, he found Annie sitting her pinto with a shotgun leveled grimly on Frank and Worm, both barrels cocked, her finger white-knuckled on the triggers. Neither man moved or spoke when Eli slid his horse to a stop, but their eyes pleaded for help, for reassurance that this crazy squaw with the face pinched in anger wouldn't coldly kill them rather than suffer the trouble of taking them along. Grass That Burns, White Feather, and Falls on the Rocks sat their ponies around the restive remuda, watching the scene before them in wide-eyed silence. It was

Annie who spoke first, in Spanish, without taking her gaze off Frank and Worm.

"The man called Reed had a short gun," she explained in a disgruntled voice. "A pistol. He had it hid under his shirt, in back. When Consuelo untied him to put him on his horse, the man called Reed pulled this pistol and put it against Consuelo's head. The man called Reed said that if we did not back away, he would kill Consuelo. The other ones, the one called Frank and the one called Worm, also asked to go, but the man called Reed only laughed. He said they could stay with the trappers, but that he would take the woman and ride away. This he did, there." She pointed with her chin toward the head of Ogden Canyon, less than a mile away. "He has the short gun," she added, "and the shotgun with two barrels that belonged to Consuelo, and one horse. These he took, but I would not let him take anything else." She lifted the muzzle of her own weapon an inch or so, to show what she meant. "They are not far away yet."

On the plain, the battle had commenced. Rifle fire crackled in the early morning air, and the hollow booms of fusils echoed back from the hills. The war whoops of the renegades and the lusty battle cries of the mountain men carried faintly into the trees. Eli glanced toward the battle, felt the quick tug of his responsibility, then shook it away. "Get going," he snapped at Annie. "Get 'em started up the pass. Your husband will catch up with you before you reach the top."

"E-Eli," Worm said, glancing nervously toward Annie and her shotgun.

"You!" Annie said sharply. "Now you will shut up!" She pointed the shotgun at Worm's belly, and the man gulped and clamped his mouth shut.

"If they try anything, kill 'em," Eli said flatly.

"You do not have to tell me this," Annie scolded. She turned and bawled a command to the others. The women kicked their ponies into action, their moccasined heels drumming as they drove the remuda out of the trees at a gallop. Annie motioned with her shotgun, and Frank and Worm spurred their horses after the remuda. Only Falls on the Rocks remained behind. She guided her pony close to Eli, her face imploring. "Let the woman go, Cutler," she said. "She will be happy with Reed, and you and I can—"

Eli's arm flashed as if of its own accord; Falls on the Rocks's head snapped back, her cheek glowing where the back of his hand had struck her. "Go help 'em with the remuda," he hissed in controlled fury. "By God, help, or get the hell out of here."

Tears welled in Falls on the Rocks's eyes, spilling down her rapidly swelling cheek. She held a hand to her face, staring at him with her big blackcherry eyes. Then, choking back a sob, she heeled her pony after the others. Grimly, Eli drove his spurs into the sorrel's flanks, racing out of the trees toward the canyon. He spotted Reed's trail easily in the snow and swung onto it, riding hard toward the narrow, sheer-walled darkness of the chasm's walls.

"Fall back!" McClure shouted. "Fall back!"

He stood with his short legs spread, the heavy saber the men in his old Dragoon outfit had dubbed "Ol' Wristbreaker" resting tip down on the snow-covered plain. Blood and bits of flesh clung to the shiny steel blade, attesting to the weapon's wicked effectiveness on the field of battle. Four of the five barrels in his pepperbox pistol still dribbled smoke, leaving him only one shot left before he was forced to begin the arduous process of reloading. He had abandoned his shotgun when his horse was shot out from under him, although it hardly mattered now. The weapon had served its purpose well, pumping two heavy charges of buckshot into the thick of Bad Gocha's warriors early in the fight. And McClure was fully convinced that it was the shotgun's sweeping path of death and destruction that had turned the tide against the Indians. In the face of its two yawning, spitting barrels, the warriors' resolve had quickly withered. Three men had been blasted out of their saddles with the shotgun's first lethal charge. Two more had died from the second; at least four had been seriously wounded.

Witnessing the shotgun's devastating effect on the Indians' courage, wrecking nearly a third of Bad Gocha's superior forces in two quick pulls of a trigger, McClure at last came to believe the story of Annie's blown fowler—the Pawnee Killer.

Yet the battle had been far from won. At least twenty warriors remained whose courage and bloodlust could not be questioned. The fighting had been fierce, an eternity of cutting and slashing, dodging lance and 'hawk, firing his pistol into body after body, until the sky itself seemed to bleed. Minutes passed like hours. Adrenaline raced along his veins like liquid fire. McClure yelled, screamed; occasionally, he laughed. If he didn't know the mountains and he didn't understand the quirky attitudes of the trappers, if the overwhelming silence and isolation of the far-flung wilderness at times made him fear insanity, he at least understood this: He was a soldier, an old soldier now, but a soldier nevertheless—as much a warrior as any man upon this field, and he reveled in the glory of battle. He was in his element here, and if his troops, this independent mob of the high lonesome, ignored most of his commands, they at least understood the intricacies of battle. So he laughed as he swept aside lance and 'hawk with his heavy saber, and grinned into the painted faces of the men he shot from their horses. No fear here, no doubt or worry. Only the bloodletting of battle, the thrill of war.

But McClure was an officer, too, and he knew that there was a time to fight and a time to retreat. With Bad Gocha's remaining warriors dropping from their ponies to take shelter in the thick sage, the time had come to fall back, to cover the retreat of the remuda, which had always been their main objective.

"Retreat!" he screamed, backing away. *"Regroup and retreat! Come on, men, fall back!"*

Pierre heard him, and rode to his side. Jorge and Clint followed. An Indian pony lunged past, trailing its long rawhide rope. McClure grabbed for it, but missed. His toe caught in a root and he fell to his hands and knees, the pepperbox skidding from his hand. Hooves drummed the frozen sod, and he looked up into the twisted, screaming face of an Indian on a big chestnut gelding.

"You!" McClure breathed. He lunged to his feet, trying to bring his saber up before Sad Smiling Man ran him down again. He cursed the weapon's awkwardness, snagging the tip in the twisted limbs of a sagebrush, and knew suddenly that he was too late, that he would never get the saber raised in time.

Then a flash of color appeared at his shoulder, and Clint was hauling his mount to a snow-showering stop. He lifted a pistol coolly, and Sad Smiling Man's look of triumph vanished. The Indian tried to swing his rifle up, but Clint pulled the trigger without hesitation. The huge .54-caliber ball slammed into Sad Smiling Man's chest, flipping him off the back of the chestnut. The horse whinnied and tried to dodge away, but McClure managed to grab the rawhide rope that Sad Smiling Man had tied around the animal's neck, tucking the loose end in under his belt in case he became unhorsed. McClure pulled the chestnut around, dragging it to him hand over hand. The animal was walleyed in fright, its head thrown high, but it still responded to McClure's hand, to the soothing words he spoke as he tried to calm the beast long enough to mount.

Silas left the pepperbox where it had fallen, buried somewhere beneath the snow. The shotgun leaned against his own horse, which was lying motionless nearby with an arrow protruding from its neck. He spurred the chestnut to the animal's side and leaned from the saddle to snatch up the shotgun. When he straightened, he saw Clint standing over Sad Smiling Man's prone form.

"Clint!" he shouted. "Clint, come on!"

But Clint ignored him. He bent over Sad Smiling Man's prone body, slapping the Indian's weakly waving arms aside. A knife appeared in Clint's hand, and McClure watched horrified as the youth slid the tip under Sad Smiling Man's scalp and began his slow circle.

The Indian screamed as Clint followed the hairline, taking more than just the topknot, that upper, palm-sized portion most scalp-takers were satisfied with. He wanted the whole thing. He wanted this man who had lured his brother away, then killed him, to understand the full intensity of the feelings that burned within him.

It was his first scalp, and he made a poor showing of it, what with the yelling and screaming and the banging of rifles all around him, but he kept after it, hacking and sawing until the flesh was circled. Then he put his moccasined foot against Sad Smiling Man's neck the way he had seen some of the old hands do after the battle with the Arapahos, grabbing the twin braids in both hands and straining upward. The scalp came away with a wet, ripping sound, popping faintly as the last of the hide pulled free of Sad Smiling Man's bony white skull. Clint stumbled back, lifting the scalp to look at it in wonder. Sad Smiling Man's eyes were wide as he watched Clint holding his hair. A pink froth had appeared at the corner of the Indian's mouth, bubbling larger with each exhalation. Clint had wanted to shake the scalp in Sad Smiling Man's face, but a weakness caught him in the stomach as he looked at the puckered flesh dotted with drops of blood that were already starting to freeze. His stomach heaved, last night's supper threatening the back of his throat. Slowly, he lowered the scalp, taking a deep, fluttery breath tinged with the acrid taste of powder smoke. The wildness he had felt when he had seen Sad Smiling Man riding Jake's horse, carrying Jake's rifle, left him. He heard McClure calling him, urging him to remount. Pierre rode forward, leading his horse. Numbly, Clint gave the scalp a quick, jerking snap to shake what blood he could off the flesh, then tucked it under his belt and resheathed his knife. He quickly reclaimed Jake's rifle and shooting bag and horn, then vaulted back into the saddle.

"Come on!" McClure ordered, riding up on Jake's chestnut. "Some of the Indians have spotted the women!"

Clint looked at Sad Smiling Man a final time, his mouth working but no words coming. He had lost a brother, and he knew a hundred scalps would never bring him back. Taking the Indian's hair from his belt, Clint tossed it onto Sad Smiling Man's chest. The Indian's fingers crabbed weakly up his stomach to claim it, a look of gratitude in his pain-racked eyes. He had his scalp; he could put it back on, on the Other Side.

Clint reined his horse around, booting it into a lope. McClure, Pierre, and Jorge were already riding toward the North Fork, racing their mounts to intercept the handful of braves who had spotted the remuda and were rushing to head it off. Grimly, Clint spurred after them.

"Come on," Pete shouted. "Let's get the hell out of here!"

He knee-guided the buckskin around, slamming his rifle's butt into an Indian's face. Charlie was cursing his mule, sawing at its reins, trying to get the panicky animal turned. Bad Gocha's renegades were breaking up rapidly now, pulling apart; some fled east toward the mouth of Middle Fork Canyon; others rode north as fast as their ponies could carry them; a few were scattering through the sage to fight on foot; but at least a dozen were running their ponies after the brigade's remuda, a thin black line moving liquidly in the west, toward Ogden Pass.

Pete saw McClure and two or three trappers racing after them, but he knew Annie and Red-Winged Woman would need more help than McClure's handful would afford. The trail over Ogden was steep and treacherous, and at this time of year the snow would be chest-deep to the horses in places. The women would need time and patience if they were to force the remuda over that wind-scoured path, more than the men had bought for them so far.

"Goddamnit, Charlie, get that mule under rein," Pete yelled.

Charlie drove his heavy-roweled Mexican spurs into the jack's ribs, drawing a sharp grunt and an angry squeal from the animal, as well as a thin stream of blood. But it did the trick. The mule lunged, then took off at a pounding run. Charlie let it go, pulling his powder horn around to reload his fusil and pistols.

Pete whirled his buckskin a final time to cover their retreat, but the battleground was suddenly empty save for the dead and the dying. The sight surprised him so much that for a moment he just sat and stared. Old Cal and Johnny rode up, both wounded. Old Cal's bald head and leathered face was sheened with blood, and the broken shaft of an arrow protruded from Johnny's hip. Yet neither man seemed near death, and it was Johnny who said, "We'd better ride, Pete. Bad Gocha's men are going to reach the women before McClure does."

Pete glanced silently at Johnny's wounds, but the half-breed shook his head. "They're too far from my heart to kill me."

"Let's go," Pete said, reining away.

It was about five miles from the brigade's camp to the base of Ogden Pass. The women had covered nearly half that distance before Bad Gocha's men spotted them. They made another mile before Annie saw that the Indians would overtake them before they reached the pass. She shouted for Red-Winged Woman, who was leading the remuda, to take them into an arroyo that snaked down from the foothills on their left. Red-Winged Woman saw the opening and understood, even though Annie had bawled her orders in Comanche. She reined her pony into the gulch, the lead animals of the remuda following unhesitatingly. The sides of the arroyo quickly steepened—not enough to keep an animal in if it wanted to escape, but enough to offer some control and protection for a short time. Annie motioned her prisoners to the side of the arroyo's mouth while the horses and mules streamed past, the dogs yammering at the heels of the remuda like darting flies.

When the outfit was safely sheltered behind the first bend, Annie pointed at Worm, then Frank, with the muzzle of her shotgun—a silent order to dismount. Both men slid from their saddles without argument, stepping away from their horses and standing uncertainly with their legs splayed, their eyes pleading. Worm kept glancing over his shoulder at the approaching Indians, whimpering softly.

"What are you gonna do?" Frank asked hoarsely. "You gonna kill us, or let us help you fight?"

Annie flicked a quick look at the closing warriors. They were only a few hundred yards away now, no more than a quarter of a mile, separated by the timbered course of North Fork. They would be upon them within minutes, and Annie knew the women wouldn't be able to hold them back long. Her shotgun was a close-range weapon. It wouldn't stop a band of charging Indians at two hundred yards the way a rifle would, and it wouldn't have much effect on a dozen men once they got close, not if they scattered to come in on her from all sides.

"Best give us our rifles, woman," Frank said tautly. "We're on your side in this."

But Annie didn't trust the two men. She wouldn't trust her back to them, and she wouldn't trust the lives of her friends to them, either. Red-Winged Woman appeared suddenly at the mouth of the arroyo, and Annie shouted, "Bring their rifles."

Red-Winged Woman hurried away without comment, returning seconds later with the pair's two long guns.

"Knock the flint out of them," Annie ordered.

"*Gawddamnit, woman,*" Frank bellowed. "They won't fire without a flint."

"Put new flint in," Annie said in English. "Out there." She motioned toward the sloping bench that separated them from the North Fork.

"There ain't gonna be time," Frank said desperately. "Do you understand, you dumbassed squaw?"

Annie smiled tightly, laying her cheek against the shotgun's stock. "Yes. Dumbass squaw understands plenty good. But dumbass squaw holds shotgun. You go. Now."

Red-Winged Woman tossed them their rifles. "What about our bags?" Frank said. "Our powder horns? Goddamnit, you're sending us to our deaths this way."

"Maybe there," Annie said, nodding toward the open ground. Then she cocked the shotgun's right hammer. "You bet, you stay here."

"Sonofabitch," Frank muttered, reaching down and snatching up a rifle. Worm looked at him in confusion. "Frank," he said. "That's my rifle."

"Shuddup, Worm," Frank growled. He turned toward the slope, took a deep breath, then sprinted toward the river.

"Frank?" Worm called. "What am I supposed to do?"

But Frank wasn't listening. He was racing for the trees lining the banks of the North Fork, intent upon reaching their shelter before Bad Gocha's warriors spotted him through the trees. It was a futile effort, though. He hadn't covered half the distance before a Navajo on a bay burst up out of the brush along the North Fork and spotted him. As the Navajo veered his pony toward him, Frank skidded to a stop and threw the rifle to his shoulder. The Indian, thinking the weapon was loaded, swerved his pony away, dropping low along the side of the bay's neck to hang there by an arm and a heel. Frank lowered his rifle and made another mad dash for the river, but the Navajo came after him, his lance sloped toward Frank's shoulders. At the last minute, Frank dodged to the side, spinning and swinging his rifle like a club.

The rifle's solid maple stock struck the Indian in the chest, slamming him off his horse. Before he could rise, Frank was on top of him, hammering at his head with the brass butt of his rifle. When he was sure the Indian was dead, he threw the rifle away and picked up the Navajo's lance and knife. More warriors came surging up from the creek, spotting him immediately. They turned their ponies toward him, screaming their war cries. Frank darted toward the river once more, but it was still too far away. He slid to a stop as the Indians closed, lifting his lance. The first warrior rode wide around him. Another veered to the opposite side. Frank tried to cover both, but he couldn't get the lance back in time to ward off the third man. Even from the arroyo, a good hundred yards away, Annie heard the sharp smack of the Indian's war club on Frank's head, heard its ripe melon *pop,* and watched the blood and bits of hair and brain fan across the sky.

Frank crumpled silently to his knees, what was left of his head tipping back from a broken neck onto his shoulder blades.

Worm looked at Annie in confusion. "I can't go out there," he said. "Them Injuns is gonna kill me if I do."

Annie waved the shotgun at him, her voice cold. "You go. Maybe Blossom, Magpie, Little Pete, they live then."

"But they're gonna kill me," Worm whined.

"You go," Annie ordered.

Slowly, his simple mind refusing to comprehend it all, Worm turned and plodded toward the Indians standing over Frank's body. He stumbled often, and looked neither right nor left. Annie heard his plaintive voice, like a small child's who didn't want to be sent to his robe, although she couldn't make out the words. It didn't matter now. More Indians had appeared, but rather than rushing the arroyo, they gathered at Frank's body, watching silently as Worm tripped and lurched toward them. Annie saw nervousness ripple through the knot of warriors. She understood their fear. She felt it herself as she watched the man called Worm walk unarmed toward Bad Gocha's men, his simple mind shattered now by fear. Slowly, one of the Indians began to back away. Others followed, abandoning Frank's body without attempting to retrieve the scalp, afraid now of this ghostly specter of death that walked toward them, afraid to touch the body at their ponies' feet for fear that whatever spirit had guided this man into insanity might be lurking nearby, intent on claiming another victim. The image of Worm, forever out there, somewhere, forever stumbling toward them, haunting their dreams, was too much for their superstitious minds. Better to let this one go, they thought, better to rid themselves of the evil magic that guided him toward them. Better to let Bad Gocha extract his own revenge on the man called Reed. Today, with such tortured spirits roaming the broad white plain, was not a good day to die.

Bad Gocha sat in the snow near the mouth of the middle fork canyon of the Crippled Elk River and steeled his features against any expression of pain or humiliation. Below him, in the trees along the river bottom, his men were starting to come together at last. Many rode hunched in their saddles with pain, their clothes bloody from wounds received in the battle with the mountain men. A few reeled as if drunk, barely hanging on.

Bad Gocha's lips thinned in rage as he watched the defeated warriors slink into the trees. Whenever one of them looked his way or acted as if he wanted to approach the renegade chief, Bad Gocha glared until that man averted his eyes or turned away.

Bad Gocha lifted his gaze to the broad plain to the west, and the thin line of trees and brush that marked the north fork of the Crippled Elk. A fresh wave of anger washed through him as he watched the clumps and clusters of horsemen riding toward him, so tiny in the distance that even three or four riding together looked like little more than a scrub pine skittering across the snow. But even from here, Bad Gocha knew the horsemen were his and that the battle was lost. The mountain men had fought too fearlessly, too savagely, like demons bent on the destruction of everything that lay within their reach. In the face of such ferociousness Bad Gocha's own will had quickly crumbled. Although he had attempted to kill only one man, he had failed even in that. And when the mountain man's horse whirled and kicked his own pony, breaking its leg, Bad Gocha knew that today was not a good day to die, that the spirits upon which he depended so heavily for his own personal medicine had deserted him.

He sighed as that thought crossed his mind. It was not the first time he had experienced that hollowness of his soul that told him he rode alone, without the guidance of Man Above, or the kinship of the wind and the sun and the rocks. But it would return. It always did, with time.

Bad Gocha stood abruptly, masking the lance of pain that stabbed his knee. He had wrenched the joint when his pony fell, and barely managed to pull himself free of the screaming animal. Luckily, Running Otter had been blasted out of his saddle by a heavy lead slug just as Bad Gocha gained his feet. He had snatched the reins from the clutching fingers of the dying man and scrambled awkwardly onto the panther-hide saddle. Bad Gocha had stared down only briefly into the dark, liquid eyes of Running Otter. Then he'd jerked the pony around and slammed his quirt down hard on the base of the animal's tail. The horse jumped, then lit into a run. Bad Gocha spotted a gap in the battle, the broad mouth of the middle fork of the Cripple Elk River beyond it. He raced the pony toward it, abandoning the field to those whose medicine remained strong.

It angered him now to realize that, without him, his men had been unable to defeat the fewer numbers of white-eyes, but in a way, it made him proud, too. He would remind them often of the successes the renegades had enjoyed under his leadership, and lose no opportunity to rub their noses in the failure they had suffered here today, once he left the battle.

Bad Gocha limped down the slope to the pony that had once belonged to Running Otter, using the side of the hill to help him mount. In the saddle, he motioned for the others to get ready to ride. His gaze strayed over those who were wounded the worst—Morning

Bear and Tall Horse and the stunted Navajo they called Runt—and knew some of them wouldn't make it. But the war party would not pause. The injured would have to keep up as best they could until nightfall, when Bad Gocha would order some of the unscathed warriors to bind their wounds. It was harsh, but then, life had always been harsh for the men and women of Bad Gocha's village. Lifting his hand, he gave the order to move out.

Pete slid wearily from his saddle and took Annie into his arms. She tipped her head against his chest, letting her muscles relax. He lowered his face, smelling the smell of her—the fragrance of woodsmoke and sage and wild mint, and the musky, wild odor of their life in the wilderness.

"You did good," he whispered for her ear alone.

On the plain, the Indians were riding away, splotches of color deserting the field, the battle over as abruptly as it had begun. Worm stood beside Frank's body, asking what he should do from a man who was beyond answering. And between the two rivers, Jorge, McClure, and Clint were retrieving Mateo's body before some Indian decided to come back and mutilate it. It was over . . . finished . . . the battle won, and the women—Annie—safe. Pete's arms tightened around her, squeezing. "You did real good," he murmured.

"Qué?"

CHAPTER FORTY-FIVE

There was no passage through Ogden Canyon. Even the white trappers knew that.

Surely Reed did as well.

Eli was certain Reed would turn away from the dark passage before he reached it, perhaps ducking into a side canyon that opened to the south just before the dark walls of Ogden Canyon closed in. But Reed ignored that obvious escape into the high country to the south. His trail plunged without hesitation into the river's swift current. Eli scanned the bank on both sides, but there was no sign of Reed's exit and no way he could have doubled back without Eli spotting him. He was on ahead somewhere, riding fast within the icy black waters of the river itself, riding straight toward destruction . . . unless he had a plan.

Eli paused at the head of the canyon. Tall pines grew thick as fur along the north-facing slopes of the south wall; on the north wall the slope was mostly barren save for scattered, stunted cedars clinging to the craggy cliffs. Talus slopes of knife-edged gray stones trailed down like wedding veils from the notches between the snow-frosted cliffs. A man on foot might climb out on either side if he was desperate enough, but he would never take a horse with him, and Eli couldn't imagine Reed abandoning his mount. He would need it if he escaped the canyon alive; need it all the more if he expected to elude the vengeance-filled man who followed him.

Eli let the sorrel blow there on the banks of the Ogden River— thinking now, rather than just reacting on a gut level, as he had when Red-Winged Woman first told him of Reed's abduction of Consuelo. He would have to be careful. Reed was a dangerous man, and he would be all the more dangerous if he thought he was cornered. Eli wanted to catch him before he exited the canyon if he could, but he didn't want to push him into something foolish, like killing Consuelo. Reed would want to keep her alive long enough for Eli to catch up. She would be his ticket to another horse, rifle, ammunition, if he bargained with care. Eli would have to make certain he avoided both traps.

He lifted the sorrel's reins, urging the gelding into the icy waters. It was darker here in the canyon, where the just-risen sun had not yet reached, and colder. In places he knew the sun wouldn't touch the canyon floor until June or July, and because of that the temperature was a least twenty degrees colder than it had been out on the open plain. Shelves of ice rimmed the eddies close to the banks, and the foot-deep blanket of snow on the little oxbows of timbered bottomland he passed was layered with a hard, frozen crust. The sound of the sorrel's splashing seemed to echo through the canyon before him, rising even above the sound of the river itself. He kept the horse to a walk, his gaze raking the broken slopes ahead of him. Reed could be anywhere, hidden in the deep pockets of shadows beneath the pines on his left, crouched upon some low ledge to his right, or hiding behind a cottonwood right along the river. It occurred to Eli that there was no way he could avoid a trap if Reed decided to set one for him. All he could do was ride light in the saddle, and hope he recognized it a second or two before it was sprung. The alternative was to turn back now and go around, or wait for reinforcements from the brigade—options he wasn't willing to accept.

He'd gone perhaps a mile into the canyon when he heard a faint splashing floating on the breeze above him. He stopped, trying to decide if the sound was one of nature—a waterfall or rapids—or if it was being made by Reed. He listened for a long time, canting his head first one way, then another. Finally a puzzled frown crossed his face, and he turned the sorrel to face upstream, cocking his rifle as he did. Someone was following him, the sound of his mount in the water growing louder every second.

Eli slid from the saddle and turned the sorrel broadside to the river. The shock of the frigid waters against his ankles was like the gnawing of rats, but he endured the pain without acknowledging it, leveling his rifle across the seat of his saddle and taking aim at the last elbow of the river.

The splashing grew louder. He spotted movement beyond the trees leaning over the river and tensed, but it was only Travis, riding into the open with his head hanging in defeat. Eli swore under his breath and thumbed the rifle to half-cock. The gray spotted Eli's horse and lifted its head, whinnying shrilly. Travis's head jerked up, his eyes darting wildly. Even standing square in his path, it took the youth a couple of minutes to spot Eli. When he did, and Eli was sure that everything was all right, he swung back into his saddle, waiting for Travis to catch up.

"What are you doing here?" Eli asked as Travis reined to a stop beside him.

"It's all over, Eli," Travis said, his voice close to cracking. "They're all dead."

Eli sucked his breath in, unable to believe for a moment the words Travis spilled at him.

"They was just everywhere," he went on. "Everywhere you turned. Killin' right and left. Ain't nobody stood a chance."

He had been crying, Eli saw, and now, as he retold the events he had witnessed, the tears started again, accompanied by racking sobs.

"Buck up, boy," Eli snapped, his voice raw with tortured fury. "Goddamnit, stop that blubbering! You're all right, aren't you?"

Travis sniffed, bobbing his head. "Just a cut. But the others . . . "

"Don't tell me about the others," Eli said harshly. "Just don't tell me about them." His teeth grated, and a muscle in his cheek twitched. He jerked the sorrel around. "Big Tom Reed is still ahead of us somewhere. And he still has Connie. I'm going to get her back, or die trying. You're welcome to ride along if you want."

Travis dragged a sleeve across his eyes, his breath catching as he tried to bring his sobs under control. "All right," he said.

Nodding stiffly, Eli started downstream, with Travis following. He shut all thoughts of the brigade, of his own final betrayal of them, out of his mind. Only one thing mattered now, and that still lay ahead.

Consuelo rode as if in a trance. She was unhurt save for a few small bruises, but the enormity of what had happened, and of what eventually would happen, overwhelmed her mind. She had been a captive once before, among the Navajos who had first killed her husband, then seduced her children away from her. She knew slavery; she understood its heart and soul; she knew what was in store for her mind as much as her body, and she feared that this time she would not have the strength to survive.

She had married young, as had most of her friends in El Paso del Norte, and by the time she was twenty she and her husband had had four children. They had lived along the Rio Grande, her husband one of two dozen peons who tended the sprawling vineyards of a rich landowner. It had been a hard life in all ways, marked by incredible poverty, but rich in their love for one another and for their children. It was for the children that they had decided to move to Santa Fe. It would be different there, José Aragon had promised her. They would have their own place, with goats and chickens, and maybe another burro to help haul the heavier loads. He had refused to go into debt to his patron, as most of the peons did for a few of the luxuries that El Paso had to offer, and therefore was able to quit his job with only a vicious cursing from the vineyard's foreman. Packing their few possessions on the back of a little burro along with their two youngest children, they had started northward, filled with hope for a new beginning.

But the journey had been cataclysmic in its hardships. The burro had died their first week on the trail, and their water had run out less than halfway across the *Jornada del Muerto*—the Journey of Death—that had already claimed hundreds of lives. Felicia, whom they called the Lucky One, had died first, mocking the meaning of her name. Augustin had perished next, his tiny body laid to rest beneath stones because they had been forced to leave their hoe and shovel behind with the burro, and the sun-baked land had been too hard to more than scratch at otherwise.

They would have all died if a trading caravan had not come upon them from the south, traveling from Mexico City to the country's northernmost outposts. Eventually Consuelo realized that a part of her had died within that blazing, waterless hell. Love, hope, dreams. These things she had left buried with her two youngest children, filling the void with bitterness and a smoldering contempt for José, who had proved so ill-prepared to care for his family while in pursuit of his dreams.

They settled in the hills north of Santa Fe and farmed a patch of ground that never yielded much, and cut piñon that they sold in town, making the trek weekly except when the snows were too deep. And in time she began to grow happy again. Not with the same joyful exuberance of her youth, but content. José was a good man who worked hard and who never ceased to love her. And despite the harshness of the country, her two remaining children seemed to thrive. In time they bought their goats and chickens and replaced their burro with a mule. José began to talk of trying a few grapes in the next year or two, and perhaps distilling a little wine that they could sell in Santa Fe.

The Navajo came in the spring of her twenty-third year, sweeping down the High Road between Taos and Santa Fe, killing and plundering. They arrived at the Aragon household just after dawn. José had already been at work in the cornfield, hoeing weeds among the tender spring shoots. He had tried to defend his family, but a hoe was no match for a lance, nor was a farmer any match against a score of warriors. The Navajo had laughed as they swept aside José's puny efforts at defense. Then, tiring of the sport, they casually lanced him and came on to the house. Consuelo did no better. She raced out to meet them with a skillet, and again the Navajo laughed, taunting her as they rode their ponies in circles around her, keeping just out of reach of her swinging skillet. When they tired of their game, they flicked the skillet out of her hand with the slash of a lance and jerked her to the ground with a rawhide reata. The Navajo bound her and her children like sacks of grain and slung them onto mules stolen at other small homes along the High Road.

She had remained a captive for eight years, and in that time watched the gradual assimilation of her children into a culture she grew to despise. Her son accompanied a war party of *Diné*—the Chosen Ones, as the Navajo called themselves—against the Utes the same year her daughter married a man from another clan, and Consuelo knew then that her children were lost to her forever. She had seen too many captives brought back to civilization against their will to hope that her own children would be different. So on the night of her daughter's wedding she stole a knife, a blanket, and a sack of parched corn, walking out of the village and never looking back. She knew the Navajo could have recaptured her easily, but they hadn't even afforded her that dignity. She was only a slave, and not worth the effort.

She went to Taos and began to rebuild her life. Two years later, so desperate to escape the burning loneliness of her existence, she attended a *baile,* willing to endure the condescending looks and hushed whispers of the other women and the bold stares of the men, who could only guess at what sexual secrets she had learned among the savage Navajos. She had sat alone on a bench at the back of the room, idly running her work-callused fingers over the ridges of scar tissue around her wrists, when the Americans strode in, immediately dominating the room with their presence. There had been nearly a dozen of them altogether, recently returned from the high, wild lands of the north. They were ready to spree—to drink and dance and fight and make love to the pretty *señoritas* attending the *baile*—but Consuelo had eyes for only one, the tall, brown-haired gringo with the flashing blue eyes—the one they called Eli.

And now he had failed her as well.

She felt Reed's arm around her waist, his rough, ungentle hands now and again straying over her breasts. His stubbled chin scratched the tender flesh between her neck and shoulder, and his breath rasped hoarsely in her ear. He whispered to her, telling her what he would do when there was time, what he would do to Eli if he came after her. And he told her how he would leave her when he was finished. He wanted to frighten her into submission, she knew, yet his words had no more meaning than the moaning of the wind through the rocks and trees. She was only dimly aware of his roaming hands or the hard presence of his erection against the small of her back. She no longer feared rape or beatings, since she had already given up any hope of rescue. Instead, her mind wandered back to the canyonlands far to the south, claimed by the powerful *Dine,* to an existence she had sworn she would never return to again. She remembered her life there, shivering through the frigid winter months with only the cast-off rags of others to clothe her, fighting with the dogs for bones or scraps of hide that might contain a little raw meat, sleeping outside the mud and log hogans but huddling close to them for what little warmth they might provide. She remembered the beatings, and the spitting words of the Navajo as she had learned their language, telling her to get out of the way, to leave the dogs alone, to fetch water or wood or stir the fire. And she remembered the hard, lusting looks of the men as they beckoned her into the darkness, and the scornful expressions of the women as they gave her the bitter brews that would prevent pregnancy. It had been a time of utter degradation, when the small candle of her soul had guttered and almost gone out, and she knew she could not go back to that. Not ever again. She would rather die than face even the possibility.

Reed pulled his horse to a stop, his tone of voice changing abruptly, hauling Consuelo slowly back from the fog that swirled through her mind. "Wake up, you damned bitch," Reed hissed, poking her sharply in the ribs with his thumb.

Consuelo lifted her head. The canyon had narrowed, the river funneling swiftly between two nearly sheer cliffs. In the sunless light, she saw the sawyer caught between the dark bluffs, a single large cottonwood holding a tangle of smaller trees and branches. The water rushed musically through the blockage, but a horse would never make it, and it would take an ax and most of a day for a man to chop it free.

Reed turned his horse back upstream. "Think that man-friend of yours is following?" he asked, keeping his lips nearly closed as he spoke to prevent the cold air from touching his broken tooth. "Well, I'll tell you now, it ain't gonna do no good. Not as long as I got you." They came to a flat bench of land covered with trees, and Reed urged his horse out of the river. They sat there for a couple of minutes, while Reed studied the situation. Finally he grunted. "Damnit, if I thought it was only Cutler following, I'd wait for the sonofabitch right here. But I know ol' Bad Gocha, and that coon ain't gonna let a handful of trappers slow him down much. Come on. We're gonna hoof it outta this canyon. There's a village of Utes on the other side, and if we can get there, Bad Gocha ain't likely to follow."

He slid from the saddle and hauled Consuelo roughly after him. Shoving the twin barrels of the shotgun under her chin, he growled, "Listen good, bitch, you give me any trouble climbing outta this canyon, and I'll blow your fucking head off. You savvy that?"

Consuelo nodded, but her expression never changed. Reed muttered "Jesus" and pushed her toward the north wall. "Get goin'," he ordered.

The canyon rose steeply before her, the gray stone crumbling and loose. Scrawny bushes and bunchgrass grew along the narrow ledges. She lifted her gaze to the top, towering so far above her it made her dizzy just to look at the blue of the sky.

"Move it," Reed barked, then cursed, tears coming to his eyes. He cupped his hand over his mouth, his eyes wild with rage. "I'll tell you what," he hissed. "I hope it is Cutler that follows us. I owe that bastard." He poked her with the shotgun, motioning toward the cliff.

Consuelo started to climb, placing her moccasined feet with care into the tiny crevices that seemed to open magically before her eyes. Within ten feet she was forced to use her hands, the sharp stones slicing at her mittens. They went another thirty feet and came out onto a ledge.

"Over there," Reed said, pointing to another climb to another small ledge.

They climbed rapidly, moving from ledge to ledge, and taking time to catch their breath in between. Reed's horse quickly grew small on the canyon's floor, and the sound of the river faded into the wind. They were flanked on two sides by unsettled talus slopes, following a more stable line of cliffs and ledges into the sun. They would climb ten feet or fifteen feet, then have a relatively gentle slope of an equal or shorter distance, with weeds and grass and sometimes a small cedar clinging to the shallow soil, before having to climb to the next ledge. Consuelo rarely looked down, but when she did, she couldn't help noticing how far away the canyon's floor was becoming, while the top didn't seem any nearer now than it had when they started. They were perhaps three hundred feet from the bottom when Reed grabbed her capote and forced her to stop.

"We'll take a break here," he said, panting. He leaned against the sun-warmed rock and breathed deeply through his nose. Consuelo walked to the edge of the ledge, wondering if she could see the Great Salt Lake from here, but the canyon was too winding yet, and all she saw beyond the veed notch of the canyon's mouth was the hazy blue distance. "What are you doing over there?" Reed asked suspiciously.

Consuelo came back wordlessly and sat down on a rock. Her limbs ached and her mittens were frayed from climbing. Once a stone about the size of a child's foot had come loose above her, striking her cold fingers and smashing them as they clutched at a small crevice in the cliff's face before bouncing away. Those fingers were puffy now, throbbing painfully and growing stiff. She tried to flex them, but the discomfort was too great, and she tucked them under her armpit instead, hoping the warmth of her body would ease the hurt. Reed rose after ten minutes or so, poking at her again with the shotgun. "Come on, heifer," he said. "We've got a long way to go."

They approached the next cliff almost reluctantly, but with no other alternative. "Start climbin'," Reed grunted.

Consuelo reached up, then lowered her arm.

"I said, start climbin'," Reed said impatiently.

"No."

Reed's eyes narrowed. "I can kill you here or sometime later, it doesn't make any difference to me."

"Then kill me here," Consuelo said. "I won't climb any higher."

Reed's eyes flashed anger. "There ain't nothing more bullheaded than a woman, is there? Bitch, I ain't bluffin'. You start climbin' now, or I'll—"

"*Reed!*"

Reed spun, grasping the shotgun in both hands, but the voice seemed to come from everywhere, echoing back and forth from the canyon's walls.

"Back away, Reed."

"Cutler, is that you?"

"Back away, or I'll drop you where you stand."

Reed's eyes darted, then he stepped closer to Consuelo. "I don't think so, Cutler. You would've done it already if you weren't afraid of hitting the woman."

"It's over, Reed. Throw down the shotgun."

"Come on out where I can see you, Cutler," Reed shouted. Consuelo followed his gaze to the next line of ledges and cliffs over, perhaps fifty yards away. Slowly, Eli rose from behind a rock, his rifle leveled. Behind him, Travis Ketchum stepped away from the cliff's face. Reed put his arm around Consuelo's neck, pulling her around until she stood between him and Eli. "Looks like you ain't booshway anymore, Cutler."

"Let her go, Reed. It's the only way. I'll make you a deal: You let Connie climb down, and I'll let you go free."

"Who's with you, Cutler?"

"It's just me and the boy."

"Is that true, Travis?" Reed called.

Consuelo saw Eli's look of understanding, saw Travis swing the long-barreled Kentucky toward Eli, and suddenly lunged against Reed's grip, sinking her teeth into his hand. Reed screamed and jerked his hand away. Consuelo tasted blood on her tongue as she tried to dart away. Then the shotgun roared; buckshot ripped into her flesh. She took three stumbling steps, then felt the ground give way beneath her feet. She wanted to scream as she tipped outward, but her throat suddenly constricted in fear. Wordlessly, she plunged into the abyss below.

A long silence followed Consuelo's fall. Eli heard the rattle of shale where she struck, saw her bounce out away from the talus, then plummet downward in a swirl of cloth and long black hair. He watched, frozen in horror, unable for a moment to comprehend what he saw. Then she was gone from sight, with only the sounds of a small avalanche of stones following her descent toward the canyon floor.

Slowly, he looked up. Reed was staring transfixed at the edge of the ledge where Connie had disappeared. He, too, was a long time in lifting his gaze away from the spot where she had fallen. When he looked at Eli, he shook his head in disbelief. "Gawddamn," he said as if in awe.

Eli started to bring his rifle up, but Travis stepped forward, the Kentucky's muzzle pointed at his ribs. "I can't let you do it, Eli," Travis said.

Eli looked at him. "You?" he asked.

Travis's mouth worked. His eyes, already reddened from past tears, misted over once more. "I'm sorry. I'm really sorry. I . . . Tom, he's my cousin. When I was in jail in Santa Fe, it was him that told me where to find my rifle and a horse. I would've rotted in that filthy cell if not for him."

"So you joined the brigade to slow us down?"

Travis nodded sickly. "Yeah. Tom heard about Vidales. It was the only way he'd help me bust out."

"He sounds like a good friend, too," Eli said sarcastically.

"The only one I had then," Travis said. "Damnit, now, don't you be judging me. I did the best I could."

Reed whooped behind a cupped hand. "You tell 'em, Travis." He started across the talus, picking his way with care. "Hang on to him until I get there," he shouted.

"Was it worth it?" Eli asked. "It's come to this now. Was it worth it?"

"Don't ask me that."

"Why not? It's a question you're going to be asking yourself for a long time to come. This isn't going to go away for you, Travis. I've watched you. You've got a conscience, something your cousin doesn't have. This is going to haunt you to your grave."

"Don't listen to him, Travis," Reed shouted breathlessly, edging his way cautiously across the unpredictable slope. "Kin's got to stick together. You didn't see ol' Eli bustin' you outta that *calabozo,* did you?"

"Remember the sergeant and his men that stopped us north of Taos?" Eli asked.

Travis took a deep breath, blinking rapidly.

"He was going to take you back, but you were a Cutler man then. And by God, we did more than just tell you where to find your rifle and a horse."

Travis swallowed, flicking his eyes toward Reed.

"Gawdamnit, Cutler, shut up! Travis, shut him up right now!"

"Go ahead and pull the trigger, Travis," Eli said quietly. "I reckon I'd rather be killed by you than the likes of Tom Reed."

Reed scrambled onto the ledge at last and immediately slammed the butt of his shotgun into Eli's stomach. Eli gasped, the wind driven from his lungs. His rifle dropped clattering to the ledge. Reversing the shotgun and cocking the unfired barrel, Reed laughed. Leaning forward, he slid Eli's rifle toward him. "You ain't such a big man after all, are you, Cutler? You and Girardin both, actin' like your shit don't stink. But when it came right down to it, neither one of you were a match for ol' Tommy Reed, were you?"

Gasping, red-faced, Eli forced himself to stand straight. "So . . . what now . . . Reed? You got what you . . . wanted."

"The hell!" Reed shouted loudly enough to bounce his voice off the far wall, his eyes tearing almost unnoticed from the pain of his broken tooth, "I lost a fortune in furs, thanks to you. I lost damn near everything."

"So what now?"

Reed smiled. "Now you die." He shouldered the shotgun.

"Tom," Travis said uncertainly, swinging his rifle around to cover his cousin. "Don't."

"Shut up," Reed growled. "I oughta use this on you. I thought I told you to make sure they didn't get here."

"I tried, damnit."

"Well, you didn't try hard enough, did you? 'Cause look what happened. Everything's gone to hell because you were too chicken-shit to do what I told you."

"I didn't want to, Tom. I did what I could, but I couldn't kill Eli or Mr. McClure."

"*Mister* McClure? Christ, you are a worthless piece of shit, aren't you?"

Travis looked desperately at Eli. "I killed Juan Vidales. I admit that. But I didn't know you then. I didn't know anyone except Jake and Clint. I didn't want to kill Cork-Eye. That was an accident. He caught me . . . the fire . . . the trade goods."

"Shut up," Reed said bluntly. He smiled, turning back to Eli. "Kiss your ass good-bye, Cutler."

"Tom! No!"

Reed aimed the shotgun at Eli's face, grinning broadly down the twin barrels. His finger tightened on the trigger, and Eli braced himself for the shotgun's blast. But before Reed could squeeze the trigger, Travis's Kentucky cracked sharply. Reed howled and spun away, the shotgun flying from his grasp. It landed butt-first on the talus slope, the fall jolting the trigger. The gun roared, spitting buckshot harmlessly skyward. Reed whirled, his eyes crazy. Blood dripped from his hand where the shotgun's splintered forestock had pierced his flesh. He reached inside his coat and pulled the hideaway gun from his belt. Travis's eyes widened as Reed thrust the pistol toward him. "Tom! No!"

Reed fired without hesitation, the ball staggering Travis, dropping him to his knees. Eli lunged, knocking the pistol aside and slamming his shoulder into Reed's chest. Reed grunted as Eli drove him back against the face of the cliff, then brought the pistol down hard on top of Eli's shoulder. Pain lanced through Eli's body. Reed's knee drove into his stomach. His legs buckled and he fell to the ledge. He tried to roll away, but in his pain he lost all sense of direction. Reed slid a knife from his belt, and Eli recognized it as Consuelo's. Reed straddled Eli's body, the knife flashing downward. Eli managed to parry the thrust. The knife skidded across his cheek, slicing the lobe of his ear. He threw himself sideways, against Reed's knee. Reed cried out as he tumbled to the ledge. Eli clawed at his coat, his fingers clutching at the checkered grip of his pistol. Reed rolled away and to his feet in one catlike motion. He held the knife in his right hand, the blade turned up. "I'm gonna cut you like a hog, Cutler," he rasped past his broken tooth. "I'm gonna—"

Eli's pistol roared. The ball took Reed squarely in the chest, flinging him backward. He landed on the edge of the ledge, but the momentum of the bullet's impact slid him over. Eli watched him slide out of sight, heard the rattle of stones as Reed's shattered body struck the talus slope, the grating slide of the avalanche that dragged him toward the canyon floor.

CHApter Forty-six

Travis's face was white as Eli knelt over him. His hand reached out to grasp Eli's. "Eli . . . " Tears came to his eyes, flowing unchecked down his smooth, tanned cheeks. "I'm . . . I'm sorry. Please, God, I'm sorry . . . "

Eli pulled his hand away numbly. "We'll talk about it later," he said, pulling Travis's capote aside to examine the wound. Reed's ball had taken him high in the shoulder, the wound concaved, the flesh around it already turning a deep purple. Gently, Eli lifted him up to view his back. The ball hadn't gone all the way through, but he could see it clearly under the lumped, bruised flesh. He laid Travis back and drew his knife.

"You gonna kill me?" Travis asked weakly.

"Not yet." Eli pulled his shirt out of his britches and sliced off the long tail. He bound Travis's wound as best he could considering the awkward location, then rocked back on his heels. "You'll live," he said flatly. "If you don't fall on the way down." He got his shoulder under Travis's arm and lifted the youth to his feet. He half carried him to the edge of the ledge, then said, "This isn't going to be easy. We'll have to take our time, and rest whenever you get tired."

"I'll be all right," Travis said. He looked at Eli, his tears drying at last. "I just want you to know, it'll be fine with me if you want to hang me when we get down."

Eli stared at him for a moment, then laughed. "You do beat all, kid. Hell, no, I ain't gonna carry you down off this cliff just to hang you. Now come on. We've got a lot to do."

It was a nightmare going down. Travis's shoulder was all but useless, and waves of pain washed through his body. Sweat dripped off his face, and twice he had to stop to vomit. But they made it, a little more bruised and a little bloodier than when they started, but alive. Eli led Travis to where their horses were tethered, and kicked the snow away from the base of a tree. He put his greatcoat around Travis's capote and helped him sit down, his back to the tree.

"You going to be all right here for a spell?" Eli asked.

"Sure, I'll be fine. Where are you going?"

Eli looked back to the cliff, his gaze sweeping the gray slope but not finding what he sought. "I've got some unfinished business to attend to," he said quietly.

"Connie?"

"Yeah." He left both rifles with Travis and got his horse. "I'll be back as soon as I find her," he told Travis.

Leading the sorrel, Eli walked slowly through the canyon's shadows, scanning the slope above him for Consuelo's body. He tried not to think beyond the next minute, the next dragging step. He should be planning ahead, he knew, mapping out his next move. Travis had told him the brigade had been wiped out. That meant that Bad Gocha was probably tracking them now. Even if he wasn't, there were hundreds of miles between him and the nearest form of civilization, weeks of travel without supplies, hampered even further by a wounded man. These were all things to consider, yet none of them seemed important. He wanted only to bury Consuelo, to hide her body where Bad Gocha would never find it.

"So, you have come at last?"

Eli jerked to a stop, his hand going to the pistol in his belt, realizing even as he grabbed for it that he had forgotten to reload. His gaze darted through the deeper shadows, probing for the source of the voice. Then his eyes found her, and for a moment he could only stare. Consuelo smiled weakly. "Do not worry, Eli. I am not a ghost," she whispered.

"Connie?"

"*Sí*. Alive, but not so well."

Eli dropped the sorrel's reins and ran to her side. She was lying on her stomach in the snow at the base of the slope, her face bleeding, her left arm bent back in an impossible angle. He put his hand on her shoulders, but was afraid to move her. "How bad are you hurt?" he asked.

"Very bad, I think." She swallowed, blinking. "Turn me over, Eli. I want to look at the sky."

As gently as possible, Eli rolled her over. A small whine of pain escaped her lips as her broken bones grated against one another. She shut her eyes until it passed, then let them flutter open. "Reed?"

"He's dead."

"Good. That is good."

"Where are you hurt?" he asked.

"The arm. My cheek. Some ribs. These are broken, I think. I am shot, too, but not so bad." She tried to chuckle. "Reed was a poor shot."

Eli found the wounds, two small punctures in her side. "Maybe . . . " he said.

"I think so," she said, smiling. "If you do not rush so much anymore."

"God, Connie. I thought you were dead."

"Almost, Eli. Almost. But not yet." She reached up with her good hand to touch his face. "By the way, did I tell you that I love you?"

EPILOGUE

Sylvester Girardin remained motionless in his chair as Eli paused to take a drink. The old Frenchman's half-lidded gaze lingered on his desktop. His thin, angular face seemed strangely calm in the wake of Eli's news, the expression of a man contemplating bedtime, or an after-dinner cigar, not that of someone who had just learned that his son had indeed been murdered, and that the murderer had been brought to a swift and brutal justice somewhere in the middle of the cold depths of the Rockies. It was almost a full minute before Girardin lifted his eyes from the clutter atop his desk. The corners of his lips tilted upward in a sad, conceding smile. "I suppose I knew it was true all along," he said gently. "But I wanted it verified. And I wanted Tom Reed to pay for his horrendous treachery, not only to the G.S.&T., but for what he did to me—and my son. You are certain of Reed's death?"

"Yes," Eli replied. "I went back up to check the body a couple of days later, to be sure." He sat in the same upholstered chair where he had sat nearly a year ago, a glass of wine in one hand, a cigar in the other. He wore his father's old broadcloth suit and a new linen shirt, loose at the neck. From the open window, the bright July sun poured a buttery light into the tiny office. The sounds of the St. Louis wharves rose faintly on the muggy air, and from somewhere downriver a steamboat announced its arrival with a shrill blast of its whistle.

"Good," Girardin answered in a musing tone, turning his attention momentarily toward the window and the still, lacy curtains. Then his head jerked back and his eyes narrowed into shards of black flint. "You didn't bury him, did you?"

"No. We didn't bury him."

There was a slight, almost imperceptible sagging of Girardin's shoulders, a long, ragged exhalation. His gaze darted once around the room, then came back to Eli. And then it was over. The pain of his son's death, the long months of waiting, it all disappeared behind the impenetrable facade of a businessman, the way a lamplit room disappeared from a darkened street when the shades were drawn. He took a puff from his cigar and jetted the smoke toward the ceiling, then sipped from his wine. Touching his cheek with a finger, he said, "Your scar, that's new. Is it from Reed's knife?"

"Yes." There were, Eli thought, quite a few scars from his encounter with Reed, but not all of them were visible to the naked eye.

"Tell me the rest," Girardin went on. He tapped a stack of papers on his desktop with a thin, elegantly ringed finger. "I've perused Mr. McClure's dispatches, of course, but his journal was somewhat vague after your recovery of the stolen furs. You wintered on the Salt Lake, near a village of Utes. And Consuelo . . . ?"

Eli's thoughts turned inward, backtracking over the long, hard miles, the endless months. He had been like a man in a stupor during those first few hours in Ogden Canyon. Consuelo had been badly injured, near death, and Travis, wounded, nearly delirious with fever and defeat, had been no help at all. Eli had reloaded all of the weapons he had, then quickly moved Travis downcanyon to Consuelo's side. He had intended to throw up a makeshift camp, surrounding it with a cramped breastworks from which he would fight Bad Gocha's men. But he had hardly started before he heard the crunch of frozen snow breaking under the hooves of several horses. Cursing desperately, he threw himself behind a fallen log and leveled his rifle on the nearest bend of the canyon. He almost fired as the first horseman rounded the bend, but jerked his finger away from the trigger at the last instant.

Pete rode in the lead, his rifle butted to his thigh. Clint and Pierre followed. They came slowly, warily, spread out so that an ambush wouldn't catch all three men in the same volley.

Eli stared, dumbfounded. Travis' declaration that the entire brigade had been wiped out by the renegades gripped him so strongly that for a moment he couldn't comprehend what he was seeing. He moved the hammer on his rifle to half-cock and stood up. Pete yanked his buckskin to a halt, and Pierre swore sharply. For a brief moment, no one spoke. Then Pete smiled his slow smile and spurred his horse forward, kicking up a shower of snow. He pulled to a stop at Eli's side and leaped from the saddle, his gaze going beyond him, searching out Consuelo.

"She all right?" he asked, spotting her lying wrapped in blankets near the base of the canyon's wall.

"The others?" Eli said blankly, watching Clint and Pierre jog their mounts in.

"We made it," Pete said. His gaze strayed uncertainly to Travis. "Mateo . . ." He let what he was going to say drift off.

Eli also looked at Travis, but the young man's story—stories—were too much to think about now. There was still too much to be done. "Connie's badly hurt," he told Pete and the others. "We need to take care of her wounds, and get her warm."

While Pierre quickly kindled a roaring blaze and Clint cut pine boughs for a bed, Eli and Pete readied Consuelo. The four men lifted her away from the rough ground at the bottom of the steep slope on a blanket and deposited her on the springy boughs next to the fire. They did what they could for her wounds, binding the broken ribs in strips of leather cut from Eli's buckskin jacket, and splinting her arm with a cast made from cottonwood bark. The two wounds caused by Reed's buckshot were ugly, but not serious. They fingered salve on both the entrance and exit wounds, and bound them in cloth. Her cheek was the most difficult to bandage. Pete sewed the gash up as best he could with needle and sinew, then smeared salve over the suture before wrapping the lower portion of her face with soft cotton cut from a spare shirt. Two days later they took her out of the canyon on a travois cushioned with shaggy buffalo robes, to the camp the brigade had made along the North Fork of the Ogden River. A week after that, they moved the entire outfit over Ogden's Pass to the milder climes along the Wasatch Front. They settled near the forks of the Ogden and Weber Rivers for the winter, and Eli purchased a small deerskin lodge from a village of Utes camped several miles below them.

By Christmas, Consuelo was sitting up and feeding herself. She ventured outside for the first time on New Year's Day, and after that her progress quickened. Now only the scars remained, the scars and the nightmares.

Eli looked up. July sweat trickled from his brow, dampened the collar of his shirt. "She recovered," he said simply.

"And of the others?" Girardin asked. "You mentioned that Johnny Two-Dogs and Caleb Underwood were injured in the battle with Bad Gocha's warriors."

Eli took a sip of his wine, wishing he had asked for bourbon instead. He said, "Old Cal wasn't hurt bad at all, just a cut across his scalp from a tomahawk. A lot of blood, but the wound itself was shallow. Johnny had three wounds. Two were minor, the third was an arrow in his hip. The shaft came out all right, but the head remained stuck in the bone. It's still there, but he's getting around fine. Johnny won't be the first man to die of old age with an arrowhead in him from his wilder days." He smiled. "Of course, he has some help now. Falls On The Rocks moved her things in with him during the winter. They were still together when the outfit reached Taos in June.

"We buried Mateo in the cache, rather than try to dig a new hole in the frozen ground. We left Frank for the wolves, and Reed for the vultures. Worm recovered somewhat, but no one knew what to do with him, so we just turned him loose. He said he was going back to Mexico, but I wouldn't count on him finding his way without someone's help. Worm . . ." Eli hesitated, then shook his head. "The man was buffalo witted, no one would deny that. I don't think he had any idea that what he was doing with Tom Reed and Frank was wrong. Frank was his partner. Worm followed his lead. I reckon that was good enough for him."

Girardin remained silent while Eli took a prolonged breath, then another sip of wine. It was obvious that Girardin wanted to know it all, everything that had happened, and why. But how did he go about telling Girardin everything when he hadn't been there? Eli wondered. How did he explain what he didn't fully understand himself?

They had let Travis live, and not even Old Cal, who had probably put a dozen men under without remorse, had called for his scalp. It had been an odd thing to see, Eli thought, harking back to those first hectic days after their battle with Bad Gocha's men. Everyone thought the renegades would strike again, and the nerves of the men had been stretched as taut as a drum's head as the brigade waited for Consuelo to heal enough to tackle Ogden's Pass. Travis had been too weak to help himself at first, although he healed quicker than Connie. For some reason Eli didn't quite understand even now, he had withheld the information of Travis' double-cross from the others. As it turned out, word had quickly spread through the brigade. His cowardice in the face of Bad Gocha's warriors had been the first to surface. Other things hadn't added up as well, and the mutterings grew—where had Travis been the night the tack had been slashed the mules hamstrung back in the village of Río Colorado? Where had he been the night Juan Vidales was killed, and the night Cork-Eye was knifed and the trade-goods tent burned? In the face of an impending attack, the men's tempers had darkened. But before the situation could explode, Travis himself came forward, hobbling out of his shelter one evening at supper time and confessing everything. He stood in the deepening twilight with his head bowed and his shoulders slumped, his voice shaky with emotion. Tears streaked his cheeks by the time he finished, but he asked for neither pity nor understanding, he had merely stood there in the growing silence after he'd finished, and when no one said a word, had hobbled back to his bed to await whatever punishment the brigade decided on.

In the weeks that followed Eli had decided it was Travis' quiet courage in facing up to the men that saved him. Had the youth denied anything; had he waited for someone else to call him on it; had he attempted to lie or bluff his way out of trouble, or tried for sympathy, the mountaineers probably would have shot him there, along North Fork.

"You allowed him to leave unpunished?" Girardin said, surprised.

Eli let his breath go with a great expulsion of air. "He was a broken man, Mr. Girardin. He'd lied to me and deserted his outfit in the middle of a fight. He was finished in the mountains, and he knew it. Johnny Two-Dogs drew him a map after he'd recovered from his cousin's bullet, showing him how to get back to the States following the Platte. He left in February, and I haven't heard whether he made it or not. He had some pretty rough country to travel through alone, country claimed by the Cheyenne, the Arapaho, the Rees, and the Pawnees. My guess is that he didn't make it, but he might have. Despite what he thought of himself, despite what he did, he was a pretty brave man. Just . . . confused, I guess. He ran from Bad Gocha's warriors, but he was almost foolishly brave against the Arapahos. He killed Juan Vidales and Cork-Eye Weathers, but he saved my life when Big Tom Reed was about to kill me.

"His brother was killed on the Mississippi some time back. I guess he was there when it happened, but didn't do anything to stop it. From what he told me, I'm not sure he could've done anything, but it was obvious the incident . . . tortured him. McClure wanted him brought back in chains, of course, but I left it up to the boys. They said let him go."

Girardin was silent for a couple of minutes. Then, "I'm not sure I agree with your decision, but I wasn't there. You were, and sometimes a leader must bow to the wishes of his men or risk a general mutiny. I will assume that that was the case in this instance. However, to satisfy my own curiosity, I will have my agent in Fort Smith send a man to Hanging Creek Falls to inquire as to whether young Ketchum returned there or not."

"You won't let it drop?"

"Not without further inquiry." Girardin's voice hardened. "Travis Ketchum murdered two men in my employ, and jeopardized the success and safety of the brigade, Mr. Cutler. If he survived his trek across the plains, he'll have to answer for that."

Eli nodded. Although he didn't like it, he understood Girardin's position. Juan Vidales had left a wife and son back in Mexico. Cork-Eye, for better or worse, had been an employee of the G.S.&T. A man like Girardin couldn't afford the luxury of ignoring what Travis had done, no matter what the circumstances. Not in a cutthroat business like the fur trade.

The old man's expression softened. "I will take your concern for Mr. Ketchum into consideration," he promised. "Whatever punishment he is dealt, I will assure you today that it will be fair."

"Thank you," Eli said quietly. A moment of silence followed Eli's reply. Finally, Girardin cleared his throat.

"The French-Canadian," he prodded. "What was his name . . . ?"

"Remi . . . Remi LeBlanc."

"Yes, of course, LeBlanc. He found you at winter quarters, then?"

Sadness momentarily clouded Eli's face. "Yeah, near green-up time, it was. He came riding in on the same little paint horse he'd almost eaten last winter. He's a tough old bird, although I doubt if he'll ever trap again. His ankle wouldn't take the icy waters." Eli's gaze took on a faraway cast, his thoughts drifting backward like the floating of cottonwood fluff on a summer's breeze. It had been late February when Remi appeared as if from the grave. Perhaps, considering the way Jake Orr had turned out, Eli shouldn't have been that surprised to see Remi riding into camp. But no one save maybe Clint had even considered that Jake might have lied about Remi's fate back in the canyonlands. To abandon a partner that way was just about inconceivable as far as the old hands were concerned; Jake's

fear of the mountains had made the possibility seem even more re-
mote.

They had been slowly readying themselves for the spring hunt
when Remi showed up. Annie spotted him first, a lone rider sitting
his horse on the bench above the Weber River. Eli, squatting next to
McClure by the fire and going over their plans for the coming season of trapping, had looked up at Annie's shout. He spotted the
horseman immediately, silhouetted against the barren, snow-covered
crags of the Wasatch.

"Who is it?" McClure asked, squinting into the blaze of reflected
sunlight. "One of ours?"

"No," Eli said, feeling even then the tug of something familiar in
the way the man sat his horse, the splotchy colors of the mount itself.
It was Pete who put it into words.

"Hell, ain't that Remi's mare?"

"Damn if it ain't," Eli said, surging to his feet. "And
damn . . . damn if that doesn't look like . . ."

He heard Annie and Red-Winged Woman gasp, then start to wail,
the sound starting out low and climbing steadily. Soon Falls On The
Rocks and Grass That Burns also took up the keening, swaying on
their feet, dropping what they were doing.

"What the . . . !" McClure exclaimed, scrambling to his feet and
staring at the women.

"They think it's a ghost," Eli explained. "A specter that's come
back from the Other Side to haunt us, or come for revenge." An in-
voluntary shiver ran down his spine. For a second, for a brief, chill-
ing second, he wondered if they were right. Then the rider booted his
horse toward the lip of the bench and started down the steep bank in
an explosion of sparkling, half-frozen snow. By the time he reached
the bottom, Eli was certain. "I'll be goddamned," he breathed, then,
his voice rising, "Pete, shut them women up. It's Remi, by God, *it's
Remi!*"

They converged toward the edge of camp. Most of the outfit was
on hand; only a few were out hunting, or visiting in the Ute village.
The women continued to wail, but softened their voices at the angry
commands of their men. An excited babble passed through the trappers, but died as Remi splashed his mount across the Weber and
drew up. Eli swallowed hard at the sight. If not for the horse, he wondered if he would have even recognized the man sitting before them.

Remi looked smaller than he remembered, gaunt as a winter-hungry wolf. His face was thin, the cheeks hollowed, as if maybe he had lost some teeth along the way, and his once thick, dark hair had gone limp and gray. But it was his eyes that struck Eli the hardest. Gone was the impish sparkle of old; in their place was a pair of black pits, like the hollow sockets of a skull. Remi carried a fusil across the bows of his saddle. He shook the mitten off his right hand as those hate-filled eyes swept the camp, and thumbed the big sidehammer back to full-cock.

"Where is he, Eli?" Remi croaked.

Eli sighed. "He's gone under, Remi. Up on the Bear River. He was killed by a renegade."

Confusion crossed Remi's face. His gaze darted from man to man, then rose to the cluster of lodges behind them.

"Jake's not here," Pete said gently. "I'm sorry, ol hoss."

"Non," the French-Canadian rasped in disbelief. "This cannot be true." He looked at Eli, and the hardness of his eyes seemed to crack. Watching Remi's reaction, seeing it in that brief moment of clarity that comes to all men occasionally, Eli felt his heart wretch. Finally, Remi nodded. His shoulders sagged in resignation. "Then his soul lives with Satan."

"Yes," a voice said from behind Eli, and Clint Orr shoved forward, his voice choked with emotion. "Jake is dead, Remi, and gone to hell. There was no other way, not for Jake."

"Oui," Remi acknowledged. "But I will meet him there, in time, and then we will settle this thing between us."

Girardin's chuckle broke into Eli's reminiscing. "It must have been quite a shock," he said.

Eli smiled wanly. "Yes, it was. It was, indeed." He cleared his throat and went on. "Remi'd fallen in with Bill Byrum and Curly Jamison, the two Smith, Jackson and Sublette trappers we met in Brown's Hole. I reckon he was more dead than alive by that time, but he pulled through. He was changed, though . . . different. He ain't the same man at all."

"An ordeal like that, who could be?" Girardin said.

He straightened in his chair, his voice turning suddenly brisk. "Come the spring season, we trapped the Bear and its tributaries, then moved south of the Uintas and on down along the Yampa. We came back down to Taos through Bayou Salade. Pete Meyers and

Charlie Williams left us there, after selling us their furs at a good price. They went back north, while we continued toward Taos." Eli smiled fleetingly. "Charlie aims to steal his appaloosa back from the Blackfeet, and if I were a betting man, I'd bet good money that the next time I see him, he'll be riding it."

"I sense the challenge of a wager in your words, Mr. Cutler, but I think I'll decline. Tell me about the rest of the brigade."

Eli went on, speaking rapidly now, wanting to finish this up, to get on with the business he had to attend to in St. Louis. He knew this was only the first of numerous meetings Girardin would want, but they had covered a lot of ground for such a short time. Eli figured the rest could wait until another day.

"We had a good spring hunt, and no trouble with brownskins to speak of. Ran into another little bunch of Arapahos over in New Park, but they weren't much of a fight. Someone took a potshot at Jorge while he was watching the remuda one evening. It was too late to track him down that night, but some of the boys went out the next day and found his trail. Old Cal thought it was a Cheyenne pony, but no one else was sure. Whoever it was, he was making tracks for the plains. I didn't see any sense in following.

"A rabid wolf got in with the remuda one night and bit two of the mules, but Clint killed the wolf before it did any more damage. When we got back to Taos, McClure contracted with a Mexican freighter to haul your furs to St. Louis. I came along to make sure there wasn't any trouble."

"A relatively uneventful spring hunt, then?"

Eli nodded. "Nothing out of the ordinary."

"A shame Bad Gocha escaped. But then, his kind often does."

"He'll answer for what he's done sooner or later," Eli said. "Too many people, both Indian and white, are looking for his scalp now."

"Let us hope it is sooner, rather than later," Girardin said grimly. "Now tell me of the authorities in Santa Fe? There was some question regarding the legality of your license, was there not?"

"It had all blown over by the time we got back. McClure greased a few pockets with *pesos,* and they were all smiles again. I don't reckon the Mexican government'll give you any trouble on account of us throwing down on that sergeant outside of Taos. As far as Ketchum, well, that's their concern now."

Girardin seemed to beam. "Then all is in order for next winter's hunt?"

"As much as it'll ever be. McClure is already getting the necessary permits together to take another outfit out, if that's where your stick floats."

"It is," Girardin replied. "Most assuredly, it is." He was quiet for a moment, thinking. Then he touched the pile of letters and Silas McClure's ledger on the cluttered desk in front of him. "Mr. McClure speaks very highly of you and your abilities. Despite some hesitation early on, he seems to have come around to your side completely. I have known Silas for a number of years now, and I respect his judgment. I offered you a partnership if you were successful, and a percentage of the profits. I am a man of my word. Three percent of the season's catch will be put in a bank draft in your name as soon as the furs are graded. Now, what do you think of a partnership?"

Eli hesitated, then ground the stub of his cigar out in the ash stand. "The offer is generous, Mr. Girardin," he said finally. "But I reckon I'll have to pass. St. Louis is a mite too tame for me."

For the first time since Eli had known him, Sylvester Girardin looked stunned. Then he tipped his head back in laughter. "Forgive me, Mr. Cutler, but you are the first man I've heard refer to St. Louis as 'tame.' I'm afraid I have been out of the borderlands too long. But that opinion is neither here nor there, and frankly, I'm glad you feel that way. I think the offer of a partnership is still possible. A junior partnership, of course, but one centered in the Rockies. I do want to put another outfit in the mountains this fall, one much larger than that which you took out last year. At least thirty full-time trappers, and whatever number of swampers and mule skinners you deem necessary. One exception, though. You'll have to find another clerk. I want Silas McClure to remain in Santa Fe to begin groundwork on opening a store there for me next summer. Other than that, you may hire whomever you wish, with the same financial arrangements between us as last year. Your salary, plus three percent of the profits that you bring in."

A slow smile spread across Eli's face. "I reckon that sounds mighty fine, Mr. Girardin. I have a little business to transact in Taos before we put out, but I don't see why I can't complete it before the fall season."

"Consuelo?"

"Yes, sir. Connie and I are going to get married. I'll have to convert to Catholicism and take up Mexican residency to make it legal, but I don't foresee any trouble in that."

"Congratulations," Girardin said. "She sounds like a remarkable woman, Eli. I shall look forward to meeting her someday."

"Perhaps you will, if you ever come to Taos. I doubt if I'll ever get her farther away from her new home than maybe Santa Fe once in a while."

"A new home?" Girardin cocked an eyebrow.

"A new home," Eli returned. "A nice, new home, and a hired woman to help with the cooking and cleaning." His grin broadened. "To help with the young'un, too, when it comes. That's why I'm not going to stay long in St. Louis. I want to be back in Taos when he's born."

Laughing pleasantly, Girardin raised his glass. "This deserves a toast. To the son of Eli and Consuelo Cutler. May he have his father's courage, and his mother's fortitude."

Eli lifted his wine. *"Bueno!"* he said.

RUNNING FROM THEIR PASTS, CAUGHT UP IN THEIR OWN WARS, THEY CAME TOGETHER AT THE CONTINENTAL DIVIDE . . .

★

ELI CUTLER: He led his ragged company from Taos in pursuit of a killer and the truth. But when the dying was done, it would all be about a woman.

MATEO CHAVEZ: He came from a family of ciboleros, Mexican buffalo hunters, fleeing the rage of his father, pursued by a killer, and tormented by the seething anger in his own heart.

TRAVIS KETCHUM: He was raised in a one-room cabin in Arkansas, and saw his brother die in the muddy Mississippi. Now the daring young mountain man was following his own river of tears and shame.

CORK-EYE WEATHERS: He claimed his scarred face was the work of a Blackfoot tomahawk. But the mountain men knew him as a coward who would get somebody killed. They just didn't know who . . .

REMI LEBLANC: The French Canadian trapper had never walked away from a wager in his life. Now he will be plunged into a lonely odyssey in a trackless wilderness.

★

"A RUGGED ADVENTURE THAT TAKES THE READER STRAIGHT INTO MAJESTIC VISTAS AND AMONG FIERCE, PROUD PEOPLE."

—John Legg, author of *The Mountain Country Trilogy*

"FANDANGO IS A WINNER. . . . [There is] a wealth of historical fact interwoven in a plot filled with a cast of spirited, colorful characters."

—Johnny Quarles, author of *Fool's Gold* and *Spirit Trail*